THE
BUMPER
BIGGLES
BOOK

THE BUMPER BIGGLES BOOK

Five Adventures of the Intrepid Aviator

CAPTAIN W. E. JOHNS

CHANCELLOR PRESS

Biggles, Pioneer Air Fighter was first published in Great Britain in 1932 by
John Hamilton Ltd, London under the title *The Camels Are Coming*, and
subsequently by Purnell Books
Copyright W. E. Johns (Publications) Ltd

Biggles Flies South was first published in Great Britain in 1938 by
Oxford University Press, London and subsequently by Hodder & Stoughton Ltd
Copyright W. E. Johns (Publications) Ltd

Biggles in the Orient was first published in Great Britain in 1945 by
Hodder & Stoughton Ltd, London
Copyright W. E. Johns (Publications) Ltd

Biggles Defies the Swastika was first published in Great Britain in 1941 by
Oxford University Press, London and subsequently by Hodder & Stoughton Ltd
Copyright W. E. Johns (Publications) Ltd

Biggles in the Jungle was first published in Great Britain in 1942 by
Oxford University Press, London and subsequently by Hodder & Stoughton Ltd
Copyright W. E. Johns (Publications) Ltd

This collected edition first published in Great Britain in 1983 by
Chancellor Press
59 Grosvenor Street
London W1

© 1983 Arrangement and Design Octopus Books Ltd

All Rights Reserved

ISBN 0 907486 32 0

Printed in Czechoslovakia
50 522

CONTENTS

BIGGLES

PIONEER
AIR FIGHTER

ABOUT PIONEER AIR COMBAT

by Captain W. E. Johns

CAPTAIN JAMES BIGGLESWORTH is a fictitious character, yet he could have been found in any R.F.C. mess during those great days of 1917 and 1918 when air combat had become the order of the day and air duelling was a fine art.

To readers who are unfamiliar with the conditions that prevailed in the sky of France during the last two years of World War I, it may seem unlikely that so many adventures could have fallen to the lot of one man. In these eventful years, every day—and I might almost say every hour—brought adventure, tragic or humorous, to the man in the air, and as we sat in our cockpits warming up our engines for the dawn 'show', no one could say what the end of the day would bring, or whether he would be alive to see it.

Again, it may seem improbable that any one man could have been involved in so many hazardous undertakings, and yet survive. That may be true; sooner or later most war pilots met the inevitable fate of the flying fighter. I sometimes wonder how any of us survived, yet there were some who seemed to bear a charmed life. William Bishop, the British ace, Rene Fonck, the French ace and prince of air duellists, and, on the other side, Ernest Udet, and many others, fought hundreds of battles in the air and survived thousands of hours of deadly peril. Every day incredible deeds of heroism were performed by pilots whose names are unknown.

Nowhere are the curious whims of Lady Luck so apparent as in the air. Lothar von Richthofen, brother of the famous ace, shot down forty British machines and was killed in a simple cross-country flight. Nungesser, the French champion of forty-five air battles, was drowned, and McKeever, Canadian ace of thirty victories, was killed in a skidding motor-car. Captain 'Jock' McKay, of my squadron survived three years' air warfare only to be killed by 'archie' an hour before the Armistice was signed. Lieutenant A. E. Amey, who fought his first and last fight beside me, had not even unpacked his kit! I have spun into the ground out of control yet lived to tell the tale. Gordon, of my squadron, made a good landing, but bumped on an old road that ran across the aerodrome, turned turtle, and broke his neck.

Again, should the sceptic think I have been guilty of exaggeration, I would say that exaggeration is almost impossible where air combat is concerned. The speed at which a dog-fight took place and the amazing manner in which machines appeared from nowhere, and could disappear, apparently into thin air, was so bewildering as to baffle description. It is beyond my ability to convey adequately the sensation of being one of ten or a dozen machines, zooming, whirling, and diving among the maze of pencil-lines that marked the track of tracer bullets. One could not exaggerate the horror of seeing two machines collide head-on a few yards away, and words have yet to be coined to express that tightening of the heart-strings that comes of seeing one of your own side roaring down in a sheet of flame. Seldom was any attempt made by spectators to describe these things at the time; they were best forgotten.

It is not surprising that many strange incidents occurred, incidents that were never written down on combat reports, but were whispered in dim corners of the hangers while we were waiting for the order to start up, for the 'late birds' to come home to roost. It was 'H', a tall South African S.E. pilot, who came in white-faced and told me he had just shot down a Camel by mistake. It was the Camel pilot's fault. He playfully zoomed over the S.E., apparently out of sheer lightheartedness. 'H' told me that he started shooting when he saw the shadow; he turned and saw the red, white and blue circles, but it was too late. He had already gripped the Bowden control and fired a burst of not more than five rounds. He had fired hundreds of rounds at enemy aircraft without hitting one, but the Camel fell in flames. He asked me if he should report it, and I, rightly or wrongly, said no, for nothing could bring the Camel back. 'H' went West soon afterwards.

Almost everybody has heard the story told by Boelike, the

German ace, of how he once found a British machine with a dead crew flying a ghostly course amid the clouds. On another occasion he shot down an F.E., which, spinning viciously, threw its observer out behind the German lines and the pilot behind the British lines. What of the R.E.8 that landed perfectly behind our lines with the pilot and observer stiff and stark in their cockpits! The R.E.8 was not an easy machine to land at any time, as those who flew it will remember.

Rene Fonck once shot down a German machine which threw out its pilot; machine and man fell straight through a formation of Spads below without touching one of them! The German pilot was Wissemann, who had just shot down Guynemer, Fonck's friend and brother ace, but he did not know that at the time. The coincidence is worth noting. Madon, another ace, once attacked a German two-seater at point-blank range—his usual method. A bullet struck the goggles off the Boche observer and sent them whirling into the air; Madon caught them on his wires and brought them home. When Warneford shot down his Zeppelin, one of the crew jumped from the blazing airship, and after falling for a distance generally believed to be about 200 feet, crashed through the roof of a convent and landed on a bed that had just been vacated by a nun. He lived to tell the tale.

One could go on with such stories indefinitely, but these should be sufficient to show that, in the air at least, truth is stranger than fiction.

Many of the adventures that are ascribed to Biggles did actually occur, and are true in their essential facts. Students of air history may identify them. In some cases the officers concerned are still alive and serving in the Royal Air Force.

Finally, I hope that from a perusal of these pages a younger generation of air fighters may learn something of the tricks of the trade, of the traps and pitfalls that beset the unwary, for I fear that many of the lessons which we learned in the hard school of war are being rapidly obscured by the mists of peace-time theory. In air-fighting, one week of experience is worth a year of peace-time practice. In peace a man may make a mistake—and live. He may not even know of his mistake. If he makes that same mistake in war—he dies, unless it is his lucky day, in which case the error is so vividly brought to his notice that he is never guilty of it again.

No one can say just how he will react when, for the first time, he hears the slash of bullets ripping through his machine. The sound has turned boys into grey-faced men, and even hardened campaigners who learnt their business on the ground have felt their lips turn dry.

In the following pages certain expressions occur from time to time in connection with the tactics of air combat which may seem to the layman to be out of proportion to their importance. For instance, he will read of 'getting into the sun'. It is quite impossible for anybody who does not fly to realise what this means and how utterly impossible it is to see what is going on in that direction, particularly when the sun is low and one is flying west. To fly into the face of the setting sun can be uncomfortable at any time, but the strain of trying to peer into the glare, knowing that it may discharge a squadron of enemy aircraft at any moment, becomes torture after a time.

It should also be remembered that an aeroplane is an extremely small vehicle and difficult to see. When one is on the ground it is the noise of the engine that almost invariably first attracts attention, and but for the unmistakeable telltale hum, few would be seen at all. In the air, the roar of one's own engine drowns all other sound, and one is therefore dependent upon sight alone for detecting the presence of other aircraft. This fact should be borne in mind when reading stories of the air, and particularly of air combat.

Constant reference is also made to 'archie'. Most people know by now that this was not an old friend whom we called by his Christian name. There was nothing friendly about archie. On the contrary, it often bit you when you were least expecting it, but on the whole its bark was worse than its bite. Archie was the war-pilot's nickname for anti-aircraft gun-fire. During the war, archie batteries stretched from the North Sea to the Swiss frontier; its appearance in the sky was accepted as a matter of course, and dodging it was part of the daily round. After a time one became accustomed to it and ignored it unless it was very bad.

HOW BIGGLES WAS 'BORN'

THESE stories of World War I were written about a character whose exploits—little suspected by me at the time—were to continue to the present day. They were written for a magazine of which I was the editor, and apart from the entertainment of the reader, had the more serious purpose of presenting a picture of war flying as it was in its infancy. It seems unlikely that anyone could have suspected the developments that were to follow and astonish us in World War II.

In the 1914 war, flying began with pilots trying to drop stones on each other. The pistol followed, then the carbine, and the first casualties occurred. The next step was an ordinary ground machine-gun. Later, this was fixed to the machine. A great stride was made when a timing gear was produced to allow first one, then two, machine-guns to fire forward through the airscrew—at that time incorrectly called a propeller. Even in 1918 armament was still primitive compared with the types that fought in the Battle of Britain. Air combat was mostly a matter of 'catch as catch can', with every man for himself. Tricks and ruses were common. Discipline was casual, for the senior officers of the R.F.C. had not had time to grow old.

In short, it was the era of experiment, of trial and error. But it was from the apparently irresponsible behaviour of the pilots of the Kaiser's war that the traditions of the air service emerged. Discipline, speed and striking power may have been stepped up, but the human factor is the same.

W.E.J.

GLOSSARY OF TERMS

Altimeter: The instrument used for determining the height of an aeroplane. It is not unlike a barometer, and is set in the instrument board.

Ammonal: A very powerful explosive. It was used in Mills bombs.

Archie: The old Royal Flying Corps expression for anti-aircraft gun-fire. In World War II it became 'flak'.

'Blipping': The art of opening the throttle of a rotary engine in short, sharp bursts to keep it 'alive'.

Bomb-Toggle: The bomb release handle.

Bowden Lever: The machine-guns of certain aeroplanes were fired by depressing a lever on the joystick. Sometimes a thumb button was used in the top of the joystick. Other methods were also employed according to the type of machine.

Brass-Hats: A common expression meaning staff officers, no doubt originating from the gold device on the peaks of their caps—often referred to as 'bananas'.

Bristol Fighter: A famous type of two-seater British all-purpose aeroplane.

Buckingham: A type of incendiary bullet, calculated to set fire to anything it hit. They were used chiefly against lighter-than-air craft in order to set fire to the hydrogen gas with which these were inflated.

Camouflage: A word coined from the French, meaning 'to conceal', 'disguise', or make a thing look like something it was not. Many different forms of camouflage were employed during the war. Imitation grass mats, spread above guns, was known as camouflage. The paintings of buildings, hangars and guns in sections of different colours, in order to break up their outlines, was also known as camouflage.

Centre Section: That part of the top plane of an aeroplane which comes immediately over the fuselage, and to which the wings themselves are joined.

Circus: Formations of enemy aeroplanes were commonly called circuses; often they were known by the name of the leader: thus 'Richthofen's circus'.

Cooper Bombs: Special bombs generally reckoned to weigh twenty pounds, although as a matter of fact they usually weighed about twenty-five pounds; often carried by single-seat fighters under the wings, four each side.

Deflection: The allowance made when shooting at a moving target. Briefly, it means shooting at the place where the target is expected to be when the missile reaches it.

Double-Frontiers: In order to prevent prisoners of war from escaping, the Germans, in many places, arranged artificial or false frontiers in order to lead escaping officers to believe that they had entered another country, whereas in fact they had not.

Fanning (Down): An R.F.C. expression for blowing up with bombs. Things were fanned down, not blown up.

Flaming Onions: Missiles used by the Germans against aeroplanes in World War I. The weapons that fired them remained a mystery until the end of the war. They appeared in a series of glowing balls of fire that rose vertically from the ground.

Flying Wire: Broadly speaking, the wings of biplanes were braced with two sorts of wires, flying wires and landing wires. Flying wires hold the wings in position in the air; landing wires take the weight of the wings when the machine is standing on the ground.

Hannoverana: An efficient type of German two-seater, 1917–18.

Inclinometer: An instrument very much like a spirit-level, set across the instrument board, the position of the bubble showing if the machine is flying level, or banking.

M.O.: Medical Officer.

'Nines': De Havilland 9s, famous 2-seater bombers, 1917–18.

Parachute Flares: Bright lights which had a parachute attachment in order that they should sink slowly to the ground. They were used by aeroplanes to illuminate the ground below them while night-flying.

Pour Vous: Words supposed to resemble the noise made by the German Mercédès aero engine.

Rocking Wings: The signal usually employed (before the days of radio) by the leader of a formation to indicate that enemy aircraft were in sight or that he was going to attack.

Rumpler: A German two-seater aeroplane used in large quantities during the war.

'Sausage': Kite balloons were sometimes called 'sausages'. German balloons were sometimes referred to as *Drachens.*

'Shoot' (Artillery): A machine spotting for the artillery was said to be doing a 'shoot'.

Sidcot (suit): A thick, padded overall garment worn by pilots.

Smudge Fire: A small fire usually kept alight on aerodromes to show landing machines the direction of the wind.

Spandaus: Many German machine-guns and bullets were made at Spandau, Germany. For this reason German machine-guns were often referred to as Spandaus.

Tarmac: The paved area in front of the hangars.

Triplane: An aeroplane having three wings is a triplane. During the war it usually meant the Fokker triplane; also called 'Tripehound'. Sopwith triplanes were used by the British.

Very Pistol: A short, large-bore pistol used for firing signal lights.

THE CARRIER

CAPTAIN BIGGLESWORTH, of Squadron No. 266, R.F.C., sat shivering in the tiny cockpit of his Camel at rather less than 1,000 feet above the allied reserve trenches. It was a bitterly cold afternoon; the icy edge of the February wind whipped round his face and pierced the thick padding of his Sidcot suit as he tried to snuggle lower in his 'office'.

The little salient on his right was being slowly pinched out by a detachment of infantry; to Biggles it seemed immaterial whether the line was straightened out or not; a few hundred yards one way or the other was neither here nor there, he opined. He was to change his mind before the day was out. Looking down, he could see the infantry struggling through the mud from shell-hole to shell-hole, as inch by inch they drove the enemy back.

Squadron orders for the day had been to help them in every possible way by strafing back areas with machine-gun fire and 20-lb. Cooper bombs to prevent the enemy from bringing up reinforcements. He had been at it all morning, and as he climbed into his cockpit for the afternoon 'show', he anticipated another miserable two hours watching mud-coated men and lumbering tanks crossing no-man's-land, as he dodged to and fro through a venomous fire from small-arms, field-guns and archie batteries.

He was flying a zig-zag course behind the British lines, keeping a watchful eye open for the movements of enemy troops, although the smoke of the barrage, laid down to protect the advancing troops, made the ground difficult to see. It also served to some extent to conceal him from the enemy gunners. From time to time he darted across the line of smoke and raked the German front line with bullets from his twin Vickers guns. It was a highly dangerous, and, to Biggles, an unprofitable pursuit; he derived no sense of victory from the performance, and the increasing number of holes in his wings annoyed him intensely. 'I'll have one of those holes in *me* in a minute,' he grumbled.

Crash! Something had hit the machine and splashed against his face, smothering his goggles with a sticky substance.

'What's happened now?' he muttered, snatching off the goggles. His first thought was that an oil lead had been cut by a piece of shell, and he instinctively throttled back and headed the Camel nose down, farther behind his own lines.

He wiped his hand across his face and gave a cry of dismay as it came away covered in blood. 'My gosh! I'm hit,' he thought, and looked anxiously below for a suitable landing-ground. He had little time in which to choose, but fortunately there were many large fields handy, and a few seconds later the machine had run to a standstill in one of them. He stood erect in the cockpit and felt himself all over, looking for the source of the gore. His eye caught a sight of a cluster of feathers stuck on the centre section bracing wires, and he sank down limply, grinning sheepishly.

'Holy mackerel,' he muttered, 'a bird! So that was it!' Closer investigation revealed more feathers and finally he found a mangled mass of blood and feathers on the floor of the cockpit. 'The propeller must have caught it and chucked what was left of it back through the centre section into my face,' he mused. 'Looks like a pigeon. Oh, well!'

He made to throw it overboard, when something caught his eye. It was a tiny tube attached to the bird's leg.

'A carrier pigeon, eh?' He whistled. 'I wonder if it is one of ours or a Boche?'

He knew, of course, that carrier pigeons were used extensively by both sides, but particularly by the Allies for the purpose of conveying messages from spies within the occupied territory.

Sitting on the 'hump' of his Camel, he removed the capsule and extracted a small flimsy piece of paper. One glance at the jumbled lines of letters and numbers was sufficient to show him that the message was in code.

'I'd better get this to Intelligence right away,' he thought, and looked up to see an officer and several Tommies regarding him curiously from the hedge.

'Are you all right?' called the officer.

'Yes,' replied Biggles. 'Do you know if there is a field-telephone anywhere near?'

'There's one at Divisional Headquarters—the farmhouse at the end of the road,' was the answer.

'Can I get through to 91st Wing from there?'

'I don't know.'

'All right; many thanks,' called Biggles. 'I'll go and find out. Will you keep an eye on my machine? Thanks.'

Five minutes later he was speaking to Colonel Raymond at Wing Headquarters, and after explaining what had happened, at the Colonel's invitation read out the message letter by letter. 'Shall I hold on?' asked Biggles at the end.

'No; ring off, but don't go away. I'll call you in a minute or two,' said the Colonel crisply.

Five minutes passed quickly as Biggles warmed himself by the office fire, and then the phone bell rang shrilly.

'For you, sir,' said the orderly, handing him the instrument.

'Is that you, Bigglesworth?' came the Colonel's voice.

'Yes, sir.'

'All right; we shan't want you again.'

'Hope I brought you good news,' said Biggles, preparing to ring off.

'No, you brought bad news. The message is from one of our fellows over the other side. The machine that went to fetch him last night force-landed and killed the pilot. That's all.'

'But what about the sp—man?' asked Biggles, aghast.

'I'm afraid he is in a bad case, poor devil. He says he is on the north side of Lagnicourt Wood. The Huns have got a cordon of troops all round him and are hunting him down with dogs. He's heard them.'

'How awful!'

'Well, we can't help him; he knows that. It will be dark in an hour and we daren't risk a night landing without looking over the ground. They'll have got him by tomorrow. Well, thanks for the prompt way you got the message to us. By the way, your

M.C. is through; it will be in orders tonight. Goodbye.' There was a click as the Colonel rang off.

Biggles sat with the receiver in his hand. He was not thinking about the decoration the Colonel had just mentioned. He was visualizing a different scene from the one that would be enacted in mess that night when his name appeared in orders on the notice-board. In his mind's eye he saw a cold, bleak landscape of leafless trees through which crawled an unkempt, mud-stained, hunted figure, looking upwards to the sky for the help that would never come. He saw a posse of hard-faced, grey-coated Prussians holding the straining hounds on a leash, drawing ever nearer to the fugitive. He saw a grim, blank wall against which stood a blind-folded man—the man who had fought the war his own way, without hope of honour, and had lost.

Biggles, after two years of war, had little of the milk of human kindness left in his being, but the scene brought a lump into his throat. 'So they'd leave him there, eh?' he thought. 'That's Intelligence, is it?' He slammed the receiver down with a crash.

'What's that, sir?' asked the startled orderly.

'Go to blazes,' snapped Biggles. 'No, I didn't mean that. Sorry,' he added, and made for the door.

He was thinking swiftly as he hurried back to the Camel. 'North edge of Lagnicourt Wood, the Colonel said; it's nearly a mile long. I wonder if he'd spot me if I got down. He'd have to come back on the wing—it's the only way, but even that's a better chance than the firing party'll give him. We'll try it, anyway; it isn't more than seven or eight miles over the line.'

Within five minutes he was in the air heading for the wood, and ten minutes later, after being badly archied, he was circling over it at 5,000 feet.

'They haven't got him yet, anyway,' he muttered, for signs of the pursuit were at once apparent. Several groups of soldiers were beating the ditches at the west end of the wood and he saw hounds working along a hedge that ran diagonally into its western end. Sentries were standing at intervals on the northern and southern sides. 'Well, there's one thing I can do in case all else fails. I'll lay me eggs first,' he decided, thinking of the two

Cooper bombs that still hung in their racks. He pushed the stick forward and went tearing down at the bushes where the hounds were working.

He did a vertical turn round the bushes at fifty feet, levelled out, and, as he saw the group just over the junction of his right-hand lower plane and the fuselage, he pulled the bomb-toggle, one—two. Zooming high, he half rolled, and then came down with both Vickers guns spitting viciously. A cloud of smoke prevented him from seeing how much damage had been done by the bombs. He saw a helmeted figure raise a rifle to shoot at him, fall, pick himself up, fall again, and crawl into the undergrowth. One of the hounds was dragging itself away. Biggles pulled the Camel up, turned, and came down again, his tracer making a straight line to the centre of the now clearing smoke. Out of the corner of his eye he saw other groups hurrying towards the scene, and made a mental note that he had at least drawn attention to himself, which might give the spy a chance to make a break.

He levelled out to get his bearings. Left rudder, stick over, and he was racing low over the wood towards the northern edge. At thirty feet from the ground he tore along the side of the wood, hopping the trees and hedges in his path. There was only one field large enough for him to land in; would the spy realise that, he wondered, as he swung round in a steep climbing turn and started to glide down, 'blipping' his engine as he came.

He knew that he was taking a desperate chance. A bad landing or a single well-aimed shot from a sentry when he was on the ground would settle the matter. His tail-skid dragged on the rough surface of the field; a dishevelled figure, crouching low, broke from the edge of the wood and ran for dear life towards him. Biggles kicked on rudder and taxied, tail up, to meet him, swinging round while still thirty yards away, ready for the take-off. A bullet smashed through the engine cowling; another struck the machine somewhere behind him.

'Come on!' he yelled frantically, although it was obvious that the man was doing his best. 'On the wing—not that—the left one—only chance,' he snapped.

The exhausted man made no answer, but flung himself at full length on the plane, close to the fuselage, and gripped the leading edge with his bare fingers.

'Catch!' cried Biggles, and flung his gauntlets on to the wing within reach of the fugitive.

Bullets were flicking up the earth about them, but they suddenly ceased, and Biggles looked up to ascertain the reason. A troop of Uhlans were coming down the field at full gallop, not a hundred yards away. Tight-lipped, Biggles thrust the throttle open and tore across the field towards them. His thumbs sought the Bowden lever of his Vickers guns and two white pencil lines of tracer connected the muzzles with the charging horsemen.

A bullet struck a strut near his face with a crash that he could hear above the noise of his engine, and he winced. Zooming high, he swung round towards the lines.

'I've got him—I've brought it off!' hammered exultantly through his brain. 'If the poor fellow doesn't freeze to death and fall off I'll have him home within ten minutes.' With his altimeter needle touching 4,000 feet, he pulled the throttle back and, leaning out of the cockpit, yelled at the top of his voice, 'Ten minutes!' A quick nod told him the spy had understood.

Biggles pushed the stick forward and dived for the line. He could feel the effect of the 'drag'[1] of the man's body, but as it counterbalanced the torque[2] of his engine to some extent it did not seriously interfere with the performance of the machine.

He glanced behind. A group of small black dots stood out boldly against the setting sun. Fokkers!

'You can't catch me, I'm home,' jeered Biggles pushing the stick further forward.

He was down to 2,000 feet now, his air-speed indicator showing 150 m.p.h.; only another two miles now, he thought with satisfaction.

Whoof! Whoof! Whoof! Three black clouds of smoke

---

[1] *'Drag': head resistance.*

[2] *Torque: the reaction of a propeller, which tends to turn an aeroplane in the opposite direction to which the propeller is turning.*

blossomed out in front of him, and he swerved. Whoof!—Spang! Something smashed against the engine with a force that made the Camel quiver. The engine raced, vibrating wildly, and then cut out dead. For a split second Biggles was stunned. Mechanically he pushed his stick forward and looked down. The German support trenches lay below.

'My gosh! What luck; I can't do it,' he grated bitterly. 'I'll be three hundred yards short.'

He began a slow glide towards the Allied front line, now in sight. At 500 feet, and fast losing height, the man on the wing twisted his head round, and the expression on his face haunted Biggles for many a day. A sudden thought struck him and an icy hand clutched at his heart.

'By heavens! I'm carrying a professed spy; they'll shoot us both!'

The ground was very close now and he could see that he would strike it just behind the Boche front line. 'I should think the crash will kill us both,' he muttered grimly, as he eyed the sea of shell-holes below. At five feet he flattened out for a pancake landing; the machine started to sink, slowly, and then with increasing speed. A tearing, ripping crash and the Camel closed up around him; something struck him on the head and everything went dark.

'Here, take a drink of this, young feller—it's rum,' said a voice that seemed far away.

Biggles opened his eyes and looked up into the anxious face of an officer in uniform and his late passenger.

'Who are you?' he asked in a dazed voice, struggling into a sitting position and taking the proffered drink.

'Major Mackay of the Royal Scots, the fust of foot, the right of the line and the pride of the British Army,' smiled his *vis-à-vis*.

'What are you doing here—where are the Huns?'

'We drove 'em out this afternoon,' said the Major, 'luckily for you.'

'Very luckily for me,' agreed Biggles emphatically.

2

SPADS AND SPANDAUS

BIGGLES looked up from his self-appointed task of filling a machine-gun belt as the distant hum of an aero engine reached his ears; an S.E.5, flying low, was making for the aerodrome. The Flight-Commander watched it fixedly, a frown deepening between his eyes. He sprang to his feet, the loose rounds of ammunition falling in all directions.

'Stand by for a crash!' he snapped at the duty ambulance driver. 'Grab a Pyrene, everybody,' he called; 'that fellow's hit; he's going to crash!'

He caught his breath as the S.E. made a sickening flat turn, but breathed a sigh of relief as it flattened out and landed clumsily. The visiting pilot taxied to the tarmac and pushed up his goggles to disclose the pale but smiling face of Wilkinson, of 287 Squadron.

'You hit, Wilks?' called Biggles anxiously.

'No.'

Biggles grinned his relief and cast a quick, critical glance at the machine. The fabric of the wings was ripped in a dozen places; an interplane strut was shattered, and the tail-unit was as full of holes as the rose of a watering-can.

'Have you got a plague of rats or something over at your place?' he inquired, pointing at the holes. 'You want to get some cats.'

'The rats that did that have red noses, and it'll take more than cats to catch 'em,' said Wilkinson meaningly, climbing stiffly out of the cockpit.

'Red noses, did you say?' said Biggles, the smile fading from his face. 'You mean—'

'The Richthofen crowd have moved down, that's what I mean,' replied Wilkinson soberly. 'I've lost Browne and Chadwicke, although I believe Browne managed to get down just over our side of the line. There must have been over twenty Huns in the bunch we ran into.'

'What were they flying?'

'Albatrosses. I counted sixteen crashes on the ground between Le Cateau and here, theirs and ours. There's an R.E.8 on its nose between the lines. There's a Camel and an Albatross piled up together in the Hun front-line trench. What are we going to do about it?'

'Pray for dud weather, and pray hard,' said Biggles grimly. 'See any Camels on your way?'

Wilkinson nodded. 'I saw three near Mossyface Wood.'

'That'd be Mac; he's got Batty and a new man with him.'

'Well, they'll have discovered there's a war on by now,' observed Wilkinson. 'Do you feel like making Fokker fodder of yourself, or what about running down to Clarmes for a drink and talk things over?'

'Suits me,' replied Biggles. 'I've done two patrols today and I'm tired. Come on; I'll ask the C.O. if we can have the tender.'

Half an hour later they pulled up in front of the Hôtel de Ville, in Clarmes. In the courtyard stood a magnificent touring car which an American staff officer had just vacated. Lost in admiration, Biggles took a step towards it.

'Thinking of buying it?' said a voice at his elbow.

Turning, Biggles beheld a captain of the American Flying Corps. 'Why, are you thinking of selling it?' he asked evenly.

As he turned and joined Wilkinson at a table, the American seated himself near them. 'You boys just going to the line?' he asked. 'Because if you are I'll give you a tip or two.'

Biggles eyed the speaker coldly. 'Are you just going up?' he inquired.

'Sure,' replied the American. 'I'm commanding the 299th Pursuit Squadron. We moved in today—we shall be going over tomorrow.'

'I see,' said Biggles slowly; 'then I'll give *you* a tip. Don't cross the line under fifteen thousand.'

The American flushed. 'I wasn't asking you for advice,' he snapped; 'we can take care of ouselves.'

Biggles finished his drink and left the room.

'That baby fancies himself a bit,' observed the American to

Wilkinson. 'When he's heard a gun or two go off he won't be so anxious to hand out advice. Who is he?'

'His name's Bigglesworth,' said Wilkinson civilly. 'Officially, he's only shot down twelve Huns and five balloons, but to my certain knowledge he's got several more.'

'That kid? Say, don't try that on me, brother. You've got a dozen Huns, too, I expect,' jibed the American.

'Eighteen, to be precise,' said Wilkinson, casually tapping a cigarette.

The American paused with his drink halfway to his lips. He set the glass back on the table. 'Say, do you mean that?' he asked incredulously.

Wilkinson shrugged his shoulders, but did not reply.

'What did he mean when he said not to cross the line under fifteen thousand?' asked the American curiously.

'I think he was going to tell you that the Richthofen circus had just moved in opposite,' explained Wilkinson.

'I've heard of that lot,' admitted the American. 'Who are they?'

Wilkinson looked at him in surprise. 'They are a big bunch of star pilots each with a string of victories to his credit. They hunt together, and are led by Manfred Richthofen, whose score stands at about seventy. With him he's got his brother, Lothar— with about thirty victories. There's Gussmann and Wolff and Weiss, all old hands at the game. There's Karjust, who has only one arm, but shoots better than most men with two. Then there's Lowenhardt, Reinhard, Udet and—but what does it matter? A man who hasn't been over the line before meeting that bunch, has about as much chance as a rabbit in a wild-beast show,' he concluded.

'You trying to put the wind up me?'

'No. I'm just telling you why Biggles said don't cross under 15,000 feet. You may have a chance to dive home, if you meet 'em. That's all. Well, cheerio; see you later perhaps.'

'It's a thundering shame,' raved Biggles, as they drove back to the aerodrome. 'Some of these Americans are the best stuff in the world. One or two of 'em have been out here for months with our own squadrons and the French Lafayette and Cigognes Escadrilles. Now their brass-hats have pulled 'em out and rolled 'em into their own Pursuit Squadrons. Do they put them in charge because they known the game? Do they? No! They hand 'em over to some poor boob who has done ten hours' solo in Texas or somewhere, but has got a command because his sister's in the Follies; and they've got to follow where he leads 'em. Bah! It makes me sick. You heard that poor prune just now? He'll go beetling over at five thousand just to show he knows more about it than we do. Well, he'll be pushing up the Flanders poppies by this time tomorrow night unless a miracle happens. He'll take his boys with him, that's the curse of it. Not one of 'em'll ever get back—you watch it,' he concluded, bitterly.

'We can't let 'em do that,' protested Wilkinson.

'What can we do?'

'I was just thinking.'

'I've got it,' cried Biggles. 'Let them be the bait to bring the Huns down. With your S.E.s and our Camels together we'll knock the spots off that Hun circus. How many S.E.s can you raise?'

'Eight or nine.'

'Right. You ask your C.O. and let me know tonight. I'll ask Major Mullen for all the Camels we can get in the air. That should even things up a bit; we'll be strong enough to take on anything the Huns can send against us. I'll meet you over Mossyface at six. How's that?'

'Suits me. I hope it's a fine day,' yawned Wilkinson.

The show turned out to be a bigger one than Biggles anticipated. Major Mullen had decided to lead the entire Squadron himself, not so much on account of the possibility of the American Squadron being massacred, as because he realised the necessity of massing his machines to meet the new menace.

Thus it came about that the morning following his conversation with Wilkinson found Biggles leading his Flight behind the C.O. On his right was 'A' Flight, led by Mahoney, and on his left 'B' Flight, with MacLaren at their head. Each Flight comprised three machines, and these, with Major Mullen's red cowled Camel, made ten in all. Major Sharp, commanding the S.E.5. Squadron, had followed Major Mullen's example, and from time to time Biggles looked upwards and backwards to where a formation of nine tiny dots, 6,000 feet above them, showed where the S.E.s were watching and waiting. A concerted plan of action had been decided upon, and Biggles impatiently awaited its consummation.

Where were the Americans? He asked himself the question for the tenth time; they were a long time showing up. Where was the Boche circus? Sooner or later there was bound to be a clash, and Biggles thrilled at the thought of the coming dog-fight.

It was a glorious day; not a cloud broke the serenity of the summer sky. Biggles kept his eyes downwards, knowing that the S.E.s would prevent molestation from above. Suddenly, a row of minute moving objects caught his eye, and he stared in amazement. Then he swore. A formation of nine Spads was crossing the line far below. 'The fools; the unutterable lunatics!' he growled. 'They can't be an inch higher than four thousand. They must think they own the sky, and they haven't even seen us yet. Oh, well, they'll wake up presently, or I'm no judge.'

The Spad Squadron was heading out straight into enemy sky, and Biggles watched them with amused curiosity, uncertain as to whether to admire their nerve or curse their stupidity. 'They must think it's easy,' he commented grimly, as his lynx-eyed leader altered his course slightly to follow the Americans.

Where were the Huns? He held his hand, at arm's length, over the sun, and extending his fingers squinted through the slits between them. He could see nothing, but the glare was terrific and might have concealed a hundred machines.

'They're there, I'll bet my boots,' muttered the Flight-Commander; 'they are just letting those poor boobs wade right into the custard. How they must be laughing!'

Suddenly he stiffened in his seat. The major was rocking his wings—pointing. Biggles followed the outstretched finger and caught his breath. Six brightly painted machines were going down in an almost vertical dive behind the Spads. Albatrosses!

He lifted his hand high above his head, and then, in accordance with the plan, pushed the stick forward and, with Batson and Healy on either side, tore down diagonally to cut off the enemy planes. He knew that most of the Hun circus was still above, somewhere, waiting for the right moment to come down. How long would they wait before coming down, thus bringing the rest of the Camels and S.E.s down into the mix-up with them? Not long, he hoped, or he might find his hands full, for he could not count upon the inexperienced Spad pilots for help.

The Spad Squadron had not altered its course, and Biggles' lip curled as he realised that even now they had not seen the storm brewing above them. Ah, they knew now! The Albatrosses were shooting, and the Spads swerved violently, like a school of minnows at the sudden presence of a pike. In a moment formation was lost as they scattered in all directions. Biggles sucked in his breath quickly as a Spad burst into flames and dropped like a stone. He was among them now; a red-bellied machine appeared through his sights and he pressed his triggers viciously, cursing a Spad that nearly collided with him.

A green Albatross came at him head-on, and, as he charged it, another with a blue-and-white checked fuselage sent a stream of tracer through his top plane. The green machine swerved and he flung the Camel round behind it; but the checked machine had followed him and he had to pull up in a wild zoom to escape the hail of lead it spat at him.

'Strewth!' grunted Biggles, as his wind-screen flew to pieces. 'This is getting too hot. My gosh! what a mess!'

A Spad and an Albatross, locked together, careered earthwards in a flat spin. A Camel, spinning viciously, whirled past him, and another Albatross, wrapped in a sheet of flame, flashed past his nose, the doomed pilot leaping into space even as it passed.

Biggles snatched a swift glance upwards. A swarm of Albatrosses were dropping like vultures out of the sky into the fight; he had a fleeting glimpse of other machines far above and then he turned again to the work on hand. Where were the Spads? Ah, there was one, on the tail of an Albatross. He tore after it, but the Spad pilot saw him and waved him away. Biggles grinned. 'Go to it, laddie,' he yelled exultantly, but a frown swept the grin from his face as a jazzed machine darted in behind the Spad and poured in a murderous stream of lead. Biggles shot down on the tail of the Hun. The Spad pilot saw his danger and twisted sideways to escape, but an invisible cord seemed to hold the Albatross to the tail of the American machine. Biggles took the jazzed machine in his sights and raked it from end to end in a long deadly burst. There was no question of missing at that range; the enemy pilot slumped forward in his seat and the machine went to pieces in the air.

The Spad suddenly stood up on its tail and sent two white pencils of tracer across Biggles' nose at something he could not see. A Hun, upside down, went past him so closely that he instinctively flinched.

'Holy smoke!' muttered Biggles. 'He saved *me* that time; that evens things up.'

His lips closed in a straight line; a bunch of six Albatrosses were coming at him together. Biggles fired one shot, and went as cold as ice as his gun jammed. Bullets were smashing through his machine when a cloud of S.E.s appeared between him and the Hun, and he breathed again.

'Lord, what a dog-fight,' he said again, as he looked around to see what was happening. Most of the enemy planes were in full retreat, pursued by the S.E.s. Two Camels and two Albatrosses were still circling some distance away and four more Camels were rallying above him. Biggles saw the lone Spad flying close to him. Seven or eight crashed machines were on the ground, two blazing furiously, but whether they were Spads or Camels he couldn't tell.

He pushed up his goggles and beckoned to the Spad pilot, whom he now recognised as his acquaintance of the previous day, to come closer.

The American waved gaily, and together they started after the Camels, led by Major Mullen's red cowling, now heading for the line.

Biggles landed with the Spad still beside him; he mopped the burnt castor-oil off his face and walked across to meet the pilot. The American held out his hand. 'I just dropped in to shake hands,' he said. 'Now I must be getting back to our field to see how many of the outfit got home. I'd like to know you better; maybe you'll give me a tip or two.'

'I can't tell you much after what you've seen today,' laughed Biggles, turning to wave to an S.E.5, which had swung low over them and then proceeded on its way.

'Who's that?' asked the American.

'That's Wilks, the big stiff you saw with me yesterday,' replied Biggles. 'He's a good scout. He'll be at the Hôtel de Ville tonight for certain; so shall I. Do you feel like coming along to tear a chop or two?'

'Sure,' agreed the Spad pilot enthusiastically.

3
THE ZONE CALL

'OH, my batman awoke me from my bed;
I'd had a thick night and I'd got a sore head;
   So I said to myself,
   To myself, I said,
Oh, I haven't got a hope in the mo-orning.

So I went to the sheds to examine my gun,
And then my engine I tried to run,
   But the revs she ga-ave.
   Were a thousand and one.
So I hadn't got a hope in the mo-orning.'

The words of the old R.F.C. song, roared by forty youthful voices to the tune of 'John Peel', drowned the accompaniment of the cracked mess piano in spite of the strenuous efforts of the pianist to make his notes audible.

Biggles pushed the hair off his forehead. 'Lord, it's hot in here; I'm going outside for a breath of air,' he said to Wilkinson of 287

Squadron, who had come over for the periodical party.

The two officers rose and strolled slowly towards the door. It was still daylight, but a thick layer of thundercloud hung low in the sky, making the atmosphere oppressive.

> 'Oh, we were escorting "twenty-two,"
> Hadn't got a notion what to do,
>   So we shot down a Spa-ad,
>   And an S.E. too,
> For we hadn't——'

'Stop!' Biggles had bounded back into the centre of the room and held up his arms for silence. 'Hark!'

At the expression on his face a sudden hush fell upon the assembly, and the next instant forty officers had stiffened into attitudes of tense expectancy as a low vibrating hum filled the air. It was the unmistakable 'pour-vous' of a Mercédès aero-engine, low down, not far away.

'A Hun!' The silence was broken by a wild yell and the crash of fallen chairs as Biggles darted through the open door and streaked like a madman for the sheds, shouting orders as he went. The ack-emmas had needed no warning; a Camel was already on the tarmac; others were being wheeled out with feverish speed. Capless and goggleless, tunic thrown open at the throat, Biggles made a flying leap into the cockpit of the first Camel, and within a minute, in spite of Wilkinson's plaintive 'Wait for me', was tearing down-wind across the sun-baked aerodrome in a cloud of dust.

He was in the air, climbing back up over the sheds, before the second machine was ready to take off. The clouds were low, and at 1,000 feet the grey mist was swirling in his slipstream. He could no longer hear the enemy plane, for the roar of his Bentley Rotary drowned all other sound. He pushed his joystick forward for a moment to gather speed and then pulled it back in a swift zoom. Bursting out into the sunlight above he literally flung the machine round in a lightning righthand turn to avoid crashing into a Pfalz scout, painted vivid scarlet with white stripes behind the pilot's seat.

'My gosh!' muttered Biggles, startled. 'I nearly rammed him.'

He was round in a second, warming his guns as he came. The Pfalz had turned, too, and was now circling erratically in a desperate effort to avoid the glittering pencil lines of tracer that started at the muzzles of Biggles' guns and ended at the tail of the Boche machine. The German pilot made no attempt to retaliate, but concentrated on dodging the hail of lead, waving his left arm above his head. Biggles ceased firing and looked about him suspiciously, but not another enemy machine was in sight.

'Come on; let's get it over,' he muttered, as he thumbed his triggers again; but the Boche put his nose down and dived through the cloud, Biggles close behind him.

They emerged below the cloud bank in the same relative positions, and it at once became obvious that the German intended to land on the aerodrome, but a brisk burst of machine-gun fire from the Lewis guns in front of the mess caused him to change his mind; instead, he hopped over the hedge and made a clumsy landing in the next field. Biggles landed close behind him and ran towards the pilot, now struggling to get a box of matches from his inside pocket to fire the machine.

Biggles seized him by the collar and threw him clear.

'Speak English?' he snapped.

'Yes.'

'What's the matter with you? Haven't you got any guns?' sneered the British pilot, noting the German's pale face.

'Nein, no guns,' said the German quickly.

'What?'

The German shrugged his shoulders and pointed. A swift glance showed Biggles that such was indeed his case.

'Great Scott!' he cried, aghast. 'You people running short of weapons or something? We'd better lend you some.'

'I vas lost,' said the German pilot resignedly. 'I am to take a new Pfalz to Lille, but the clouds—I cannot see. The benzine is nearly finished. You come—I come down, so.'

'Tough luck,' admitted Biggles as a crowd of officers and ack-

emmas arrived on the scene at the double. 'Well, come and have
a drink—you've butted into a party.'

'Huh! No wonder your crowd scores if you go about shooting
at delivery pilots,' grinned Wilkinson, who had just landed.

'You go and stick your face in an oil sump, Wilks,' cried
Biggles hotly. 'How did I know he hadn't any guns?'

Biggles sprang lightly from the squadron tender and looked at
the deserted aerodrome in astonishment. It was the morning
following his encounter with the unarmed Pfalz. For some days
a tooth had been troubling him, and on the advice of the
Medical Officer he had been to Clarmes to have the offending
molar extracted. He had not hurried back, as the M.O. had
forbidden him to fly that day, and now he had returned to find
every machine except his own in the air.

'Where have they all gone, Flight?' he asked the Flight-
Sergeant.

'Dunno, sir. The C.O. came out in a hurry about an hour ago
and they all went off together,' replied the N.C.O.

'Just my luck,' grumbled Biggles. 'Trust something to happen
when I'm away for a few hours! Oh, well!'

He made his way to the Squadron office, where he found
Tyler, commonly known as 'Wat', the Recording Officer, busy
with some papers.

'What's on, Wat?' asked Biggles.

'Escort.'

'Escorting what?'

'You remember that Hun you got yesterday?'

Biggles nodded.

'Well, apparently he was three sheets in the wind when Wing
came and fetched him. He blabbed a whole lot of news to the
Intelligence people. This is what he told 'em. He said that three
new Staffels were being formed at Lagnicourt. A whole lot of
new machines were being sent there; in fact, when he was there
two days ago, over thirty machines were being assembled.'

'Funny, him letting a thing like that drop,' interrupted
Biggles. 'He didn't strike me as being blotto, either. He drank

practically nothing.'

'Well, Wing says he was as tight as a lord, and bragged that the three new circuses were going to wipe us off the map, so they decided to nip the plot in the bud. They've sent every machine they can get into the air with a full load of bombs to fan the whole caboodle sky-high—all the Fours, Nines, and Biffs[1] have gone and even the R.E.8s they can spare from Art. Obs.[2] Two-eight-seven, two-nine-nine and our people are escorting 'em.'

'Well, they can have it,' said Biggles cheerfully. 'Escorting's a mouldy business, anyway. Thanks, Wat.'

He strolled out on to the aerodrome, gently rubbing his lacerated jaw, and catching sight of the German machine now standing on the tarmac made his way slowly towards it. He examined it with interest, for a complete ready-to-fly-away Boche machine was a *rara avis*. He slipped his hand into the map case, but the maps had been removed. His fingers felt and closed around a torn piece of paper at the bottom of the lining; it was creased as if it had been roughly torn off and used to mark a fold in a map. Biggles glanced at it disinterestedly, noting some typewritten matter on it, but as it was in German and conveyed nothing to him he was about to throw it away when the Flight-Sergeant passed near him.

'Do you speak German, Flight?' called Biggles.

'No, sir, but Thompson does; he used to be in the Customs Office or something like that,' replied the N.C.O.

'Ask him to come here a minute, will you?' said Biggles.

'Can you tell me what that says?' he asked a moment later, as an ack-emma approached him and saluted.

The airman took the paper and looked at it for a minute without speaking. 'It's an extract from some orders, sir,' he said at length. 'The first part of it's gone, but this is what it says, roughly speaking: "With effect"—there's a bit gone there—"any flieger"—flyer, that is—"Falling into the hands of the enemy will therefore repeat that three Jagdstaffels are being

---

[1] *Bristol Fighters.*

[2] *Artillery Observation.*

assembled at Lagni——" Can't read the place, sir. "By doing so, he will be doing service by assisting"—can't read that, sir. It ends, "Expires on July 21st at twelve, midnight. This order must on no account be taken into the air." That's all, sir.'

'Read that again,' said Biggles slowly.

After the airman had obeyed, Biggles returned to the Squadron office deep in thought. He put a call through to Wing Headquarters and asked for Colonel Raymond.

'That you, sir? Bigglesworth here,' he said, as the Colonel's crisp voice answered him. 'About this big raid, sir. Do you mind if I ask whether you know for certain that these Boche machines are at Lagnicourt?'

'Yes; we made reconnaissance at dawn, and the observer reported several machines in various stages of erection on the tarmac. Why do you ask?'

'I've just found a bit of paper in the Pfalz that Boche brought over. I can't read it because it's in German, but I've had it translated, and it looks as if that Hun had orders to tell you that tale. Will you send over for it?'

'I'll send a messenger for it right away, but I shouldn't worry about it; the Huns are there; we've seen them. Goodbye.'

Biggles hung the receiver up slowly and turned to Wat, who had listened to the conversation.

You'll get shot one day ringing up the Wing like that!' he said reprovingly.

'It would be a deuce of a joke to send forty machines to drop twenty thousand quid's worth of bombs on a lot of obsolete spare parts,' mused Biggles. 'But there's more in it than that. The Boche want our machines out of the way. Why? That's what I want to know. Lagnicourt lies thirty miles north-west of here. I fancy it wouldn't be a bad idea if somebody went and had a dekko what the Huns were doing in the north-east. Even my gross intelligence tells me that when a Hun is told what he's got to say when he's shot down there's something fishy about it.'

'The M.O. says you're not to fly today,' protested the R.O.

'Rot! What the deuce does he think I fly with, my teeth?' asked Biggles sarcastically. 'See you later.'

Within ten minutes Biggles was in the air, heading into the blue roughly to the north-east of the aerodrome. An unusual amount of archie marked his progress and he noticed it with satisfaction, for it tended to confirm his suspicions.

'What ho!' he addressed the invisible gunner. 'So you don't want any Peeping Toms about today, eh?' Want to discourage me.'

The archie became really hot, and twice he had to circle to spoil the gunner's aim. He kept a watchful eye on the ground below, but saw nothing unusual.

He passed over an R.E.8 spotting for the artillery, manfully plodding its monotonous figure-of-eight 3,000 feet below, and nodded sympathetically. Presently he altered his course a little westerly and the archie faded away. 'Don't mind me going that way, eh? Well, let's try the other way again,' he muttered. Instantly the air was thick with black, oily bursts of smoke, and Biggles nodded understandingly. 'So I'm getting warm, am I?' he mused. 'They might as well say so; what imaginations they've got.'

Straight ahead of him, lying like a great dark green stain across the landscape, lay the forest of Duvigny. Keeping a watchful eye above for enemy aircraft, he looked at it closely, but there was no sign of anything unusual about its appearance.

'I wonder if that's it?' he mused, deep in thought. 'I could soon find out; it's risky, but it's the only way.'

He knew what all old pilots knew, a trick the German pilots had learned early in the war, when vast numbers of Russian troops were concealed in the forests along the north-German frontier; and that was, that if an enemy plane flew low enough, the troops, no matter how well hidden, would reveal their presence by shooting at it. Not even strict orders could prevent troops from firing at an enemy aeroplane within range.

He pushed his stick forward and went roaring down at the forest. At 1,000 feet he started pulling out, but not before he had seen several hundred twinkling fireflies among the greenery. The fireflies were, of course, the flashes of rifles aimed at him. In one place a number of men had run out into a little clearing and started firing, but an officer had driven them back.

'So that's it, is it?' muttered Biggles, thrilling with excitement.
'I wonder how many of them there are.'

Time and time again he dived low over different parts of the
forest and each time the twinkling flashes betrayed the hidden
troops. His wings were holed in many places, but he heeded
them not. It would take a lucky shot from a rifle to bring him
down.

'My gosh!' he muttered, as he pulled up at the far end of the
forest, after his tenth dive. 'The wood's full of 'em. There must
be fifty thousand men lying in that timber, and it's close to the
line. They're massing for a big attack. What did those orders
say? July 21st? That's tomorrow. They'll attack this afternoon,
or at latest tonight. I'd better be getting out of this. So that's why
they didn't want any of our machines prowling about.'

He made for the line, toying with the fine adjustment to get
the very last rev. out of his engine. He could see the R.E.8 still
tapping out its 'G.G.' (fire) signal to the gunners and marking
the position of the falling shells, and the sight of it gave him an
idea. The R.E.8 was fitted with wireless; he was not. If only he
could get the pilot to send out a zone call on that wood, his work
was done.[1]

Biggles flew close to the R.E.8, signalling to attract attention.
How could he tell them, that was the problem? He flew closer
and gesticulated wildly, jabbing downwards towards the wood,
and then tapping with his finger on an invisible key. The pilot
and observer eyed him stupidly and Biggles shrugged his

[1] *A Zone Call was a special call from an aircraft to the artillery and was only used in very
exceptional circumstances. When the zone call was tapped out by the wireless operator it
was followed by the pin-point of the target. Military maps were divided into squares and
smaller squares, each square numbered and lettered. By this means it was possible to name
any spot on the map instantly. When a zone call was sent out, every weapon of every calibre
within range, directed rapid fire on the spot, and this may have meant that hundreds of guns
opened up at once on the same spot. The result can be better imagined than described.
Obviously such treatment was terribly expensive, costing possibly £10,000 a minute while it
lasted, and only exceptional circumstances, such as a long line of transport, or a large body
of troops, warranted the call. There was a story in France of a new officer who, in
desperation, sent out a zone call on a single archie battery that was worrying him. He was
court-martialled and sent home.*

shoulders in despair. Then inspiration struck him. He knew the morse code, of course, for every pilot had to pass a test in it before going to France. He flew close beside the R.E.8, raised his arm above his head and, with some difficulty, sent a series of dots and dashes. He saw the observer nod understandingly and grab a notebook to take down the message. Biggles started his signal. Dash, dash, dot, dot—Z, dash, dash, dash—O, dash, dot—N, dot—E. He continued the performance until he had sent the words, 'Zone Call, Wood,' and then stabbed viciously at the wood with his forefinger. He saw the observer lean forward and have a quick, difficult conversation with the pilot, who nodded. The observer raised both thumbs in the air and bent over his buzzer. Biggles turned away to watch the result.

Within a minute he saw the first shell explode in the centre of the wood. Another followed it, then another and another. In five minutes the place was an inferno of fire, smoke, flying timber and hurtling steel, and thousands of figures, clad in the field-grey of the German infantry, were swarming out into the open to escape the pulverizing bombardment. He could see the officers attempting to get the men into some sort of order, but there was no stemming that wild panic. They poured into the communication trenches, and others, unable to find cover, were flinging away their equipment and running for their lives.

'Holy mackerel, what a sight!' murmured Biggles. 'What a pity the Colonel isn't here to see it.'

A Bristol Fighter appeared in the sky above him, heading for the scene of carnage. The observer was leaning over the side and the pilot's arm was steadily moving up and down as he exposed plate after plate in his camera.

'He'll have to believe me when he sees those photographs, though,' thought Biggles. 'Well, I should think I've saved our chaps in the line a lot of trouble,' he soliloquised, as he turned to congratulate the R.E.8 crew, but the machine was far away. Biggles' Camel suddenly rocked violently and he realised the reason for the R.E.8's swift departure. He was right in the line of fire of the artillery and the shells were passing near him. He put his nose down in a fright and sped towards home in the wake of the R.E.8.

He landed on the aerodrome to find the escorting Camels had returned, and the pilots greeted him noisily.

'Had a nice trip, chaps?' inquired Biggles.

'No,' growled Mahoney; 'didn't see a Hun the whole way out and home. These escorts bore me stiff. What have you been doing?'

'Oh, having a little fun and games on my own.'

'Who with?'

'With the German Army,' said Biggles lightly.

4
THE DECOY

BIGGLES landed and taxied quickly up to the sheds. 'Are Mr. Batson and Mr. Healy home yet?' he asked the Flight Sergeant, as he climbed stiffly from the cockpit. 'We got split up among the clouds near Ariet after a dog-fight with a bunch of Albatri.'

'Mr Healy came in about five minutes ago, sir; he's just gone along to the mess, but I haven't seen anything of Mr. Batson,' replied the N.C.O.

Biggles lit a cigarette and eyed the eastern sky anxiously. He was annoyed that his flight had been broken up, although after a dog-fight it was no uncommon occurrence for machines to come home independently. He breathed a sigh of relief as the musical hum of a Bentley Rotary reached his ears, and started to walk slowly towards the mess, glancing from time to time over his shoulder at the now rapidly approaching Camel. Suddenly he paused in his stride and looked at the wind-stocking.

'What's the young fool doing, trying to land cross-wind?' he growled, and turned round to watch the landing.

The Camel had flattened out rather too high for a good landing, and dropped quickly as it lost flying speed. The machine bumped—bumped again as the wheels bounced, and then swung round in a wide semi-circle as it ran to a standstill not fifty yards away.

Biggles opened his mouth to shout a caustic remark at the pilot, but his teeth suddenly closed with a snap, and the next instant he was running wildly towards the machine, followed by the Flight-Sergeant and several ack-emmas. He reached the Camel first, and, foot in the stirrup, swung himself up to the cockpit; one glance and he was astride the fuselage and unbuckling the safety-belt around the limp figure in the pilot's seat.

'Gently, Flight-Sergeant, gently,' he said softly, as they lifted the stricken pilot from his seat and laid him carefully on the grass. Biggles caught his breath as he saw an ugly red stain on his hand that had supported the wounded pilot's back. 'How did they get you, kid?' he choked, dropping on to his knees and bending close over the ashen face.

'I—got—the—bus—home—Biggles,' whispered Batson eagerly.

'Sure you did,' nodded Biggles, forcing a smile. 'What was it, laddie—archie?'

The pilot looked at his Flight-Commander with wide-open eyes. 'My own fault,' he whispered faintly . . . 'I went down— after Rumpler—with green—tail. Thought I'd—be—clever.' He smiled wanly. 'Albatrosses—waiting—upstairs. It was— trap. They got me—Biggles. I'm going—topsides.'

'Not you,' said Biggles firmly, waving away Batson's mechanic, who was muttering incoherently.

'It's getting dark early; where are you—Biggles——? I can't see you,' went on the wounded man, his hand groping blindly for the other pilot.

'I'm here, old boy. I'm with you; don't worry,' crooned Biggles, like a mother to an ailing child.

'Not worrying. Get that—Rumpler—for me—Biggles.'

'I'll get him, Batty; I'll get the swine, never fear,' replied Biggles, his lips trembling.

For a minute there was silence, broken only by the sound of a man sobbing in the distance. The wounded pilot opened his eyes, already glazed by the film of death.

'It's getting—devilish—dark—Biggles,' he whispered

faintly, 'dev—lish—da—ark——'

The M.O. arrived at the double and lifted Biggles slowly, but firmly, to his feet. 'Run along now, old man,' he said kindly, after a swift glance at the man on the ground. 'The boy's gone.'

For a moment longer Biggles stood looking down through a mist of tears at the face of the man who had been tied to him by such bonds of friendship as only war can tie.

'I'll get him for you, Batty,' he said through his teeth, and turning, walked slowly towards the sheds.

The Rumpler with the green tail was an old menace in the sky well known to Biggles. Of a slow, obsolescent type, it looked 'easy meat' to the beginner unaware of its sinister purpose, which was to act as a tempting bait to lure just such pilots beneath the waiting Spandau guns of the shark-like Albatrosses. Once, many months before, Biggles had nearly fallen into the trap. He was going down on to an old German two-seater when a premonition of danger made him glance back over his shoulder, and the sight that greeted his eyes sent him streaking for his own side of the line as if a host of devils were on his tail, as, indeed, they were.

Such death-traps were fairly common, but they no longer deceived him for an instant. 'Never go down after a Hun,' was the warning dinned into the ears of every new arrival in France by those who knew the pitfalls that awaited the unwary—alas, how often in vain.

So the old pilots, who had bought their experience, went on, and watched the younger ones come and go, unless, like Biggles, they were fortunate enough to escape, in which case the lesson was seldom forgotten.

And now the green-tailed Rumpler had killed Batty, or had led him to his doom—at least, that was what it amounted to; so reasoned Biggles. That Batson had been deceived by the trap he did not for one moment believe. The lad—to use his own words—'tried to be clever', and in attempting to destroy the decoy had failed, where failure could have only tragic results; and this was the machine that Biggles had pledged himself to destroy.

He had no delusions as to the dangers of the task he had undertaken. Batson's disastrous effort was sufficient proof of that. First, he must find the decoy; that should not be difficult. Above it, biding their time, would be the school of Albatrosses, eyes glued downwards, waiting for the victim to walk into the trap.

Biggles sat alone in a corner of 'C' Flight hangar and wrestled with the problem, unconscious of the anxious glances and whispered consultations of his mechanics. The death of Batson had shaken him badly, and he was sick, sick of the war, sick of flying, sick of life itself. What did it matter, anyway, he mused. His turn would come, sooner or later, that was certain. He didn't attempt to deceive himself on that point. He made up his mind suddenly and called the Flight-Sergeant to him in tones that brooked no delay.

'Let's go and look at Mr. Batson's machine,' he said tersely.

'I have examined it, sir,' said the N.C.O. quickly. 'It's still O.K. Hardly touched; just one burst through the back of the fuselage, down through the pilot's seat and through the floor.'

'Good. I'll take it,' said Biggles coldly. 'Come and give me a swing.'

'But you're not going to—not going——?'

'Do what you're told,' snapped Biggles icily. 'I'm flying that machine from now on—until——' Biggles looked the Flight-Sergeant in the eyes—'until—well, you know——' he concluded.

The N.C.O. nodded. 'Very good, sir,' he said briskly.

Five minutes later Biggles took off in the dead pilot's Camel; the Flight-Sergeant and a silent group of ack-emmas watched his departure. 'Mad as a 'atter. Gawd 'elp the 'Un as gets in 'is way today,' observed a tousle-headed Cockney fitter.

'Get back to your work,' roared the Flight-Sergeant. 'What are you all gaping at?'

Major Mullen hurried along the tarmac. 'Who's just taken off in that machine, Flight-Sergeant?' he asked curtly.

'Mr. Bigglesworth, sir.'

The C.O. gazed after the rapidly-disappearing Camel sadly. 'I see,' he said slowly, and then again, 'I see.'

The finding of the green-tailed Rumpler proved a longer job than Biggles anticipated. At the end of a week he was still searching, still flying Batson's machine, and every pilot within fifty miles knew of his quest. Major Mullen had protested; in fact, he had done everything except definitely order Biggles out of the machine; but, being a wise man and observing the high pressure under which his pilot was living, he refrained from giving an order that he knew would be broken. So Biggles continued his search unhindered.

The Rumpler had become an obsession with him. For eight hours a day he hunted the sky between Lille and Cambrai for it, and at night, in his sleep, he shot it down in flames a hundred times. He had become morose, and hardly even spoke to Mac or Mahoney, the other Flight Commanders, who watched him anxiously and secretly helped him in his search. He was due for leave, but refused to accept it. He fought many battles and, although he hardly bothered to confirm his victories, his score mounted rapidly. His combat reports were brief and contained nothing but the barest facts.

No man could stand such a pace for long. The M.O. knew it, but did nothing, although he hoped and prayed that the pilot might find his quarry before his nerves collapsed like a pack of cards.

One morning Biggles had just refuelled after a two-hour patrol, and was warming up his engine again, when a D.H.9 landed, and the observer hurried towards the sheds. Dispassionately, Biggles saw him speak to the Flight-Sergeant and the N.C.O. point in his direction. The observer turned and crossed quickly to the Camel.

'Are you Bigglesworth?' he shouted above the noise of the engine.

Biggles nodded.

'I hear you're looking for that green-tailed Rumpler?'

Biggles nodded again eagerly.

'I saw it ten minutes ago, near Talcourt-le-Chateau.'

'Thanks,' said Biggles briefly, and pushed the throttle open. He saw the Rumpler before he reached the lines; at least, he saw the wide circles of white archie bursts that followed its wandering course. The British archie was white, and German archie black, so he knew that the plane was a German and from its locality suspected it to be the Rumpler. A closer inspection showed him that his supposition was correct. It was just over its own side of the lines, at about 8,000 feet, ostensibly engaged on artillery observation. Biggles edged away and studied the sky above it closely, but he could see nothing. He climbed steadily, keeping the Boche machine in sight, but making no attempt to approach it, and looked upwards again for the escorting Albatrosses which he knew were there; but he was still unable to discover them.

'If I didn't know for certain that they were there, I should say there wasn't a Hun in the sky,' he muttered, as he headed south-east, keeping parallel with the trenches. With his eye still on the Rumpler he could have named the very moment when the Boche observer spotted him, for the machine suddenly began to edge towards him as though unaware of his presence, and seemingly unconsciously making of itself an ideal subject for attack by a scout pilot.

To an old hand like Biggles the invitation was too obvious, and even without his knowledge of the trap the action would have made him suspiciously alert. Unless he was the world's worst observer, the man in the back seat of the black-crossed machine would not have failed to see him, in which case he should have lost no time in placing as great a distance as possible between himself and a dangerous adversary; for the first duty of a two-seater pilot was to do his job and get home, leaving the fighting to machines designed for the purpose. Yet there was an old and comparatively unmanoeuvrable machine deliberately asking for trouble.

'Bah!' sneered Biggles, peeved to think he had been taken for a fool. 'Will you step into my parlour?' said the spider to the fly. Yes, you hound, I will, but it won't be through the front door.'

He looked upwards above the Rumpler, but the sun was in his eyes, so he held on his way, still climbing, and had soon left the Boche machine far below and behind him.

At 15,000 feet Biggles started to head into enemy sky, placing himself between the sun and the Rumpler, now a speck in the far distance. His roving eyes suddenly focused on a spot high above the enemy plane.

'So there you are,' he muttered grimly. 'How many? One—two—three'—he shifted his gaze still higher—'four—five—six—seven. Seven, in two layers, eh? Ought to be enough for a solitary Camel. Well, we'll see.'

He estimated the lowest Albatrosses to be at about his own height. The other four were a couple of thousand feet higher. With the disposition of the trap now apparent he proceeded in accordance with the line of action upon which he had decided. He had already placed himself 'in the sun', and in that position it was unlikely that he would be seen by any of the enemy pilots. He continued to climb until he was above the highest enemy formation, and then cautiously began to edge towards them, turning when they turned and keeping in a direct line with the sun.

He felt fairly certain that the crew of the Rumpler would ignore the possibility of danger from above on account of the escorting Albatrosses, and the pilots of the enemy scouts would have their eyes on the machine below. Upon these factors Biggles planned his attack. If he was able to approach unseen he would be able to make one lightning attack almost before the Huns were aware of his presence. If he was seen, his superior altitude should give him enough extra speed to reach the lines before he was caught.

He knew he would only have time for one burst at the Rumpler. If he missed there could be no question of staying for a second attempt, for the Albatrosses would be down on him like a pack of ravening wolves. The Rumpler was now flying almost directly over no-man's-land, and Biggles edged nearer, every nerve quivering like the flying wires of his Camel.

The decoy, confident of its escort, was slowly turning towards the British lines, and this was the moment for which Biggles had been waiting, for the end of his dive would see him over his own lines—either intact or as a shattered wreck. His lips were set in a straight line under the terrific strain of the impending action as he swung inwards until the Albatrosses were immediately between him and the Rumpler, and then he pointed his nose downwards. 'Come on, Batty, let's go,' he muttered huskily, and thrust the stick forward with both hands.

The top layer of Albatrosses seemed to float up towards him. Five hundred feet, one hundred feet, and still they had not seen him; he could see every detail of the machines and even the faces of the pilots. He went through the middle of them like a streak of lightning—down—down—down—he knew they were hard on his heels now, but he did not look back. They would have to pull out as he went through the second layer—or risk collision.

'Come on, you swine,' he rasped through set teeth, and went through the lower Albatrosses like a thunderbolt.

The Rumpler lay clear below; he could see the observer idly leaning over the side of the fuselage watching the ground. He took the machine in his sights, but held his fire, for he was still too far off for effective shooting. Down—down—down—a noise like a thousand devils shrieking in his ears, his head jammed tight against the head-rest under the frightful pressure.

At 200 feet he pressed his triggers, and his lips parted in a mirthless smile as he saw the tracers making a straight line through the centre of the Boche machine. The observer leapt round and then sank slowly on to the floor of the cockpit. The nose of the Rumpler jerked upwards, an almost certain sign that the pilot had been hit.

Biggles held his fire until the last fraction of a second, and only when collision seemed inevitable did he pull the stick back. His under-carriage seemed to graze the centre section of the Rumpler as he came out, and he bit his lips until the blood came as he waited for the rending crash that would tell him that his wings had folded up under the pressure of that frightful zoom. Before he had reached the top of it he had thrust the stick forward again and was zig-zagging across his own lines.

For the first time since he had started that heart-bursting dive he looked back. The Rumpler was nowhere in sight, but an involuntary yell broke from his lips as his eyes fell on two Albatrosses, one minus its top-plane, spinning wildly downwards; whether as the result of a collision or because they had cracked up in the dive he neither knew or cared. The five remaining Albatrosses were already turning back towards their own lines, followed by a furious bombardment of archie.

Where was the Rumpler? He looked downwards. Ah! He was just in time to see it crash behind the British front-line trench. Tiny ant-like figures were already crawling towards it, some looking upwards, waving to him.

Biggles smiled. 'Given the boys a treat anyway,' he thought, as he pushed up his goggles and passed his hand wearily over his face. A sound like a sob was drowned in the drone of the engine. 'Well, that's that,' he said to himself, and turned his nose for home.

The following morning, as the Sergeant-Major in charge of the burying party at Lagnicourt Cemetery entered the gate, his eye fell on a curious object that had been firmly planted on a new mound of earth, at the opposite end to the usual little white cross.

'What the devil's that thing, Corporal?' he said. 'It wasn't there yesterday, I'll swear.'

The Corporal took a few steps nearer.

'That's where they planted that R.F.C. wallah last week, Sergeant-Major,' he replied. 'Looks to me like a smashed aeroplane propeller.'

'All right, let it alone. I expect some of his pals shoved it there. For-ward—ma—arch!'

5

THE BOOB

MAHONEY, on his way to the sheds to take his Flight off for an early Ordinary Patrol, paused in his stride as his eye fell on Biggles leaning in an attitude of utter boredom against the doorpost of the officers' mess.

'Why so pensive, young aviator?' he smiled. 'Has Mr. Cox grabbed your pay to square up the overdraft?' he added, as he caught sight of an open letter in the other's hand.

'Worse than that; much, much worse,' replied Biggles. 'Couldn't be worse, in fact. What do you think of this?' He held out the letter.

'I haven't the time to read it, laddie. What's the trouble?'

'Oh, it's from an elderly female relative of mine. She says her son—my cousin—is in the R.F.C. on his way to France. She's pulled the wires at the Air Board for the Pool to send him to 266, as she feels sure I can take care of him. She asks me to see that he changes his laundry regularly, doesn't drink, doesn't get mixed up with the French minxes, and a dozen other "doesn'ts." My gosh! it's a bit thick; what does she think this is—a prep. school?'

'What's he like?'

'I don't know, it's year since I saw him; and if he's anything like the little horror he was then heaven help us—and him. His Christian names are Algernon Montgomery, and that's just what he looked like—a slice of warmed-up death wrapped in velvet and ribbons.'

'Sounds pretty ghastly. When's he coming?'

'Today, apparently. His name's on the notice-board. The old girl had the brass face to write to the C.O., and he's posted him to my Flight—in revenge, I expect.'

'Too bad,' replied Mahoney, sympathetically. 'Well, go and get the letter done, telling her how bravely he died, and forget about it. There comes the tender now—see you later.'

Biggles, left alone, watched the tender pull up and discharge two new pilots and their kit; he had no difficulty in recognizing his new charge, who approached eagerly.

'You're Biggles—aren't you? I know you from the photo at home.'

The matured edition of the youth was even more unprepossessing than Biggles expected. His uniform was dirty, his hair long, his face, which wore a permanent expression of amused surprise, was a mass of freckles.

'My name's Captain Bigglesworth,' said the Flight-Commander coldly. 'You are posted to my Flight. Get your kit into your room, report to the Squadron office, and then come back here; I want to have a word with you.'

'Sorry, sir,' said Algernon apologetically; 'of course, I forgot.'

A few minutes later he rejoined Biggles in the mess. 'What'll you have to drink?' invited Biggles.

'Have you any ginger ale?'

'I shouldn't think so,' replied Biggles. 'We don't get much demand for it. Have you any ginger ale, Adams?' he asked the mess waiter. 'I'll have the usual.'

'Yes, sir, I think I've got one somewhere, if I can find it,' replied the waiter, looking at the newcomer curiously.

'Sit down and let's talk,' said Biggles, when the drinks had been served. 'How much flying have you done?'

'Fourteen hours on Avros and ten on Camels.'

'Ten hours, eh?' mused Biggles. 'Ten hours. So they're sending 'em out here with ten hours now. My gosh! Now listen,' he went on; 'I want you to forget those ten hours. This is where you'll learn to *fly*—they can't teach you at home. If you live a week you'll begin to know something about it. I don't want to discourage you, but most people who come out here live on an average twenty-four hours. If you survive a week you're fairly safe. I can't teach you much; nobody can; you'll find things out for yourself. First of all, never cross the line alone under 10,000 feet—not yet, anyway. Never go more than a couple of miles over unless you are with a formation. Never go down after a Hun. If you see a Hun looking like easy meat, make for home, and if that Hun fires a Very light, kick out your foot and slam the stick over as if somebody was already shooting at you. Act first and think afterwards, otherwise you may not have time to act. Never leave your formation on any account—you'll never get back into it if you do, unless it's your lucky day; the sky is full of Huns waiting to pile up their scores and it's people like you that make it possible. Keep your eyes peeled and never stop looking for one instant. Watch the sun and never fly straight for more than two minutes at a time if you can't see what's up in the sun. Turn suddenly as if you've seen something—and you may see something. Never mind archie—it never hits anything. Watch out for balloon cables if you have to come home under 5,000. If a Hun gets on your tail, don't try to get away. Go to him. Try to bite him as if you were a mad dog; try to ram him—he'll get out of your way then. Never turn if you are meeting a Hun head-on; it isn't done. Don't shoot outside 200 feet—it's a waste of ammunition. Keep away from clouds, and, finally, keep away from balloons. It's suicide. If you want to commit suicide, do it here, because then someone else can have your bus. If you see anything you don't understand, let it alone; never let your curiosity get the better of you. If I wave my hand above my head—make for home. That means everbody for himself. That's all. Can you remember that?'

'I think so.'

'Right. Then let's go and have a look at the line and I'll show you the landmarks. If I shake my wings it means a Hun—I may go for it. If I do, you stay upstairs and watch me. If anything goes wrong—go straight home. When in doubt—go home, that's the motto. Got that?'

'Yes, sir.'

They took off together and circled over the aerodrome, climbing steadily for height; when his altimeter showed 6,000 feet Biggles headed for the line. It was not an ideal day for observation. Great masses of detached cumulus cloud were sailing majestically eastward and through these Biggles threaded his way, the other Camel in close attendance. Sometimes through the clouds they could see the ground, and from time to time Biggles pointed out salient landmarks—a chalk-pit—stream—or wood. Gradually the recognisable features became fewer until they were lost in a scene of appalling desolation, criss-crossed with a network of fine lines scarred by pools of stagnant water.

Biggles beckoned the other Camel nearer and jabbed downwards. Explanation was unnecessary. They were looking down at no-man's-land. Suddenly Biggles rocked his wings violently and pointed, and without further warning shot across the nose of the other Camel and dived steeply into a cloud. He pulled out underneath and looked around quickly, but of his companion there was no sign. He circled the cloud, climbing swiftly, and looked anxiously to right and left, choked back an expletive as his eye fell on what he sought. Far away, almost out of sight in the enemy sky, were five straight-winged machines; hard on their heels was a lone machine with a straight top wing and lower wings set at a dihedral angle—the Camel.

'The crazy fool!' ground out Biggles, as he set off in pursuit; but even as he watched, the six machines disappeared into a cloud and were lost to view. 'I should say that's the last anyone will see of Algernon Montgomery,' muttered Biggles philosophically, as he climbed higher, scanning the sky in the direction taken by the machines, but the clouds closed up and hid the earth from view, leaving the lone Camel the sole occupant of the sky. 'Well, I might as well go home and write that letter to his mother, as Mahoney said,' mused the pilot. 'Poor little devil! After all I told him, too. Well——!' He turned south-west and headed for home, flying by the unfailing instinct some pilots seem to possess.

Major Mullen, MacLaren and Mahoney were standing on the tarmac when he landed. 'Where's the new man, Biggles?' said Major Mullen quickly.

'He's gone,' said Biggles slowly as he took off his helmet. 'I couldn't help it. I told the young fool to stick to me like glue. We were just over the line when I spotted the shadows of five Fokkers on the clouds; I gave him the tip and went into the cloud, expecting him to follow me. When I came out he wasn't there. I went back and was just in time to see him disappearing

into Hunland on the tails of the five Fokkers. I spent some time looking for him, but I couldn't find him. Could you believe that a—bah!—it's no use talking about it. I'm going for a dr——
Hark!' The hum of a rotary engine rapidly approaching sent all eyes quickly upwards.

'Here he comes,' said Biggles frostily. 'Leave this to me, please, sir. I've something to say to him.'

The Camel landed and taxied in. The pilot jumped out and, with a cheerful wave of greeting, joined Biggles on the tarmac.

'I've——'

'Never mind that,' cut in Biggles curtly. 'Where do you think you've been?'

'I saw the Huns—I was aching to have a crack at them—so I went after them.'

'Didn't I tell you to stay with me?'

'Yes, but——'

'Never mind "but"; you do what you're told or I'll knock heck out of you. Who do you think you are—Billy Bishop or Micky Mannock, perhaps?' sneered Biggles.

'The Huns were bolting——'

'Bolting my foot; they hadn't even seen you. If they had you wouldn't be here now. Those green-and-white stripes belong to von Kirtner's circus. They're killers—every one of 'em. You poor boob.'

'I got one of them.'

'*You what?*'

'I shot one down. I don't think he even saw me, though. I got all tangled up in a cloud, and when I came out and looked up, his wheels were nearly on my head. I pulled my stick back and let drive right into the bottom of his cockpit. He went down. I saw the smoke against the clouds.'

Biggles subjected the speaker to a searching scrutiny. 'Where did you read that tale?' he asked slowly.

'I didn't read it, sir,' said the new pilot, flushing. 'It was near a big queer-shaped wood. I think I must have been frightfully lucky.'

'Lucky!' ejaculated Biggles sarcastically. 'Lucky! Ha, ha!

Lucky! You don't know how lucky you are. Now listen. If ever you leave me again I'll put you under close arrest as soon as your feet are on the ground. Whatever happens, you stick to me. I've other things to do besides write letters of condolence to your mother. All right, wash out for today.'

Biggles sought Major Mullen and the other Flight-Commander in the Squadron office. 'That kid got a Hun or else he's the biggest liar on earth.'

'The liar sounds most likely to me,' observed MacLaren.

'Oh, I don't know; it has been done,' broke in Major Mullen; 'but it does seem a bit unlikely, I'll admit.'

The new pilot entered to make his report, and Biggles and MacLaren sauntered to the sheds. 'Wait a minute,' said Biggles suddenly. He swung himself into the cockpit of the Camel which had been flown by the new pilot. 'Well, he's used his guns anyway,' he said slowly, as he climbed out again. 'I'll take him on the dawn patrol with Healy in the morning. He's not safe alone.'

Biggles, leading the other Camels, high in the early morning sky, pursed his lips into a soundless whistle as his eyes fell on a charred wreck at the corner of Mossyface Wood.

'So he got him all right,' he muttered. 'The kid was right. Well, I'm dashed!'

A group of moving specks appeared in the distance. He watched them closely for a moment, then he rocked his wings and commenced a slow turn, pointing as he did so to the enemy machines which were coming rapidly towards them. He warmed his guns, stiffened a little in his seat, and glanced to left and right to make sure that the other two Camels were in place. He saw a flash of green-and-white on the sides of the enemy machines as they swung round for the attack, and he unconsciously half-glanced at the new pilot.

'You'll have the dog-fight you were aching for yesterday,' was his unspoken thought.

The Fokkers, six of them, were slightly above, coming straight on. Biggles lifted his nose slightly, took the leader in his sights, and waited. At 200 feet, still holding the Camel head-on to the other machines, he pressed his triggers. He saw the darting, jabbing flame of the other's guns, but did not swerve an inch. Metal spanged on metal near his face, the machine vibrated, and an unseen hand plucked at his sleeve. He clenched his teeth and held his fire. He had a swift impression of two wheels almost grazing his top plane as the first Fokker zoomed.

Out of the corner of his eye he saw Healy's tracer pouring into the Fokker at his right, and a trail of black smoke burst from the engine. Neither machine moved an inch. There was a crash which he could hear above the roar of his own engine as the Camel and the Fokker met head-on. A sheet of flame leapt upwards.

'Healy's gone—that's five to two now—not so good.'

He did a lightning right-hand turn. Where was Algernon? There he was, still in position at his wing-tip. The Huns had also turned and were coming back at them.

'Bad show for a kid,' thought Biggles, and on the spur of the moment waved his left hand above his head. The pilot of the other Camel was looking at him, but made no move.

'The fool, why doesn't he go home?' Biggles muttered, as he took the nearest Fokker in his sights again and opened fire. The Hun turned and he turned behind it, and the next second all seven machines were in a complete circle. Out of the corner of his eye Biggles saw the other Camel on the opposite side of the circle on the tail of a Hun.

'Why doesn't he shoot?' Biggles cursed blindly.

He pulled the stick back into his right side and shot into the circle, raking the Fokker that had opened fire on the other Camel. It zoomed suddenly, and as Biggles shot past the new pilot he waved his left arm.

He saw Algernon make a turn and dive for the line. A Fokker was on his tail instantly and Biggles raked it until it had to turn and face him. He half-rolled as a stream of lead zipped a strip of fabric from the centre section and went into a steep bank again to look at the situation.

He was alone, and there were still four Fokkers. For perhaps a minute each machine held its place in the circle, and then the Fokkers began to climb above him. Biggles knew that he was in an almost hopeless position, and he glanced around for a cloud to make a quick dash for cover, but from horizon to horizon the sky was an unbroken stretch of blue. The circle tightened as each machine strove to close it. The highest Fokker turned suddenly and dived on him, guns spitting two pencil lines of tracer. Biggles crouched a little lower in the cockpit. Two more of the Fokkers were turning on him now, and he knew that it was only a question of time before a bullet got him or his engine in a vital part.

Already the Camel was beginning to show signs of the conflict. 'Gosh! What's that?' Biggles almost stalled as another Camel shot into the circle. It did not turn as the others, but rushed across the diameter, straight at a Fokker which jerked up in a wild zoom to avoid collision. The Camel flashed round— not in the direction of the circle, but against it, and Biggles stared open-eyed with horror as the other Fokkers shot out at a tangent to avoid disaster.

'Great Scott! What's he doing?' he muttered as he flung his own machine on its side to pass the other Camel. He picked out a Fokker and blazed at it. Where were the others? They seemed to be scattered all over the sky. The other Camel was circling above him. 'We'll get out of this while the going's good,' he muttered grimly, and waved his hand to the other pilot. Together they turned and dived for the line.

Biggles landed first and leant against the side of his machine to await the new pilot. For a moment he looked at him without speaking.

'Listen, laddie,' he said, when the other had joined him. 'You mustn't do that sort of thing. You'll give me the willies. You acted like a madman.'

'Sorry, but you told me to go for 'em like a mad dog. I thought that's what I did.'

Biggles looked at the speaker earnestly. 'Yes,' he grinned: 'that's just what you did, but why didn't you do some shooting! I never saw your tracer once.'

'I couldn't.'

'Couldn't?'

'No—my gun jammed.'

'When?'

'It jammed badly with a bulged cartridge in that first go, and I couldn't clear it.'

Biggles raised his hand to his forehead. 'Do you mean to say you came back into that hell of a dog-fight with a jammed gun?' he said slowly.

'Yes. You said stick with you.'

Biggles held out his hand. 'You'll do, kid,' he said. 'And you can call me Biggles.'

6

THE BATTLE OF FLOWERS

THE summer sun was sinking in the western sky in a blaze of crimson glory as Biggles, with his flying kit thrown carelessly over his arm, walked slowly from the sheds towards the officers' mess. At the porch he paused in his stride to regard with wonderment the efforts of a freckle-faced youth, who, regardless of the heat, was feverishly digging up a small square patch of earth some thirty feet in front of the mess door.

'What the deuce are you doing, Algy?' he called cheerfully. 'Making a private dugout for yourself?'

'No,' replied Algernon Montgomery, straightening his back with an obvious effort and wiping the perspiration off his brow with the back of his hand. 'I'm making a garden. This dust-smitten hole wants brightening up.'

'You're what?' cried Biggles incredulously.

'Making a garden, I said,' responded Algy shortly, resuming his task.

'Good Lord! What are you going to sow, or whatever you call it?'

'I've got some sunflowers,' replied Algy, nodding towards a

newspaper package from which some wilted sickly green ends protruded.

'Sunflowers, eh?' said Biggles, curiously, advancing towards the scene of action. 'They ought to do well. But why not plant some bananas or pineapples, or something we could eat?'

'It isn't hot enough for bananas,' said Algy, between breaths. 'They were all I could get, anyway.'

'Not hot enough?' answered Biggles. 'Holy mackerel! It feels hot enough to me to grow doughnuts.'

Algy dropped his spade and drew one of the seedlings gently from the package.

'Do you mean to tell me that you are going to stick that poor little thing in that pile of dust? I thought you said you were going to brighten things up,' said Biggles slowly.

'That'll be ten feet high presently,' said Algy confidently, scratching a hole in the earth and dropping the roots in.

'Ten feet! You mean to tell me that little squirt of a thing's got a ceiling of ten feet? Why, he's stalling already. Bah! You can't kid me. Straighten him up. You've got him a bit left wing low.'

'You push off, Biggles; I want to get these things in before dark,' cried Algy hotly. 'They've got to have some water yet.'

'They look to me as if a double brandy would do them more good,' retorted Biggles as he turned towards the mess. 'So long, kid—see you later. You can lie up in the morning. I'll take Cowley and Tommy on the early show.'

Three hours later Biggles pushed his chair back from the card-table in the anteroom. 'Well, I'm up five francs,' he announced, 'and now I'm going to roost. I'll——'

A voice from the doorway interrupted him. It was Algy.

'Here, chaps,' he called excitedly. 'Come and look at this— quick, before it goes.'

'He wants us to go and watch his posies sprouting in the moonlight, I expect,' grinned Biggles at Mahoney and Mac-Laren, who were leaning back in their chairs. He turned towards the door, but as his eye fell on a window which had been flung wide open to admit as much air as possible, he stopped abruptly. 'What the . . .?' he ejaculated, and sprang towards the door. The crash of falling chairs announced that the others were close behind him.

At the open doorway he stopped and looked up. A hundred feet above, a brilliant white light was sinking slowly earthwards, flooding the mess and the surrounding buildings with a dazzling radiance. A faint whistling sound, increasing in volume, became audible.

'Look out!' yelled Biggles and, covering twenty yards almost in a bound, dived headlong into a trench which surrounded a nearby Nissen hut. The whistle became a shrieking wail. 'Look where you're coming,' protested Biggles, as a dozen bodies thudded into the trench, one landing on the small of his back. 'Where's——?' His voice was lost in a deafening detonation; a blinding sheet of flame leapt upwards.

'If they've knocked my drink over——' snarled Mahoney, struggling to get out of the trench.

'Come back, you fool,' yelled Biggles, hanging on to his foot. 'Here comes another—get down.'

Bang! Another terrific explosion shook the earth, and falling debris rattled on the tin roof beside them. The roar of an aero-engine almost on their heads, but swiftly receding, split the air.

'All right, chaps, he's gone,' said Biggles, scrambling out of the trench. 'Don't step on my cigarette-case, anybody; I've dropped it somewhere. By thunder, he nearly caught us bending! To the deuce with these new parachute flares; they don't give you a chance.'

'I hope he hasn't knocked our wine store sideways, like somebody did to 55 the other day,' grumbled Mahoney. 'Hello! The searchlights have got him. Just look at that stinking archie; I wouldn't be in that kite for something.'

All eyes were turned upwards to where a black crossed machine was twisting and turning in the beams of three searchlights which had fastened upon it. The air around was torn with darting, crimson jets of flame.

'He'll get away; they always do,' said MacLaren with deep disgust, making his way towards the mess.

'Well, I hope he does; he deserves to. I'd hate his job,' observed Biggles philosophically.

'Where's Algy?'

'I expect the kid's gone to see if his plantation's all right,' replied Mahoney. 'Well, good night, chaps—good night, Biggles.'

'Cheerio, laddie.'

Ten minutes later there was a knock on Biggles' door, and in reply to his invitation a wild-eyed, freckle-faced youth thrust his head inside. He seemed to be labouring under some great emotion.

'What—what was that?' he gasped.

Biggles grinned. 'Hannoverana—didn't you see it in the beam?' he replied. 'There's no harm done.'

'Where did that dirty dog come from, do you think?' choked Algy.

'Aerodrome 29, I expect; they are the only Hannovers near here. Must have crossed the line at twenty thousand and glided down with his engine off,' replied Biggles.

'Where's Aerodrome 29?'

'Oh, go to the map-room and find out; it's time you knew. There are some photos there, too. Push off. I'm tired and I'm on the early show.'

Algy stood for a moment breathing heavily, staring at his flight-commander, and then abruptly slammed the door.

Biggles scarcely seemed to have closed his eyes when he was awakened by the ear-splitting roar of an engine. It was still dark. He grabbed his luminous watch and looked at the time—it was 3.30. 'What the dickens—?' he croaked, springing out of bed. He reached the window just as the dim silhouette of a Camel passed overhead. He flung on a dressing-gown and raced along the sun-baked path to the sheds. 'Who's that just gone off?' he called to a tousle-headed ack-emma who was still staring upwards with a vacant grin on his face.

'Alger—sorry, sir—Mr.——'

'Never mind,' snapped Biggles, overlooking the breach of

respect. 'I know. Where's he gone—did he say?'

'No, sir, but I saw him marking up his map. He took eight Cooper bombs.'

'What did he mark on his map?' snapped Biggles.

'Aerodrome 29, sir.'

Biggles swung on his heel and tore back towards the huts. He shook and pummelled the life into Cowley and Thomas. 'Come on,' he said tersely; 'jump to it. Algy's gone off his rocker—he's shooting up 29 alone. Let's get away.'

Sidcots were hastily donned over pyjamas, and within five minutes three machines were in the air heading for the line. The sun was creeping up over the horizon when Biggles, at 5,000 feet, waved to the other two pilots and, leaning over the side of his cockpit, pointed downwards. Far below, a tiny moving speck was circling and banking over a line of hangars. A cloud of white smoke arose into the air. Tiny ant-like figures were running to and fro.

'The fool, the crazy lunatic!' gasped Biggles, as he pushed the stick forward and went roaring down with the others behind him.

At 500 feet a row of holes appeared like magic in his wing and he sideslipped violently. He levelled out and poured a stream of tracer at a group of figures clustered around a machine-gun. A green machine was taking off cross-wind; he swung down behind it and raked it with a stream of lead. The gunner in the rear seat dropped limply and the machine crashed into the trees at the far end of the aerodrome. The air was full of the rattle of guns and an ominous *flack! flack! flack!* behind warned him that it was time to be leaving.

He looked around for Algy, and, spotting him still circling, zoomed across his nose, frantically waving his arm above his head.

'If he doesn't come now he can stay and get what he deserves,' muttered Biggles, as he shot over the edge of the aerodrome.

He looked behind. To his relief three Camels were on his tail, so, climbing swiftly for height, he headed back towards the lines.

'I'll see him back home and then go straight on with the

morning show,' he mused a few minutes later as they raced
across the lines in a flurry of archie. He landed and leaned
against the side of the Camel while he waited for the others to
come in. Another Camel touched its wheels gently on the
aerodrome and finished its run not twenty yards away.

Algy sprang out of the cockpit and ran towards him. 'I got
it—I got it!' he shouted exultantly as he ran.

'Who do you think you are?' snapped Biggles. 'Archimedes?'

'I got four hits out of eight,' cried Algy joyously.

'You got nothing—I had a good look. You didn't touch a
single hangar,' growled Biggles.

'Hangar—hangar—?' replied Algy stupidly. 'Who's talking
about hangars?'

'I am; what else do you suppose?'

'Hangars, be dashed!' cried Algy. 'I mean their geraniums!'

'Germaniums—germaniums——? Am I going crazy? What
are you talking about—germaniums?'

'Raniums—raniums—N—N——! Good Lord, did you
never hear of geraniums? They had a bed full of geraniums and
calceolarias.'

'Calcium—calcium——' Biggles took a quick step backwards and whipped out his Very pistol. 'Here, stand back, you,
or I'll shoot. You're daft.'

'Daft be dashed! I mean flowers—I've scattered their blinking geraniums all over the aerodrome.'

Biggles stared at him for a moment, his jaw sagging foolishly.
'Do you mean to tell me you've been to that hell-hole, and
dragged me there, to bomb a perishing flower-bed?'

'Yes, and I've made a salad of their lettuce-patch,' added
Algy triumphantly.

'But why? What have the lettuces done to you?'

'Done to me? Haven't you seen what that swine did to my
sunflowers last night?'

Biggles swung round on his heel as enlightenment burst upon
him. At the spot where Algy's flower-bed had been yawned a
deep round hole.

THE THOUGHT-READER

THE summer sun blazed down in all its glory from a sky of cloudless blue. Biggles, his head resting on his hands, lay flat on his back in a patch of deep, sweet-scented grass in a quiet corner of the aerodrome, and stared lazily at a lark trilling gaily far above. The warmth, the drowsy hum of insects, and the smell of the clean earth were balm to his tired body. For since the disaster which had robbed his squadron of two thirds of its machines he had been doing three patrols a day. New Camels had now arrived, however, and at the commanding officer's suggestion he was taking things quietly for a few days.

The war seemed far away. Even the mutter of guns along the Line had died down to an occasional fitful salvo. France was not such a bad place, after all, he decided, as he glanced at his watch, and then settled himself again in the grass, his eyes on the deep-blue sky.

A little frown puckered his brow as he heard the soft swish of footsteps approaching through the grass, but he did not move. The footsteps stopped close behind him.

'You taking up star-gazing?' said a voice. It was Algy's.

'I should be if there were any to gaze at. You ought to know, at your age, that they only come out at night,' replied Biggles coldly.

'You'll be boss-eyed staring up that way,' warned Algy. 'Do you expect to see something, or are you just looking into the future?'

'That's it,' agreed Biggles.

'What's it?' asked Algy.

'I'm looking into the future. I can tell you just what you'll see up there in exactly three and a half minutes time.'

'You're telling me!' sneered Algy. 'You mean a nice blue sky!'

'And something else,' replied Biggles seriously. 'I've been doing a bit of amateur astrology lately, and I'm getting pretty good at it. I can work things out by deduction. My middle name ought to have been Sherlock—Sherlock Holmes, you know, the famous detective!'

'Well, do your stuff,' invited Algy. 'What are you deducing now?'

Biggles yawned, and said: 'In one minute you'll see a Rumpler plane come beetling along from the south-east at about ten thousand feet. Our people will archie him, but they won't hit him. When he gets over that clump of poplars away to the right he'll make one complete turn, and then streak for home, nose down, on a different course from the one he came by.'

'This sun has given you softening of the brain,' declared Algy. 'What makes you think that, anyway?'

'I don't have to think—I know!' replied Biggles. 'I've got what is known as second sight. It's a gift that——'

'Come, come, Bigglesworth,' broke in another voice. 'You can't get away with that!'

Biggles raised himself on his elbow, and found himself looking into the smiling face of Colonel Raymond, of Wing Headquarters.

'Sorry, sir!' he gasped, struggling to get to his feet, 'I thought Algy was by himself.'

'All right—lie still, don't let me disturb you. I was just looking around—Hark!'

A faint drone became audible high overhead, and three pairs of eyes turned upwards to a tiny black speck heading up from the south-east. Although small, it could be recognised as a German aeroplane, a Rumpler.

Whoof! Whoof! Whoof!

Three little fleecy white clouds blossomed out some distance behind it as the British anti-aircraft gunners took up the chase.

Biggles glanced at the others out of the corner of his eye, and their expressions brought a quick twitch of amusement to the corners of his lips. His smile broadened as the Rumpler held on its way until it was almost exactly above the group of poplars to which he had referred. Then, very deliberately, it made a complete circle and raced back, nose-down, towards the Lines on a different course.

'Not a bad forecast for an amateur!' observed Biggles calmly. 'Pretty good!' admitted Algy reluctantly. 'Maybe you know why he's flying in that direction now?'

'I do,' replied Biggles. 'It's a matter of simple deduction. He's going that way because if he followed his own course back he'd just about bump into Mahoney's flight coming in from patrol. He knows all about that, and as he doesn't fancy his chances with them he's steering wide of them.'

The enemy Rumpler was almost out of sight now, and the drone of its engine was gradually drowned by others rapidly approaching. Following the course by which the Rumpler pilot had crossed the Lines came three British Camels, straight towards the aerodrome.

'I told you my middle name ought to have been Sherlock!' grinned Biggles.

'Good show, Bigglesworth!' said the Colonel. 'I must say that was very neat. Tell us how you knew all this.'

'Oh, sir!' replied Biggles reprovingly. 'Fancy asking a conjurer to show you how he does his tricks! It isn't done.'

'But I'm very interested,' protested the Colonel.

'So am I, to tell you the truth, sir!' Biggles replied. 'You know as much as I do now, but I figure it out this way. The average German hasn't very much imagination, and he works to a timetable, like a clock. I've been over here for the last two days at this time, and on both occasions that Rumpler has turned up and done exactly the same thing. Well, when I put my ear to the ground a little bird tells me that what a Hun does twice he'll do three times—and he'll keep on doing it until someone stops him. Maybe I shall have to stop him. If you ask me why he comes over here you've got me. I don't know. But I should say he comes over to look at something. He doesn't just come over on an ordinary reconnaissance. He's sent to look at something which he can see from that position where he turned over the poplars. Having seen it, he beetles off home. I may be wrong, but even my gross intelligence tells me he doesn't come over here just for fun. I must confess I'm getting a bit curious. What Huns can see I ought to be able to see.'

'That's what I was thinking,' agreed the Colonel. 'The Huns seem to be seeing quite a lot of this sector, too, of late. A week ago an artillery brigade took up a position in the sunken road at Earles. They were well camouflaged and could not have been seen from above, yet they were shelled out of existence the same night. That wasn't guesswork. We had to have some guns somewhere, so a couple of days ago we brought up a heavy naval gun, and sank it in a gun-pit behind that strip of wood on the Amiens road. It was perfectly concealed against aerial observation, yet by twelve noon the Boche artillery were raking that particular area and blew it to pieces. That wasn't guesswork, either. Then some ammunition lorries parked behind the walls of the ruined farm at Bertaple—the same thing happened to them. Now you know what I mean when I say that the Boche has been looking pretty closely at this sector.'

'Someone's been busy, that's certain,' agreed Biggles.

'I wish you'd have a look round,' the Colonel went on. 'I don't know what to tell you to look for—if I did, there would be no need for you to go. You'll have to put two and two together, and you're pretty good at that!'

'Don't make me blush in front of Algy, sir!' protested Biggles, grinning. 'Right-ho; I'll beetle around right away and see if I can see what the gentleman in the Rumpler saw!'

Half an hour later, Biggles was in the air flying over exactly the same course as that taken by the Boche machine, and as he flew he subjected the ground below to a searching scrutiny. Reaching the spot where the Rumpler had turned, he redoubled his efforts, studying the landscape road by road and field by field.

There was a singular lack of activity. Here and there he saw small camps where British battalions from the trenches were resting. He picked out a wrecked windmill, minus its arms, an overturned lorry, and a dispatch-rider tearing along a road in a cloud of dust. One or two small shell-torn villages came within his range of vision, and a farm-labourer harvesting his corn, piling the sheaves into shocks, regardless of the nearness of the firing-line. Shell-holes, both old and new, could be seen dotted about the landscape, but he could not see a single mark likely to be of interest to, or which might be taken as a signal for, the enemy. He saw the place, where the artillery brigade had been shelled, and he turned away, feeling depressed.

For an hour or more he continued his quest, but without noting anything of interest. And then, in not too good a humour, he returned to the aerodrome.

Colonel Raymond was talking to Major Mullen when he landed.

'Well, Sherlock,' called the Colonel, 'what's the latest?'

'Nothing doing, sir,' replied Biggles shortly. 'But I haven't given up hope. I hope to pass the time of day with that Rumpler pilot tomorrow, anyway!'

The following morning he was in the air in ample time to intercept the Boche machine. In fact, he had deliberately allowed himself a wide margin of time in order to make a further survey of the ground which appeared to be the object of the enemy plane's daily visit, and towards which he now headed. Reaching it, he gave a grunt of annoyance as his probing eyes searched the earth below. Everything was just the same—the same lonely farm-labourer was still harvesting his corn.

Flying lower, he saw, farther on, a large body of British troops—a brigade, he judged it to be—lying fairly well concealed along the edge of a wood, no doubt awaiting their turn to move up to the trenches. He wondered vaguely whether the prying eyes in the Rumpler would see them, but he decided not, both from the fact that the machine would be too high up and would hardly be likely to venture so far over the British Line.

He glanced at the watch on his instrument-board and saw that he still had a quarter of an hour to wait for the Rumpler, assuming it came at the same time as before.

'Well, I might as well be getting plenty of height,' he mused, as he tilted the nose of the Camel upwards, glancing down for a final survey of the ground as he did so.

His eye fell on the labourer, still working at his harvest. It

seemed to Biggles that he was working unnecessarily fast, and a
frown lined his brow as he looked around the sky to see if there
were any signs of an impending storm to account for the man's
haste. But the sky was an unbroken blue canopy from horizon to
horizon. He looked back at the man on the ground, and, leaning
over the side of the cockpit to see better, he stared at the field and
the position of the shocks of corn with a puzzled expression on his
face. It struck him that, in spite of the man's haste in moving the
corn, the shocks were as numerous as they had been the previous
day. They only seemed to have moved their positions, and they
now formed a curious pattern, quite different from the usual
orderly rows.

'So that's your game, is it?' Biggles muttered, after a quick
intake of breath, as he realised the significance of what he saw.

His eyes followed a long line of sheaves pointing in the
direction of the concealed infantry, and a number of isolated
shocks which probably indicated the distance they were away,
and so disclosed their position to the German aerial observer!

Biggles' brain raced swiftly. What should he do? There were
several courses open to him. He might proceed with his original
plan and shoot down the Rumpler. That would at least prevent
the information from reaching the German gunners.

But suppose he failed? Suppose the Boche shot him down?
He did not anticipate such a catastrophe, nor did he think it
likely, but it was a possibility. His engine might be damaged,
when he would be forced to land, in which case there was
nothing to prevent the Rumpler from reaching home. He might
have engine trouble and have to force-land, anyway, and he
shuddered to think of the consequences, for he had not the
slightest doubt but that the British infantry would be annihi-
lated by the guns of the German artillery.

Another plan would be to return to the aerodrome, ring up
Colonel Raymond, at Wing Headquarters, and tell him what he
had discovered. The Colonel could then send a message to the
brigade warning them to shift their position before the bombardment started.

'No,' he decided: 'that won't do.' It would take too long. It would allow the Boche plane ample time to return home and start the enemy gunners on their deadly work before the message could reach the brigade.

The only really sure plan seemed to be to land and destroy the tell-tale signal before the Boche plane came over. If he could do that quickly he might still have time to get off again and get the Rumpler when it arrived.

'Yes,' he thought; 'that's the safest way!' There was still ten minutes to go before the Rumpler was due to appear on the scene.

Having made up his mind, he sideslipped steeply towards the ground near to where the supposed peasant was at work. The fact that he was unarmed did not worry him. After all, there was no reason to suppose that the spy would suspect he had been discovered—his method of conveying information to the enemy was so simple and so natural that nothing but a fluke or uncanny perception could detect it.

It was improbable that a roving scout pilot would even pass over the field so far behind the Lines, much less suspect the sinister scheme. But the improbable had happened, and Biggles, as he swooped earthwards, could not help admiring the ingenuity of the plan.

He did not risk a landing on the stubble of the cornfield, but dropped lightly to earth on a pasture a short distance away. Climbing from the cockpit, he threw his heavy flying-coat across the lower wing and started off at a steady trot towards the cornfield. As he neared it he slowed down to a walk in order not to alarm the spy, and made for a gate leading into the field. He saw the supposed labourer, dressed in the typical blue garb of a French peasant, still carrying the sheaves of corn, and he smiled grimly at his thoroughness. For the labourer did not so much as glance up when a distant deep-toned hum announced the approach of his confederate, the Rumpler.

He saw Biggles coming towards him and waved gaily.

'*Bonjour, m'sieur le capitan!*' he cried, smiling, and the pilot was too far away to see the curious gleam in his eyes.

'*Bonjour, m'sieur!*' echoed Biggles, still advancing.

He was still about twenty yards away when he saw the peasant's hand move quickly to his pocket, and then up. Before he even suspected the other's purpose, a deafening roar filled Biggles' ears, and the world seemed to blow up in a sheet of crimson and orange flame that slowly turned to purple and then to black.

As he pitched forward limply on his face, Biggles knew that the spy had shot him!

Biggles' first conscious realisation as he opened his eyes was a shocking headache. He tried to raise his arm to his head to feel the extent of the damage done by the spy's bullet, but his arm seemed to be pinned to his side. It was dark, too, and an overwhelming smell of fresh straw filled his nostrils, seeming to suffocate him. He saw some narrow strips of daylight in the darkness, and it took him several minutes of concentrated thought to realise that he was buried under a pile of corn-sheaves.

With a mighty effort that seemed to burst his aching head, he flung the sheaves aside and rolled out into the open, blinking like an owl in the dazzling sunlight. He struggled to his feet, and, swaying dizzily, looked about him. Apparently he was at the very spot where he had fallen; everything was precisely the same except that the spy had just flung the sheaves of corn over the pilot's unconscious body to conceal it from any casual passersby, and then had made his escape.

Biggles wondered how long he had been unconscious, for he had no means of knowing; his watch was on the instrument-board of the Camel. From the position of the sun, however, he decided that it could not have been very long, but ample for the Rumpler pilot to read the message and return. At least, the machine was nowhere in sight, and he could not hear the sound of its engine. He tried to think, raising his hand to his aching head and looking aghast at his red-stained fingers when he took it away.

Suddenly he remembered the infantry, and with a shock he recalled the perilous position in which they must now be placed. He must get in touch with the brigade, was the thought that

hammered through his brain. The inevitable artillery bombardment had not yet started, and he might still be in time to save
them!

The sudden splutter of a motor-car engine made him swing
round, and he was just in time to see a rather dilapidated old
Renault car, with the spy at the wheel, disappearing out of the
yard of the small farmhouse a short distance away, to which the
cornfield evidently belonged. At the same time a thick column of
smoke began to rise from the farm itself, and he guessed that the
spy had set fire to the place to destroy any incriminating
documents or clues he might have left behind in his hurried
departure.

Biggles' lips set in a straight line, and his eyes narrowed.

'You aren't getting away with that!' he snarled, and started
off at a swaying run towards the place where he had left his
Camel, breathing a sigh of relief when he saw it was still there.

He paused for an instant at a ditch to soak his handkerchief
and bind it round the place on the side of his head where the
spy's bullet had grazed it.

'If I ever get a closer one than that it will be the last!' he
muttered grimly, as he realized what a close shave he had had.
Indeed, the spy must have thought he had killed him, he
reflected, or he would not have left him to tell the tale.

He climbed into the cockpit, and, after a swerving run,
somehow managed to get the machine off the ground and
headed towards the road down which the spy had disappeared.
He saw the car presently, and the long cloud of dust hanging in
the air behind it, and he flung the Camel at it viciously, knowing
that he had no time to lose. He knew he ought to go straight to
the infantry brigade and sound the warning, but his blood was
up and he could not bear to think the spy might escape to
continue his dangerous work elsewhere. In any case, he thought,
as he tore down the road just above the column of dust, the
Rumpler pilot could scarcely have reached home yet, for the fact
that he—Biggles—had caught the spy in the act of escaping
indicated that he had not been unconscious for more than a few
minutes. His lips parted in a mirthless smile as he saw the

fugitive look back over his shoulder at the pursuing demon on his trail, and the car leaped forward as the spy strove to escape by increasing his speed.

Biggles laughed. The idea of any vehicle on the ground leaving his Camel, which was doing 140 miles an hour, struck him as funny. But the smile gave way to the cold calculating stare of the fighting airman as the Camel drew swiftly into range, and Biggles' eyes sought his sights.

Rat-tat-tat-tat-tat! The twin Vickers guns began their song. The end came suddenly. Whether he hit the driver, or burst a tyre, or whether it was simply the result of the driver trying to take a bend at excessive speed, Biggles did not know, nor did he stop to ascertain. The car seemed suddenly to plough into the road, and a great cloud of dust arose above it. The bodywork, with a deliberation that was appalling to watch, seemed slowly to spread itself over the landscape. A solitary wheel went bounding along the road. A tongue of flame licked out of the engine, and in a moment all that was left of the wreck was concealed under a cloud of smoke.

Biggles grimaced at the unpleasant sight, and circled twice to see if by some miracle the driver was still alive. But there was a significant lack of movement near the car, and he shot off at a tangent in the direction of the infantry encampment.

He had made a bad landing, excusable in the circumstances, in an adjacent field, and ran quickly towards a group of officers whom he saw watching him.

'I must speak to the Brigadier at once!' he cried, as he reached them.

'Did no one teach you how to salute?' thundered an officer who wore a major's crown on his sleeve.

Biggles flushed, and raised his hand smartly to the salute, inwardly fuming at the delay.

'I must speak to the Brigadier or the Brigade-major at once!' he repeated impatiently.

A major, wearing on his collar the red tabs of a staff-officer, hurried up and asked: 'Are you the officer who just flew low over——'

'Do you mind leaving that until later, sir?' ground out Biggles. 'I've come to tell you to move your men at once. I——'

'Silence! Are you giving *me* orders?' cried the Brigade-major incredulously. 'I'll report you for impertinence!'

Biggles groaned, then had an inspiration.

'May I use your telephone, sir? It's very urgent!' he asked humbly.

'You'll find one at Headquarters—this way!'

In the Brigade Headquarters, Biggles grabbed the telephone feverishly. The Brigade-major and an orderly-officer watched him curiously. In a few moments he was speaking to Colonel Raymond at Wing Headquarters.

'Bigglesworth here, sir!' he said tersely. 'I've found what you were looking for. That Boche came over to pick up a message from a spy who has signalled to the German gunners the position of the brigade from whose headquarters I am now speaking— yes, sir—that's right—by the side of the wood about two miles east of Buell. Yes, I've tried to tell the people here, but they won't listen. I killed the spy—he's lying under the wreckage of his own car on the Amiens road. Yes, sir—I should say the bombardment is due to start any minute.'

'What's that—what's that?' cried a voice behind him.

Biggles glanced over his shoulder and saw the Brigadier watching him closely.

'Just a moment, sir,' he called into the telephone, and then, to the Brigadier: 'Will you speak to Colonel Raymond, of 51st Wing Headquarters, sir?'

The Brigadier took the instrument and placed the receiver to his ear. Biggles saw his face turn pale. An instant later he had slammed down the receiver and ripped out a string of orders. Orderlies dashed off in all directions, bugles sounded, and sergeant-majors shouted.

Ten minutes later, as the tail of the column disappeared behind a fold in the ground to the rear, the first shell arrived. A salvo followed. Presently the earth where the British camp had been was being torn and ploughed by flame and hurtling metal.

Biggles ran through the inferno of flying earth and shrapnel to where he had left the Camel. The pain in his head, forgotten in the excitement, had now returned with greater intensity, and as he ran he shut his eyes tightly, fighting back the wave of dizziness which threatened him.

'I must have been barmy to leave the bus as close as this,' he thought. 'She's probably been blown sky-high by this time.'

There was reason for his concern, for the enemy shells were falling uncomfortably near the field where he had left the machine. But the Camel was intact when he reached it, although the ploughed-up ground which he had looked upon as a possible take-off showed how narrowly some of the shells had missed it.

Biggles scrambled into the cockpit and revved up the engine, then kicked hard at the rudder-bar to avoid the edge of a shell-hole as the machine lurched forward. Bumping and swaying on the torn ground, the Camel gathered speed.

'I'll have the undercarriage collapsing if I can't get off soon,' Biggles muttered, and eased back the joystick.

For a few moments the wheels jolted on the rough earth, then a bump bigger than usual threw them into the air.

As he landed at Maranique, Wat Tyler, the Recording Officer, handed him a signal.

'From Wing,' he said. 'What have you been up to now?'

Biggles tore the envelope open and smiled as he read: 'Good work, Sherlock!' The initials below were Colonel Raymond's.

8
BIGGLES FINDS HIS FEET

CRUISING over the Somme, France, at fifteen thousand feet, Biggles paused for a moment in his unceasing scrutiny of the sky to glance downwards. The smoke from a burning farmhouse caught his eye, and a little frown of anxiety lined his forehead as he noticed that the smoke was rolling along the ground towards Germany at an angle which could only mean that a very high wind was blowing.

He swung his Camel round in its own length, the frown deepening with anxiety as he realised for the first time that he was a good deal farther over the Lines than he imagined.

'It'll take me half an hour to get back against this wind. I must have been crazy to come so far over,' he thought, as he pushed his joystick forward for more speed.

The archie bursts that had followed him on his outward passage with indifferent results now began to creep closer as the Camel offered a less fleeting target. The pilot was forced to change direction in order to avoid their unwelcome attentions.

'I must have been crazy,' he told himself again angrily, as he swerved to avoid a cluster of ominous black bubbles that had appeared like magic in front of him. 'I ought to have spotted that the wind had got up. But how was I to know it was going to blow a gale?'

Under the forward pressure on the joystick, his height had dropped to ten thousand feet by the time the white scars of the shell-torn trenches came into view. Suddenly he stiffened in his seat as a faint but unusual noise reached his ears. Underlying the rhythmic hum of his Bentley engine was a persistent *tick-a-tack—tick-a-tack*.

With a grim suspicion forming in his mind, he glanced back over his shoulder. Along his line of flight, stretching away behind him like the wake of a ship, was a cloud of pale-blue smoke, and he knew beyond doubt that his engine was giving trouble.

He turned quickly to his instrument-board and confirmed it. The engine revolution counter had fallen to nearly half its normal revs. He looked over the side, now thoroughly alarmed, to judge his distance from the Lines. He decided, with a sigh of relief, that he might just reach them provided the trouble did not become worse. But in this he was doomed to disappointment, for hardly had the thought crossed his mind than there was a loud explosion, a streamer of flame leapt backwards from the whirling rotary engine, and a smell of burning oil filled his nostrils. Instantly he throttled back, preferring to land behind the German Lines rather than be burnt to a cinder in the air.

He lost height rapidly, and fixed his eyes on the Lines in an agony of suspense. Fortunately, the sky was clear of enemy machines, a fact which afforded him some consolation, for he would have been in a hopeless position had he been attacked. Still gliding, he moistened his lips, and tried opening the throttle a trifle. But the flames reappeared at once, and he had no alternative but to resume his former gliding angle.

The Lines were not much more than a mile away now, but his height was less than a thousand feet, a fact that was unpleasantly impressed upon him by the closeness of the anti-aircraft gun-fire. An ominous crackling, too, warned him that the enemy machine-gunners on the ground were also making good shoot-ing at the struggling machine. To make matters worse, there seemed to be a battle raging below. Clouds of smoke, stabbing spurts of flame, and leaping geysers of mud told a story of concentrated bombardment on both sides of the Lines. More than once the Camel rocked violently as a big projectile from the thundering howitzers hurtled by.

Biggles crouched a little lower in the cockpit, looking swiftly left and right, hoping to ascertain his position. But he was now too low to distinguish anything except the churning inferno of smoke and mud. A battered tank, its nose pointing upwards like that of a sleeping lizard, loomed up before him and he kicked the rudder desperately to avoid it. Barbed wire, tangled and twisted, was everywhere. Mud, water, and bodies in khaki and field-grey were the only other things he could see.

There was no question of choosing a place to land—everywhere was the same, so there was no choice. There came a deafening explosion, the Camel twisted into a sickening side-slip, and, with a crash of rending timbers, struck the upright post of some wire entanglements.

Biggles' next conscious recollection was of digging feverishly in the mud under the side of his now upside-down machine in order to get clear, and then staring stupidly at the inferno raging about him. In which direction lay the British Lines? He had no idea, but the vicious rattle of a machine-gun from somewhere near at hand, and the shrill whang of bullets striking his machine, brought him back from his semi-stunned condition with a rush, and suggested the immediate need for cover.

About twenty yards away a huge shell-crater yawned invitingly, and he leapt towards it like a tiger. A bullet clutched at the sleeve of his coat as he plunged through the mud, and he took the last two yards in a wild leap. His foot caught on the serrated rim of the crater and he dived headlong into the stagnant pool of slime at the bottom. Scrambling out blindly, he slipped and fell heavily on something soft.

'Now, then, look where you're comin' to, can't you! What's the 'urry?' snarled a Cockney voice.

Biggles blinked and wilted into a sitting position in the soft mud on the side of the hole. On the opposite side sat a Tommy, caked with mud from head to foot, a drab and sorry spectacle; upon his knee, from which he had cut away a portion of his trousers, was a red-stained bandage which he had evidently just finished tying.

'Was I in a hurry?' inquired Biggles blandly, regarding the apparition curiously. 'Well, I may have been,' he confessed. 'This isn't the sort of place to dawdle on an afternoon's stroll— at least, it didn't strike me like that. Where are we, and what's going on?' he asked, ducking instinctively as a shell landed just outside the crater with a dull *whoosh*.

'What did you want to land 'ere for? Ain't it bad enough upstairs?' snorted the Tommy. 'Life won't be worth livin' 'ere in 'arf a minute, when they start puttin' the kybosh on your aeroplane.'

'I didn't land here because I was pining to see you, so don't get that idea,' grinned Biggles. 'Where are we—that's what I want to know.'

'About in the middle, I should think,' growled the Tommy.

'Middle of what?' asked Biggles.

'The war, of course!' was the reply.

'Yes, I can see that,' admitted Biggles. 'But whereabouts are our troops, and where's the enemy?'

The soldier jerked his thumb over his shoulder and then jabbed it in the opposite direction.

'There and there, or they was last time I saw 'em, but they might be anywhere by now. You know, mate, my missus, she says to me, "Bert," she says——'

'Is your name Bert?' asked Biggles, to stop the long oration he could see was coming.

'Yes. Bert Smart, 'A' Company, Twenty-third London,' replied the soldier.

'Nice name!' said Biggles.

'What's the matter with it?' growled the Tommy.

'Nothing! I said it was a nice name—nice and easy to remember!' protested Biggles.

'I thought you was pulling my leg!' growled Bert suspiciously.

'Oh, no, I wouldn't do that!' exclaimed Biggles, repressing a smile with difficulty. 'But what about getting out of here?'

'Well, I ain't stoppin' you, am I?' said Bert. 'If you don't like my blinkin' society——'

'It isn't that!' broke in Biggles quickly, a broad grin on his face. 'I'd like to sit and chat to you all day—but not here!'

'Well, it's better than chargin' up and down, with people stabbin' at you, ain't it?' asked Bert. 'If you wants to go, there's a sap just behind you what leads to our Lines.'

'A sap?' queried Biggles.

'Yes, sap!' said Bert. 'S-A-P—stuff what they put in trees— you know—trench, if you like. I wish I could come with you. Jerry'll be coming back in a minute, I expect. This is 'is property. We'd just driven 'im out when I copped this one in my knee and down I goes. Blighty one, I 'opes. As my missus says, "Bert," she says——'

'Hold hard!' cried Biggles. 'Let's leave what she says till another day. Can you walk?'

'With no blinkin' knee-cap?' asked Bert. 'No! And I can't 'op neither, not in this muck! What do you think I am—a sparrer?'

'No. I can see you're no sparrow,' replied Biggles looking at the man's thirteen-stone bulk. 'And I'm no Samson to carry you, much as I should like to. I'll nip across and tell our fellows you're here. Then we'll come and fetch you.'

'You'll fetch me?' repeated Bert.

'Yes,' said Biggles.

'No sprucing?' asked the wounded man.

'What's that?' asked Biggles, with a start.

'Kiddin'. I mean, do you mean it?' explained Bert.

'Of course I mean it!' replied Biggles.

'Well, you're a toff! All right; I'll wait 'ere!'

'That's right; don't run away!' grinned Biggles. 'Where's that sap you were talking about?'

'Straight over the top, about twenty yards 'arf left,' replied Bert, pointing.

Biggles peeped stealthily over the rim of the crater. In all directions stretched a wilderness of mud and water in which barbed wire, tin helmets, rifles and ammunition-boxes lay in hopeless confusion. A bullet flipped through the ooze not an inch from his face, and he bobbed down hurriedly. But he had seen the end of the shell-shattered trench.

Turning, he looked down at Bert, whose face had turned chalky-white, and Biggles knew that in spite of his casual pose the Tommy was badly wounded, and would soon die from loss of blood if medical aid was delayed.

'Stick it, Bert, I shan't be long!' he called, dragging off his coat and throwing it to the wounded man. 'Put that over you; it'll keep you warm.' Then he darted for the end of the trench.

A fusillade of shots and the chatter of a machine-gun greeted him as, crouching low, he staggered heavily through the clinging mud. Out of the trench, as he neared it, the point of a bayonet rose to meet him, but with a shrill yell of 'Look out!' he leapt aside and then flung himself into the trench.

At the last moment he saw an infantry colonel who was talking to another officer at the end of a communication trench. He did his best to avoid them, but his foot slipped on the greasy parapet, and like a thunderbolt he struck the colonel in the small of the back. All three officers sprawled in the mud at the bottom of the trench.

The colonel was up first. Jamming a mud-coated monocle into his left eye, he glared at Biggles furiously.

'Where the dickens have you come from?' he snarled.

'My Camel landed me in this mess,' complained Biggles bitterly.

The colonel started violently.

'Camel?' he gasped. 'Have they brought up the Camel Corps?'

'That's right. That's why everyone's got the "hump"!' punned Biggles sarcastically. 'A Camel's an aeroplane in this war, not a dromedary!'

Further explanations were cut short by a shrill whistle and a cry of 'Here they come!'

'Who's coming?' cried Biggles anxiously to a burly sergeant who had sprung to the fire step and was firing his rifle rapidly.

'Father Christmas! Who do you think? 'Uns—the Prussian Guard—that's who!' snapped the N.C.O.

'Huns! Give me a rifle someone!' pleaded Biggles.

A bomb burst somewhere near at hand, filling the trench with a thick cloud of acrid yellow smoke, and he grabbed, gasping and choking, at a rife that leaned against the rear wall of the trench. The din of war was in his ears—the incessant rattle of rifles, the vicious crackle of machine-guns, the dull roar of heavy artillery, and the stinging crack of hand-grenades. Near at hand someone was moaning softly.

Above the noise another voice was giving orders in a crisp parade-ground voice:

'Here they come, boys—take it steady—shoot low—pick your man!'

With his head whirling, Biggles clambered up the side of the trench, still grasping his mud-coated rifle.

'Hi! Where are you going, that man? Get down, you fool!' yelled a voice.

Biggles hesitated. From the parapet he could see a long struggling line of men with fixed bayonets approaching his position at a lumbering trot. Then a hand seized his ankle and jerked him back into the trench. He swung round and found himself staring into the frowning face of the colonel, the monocle still gleaming in his eye.

'Who are you pulling about?' snarled the Camel pilot.

'What do you think you're doing?' grated the staff officer.

'I'm going to fetch Bert!' snapped Biggles.

The colonel started.

'Bert? Bert who?' he asked.

'Bert, of the Twenty-third Londons,' replied Biggles. 'He's a pal of mine, and he's out somewhere in the middle by himself.'

'In the middle?' repeated the staff officer.

'Yes!' snapped Biggles. 'In the middle of the war, he says, and I reckon he's about right!'

'You're crazy!' said the colonel. 'I can't bother about individuals—and I order you to stay where you are!'

'Order me!' stormed Biggles. 'Who do you think I am? I'm not one of your mob; I'm a flyer——'

'I don't care tuppence who you are!' replied the other. 'You're about as much good to me as a sick headache. I haven't time to argue. Another word from you, and I'll put you under close arrest for insubordination under fire!'

Biggles choked, speechless, knowing in his heart that the senior officer was well within his rights.

An orderly tumbled into the trench and handed the colonel a note. He read it swiftly, nodded, and then blew his whistle.

'"A" Company, retire! "B" Company, stand fast!' he ordered crisply. And then, turning to the sergeant. 'The Boche are in on both flanks,' he went on quickly. 'Get "A" Company back as fast as you can. "B" Company will have to cover them. And you'd better get back, too!' he snapped, turning to Biggles, who, a moment later, in spite of violent protests, found himself slipping and stumbling up a narrow, winding trench.

'But what about Bert?' he pleaded to the sergeant in front of him.

'Can't 'elp 'im. We're in the soup as it is!' snarled the N.C.O.

'The trouble about this foot-slopping game is the rotten visibility!' growled Biggles. 'It's worse than flying in clouds. No altitude, no room to move—no nothing! You blokes might call this a dog-fight, but I call it a blooming worm-fight! A lot of perishing rabbits, that's all you are, bobbing in and out of holes!'

His remarks were cut short by an explosion that filled the air with flying mud and half-buried him. He struggled to his feet, to see a white-faced orderly talking rapidly to the sergeant and pointing in rapid succession to each point of the compass.

'Surrounded, eh?' said the sergeant.

'What with?' asked Biggles breathlessly.

The sergeant eyed him scornfully.

'Mud!' he said. 'Mud and blood and 'Uns! You ought to 'ave stayed upstairs, young feller. We're in the blinking cart, and no mistake. The 'Uns are coming in on both flanks!'

'But I'm due for another patrol at six!' protested Biggles, aghast.

'You'll be patrolling the Milky Way by that time, me lad!' observed the sergeant bitterly.

Biggles turned to the orderly.

'Are you a messenger?' he said.

'I'm a runner,' replied the lad.

'Well, let's see you do a bit of running!' snapped Biggles crisply, whipping out his notebook and writing rapidly. 'You run with that,' he went on, handing the orderly a note. 'Get through the Huns somehow, and don't stop for anyone. Grab the first motor-cyclist you see, and tell him it's urgent!'

'What's the big idea?' asked the sergeant, as the runner departed at the double.

'I'm just saying goodbye to all kind friends and relations,' grinned Biggles. 'Hallo, here's old glass-house turned up again!'

The colonel, followed by a line of dishevelled, mud-coated men, staggered wearily up the communication trench.

'Line the parapets both sides!' he shouted. 'We'll get as many of them as we can before they get us! Get that gun, someone,' he snapped, pointing to a Vickers gun which, with its crew dead behind it, pointed aimlessly into the sky. 'Is there a machine-gunner here?'

'I should say so!' cried Biggles joyfully.

He dragged the gun, with its heavy tripod, clear of the mud, and mounted it on the parapet. A line of grey-clad men in coal-scuttle steel helmets was advancing stealthily up a nearby trench, and Biggles' lips parted in his famous fighting smile as he seized the spade-grips of the gun, thumbs seeking the trigger. *Rat-tat-tat-tat-tat! Rat-tat-tat-tat-tat!*

The grey line wilted and sagged.

'Fill some more belts for me!' shouted Biggles, ducking as a bullet cut through the loose flap of his flying helmet.

'Here, stick that on your head!' cried the colonel, passing him a steel helmet. 'Can you see anything?' he went on, crawling up beside him.

'I can,' replied Biggles shortly. 'Huns to the right of us, Huns to the left of us—and Huns blinking well above us! Look at that nosy parker!' he snarled, jerking his thumb upwards to where an Albatross had appeared like magic in the sky, guns spouting lead into their trench.

Biggles flung himself on his back and jerked the muzzle of his gun upwards. He knew what few infantrymen knew—the distance it is necessary to shoot in front of a rapidly-moving target in order to hit it. He aimed not at the machine, but well in front of it on its line of flight. He pressed the double thumb-piece. A stream of lead soared upwards.

The German pilot was either careless or a novice, for he did not trouble to alter his course in conditions where straight flying was almost suicidal. Straight into Biggles' line of fire he flew. The watchers in the trench saw the black-crossed machine swerve, and then, with engine roaring full on, plunge downward into the sea of mud. They could hear the crash above the noise of the battle.

'Got the blighter!' chuckled the sergeant. 'Good shooting, sir!'

'Oh, I hope he didn't land on top of poor old Bert!' gasped Biggles. 'He must have been mighty close. I can see his tail sticking up near my Camel. I wonder will that one count on my score?' he asked the colonel. 'Although I don't suppose they'll believe it, anyway.'

'I'll confirm it,' said the colonel vigorously; 'that is, if we get out alive. We're in a nasty hole!'

'So I see,' retorted Biggles, taking him literally. 'And I don't think much of it. I'm no mole. I like doing my fighting sitting down, and where I can see what's going on.'

'I'm afraid we haven't a hope,' went on the colonel casually. 'The brigadier won't risk the brigade up here in broad daylight to get us out. We're for it, unless a miracle happens—and the day of miracles has passed.'

'Don't you be too sure about that,' returned Biggles, spraying a group of sprawling Boche with bullets. 'What about those?' he added, jerking his thumb upwards.

The colonel cocked his eye towards a little cluster of black specks that had appeared high in the blue.

'What can they do?' he asked.

'Do? You watch 'em and see!' said Biggles. 'Give me a Very pistol, so that I can fire a light to show them where we are.'

'Who are they?' asked the other.

'Friends of mine,' replied Biggles. 'I sent them word by a runner that their services were urgently required, and unless I'm very much mistaken the boys in this trench are going to see a treat for tired eyes. That's Mahoney in front—you can spot his machine a mile off. And that's Mac over on the left.'

'Oh!' he went on incredulously. 'What's all this coming behind them? A squadron of S.E.s, with old Wilks leading! The C.O. must have phoned 287 Squadron after he got my message,' he grinned, and let out a shrill whoop of triumph. 'Here, we'd better bob down a bit, or we're likely to stop something,' he went on. 'I've an idea that this locality is going to be a pretty warm spot for the next few minutes when those lads start doing their stuff. Oh—look at that!'

'That' was a line of Camels that plunged down out of the blue and scoured the ground with double lines of glittering tracer bullets. Straight along the war-torn earth they roared, guns rattling, bullets stuttering a deadly tattoo on the ground. At the end of their dive the Camels soared upwards to let the S.E.s go by, and then, after a steep, stalling turn, came down again, raking the earth with streams of lead. The colonel watched in stupefied amazement. Biggles slid down the parapet and caught the sergeant by the sleeve.

'Now, sergeant,' he said tersely, 'I've got you out of a hole, and I want you to help me get someone else out of one.'

'You bet I will!' cried the N.C.O. delightedly.

'Come on then!' cried Biggles, darting down the trench towards the old front line that had been their original position. Reaching it, he did not stop, but slithered across the intervening stretch of mud towards the crater near the crashed Camel. Bullets zipped and whined about them, and Biggles had a fleeting glimpse of a grey-clad figure rising about thirty yards in front of him, one arm raised in the act of throwing. Instinctively he flung himself full-length in the mud, dragging the sergeant with him. A moment later, a roar to their left, accompanied by a flame-hearted explosion, told them where a hand-grenade thrown by the German had struck.

Almost before the flurry of the explosion had subsided, Biggles was on his feet again, the sergeant following closely at his heels. Scrambling and slithering over the ground, they made a few more paces' headway. Then again that grey-clad figure rose up, and again the arm swung. But this time the grenade was not thrown. From somewhere behind them came a sharp crack of a rifle, and the German bomb-thrower sagged in mid-air in the very act of throwing.

It was the Britishers' chance—and they took it. Crouching low, they sped across to the crater where Bert was waiting, and scrambled down beside the wounded man.

Bert was sitting just as he had left him, calmly smoking a cigarette.

'Here you are!' he cried. 'I thought you'd gone without me. When I tell my missus about this she'll say, "Bert," she'll say—'

Biggles seized him unceremoniously by the scruff of the neck.

'Take his feet, sergeant,' he panted; and together they bore the wounded man to the rear.

They found the colonel where they had left him.

'What are you up to?' he shouted, as Biggles and the sergeant came into view with their burden. 'I've been waiting for you. Couldn't make out where you'd disappeared to. The machines have opened up the communication trenches, and we can get through now. We'd better be going.'

Half an hour later, Biggles was washing the grime of war from his face in a headquarters dug-out behind the support trenches. The senior officer, monocle still in place, was talking.

'It was jolly smart of you to hold up the Boche advance by conjuring up those machines,' he said.

'Boche advance? I didn't know they were advancing,' replied Biggles. 'All directions looked alike to me.'

'Then what on earth did you do it for?' cried the Colonel.

'So that I could go and fetch Bert. What else do you think? I promised him I would, so I had to,' replied Biggles, grinning broadly.

9
THE BOMBER

BIGGLES, cruising along the line on a dawn patrol, pressed on the rudder-bar with his left foot as his ever-searching eyes fell on a line of white archie bursts to the south-east, far over the British lines. The colour of the bursts told him at once that the shells were being fired by British guns, for German anti-aircraft gunfire was usually black. It could only mean that one or more enemy machines were in the vicinity, an event sufficiently unusual to intrigue him immensely.

'I must look into this,' was his unspoken thought as he headed his Camel along a course which would intercept the target of the rapidly-lengthening line of archie bursts.

A small, black speck, well in front of the foremost bursts, soon became visible and his curiosity increased, for the machine was of a type unknown to him. As he drew nearer a puzzled frown lined his forehead.

'I don't believe it; it can't be true,' he murmured at last, when only a few hundred yards separated him from his objective.

The anti-aircraft fire ceased when the gunners observed his presence, and Biggles closed rapidly with the other machine, which with sublime indifference continued on its way, without paying the slightest attention to him. Large Maltese crosses on the tail and fuselage left no doubt as to its nationality.

It was the largest aeroplane Biggles had ever seen. He noted two engines, one on each side of the fuselage, and raked his memory for some rumour or gossip by which he could identify it.

'It isn't a Gotha,' he mused. 'Dashed if I know what it is; but I'll bet she carries a tidy load of eggs.'

Almost unconsciously he had been edging nearer to the nose of the big machine as he inspected it, but a sudden burst of fire from the gunner in the nacelle, and an ominous *flack! flack! flack!* behind warned him that the crew were on the alert and well prepared to receive him. He made a lightning right-hand turn, and as he flashed back past the bomber a murderously accurate burst of fire from the rear gunner startled him still further.

'Strewth!' swore Biggles. 'This is a bit hot.'

The big machine had not moved an inch from its course, and to be thus treated with contempt annoyed him intensely. They were rapidly approaching the Lines and if he was to prevent the return of the bomber to its aerodrome, something would have to be done quickly.

Biggles swept to the rear of the machine, muttering again as the Camel bumped violently in the slipstream of the two engines.

'All right, let's see how you like this one,' he snapped angrily, and put his nose down in a steep dive. He was following the usual practice of attacking a two-seater, judging his speed and distance to bring him up under the elevators of the enemy machine, out of the field of fire of both gunners.

The attack was perfectly timed and the Camel soared up like a bird immediately under the big fuselage. Biggles glanced through the sights and took the bomber at where he judged the pilot's seat to be, withholding his fire until the Camel was almost at stalling point in order to make certain of his aim. What happened next occurred with startling rapidity. The muzzles of a pair of twin Parabellum guns slid out of a trap-door in the floor of the bomber and the next instant a double stream of lead was shooting the Camel to pieces about him. *Flack! Flack! Whang! Whang!* sang the bullets as they bored through fabric and metal.

Biggles, shaken as never before in all his flying experience, kicked out his left foot spasmodically and flung the stick over and back into his stomach. The Camel whirled over and fell into a dive; the 150 h.p. Bentley Rotary coughed once—twice—and then cut out altogether. The propellor stopped dead and the thoroughly alarmed pilot started to glide earthwards with the rapidly-diminishing hum of the bomber's engines in his ears.

Biggles pushed up his goggles and looked downwards, and then up at the fast disappearing Boche machine.

'Phew!' he breathed soberly. 'That'll stop me laughing in church in the future. What a trap. Who would have guessed it? Well, we live and learn,' he concluded bitterly, and turned his attention to the inevitable forced landing. He anticipated no difficulty, for he had ample height from which to choose a landing ground. 'Thank goodness I'm over my own side of the line,' he mused philosophically, as he slowly lost height.

He could not get to his own aerodrome, at Maranique, but 287 Squadron might just be reached, and although he did not look forward with any degree of pleasure to the inevitable jibes of the S.E.5 pilots it was better than risking damaging the machine in an open field.

He made a good landing in the middle of the aerodrome and sat up on the 'hump' of the Camel to await the arrival of the mechanics to tow the machine to the tarmac, where a group of cheering pilots awaited him.

'Get stung, Biggles?' yelled Wilkinson, the good-natured flight-commander.

'I got stung all right,' acknowledged Biggles ruefully. 'That kite's got more stings than a hornet's nest. What is it, anyway?'

'That's our pet Friedrichshafen. Come and have a drink while we ring up your old man and tell him you're O.K., and I'll tell you about it,' said Wilks, linking his arm through that of the Camel pilot's.

'Have you had a go at it?' inquired Biggles.

'Me? We've all had a go at it. It comes over just before dawn nearly every day, lays its eggs, and beetles home about this time.'

'And so you mean to say that you can't stop it?' exclaimed
Biggles incredulously.

Wilkinson shrugged his shoulders. 'You didn't do a lot
yourself, did you? The only thing that did any stopping was your
cowling, by the look of jt. It's as full of holes as a colander. It'd be
easier to sink a battleship than that flying arsenal. There isn't a
blind spot anywhere that we've discovered; the usual weak spots
aren't weak any longer. They just plaster you whichever way
you come—oh! I know. Twin mobile guns'll beat fixed guns any
day. I'm not aching to commit suicide, so I let it alone, and
that's a fact. There was a rumour that Wing had offered three
pips to anybody who got it. Lacie of 281 had a go, and went
down in flames. Crickson of 383 had a stab at it in one of the new
Dolphins, and it took a week to dig him out of the ground. Most
people keep their distance now and watch archie do its stuff; but
they couldn't hit a Zeppelin at fifty yards. Guns[1] reckons that the
Friedrichshafen costs our people, who are paying for the War,
five thousand pounds a day for archie ammunition, and I reckon
he isn't far out.'

'I see,' said Biggles thoughtfully. 'Well, I'll be getting back if
you can find me transport. I'll come back for the Camel later on.
Cheerio, Wilks.'

'Cheerio, Biggles. Keep away from that Hun till the first of the
month. I'll send you a wreath, but I'm broke till then.'

'Yes? Well, don't chuck your money away on losers. What
you'll need is a pair of spectacles next time I meet that Hun.'

After seeing the damaged Camel brought home, and the
ignition lead which had caused the engine failure repaired,
Biggles spent the evening with a lead pencil and some paper,
making drawings of the big bomber as he remembered it. He
marked the three guns and drew lines and circles to represent
the field of fire covered by each. He quickly discovered that
what Wilkinson had told him concerning the guns covering all
angles of approach was correct, and ordinary attack was almost

---

[1] *'Guns' was the usual squadron nickname for the gunnery officer.*

useless, and certainly very dangerous.

The old weakness in the defence of all big machines, which was underneath the fuselage, did not exist. The only possible spot which could be regarded as 'blind' was immediately under the nacelle, and even so he would be exposed to the fire of at least one of the gunners while he was manoeuvring into that position. He considered the possibility of dropping bombs, but discarded it as impracticable. If he dropped the bombs over his own side of the line and missed, the people down below would have something to say about it, and it was hardly likely that he would be allowed to go about it unmolested over the German side.

No! The only chance was the spot under the nacelle and then use a Lewis gun which fired upwards through his centre section. He did not usually carry this weapon, and he infinitely preferred head-on tactics with his double Vickers guns. Not entirely satisfied with the result of his calculations, he gave instructions for the Lewis gun to be fitted, told his batman to call him an hour before dawn, and went to bed.

It was still dark when, with his flying coat and boots over his pyjamas, he climbed into the cockpit of his Camel the following morning. He felt desperately tired and disinterested in the project, and half regretted his decision to pursue it, but once in the air he felt better.

It was a glorious morning. A few late stars still lingered in the sky; to the east the first gleam of dawn was lightening the horizon. He pointed his nose and cruised steadily in the direction of his encounter of the preceding day, climbing steadily and inhaling the fresh morning air. As he climbed, the rim of the sun, still visible to those below, crept up over the skyline and bathed the Camel in an orange glow. Around and below him the earth was a vast basin of indigo and deep purple shadows, stretching, it seemed, to eternity. He appeared to hang over the centre of it, an infinitesimal speck in a strange world in which no other living creature moved. The sense of utter loneliness and desolation, well known to pilots, oppressed him, and he was glad when six D.H.9s, which had crept up unseen from the void beneath, gleamed suddenly near him like jewels on velvet as the rays of the sun flashed on their varnished wings. He flew closer to them and waved to the observers leaning idly over their Scarff rings.[1] The Nines held on their way and were soon lost in the mysterious distance. Biggles idly wondered how many of them would come back. The dome above him had turned pale-green, and then turquoise, not slowly, but quickly, as if hidden lights had been switched on by the master of a stage performance.

'And this is war!' mused the pilot. 'It's hard to believe—but unless I'm mistaken here it comes,' he added, as his eye caught a cluster of tiny sparks in the far distance at about his own height. 'Good morning, Archibald, you dirty dog,' he muttered, as he eyed the approaching flashes, at the head of which he could now discern the silhouette of the big bomber. He swiftly closed the distance between them, warming his guns as he went, and the answering stream of tracer from the forward guns of the bomber brought a faint smile to his lips. There was no chance of approaching unobserved and he had not attempted it. He circled slowly 500 feet above the big machine and looked down; the gunner in the rear cockpit gave him a mock salute, and waved back.

He wasted no further time on pleasantries, but dived steeply, still well outside effective range. Down and down he went until he was well below the bomber and then slowly pulled the stick back; the bomber seemed to be dropping out of the sky on to him. He was coming up under the nacelle and his eyes were glued to the trap-door, through which he could see the crouching gunner. A spurt of flame leapt outwards towards him and the ominous tell-tale *flack! flack!* behind and on each side told that the gunner was making good shooting. A moment later he was flying on even keel not more than twenty feet below the nacelle and in the same direction as the other machine.

Something seemed to drop off the bomber and whizz past him; he looked upwards with a start, in time to see another bomb swing off the bomb-rack and hurtle past dangerously

---

[1] *Gun-mountings.*

near. He looked along the line of racks, but could see no more bombs, which relieved him greatly, for he had entirely over-looked the fact that the bomber might not have laid all its eggs. He could see the face of the forward gunner peering over the side, looking at him, and a quick glance astern revealed spasmodic bursts of tracer passing harmlessly under the tail of the Camel. Satisfied that the gunner could not reach him, he took the joystick between his knees and seized his top gun, left hand grasping the spade grip and right forefinger curled around the trigger. *Rat-tat*—— He muttered as he struggled to clear the jammed gun. Why did guns always jam at the crucial moment?

The bomber was turning now and he had to grab the stick with one hand to keep his place. He stood up in the cockpit and hammered at the ammunition drum with his fist. He tried the trigger, found the gun was working and dropping back into his seat, just had time to push the stick forward as the bomber came down on him as its pilot tried to tear his wing off with its under-carriage. He side-slipped in a wild attempt to keep in position, but his windscreen flew to pieces as a stream of tracer from the rear gun caught him. He dived frantically away, kicking alternate feet as he went to spoil the gunner's aim.

Safely out of range, he pushed up his goggles and wiped his forehead. 'Dash this for a game,' he moaned, 'but for that jam I'd have had him then.'

He glanced down and was horrified to see that they were already over the enemy's lines. He tested his top gun to make sure that it was working and then savagely repeated his manoeuvre to come up underneath the bomber. He held his breath as he ran the gauntlet of the gunners again, and then at point-blank range he dropped the stick, seized the gun and pressed the trigger.

There was no mistake this time. He held the burst until the Camel began to fall away from under him and then he dropped back into his seat, grabbing wildly at the stick as the machine went into a spin, bracing himself with all his strength against the sides of the cockpit to prevent himself being thrown out.

'By gosh! That's all I want of that,' he muttered, as he got the machine under control and looked around for the bomber.

It was steering an erratic course for the ground, obviously in difficulties. He dived after it and noticed that the rear gunner's cockpit was empty.

I've hit the pilot, and the observer is trying to get the machine down,' he decided instantly, and a closer view confirmed his suspicions, for he could see the observer holding the joystick over the shoulder of the limp figure of the pilot. 'I hope he manages it,' thought Biggles anxiously, and held his hand up to show that they had nothing more to fear from him, afterwards circling round to watch the landing. It was a creditable effort; the big machine flattened out, but failed to clear a line of trees; Biggles almost fancied he could hear the crash as it settled down in a pile of torn fabric and splintered wood.

'I'll have to go and tell Wilks about this,' said Biggles to himself, as he steered a course for the S.E.5 aerodrome. 'He'll be tickled to death!'

10

ON LEAVE

BIGGLES, glanced up carelessly at the noticeboard in passing; a name caught his eye and he took a step nearer. The name was his own. He read:

Captain J.C. Bigglesworth: posted to 69 F.T.S. Narborough. W./48 P./1321.

For a full minute he looked at the notice uncomprehendingly, and as its full significance dawned upon him strode purposefully to the Squadron office.

'Yes, Biggles?' said Major Mullen, glancing up from his desk. 'Do you want to see me?'

'I see I'm posted to Home Establishment,' replied Biggles. 'May I ask why?'

The C.O. laid down his pen, crossed the room and laid a fatherly hand on the flight-commander's shoulder. 'I'm sorry, Biggles,' he said simply, 'but I've got to send you home. Now listen to me. I've been out here longer than you have. I know every move in the game; that's why I'm commanding 266. I know when a man's cracking up; I saw you start weeks ago; when Batson went west you were at breaking-point. Now, remember, I'm telling you this for your own good—not to hurt your feelings. I think too much of you for that. If I thought less of you, why, I'd leave you here to go on piling up the score in the Squadron "game book". If you did stay here, you wouldn't last a month. You'll be caught napping; you'll stall taking-off, or you'll hit a tree coming in. Cleverer pilots than you have gone out that way. You can't help it and you can't stop it. No one can stand the pace for ever. This game makes an old man of a young one without him knowing it. That's the truth, Biggles. You've got to have a rest. If you don't rest now you'll never be able to rest again. You are more use to us alive than dead; put it that way if you like. That's why I put your posting through.'

'But can't I have a rest without being posted?' said Biggles bitterly.

'No; I have asked you to take some leave. The M.O. has asked you, and I've heard Mac and Mahoney telling you to—they've both been on leave and it's done them a power of good.'

'All right, sir. I'll go on leave if you'll cancel the posting. It would kill me to hang about an F.T.S.[1]'

'Very well. Fill in your application. Ten days, with effect from tomorrow. I'll send it to Wing by hand right away. You stay on the strength of 266.'

'I've only one other thing to ask, sir. May I fly home?'

'There you go, you see. You can't leave it alone. Well, you might get a lift with a ferry pilot from Bourget. How's that?'

'Not for me,' said Biggles firmly. 'I'm not trusting my life to any ferry pilot. I'll fly myself in a Camel.'

'How am I going to account for the Camel if you break it up?'

'Break it up! I don't break machines up.'

'You might.'

'Well, send one back for reconditioning. I'll take it.'

[1] *Flying Training School.*

'All right,' said the C.O. after a brief pause. 'It's against regulations and you know it. Don't come back here without that Camel, that's all.'

'Very good, sir.'

Biggles saluted briskly and departed.

Major Mullen turned to 'Wat' Tyler, the Recording Officer, who had been a witness to the scene, and deliberately winked. 'You were right, Tyler,' he smiled. 'That posting worked the trick; that was the only way we would have got him to take some leave.'

Early the following morning Biggles, in his best uniform, took off and steered a course for Marquise, where he proposed to refuel before crossing the Channel. He eyed the enemy sky longingly, but true to his word to the C.O. held firmly to his way. The trip proved uneventful, and midday found him lunching in the officers' mess at Lympne. He reported to the officer commanding the station, presenting his movement order, saw his machine safely in a hangar, and went on to London by train. Arriving home, he discovered the house closed; he telephoned a friend of the family, only to find out that his father and brother, his only living relations, were in the Army and 'somewhere in France'.

'Well, that's that,' said Biggles, as he hung up the receiver. 'I might have known they would be.'

For a week he hung about town, thoroughly bored, doing little except drift between his hotel and anywhere he thought he might strike somebody he knew, home on leave from the Front. The weather was cold and wet and he looked forward joyfully to his return to the Squadron. And then, walking down Shaftsbury Avenue, he met Dick Harboard, his father's greatest friend and business associate. Over some coffee Biggles briefly explained his position, bitterly lamenting the time he was wasting when he might be doing something useful in France.

'I'm sick of loafing about here,' he concluded. 'London is getting me down fast. I hate the sight of the place, but there's nowhere else to go.'

'Why not come down to my place for the rest of your time.

I've a shooting party down for the week-end. Mixed crowd, of course—some funny people have got the money these days—but it can't be helped. What about it?'

'Where is your place?'

'Felgate, in Kent—near Folkestone.'

'Folkstone is near Lympne, isn't it?'

'Next door to it. Why?'

'Oh, I just wondered,' said Biggles vaguely. He did not think it worth while explaining that he had a machine at Lympne and had visions of putting in a few hours' flying-time if the weather improved.

'Good enough,' said Harboard as they parted. 'I shall expect you tonight in time for dinner.'

'I'll be along,' agreed Biggles. 'I'll come down in mufti, I think, and forget the war for a bit. Cheerio—see you later.'

Biggles, clad in grey flannels and a sweater, deep in a novel from his host's library, paused to pull his chair a little nearer to the hall fire. It was bitterly cold for the time of the year; lowering skies and a drizzle of rain had put all idea of flying out of his head, and he settled down for a comfortable spell of reading.

He frowned as the door opened to admit a party of men and girls whose heavy boots and mackintoshes proclaimed them to be a shooting party, bound for the fields. At their head was Frazer, a big, florid, middle-aged man to whom Biggles had taken an instant dislike when they had been introduced the previous evening. Biggles did not like the easy air of familiarity with which he had addressed him. His loud, overbearing manner, particularly when there were women present, irritated his frayed nerves. He had noticed on arrival that none of the party was in uniform, and he wondered vaguely why a man of such obviously splendid physique as Frazer was not in the Army; to save any possible embarrassment he had asked to be introduced as Mr. Bigglesworth. He was not left long in wonder, for Frazer, tapping his chest ruefully with his forefinger, complained at frequent intervals of the weak heart that kept him at home and thus prevented him from showing in actual practice how the war could be ended forthwith. The fact that he was obviously making a lot of money out of the war did nothing to lessen Biggles' irritation, and these were the reasons why he had decided to remain in the hall with a book rather than have to suffer the fellow's society with the shooting party.

'Well, well,' observed Frazer in affected surprise, with his eyes on the slippers on Biggles' feet. 'Not coming out with the guns?'

'No, thanks,' replied Biggles civilly.

'Huh! I should have thought a bit of exercise would have done you good; a shot or two at the birds will get your eye in for when you join the Army.' The sneer behind the words was unmistakable.

'It's too confoundedly cold, and I hate getting my feet wet,' said Biggles quietly, keeping his temper with an effort.

'I can't understand you young fellows,' went on Frazer, when the snigger that had followed Biggles' words had subsided. 'Anyway, I should have thought there were plenty of things you could do with a war on besides rotting over a fire.'

Again the inference was obvious, and Biggles choked back a hot retort. 'Bah! Why argue,' was his unspoken thought. The man was in his element, holding the floor; well, let him. He eyed Frazer coldly, without answering, and it may have been something in his eye that caused Frazer to shift uneasily and turn to the outside door.

'Well, let's get along, folks,' he said loudly. 'Somebody has got to keep the home fires burning, I suppose,' was his parting shot as the door closed behind them.

Biggles, left alone, smiled to himself for a moment, and then settled down to his book. The telephone in the next room shrilled noisily—again, and yet again, and Biggles breathed a prayer of thankfulness when he heard Lea, the butler, answer it. He was half-way through the first chapter of his book when the phone again jarred his nerves with its insistent jangle. He laid down his book with a weary sigh. 'My gosh! I can't stand this infernal racket,' he muttered, and looked up to see Lea standing white-faced in the doorway.

'What's the matter, Lea?' he asked irritably. 'Is the house on fire or something?'

'No, sir; but Mr. Harboard is out. He is the chief Constable, you know, and they say that two German seaplanes are bombing Ramsgate.'

'What?' Biggles leapt up as if he had been stung by a hornet. 'Say that again.'

'Two German seaplanes——'

Biggles made a flying leap to the window and cast a critical eye at the sky. The rain had stopped and small patches of blue showed through the scudding clouds.

'Quick!' he snapped, every nerve tingling with excitement. 'Get the car round.'

The butler, shaken from his normal sedate bearing by the brisk command, departed almost at a run.

'Get me to Lympne as quickly as you can; put your foot down and keep it down,' Biggles told the chauffeur a few minutes later, as, with flying-coat, cap and goggles over his arm, he jumped into the big saloon car.

For fifteen minutes Biggles fretted and fumed with impatience as the car tore through the narrow Kentish lanes.

'Go on,' he shouted, when they arrived at the aerodrome, 'straight up to the hangar.'

The guard at the gate challenged him, but Biggles yelled him aside with a swift invective.

'Get that Camel out of No. 3 shed,' he snapped at a group of idling mechanics. 'Number 9471—jump to it!' and then he burst into the C.O.'s office.

'Captain Bigglesworth, 266 Squadron, on leave from overseas, sir. You remember I reported last week?'

'Oh, yes, I remember,' said the C.O. 'What's the hurry?'

'Two Huns are bombing Ramsgate—I'm going for them. I've got ammunition—and I had two belts put in in case I ran into anything coming over.'

'But——'

Biggles was already on his way; he took a flying leap into the cockpit.

'Switches off, petrol on,' sang out the ack-emma.

'Petrol on,' echoed Biggles.

'Contact!'

'Contact!'

The Bentley started with a roar and sent a cloud of smoke whirling aft in the slipstream. He adjusted his goggles, waved the chocks away, and a few minutes later was in the air heading N.N.W., with the coastline cutting across the leading edge of his starboard wing. He had no maps, but he estimated the distance to Ramsgate to be about fifteen to twenty miles, not more; with the wind under his tail he should be there in less than ten minutes. Deal was on his starboard quarter now, and Sandwich loomed ahead; in the distance he could see the sweep in the coast where the North Foreland jutted out.

He had been flying low in order to watch the landmarks, but now he pulled the joystick back and climbed through a convenient hole in the clouds. Above, the cloud-tops were bathed in brilliant sunshine, and, still climbing, he looked eagerly ahead for the enemy machines. The only machine he could see was an old F.E. circling aimlessly some distance inland, so he pointed his nose north-west and headed out to sea in an endeavour to cut the raiders off should they have started on the homeward journey.

For a quarter of an hour he flew thus, peering ahead and around him for the hostile machines. Doubts began to assail him. Suppose the whole thing was a wild rumour? What a fool he had been not to get some reliable information before he started. His altimeter was registering 10,000 feet; the clouds through which he could occasionally see patches of grey sea, were far below.

He commenced a wide circle back towards land, noting that he had already ventured much too far away to be safe should his engine give trouble. He throttled back to three-quarters and for a few minutes cruised quietly in a due easterly direction, touching his rudder-bar from time to time to permit a clear view ahead.

A movement—or was it instinct—made him glance to the north. Far away, flying close together, were two machines—seaplanes. He was round in an instant heading north-west to cut them off. Five minutes later he could see that he would catch them, for they were appreciably nearer. He could tell the moment they saw him, for they turned in a more northerly direction away from him and put their noses down for more speed. A few minutes later he could see the black crosses and the gunners standing up waiting to receive him.

'Well,' mused Biggles, 'this is no place to mess about in a Camel. If I run out of fuel, or if they get a shot in my tank, I'm sunk. I must have been crazy to come right out here. It's neck or nothing if I'm going to do anything. Here goes.'

He pushed his nose down for speed and then pulled up in a steep zoom under the elevators of the nearest machine; but the pilot had seen his move and swung broadside on and exposed him to the full view of his gunner, who at once opened fire; but his shooting was wild, and Biggles could see his tracer passing harmlessly some distance away. The Camel pilot deliberately hung back until the other had emptied his drum of ammunition and started to replace it with a new one; then he zoomed in to point-blank range, and, knowing that he might not get such another opening, held his fire until his sights were aligned on the forward cockpit, and then pressed his triggers.

The nose of the Brandenburg seaplane tilted sharply upwards, and then dropped; the machine made an aimless half-turn that quickly became a spin as the nose dropped, and then whirled downwards with the engine still at full throttle.

Biggles fell off on to his wing and peered through his centre section for the second seaplane. For a moment he could not see it, and when he did spot it it was going down in a steep dive towards the clouds.

'Looks as if he's lost his nerve,' muttered the Camel pilot, as he pushed his stick forward and went down like a thunderbolt in the wake of the diving German.

He opened fire some distance away at a range which he knew quite well could not be effective unless a lucky shot found its mark, but he did it with the deliberate intention of rattling an obviously nervous foe.

The Brandenburg dropped tail-up into the cloud-bank and

Biggles carefully followed it; he found it again just below the clouds and resumed the chase. Just ahead, a wide patch of blue sky showed through a gap in the cloud, and Biggles closed in quickly, but the German swung round in obvious indecision.

'The fool can't be thinking of trying to land,' thought Biggles in astonishment, and fired a series of short bursts to confuse his opponent still more.

But the German had had enough, and apparently having no wish to share the fate of his companion, cut off his engine and commenced to glide down towards the water.

A new possibility occurred to Biggles. 'If he gets that kite down on the water safely the gunner might be able to hold me off.' A floating target would be more difficult to hit than one in the air, for he dare not risk overshooting his mark. 'Well, I've got to cramp his style,' thought Biggles, and he dived recklessly at the seaplane, guns streaming tracer, to which, to his surprise, the enemy gunner made no reply. 'What a gutless hound,' he thought. 'Hullo—there he goes!'

The Brandenburg pilot, in his haste to get out of that withering blast of lead, had tried to land too fast; the floats struck the surface of the sea with a terrific splash; the nose buried itself under the water and the tail cocked high into the air. Biggles watched both occupants climb along the elevators, and, circling low, pointed in the direction of the shore, in the hope that they would realize that he had gone for help.

'You are wanted on the phone, sir,' said Lea, the butler, apologetically.

It was late in the afternoon. Biggles put down his book and hurried to the instrument, for he was expecting the call, and anxious to hear the fate of the two German airmen. He picked up the receiver.

'Major Sidgrove speaking, from Lympne,' said a voice.

'Captain Bigglesworth here, sir,' replied Biggles.

'Good show, Bigglesworth; we found both machines in the sea. The crew of the first were both dead—gunshot wounds— but the others were all right except for shock and exposure.

Rather funny; the pilot had a brace of beautiful black eyes that the observer had given him. The pilot was an N.C.O. under the command of an officer in the rear seat; the Germans fly like that, you know.'

Biggles knew well enough, but he made no comment.

'Apparently it was the pilot's first show,' went on the Major, 'and when you started shooting he went to bits. He made for the water with the officer beating hell out of him and yelling for him to get into the clouds. He was swiping him over the nut instead of shooting at you. I've never seen a man so peeved in my life. Well, that's all. I thought you'd like to know. I've forwarded your report to the Ministry. They've been on the phone wanting to know what the dickens you were doing at Lympne, where you got the Camel, who gave you instructions, and goodness knows what else! They seem more concerned about that than about the two Huns—they would be! I expect they'll send for you during the next day or two; where can I get hold of you if they do?'

'Maranique,' replied Biggles shortly. 'I'm going back tomor-row. Many thanks, Major; goodbye.'

Biggles hung up the receiver and returned to the hall. The door opened and the shooting party, covered with mud, entered. Frazer looked at Biggles in undisguised disgust.

'Still keeping the fire warm,' he sneered. 'You should have been with us; we've had great sport.'

'So have I,' said Biggles softly.

'I got in some pretty shooting,' continued Frazer.

'Funny; so did I,' said Biggles, smiling faintly.

'You! Why, you haven't been out. I can't understand why some people are so careful about their skins.'

One of the girls came forward.

'There,' she said. 'I've brought you a little souvenir.' She laid a small white feather on the table.

'Thanks,' said Biggles evenly. 'I've always wanted a feather in my cap. I've got one today.'

Mr. Harboard bustled into the room.

'What's that—what's that—feather in your cap? I should say it will be. I shouldn't be surprised if you got the D.S.O. Well done, my boy; you deserve it.'

'D.S.O.—D.S.O.——?' echoed Frazer stupidly. 'What the devil for?'

'Haven't you heard?'

'Oh, cut it out, sir,' protested Biggles.

'Cut it out, be blowed. I'm proud to have you under my roof and I want everybody to know it.' He turned to the others. 'He's just shot down a couple of Hun bombers in the sea, after they bombed Ramsgate.'

A silence fell that could almost be felt.

'Who—who is he?' blurted out Frazer, at last, nodding towards Biggles, who was lighting a cigarette. 'He's not *the* Bigglesworth—the fellow we read about in the papers—the flyer—is he?'

'Of course he is; who else did you think he was?' cried Harboard in astonishment.

'Well,' said Frazer quietly, 'I'll be getting along. I've just had a phone call calling me up to Newcastle in the morning. I'll have to start tonight to catch my train.'

'That's all right,' said Biggles cheerfully. 'Stay the night and I'll fly you up in the morning. I can get a Bristol from Lympne.'

'No thanks,' cried Frazer firmly.

'I can't understand some people,' said Biggles softly, as he turned towards the library, 'being so careful about their skins.'

11

FOG!

FOG, mist, and still more mist. Biggles crouched lower in his cockpit as the white vapour swirled aft, and wished he had taken Major Sidgrove's advice and waited at Lympne until it had lifted.

'It will clear as the sun comes up,' he had told the Major, optimistically, as he took off.

He was anxious to get back to the Squadron, and although visibility on the ground had not been good he did not think it was so bad as it proved to be in the air. At 500 feet the ground was completely hidden from view, but a glance at the compass told him that he was heading towards the French coast.

'What a day!' he muttered, and climbed steadily to get above the opaque curtain. At 5,000 feet the mist began to thin and the sun showed wanly as a pale white orb; when his altimeter told him that he was 6,000 feet above the earth, he emerged into clear sunshine with a suddenness that was startling.

'I've a poor chance of finding the aerodrome if this stuff doesn't lift,' he told himself as he skimmed along just above the pea-soup vapour.

For an hour he followed his course, peering below anxiously for a break in the mist to show him his whereabouts, but in vain.

'Well, I'd better go down and see where I am,' he muttered. He throttled back and slid once more into the bank of clammy moisture. He was flying blind now, hoping against hope that the mist would thin out before he reached the ground; if it didn't, well, he would probably crash, that's all there was to it; but sooner or later he would have to come down, and he preferred to do it now rather than when he was getting short of fuel.

He kept a watchful eye on the altimeter. 2,000—1,000— 500—— 'I'll be into the carpet in a minute,' was his unspoken thought.

He went into a shallow glide, peering below anxiously, praying that his altimeter was functioning properly and that he would not crash into a church tower or a tree. Something dark loomed below and for a minute he could not make out what it was.

'Strewth! It's the sea!' he ejaculated, and thrusting the throttle wide open he began climbing swiftly. For a moment the discovery left him stunned. 'Where the deuce have I got to?' he said to himself, half in anger and half in fright; 'I ought to have crossed the coast half an hour ago. This compass is all wrong, I expect.'

He climbed above the mist and for another fifteen minutes flew south and then dropped down again. Something dark reared up in front of him and he zoomed swiftly to avoid hitting a tree, but an exclamation of relief escaped his lips as he saw that he was, at least, over terra firma.

'What a day!' he muttered again, and once more climbed up above the swirling fog, realizing that if conditions did not improve he would be lucky to get down without damaging the machine and possibly himself. In all directions the fog stretched in an unbroken sea of glistening white. 'This is no use,' he mused; 'I'd better find out where I am—it might as well be now as later on.'

He throttled back once more and commenced another slow glide towards the ground. At 500 feet he could just see what appeared to be open fields below. He S-turned, almost at stalling point, keenly alert for any possible obstruction. When he was satisfied that all was clear he tipped up his wing and side-slipped down; he levelled out, switched off the ignition, and a moment later ran to a standstill not ten yards from a thick hedge. For a few moments he sat contemplating his predicament, and then climbed slowly out of the cockpit.

'I suppose all I can do is to walk until I find a house or somebody who can tell me where I am,' he reflected ruefully, as, pushing up his goggles and loosening his throat-strap, he set off at a steady pace across the field. He was glad of his short, leather coat, for the ground-mist was cold and clammy. A hedge loomed up in front of him and he faced it blankly. 'Which way now?' he asked of himself. He thrust his hand in his trouser-pocket and pulled out a coin. 'Heads left, tails right,' he muttered. 'Heads, eh? Left it is then'; and he once more set off parallel with the hedge. A hundred yards and another hedge appeared dimly in front of him. 'Let's have a look what's over the other side,' he muttered, as he took a flying leap and landed on top of it. A sunken road, or, rather, a cart-track, lay before him. 'I wish this infernal mist would clear,' he thought petulantly, as he set off down the road. 'Hullo! Here's signs of life, anyway.' On his right was a row of poles which reminded him of the hop-fields he had often seen in Kent; a thick layer of greenery was spread over the tops of the wires that connected them. 'Don't tell me I'm back home again,' he said, aghast. 'No, by thunder; it's camouflage!'

He paused in his stride to survey what was the finest and certainly the largest piece of camouflage he had ever seen. Below it the ground fell away suddenly into a steep dip, and across the intervening vally stretched row after row of posts, criss-crossed at the top with wires, and the whole covered with a layer of drab green canvas and imitation grass.

'Whew!' he whistled. 'Whatever's under that would take a bit of spotting from the air.' He bent down and peered below the concealing canopy, but could only see what appeared to be a number of grey cisterns and cylinders. 'Beats me,' he muttered, as he continued his walk. 'Well, here's someone coming, anyway, so we'll soon know.'

On the left a gate opened into the field he had just left, and he leaned against it carelessly, awaiting the arrival of the owners of the approaching footsteps.

'It sounds like troops,' was his unspoken thought as he lit a cigarette and gazed pensively into the grey mist that hung like a blanket over the field.

The footsteps of marching men were close now, and he turned casually in their direction. The sight that met his eyes seemed to freeze his heart into a block of ice. The shock was so great that he did not move, but stood rigid as if he had been transformed into a block of granite. Out of the mist, not ten yards away, straight down the middle of the road, marched a squad of grey steel-helmeted German soldiers, an N.C.O. at their head.

Biggles looked at them with a face of stone, praying that they would not hear the tumultuous beating of his heart. There was a sharp word of command; as in a dream he saw the N.C.O.'s hand go up in salute, and his return of the salute was purely automatic. Another word of command and the troops had disappeared into the mist.

For a full minute Biggles gazed after them, utterly and completely stunned, and then a thousand thoughts flooded into his brain at once. Nauseating panic seized him, and he ran to and fro in agitated uncertainty. Never before had he experienced anything like the sensation of helplessness that possessed him now.

'Steady, steady, you fool!' he snarled, as he fought to get a grip on himself. 'Think—think!'

Sanity returned at last and he listened intently. In the distance someone was hammering metal against metal. *Clang! Clang! Clang!* boomed the sound dully through the enveloping mist.

They took me for one of their own pilots—of course they would. Why should they expect a British pilot to be standing gaping at them? Thank goodness I had my coat on, were thoughts that rushed through his mind.

A little farther down the road a large notice faced him, and he wondered how he had failed to see it before.

ACHTUNG! LEBENSGEFAHR

CHLORGASANSTALT

EINTRITT STRENG VERBOTEN

Chlorgasanstalt! Gas! In an instant he understood everything; the camouflage covered a Hun gas-manufacturing plant.

'I'll be getting out of this,' he muttered, and, vaulting over the gate, set off at a run across the field in the direction of the Camel. Another hedge faced him; he struggled through it and found himself in a field of roots. 'This isn't it,' he muttered hoarsely, and realised with horror that he had lost his sense of direction. He clambered back into the field he had just left and raced down the side of the hedge, pulling up with a cry of despair as the edge of the wood suddenly faced him.

He knew he was lost. 'Curse this fog; where am I?' he groaned out viciously. It was suddenly lighter and he glanced upwards; the mist was lifting at last, slowly, but already he could see the silvery disc of the sun. 'The Boche'll see the Camel as soon as I shall,' he pondered, hopelessly, 'and the farther I go now the farther I shall get away from it. If they spot it, I'm sunk.'

Another thought occurred to him—what of his discovery? Quite apart from saving his own skin he was now in possession of information which the Headquarters Staff would willingly give fifty officers to possess—the whereabouts of the German gas supply dump.

'If I do get away I can't tell them where it is,' he mused; 'I don't know where I am to within a hundred miles. Dash that compass!'

He started; someone was coming towards him. He dived into the undergrowth and crouched low, scarcely daring to breathe. The newcomer was a Belgian peasant, garbed in the typical garments of a worker on the land; in his hand he carried a hedger's hook. He was a filthy specimen of his class, dirty and unshaven, and Biggles watched him anxiously as he plodded along muttering to himself, glancing from time to time to left and right.

'I wonder if I dare risk speaking—if he would help me?' thought Biggles.

But the risk was too great and he dismissed the idea from his mind. The peasant was opposite him now, snivelling and wiping his nose on the back of his hand. He stopped suddenly and listened intently.

'Where are you?'

The words, spoken in English in a quick sibilant hiss from somewhere near at hand, stunned Biggles into a frozen state of immobility for the second time within a quarter of an hour. His heart seemed to stop beating and he felt the blood drain from his face. Who had spoken? Had anybody spoken—or had he imagined it? Were his nerves giving out? He didn't know, but he bit his lip to prevent himself crying out.

'Where are you?'

Again came the words in a low penetrating whisper, but in an educated English voice.

'Here,' said Biggles involuntarily.

The peasant swung round on his heel and hurried towards him. 'Your machine is in the next field,' he said quickly; 'hurry up, you've no time to lose. Fifty yards—look out—get down!'

Biggles flung himself back into the undergrowth and pressed himself into the bottom of the ditch that skirted the wood. The peasant's hook flashed above him and a tangle of briars covered him. Through them Biggles could just see the Belgian lopping at the hedge unconcernedly, muttering to himself as he did so.

Guttural voices jarred the silence somewhere near at hand and a group of German soldiers, carrying mess tins, loomed into his field of vision. Without so much as a glance at the hedge-trimmer they passed on and were swallowed up in the mist.

'Quick now,' said the voice again; 'run for it. There's an archie battery fifty yards down there—you were walking straight into it; I saw you land, and I've been chasing you ever since.'

'What about the gasworks?' said Biggles irrelevantly.

The pseudo-Belgian started violently. 'What gasworks?' he said, in a curiously strained voice.

'The Hun gas dump,' replied Biggles.

'Where is it?'

'Just across there at the corner of the wood; it's well camouflaged.'

'Great heaven! You've stumbled on the thing I've been looking for for three weeks. Get back and report it in case I am taken before I can loose a carrier pigeon. Here comes the sun— turn right down the hedge, fifty yards, then get through the hedge and you will see the machine in front of you.'

'Where am I now?' inquired Biggles.

'Thirty kilos north-west of Courtrai—one mile due east of Berslaade.'

'Aren't you coming? I can take you on the wing.'

'No; I'll stay here and see what damage the bombers do.'

'What's your name?' asked Biggles quickly.

'2472,' replied the other, with a queer smile.

'Mine's Bigglesworth—266 Squadron. Look me up sometime—goodbye.'

A swift handshake and Biggles was sprinting down the side of the hedge in the direction indicated by his preserver.

'Gosh! What jobs some people have to do. I wouldn't have that fellow's job for a million a year and a thousand V.C.s,' thought Biggles as, fifty yards down the hedge, he crawled through a convenient gap.

As he sprang erect the mist rolled away as if a giant curtain had been drawn, and the sun poured down in all its autumnal glory. There, ten yards away, stood the Camel, and beside it two German soldiers. They carried mess tins, and were evidently two of the party he had seen a few moments before.

With a bound, almost without pausing to think, Biggles was on them. The Germans swung round in alarm as they heard his swift approach, but Biggles held all the advantages of surprise attack. The first went down like a log before he had time to put his hands up as his jaw stopped a mighty swing from Biggles' right; the iron mess-tin rolled to one side as he fell. Biggles snatched it up by the strap and swung it with all his force straight at the head of the other German. It caught the man fairly and squarely on the temple and he dropped with a grunt like a pole-axed bullock. The whole thing was over almost before Biggles had realised the danger. With feverish speed he sprang to the cockpit of the Camel, switched on, turned the petrol on, and opened the throttle a fraction. Dashing back to the front of the machine he paused to feel the cylinders of the Bentley engine. They were not yet cold. He seized the propeller and whirled it with all his strength, almost falling backwards as it started with a roar. He tore madly round the wing and literally fell into the cockpit; once there, all his old confidence returned in a flash and he looked eagerly around. Behind him the field stretched open for take-off; in the far corner some men were running, pointing at him as they ran. He 'blipped' the engine with the rudder hard over, almost swinging the Camel round on its own axis, and for the first time since he realized he was in enemy country he breathed freely. He pushed the throttle open and tore across the field like a blunt-nosed bullet; a moment later he was in the air heading for the line, with the landscape lying clear and plain below him.

A stab of orange flame and a cloud of black smoke blossomed out in front of him, another, and another, and Biggles twisted like a snipe to throw the archie gunners off their mark. Strings of 'flaming onions' shot past him and the sky was torn with fire and hurtling metal.

'They're taking good care no one comes prowling about here for long,' he observed, as he kicked out first one foot and then the other to maintain his erratic course in order to confuse the batteries below. He was glad when the storm died down behind him. He surveyed the sky ahead intently. 'They saw me take off and they'll phone every aerodrome between here and the line to be on the look-out for me,' he told himself.

With his nose slightly down and engine at full throttle he sped onwards. An aerodrome appeared ahead; he could see little ant-like figures running around the black-crossed machines which stood on the tarmac. Something struck the Camel with a vibrating *sprang-g-g*, and he knew the machine-gunners were busy. He put his nose down in a fury and swept across the hangars with his guns spurting a double stream of tracer, and laughed as he saw the figures below sprinting for cover. He zoomed up and roared on without waiting to see what damage he had done.

A Fokker triplane, looking like a Venetian blind, flashed down on his flank and the sight sent him fighting mad. The Camel made the lightning right-hand turn for which it was famous and the twin Vickers guns on the cowling poured a stream of bullets through the Fokker's centre section. The Boche machine lurched drunkenly and plunged down out of sight below. Biggles continued his way without another glance. Far away to his left he could see a formation of straight-winged machines heading towards him, and he swept still lower, literally hopping the trees and hedges that stood in his path. The pock-marked desolation of the trenches appeared below and Biggles thrilled at the sight; he shot across them at fifty feet, wondering vaguely where all the bullets that were being fired at him were going.

He was over his own side of the lines now, and he sagged lower in the cockpit with relief as he passed the balloon line. Ten minutes later he landed at Maranique. Major Mullen was standing on the tarmac and came to meet him as he taxied in.

'You've got back, then, Biggles—had a good leave?'

'Fine, sir, thanks,' responded Biggles.

'It's been pretty thick here. What time did you leave this morning?'

'Oh, about sixish.'

'Then you must have called somewhere on the way—I hope they gave you a good time?'

'They did that,' grinned Biggles as he climbed out of the cockpit.

Major Mullen eyed his mud-plastered boots and coat with astonishment. 'Good Lord!' he cried. 'Where the deuce have you been?'

'On leave, sir,' smiled Biggles innocently. 'But I've got an urgent message for H.Q.'

In a few words he described his adventures of the morning, and ten minutes later his written report was on its way by hand to Headquarters. One thing only he omitted—his finding of the gas plant. He reported its position, but the credit for that discovery he left to '2742'.

'That's the least I can do for him,' decided Biggles.

12

AFFAIRE DE COEUR

BIGGLES hummed cheerfully as he cruised along in the new Camel which he had just fetched from the Aircraft Park.

'Another five minutes and I shall be home,' he thought, but fate willed otherwise. The engine coughed, coughed again, and, with a final splutter, expired, leaving him with a 'dead' prop. He exclaimed softly, pushed the joystick forward, and looked quickly around for the most suitable field for the now inevitable forced landing.

To the right lay the forest of Clarmes. 'Nothing doing that way,' he muttered, and looked down between his left wings. Ah! there it was. Almost on the edge of the forest was a large pasture, free from obstruction. The pilot, with a confidence born of long experience, side-slipped towards it, levelled out over the hedge and made a perfect three-point landing.

He sat in the cockpit for a minute or two contemplating his position; then he yawned, pushed up his goggles and prepared to take stock of his immediate surroundings. He raise his eyebrows appreciatively as he noted the sylvan beauty of the scene around him. Above, the sun shone from a cloudless blue sky. Straight before him a low lichen-covered stone wall enclosed an orchard through which he could just perceive a dull red pantiled roof. To the right lay the forest, cool and inviting. To the left a stream meandered smoothly between a double row of willows.

'Who said there was a war on?' he murmured, lighting a cigarette, and climbing up on to the 'hump' of his Camel, the better to survey the enchanting scene. 'Well, well, let's see if anyone is at home.'

He sprang lightly to the ground, threw his leather coat across the fuselage, and strolled towards the house. An old iron gate opened into the orchard; entering, he paused for a moment, uncertain of the path.

'Are you looking for me, monsieur?' said a musical voice.

Turning, he beheld a vision of blond loveliness, wrapped up in blue silk, smiling at him. For a moment he stared as if he had never seen a woman before. He closed his eyes, shook his head, and opened them again. The vision was still there, dimpling.

'You were looking for me, perhaps?' said the girl again.

Biggles saluted like a man sleep-walking.

'Mademoiselle,' he said earnestly, 'I've been looking for you all my life. I didn't think I'd ever find you.'

'Then why did you land here?' asked the girl.

'I landed here because my mag. shorted,' explained Biggles.

'What would have happened if you had not landed when your bag shorted?' inquired the vision curiously.

'Not bag—mag. Short for magneto, you know,' replied Biggles, grinning. 'Do you know, I've never even thought of doing anything but land when a mag. shorts; if I didn't, I expect that I should fall from a great altitude and collide with something substantial.'

'What are you going to do now?'

'I don't know—it takes thinking about. It may be necessary for me to stay here for some time. Anyway, the war will still be on when I get back. But, pardon me, mademoiselle, if I appear impertinent; are you English? I ask because you speak English so well.'

'Not quite, monsieur. My mother was English and I have been to school in England,' replied the girl.

'Thank you, Miss—er——'

'Marie Janis is my name.'

'A charming name more charming even than this spot of heaven,' said Biggles warmly. 'Have you a telephone, Miss Janis? You see, although the matter is not urgent, if I do not ring up my Squadron to say where I am someone may fly around to look for me,' he explained.

The thought of Mahoney spotting his Camel from the air and landing did not, in the circumstances, fill him with the enthusiasm one might normally expect.

'Come and use the telephone, M'sieur le Capitaine,' said the girl, leading the way. 'May I offer you *un petit verre?*'

'May you?' responded Biggles, warmly. 'I should say you may!'

Five hours later Biggles again took his place in the cockpit of the Camel, which a party of ack-emmas had now repaired. He took off and swung low over the orchard, waving gaily to a slim blue-clad figure that looked upwards and waved back.

Rosy clouds drifted across the horizon as he made the short flight back to the aerodrome.

'That girl's what I've been reading about,' he told himself. 'She's the "Spirit of the Air", and she's going to like me an awful lot if I know anything about it. Anyway, I'd be the sort of skunk who'd give rat poison to orphans if I didn't go back and thank her for her hospitality.'

Biggles, a week later, seated on an old stone bench in the orchard, sighed contentedly. The distant flickering beam of a searchlight on the war-stricken sky meant nothing to him; a little head, shining whitely in the moonlight, nestled lightly on his sleeve. In the short time that had elapsed since his forced landing he had made considerable progress.

'Tell me, Marie,' he said. 'Do you ever hear from your father?'

'No, m'sieur,' replied the girl sadly. 'I told you he was on a visit to the north when war was declared. In the wild panic of the Boche advance he was left behind in what is now the occupied territory. Communication with that part of France is forbidden, but I have had two letters from him which were sent by way of England by friends. I have not been able to tell him that mama is—dead!'

Tears shone for a moment in her eyes, and Biggles stirred uncomfortably.

'It is a hell of a war,' he said compassionately.

'If only I could get a letter to him to say that mama is dead and that I am looking after things until he returns I should be happy. Poor Papa!'

'I suppose you don't even know where he is?' said Biggles sympathetically.

'But yes,' answered the girl quickly; 'I know where he is. He is still at our friend's chateau, where he was staying when the Boche came in.'

'Where's that?' asked Biggles in surprise.

'At Vinard, near Lille; le Chateau Borceau,' she replied. 'But he might as well be in Berlin,' she concluded sadly, shrugging her shoulders.

'Good Lord!' ejaculated Biggles suddenly.

'Why did you say that, monsieur?'

'Nothing—only an idea struck me, that's all,' said Biggles. 'Tell me.'

'No. I'm crazy. Better forget it.'

'Tell me—please.'

Biggles wavered. 'All right,' he said. 'Say "please Biggles," and I'll tell you.'   ·

'Please, Beegles.'

Biggles smiled at the pronunciation. 'Well, if you must know,' he said, 'it struck me that I might act as a messenger for you.'

'Beegles! How?'

'I had some crazy notion that I might be able to drop a letter from my machine,' explained Biggles.

'*Mon dieu!*' The girl sprang to her feet in excitement, but

Biggles held her arm and pulled her towards him.

For a moment she resisted, and then slipped into his arms. 'Beegles—please.'

'Marie,' whispered Biggles, as their lips met. Then, his heart beating faster than archie or enemy aircraft had ever caused it to beat, he suddenly pushed her aside, rose to his feet and looked at the luminous dial of his watch. 'Time I was getting back to quarters,' he said unsteadily.

'But, Beegles, it is not yet so late.'

Biggles sat down, passed his hand over his face, and then laughed. 'My own mag. was nearly shorting then,' he said.

They both laughed, and the spell was broken.

'Tell me, Beegles, is it possible to drop such a letter to Papa?' said the girl presently.

'I don't know,' said Biggles, a trifle anxiously. 'I don't know what orders are about that sort of thing, and that's a fact. There wouldn't be any harm in it, and they wouldn't know about, it, anyway. You give me the letter and I'll see what I can do.'

'Beegles—you——'

'Well?'

'Never mind. Come to the house and we will write the letter together.'

Hand in hand they walked slowly towards the house. The girl took a writing-pad from a desk and began to write; the door opened noiselessly and Antoine, Marie's elderly manservant, appeared.

'Did you ring, mademoiselle?' he asked.

'Merci, Antoine.'

'Do you know,' said Biggles, after the man had withdrawn, 'I don't like the look of that bloke. I never saw a nastier-looking piece of work in my life.'

'But what should I do without Antoine, and Lucille, his wife? They are the only two that stayed with me all the time. Antoine is a dear; he thinks only of me,' said the girl reproachfully.

'I see,' said Biggles. 'Well, go ahead with the letter.'

The girl wrote rapidly.

'Look,' she smiled when it was finished. 'Read it and tell me if you do not think it is a lovely letter to a long-lost father.'

Biggles read the first few lines and skipped the rest, blushing. 'I don't want to read your letter, kid,' he said.

Marie sealed the letter, addressed it, and tied it firmly to a small paperweight. 'Now,' she said; 'what can we use for a banner?'

'You mean a streamer,' laughed Biggles.

'Yes, a streamer. Why! Here is the very thing.' She took a black-and-white silk scarf from the back of a chair and tied the paperweight to it. 'There you are, *mon aviateur*,' she laughed. 'Take care; do not hit Papa on the head or he will wish I had not written.'

Biggles slipped the packet into the pocket of his British 'warm' and took her in his arms impatiently.

Arriving at the aerodrome he went to his quarters and flung the coat on the bed, and then made his way across to the mess for a drink. As the door of his quarters closed behind him, two men—an officer in uniform and a civilian—entered the room. Without a moment's hesitation the civilian picked up the coat and removed the letter from the pocket.

'You know what to do,' he said grimly.

'How long will you be?'

'An hour. Not more. Keep him until 11.30, to be on the safe side,' said the civilian.

'I will,' replied the officer, and followed Biggles into the mess.

Biggles, humming gaily, headed for home. His trip had proved uneventful and the dropping of Marie's letter ridiculously simple. He had found the chateau easily, and swooping low had seen the black-and-white scarf flutter on to the lawn. Safely back across the line he was now congratulating himself upon the success of his mission. S.287, the neighbouring S.E.5 Squadron, lay below, and it occurred to him to land and pass the time of day with them.

Conscious that many eyes would be watching him, he sideslipped in and flattened out for his most artistic landing. There was a sudden crash, the Camel swung violently and tipped up on to its nose. Muttering savagely, he climbed out and surveyed the damage.

'Why the deuce don't you fellows put a flag or something on this sunken road?' he said bitterly to Wilkinson and other pilots who had hurried to the scene; he pointed to the cause of his misadventure. 'Look at that mess.'

'Well, most people know about that road,' said Wilkinson. 'If I'd have known you were coming I'd have had it filled in altogether. Never mind; it's only a tyre and the prop. gone. Our fellows will have it right by tomorrow. Come and have a drink; I'll find you transport to take you home. The C.O.'s on leave, so you can use his car.'

'Righto, but I'm not staying to dinner,' said Biggles emphatically. 'I'm on duty tonight,' he added, thinking of a moonlit orchard and an old stone seat.

It was nearly eight o'clock when he left the aerodrome, seated at the wheel of the borrowed car. He had rung up Major Mullen and told him that he would be late, and now, thrilling with anticipation, he headed for the home of the girl who was making his life worth living and the war worth fighting for.

The night was dark, for low clouds were drifting across the face of the moon; a row of distant archie-bursts made him look up, frowning. A bomb raid, interrupting the story of his successful trip, was the last thing he wanted. His frown deepened as the enemy aircraft and the accompanying archie drew nearer.

'They're coming right over the house, confound 'em,' he said, and switching off his lights raced for the orchard. 'My gosh, they're low!' he muttered, as he tore down the road, the roar of the engines of the heavy bombers in his ears. 'They're following this road, too.' He wondered where they were making for, trying to recall any possible objective on their line of flight. That he himself might be in danger did not even occur to him. He was less than five miles from the house now and taking desperate chances to race the machines. 'The poor kid'll be scared stiff if they pass over her as low as this.'

With every nerve taut he tore down the road. He caught his

breath suddenly. What was that? A whistling screech filled his ears and an icy hand clutched his heart. Too well he knew the sound. *Boom! Boom! Boom!* Three vivid flashes of orange fire leapt towards the sky. *Boom! Boom! Boom!*—and then three more.

'What are they fanning, the fools? There is only the forest there,' thought Biggles, as, numb with shock, he raced round the last bend. Six more thundering detonations, seemingly a hundred yards ahead, nearly split his eardrums, but still he did not pause. He tried to think, but could not; he had lost all sense of time and reason. He seemed to have been driving for ever, and he muttered as he drove. Searchlights probed the sky on all sides and subconsciously he noticed that the noise of the engines was fading into the distance.

'They're gone,' he said, trying hard to think clearly. 'What if they've hit the house?'

He jammed on his brakes with a grinding screech as two men sprang out in front of the car as he turned in the gates; but he was not looking at them. One glance showed him that the house was a blazing pile of ruins. He sprang out of the car and darted towards the conflagration, but a hand closed on his arm like a vice.

Biggles, white-faced, turned and struck out viciously. 'My girl's in there,' he muttered.

A sharp military voice penetrated his stunned brain. 'Stand fast, Captain Bigglesworth,' it said.

'Let me go,' snarled Biggles, struggling like a madman.

'One more word from you, Captain Bigglesworth, and I'll put you under arrest,' said the voice harshly.

'You'll what?' Biggles turned, his brain fighting for consciousness. 'You'll what?' he cried again incredulously.

He saw the firelight gleam on the fixed bayonets of a squad of Tommies; Colonel Raymond of Wing Headquarters and another man stood near them. Biggles passed his hand over his eyes, swaying.

'I'm dreaming,' he said; 'that's it, dreaming. What a nightmare! I wish I could wake up.'

'Take a drink, Bigglesworth, and pull yourself together,' said Colonel Raymond, passing him a flask.

Biggles emptied the flask and handed it back.

'I'm going now,' said the Colonel. 'I'll see you in the morning. This officer will tell you all you need to know,' he concluded, indicating a dark-clad civilian standing near. 'Good night, Bigglesworth.'

'Good night, sir.'

'Tell me,' said Biggles, with an effort, 'is she—in there?'

The man nodded.

'Then that's all I need to know,' said Biggles, slowly turning away.

'I'm sorry, but there are other things you will have to know,' returned the man.

'Who are you?' said Biggles curiously.

'Major Charles, of the British Intelligence Service.'

'Intelligence!' repeated Biggles, the first ray of light bursting upon him.

'Come here a moment.' Major Charles switched on the light of his car. 'Yesterday, a lady asked you to deliver a message for her, did she not?' he asked.

'Why—yes.'

'Did you see it?'

'Yes!'

'Was this it?' said Major Charles, handing him a letter.

Biggles read the first few lines, dazed. 'Yes,' he said; 'that was it.'

'Turn it over.'

Unconsciously Biggles obeyed. He started as his eyes fell on a tangle of fine lines that showed up clearly. In the centre was a circle.

'Do you recognise that?'

'Yes.'

'What is it?'

'It is a map of 266 Squadron aerodrome,' replied Biggles, like a child reciting a catechism.

'You see the circle?'

'Yes.'

'The Officers' Mess. Perhaps you understand now. The letter you were asked to carry had been previously prepared with a solution of invisible ink and contained such information that, had you delivered it, your entire squadron would have been wiped out tonight, and you as well. The girl sent you to your death, Captain Bigglesworth.'

'I'll not believe it,' said Biggles distinctly. 'But I did deliver the letter, anyway,' he cried suddenly.

'Not this one,' said Major Charles, smiling queerly. 'You delivered the one we substituted.'

'Substituted?'

'We have watched this lady for a long time. You have been under surveillance since the day you force-landed, although your record put you above suspicion.'

'And on the substituted plan you marked her home to be bombed instead of the aerodrome?' sneered Biggles. 'Why?'

Major Charles shrugged his shoulders. 'The lady was well connected. There may have been unexpected difficulties connected with an arrest, yet her activities had to be checked. She had powerful friends in high places. Well, I must be going; no doubt you will hear from Wing in the morning.'

Biggles walked a little way up the garden path. The old stone seat glowed dully crimson. 'Bah!' he muttered, turning. 'What a fool I am. What a hell of a war this is.'

He drove slowly back to the aerodrome. On his table lay a letter. Ripping it open eagerly, he read:

Darling,
    I have something important to ask you—something you must do for me. Tonight at seven o'clock I will come for you. It is important. Meet me in the road by the aerodrome. I will be very kind to you, my Biggles.

                                                    MARIE.

Biggles, with trembling hands, sat on the bed and re-read the letter, trying to reason out its purpose. 'She timed the raid for eight,' he said to himself, 'when all officers would be dining in the mess. She knew I should be there and wrote this to bring me out. She knew I'd never leave her waiting on the road—that was the way of it. She must have cared, or she wouldn't have done that. When I didn't come she went back home. She didn't know I hadn't seen her letter—how could she? Now she's dead. If I hadn't landed at 287 I should be with her now. Well, she'll never know.'

He rose wearily. Voices were singing in the distance, and he smiled bitterly as he heard the well-remembered words:

> 'Who minds to the dust returning,
>   Who shrinks from the sable shore,
> Where the high and haughty yearning
>   Of the soul shall be no more?
>
> So stand by your glasses steady,
>   This world is a world of lies;
> A cup to the dead already,
>   Hurrah! for the next man who dies.'

A knock at the door aroused him from his reverie. An orderly of the guard entered.

'A lady left this for you,' he said, holding out a letter.

'A lady—when?' said Biggles, holding himself in hand with a mighty effort.

'About ten minutes ago, sir. Just before you came in. She came about eight and said she must see you, sir, but I told her you weren't here.'

'Where is she now?'

'She's gone, sir; she was in a car. She told me to bring the letter straight to you when you returned, sir.'

'All right—you may go.'

Biggles took the letter, fighting back a wild desire to shout, opened it, and read:

Goodbye, my Biggles.

You know now. What can I say? Only this. Our destinies are not always in our own hands—always try and remember that, my Biggles. That is all I may say. I came tonight to take you away or die with you, but you were not here. And remember that one thing in this world of war and lies is true; my love for you. It may help, as it helps me. Take care of yourself. Always I shall pray for you. If anything happens to you I shall know, but if to me you will never know. My last thought will be of you. We shall meet again, if not in this world then in the next, so I will not say goodbye.

Au revoir,

MARIE.

'And they think she's dead,' said Biggles softly. 'She risked her life to tell me this.'

He kissed the letter tenderly, then held it to the candle and watched it burn away.

He was crumbling the ashes between his fingers when the door opened, and Mahoney entered. 'Hullo, laddie, what's wrong; had a fire?' he enquired.

'Yes,' replied Biggles slowly; 'foolish of me; got my fingers burnt a bit, too.'

13

THE LAST SHOW

In the days that followed the tragic *affaire*, Biggles flew with abandon and with such an utter disregard of consequences that Major Mullen knew that if he persisted it could only be a matter of time before he 'failed to return'. The C.O. had not mentioned the affair of the girl to him, but Biggles knew that he must be aware of the main facts of the case, or he would certainly have asked him why he had been called to Headquarters.

However much the Major knew he said nothing, but he watched his flight-commander's behaviour with deep-rooted anxiety. He called MacLaren and Mahoney into his office to discuss the matter with them.

Mahoney nodded sympathetically as he listened to the C.O.'s plaint. 'Biggles is finished unless he takes a rest,' he said. 'He's drinking, and you know what that means—he's going fast. Of course, a fellow doesn't get drunk when he's in the state Biggles is in. It's no use talking to him—you know that as well as I do. He's got to the stage when he takes advice as a personal affront against his flying. It's a pity, but most of us go that way at the end, I suppose. Newland, of 287, told me confidentially the other day that a blue pigeon follows him in the air wherever he goes, and he meant it.'

'Well, I shall have to send him home, whether he likes it or not,' went on the Major, 'but it will break his heart if I don't find a good excuse. Now look, you fellows. I've got to send somebody home to form a new Squadron—of Snipes, I believe—and bring it over. You are both senior to Bigglesworth; you are both due for promotion. I shall be going to Wing in a week or two, I hear, so one of you will have to take over 266. Do you mind if I send Bigglesworth home for the new Squadron?' The C.O. looked at the two captains apologetically.

'Not me, sir,' said Mahoney instantly.

'Nor I, sir,' echoed MacLaren.

'Thank you. That's what I wanted to know,' said the Major. 'I'll send him home, then. Where is he now?'

'He's in the air,' replied Mahoney. 'He's never on the ground. Goodness knows where he goes; it must be miles over; I never see him on patrol.'

The C.O. nodded, 'Well, he can't get away with that much longer. They're bound to get him. By the way, there's a big show tomorrow—it will be in orders tonight. You'd better have a good look round your machines.'

Biggles, cruising at 18,000 feet, turned in the direction of Lille without being really conscious of the fact. He surveyed the surrounding air coldly and dispassionately for signs of enemy aircraft, but except for a formation of Bristol Fighters homeward bound, far below, the sky was empty. His thoughts wandered back to the girl who had come into his life. Where was she now? Where had she gone on that tragic night of disillusionment? Had she been caught? That was the thought that made the day a torture and the night a horror. He visualized her in the cold-grey of dawn with a bandage over her eyes facing a firing party in some gloomy French prison.

A volley of shots rang out, something jerked the rudder-bar from his feet and brought him back to the realities of life with a start.

He half-rolled and looked around; a Hannoverian was rapidly receding into the distance. He frowned at it in surprise and consternation. 'Good Lord! I must have nearly flown into it without seeing it, and the observer had a crack at me as he went by,' he mused. 'If it had been a D.VII——' He shrugged his shoulders. What did it matter—what did anything matter?

He looked downwards to pick up his bearings; the landscape was familar, for he had seen it a dozen times during the past week. To the left lay Lille, the worst hot-bed of archie in the whole of France. On his right a narrow, winding road led to the village of Vinard and the Chateau Boreau—his only link with Marie. She might even be there now—the thought occurred to him for the first time. How could she have reached it? Spies went to and fro across the line, he reflected; nobody knew how, except the chosen few whose hazardous business it was. He looked around the sky, but could see nothing; he put the stick forward and commenced to spiral down in wide circles.

At 5,000 feet he hesitated. Dare he risk losing any more height? He looped, half-rolled, came out and looped again, half-rolling off the top of it. Then he spun. He came out at 2,000 feet and studied the chateau intently. No one was in sight—yes—his eye caught a movement at the end of the garden and he glided lower. He knew that he was taking a foolish risk, but his curiosity overcame his caution.

Someone was waving—what? He put his nose down in a swift dive and then zoomed upwards exultantly, his heart beating tumultuously. Had his eyes betrayed him or had he seen a blue-clad figure waving a blue-and-white scarf? He looked back; the

blue-and-white scarf was spread on the lawn. He turned the
Camel in the direction of the line and raced for home, his mind
in a whirl.

'I'm mad,' he grated between his clenched teeth. 'She must be
a spy or she wouldn't be there.' The thought seemed to chill him,
and only then did he realize that he still hoped that the
authorities were mistaken in their belief that she was engaged in
espionage.

Doubts began to assail him. Had he really seen her—or had it
been a trick of the imagination? It might have been someone
else; he was too far away to recognize features.

'She's a spy anyway. I must be stark, staring mad,' he told
himself, as he dodged and twisted away from a close salvo of
archie.

Half-way home he had the good fortune to fall in with a
formation of S.E.5s, to which he attached himself. Safely over
the lines he waved them farewell and was soon back at
Maranique. He made his way to the mess and thrust himself into
a group of officers clustered around the noticeboard.

'What's on, chaps?' he asked.

'Big show tomorrow, Biggles,' replied Mahoney.

'What is it?'

'Escort—a double dose. Eighteen "Nines" are bombing
Aerodrome 27 in the morning and the same lot are doing an
objective near Lille in the afternoon. We and 287 are escorting.
287 are up in the gallery, and we're sticking with the formation.
Rendezvous over Mossyface at 10,000 feet at ten ack-emma.'

'Great Scott! Have they discovered the German Headquarters
Staff or something?'

'Shouldn't be surprised. Must be something important to do
the shows. The Aerodrome 27 show was on first—and the
second show came through later. They must be going to try and
blot something off the map; the idea's all right if the bombers
could only hit the thing.'

Biggles nodded moodily, for the show left him unmoved.
Escort was a boring business, particularly in his present state of
mind. Later in the evening another notice was put on the board,

which was greeted with loud cheers. Biggles forced his way to the front rank of the group and read:

Promotions
Act. Cpt. J. Bigglesworth, M.C., to Major, W.E.F. 10.11.18 (Authority) P.243/117/18.

Postings
Major J. Bigglesworth, from 266 Squadron to Command 319 Squadron. H.E., W.E.F. 11.11.18. P.243/118/18.

Biggles looked at the notice unbelievingly. He turned to Major Mullen, who had just entered.

'So I'm going home, sir,' he said in a strained voice.

'Yes, Bigglesworth. Wing wants you to fetch 319 out. I believe you're getting Snipes—you'll be able to make rings round Camels.

'Camels are good enough for me,' protested Biggles. 'That's the trouble with this infernal war. People are never satisfied. Let us stick to Camels and S.E.s and let the Boche have their D. Sevens, instead of all this chopping and changing about. I've heard a rumour about a new kite called a Salamander that carries a sheet of armour plate. Why? I'll tell you. Some brass-hat's got hit in the pants and that's the result. What with sheet iron, oxygen to blow your inside out, and electrically heated clothing to set fire to your kidneys, this war is going to bits.'

'You'll talk differently when you get your Snipes,' laughed the Major.

'Orders say I'm to move off tomorrow.'

'Yes, that's right.'

'Good. You can give my love to the Huns at Aerodrome 27 and—what's the name of the other target they're going to fan down?'

'Oh, it's a new one to me,' replied the Major. 'Place near Lille—Chateau Boreau or something like that—cheerio—see you later.'

It was as well that he did not pause to take a second glance at his flight-commander's face, or he might have asked awkward questions. For a full minute Biggles remained rooted to the spot with the words ringing in his ears.

'Chateau Boreau, eh?' he said, under his breath. 'So they know about that. How the deuce did those nosy-parkers on Intelligence find that out?' he muttered bitterly.

Mahoney slapped him on the back. 'Have a drink, Biggles?' he cried.

Biggles swung round. 'Go to—— No, I didn't mean that, old lad,' he said quickly. 'I was a bit upset at leaving the Squadron. Sorry—what are you having, everybody?' he called aloud. 'Drinks are on me tonight.'

Dinner was a boisterous affair; the usual farewell speeches were made and everybody was noisily happy. Biggles, pale-faced, with his eyes gleaming unnaturally, held the board.

'So tomorrow I am doing my last show,' he concluded.

The C.O. looked up quickly. 'But I thought you were going in the morning,' he exclaimed in surprise.

'In the afternoon, if you don't mind, sir,' answered Biggles. 'I must do one more show with 266.'

Major Mullen nodded. 'All right,' he said; 'but don't take any chances,' he added. 'I ought to pack you off in the morning really.'

Biggles spent a troubled and restless night. Why he had asked to be allowed to fly with the morning show he hardly knew, unless it was to delay departure as long as possible. He racked his brain to find an excuse to postpone it until the evening in order to learn the result of the bombing of the Chateau. If he was unable to do that, he had decided to ask Mac or Mahoney to try to send him copies of the photographs of the bomb-bursts.

Thinking things over, he realised that his first fears that the Chateau was to be bombed because Intelligence had learned that Marie had made her way there were unfounded. It was far more likely that they had known for some time that the building housed certain members of the German Headquarters or Intelligence Staff, and the recent trouble had simply served to expedite their decision to bomb it.

What could he do about it? Nothing, he decided despairingly, absolutely nothing. It crossed his mind that he might drop a message of warning, but he dismissed the thought at once, because such an act would definitely make him a traitor to his own side. The thought of returning to England and leaving the girl to her fate without lifting a finger to save her nearly drove him to distraction. After all, the girl had tried to save him when the position had been reversed!

He was glad when his batman brought him early morning tea, and he arose, weary and hollow-eyed. Ten o'clock found him in the air heading for the line and the Boche aerodrome at Lille. Behind him were Cowley and Algernon Montgomery. On his left were the bombers, the sun flashing on their varnished wings, the observers leaning carelessly on their Scarff rings. Beyond was Mahoney and 'A' Flight. Somewhere in the rear was MacLaren and 'B' Flight, while two thousand feet above he could see the S.E.5s.

'What a sight,' thought Biggles, as his eyes swept over the thirty-six machines; 'it will take a Hun with some nerve to tackle this lot.'

The observer in the nearest 'Nine' waved him, crossed his fingers and pointed. Biggles, following the direction indicated, saw half-a-dozen Fokker Triplanes flying parallel with them. Presently they turned away and disappeared into the distance. The observer waved and laughed and held out his hands with the thumbs turned up.

'Yes,' agreed Biggles mentally; 'they spotted the S.E.s up top. They've thought better of it, and I don't wonder.'

He was sorry that the Huns had departed, for he was aching for action. For three-quarters of an hour they flew steadily into enemy sky, and then the leader of the bombers, conspicuous by his streamers, began to turn.

'He's coming round into the wind,' thought Biggles. 'We must be over the objective.'

He looked down and beheld the aerodrome. He looked up again just in time to see the leader fire a green Very light. Eighteen 112-lb bombs swung off their racks into space.

A moment later a second lot of eighteen bombs followed the first. Keeping a watchful eye on his position in the formation Biggles snatched quick glances at the earth below. What a time it seemed to take the bombs to reach the ground.

'Dash it, they can't all be duds,' he muttered. 'Ah, there they go!'

A group of smoke-bursts appeared on the aerodrome, and, a moment later, another group.

The second lot were better than the first. One bomb had fallen directly on to a hangar, one had burst among the machines on the tarmac, and another had struck some buildings just behind. The rest of the bombs had scattered themselves over the aerodrome.

'There will have to be a lot of spade work there before anybody will try any night-landings,' grinned Biggles, as he visualised the havoc the bombs had caused to the surface of the aerodrome.

The faint crackle of guns reached his ears above the noise of the engines; he looked quickly over his shoulder and caught his breath as his eyes fell on a mixed swarm of Fokker D.VIIs and Triplanes coming down almost vertically on the rearmost 'Nines'. The gunners in the back seats were crouching low behind their Lewis guns. For a brief moment, as the enemy came within range, the air was full of sparkling lines of tracer, and then the Fokkers disappeared through and below the bombers.

He saw MacLaren's machine wallow for a moment like a rolling porpoise, and then, with the rest of his Flight, plunge down in the wake of the enemy machines.

'Suffering heavens! There must be thirty of them, and they mean business, coming in like that,' thought Biggles, as he rocked his wings and roared down into the whirling medley below. A red-painted machine crossed his sights and he pressed his triggers, but had to jerk round in a steep bank to avoid colliding with the first of the S.E.s which were coming down from above. He glanced around swiftly. The air about him was full of machines, diving, zooming and circling; the bombers had held on their course and were already a mile away.

He flung his Camel on the tail of a blue-and-white Fokker, and the same instant there was a splintering jar as something crashed through his instrument board. A burning pain paralysed his leg, and he twisted desperately to try to see his opponent. Huns were all round him shooting his machine to pieces. He pulled the joy-stick back into his stomach and zoomed wildly. A Fokker flashed into his sights; he saw his tracer pour straight through it; the pilot slumped forward in his seat and the nose of the machine went down in an engine stall as the withering blast of lead struck it.

Something lashed the Camel like a cat-o'-nine-tails; he felt the machine quiver, and the next moment he was spinning, fighting furiously to get the machine on an even keel. A feeling of nauseating helplessness swept over him as he realized that the Camel was not answering to the controls.

Something strange seemed to be whirling on the end of his wing-tip, and he saw it was an aileron, hanging by a single wire. He kicked on the opposite rudder and the nose of the Camel came up.

'If I can only keep her there,' was the thought that flashed through his brain; but another burst of fire from an unseen foe tore through his centre section and he instinctively kicked out his right foot. The Camel spun again at once. He was near the ground now and he fought to get the nose of the machine up again, but something seemed to have gone wrong with his leg. He couldn't move it.

Biggles knew his time had come. He knew he was going down under a hail of lead in just the same way as he had seen dozens of machines going down, as he himself had sent them down. He knew he was going to crash, but the knowledge left him unmoved. A thousand thoughts crowded into his mind in a second of time that seemed like minutes; in that brief moment he thought of a dozen things he might do as the machine struck.

The nose of the Camel half came up—slowly—and the machine stopped spinning.

The Camel was side-slipping steeply to the right now, nose down, on the very verge of another spin that would be the last.

The joystick was back in his left thigh and he unfastened his belt and twisted in his seat to get his right foot on the left side of the rudder, but it had no effect. A row of poplars appeared to leap upwards to meet him; he switched off the ignition with a lightning sweep of his hand, lifted the knee of his unwounded leg to his chin, folded his arms across his face and awaited the impact.

There was a splintering, rending crash, like a great tree in a forest falling on undergrowth. With the horror of fire upon him he clawed his way frantically out of the tangled wreck and half-rolled and half-crawled away from it. He seemed to be moving in a ghastly nightmare from which he could not awake. He became vaguely aware of the heat of a conflagration near him; it was the Camel, blazing furiously. Strange-looking soldiers were running towards him and he tore off his blood-stained goggles and stared at them, trying to grasp what had happened and what was happening.

'I'm down,' he muttered to himself in a voice which he hardly recognised as his own. 'I'm down,' he said again, as if the sounds of the words would help him to understand.

The German soldiers were standing in a circle around him now, and he looked at them curiously. One of them stepped forward, '*Schweinhund flieger!*' he grunted, and kicked him viciously in the side.

Biggles bit his lip at the pain. The man raised his heavy boot again, but there was a sudden authoritative word of command and he stepped back hastily. Biggles looked up to see an officer of about his own age, in a tight-fitting pale-grey uniform, regarding him compassionately. He noted the Pour-le-Merite Order at his throat, and the Iron Cross of the First Class below.

'So you have had bad luck,' he said, in English, with scarcely a trace of accent.

'Yes,' replied Biggles with an effort, forcing a smile and trying to get on his feet. 'And I am sorry it happened this morning.'

'Why?'

'Because I particularly wanted to see a raid this afternoon,' he answered.

'Yes? But there will be no raid this afternoon,' replied the German, smiling.

'Why not?'

The German laughed softly. 'An armistice was signed half an hour ago—but, of course, you didn't know.'

BIGGLES

FLIES
SOUTH

I
'THE KING HAS SPOKEN'

MAZEUS, son of Hystomannus, leaned against the warm trunk of a royal palm and regarded with brooding eyes the endless sands that rolled away from his feet to the far horizon. What lay beyond that mysterious belt of purple-blue that veiled the distance, he wondered. What strange beasts dwelt there? Perhaps those legendary monsters of which he had heard so much, the unicorn and camelopard. He thrilled at the thought of beholding them in the flesh, for Mazeus was young, barely sixteen years of age, and this was his first campaign with the mighty Persian host in which his father was a Captain of the Royal Guard, now encamped on the Oasis of Khargah, in Upper Egypt, the sinister land of that potent god-head, Ra.

The year was 525 B.C., nearly five centuries before the Roman Caesar landed on the shores of barbaric Britain. Cambyses, conquering son of Cyrus the Great, founder of the Persian Empire, was on the march, adding more and more territory to his wide-spread kingdom. Egypt had fallen under the pikes and scimitars of his armoured warriors, and he had celebrated the event by destroying the sacred Apis and plundering the temples of the high priests. And now he paused at the oasis to refresh his troops, before moving on to conquer new worlds.

But strange rumours were current in the camp. With bated breath the superstitious soldiers told of strange signs and stranger portents, of crafty sorcerers caught in the act of casting spells, and fanatic necromancers who died with a curious light of triumph in their eyes; of pillars of smoke that rose from the desert by day and mystic fires that blazed in the heavens by night. Yet, when the furious Persian scouts had galloped out, they found— nothing. Some spoke of evil shapes seen slinking in the dunes, of double-headed cats, men with heads like dogs', and other horrors never seen before; yet not one could they slay. One archer vowed that he had seen his arrow pass through the body of a twin-faced hawk, yet it did not fall, and a slinger claimed that his stone had bounded from a hydra-headed snake which vanished on the open sand where there was not a hole, or bush, or any other hiding-place. It was all very mysterious.

Mazeus turned from his musings and saw his father striding through the serried ranks of resting men; his face was grave, and Mazeus felt a thrill of apprehension, for his father had been in council with the king.

'What news, O Father?' he asked, as the bearded captain reached their silken tent.

Within the restful shade Hystomannus placed his hands upon the shoulders of his son, a gesture of affection seldom shown. 'You were over young for this campaign,' he said thoughtfully. 'Would that I had left you with your mother in Persepolis.'

'Over young, sir?' cried Mazeus in surprise. 'Why, all the sons I know, many much younger than I, have been to war.' Which was true, for in those distant days boys were trained in the use of arms as soon as they could bear them.

'That may be so,' answered his father moodily, mopping the perspiration from his face with a towel. 'But this is different.'

'How so, my Father? Have I not acquitted myself in battle?'

'Yes—yes. But now—I do not know. These pagan gods— within my heart there is a fear that neither common sense nor reason can dispel.'

'You mean—the king has spoken?'

'Yes. And he acts against the advice of all of us. This passion for strife is going to his head, I fear, until he knows not where to stop.'

'You mean—he will go on?'

'When the sun goes down we march—forward.'

Mazeus's dark eyes opened wide. 'Forward!'

Hystomannus pointed a finger at the shimmering, sun-scorched sand. 'There lies our path,' he said grimly.

'For what purpose, Father? Have we not enough plunder already?'

'More than enough; but Cambyses swears to sack the Temple and destroy the outlandish gods at Ammon. Rumours have reached him of this place, which is near a citadel called Siwah, the home of all the witchcraft in this thrice-accursed land, where none can quench his thirst although his body boils inside his armour. It is there, so 'tis said, the lying priests consult their Oracle.'

'How far is it?'

'No man can say. It lies out in the unknown desert, that is all we know.'

'Cannot a guide be found?'

'They prefer to die in agony rather than speak.'

'But what of those who led us here from Memphis and Djebel Dakrour?'

'They will go no farther. They say their feet are tied and their lips are sealed by Ra.'

'Can no way be found to make them open them?'

'None—we have tried them all, you may be sure,' said Hystomannus dryly.

'Yet still we go?'

'Yet still. And now you know what I mean when I say that this is different.'

'I will go and sharpen my lance,' smiled Mazeus.

His father shook his head. 'The enemies that we shall have to face will not be those of flesh and blood. Didst ever see me flinch before stones or flying steel?'

'Never, my Father.'

'There are worse things in the wilderness: such things as thirst, heat, dust-devils that sweep across the sand and carry all before them. No sword can hold such things in play, no shield can stem their rush.'

'Father! It is not like you to talk this way,' cried Mazeus in alarm.

'I know, I know.' Hystomannus shook himself almost savagely. 'It is these accursed priests,' he muttered. 'We have destroyed their gods, and in the night strange voices say they will destroy us, too.'

Mazeus smiled, a little nervously, perhaps. 'We shall see. How many men are going on this expedition?'

'Fifty thousand.'

'You mean——?'

'The army marches forward as the sun goes down. Come, let us prepare.'

2

THE DESERT ANSWERS

THUS, as the sun went down in a blaze of crimson glory, the mightly Persian host marched out in martial splendour: Parthian pikemen, Mardian archers, Scythian cavalry, Medes and Susians, slingers, bow-men, horse and foot, chariots and baggage-wagons—all moved out across the quivering dunes, confident of victory, never having known defeat.

Mazeus, with his lance at rest, rode beside his father near the royal wardrobe chest, which rested in a chariot beside the records of the historians who accompanied the king so that the story of his prowess might be told. Around this chariot rode the Royal Guard, drawn from the highest born in the noble city of Persepolis.

Swiftly the rim of the sun melted into the sand; the moon came up and a myriad stars blazed down from the sky of purple velvet, while along the line of marching men arose such sounds as the dunes had never heard before; the dull rumble of a hundred thousand feet, the musical jingle of arms and accoutrements, the creaking of wagons, the groans of toiling slaves, and the cracking of the whips of their taskmasters.

For three long days and nights the army wound like a gigantic serpent across the brooding sand, halting when the sun was high, the soldiers seeking in vain for shelter where there was none; for not a tree, not a bird, not an animal or blade of grass, nor any other living thing broke the eternal monotony of sand, sand, and still more sand. Yet ever in the distance strange wraiths of smoke pointed upwards to the heavens like accusing fingers, while at night unearthly fire was seen to flicker in the dunes. And the marching men marched on in silence, avoiding each other's eyes, for in their hearts was fear.

On the evening of the third day, soon after the army had resumed its march, an excited murmur ran along the line. Hills could be seen ahead, so it was said, and the men were as cheered as shipwrecked mariners when a coast is seen. Mazeus rode forward to the top of a towering dune and looked long and steadily at the line of jagged peaks, which, like a row of broken teeth, rose stark and clear into the sky. They were, he judged, still twenty miles away, but dawn should see the weary soldiers resting in their shade. He paused for a moment to watch the army winding through the sands, then he galloped back to his father to report.

It was nearly four hours later when he noticed, with more curiosity than alarm, that the moon had changed its colour. No longer was it an orb of gleaming silver; it had turned a creamy tint, almost golden; it appeared to be much larger, too, and misty at the edges. He called his father's attention to it, but all he got by way of answer was a curt 'Ride on!'

Another hour passed, and he saw that the moon had become a dullish, orange globe, a phenomenon he had never seen before. He noticed, too, that the pace of march had been increased, and that unusual noises now arose from the winding train behind. The crack of whips came faster, and the hoarse cries of the chariot-drivers were nearly drowned in the plaintive groaning of the camels. A breath of wind played for a moment on his cheek, but it brought him no refreshment, for it was as hot as if it had been breathed from the heart of a live volcano, and a thrill of apprehension swept through him.

'What means this speed, O Father?' he asked wonderingly, and then ran his tongue over his teeth, for there seemed to be some grit on them, which grated as he spoke.

'A storm is coming,' was the brief reply. 'Look at the moon.'

Mazeus turned, and caught his breath when he saw that it had turned dull brown, with edges blurred, as though a veil were being drawn across it. 'You mean a sand-storm?' he asked easily, for now he felt no fear, having seen such things before.

'Yes. Ride nearer to the chariot.'

'It will overtake us, you think, before we reach the hills?' questioned Mazeus, pressing his left leg against his horse's flank to move it nearer to the chariot.

'It will.'

'But we cannot be far away now.' As he spoke Mazeus turned again in the saddle, eyes seeking the moon, but now in vain. The column moved through a world of utter darkness.

'Tie your scarf across your mouth and keep close by my side,' his father told him, and a moment later came the wind.

At first it came quite quietly, a gentle sigh, a moan that crept across the wilderness; but then there came a gust, a howl, a searing, scorching blast, bringing with it a cloud of sand that stung and smarted like the bites of countless ants.

Mazeus bowed his head and swiftly tied his scarf about his mouth, at the same time fighting to check his plunging steed, in such darkness as he had never known. Where was the chariot? He moved, as he thought, towards it, but it was not where he had imagined it to be. Faintly, above the scream of the wind, he heard the groans of slaves and the cursing of the soldiers he could not see. Panic clutched his heart. Where was his father? 'Father!' he cried, but the blast, with a shriek of triumph, tore the word from his lips and flung it in the air. 'Father!' he called again, shortening his reins to control his frenzied mount. The animal, sensing his fear, reared high, then plunged. The rein snapped like a piece of cotton, and in an instant the maddened creature was racing before the storm.

Blindly, gasping for breath, Mazeus clung to the saddle with his left hand, still gripping in his right, perhaps from force of habit, his lance, for to lose a weapon in Cambyses' army meant, for the loser, death. And as he rode a thousand demons seemed to clutch him, tearing at his clothes, snatching at his body, scouring his face and hands with sand until they bled. Where he was going, in what direction, he did not know; he only knew that the sand was choking him to death; for he had to breathe, and every time he drew a breath, by nose or mouth, the tiny grains poured in and clogged his throat and lungs.

He was reeling in the saddle when the horse fell, with an

almost human scream of terror. Thrown clear, he rose at once,
groping for the animal. But it had gone. For a moment or two he
stood still, appalled by the calamity, then he began to run. But
he seemed to be staggering through a roaring tide which,
snatching at his ankles, dragged him down. He fell, rose, and fell
again, hardly knowing that he did. 'It is the end of the world,' he
thought, in a vague, bewildered way as he blundered on only to
fall again. This time he remained rigid, his questing hands
feeling the earth beneath him. It was no longer sand. It was
rock. He had reached the hills! Gradually, like a blind man on a
strange road, he felt his way along it until he found the thing he
sought, a cleft, a fault in the rocky *massif*, and into it he tumbled.
The sand poured in, but it was not so bad as it was outside, and
gradually the storm began to wane.

Came dawn, and he crawled wearily from his refuge, his face
all raw and his dry lips cracked and bleeding. A dreadful thirst
consumed him and he knew that he must drink or die. No longer
could he remove the cloying sand from his mouth. The army?
Yes, some one would see him when he raised his lance. Forcing
open his aching eyes, he looked out across the desert, but all that
met his gaze was sand, billowing yellow dunes of sand as far as
the eye could see. Behind him was the mountain, grim and stark,
as relentless as death itself. At first he did not understand. Where
was the army? The thought repeated itself again and again in his
reeling brain. Where could it have gone in so short a time? One
thing alone was certain: it was not there.

He was not to know that nearly all the mighty Persian host,
fifty thousand horse and foot, horses, carts, and chariots, lay
buried in the sand not a mile from where he swayed, so that
neither pike nor lance, wheel nor standard remained to mark its
mile-square tomb.

'My father will come back,' he thought desperately. 'He will
come back to seek me. I must make a mark that he will see. My
lance!' Weakly, the dunes rocking before his eyes, he picked up
the weapon and drove the handle deep into the sand, so that the
point was skyward. This done, he lay down to wait.

The sun soared upwards, driving bars of living fire into the sterile earth. Silence reigned, the awful silence of the uttermost wilderness. The rays crept round the rock and played upon the huddled body that lay at the foot of the lance. It did not move. It would never move again, for the spirit of Mazeus, son of Hystomannus, the last survivor of Cambyses' Royal Guard, had gone to seek its comrades in the cloudless blue, above the eternal sand.

3
THE MOONLIGHT ASSASSIN

MAJOR JAMES BIGGLESWORTH better known to his friends as Biggles, folded up the map he had been studying and put it on the paved terrace near the feet of the long cane-chair in which he was sitting.

'No,' he said, for the benefit of Ginger Hebblethwaite, who was standing near him. 'Quite definitely, no. Algy will bear me out—if he is capable of bearing anything—that when we started on this trip it was agreed that we should fly direct to Capetown without any intermediate meandering. Yet here we are, rather less than half-way, and you want to fly off, literally, at a tangent. My answer is, unless any insuperable obstacle arises to prevent me from getting there, I am going to Capetown and nowhere else.'

'Good enough, chief,' agreed Ginger, with just a hint of disappointment in his voice. 'It was only a suggestion, you know——'

'Yes, I know all about your suggestions. Say no more. The matter is closed.' Biggles settled back in his chair and reached for the iced drink that stood on a small table near his elbow.

'Picture of a Great White Chief putting his foot down,' murmured the Honourable Algernon Lacey, more often known as Algy, catching Ginger's eye and smiling at his discomfiture.

The three airmen were in Egypt, where they had arrived a few days earlier after an uneventful flight from England in one of the new 'Tourer' twin-engined sports aeroplanes which had been acquired for the purpose.

The reason for the trip was quite a prosaic one. Major Mullen, Biggles's old C.O. in Number 266 Squadron, R.F.C., now a high official in South African civil aviation, had conceived the idea of a Squadron Reunion Dinner; but as many of the old members of the Squadron were now in Africa, in his service, it was decided that it would be more convenient for the majority if the dinner was held in Capetown instead of London. This information, together with an invitation, had been sent to Biggles, who, having little to do at the time, had decided to accept, taking his two friends with him as guests. Naturally, it did not occur to him to travel any way other than by air, so a new machine had been purchased with the idea of making the occasion something of a pleasure cruise.

They had started with plenty of time at their disposal in order to make the journey in easy stages, which would allow them to see something of the places of interest on the route, and up to the time they reached Egypt this programme had been adhered to. They were now in Cairo, and had, in fact, been there for three days, leaving their machine at Heliopolis Aerodrome while they explored the ancient city.

Ginger, however, either because he found the slow progress somewhat irksome, or possibly because he was never so happy as when he was in the air, had lately formed a habit of suggesting minor expeditions by air, and it was such a proposal that he had just put forward. For reasons best known to himself—for he had not had time to disclose them—he had suddenly decided that he would like to see Jerusalem, and it was on this question that Biggles had given his decision.

They were staying at one of the lesser-known hotels on the outskirts of the city, partly because it was inexpensive, and partly because Biggles preferred to keep away from the usual tourist crowd with their clicking cameras and swarms of *baksheesh*-seeking natives. The hotel was, moreover, a small one, and they were not disappointed when they found that they had it almost to themselves. Night had fallen and they were sitting outside on the terrace under the gleaming Egyptian moon, enjoying a rest after a rather tiring day of 'seeing the sights.'

'So you're thinking of moving on tomorrow?' murmured Algy, glancing at Biggles.

'I think so. I fancy we have seen all that is likely to interest us here. We'll push on to Khartoum; there are one or two R.A.F. fellows stationed there whom I should like to look up.'

'Suits me,' agreed Algy. 'Anything for a quiet life. I find it curiously refreshing to be able to drift along like this, in our own time, instead of roaring about on some crazy business.'

Ginger wrinkled his nose but said nothing, and presently turned his attention to a particularly large white moth wheeling in erratic flight among the orange trees that stood at intervals in the garden, which began where the terrace ended. In many respects he was now grown up, but he had not yet lost the boyish desire to chase an attractive butterfly. Picking up his sun helmet in lieu of a net, and keeping as far as possible in the inky shadow of a group of fern-palms, he began a cautious advance towards his quarry; but he had not taken more than a dozen paces when he saw something that caused him to halt, tense and alert, the moth forgotten. Some twenty yards to his right a low white wall separated the garden from the road on which the hotel was situated; a line of tall date-palms followed the wall, and through their graceful fronds the moon cast a curious lattice-like pattern of black-and-white bars that fell across the dappled flower-beds, the sandy paths, and the wall beyond. Along the inside of the wall, ghostly in the silvery half-light, was creeping the white-robed figure of a native. The criss-cross shadows of the palm fronds fell across his sheet-like *burnous* so that he appeared to be gliding behind the bars of a cage; and so silent and furtive were his movements that it was at once apparent that his purpose was not a lawful one.

At this juncture it is probable that Ginger would have denied that his interest was anything more than natural curiosity. He had travelled far, and in strange lands, and the mere unexpected appearance of a soft-footed native no longer aroused in him the instinctive suspicion, and possible apprehension, that it does in most Europeans when first they find themselves in a land where the native population is 'coloured'. Yet there was at once something so sinister about the actions of the intruder—for Ginger's common sense told him that the man would not behave thus were he not trespassing—that he felt his nerves tighten in expectation of something that was about to happen.

Making no more noise than the object of his suspicion, he took a pace or two nearer and placed his helmet on the ground. A swift glance in the direction of the terrace revealed Biggles and Algy still sitting where he had left them; the faint murmur of their voices reached him, and he would have attracted their attention had it been possible without alarming the man who was still creeping stealthily along the inside of the wall. Reaching the wrought-iron gate that gave access to the road from the garden, the intruder stopped, and it was at that moment that Ginger had his first suspicion of his purpose. He saw the moonlight glint dully on something that he held in his right hand, and an instant later he heard footsteps beyond the wall, as though someone was approaching the gate from the outside.

The inference was immediately apparent. A visitor was about to enter the hotel by the garden gate, and the man inside was stalking him with murderous intent.

Ginger, with the idea of frustrating this, at once started forward, and he was just in time to avert a tragedy. The garden gate swung inward, and a slim figure in European clothes, but wearing the customary *tarboosh* of the better-class Egyptian, appeared in the opening. At that moment the assassin made his attack, but Ginger, seeing what was about to happen, and perceiving that he could not reach the gate in time, had uttered a shout of warning; and there is no doubt that his prompt action saved the newcomer's life, for the cry had its effect on both actors in the drama. The figure in the *tarboosh* jumped aside, and his aggressor hesitated momentarily in making his stroke.

By this time Ginger was less than half a dozen paces away, and his swift approach was heard. Even so, the assassin made a last desperate attempt to achieve his purpose; he made a cat-like spring, but the other was as quick, and warded off the gleaming blade by an upward sweep of his arm. The attacker, seeing that Ginger was now almost upon him, and noting, no doubt, that he was a white man, darted through the gate and fled.

Ginger, knowing the futility as well as the danger of pursuit, did not attempt it, but contented himself with flinging a stone, which he snatched from the top of the wall, at the flying figure. It missed its mark, however, so with a grunt of chagrin he turned back to the gate, to find that Biggles and Algy had arrived on the scene.

'What's going on?' asked Biggles sharply.

'A fellow tried to knife this chap,' answered Ginger briefly, indicating the newcomer, who was standing near the wall with one arm resting against it. 'Jolly near got him, too,' he added, noting that the man he had saved was also a native.

Biggles's keen eyes evidently saw something that Ginger's did not, for he took a quick pace forward. 'Did he touch you?' he asked the stranger.

'It is nothing,' was the quiet answer, spoken in perfect English. 'My arm—a scratch—nothing more.'

'You had better come up into the light and let us have a look at it,' suggested Biggles in a friendly tone.

'Thank you. You are most kind,' was the soft answer, and the four of them walked quietly to the terrace.

'My word! You had a close squeak, and no mistake,' observed Biggles, as the stranger exhibited a slashed sleeve and a bloodstained hand. 'Algy, slip in and get a towel or something. Better ask the manager to come along, too.'

'No, say nothing,' put in the stranger quickly. 'It will be better so.'

'Well, it's your affair,' agreed Biggles as Algy hurried away on his errand.

While they were waiting for him to return, Ginger had a good look at the man he had saved. He was, as he had already observed, a native, but obviously one of the better class, and his skin was not much darker than that of a sun-burned white man. He was young, no older than himself, with finely cut features and soft, intelligent eyes. His clothes were of good quality, and might have been made in London; indeed, but for his distinguishing *tarboosh*, he might have passed for a European.

Algy soon returned with two soft linen face-towels. With one of these Biggles cleaned the wound, and with the other, folded in the manner of a bandage, he bound it up. Fortunately, as the victim had stated, it was little more than a scratch, and he smiled apologetically as Biggles gave him medical attention.

'Does this sort of thing often happen to you?' inquired Biggles. 'If it does, the sooner you provide yourself with a suit of armour, or a bodyguard, the better. You might not be so lucky next time.'

'It has never happened to me before,' was the candid reply.

'Are you feeling all right now?' Biggles asked the question in a manner which suggested politely that the wounded man was free to proceed on his errand if he so wished.

'Quite all right thanks to you,' was the quiet answer. But the stranger made no move to depart.

There was rather an embarrassing silence in which Biggles lit a cigarette.

'You were coming to the hotel, weren't you?' inquired Ginger, more for the sake of saying something than inquisitiveness.

The answer took them all by surprise. 'Yes, I was coming to see you,' said the young Egyptian quietly, looking at Biggles.

'To see *me*?' Biggles was frankly astonished.

'Yes—you are Major Bigglesworth, are you not?'

Biggles looked at their guest with renewed interest. 'Yes, that is my name,' he admitted. 'Sit down if you have something to tell me.'

'Thanks. I will, if you don't mind. The shock of the attack has left me a little—how do you say?—shaken.'

There was another short silence while the visitor seated himself, and the airmen waited for him to continue.

'My name is Kadar Alloui Bey,' he said at last, in a manner which suggested that it might mean something to his listeners.

Biggles shook his head. 'Do not think me discourteous, but I am afraid I must confess that your name means nothing to me.'

'No—of course, you are a stranger here. My father's name is not unknown in Cairo.'

'I see,' returned Biggles awkwardly. 'You came to see me about something?' he prompted.

'Yes. The circumstances of my arrival have made my mission rather difficult, but—you are an air pilot, I believe?'

'That is correct,' admitted Biggles, wondering what was coming next.

The other coughed nervously. 'I was coming here to ask you if you would care to sell me your aeroplane.'

Biggles stared. 'Sell you my aeroplane?' he repeated wonderingly.

'Yes, I have urgent need of one.'

'But couldn't you get one here—I mean, through the usual channels? Haven't Misr Airwork got one for disposal?

'No, unfortunately. As far as I can discover there is not an aeroplane for sale in Egypt—at least, not of the sort I require. You see, I need a large one, and all the large ones are in use on the air routes. Owing to the air expansion in England there are no civil aeroplanes to spare; even the air line companies need more than they have, for they are running to capacity on every service.'

'I see. Well, I'm afraid we need ours. In any case, do you know what an aeroplane costs?' Biggles asked the question seriously, feeling sure that the young Egyptian must be unaware of the cost of a large modern aeroplane, and that when he was better informed he would soon give up the idea of buying one.

'A twin-engined tourer such as yours costs, I believe, eight thousand pounds. Had you been here on business I was prepared to offer ten thousand pounds for it,' was the calm answer.

Biggles could hardly believe his ears. 'You are right about the price,' he confessed. 'Still, I am afraid I cannot part with my machine. All the same, we are in no great hurry, and if you want a lift somewhere it might be arranged. In face, under certain conditions, if your purpose is really urgent—which apparently it is—I would be prepared to let you charter it for a couple of days.'

The other shook his head and smiled as he stood up. 'Thank you. That is very generous of you, but I am afraid that would be no use. I should need it for some time, and it might take me a little while to find a pilot.'

'I see. You can't fly yourself?'

'No. I was in rather a difficult position. It was no use my engaging a pilot before I had an aeroplane. Had I been able to buy one, my intention was then to find a pilot to fly it for me, to take me to the place I wish to visit.'

'I understand,' said Biggles slowly. 'I am sorry, but I am afraid we can't do anything about it. As a matter of detail, we are on our way to Capetown. If your objective lies in that direction, we shall be happy to give you a lift.'

'No, I fear that would not do, thank you all the same,' answered the young Egyptian rather sadly. 'I am sorry to have taken up your time. Never mind; perhaps it would be better if I abandoned my project.'

A new thought struck Biggles. 'Was the project you mention the reason for the attack made on you just now?'

'Undoubtedly,' was the instant reply. 'I think it would be safe to say that it was in order to prevent my reaching you that I was waylaid. There could be no other reason. I knew I was being watched, but I did not think my enemies would go as far as to try to murder me.'

'Somebody must be very anxious to keep you in Cairo,' smiled Biggles.

'Yes, very anxious, and I think I know who it is. But there, as I say, no doubt he will leave me alone when it becomes known that I have abandoned my proposed quest.'

The final word made Ginger prick up his ears. 'Quest?' The word was a naïve question.

Biggles frowned. 'Don't be inquisitive,' he admonished him.

Their guest smiled. 'It is no secret,' he said. 'Yes, I suppose one would call it a quest. I have spent some years preparing for it, so it is rather disappointing to have to give it up. Still, we must learn to accept these things as they come.'

'You speak English very well,' said Biggles, changing the subject.

'That is not surprising, considering that I was at school in England for seven years,' was the unexpected reply.

'The dickens you were!'

'What was this quest you were projecting?' persisted Ginger.

'I am afraid it is rather a long story.'

'Well, the night is young,' declared Biggles. 'I can't make any promises, but if you feel like telling us something more about it, perhaps——'

'I will tell you with pleasure, because I know without being told that you will respect my confidence. Much of my information is common property, but there are some things——'

'Shall we sit down and have some coffee?' suggested Biggles.

'Thank you, you are most hospitable.'

'Ring the bell, Ginger,' ordered Biggles.

4

KADAR'S STORY

WHEN they were all comfortably settled and a native servant had placed coffee on a brass-topped table between them, Biggles looked at their guest, 'Go ahead,' he invited.

The young Egyptian leaned forward, his dark eyes keen with eagerness. 'In the first place,' he began, 'as I tell my story I want you to bear in mind two things: one is that this subject on which I am going to speak has a peculiar fascination for me—I mention that to account for what may seem a disproportionate enthusiasm on my part. Secondly, my father was, until he retired a few years ago, an honorary assistant curator of antiquities at the Cairo Museum, where, as you probably know, the most famous relics of ancient Egypt are kept. Naturally, he taught me much, and that is why I am well informed on a subject which, to most people, is of no importance. Have you ever heard of the Lost Oasis?'

'Vaguely,' answered Biggles, wrinkling his forehead.

'I know a little about it,' put in Ginger, somewhat to the others' surprise.

'How did you learn about it?' inquired Biggles curiously.

'I remember reading something about it in a paper called *Popular Flying*,' explained Ginger.

'That is correct. I read the article myself,' declared Kadar Alloui. 'In fact, I cut it out, and have it here in my pocket. It deals with the last attempt to locate the oasis, the expedition being made by air. I think it would be a good thing if I read it to you, because that will tell you, more or less officially, how the matter has been left. But before doing that I must ask another question. It is not necessarily associated with the Lost Oasis, but—well, it may be. One must consider both questions to gather the full significance of my proposed quest. Did you, when you were at school, or since, hear the name Cambyses?'

'Wasn't he a general who got lost in the desert, or something of the sort?' answered Biggles.

'Yes. That is more or less correct, but what actually happened was this. In the year five hundred and twenty-five B.C., Cambyses, the son of Cyrus, the founder of the great Persian Empire—the greatest empire in the world at that time— conquered Egypt. He destroyed the Egyptian gods, and, to complete all, he decided to plunder Jupiter Ammon, a famous sanctuary situated near the Oasis of Siwah. I must tell you about this temple of Ammon, which was then the centre of the great Ammonite kingdom. At the time of which we are speaking, and for many centuries later, it was the most celebrated place of pilgrimage in the world, on account of its Oracle. In other words, the high priests claimed to be able to tell the fortunes of those who went there to consult them. Many people still believe in fortune-tellers, so it is not hard to imagine that the Temple of Ammon flourished in those superstitious days. Everyone be-lieved in its power, and everyone who could afford it went there to learn his fate. You must understand that it was not then so inaccessible as it is now. It stood at the crossroads of the two great African caravan trails—perhaps the oldest roads in the world. Alexander the Great went there to consult the Oracle. So did Hannibal, the famous Carthaginian general: he made a special journey there to ask what would happen if he made war on the Romans. Croesus, the man of fabulous wealth, went there, as did many other kings and princes. This, then, was the shrine that Cambyses proposed to plunder, and we need not wonder why. There must have been vast wealth stored there; indeed, there are still many legends of treasures hidden beneath the crumbling stones.'

'Then it is still there?' put in Biggles.

'Oh, yes, although the temple is now in ruins. But we will return to that presently. Cambyses' army left the Oasis of Khargah, but it never reached Ammon. Nothing more was ever heard of it. Not a man returned. That night the army disappeared as completely as if the earth had opened and swallowed it up—as indeed, in a way, no doubt it did. And this brings us to the Lost Oasis, named, some say, Zenzura.

'Whether or not this Oasis really exists no man can say, yet it would be a strange thing, would it not, if a name could exist without foundation? From time to time through the ages there have come out of the desert strange rumours of an Oasis, and ruined cities, far away in the heart of the dreaded Libyan sands, known to the Tuareg Arabs as the Region of Devils. If you will look at a map of Africa you will see that all that area is left white, without a mark of any sort on it, unless it be the intriguing word "unknown". Certainly no white man has ever crossed it. Yet rumours of a mysterious oasis have persisted, and that is not all. The Tuaregs, the cruel nomads of the desert, even tell of a strange white race that live there. If that seems hard to believe, remember that there is a race of white Arabs farther west, in the heart of the Sahara, the descendants, it is generally believed by scientists, of a lost party of Phoenicians. As you probably know, the Phoenician civilization of North Africa was one of the greatest in the early days of the world. When, as I say, one remembers this, there would not appear to be any reason why, if there is an oasis far out in the desert, it should not be peopled by the descendants of the survivors of Cambyses' ill-fated army. Whatever the disaster was that overwhelmed it, one would expect some to escape, possibly the scouts or advance guards. If some of these did, in fact, reach an oasis in the heart of the great sands, they would have to remain there. It would be impossible for them to get back to civilization. They would be marooned more effectively than mariners on a desert island. On an island there is always a chance, however remote, that a ship will one day call, but the fiery heart of the Libyan Desert is perhaps the one place on earth where no one has ever gone, or is likely to go. There could be no hope of rescue, for not even the most daring explorer would venture there. It is rock, sand and desolation unutterable. Nothing more. It never rains——'

'You don't mean that literally, do you?' interrupted Biggles.

'It is hardly a mis-statement,' was the firm reply. 'The people who live on the fringe of the sands say that no rain has fallen there for more than three hundred years.'

'Not exactly the spot to open a barometer shop,' remarked Ginger.

Kadar saw no humour in the observation. 'It would be a bad place,' he said seriously. 'From day to day, from month to month, and from year to year, you can always be quite sure that tomorrow will be as yesterday; cloudless, and of such heat as is scarcely possible to imagine. What would you call a hot day in England?'

'A shade temperature of about eighty degrees Fahrenheit is reckoned to be hot,' answered Biggles. 'Ninety degrees is a rarely experienced heat-wave.'

'Then try to imagine what *a hundred and fifty degrees* in the shade would be like—that is, if there *was* any shade.'

'Phew!' exclaimed Ginger.

'This doesn't happen to be the place you propose visiting, I hope?' murmured Biggles dryly.

'Yes, this is the place.'

'I see,' nodded Biggles. 'Go on. What about that cutting you were going to read?'

Kadar took out his note-case, selected a clipping from among several, and smoothed out the creases. 'This article is entitled "The Lost Oasis, or, Has Aviation Solved an Age-Old Riddle of the Sands?"' he continued. 'The early part of it deals with the historical facts which I have already given you. It goes on to say:

"Quite recently Sir Robert Clayton and Mr. L. E. de Almasy carried out a flight of exploration in a Moth over this region, and discovered what may prove to be the Lost Oasis of Zenzura. They were accompanied by Mr. P. A. Clayton, of the Egyptian Government Desert Survey, and Squadron-Leader Penderel, R.A.F., in a Vickers Victoria twin-engined Troop Carrier. They made their base at Khargah Oasis (from which Cambyses' ill-fated army set forth) and flew over a large plateau known as Gilf el Kebir, in the direction of Kufra. Khargah is about three hundred and seventy-five miles south of Cairo.

"Running eastwards through this plateau, Sir Robert and his companions sighted a large and fertile *wadi*, or valley. Photographs were taken from the air, and enlargements distinctly show a white spot among the trees which is believed to be a hut. This discovery suggests that the *wadi* was recently inhabited, and tends to confirm the belief that it is identical with the Lost Oasis of Zenzura."

'The rest of the article,' continued Kadar, 'consists of a narrative by Sir Robert Clayton setting out particulars of the ground organization. He concludes by saying:

"Although we were able to fly over what we considered to be our object, we were forced to return to our base three days later, as the expedition had been timed to turn back on that day and no further supplies had been provided."

'The remainder of the article deals only with the prospects of future expeditions,' concluded Kadar, looking up from the paper.

'What date was that?' asked Biggles.

'It was some time ago,' replied Kadar. 'The article appeared in the August 1932 issue of the paper, so presumably the expedition was just before that time.'

'And this was the sort of trip you were hoping to make?' suggested Biggles.

'Yes,' confessed Kadar, folding up the cutting and putting it back into his pocket.

'How exactly did you propose to go about it?'

'I am coming to that,' answered Kadar. 'Ever since I was a

small boy the problem of the Lost Oasis has fascinated me. Can you wonder? Even if the Oasis does not exist, somewhere out in the sands lie the mummified remains of an army, with its weapons, armour, chariots and baggage, just as it took the field nearly two thousand five hundred years ago. What a find that would be for an archaeologist—or anyone else, for that matter, since there is certain to be much of value there. And that brings me, I suspect, to the reason for the attack made on me just now. You will believe me, I hope, when I say that my interest is entirely in the historical aspect, and that it was solely in the hope of throwing fresh light on the world's history that my father agreed to finance an expedition into the desert—not necessarily by air, or course. I have only contemplated that during the last few days. But the question of possible wealth hidden in the sands is not to be ignored. Legend has it that the chariot carrying Cambyses' treasure-chest was lost with the army, and, frankly, I think it is more than likely that it was. Be that as it may, from time to time jewels—mostly uncut emeralds and rubies—have reached Cairo and Alexandria from a mysterious source. They appear to pass through several hands, and no one knows where they come from. You will agree, I think, that it would not be straining the imagination very hard to suspect that they are coming out of the desert, and that the source is either Jupiter Ammon or the final resting-place of the Persian host. It was in the hope of being able to learn something about this fount of wealth that I have made three journeys into the desert, in disguise, for should my supposition prove correct, then I should soon be on the trail of things far more important to me than mere money.'

'Did you gather any information?' asked Biggles, almost eagerly.

'A little. My task was a difficult one. You see, I know the Bedouin too well to make the fatal mistake of asking questions. But they are born gossipers—as is only natural, for they have no other means of spreading information—and I hoped, by listening, to pick up any rumours that were current concerning the mysterious jewels, the lost army, or the Lost Oasis. As I say, I

learned a little, and it may have been due to the fact that I made
no secret of it that my plans have now miscarried.'

'Is it expecting too much to ask what you discovered?'
inquired Biggles.

'Not in the least,' was the frank reply. 'Actually, all I
discovered in substance was an inscription on a stone, the
existence of which was reported to me by a friendly Bedouin who
suspected my mission. I did not see the stone myself, for I was not
equipped for such a journey as would have been entailed, but he
went out and made a copy of it on paper. Inscribed stones,
ruined buildings, and aqueducts occur over the whole of what is
now the Libyan and Sahara deserts, relics of the great
civilizations that existed there in the dim past; but one glance at
the inscription brought to me by the Arab was enough to excite
me, for the characters were cuneiform letters. A translation told
me that the Persian army had actually passed the spot where the
stone was found. That was one thing. The second item of
importance was a story told to me by a very old man at the Oasis
of Siwah. He said he was more than a hundred years old, and it
may have been true. He told me that when he was a young man
he was out on a raid, and in the darkness of the night he became
lost. He was lost for three days. On the second day, by which
time he was suffering greatly from thirst, he saw a spear, or
lance, of a type which he had never seen before, sticking up out
of the sand near some barren hills. The handle was made of a
dark-coloured wood unknown to him and reinforced with
carved brasswork.'

'Did he collect it?' asked Biggles.

'Unfortunately, no. Such was his plight that the last thing he
thought of was to burden himself further; so he left the lance
where it was, intending to return for it later should he manage to
get back to his friends. He did, in fact, get back, but the tribe
shortly afterwards moved its tents so that he had no opportunity
of fetching the lance. Still, it is something to know it is there, for
where there is one it is more likely there will be others. The
description given by the Arab makes it almost certain that the
lance was of Persian origin. What is even more important is that

the two clues, the inscribed stone and the lance, give me the Persian line of march.'

'So the Arab told you where the lance could be found—or where he saw it?'

'Yes, as far as description is possible in the desert, where there is seldom anything to describe. Fortunately, as I have told you, the weapon happened to be at the base of some rocky hills, so that should greatly facilitate a search. And, I may say, the area is the one through which Cambyses' army might easily have marched; that is to say, it is not far south of a straight line taken between Khargah and Jupiter Ammon. You will remember that Khargah was the point of departure, and Jupiter Ammon, which is close to the Oasis of Siwah, the objective.'

'This Oasis of Siwah?' queried Biggles. 'Is it inhabited?'

'Certainly.'

'Are the people savage?' asked Ginger curiously.

'They are not exactly friendly, but one would not call them dangerous. Until recently it would have been certain death for a stranger, particularly a Christian, to go there. All the explorers who reached the place in the last century were ill treated; in fact, few escaped with their lives. But allow me to return to the matter of this information which I discovered, for the most important development is yet to come.

'On all my journeyings, sooner or later I came up against what I can only describe by using the French word *impasse*. I could get no farther. Something was there, I felt, but it ever escaped me. At first I put it down to a natural reticence on the part of the Arabs, but in the end I became convinced that it was organized opposition to my plans; and this was borne out in a curious way when, not long ago, I announced my definite intention to proceed.' Kadar broke off and glanced around nervously. When he resumed he did so in a low voice.

'A man came to see me,' he went on softly. 'He is a man well known in Cairo, affluent and influential. He is neither English nor Egyptian. He is, I think, half Turkish and half Greek—but that does not really matter. He came to see me and, much to my surprise, offered to finance my expedition under certain conditions, which were, briefly, that we should retain for our own use anything of value that we discovered. Naturally, I would have nothing to do with such a proposal, which was, not to mince words, dishonest. I must explain, in case you do not know, that every antiquity now found in Egypt becomes automatically the property of the Government, which is only right and proper, or Egypt would soon be denuded of the treasures of her romantic past. Most of the finds go into the museum here in Cairo, or Alexandria; some are distributed to other museums, such as your British Museum in London. Naturally, the finder is recompensed for his trouble. So now you see how distasteful this man's proposal was to me. In any case, I do not like him. He is not a man whom one could trust. Well, that was all. He went away and I heard no more, but I have felt a sinister influence opposing all my plans. My own opinion is, although I would not dare to say this in public, that Zarwan—his name is Fuad Zarwan, by the way—is behind these jewel finds. He finances the Tuareg, and they, from a secret source, bring him what they find.'

'A profitable business,' murmured Biggles.

'Very profitable indeed,' agreed Kadar. 'But to conclude. The affair took rather a disconcerting turn the other night when all my notes and plans were stolen. Actually, the loss was not vital because I had memorized everything, but it means that whoever stole my plans and notes now knows as much as I do. It was possibly in order to make himself the sole possessor of the information that the thief attempted to take my life.'

'Well, this is all very interesting,' said Biggles quietly. 'Your idea was originally, I take it, to lead an expedition into this mysterious land in search of the Lost Oasis?'

'Yes, the Oasis was my chief objective, firstly to settle any doubts as to whether or not there is such a place, and if there is, to try to discover if the inhabitants—if there are any—are descendants of the survivors of Cambyses' army. Failing to find the Oasis, I hoped to find the spot where the Persian army perished. But my plans having been stolen, assuming that the thief would try to take advantage of his knowledge, it seemed to me that my only chance of reaching the spot first would be to fly there.'

'You do not mean that you hoped to fly straight there and back?'

'Oh, no. I should establish a base at Semphis, which is a small, uninhabited oasis to the west of the large oasis of Dakhel, on the fringe of the great desert. It lies between Khargah and Ammon, and must be on, or near, the line of march of Cambyses' army.'

'What about petrol and stores? Quite a lot of things would be required.'

'My intention was to send a caravan on with them to Semphis. Having established a base there, I could then explore the surrounding country at leisure.'

'Such an organization would cost a lot of money,' declared Biggles dubiously.

'My father was prepared to finance me. He is as interested as I am, and he is not a poor man.' Kadar made the statement quietly, without any hint of pride or vanity.

'I see.' Biggles stroked his chin thoughtfully while Ginger watched him expectantly. Algy lit a cigarette.

The young Egyptian stood up. 'Well, I must be returning home,' he announced. 'My father will be wondering what has become of me.'

'Just a minute.' There was a peculiar smile on Biggles's face as he said the words. 'Your story has interested me very much indeed. I am always sorry to see thieves get away with anything. Let me think about this. Perhaps we shall be able to come to some arrangement after all. Come back in the morning and I will give you my views on it.'

5

ZARWAN CALLS

After Kadar had gone Algy turned an accusing eye on Biggles. 'I thought we were going straight to Capetown,' he scoffed.

Biggles smiled. 'To tell you the honest truth, I was very much taken with that lad's story,' he confessed. 'I like his straightforward manner, too. This delving into the dark pages of history is extremely fascinating, and it would be rather gratifying to contribute something to archaeological research—quite apart from which there would be some satisfaction in doing the thieves who stole the lad's plan out of what they hope to gain.'

'And get knifed for our trouble,' growled Algy. 'We seem to do nothing but dash about the world crashing into other people's affairs. This trip will cost a pretty penny, I imagine.'

'The boy's father will pay expenses, no doubt. You heard what he said. If it costs nothing, as we have a little time on our hands——'

'You've decided to go?'

'I haven't definitely made up my mind yet.'

Algy yawned. 'Well, I suppose we may as well go there as anywhere,' he agreed. 'I've always wanted to have a look at the inside of a real, first-class desert.'

'If we go with this lad you're likely to get your wish,' Biggles told him. 'Pass me that map, will you? I'd like to get an idea of where this place——' He broke off abruptly, staring at a man who was standing near them on the terrace. So quiet had been his arrival that Biggles had no idea of his presence; nor could he imagine how he had appeared without being heard.

The others had turned at Biggles's unaccountable silence, and, seeing the man standing there, Algy got up belligerently, for if there was one thing he could not tolerate it was eavesdropping.

Apparently the newcomer sensed this in his manner, for he moved forward into the light, revealing himself to be a middle-aged man of undoubted eastern extraction notwithstanding the fact that he was dressed in expensive European clothes. He was short and inclined to corpulency, but this in no way impeded his movements, for they were made with the smooth grace of a cat. His skin was dark, as were his eyes, which, like those of many orientals, appeared to be heavy and curiously expressionless. He was clean-shaven, and his regular although somewhat rounded features might almost have justified his being described as good-looking; but there was something smugly self-satisfied and well-fed about his expression, and, as Algy afterwards put it, one felt that if one stroked him he would purr. He was, in fact, of a type common in the Middle East, where east and west are all too often blended with unfortunate results.

Biggles spoke first. 'Are you looking for me, by any chance?' he asked curtly.

The man bowed, and his right hand touched his heart with an obsequious gesture. 'Have I the honour of addressing the celebrated Major Bigglesworth?' he inquired suavely.

'My name is Bigglesworth, if that's what you mean,' answered Biggles coldly.

'Ah! Permit me to present myself. Fuad Zarwan, Esquire, at your service.' As the man spoke he bowed again in a manner that made Biggles long to kick him. 'I fear with deep regret that your privacy has been disturbed tonight,' he continued smoothly.

'Even if it has, I do not see that you have any cause either for fear or regret,' Biggles told him frankly.

The man moved nearer. 'Pardon me, sirs,' he almost crooned.

'What precisely is your business here?' asked Biggles in no uncertain manner.

'I have come to express my deep regret at the inconvenience you have suffered.'

'I have suffered no inconvenience, and, if I had, I cannot see that you need lose any sleep on that account,' said Biggles in a manner that would have settled an argument with an Englishman there and then.

But the Turko-Greek only smiled and took out a heavy gold cigarette-case, at the same time, with studied carelessness, allowing the light to fall on an enormous diamond ring which he wore on a rather podgy finger. 'Will you smoke?' he murmured.

If by this ostentatious display of wealth he expected to impress Biggles he was sadly in error, for the result was the reverse. And his next words, after Biggles had refused the proffered case, did nothing to calm Biggles's rising spleen.

'It is very sad about that unfortunate young man who came to see you tonight,' he observed, placing his fingers together in an attitude of prayer.

'Why sad?' asked Biggles crisply, yet not without curiosity.

The other extended the palms of his hands. 'To be insane is an unhappy state.'

'Ah!' murmured Biggles. 'I see. So he is insane?'

'At least, he suffers from strange delusions.'

'About things like lost oases?'

'Exactly.'

'Are you his guardian or something?' asked Biggles.

'No, but we do not like to see visitors—I might say guests—in our country molested by such people.'

'Just as a matter of interest, how do you know he came here to molest me?' inquired Biggles.

The other hesitated for a moment. Then he shrugged his shoulders. 'Well, you see——'

'Yes, I think I see very clearly,' said Biggles softly. Not for one moment did he believe that there was anything wrong with the young Egyptian.

'Good! I am glad,' declared Zarwan. 'You will take no further notice of his foolish ramblings, I hope?'

'None whatever,' answered Biggles with a curious smile.

The other's manner changed suddenly. 'Of course, if you seek adventure, and would like to take part in an expedition, no doubt it could be arranged.'

'You are sending one somewhere, then?'

The other nodded. 'Yes,' he said, 'and an aeroplane would perhaps be useful.'

Biggles hesitated. He had, of course, no intention of accepting the man's offer, or even considering it, but he was trying to work out the wisest policy to pursue. There was no point in deliberately making an enemy of the man, if, by pretending to play into his hands, there was a chance that he might learn something. Yet a moment's reflection was enough to convince him that such a course was unthinkable. He could not associate with a man whose very presence was distasteful. In the end he compromised. 'We are on our way to Capetown,' he said casually. 'We shall be leaving in a day or two.'

The other bowed. 'Perhaps you are wise,' he murmured.

Biggles frowned. Even if he made an enemy of him he was not prepared to accept threats from such a man. 'Just what do you mean by that?' he asked coldly.

The half-caste, with a natural but significant movement, put his hand into his breast pocket and allowed it to remain there. 'Visitors in Egypt are well advised not to become inquisitive in matters that do not concern them,' he said softly.

Again Biggles hesitated, controlling an urge to kick the man off the terrace. 'I gather that it would annoy you if we took part in another expedition.'

'It would be imprudent of you to take part in an expedition that might interfere with my own.'

Biggles kept control of himself by an effort. 'I see,' he said smiling, but there was no humour in his eyes. 'I'll bear it in mind.'

Zarwan bowed. 'It is a great relief to hear you say that,' he said glibly. 'With your permission I will now withdraw, regretting the necessity for troubling you.' He held out his hand, but Biggles was busy lighting a cigarette.

When he looked up the man had gone, so he flicked aside the spent match and turned to Algy. 'You will go a long way before you meet a nastier piece of work than that,' he said quietly. 'Did you notice the whites of his eyes? They were yellow, like those of a wolf, and never by any chance did he look any one of us straight in the face.'

'Why didn't you kick the oily-faced hog into the road?' demanded Algy hotly. 'I would have done.'

'And spent the rest of our stay in Egypt preventing people from sticking knives into us,' replied Biggles calmly. 'Oh, no. I should say that that gentleman is a knife-thrower in a big way. There was no sense in precipitating an exhibition of it; that will come soon enough, if I know my man.'

'What do you mean?'

'I mean,' answered Biggles, 'if it is all the same to you, I am going with our young Egyptian friend to help him to find

Cambyses and his merry men—or what is left of them.'

'When are you going to start—tomorrow?' asked Ginger eagerly.

Biggles smiled. 'I shouldn't think so. As they have been lost for about twenty-five hundred years, a day or two more or less shouldn't make much difference. But what about a spot of bed? It must be getting late.'

6
A DISCONCERTING DISCOVERY

FROM a height of nearly ten thousand feet Biggles looked down on a land that was old when Cambyses came to it.[1] The Nile and its clustering rice fields with their irrigation ditches had long been left behind; the groups of palms and scattered settlements had become more and more widely parted, and now the open desert lay ahead.

Nearly three weeks had elapsed since Kadar had escaped death in the garden of the hotel in Cairo, and for the little party of explorers they had been busy ones. On the morning following the affair in the hotel garden Biggles had announced his willingness to undertake the flight with Kadar provided his father was prepared to pay the expenses involved, and to this the learned Egyptian professor had readily agreed. The expenses, it transpired, were not so heavy on account of the air journey— since they already had an aircraft—as for the ground organiz- ation. Fuel and stores would be required at the proposed base at Semphis, and, quite apart from their original cost, there was the question of transport. As it happened, Kadar's plans in this respect were already made, so, three days after Biggles's decision, a caravan had departed for the rendezvous, taking such things as would be required for a two or three weeks' stay. Relieved of this responsibility, the airmen were free to make

---

[1] *Egypt had been a kingdom for over 1,600 years when it was conquered by Cambyses in 525 B.C.*

their plans, and with these they had been able to proceed carefully, for it was proposed not to start until the caravan had reached, or nearly reached, its destination. There would, of course, be no point in their doing so, for in any case they would have to await the arrival of the extra fuel before undertaking any long-distance flights.

Nothing more had been seen or heard of Zarwan, much to Biggles's surprise and relief, for, knowing the type of man he was dealing with, he was fully prepared for him to cause mischief; but in the circumstances it could only be assumed that his veiled threat had merely been bluff to try to prevent Biggles and his companions becoming interested in Kadar's undertaking. Nevertheless, they were on their guard, for Kadar was convinced that the attempt on his life had been instigated by his crafty rival. There was, however, he explained, just a slight chance that the attack had been planned by someone else. There was in Egypt, he told them, a religious sect opposed to anything in the nature of exploration; but their activities had hitherto been directed against the mercenaries who did not hesitate to despoil tombs, or even violate the bodies of the dead, for monetary gain; and in view of his sincere pursuit of knowledge he thought it most unlikely that they would offer him violence or attempt to thwart his plans.

Only one point worried Biggles, and that was the matter of landing in the desert, or coming down at other than a recognized aerodrome. While they were on the great Imperial Airways southern route down Africa, which they had followed as far as Assiut, this did not arise, but thereafter any landing was bound to be subject to a certain amount of risk. Without landing there was no means of ascertaining what the surface of the ground was like, and there was, in fact, no way of overcoming this difficulty. Biggles did not forget that while firm sand provided an excellent surface, soft sand can be fatal to an aeroplane. The machine can land, provided the sand is not too soft, but it cannot take off again, the reason being that the wheels sink into the ground and get clogged, which prevents the aeroplane getting sufficient flying speed to rise—as more than one unlucky pilot has discovered to his cost. Soft snow acts in very much the same way.

This, then, was Biggles's chief concern as he left the main air route at Assiut and, turning westwards, headed out over the open desert towards the rendezvous at Semphis. They saw nothing of the caravan, nor did they expect to, for it was coming from the other direction, via Siwah Oasis, over what is generally supposed to have been Alexander the Great's line of march.

So far the journey had been uneventful and comparatively simple. The travellers had done most of their flying in the early hours of the morning, which is the best time for flying in Egypt, as the air is apt to become very bumpy during the heat of the day.

On this, their final long run to Semphis, they had started before dawn in the hope of reaching their objective before the real heat of the midday sun made flying uncomfortable. And in this they were successful, for, shortly after the machine began to climb what seemed to be a series of invisible waves, the oasis crept up over the horizon—much to Biggles's relief, for on such a flight a slight error of judgment, or in the compass, might have tragic results.

On all sides lay the desert, a wilderness of sand, grim, stark, silent, and relentless: a place of death. No wonder the Tuareg, the fierce, veiled warriors of the desert, called it the Region of Devils, thought Ginger, as he regarded it through the cabin window with inward misgivings. As far as the eye could see stretched the sand; it seemed incredible that there could be so much. For the most part it was flat, or slightly undulating, but farther to the south it lay in great piled-up dunes, some with curling crests, like a yellow, storm-tossed sea suddenly arrested in motion. From time to time the dunes appeared to quiver as if the merciless sun, from a sky of steely blue, tormented them with its fiery rays.

Ginger shivered suddenly in spite of the heat, and turning his eyes, looked out ahead. In the clear, dry atmosphere the oasis could be seen from a great distance, how far he was able to judge from the fact that it took the Tourer nearly half an hour to reach it.

Biggles was watching the belt of palm-trees closely. As he had been given to expect, there was no sign of life, so after circling once or twice in order to try to pick out the most suitable place for a landing, he throttled back and began to glide down. If he felt any qualms he showed none, but secretly he was more than a little relieved when the wheels bumped slightly on hard ground and the machine ran to a standstill on the western edge of the fairly extensive group of palms.

Nothing, except possibly a South Sea island, lives up to its reputation more than an oasis in a desert. It is all that has been written and said of it, and the Oasis of Semphis was no exception; so it was, therefore, with considerable satisfaction that Biggles taxied the machine into the deepest shade of the palms and switched off the engines.

'Well, here we are,' he announced. 'Let's get out and stretch our legs. Phew! It's warm, isn't it? I think a little refreshment would not come amiss.'

They got out, but before doing anything else they all assisted in covering the engines, the fuselage, and the wings with the dark-green covers which had been brought for the purpose, both as a protection against the sun, and to prevent the sand from silting in. This applied particularly to the engines. This done, they quenched their thirst, and then proceeded to make camp, or rather, prepare a site, with such limited stores as they had at their disposal. This was soon done, and, the task completed, they settled down to await the arrival of the caravan.

Biggles fetched his maps, and, in close conference with Kadar, checked up the marks he had made on it, one of which, covering a fairly large area, was the most likely site of the Lost Oasis of Zenzura. Ginger, however, was soon tired of watching this; his restless spirit chafed at the delay, so he decided to pass the time by exploring the oasis. Algy, having nothing better to do, went with him.

It was not a very exciting pastime. The oasis was, as nearly as they could judge it, between two and three miles long and about half a mile wide, but there was a tiresome monotony about it.

On the outskirts it began with straggling date-palms, their sun-scorched boles rising straight out of the sand. The trees became closer together, however, and taller in habit, with frequent pendant clusters of fruit, as they neared the depression in the centre where the much-trampled water-hole was situated. Round it for some distance grew a kind of coarse grass, and in one place a fearsome growth of prickly pear raised its thick, lozenge-shaped foliage, studded with small scarlet fruits. That was all. The heat, even in the shade, was intense, and the two wanderers were soon glad to rejoin the others. Ginger, still restless, walked over to the machine, ostensibly to make sure that the dust-covers were secure, but in reality simply for something to do.

Satisfied that the covers would not move if there came a wind, he was about to turn away when his nostrils caught the faint but unmistakable smell of petrol. Standing quite still, wondering whether he should call Biggles, he distinctly heard a slight *phut.* He was on his hands and knees instantly, crawling under the centre of the fuselage, from where the sound had seemed to come. Nor was he mistaken. A few seconds later a drop of petrol splashed on the back of his outstretched had. Quickly, he scrambled out. 'Hi! Biggles!' he called urgently. 'Come here!'

Biggles dropped his map and came at a run, followed more slowly by the others. 'What is it?' he asked anxiously.

'Petrol is leaking from somewhere.'

'Where?'

'It seems to be coming out of the main tank.'

Biggles said nothing. In a moment he was under the machine, feeling the fabric on the bottom of the fuselage. Almost as quickly he scrambled out, and swinging himself up to the cockpit, looked at the petrol gauge on the instrument-board. One glance was enough. Another second and he was down. 'Bear a hand, everybody,' he snapped. 'Get that fabric off—cut it if necessary.'

A few minutes of frantic effort and the truth was revealed. The rear main tank was leaking through a small round hole in the bottom. Biggles examined it closely before plugging it with a piece of chewing-gum from the small store they carried as a thirst preventive, and then covered it with a piece of adhesive plaster from the medicine chest.[1]

'That will have to do for the time being,' he said quietly. 'We can do nothing more. If we try siphoning what little petrol we have left into another tank we shall lose most of it by evaporation.'

Algy looked at him with startled eyes. 'How much is there left?' he asked in an odd tone of voice.

Biggles hesitated for a moment. 'About half as much as we should need to get back to the nearest point of civilization,' he answered, speaking very slowly and distinctly. 'You remember that before we started I insisted that we should carry enough fuel to get us back should anything go wrong with the caravan.'

'Yes—we did that.'

'Quite. Well, as a result of this leak, I reckon we've enough petrol left, including what is in the gravity tank, for a little more than one hour's flying. We were flying over desert for more than three hours getting here. Work that out for yourself.'

'We shall be all right when the caravan arrives,' declared Ginger optimistically.

Biggles threw him a sidelong glance. 'Yes,' he said, 'we shall— provided it *does* arrive.'

'If it doesn't?' asked Kadar.

Biggles smiled faintly. 'You should know better than any one else the answer to that question. I think it would be better not to dwell on that—anyway, not until tonight, by which time the caravan should be here.'

'What an unfortunate accident,' muttered Kadar.

Biggles laughed harshly. 'Accident! That hole in our tank could only have been made with one thing, a pointed instrument; and, believe me, that couldn't happen by accident.'

---

[1] *More than one famous long-distance airman has mended a leaking tank or petrol-lead in this fashion.*

7
THE END OF THE TRAIL

THE caravan did not arrive that evening. It did not arrive that night. Nor did it arrive the next day, although just as the sun was sinking below the horizon, and the purple dusk was closing in around them, the airmen had their first glimpse of the primeval dwellers of the endless sands when a party of those mysterious, blue-veiled warriors of the desert, the dreaded Tuareg, the 'Forgotten God', came riding out of the sunset.

The airmen were sitting talking round their meagre stores on the edge of the oasis when Kadar suddenly stiffened and glanced up. 'Tuareg,' he said softly. 'Take no notice. They may mean no harm—or they may. One can never be sure.'

The others turned to look. From out of the west, looming gigantic in the half light, came a line of veiled warriors mounted on tall Mehari camels. They rode in silence, the feet of their mounts making no noise on the sand. Looking neither to right nor left, without showing by sign or movement that they had seen the hated *Roumi*, the white man—which they must have done—they passed on, as sinister, as evil, as impassive as death, their shrouded figures the embodiment of hostility and cold malevolence. Gazing straight ahead in the gathering darkness, like spectral shapes they disappeared behind a dune, leaving behind them a chill of sullen enmity.

Biggles drew a deep breath. 'It looks as if we shall have to take turns to keep guard,' he said.

But the night passed without the return of the warriors. When the dawn came they were out of sight.

The day passed, and another night; and when the following morning the long-overdue caravan was still unsighted, Biggles called a council of war, for all nerves were on edge with the anxiety of waiting.

'Well, everybody, this is the position,' he announced gravely, as they forgathered under a palm-tree near the idle machine. 'I think you all know how we are fixed, but I will just run over the situation so that there can be no misunderstanding. Our stores have not arrived. They were scheduled to be here three days ago. It is obvious, therefore, that something has gone wrong, and although it may sound pessimistic, my own feeling is that they will not now arrive at all. In the ordinary way, that need not have caused us anything worse than irritation that our plans should have miscarried, but the incident of the leaking tank has altered the position very considerably. As you know, I made allowance for the possible non-arrival of the caravan by carrying enough petrol to get us back home again independently of it. Of that spare petrol more than two-thirds has been lost in a manner which suggests foul play. The same influence might account for the non-arrival of the caravan—we do not know; but what it boils down to is this:

'In still air, we are three hours from Dakhel, and still more from Siwah, those being our nearest points of contact with the outside world. We have enough petrol for one hour's flying, so whichever way we go we shall be compelled to land more than two hundred miles from our objective. I need hardly say that such a course is utterly out of the question. It would be plain suicide. The alternative to that is, we stay here. Very well, what is the position then? We have left out of the emergency rations which we always carry three small tins of bully beef, a few biscuits, six cubes of Bovril, some chocolate, and one or two odds and ends. In short, we have enough food, used sparingly, to last for another two days. Two days, three days, or four days, it matters little; the end must be the same. Still, while we stay here we shall not die of thirst or starvation. There is water in the spring, which Kadar assures me has never been known to dry up, and there are dates on the palms. How long we can live on a diet of dates and water without going crazy, I do not know, but it is at least possible to live. Arabs exist on nothing more than that for weeks on end; whether we shall be able to remains to be seen.

'Now as far as I can see there is only one course open to us. We can't reach civilization, so we must, therefore, stay here; but before we resign ourselves to that it is possible for us to make a last attempt to get into touch with the outside world. As I have said, we still have a little petrol in the tank, enough for an hour's flying, possibly a little more, but a few minutes either way is neither here nor there. We might as well use that petrol while we have it, for in a hot dry temperature like this it will have evaporated inside a week. For desert use, petrol in cans has to be hermetically sealed; that which we bought in Cairo to go with the caravan was sealed in that way. On what petrol we have left our cruising speed gives us a range of about seventy-five miles; that is to say, we can fly seventy-five miles out and get back here. My suggestion is that we make a reconnaissance in the direction of Siwah, that being the direction from which the caravan should have come, in the hope of seeing something of it. If we find it, all so well and good; if we do not, then we must return here and resign ourselves to the inevitable. There is always a chance, of course, that, when we do not return, Kadar's father will send out a rescue party to look for us, but some time must elapse before that is likely to happen, because, as we declared our intention of being away for some weeks, we shall not be reported missing until the end of that time. Well, that's all. If any one has a better suggestion, let him make it, but I can think of nothing else myself.'

Biggles took out one of his three remaining cigarettes, broke it in halves, gave Algy one half, and then lighted both with the same match.

'It isn't much use trying to think of an alternative plan, for the simple reason that there isn't one,' declared Algy. 'The one you have suggested is the only thing we can do.'

'I've nothing to add to that,' said Ginger.

Kadar shook his head. 'Nor I, except that I am sorry to have brought you——'

Biggles waved him to silence. 'Very well, then, that's settled,' he declared.

'When do you propose to make this trip?' asked Algy.

'Now. There is no point in waiting. From the top of the palm I climbed at dawn I estimated that I could see between thirty and forty miles. The caravan was not in sight. That means that even if it is approaching it will not get here before dark. By tomorrow morning we shall have lost, due to evaporation, perhaps five per cent. of our petrol. That is why I say let us go now, and, if necessary, learn the worst at once.'

The wisdom of this plan was apparent to every one, and preparations were at once made for the trip. Every available vessel that would hold water was filled and put aboard, as well as what was left of the stores and a quantity of dates. When there was nothing more to be done the dust-covers were removed and stowed away, and the airmen took their places.

Biggles walked the entire distance of the probable run before he attempted to take off, but the sand, while soft on the surface, was firm, and there were no obstacles. Satisfied that all was well, he climbed into the cockpit, and in a few moments the Tourer was in the air, climbing into the western sky.

As the machine gained altitude all eyes looked into the direction from which the caravan should come. The quivering needle of the altimeter crept round the dial until at length it rested on the ten-thousand mark, but as far as the eye could see not a moving speck broke the surface of the silent sea of sand.

Biggles turned to Algy, who was sitting next to him. His face was grim. 'Another five minutes and we must turn back,' he said.

Algy nodded, his eyes still questing the western horizon. A moment or two later he started. 'I can see something,' he said.

Biggles gazed long and steadily ahead. 'Yes, there is something,' he agreed, 'but it doesn't move.'

'No, it's nothing alive,' returned Algy.

Another two minutes went by and Biggles spoke again. His voice was hard and dry. 'It is a caravan,' he said. 'Or the remains of one,' he added, dropping his voice.

'The remains of one—I think.'

Biggles took the throttle in his left hand, and then hesitated, uncertain as to the wisest course when so much depended on the issue. 'What shall we do?' he asked Algy. 'I ought to turn in another minute. Dare we go down? We are eighty miles from home. I shall not be able to make up any altitude that I lose.'

Algy glanced up, caught Biggles's eyes, but looked away quickly. 'Go down,' he said. 'The petrol may still be there. If it isn't, we're sunk, anyway.'

Biggles was faced with a gamble in which life was at stake, and he knew it. Upon the events of the next few minutes hung all their lives. If the sand was soft and he attempted to land on it, it would be the end beyond all possible shadow of doubt. Even if they did not land, the flight back, with the fast-dwindling petrol, would be a nightmare. Already he doubted if they could reach the oasis, although they might get within walking distance.

The noise of the engines died away suddenly as he cut the throttle, and thereby announced his decision. The Tourer's nose tilted down and the machine began to lose height; and as it went down the details of the scene on the ground grew clearer. As Algy had prophesied, it was not a caravan. It was the remains of one. Soon it became possible to distinguish objects—camels lying outstretched on the sand—saddles—bundles—garments—bodies.

'There has been dirty work done here,' muttered Algy, white-faced.

'Tuareg work, I fancy,' answered Biggles through his teeth.

'What are you going to do?'

'I must land.'

'It's a ghastly risk.'

'I know. But I must go down. Some of those poor devils may only be wounded. Again, there is just a chance that there may be some petrol in those panniers. Either way, it is a risk that we have got to take.'

Algy nodded. 'Go ahead,' was all he said.

With the wind moaning over the wings, the aeroplane swept lower. Twice Biggles circled, unable to bring himself to take the terrible risk of landing. His eyes scrutinized the ground yard by yard. It was at least clear of obstacles. The third time he clenched his teeth and glided in to land. Beads of perspiration stood out on his face, so intense was the mental strain as he flattened out. The next few seconds would decide their fate. It was queer to think of that. Five seconds. The scene became unreal—was it really happening, or was he dreaming? The muscles of his face twitched as the wheels touched and the machine quivered, and he braced himself for the inevitable somersault should the sand be soft. The wheels touched again. There was a jar as the tail wheel dragged, and the next moment the machine was running sluggishly over the ground. The sand was soft, but not too soft, although it pulled the machine up quickly.

Algy did not wait for it quite to finish its run. He opened the door, jumped out, and ran towards the scene of the tragedy. A cloud of flies (for there are flies even in the desert) rose into the air as he dashed up; then he recoiled in horror. In his life he had seen some unpleasant sights, but that which now met his eyes nearly made him ill. Still, he ran to the nearest pannier, saw that it was empty, and hurried on to the next.

A moment or two later Biggles joined him. 'Petrol,' he said tersely. 'Is there any petrol?'

Algy looked up. His face was ashen and curiously set. 'No,' he said quietly. 'Not a drop.'

8
THE HABOOB

BIGGLES waited for the others to come up. He turned to Kadar. 'This was our caravan, wasn't it?'

Unashamed tears were running down Kadar's face. 'Yes,' he answered chokingly. 'There is old Mahomout, the caravan leader. He has ridden his last trail. What can we do with them?'

'Nothing,' answered Biggles shortly. 'If any one is alive we will take him back to the Oasis, although heaven knows what we can do for him there even if we do. You'd better leave it to me to find out, although from what I can see it will be a waste of time. Are these—mutilations—Tuareg work, Kadar?'

'Yes.'

'All right. Well, we are in no case to be squeamish. Go through the panniers and collect any food you can find, also any water-skins.' Biggles turned away to commence his gruesome task.

'It is as I thought,' he said in a hollow voice, when a few minutes later he joined the others again. 'They are all dead. I wonder why the camels all seem to be in such poor condition.'

'The others will have been taken,' replied Kadar.

'They would be needed to carry the petrol,' put in Algy.

Biggles knitted his brow. 'These shocking murders may have been Tuareg work,' he muttered, 'but why should they burden themselves with petrol? What use could it be to them? My feeling is that although Tuaregs may have done the work, there was somebody else behind them. Either that or they had definite orders to take the petrol. Look, that is the way they went.' He pointed to where a broad trail of hoof-marks wound away into the dunes. 'The murderers went that way, so the Arabs we saw at the oasis could not have been responsible—that is, unless they made a detour. But we mustn't stand talking here. The sooner we get back to the oasis the better. My heavens! Isn't the heat dreadful? Did you find any food?'

Possibly on account of the tragedy, the lesser demon of heat had been temporarily overlooked, but they now began to be conscious of it.

Algy pointed to a little heap of tins. 'Those were all in the same pannier,' he said. 'I found it under one of the dead camels, which is probably why it was overlooked. There are a few tins of meat and some dried fruits.'

'We'll take them with us,' declared Biggles. 'I fancy we shall need them. Come on, let's get back. We can do nothing more here.'

They all helped to carry the salvage into the machine. As they approached it Biggles pointed to the wheels; already the tyres had half disappeared into the sand.

'She's sinking. An hour, and we should not be able to budge her,' he said. 'We shall have to watch out for that sort of thing.'

A last glance at the pitiable spectacle behind them and they took their places. The port engine roared as Biggles swung round to get into position to take off over the same ground on which he had landed. Reaching the place, he closed his eyes for a moment before choosing a mark on which to fly, for the dunes appeared to be rocking in the heat. Then, slowly, he opened the throttle. The machine surged forward, running more and more lightly as it gathered speed. It took a long run to get off, but in the end the wheels unstuck, and at a height of a few hundred feet Biggles gave a sigh of relief and turned its nose to the east.

He allowed the machine to climb up to a thousand feet, then he levelled out and throttled back to the most economical cruising speed, all the while holding the machine as steady as he could in the choppy atmosphere. The 'bumps' were almost continuous, and often so severe that it was necessary for the airmen to hold themselves in their places by gripping their seats.[1]

For perhaps five minutes these conditions prevailed, and then, without warning, the Tourer was impelled upwards to more than double its altitude by one of the most vicious 'bumps' Biggles had ever experienced. The effect was almost precisely that of going up in an express lift; but whereas a lift is seldom more than a hundred feet high, the bump in question was sustained for more than a thousand. Kadar clasped his stomach and rolled his eyes. 'I shall be sick if it does that again,' he said desperately.

Hardly were the words out of his mouth when the machine dropped several hundred feet like a stone, as if all support had

---

[1] *Bumps are caused by rising or falling currents of air which, because they are invisible, pass unnoticed by people on the ground. In point of fact, the air is far more restless than an ocean, and is rarely still except on cold, windless days. Bumps are caused by a variety of reasons. A common cause of up-currents is the wind striking against an obstacle, such as a hill, and being deflected upward. Again, the sun striking on rock heats it, and, as hot air rises, an up-current is the result. Perhaps a short distance away a down-draught (in flying parlance, a 'sinker') may be caused by cool air falling over a lake, or a shady valley into which the sun cannot penetrate. These currents or air sometimes cause partial vacuums, and further turbulence is created by the outside air rushing in to fill them. In Africa and on the North-West Frontier of India bumps can be alarming, carrying a machine up or down for two thousand feet or more, and so straining it that it has to be completely re-rigged when it lands. There is no real danger in flying in such conditions, but, naturally, it puts an extra strain on an aeroplane and makes the pilot's task a very trying one, for he must continually correcting the bumps to keep the machine on an even keel.*

been snatched from under its wings—as indeed it had. At the bottom of the bump it struck solid air again with a shock that made it quiver.

'Getting rocky,' murmured Biggles laconically to Algy, without any particular concern, for he had flown through bumps too often to be alarmed by them, and knew that in a reliable aircraft, with no risk of structural failure, there was no danger.

As he levelled out at the bottom of the bump something made him glance to the left, which, as he was flying eastward, was toward the north. For perhaps five seconds he stared unbelievingly, then he turned to Algy with an air of almost hopeless resignation.

'I don't usually give up,' he said, 'but this looks like settling any further argument as far as we are concerned.'

Algy, staring towards the northern horizon, saw a terrifying spectacle. Racing towards them, blotting out the blue sky as effectively as a thick curtain, was what appeared to be an enormous brown cloud that twisted and writhed within itself as it bore down on them. He knew what it was as well as Biggles.

'It's a *haboob*,'[1] he said calmly. 'What are you going to do about it?'

In normal circumstances only one course is open to a pilot who encounters one of these terrifying meteorological disturbances. He must go down quickly, land, turn the nose of his machine into the wind, and anchor it by tying sandbags to the wings, tail and fuselage, after which he takes refuge in or under the machine. The bags are carried empty, of course, but they are soon filled with the most common commodity in the desert. Aeroplanes of the French Air Force, and passenger machines operating in North Africa, are nearly always provided with bags for this purpose. But they adhere to regular routes, where they are soon found if for any reason the machine is unable to take off again after the storm has passed.

---

[1] Haboob. *A severe sand-storm, far worse than the more common dust-storm; it may extend from the ground to a height of 10,000 feet.*

Biggles's position was a very different one. Should he follow the usual practice and land, there was no hope of rescue in the event of his machine being damaged, as it was not unlikely to be. He was well aware of the danger of trying to get above a *haboob*, against which pilots are warned, even if his tanks had been full. Yet what else could he do? He could not hope to reach the oasis before the swirling sand engulfed him, and to run before the storm would, within half an hour, see him on the ground with empty tanks in the very worst part of the desert, perhaps the most inaccessible spot in the world, in the path of the sand demon. In the short time he had for reflection it seemed to him that his only possible hope—how slim it was he knew only too well—lay in getting above the sand, still keeping on his course, trusting either that he would get beyond the disturbed area, which seemed unlikely as he could not see the eastern extremity of it, or that the *haboob* would soon pass. With these forlorn hopes in view he shoved the throttle wide open and began to climb as steeply as his engines would take him.

He managed to reach six thousand feet before the first sharp spatter of sand struck the side of the machine. The sun had become a fast-fading orange ball. He could still see the ground dimly, as through a thick brown haze, but, even as he watched, it was blotted out, and the Tourer was alone in the heart of the storm. For a time visibility was limited to a sort of dim twilight, but as he continued to climb, listening to every beat of the engines for the first warning of seizure, it became somewhat lighter. With the needle of his altimeter registering twelve thousand feet he was almost clear, with the sky showing as a greenish ceiling; but it was on his petrol gauge that his eyes were fixed. He was still running on his main tank, but it was nearly down to zero, and he knew that at any moment the petrol supply might fail.

He had no idea of where he was because he did not know the speed of the wind that was blowing at right angles across his path of flight. He knew the compass-bearing of the oasis, but without knowing his speed of drift he could only hold his course by guesswork. He estimated the speed of the wind at fifty to sixty miles an hour, but in view of what subsequently happened it must have been considerably more than that during the worst of the storm. The ground was buried under a ten-thousand-feet-thick layer of flying sand, so what lay beneath that he did not know, although he could only assume—and hope—that it was the desert over which he had flown on the outward journey.

He had now throttled back again to the minimum speed that would keep the machine air-borne, for his chief concern was to conserve his petrol in order to remain in the air as long as possible. It may have been in some measure due to this that nearly another ten minutes elasped before a warning cough from one of his engines told him that his main tank was nearly dry. He held on until the engines began choking, and then switched over to the gravity tank, which contained, at the outside limit, enough petrol to keep them in the air for another ten minutes. A fine film of dust had settled on his lips, and he wiped them with his sleeve before turning to speak to Algy.

'I should say that we shall be extremely fortunate if we hit the ground within sight of the oasis,' he said quietly. 'If we do, I am afraid it will be more by luck than judgment. I wouldn't swear to our position to within fifty miles. The wind speed up here might be anything—anything up to a hundred miles an hour. I don't know, and it would be a clever man who could guess. I don't fancy going down into the pea-soup underneath us, but we shall have to in a minute or two.'

'Well, at least we shan't hit somebody's wireless-mast or chimney-pot,' asserted Algy optimistically.

'I only wish there was a risk of that, believe me,' murmured Biggles. 'Better tell the boys inside to be ready to jump clear when we hit. I won't guarantee to put her down the right side up in this infernal murk.'

Algy did as he was requested, and as he returned, the engines, after a choking splutter, cut out dead. The propellers stopped. The roar died away, to be replaced by the not-unmusical murmur of wind in the wires. Biggles pushed the joystick forward. The nose went down, and almost at once the brown twilight began to close in around them again. He did not speak.

The situation did not call for comment. He, Algy, and Ginger knew precisely what was happening, and what was likely to happen. They were flying blind. Presently they would reach the ground, and the violence of the impact depended on whether or not Biggles saw it. The needle of the altimeter began to creep back, 8,000 — 7,000 — 6,000.

Algy coughed, the noise seeming to be curiously loud.

The machine continued to lose height, with Biggles's eyes alternating between the false horizon on the instrument-board and the altimeter. There was no need for him to look at the speed indicator, for he could judge his approximate speed by the feel of the joystick.

They were down to a thousand feet, and Algy began looking over the side. There was still no sign of the ground, and he said so, jerking his head back sharply as a great black bulk appeared to float past them.

'What the dickens was that?' he cried sharply.

Biggles raised his eyes for an instant. 'If I didn't know better I should say it was a mountain.'

'It was!' yelled Algy suddenly. 'Look out!'

'Impossible!' snapped Biggles, and then flung the joystick over as a great sombre mass loomed suddenly in front. The machine went over on its side, but he righted it again instantly. With every nerve in his body strained to breaking-point, he swerved again as a jagged peak leapt up out of the gloom and appeared to clutch at the machine. He flashed a glance at the altimeter. As inexorable as fate the needle was creeping back — 400 — 300. His eyes switched to the darkness ahead, and then to the vague shadows underneath.

'Look out!' yelled Algy again. 'I can see the carpet.'

So could Biggles. Or he saw something, he was not sure what it was. He snatched the stick back, felt the machine falter, and waited for the stall. The crest of a solitary palm floated past his side window, then a cairn of stones. He flattened out and braced himself for the crash. *Bump!* He felt the wheels strike something solid, and knew that he had bounced. *Bang!* Again the wheels struck, and the machine reared like a bucking horse. Another brief interval, seeming like an eternity in the pent-up anxiety of the moment, and the wheels struck again. This time they held the ground, although the machine lurched sickeningly. Then came a series of minor jars, another slight bounce, and the machine ran to a standstill.

There was a moment of utter silence, almost frightening in its suddenness. Then Algy spoke.

'Well, we are at least on the ground,' he said simply. 'And that's something.'

Biggles smiled wearily. 'It's a lot,' he said as he leaned back, and Algy noticed that his face was strangely drawn.

9
LOST IN THE DESERT

'WELL, I suppose we might as well get out and see where we've arrived at,' announced Ginger.

'I fancy we shall be lucky to do that,' answered Biggles. 'In any case, we had better sit where we are until the sand settles a bit, or we shall be choked. The storm has passed, but it has left all this stuff in the air, so we had better wait for it to thin a bit.'

'Pass me a drop of water, somebody,' requested Algy.

'Go steady with it,' warned Biggles. 'We don't know where any more is coming from.'

They bore the stifling heat inside the cabin for another half hour, and then, the sand having thinned considerably, they got out and looked about them. Biggles pointed to the machine, coated with a thick layer of sand, so that the fabric resembled nothing so much as sand-paper.

'What a pretty problem that will be for some explorer in a few hundreds of years' time, wondering how an aeroplane got here,' he observed. 'He will probably pack it up and take it home and have it put under a glass case in a museum, in the same way as we should a chariot.' While Biggles had been speaking he had been looking round. 'I may be mistaken, and I hope I am, but this place doesn't strike me as being what you might call a health resort,' he concluded.

'You're right, it doesn't,' agreed Algy.

Nevertheless, they were able to judge how lucky they had been in getting down without a serious accident, for the place in which the machine had landed was a narrow *wadi*, or valley, between forbidding outcrops of rock. All around them towered gaunt, barren hills, their peaks still half obscured in a mist of sand. Rocks lay all about them. There was little else, except the floor of the *wadi*, which was a long expanse of sand that had silted in—the accumulation of years. There was no sign of life, but one or two stunted palms, their fronds brown and withered, suggested that there might be water deep down in the earth; but as there was not a blade of grass, green or otherwise, there was clearly none near the surface.

'Gosh! What a sun-smitten dustbin,' muttered Ginger disgustedly. 'I wonder what lies beyond the edge of the *wadi*. I have a feeling that there ought to be an oasis not far away.'

'And I have a feeling that if there is we shall have found what we were looking for,' returned Biggles dryly.

The others stared at him.

'You mean—the Lost Oasis?' cried Ginger.

'Why not?' continued Biggles. 'We were flying due east when the *haboob* caught us. It came from the north, therefore our line of flight must have been something south of east—say due southeast. Speaking from memory, according to my map no oasis occurs in that direction for hundreds of miles. Nor, for that matter, are there any mountains shown. If there is an oasis here it is certainly an unknown one, even if it is not the legendary Lost Oasis of—what was the name of it?—Zenzura.'

'By the head of my father, I believe you are right!' cried Kadar. 'We have found by accident what we came to look for.'

Biggles nodded. 'Well, Kadar,' he said, 'if it is, I hope you are satisfied with your find; but you'll pardon me, I hope, if I do not go into ecstasies about it. The thing that exercises my mind at the moment is not how to find the Lost Oasis, or what to do with it if we have indeed found it, but how we are going to get home again.'

'But suppose this *is* the Lost Oasis?' cried Kadar enthusiastically.

Biggles regarded him moodily. 'Suppose it is? What are you going to do with it, anyway? It's all yours as far as I'm concerned. Personally, I'd swap the lot for a tuft of nice green grass or even a bunch of stinging-nettles.'

'It is rather depressing, I must confess,' admitted Kadar, somewhat abashed.

'Depressing!' Biggles laughed harshly. 'I could find a better word than that for it.'

'I think the first thing to do is to try to ascertain if it *is* the Lost Oasis,' declared Kadar.

Biggles eyed him sadly. 'You do, do you?'

'Yes; I fancy I saw a cairn of stones farther back——'

'Listen, laddie,' interrupted Biggles. 'From what I can see of it, you are going to have plenty of time to trot about looking for heaps of stones. What we need is a nice heap of *scones*. We are not likely to get very fat on a diet of boulders, so before we start sharpening our teeth on the crusty crags of your precious oasis, let us try to find something softer. Haven't you realized yet that if we don't find water within twenty-four hours, when the sand clears and the sun comes out, we shall be frizzled like kippers on a grill? It seems to me that the sooner we start looking for something to drink and eat, the better.'

'Yes,' agreed Kadar. 'Of course. I am sorry. I was carried away by my excitement.'

'Well, calm yourself, and try to think of something to carry us away from this oven,' Biggles told him. 'That should give you something to ponder on. Well, come on, let's start exploring.'

'All of us?' asked Ginger.

Biggles thought for a moment. 'No, I don't think we'd better all go, in case a bunch of stray Tuareg drift in and steal what little food we've got. We don't want to carry it about with us, so some one had better stay here and look after things. You stay, Algy. I'll go and have a look round. Ginger can come with me; and I'd better take Kadar in case we meet any one—not that I think it's likely—because he can speak the local languages.'

'Will you take the rifle?' asked Algy. With the exception of their pistols, a rifle was the only weapon they had brought with them. They had tried to avoid unnecessary weight, but a rifle had been brought for emergencies, although Kadar had stated that it was most unlikely that it would be needed.

'No. I will leave it here with you,' replied Biggles. 'We shan't go far. We ought to be able to see quite a long way from the top of the next hill.' So saying, he slung a waterbottle over his shoulder, adjusted a pair of dark glasses with which the expedition had been equipped, without which blindness soon comes in the desert, and set off down the *wadi* with Ginger and Kadar on either side of him. They, also, wore sun-glasses.

The heat was intense. The sand that had been whirled high into the air by the *haboob* had either settled again or been drawn on by the vortex, and the sun, now immediately overhead, probed the bare, tortured earth with bars of white heat. There was no escape, for there was no shade. The rocks quivered as they flung back the heat they could not absorb, and the sandy floor of the *wadi* became a gleaming carpet that scorched the explorers' feet through the thick rope soles of their desert shoes.

Before they had reached the end of the *wadi* the sky had entirely cleared, and the depression had become a cauldron. The white glare had given way to yellow haze, distorting the rocks into fantastic shapes, and making it impossible to judge distance. The hill at the end of the *wadi* appeared to recede as they went forward, but they reached it at last, and climbed it, only to find that their view was interrupted by a slightly higher hill in front of it.

'This is awful,' muttered Ginger, who was beginning to feel the first symptoms of the dreadful desert lassitude. He felt his face curiously, wondering why he did not perspire, not realizing that the fiery heat of the desert dries all moisture as fast as it exudes through the skin.

Biggles said nothing. He went on, with gnawing anxiety in his heart. He knew that his casual remark about the necessity of finding water was literally true. If they did not find it in the next few hours, while they had the strength to search for it, they would perish.

They climbed the next hill, and Biggles's heart sank as he saw a great face of cliff in front of him, obstructing what lay beyond and forming an insurmountable obstacle. Biting his lip with vexation and disappointment, he faced to either side in turn. It was the same everywhere. Rock and sand. Nothing more. To the left of the hill, however, the ground fell away sharply into a deep gully, and towards this he turned his steps.

'You know more about this sort of thing than we do, Kadar,' he said, 'but I imagine that we should stand a better chance of finding water on the lower ground.'

'Yes, although it will be hotter.'

They went on, traversed the gully, only to find that it led into a yet deeper one. And all around was the ghastly sameness of rock and sand.

Biggles stopped. 'This is no use,' he said simply. 'We had better not go any farther without a bigger water supply, or without Algy. We've come some distance already. Let us get back and suspend operations until the sun goes down. It will be cooler after dark, and we shall be able to find our way in the moonlight.'

They went back through the gully, climbed the hill, and descended the other side, retracing their footsteps—as they thought. Suddenly Biggles stopped again. 'This isn't the hill we came up,' he said in a hard voice.

'It must be. I think we are only going down a different way,' muttered Ginger, but his voice lacked conviction.

They went on down to the bottom, where Biggles again stopped. He pointed to a huge, mushroom-shaped rock, the base of which had been worn to a mere stalk by countless centuries of erosion. 'We didn't come past that,' he said.

'I think the *wadi* is here,' suggested Kadar, in a voice that had become strangely hoarse.

Again they went forward, hurrying now, to the great cleft in the rocks which Kadar had indicated. But as they reached it they pulled up short, staring aghast at an inferno of rocks and sand which they had certainly not seen before.

Biggles passed his hand wearily over his face. He no longer attempted to deceive himself. 'We're lost,' he said simply.

'Yes, we're lost.' Kadar sat down and buried his face in his arms. 'It was my fault,' he went on miserably. 'I should have known better. The Tuareg have a saying which is taught to their children as soon as they are old enough to understand. It means, "Never leave the trail".'

'But it seems impossible that we could lose ourselves so quickly,' said Ginger.

Kadar shook his head. 'In the desert one can become hopelessly lost, and die of thirst, within a mile of camp. It has happened many times.'

'Well, there is only one thing left. Perhaps Algy will hear this.' Biggles took out his pistol, and, pointing the muzzle into the air, fired three shots at regular intervals.

If there was a reply they did not hear it. All they heard were the echoes of the shots reverberating from hill to hill until they died away in the distance. A piece of rock detached itself from a nearby cliff and fell with an astonishing amount of noise for its size. After that there was silence. Dead, utter silence. Not merely the lesser noise of civilized countries; it was a complete absence of sound.

Ginger felt a thrill of fear, nearly approaching panic. A cold hand seemed to clutch his heart. He realized that he was very thirsty, and also very tired.

'We should never have left our water-supply,' muttered Kadar.

'It isn't much use saying now what we should or should not have done,' returned Biggles bitterly. 'The question is, what are we going to do?'

The others did not answer.

'Well, it isn't much use standing here,' continued Biggles, striking at a fly that persisted in settling on his face. 'Confound these flies. Where the dickens do they come from, anyway?'

'Wherever you go in Egypt you will find "Gippy" flies,' answered Kadar wearily, as he stood up. 'Let us go back to that deep gully and see where it leads. The ground sloped downwards there, and the bottom of the depression is the most likely place to find water.'

They dragged their weary legs back up the hill, and down the other side, but there was no sign of the gully they sought.

Biggles laughed harshly, an unpleasant sound without any humour in it. 'This place is bewitched,' he muttered viciously.

'Of course it is,' returned Kadar quietly. 'Now you know why the Tuareg call this district the Region of Devils. It is full of evil spirits. It is the *djinns* who send the *haboobs*.'

Biggles unslung his water-bottle. 'There is no need for us to die of thirst before we must,' he said casually. 'A mouthful each—no more.'

The water was quite warm, and did little to slake their raging thirst, but Biggles recorked the bottle carefully. After that they went on.

They did not go in any particular direction. One way was the same as another. More and more flies appeared, until they hung in a black cloud over their heads, and although they struck at them repeatedly, they settled on eyes, nostrils, and even crawled into their ears. Once Ginger in a fury turned and slashed at them with his helmet, but it made no difference, and he stumbled on, panting.

The afternoon wore on, with the sun, a searing ball of fire, sinking all too slowly in the west. They had not the remotest idea of where they were, or even if they were walking round and round in the same area. It was all alike. Rock and sand. Never was there the slightest promise of the water they sought.

Late in the afternoon they thought they had come to a ruined town, and they ran forward eagerly, thinking that it could not have existed there without a water-supply. But it was only rocks, hundreds of tall, mushroom-shaped rocks, like a forest of gigantic toadstools; and more and more did Ginger appreciate the Tuareg description of the Region of Devils.

The heat in this petrified forest of fungi—as Biggles called it— was awful, but they stumbled on, wetting their lips at more and more frequent intervals from the fast-dwindling water-supply. It was that or madness. Already Ginger was walking through a

dim yellow world in which ghostly figures marched beside him.
Once he pulled up dead, convinced that in some mysterious way
a line of camels had suddenly appeared; but they were only
rocks, and he stumbled on, walking automatically. Presently
flecks of vivid blue began to dance before his eyes. They merged
until they became a quivering line, and he gave a shout,
thinking that it was sunlight playing of water.

Biggles turned sharply. 'What's the matter?'

'Can't you see anything ahead?' mumbled Ginger.

'No,' answered Biggles shortly. Then he laughed, a horrid
cackling sound. 'Only rocks,' he said. 'Rocks and sand.'

Ginger reeled on, knowing that he had been mistaken. He
knew, too, that he was near the end of his endurance. Biggles
realized it, and passed him the water-bottle.

Ginger shook it, and by the sound knew that it was nearly
empty. He handed it back.

'Drink it,' ordered Biggles. 'If you fall out we shall have to stay
with you.'

Ginger allowed the precious drops—barely a mouthful—to
trickle through his black, parched lips. He threw the bottle
away.

Biggles picked it up and went on.

The sun sank behind the hills; at once the heat diminished
and the relief brought a temporary respite. They came to a cliff.
There seemed to be no way through it, and Biggles was about to
turn when he saw a cave, a mere crack in the rock. 'Let's rest in
there for a minute or two,' he suggested. 'It will be cooler.'

As they reached the fissure Kadar stopped suddenly, staring
at the piled-up sand at the entrance. His eyes opened wide and
an extraordinary expression crept over his face. He closed his
eyes for a moment, shook his head, and then stared again. With
a quivering forefinger he pointed at the sand.

The others, leaning forward to look, saw a number of imprints
on the sand such as a large bird might make, and while their
weary brains were still trying to grasp the significance of the
tracks Kadar uttered a hoarse cry and rushed into the fissure.
Understanding at last, they followed. Just inside was an

unbelievable pool of pale-green water.

In a moment they had all flung themselves down and buried their faces in the cool liquid.

10

THE TOMBS OF THE DEAD

AFTER Ginger had drunk to repletion he smiled wanly and, looking about him, noted with some surprise that the silent pool was not, as he had imagined, a new discovery of their own. All around the edges of the limpid water lay signs of man's intrusion, although there was no means of knowing whether they had been there for a month, a year, a century, or even more. Date-stones, a few gnawed bones, pieces of broken ostrich-shells, and a shattered spear-haft lay on the smooth hard sand, while in a corner—a gruesome sight—against the rock wall, in a semi-reclining position, reposed a skeleton.

'That's better,' observed Biggles, sitting back. 'We found this place just about in time. Queer sort of place to find water, isn't it, Kadar?'

'No. In the desert you sometimes find water in the most surprising places. This sort of formation is not uncommon. These pools are known to all who dwell in the desert, and have been known for countless generations. This one may have been here for thousands of years.'

'But where does the water come from?' asked Ginger.

'Condensation on the hill above at certain times of the year. The moisture condenses on the rock, collects in pockets and cavities, and seeps down through the heart of the mountain— which is why it is so cool—until it arrives in an impervious basin such as this, where, since it can get no farther, it must stay.'

Nothing more was said for a minute or two. The weary travellers were content to rest in the refreshing shade. The dim, unearthly green light that diffused the fissure was a pleasant change after the glare outside. Soliloquizing, Biggles realized that men had probably rested there in the same way for countless generations, perhaps since the birth of time. At last, seeing that the dusk was gathering in the gully, he rose to his feet.

'We must try to get back to Algy,' he said, 'although how that is to be done is more than I can imagine. Having found water, and knowing what it is like to be without it, I am loath to leave it, but we cannot exist on water alone. We need food. Still, we have learned our lesson. When we leave here we will blaze a trail, either in the sand, or by marking the rocks, so that we can find our way back again.'

'I think it would be better to wait here for a little while longer,' suggested Kadar. 'We shall travel more easily by moonlight.'

'I think you're right,' admitted Biggles.

So they sat down again and waited until the moon was flooding the gully with its cool light; then they moved towards the entrance. Reaching it, Biggles was about to step forward when he hesitated, peering at the ground a short distance beyond the mouth of the cave. Then he took a pace outside and looked up.

'That's funny,' he murmured, half to himself. 'What is causing that shadow to move?'

'What shadow?' asked Ginger.

'That one.' Biggles pointed to a wide area, reaching for some distance back, where the ground was darker than elsewhere. A stain seemed to be converging slowly on the fissure, and as they stood staring a slight sound became audible. It was a faint rustling, like the autumn wind among dead leaves.

'What the dickens is it?' asked Biggles again in a perplexed voice, and with just a hint of alarm. 'It seems to be alive.' His voice trailed away.

Kadar stepped forward, peering at the edge of the moving shadow. Suddenly, as if he had been thrust violently, he stumbled backward.

'They are scorpions!' His voice was hoarse with unutterable horror and loathing.

'Scorpions!' Biggles echoed the word incredulously.

'Yes. Thousands of them. Millions of them. I didn't know that scorpions drank water, but that must be why they are coming here—unless it is for us.'

'Good heavens! Let's get out of this!' cried Ginger, his voice rising to a high crescendo.

'Yes, but where can we go?' asked Biggles desperately. 'We can't get through that lot. One scorpion sting is bad enough, without——' He dashed out and looked up the face of the cliff.

'There's no escape that way,' he muttered, hurrying back to the others at the entrance to the cave.

For a moment they stared at the slowly approaching shadow of death—for a single scorpion sting can be fatal—the leading edge of which was now not more than half a dozen paces away. Unnoticed, a few of the poisonous creatures were in advance of the rest, and Biggles jumped aside only just in time to prevent one from climbing on to his shoe. He brought his heel down viciously on the crawling horror. 'No, you don't, you brute,' he muttered, and backed away hurriedly to the rear of the cave, where he struck a match from the box which he carried in his pocket. 'Thank goodness!' he said in tones of heartfelt relief. 'There's a way through here; we'd better see how far it goes.'

The others had joined him, and now stood staring rather apprehensively at a narrow black aperture in the farthest recess of the fissure.

'Don't for heaven's sake let us get lost in here. That would be worse than being lost outside,' said Ginger anxiously.

'I'd rather be lost than eaten—anyway, by scorpions,' declared Biggles. 'I'm not staying here.' He took his note book from his pocket, and tearing out several leaves, rolled them into the form of spills. Lighting one of them with a match, he started off along the cave with the others following close behind.

He had not gone very far when the spill was knocked out of his hand, being, of course, extinguished. But before it went out he had a fleeting impression of a dark shape bearing down on it.

'What the deuce was that?' he cried, fumbling hastily for another match. In the momentary silence that followed his words, a curious, leathery, fluttering sound could be heard; it was not unlike running water in the distance.

'Bats!' said Kadar.

At that moment something hit Ginger a hard blow in the face; instinctively he struck at it, but only succeeded in barking his knuckles against the wall of the cave.

Another match flared up, disclosing a host of dim shapes passing in a steady stream down the natural corridor over their heads towards the exit. One detached itself from the rest and made a dart at the match, but Biggles was ready, and he dashed it violently against the wall with a lightning sweep of his hand. It hit the rock with a thud and fell to the ground, where it lay fluttering. An unpleasant fetid smell became noticeable, but no one commented on it.

Biggles lighted another spill and went on. 'While there's only a single corridor we can't very well lose our way, at all events,' he exclaimed hopefully. 'There may be another way out somewhere. Let's keep going. Never mind these stinking bats. First, scorpions, now bats—my word! The Tuareg knew what they were talking about when they named this place the Region of Devils.'

The sandy floor now began to rise under their feet, but the went on, sometimes striking at the bats when they came too close to be comfortable, and keeping a good look out on either side for turnings. In this way they travelled for a considerable distance, and then, with surprising suddenness, the bats all disappeared. Kadar ventured an opinion—that was probably right—that as bats feed at night they had all gone out. Anyway, they had certainly disappeared, and presently Biggles called a halt.

'I don't think we need fear the scorpions any longer,' he said, 'so the only point in going farther seems to be the hope of finding another exit—not that we shall need one if the scorpions are considerate enough to retire to wherever they came from when it gets light. By the way, we had better be careful about picking up stones, or we may get stung; if I remember rightly, that is where they like to sit. There is one thing about going on, though: as it is dark outside we might pass an exit without seeing it, so it would perhaps be a better plan to stay where we are until it gets light.'

Everyone was tired, but nobody felt particularly like resting.

They did, in fact, sit down on the sand for a time, but they soon found that in their precarious condition sleep was out of the question, so they abandoned all thought of it.

'We've been going uphill ever since we left the pool,' observed Biggles thoughtfully, 'so if we do happen to strike an opening it should be on fairly high ground, from where we ought to get a view of the surrounding country. We might possibly be high enough to spot the machine. Poor old Algy will be in a state by this time, I expect, but we can't do anything about it.'

After that another silence fell, in which Biggles passed the time usefully by folding a bunch of spills, using nearly all the pages of his note-book for the purpose. Several matches still remained in his box, and as Ginger had a petrol-lighter, there seemed to be no reason why they should run out of illumination.

'We've been to some queer places in our time, but I doubt if we ever passed a night in a stranger place than this—the middle of a mountain in an unexplored desert,' said Ginger, after a long interval.

'It will be a long time, I hope, before I pass another night in it, anyway,' replied Biggles. 'This silence gives me the jitters; it's like being in a tomb.'

Ginger shivered. 'That's a cheerful remark to make, I must say,' he returned indignantly. 'You're too near the mark to be pleasant, and I shall feel happier when I'm out of it. I'm ready to push on a bit farther if everyone else is.'

Everyone appeared to be more than willing, so they stood up and prepared to move on. Biggles struck a match, lighted a spill, and they started off, but they had not travelled very far when Biggles, who was leading, gave a sharp exclamation.

'There's something ahead,' he said. 'I can't quite make out what it is, but the cave seems to open out considerably into a sort of hall.'

A few more paces revealed that that was indeed the case, and they all stopped, staring about them in wonderment, not that they could see very much in the dim light of the flare. All they could perceive was that they were in a lofty chamber, almost like a church, the extremities of which were lost in gloom. Biggles took several new spills, opened them fanwise between his fingers, lighted them from the one already alight, and held them aloft. His eyes first went to the ceiling; then they travelled slowly down the walls.

'For a natural formation, this place seems to be extraordinarily free from stalactites and things,' he murmured. 'What the——'

There was a short silence in which they all stared at the lower part of the walls, which appeared to be hollowed out in the form of a honeycomb. In other words, they seemed to consist of a great number of small cavities, or compartments. And that was not all. There was something in each compartment.

Kadar solved the problem. 'You said just now that this place was like a tomb,' he said, instinctively dropping his voice to a whisper. 'That's exactly what it is. I have seen a place something like this before. We are in the tombs of the dead.'

Ginger experienced that unpleasant creepy feeling at the top of the spine sometimes described as the hair standing on end. 'Crumbs!' he muttered in a thin voice. 'Let's hop it.'

Biggles lighted some more spills to replace those that were nearly exhausted. 'That looks like one of the bodies fallen out,' he said, pointing to a huddled form on the floor. 'Perhaps the poor blighter was buried alive.'

Kadar, his archaeological instinct aroused, stepped eagerly towards it, but he had not taken more than two or three steps when, to the consternation of everybody, the figure suddenly sat bolt upright. The skin over its eyes rolled back, exposing the whites, and for a fleeting instant the yellow light of the flares played on a wrinkled, leathery face, a hairless head, and a thin, scraggy neck. Then, with a wild screech, the figure leapt to its feet and bounded across the floor. What became of it no one saw, for at the screech Ginger had let out a yell of horror; Kadar leapt back as though shot out of a catapult, and coming into violent contact with Biggles knocked him over, with the result that the place was plunged into darkness.

To Ginger it was a moment of supreme horror, a ghastly nightmare from which he could not awake. He could hear

Biggles muttering as he groped for his matches, but the sound was almost drowned by a terrified whimpering sound which he presently identified as coming from Kadar. Then a match flared up, revealing Biggles just scrambling to his feet, and Kadar with his arms folded over his face.

'Come on, let's get out of this perishing place,' muttered Biggles. 'I don't believe in spooks, but if this place isn't haunted I'll eat my helmet.'

The others picked themselves up, and, while they stood collecting their scattered wits, the silence was again broken, this time by a peculiar whispering sound that seemed to come from the far end of the chamber. Hardly had it died away when there was a queer swishing noise that increased rapidly in volume, and, a moment later, from the narrow cave from which the airmen had emerged burst a black torrent of bats.

For a moment Biggles stared at them uncomprehendingly, never dreaming of danger from that direction; but as one deliberately swooped at him, and another attached itself to the side of his face with its teeth and claws, he understood. He tore the repulsive creature from his face and hurled it to the ground; then, turning, he raced from the far end of the hall, shouting to the others to follow him.

They needed no second invitation, and they all bolted incontinently, to discover that the chamber diminished rapidly to a small tunnel, at the entrance of which they arrived just in time to see the mummified figure bounding along it on all fours.

'Keep going!' yelled Biggles, and, whirling round, fired two shots from his pistol into the thick of the bats that were following him, Then, lighting matches as he went, he hurried after the others, who were stumbling along by the feeble light of Ginger's petrol-lighter.

The noise made by the bats as they poured into the tunnel was incredible, and certainly alarming, and Biggles was wondering feverishly what he could do to stem the attack when a narrow slit of crimson light appeared ahead. For a second he could not imagine what it could be, but then he realized with joy that it was the dawn, and that the passage must end there. Which, in fact, it did, and the fugitives dashed out at a speed that nearly cost them their lives; for the passage terminated in the side of the hill, which, while not exactly a precipice, was too steep for safe negotiation at the pace they were travelling.

Kadar, who was in front, saw the danger first and let out a warning cry, and in a moment they were all slipping and sliding on the hill-side, grabbing wildly at anything their clutching fingers could find to check their precipitate descent. With bruised hands and torn finger-nails, they finally managed to pull themselves up, only to sit and stare in amazement at the sight that met their eyes.

'The Tuareg are right,' announced Biggles with absolute conviction. 'This is, without doubt, the Kingdom of Devils.'

I I
THE HORROR IN THE POOL

THE bats did not pursue the airmen once they were in the open. For a minute or two they hung over the mouth of the cave like a dense black cloud, making a curious twittering noise; then, as suddenly as they had appeared, they streamed back into the cave as if they were being drawn by an invisible vortex, leaving the invaders of their domain to survey the scene that lay spread out before them. This they did without speaking.

The hill on which they were seated was one of several that sloped down to a central plain, in the manner of a basin. There was nothing unusual about these hills; indeed, they were of a monotonous uniformity, consisting entirely of rock which had been burnt by the sun to a pale, slaty grey, and worn by erosion into the most fantastic shapes. It was no doubt due entirely to the natural circular water-shed thus formed that the centre of this depression was in startling contrast to the rest. It was, briefly, an oasis, and, judging by the verdancy of the palms and other foliage, one of particular fertility. In places the palms had been cleared, leaving open spaces in which flourished what appeared to be corn.

From the centre of this refreshing prospect rose an impressive, dome-shaped hill, clothed for about half its height with palms and giant cacti; but then, due possibly to the failure of the essential water, they thinned out quickly, leaving the top of the dome bare of vegetation, so that the village which surmounted it stood out in high relief.

'Village' is, perhaps, a misleading word, for it was at once clear that most of the buildings were in ruins. For the rest, it consisted of a solid bank of dwellings set in the form of terraces, bleached grey by the sun so that the small square incisions in the structures that served for windows stood out sharply. There was no movement of any sort, which suggested that the place was uninhabited; indeed, the whole atmosphere suggested desertion, desolation and decay.

'Well, there it is,' murmured Biggles at last.

'The Lost Oasis,' breathed Kadar.

'It can't be anything else, can it?'

'No. Nothing is shown here on the map.'

Biggles stood up and brushed the worst of the dust from his clothes. 'It's a pity Algy isn't with us,' he said. 'I'm afraid we are in a hopeless mess, and, frankly, I don't see how on earth we are going to get back, but it wouldn't be so bad if we were all together. We've got to make an attempt to find Algy as quickly as we can, that's certain, if for no other reason than that he probably thinks we are dead, whereas we do at least know that he is all right. At any rate, he has enough food and water to last him for some days. The thought that worries me is that he might start off to look for us, in which case he will probably get lost as we did, but without being so lucky as we were in finding water. In fact, I think it is almost a certainty that he will try to find us. Therefore, as I say, we ought to try to get back. All the same, I don't know about you fellows, but I am passing out for want of food, and to start trying to find our way back to the machine in our present state would be dangerous. That village, or whatever it is over there, can't be more than two or three miles away, so I suggest that as a first precaution we go over to it in the hope of finding some sort of food. There will certainly be dates on the trees, and if it is corn growing in those fields, which is what it looks like, then we shall at least be able to keep body and soul together. There should be water there, too. If there isn't, then the only thing we can do is to go back through the cave to where we know there is some. I think we shall have to go back that way in any case. Bats or no bats, it will probably be easier to get through the cave than climb over the top of this hill, which, when the sun gets up, will be pretty nearly red-hot. I'm no mountaineer, anyway. What's your idea of things, Kadar?'

'I agree with you. We must find food before we do anything else. It is dreadful to get weak in the desert: one so soon gives up. I've had some of it, so I know. Let's get across to the oasis and provide ourselves with some dates, if nothing else, and then try to find our way back to Algy. I don't altogether agree with you about the cave, though. This hill behind us is a high one, and it must command a wide view. I would suggest that we attempt to scale it in the hope of seeing from the top the place where we left the machine. If there is no way down the other side, then we shall have to go through the cave whether we like it or not. And as far as getting back to civilization is concerned, I may be wrong, but I have a feeling that the Arabs sometimes come here, although the place may be known only to one or two.'

'What makes you think that?' asked Biggles sharply.

'One thing only: the jewels I told you about. They must come from just such a place as this, and there can't be many such places.'

'Ah, you mean they are found in the—tombs?'

'Yes; jewels are not likely to be found anywhere in Egypt today except in tombs.'

'Well, that's hopeful, anyway,' murmured Biggles. 'But come on; if we are going across to that village the sooner we start the better, while it is still comparatively cool.'

They set off without delay, but they had not gone far when a crash somewhere above them made them look back. A great stone was bounding down the hill towards them, followed by a number of smaller ones that had evidently been disturbed by its progress.

'Look out!' shouted Biggles, throwing himself flat under an overhanging ledge, and the others crowded into the narrow haven with him.

The stone whirled over their heads and went plunging down into the depths.

'Was that an accident, or is that animated mummy we saw in the cave trying to be unpleasant?' muttered Biggles thoughtfully, as he crawled out of the refuge.

They all stared back up the hill, but there was no sign of life, so, with an occasional apprehensive glance behind them, they resumed their march.

It was soon clear that Biggles had been wrong in his estimate of the distance to the village, for what with the steepness of the hill, and the detours they were often compelled to make round difficult places, they were an hour reaching the bottom, and a further twenty minutes getting to the nearest of the palm-trees; yet the village still looked as far away as when they had started.

'I'm afraid we shall have to alter our plans,' declared Biggles. 'By the time we get to that village it will be too late to think of looking for Algy today. I suggest that we leave the place until later on. We shall have plenty of time to explore it. I can see lots of dates, so let's get a good supply and start back. Another point is, the side of the hill we came down is still in the shade; when the sun gets round a bit, later on, it will be nearly too hot to touch.'

'Yes, I think that's the best plan,' agreed Ginger. 'Let's get together and muster up all our stores before we start any exploring.'

While they had been talking Kadar had gone on ahead through the trees, and now an excited call sent the others forward at a run. They saw the reason for Kadar's excitement even before they saw him. Set amind the luxuriant palms was a large pool of clear water, gleaming like a mirror.

'This is fine,' declared Biggles enthusiastically, and, lying down at the edge, they all had a long, refreshing drink.

Ginger began stripping off his clothes, an operation which did not take him many seconds, and with a joyous yell he plunged in. But hardly had he struck the water when Biggles, who had sat down to take off his shoes preparatory to following suit, leapt to his feet as white as death.

Ginger's head came to the surface. He was grinning all over his face, and he burbled with his lips to show his contentment.

'Come out!' Biggle's cry was almost a scream.

The expression on Ginger's face altered to one of alarm in an instant, and he struck out swiftly for the bank. He knew Biggles too well to ask questions before obeying, and it was fortunate for him that it was so.

Biggles darted to the water's edge, and whipping out his automatic, endeavoured to get the sight on a long black shadow that was shooting through the water immediately behind Ginger, the displacement of water caused by its passage making a wide ripple on the surface. But he dared not shoot for fear of hitting Ginger, so he could only jump from one foot to the other in his agitation.

Ginger reached the edge of the pool a mere three yards ahead of the thing that was following him. Biggles grabbed him by the arm and literally dragged him out of the water and flung him clear. Then he sprang back himself, while Ginger scrambled madly over the sand away from the death-trap into which he had so lightheartedly jumped.

With the majestic stateliness of a battleship, an enormous crocodile surged up on to the bank and waddled forward several paces on rigid legs before it stopped, its great jaws open, and its crested back arched. And there it stood, blinking with its little eyes at the hastily-retreating airmen, and its massive tail gently stroking the surface of the water.

'Great heaven! What a horror!' gasped Biggles, for the creature was a good twenty feet long. 'How in the name of goodness did a thing like that get here?' He turned wondering eyes to Kadar, who had turned a horrible yellowish-green under his brown skin.

'I should have guessed it,' he answered severely. 'This is quite a common thing. The crocodile played a big part in the religious ceremonies of the ancients in this part of the world, as is shown by many of the old inscriptions and sculptures. Models made of gold have also been found.'

'Well, that puts an end to the bathing party,' muttered Biggles disgustedly, sitting down and fanning his face with his helmet when he saw that the crocodile attempted to come no farther ashore. 'Shall I shoot the brute?' he inquired, looking at Kadar for advice.

'Please yourself. You won't kill him with that pop-gun, though, and there seems to be no object in wounding him. Perhaps it would be better to save what few bullets we have for emergencies. Now that we know that this ugly customer is here it can do us no harm.'

Ginger was putting on his clothes with trembling fingers, regardless of the water that still glistened on his body. He was still pale from shock. 'Let's go back and find Algy,' he said bitterly. 'Scorpions in the sand, crocodiles in the drinking water, bats in the cave—I shall have bats in the belfry if this goes on.'

Keeping a watchful eye on the monster, Biggles walked farther along the pool and filled the water-bottle with fresh water. 'Let's get some dates,' he suggested dispassionately.

We shall probably find they've got poisonous bugs in them,' grumbled Ginger. Nevertheless, he swung himself up into a palm that had been blown over at an acute angle by some long-forgotten storm. Not without difficulty, he crawled into the fronds, and from there tossed down several bunches of dates into the waiting hands of those below. This done, they ate as many as they needed, and, each carrying a bunch of the fruit in his left hand, they began retracing their steps.

Ginger turned to where the crocodile was still watching them with an expression suggestive of disappointment on its face, and placing his thumb to his nose, extended his fingers. 'That to you,' he sneered.

Thereafter they began the long climb back up the hill. They started in the shade, but before they reached the entrance to the tombs of the dead the sun was striking the hill-side with its fierce rays. A quick survey disclosed a not-too-difficult way to the top of the hill, so they scrambled on towards the serrated crest that cut into the sky like a row of broken yellow teeth. Biggles was first to reach the top, and, regardless of the heat of the rock, he dropped quickly on his hands and knees when he saw the terrifying abyss that yawned before him. Peering cautiously over the edge, he saw that they were on the top of the cliff immediately above the fissure that gave access to the pool inside, a fact which he was able to ascertain from the position of the 'forest of petrified fungi', and the faint trail of footprints leading from it. All around lay spread out a wild jumble of sun-parched hills, valleys, and gorges, destitute of life, unnerving in their stark barreness. It reminded Ginger, as he crawled up and looked over the edge, of an enlarged photograph he had once seen of the moon's surface.

Yet in the distance could be seen the end of the rocks and the beginning of the open desert, and Biggles pointed it out. 'Look!' he said. 'There is the palm we nearly hit as we came down. I don't see any palms elsewhere in that direction, so it must be the place.'

'I can't see the machine,' declared Ginger.

'You couldn't expect to,' Biggles told him. 'It was so smothered up with sand that it would be hard enough to see it from a hundred yards, never mind five or six miles. Well, that is the direction we must make for.'

'Yes, that is the palm, without doubt,' put in Kadar. 'You can just see the *wadi* we walked down, this side of it.'

From their bird's-eye view it was, in fact, possible to see the tortured earth in the form of a map, and thus follow with the eyes several routes that would take them back to the place they were so anxious to reach. Biggles took out a pencil, and on one of the few remaining pages of his note-book commenced making a sketch-map, rough, but sufficient for the purpose of finding their way back to the machine. This did not occupy many minutes, and, the task completed, he backed away from the chasm and stood up.

'We can't get down the face of this cliff, that's certain,' he said, 'so, whether we like it or not, we shall have to go back through the cave.'

'What about the bats?' asked Ginger, à trifle nervously.

'We shall have to take our chance with them,' observed Biggles. 'By this time they may have settled down again and be as docile as they were when we first went into the cave. It was that bag of skin and bones that set them on to us, I'm sure.'

'There it goes now. Look!' cried Ginger excitedly, pointing a quivering forefinger at a small, brown, ape-like creature that was scrambling down the hill towards the oasis far beyond the entrance to the tombs.

'I hope he—or she—falls into the pond,' wished Ginger viciously.

'Perhaps it thinks it is following us, not knowing that we came back up here,' suggested Kadar.

'It doesn't matter much what it thinks so long as it keeps out of our way,' said Biggles. 'Frankly, I am glad it is out of the way; there is no knowing what mischief it might be up to if it found us in the cave. The place is unpleasant enough as it is, without any added complications. Come on.'

They made the best speed possible down to the entrance, and the gruesome knowledge of what it held was in some degree compensated for by the cool shade within. Just inside the entrance Biggles mustered his remaining spills, which he had thrust into his pocket when they fled before the bats, and, in spite of Kadar's protest, augmented them with some of his newspaper clippings. Thus provided with means of illumination, they started on their unpleasant journey.

Reaching the tombs, Biggles pointed, without speaking, to the walls, which were festooned with countless sleeping bats, all hanging head downwards. Placing his finger on his lips, he went on through the chamber, and breathed a sigh of relief when they reached the other cave on the opposite side. Along this they hurried, stopping occasionally to light fresh spills, and at length, without incident, they reached the silent pool, now looking indescribably beautiful in a slant of pure white sunshine. There was no sign of the scorpions, which apparently visited the pool only by night—unless it had been, as Kadar had suggested, that they were seeking human flesh—so, after a fortifying drink, they proceeded on the last part of their journey.

With the map to guide them, finding their way through the desolation became a comparatively simple matter, although they took care to mark their trail by dragging their feet through the sand, and sometimes building small cairns with pieces of loose rock.

An hour's steady plodding saw them at the end of the *wadi*, and in their anxiety they traversed it in quick time.

'I don't see him,' said Biggles anxiously, as they approached the machine. Then, raising his voice, 'Hi! Algy!' he called.

There was no answer, so they broke into a run. Panting, they reached the Tourer, still exactly as they had left it, and stared about them.

'Algy!' shouted Biggles again, but only the echoes replied.

Ginger ran to the cabin door and opened it. 'He's not here,' he said. Then he went inside. Presently he returned. 'The rifle's gone,' he said, 'but nothing else seems to have been touched.'

They called again several times, but there was no answering hail, and at length Biggles squatted on one of the undercarriage wheels in the shade afforded by the wings.

'It is as I feared,' he said quietly. 'He's gone. No doubt he went to look for us.'

'Maybe he isn't far away, and will come back presently,' suggested Ginger optimistically.

'That is the best we can hope for,' returned Biggles briefly.

12

TRAPPED

ALL through the heat of the late afternoon they waited, and experienced for the first time the full force of the desert sun. The sand shimmered and the rocks quivered like live things. The *wadi* became a furnace in which the tortured airmen could only cower under the machine, keeping life in their fast-drying bodies by taking frequent sips of water. As the sun moved round, so they moved with it, in order to keep in the narrow shade provided by the Tourer's wings, augmented by the dust-covers which they brought out of the cabin. Even so, the sand on which the sun had be playing was too hot to touch with the bare hand, and they were compelled to spread about their spare kit and sit on that. Once Ginger, driven to desperation, bolted into the cabin, but he was soon out again, declaring that the heat inside had nearly shrivelled him to a cinder.

'Whether Algy returns or not, we shan't be able to stand much of this,' declared Biggles, during one of the many silences.

'Our skins would soon peel off, and we should probably go blind,' Kadar informed them with disconcerting frankness. 'I have seen——'

'Don't tell us what you've seen,' interrupted Biggles. 'Leave us to guess. It shouldn't be difficult.'

The day wore on, and at long last came the blessed relief of dusk. With many exclamations of thankfulness, they crawled out of their retreat and surveyed the sterile scene.

'If Algy is lost, and has been out all day in that sun without water, he must be a dead man,' declared Biggles disconsolately. 'It's no use blinking at facts. Another hour of it and I should have gone crazy. It is just one of those things one has to experience to believe. I am sorry to say it, but I find it difficult to suppose that Algy will return here. It seems to me that his only chance lay in striking a pool such as we found, or the oasis. Frankly, I don't think it's much good waiting for him. In any case, I don't think we could stand another day like today. It's no use grumbling; we're here, and it looks as though we shall have to spend the rest of our lives here. Has any one any suggestions to make?'

'The only thing we can do if we wish to remain alive is to go back to the oasis,' declared Kadar emphatically.

'We might have a last look round to see if we can find Algy's tracks,' suggested Ginger. 'It seems like deserting him just to go away.'

'It will be death to remain,' returned Kadar.

'I agree with what you say about desertion, Ginger, but I feel inclined to take Kadar's advice,' said Biggles. 'There's no sense in sitting here and dying by inches while we are within reach of an oasis. We'll have a last look round to see if we can find Algy's tracks, but I don't think we shall, or we should have found them before. If he doesn't come back during the night we'll make for the oasis, starting before dawn. We'll leave some food and water here, of course, on the off-chance that he does come back, and a note saying where we have gone. I'll leave him a map, too, showing him how he can find the oasis.'

'That is the most sensible thing to do,' agreed Kadar.

In the fading light they cast about for tracks, but it was all in vain, and at last, miserable and depressed, they returned to the machine, where Biggles sorted out the meagre store of food and water, and wrote the note to Algy, which he fixed in a conspicuous place on the fuselage. This done, they all lay down to rest and get what sleep they could.

The stars were still shining brightly in the sky when Biggles started making preparations for departure, and the others rose wearily to their feet, conscious for the first time of how much energy had been taken out of them by the lack of normal food and the scorching sun. However, they joined Biggles, who was taking a last look round.

'Ready?' he asked briefly.

'Lead on,' invited Ginger, and they started off on the weary trail back to the oasis.

Fortunately their lassitude wore off as they got into their stride, for the night air was cool and invigorating, and in just over an hour, with the breath-taking desert dawn just breaking, and flooding the hill-tops with its pink radiance, they reached the face of the cliff through which they would have to pass. They approached it cautiously, for they had not forgotten the scorpions. They saw several stray ones, which reared up and waved their tiny but formidable lobster-like claws at them, but there was no mass formation such as they had seen on the occasion of their first visit.

'I should say they scatter to their respective dug-outs as soon as it begins to get light,' opined Biggles. 'Watch you step, everybody. A scorpion sting would just about put the tin hat on things.'

A few stray bats were drifting into the cave, but they did not appear to be vicious, so the airmen ignored them and continued on their journey. Biggles had brought with him a good supply of paper, which had been used for wrapping odd articles in the machine, so with a bright torch held aloft they made good progress. There was an anxious moment or two as they passed through the tombs of the dead, for a few of the bats, disturbed, no doubt, by the unusual light, seemed inclined to protest against the intrusion; but the airmen hurried on, and soon found themselves on the side of the hill that overlooked the oasis. They made a thorough scrutiny of the landscape in the hope of seeing Algy before they moved on, but there was no sign of life anywhere, so they set off down the hill.

'I wonder what became of our friend with the wrinkled countenance?' asked Ginger.

'If we see her—I say "her" because I fancy it is a woman—we might try to catch her,' suggested Kadar. 'She ought to be able to tell us something about the place, and whether anybody ever comes here.'

'That's a good idea, although I'd as soon try to catch a wild cat,' asserted Biggles, as they approached the pool among the palms, where they proposed to refill the water-bottle, which had been emptied during the march.

Biggles suddenly caught Kadar by the arm. 'I don't think we need find the old hag to ask if any one comes here,' he said crisply, throwing swift glances to left and right. 'Look! that answers the question. I swear those weren't here yesterday.' He pointed to a group of four marks in the soft sand near the edge of the pool. Unmistakably they had been made by a camel.

Kadar caught his breath sharply, but then nodded as if he understood. 'It is more than likely that they were made by some stray animal,' he said. 'Camels are always wandering away from camps. They have wandered away for thousands of years, yet for some curious reason the Arabs never seem to think of tethering them. Also, a camel can sense water at an enormous distance, and if one is lost anywhere in the district it would make for this pool as a homing pigeon makes for its loft.'

'You know more about this sort of thing than we do, so maybe you are right,' admitted Biggles. 'All the same, we had better keep our eyes skinned. It would be a bad spot to bump into a bunch of Tuareg.'

There was no sign of the dreadful guardian of the pool, so they drank, and after a short rest, during which they ate a few dates, they pushed on towards their objective, wondering what surprises it held in store.

On nearer approach they found that the cacti formed a circular belt just below the summit of the mound on which the village was situated, and so regular was it in its formation that it had obviously been planted by human agency, doubtless as a barrier, in the same way as barbed wire is used in modern warfare. But that, clearly, had been long ago, for much of the monstrous growth was dead and withered, and the airmen had no difficulty in finding a way through it.

'This is the most exciting moment of my life,' announced Kadar, as the approached the grey, weather-worn houses. 'This discovery will cause a tremendous sensation when we get back.'

'*When* we get back,' murmured Biggles dryly.

They soon discovered that the village was, in fact, a citadel, built on the very summit of the mound, with smooth bare walls presented to possible invaders. Unable to find a way up, they could only walk along the base of what was, in effect, a rampart, and in this way they presently came to the entrance which they knew must exist. It was a dark, forbidding portal, medieval in its conception and Moorish in construction, having the customary high, pointed arch.

Biggles looked at Kadar questioningly before going on. 'Don't you think we are taking a bit of a chance, strolling into a place like this without knowing if any one is inside?' he asked quietly.

'Had there been any one here they could not have failed to see us, in which case either they would have come to meet us or prepared a reception, hostile or otherwise. Look at the track. Does it look as if it is ever used? I should say there has been no one here for many years.'

Biggles looked down and saw that what Kadar had said was

true. 'What about that corn we saw from the hill-top?' he reminded him.

'If it had once been planted here, and apparently it was, it would go on sowing itself for years,' declared Kadar confidently.

Biggles shrugged his shoulders. 'Well, I suppose you know best,' he said dubiously. 'Anyway, having come so far, we might as well go the whole way. I had a sort of uneasy feeling come over me, that's all.'

Passing through the archway, looking about them expectantly, they found themselves in a wide area, better described, perhaps, as an extensive courtyard, except that it was not paved. It had evidently been a sort of main square, a general assembly place for the people who had once lived there, for a number of crumbling stone seats occurred at intervals around the outside. In the centre was what obviously was the superstructure of a well, and automatically the airmen made their way towards it.

'When you come to think about it, there was bound to be water in here somewhere, otherwise the people could not have survived a siege,' observed Biggles.

But Kadar was not listening. Trembling with excitement, he was examining an inscription which had been carved round the plinth of the wellhead. 'It's Persian!' he exclaimed in a voice vibrant with emotion.

'Never mind about that now; let us go on a bit farther,' suggested Biggles. 'As we are fixed, it looks as if you will have the rest of your life to translate that in.'

Many streets led off the main square, but there was little to choose between them. None was any wider than a footpath. Towards one of these they made their way, often stepping aside to avoid large colonies of black ants that hurried about their business. In one place Kadar pointed to a little snake that lay curled up, watching them with tiny sparkling eyes.

'Don't step on one of those,' he said earnestly.

'Is it a poisonous sort?' asked Biggles.

'Yes. It's a *nadjda*, the little Egyptian cobra. Some scientists think that it is the asp with which, it is said, Cleopatra, Queen of Egypt, committed suicide.'

'You have some pleasant little creatures in this country of yours, Kadar,' smiled Biggles, as he stepped into the first house they came to. There was no door, but the remains of a rush mat, lying where it had fallen, suggested that as a curtain it had once served the purpose of one.

It was gloomy inside, not that there was very much to see. A great earthenware jar stood in one corner; beside it was an old-fashioned flail. A soft thud startled them, but it was only another *nadjda* that had fallen from the roof. It lay where it fell, its little forked tongue flicking in and out with lightning speed.

The airmen looked up. At first they could see nothing but rotting rafters, made of split palms; but presently, as their eyes grew accustomed to the dim light, they could make out a multitude of what looked like little twin stars.

Biggles was the first to realize that they were eyes, and he stepped back hastily as another *nadjda* thudded to the floor. 'Great Scott!' he gasped, 'the place is alive with snakes!'

There was a wild stampede for the door, and the airmen burst out into the sunshine, where they stood blinking in the bright light. Then they stiffened, while a strange silence fell. Standing in a half circle round the doorway were a dozen or more swathed Tuareg, only their cold, hostile eyes showing above their indigo-tinted veils. There they stood, appraising the airmen with a curious indifference, as they covered them with long, antiquated rifles. Their camels stood in a group near the well, from which direction another figure, draped in an Arab *burnous*, now approached. Pushing his way through the motionless Tuareg, the newcomer threw his *kafieh* aside, disclosing his face. It was Zarwan.

Biggles looked at him. He looked at the rifles covering them, and knew that resistance was useless. One movement towards his pistol would be answered by a dozen rifles—more, in fact, since several other Tuareg were now coming towards the spot.

Zarwan's sleek features broke into a crafty smile, but his eyes were cold. 'So!' he purred, 'we meet again.'

'Well, what about it?' asked Biggles.

Zarwan's smile faded, and his eyes glinted. 'Presently I will show you,' he said smoothly.

'You don't happen to have a drink of water on you, do you?' asked Biggles, who was really thirsty.

Zarwan eyed him malevolently. 'No,' he murmured evenly. 'The first rule in the desert is not to waste water. It would be wasting it to give it to you, for the short time that you will need it.'

'I see,' said Biggles coolly, his eyes flashing round the Tuareg, who, while Zarwan was speaking, had been edging nearer. Then he shrugged his shoulders, realizing that resistance would be tantamount to suicide, for the muzzles of a score of rifles were almost touching him. As a result of experience, he was a firm believer in the old adage, 'While there is life there is hope', and he could see no point in throwing away their lives uselessly. His common sense told him that they would be riddled with bullets before they could even draw their weapons. He did not, of course, know Zarwan's methods, or it may have been that he would have chosen this course.

The Tuareg made a sudden rush, and rough hands were laid on them. Kadar, perhaps suspecting what was in store for them, made a gallant but foolish attempt to break free, but he went down under a hail of blows. As he fell he shouted something evidently intended for Biggles's and Ginger's benefit, but in his excitement he lapsed into his own tongue, and so the warning passed unheeded.

Leather cords, such as those used for securing baggage on camels, were slipped over their wrists and ankles, and presently they all lay on the ground, trussed like fowls prepared for the oven, and as helpless.

Zarwan pushed his way to the front and smiled down at them, kicking Biggles in the ribs as he spoke in his soft, sibilant voice. 'So I am the oily-faced hog?' he sneered. 'You thought you could threaten me.' His voice rose to a thick husky note as his temper got the better of him, and little flecks of foam appeared at the corners of his mouth. Then, suddenly, as if he could not bear to delay his revenge a moment longer, he said something swiftly to the Arabs in a language neither Biggles nor Ginger understood, although Kadar may have done.

Instantly the three of them were seized and dragged to the centre of the courtyard where, with the Tuareg chattering like a lot of excited monkeys, their bonds were removed and re-adjusted. Camel pegs were driven into the ground, four to each of them, and to these their wrists and ankles were made fast so that they lay on their backs in the position known as spread-eagled.

Biggles bit his lip, regretting bitterly that he had not chosen the easier way out, but even then he did not know the worst. A grinning Arab appeared with a small goat-skin in his hand, from the mouth of which oozed a sticky substance.

Kadar knew only too well what was happening, for the torture of the ants is as old as the very hills in Egypt and the Sudan.

'It is wild honey,' he muttered hoarsely. 'They lay a trail of it to the ants' nest. It——' There came the sound of a blow and his voice ended abruptly.

Biggles ground his teeth, as much with impotent fury as fear, but he was powerless.

Their work complete, the Tuareg, with Zarwan slightly in front, formed a rough circle round their victims and prepared to watch their death agonies.

A moment later something nipped Biggles's ankle so sharply that, unprepared as he was, he winced, and jerked his leg violently but uselessly against its peg—an involuntary movement that brought a rasping laugh from Zarwan. Biggles felt the insect that had bitten him crawling up his leg, but already his brain was reeling from the blinding glare of the sun.

'Don't worry, you fellows,' he said quietly, 'it will soon be over.'

WHAT HAPPENED TO ALGY

If the previous twenty-four hours had been full of adventures for Biggles and his two companions, Algy had also had his share; perhaps more than his share, for, being alone, he had no one to consult, in addition to which, as Biggles had feared, he had been consumed with anxiety on their behalf.

After watching Biggles and the others out of sight up the *wadi*, he had returned to the machine to kill time as well as he could pending their return. He cleaned the rifle and got out a few clips of cartridges, not for any definite reason, but in order to be ready in the unlikely event of their being needed. Then he lay down under the wing to rest.

Utter silence reigned. With his chin cupped in the palms of his hands, he stared at the colourless landscape around him, an undulating expanse of grey without anywhere offering rest for the eyes. There was no definite configuration, no scene to remember; nothing to break the monotony of rock and sand. A brooding, indefinable atmosphere of remote antiquity dominated everything, as if the overwhelming solitude was peopled by the spirits of a long-forgotten past. The only thing that moved was the sun, and from time to time Algy was compelled to change his position to keep clear of its burning rays.

The time passed slowly; how slowly he did not know, for his watch had stopped and he was too tired to look at the watch on the instrument-board. Once or twice he nearly dozed, but, remembering his duty, he forced himself to keep awake.

He was not conscious of the moment when he first began to feel uneasy. He stared up the *wadi*, wishing his companions would come back, for he felt that the breathless hush was getting on his nerves. Then he realized that he had been watching for them for some time, and that he was getting worried, and with the knowledge a sudden pang of anxiety swept over him. Could anything have happened? It hardly seemed possible. There was just a chance, of course, that they might lose their way, but

Biggles was not the sort of fellow to do that. Thus he comforted himself, but still they did not come. Once a distant echo reached his ears, but it was so faint that he could not make out what it was, nor could he locate the direction from which it had come, and in the end he dismissed it from his mind, putting the cause down to a piece of falling rock.

But when the sun began to sink over the sky-line of the distant hills, and still they had not returned, his anxiety grew to real alarm; not only on their account, but on his own, for he knew that he would not be able to endure the solitude alone without going mad. He climbed the nearest hill, but could see nothing of them. He shouted, and listened for a reply, but none came— except the mocking echoes. Depressed, he returned to the machine, wondering if he ought to go to look for them. It was a difficult problem. If he left the spot, and they returned during his absence, they would probably go off to look for him. After that anything might happen. Both he and the others might wander about the hills until they died from exhaustion without finding each other again.

Came night, and he sat down on one of the undercarriage wheels to wait, but he could not remain still. He drank sparingly of the water, ate a biscuit or two, and then paced up and down. The hours went by, each one as it passed leaving him more and more depressed. The silence was awful. The desert was awful. Everything was awful, he decided miserably. What fools they had been to listen to the crazy young Egyptian and his crazy scheme. Thus he thought bitterly as he paced up and down the deserted *wadi*. No longer did he attempt to deceive himself. Something must have happened. Not willingly would they have left him for so long.

His heart gave a great leap as a distant sound reached his ears. At last! Yet, strangely enough, the sound seemed to come from the desert and not from the far end of the *wadi*. For what purpose could they have gone into the desert? It was absurd. Nothing could have induced them to go out into that dreadful waste of sand. Again the sound reached his ears, and he knew beyond doubt that it could only have been made by a human being.

Grabbing the rifle, he ran down the *wadi* towards the open sand, and then climbed up on a piece of rock in order to get a wider view.

The sight that met his gaze was so unexpected that at first he thought the desert was playing tricks with his eyes. In the bright moonlight, moving slowly in single file towards the hills, and not more than two or three miles away, was a long line of camels. A caravan!

His first impulse was to rush out and hail it, but then he remembered the Tuareg and hung back in a quandary. If the newcomers were the dreaded desert warriors it were better to keep clear of them, he thought. Had Kadar been there it would have been different, for he was, after all, of the country, and he could speak their language. He might have arranged with them to take a message to Siwah, or some such place. But in the circumstances it would be asking for trouble to expose himself, a hated *Roumi*, to them. Yet suppose it was a proper caravan? To let it disappear might be to lose a chance that would not occur again. It was very hard to know what to do for the best.

In the end he decided on a sort of compromise. The best plan, he thought, was, as a first precaution, to try to find out who the riders were, after which he would know better what to do. There was plenty of cover, and in any case they would hardly be expecting any one in such a place. So, with this scheme in view, taking care to keep out of sight, he began walking along the fringe of the rocks on a course that would intercept the caravan when it reached the hills. It was an eerie experience, this stalking of mysterious black shadows in the moonlight, and more than once he wished fervently that the others were with him.

It was while he was creeping round a buttress of rock that he found the lance. It gave him a queer shock. He had been compelled to round the buttress for the reason that a hill towered high at that point, and it would have been dangerous, if not impossible, to climb it. Keeping close to the still warm rock, he saw the point of something sticking out of the sand just in front of him. At first he thought it was a twig, but an instant later he realized that that was impossible, for where there were no trees there could be no twigs. Putting out his hand, he touched it, and then he knew at once what it was. Slowly he allowed his hand to slide down the point, and the carved metal-work touched a chord in his memory. The lance was buried deeply, so deeply that little more than the point protruded, for the sand had silted up around it, which no doubt accounted for its remaining in such a position. He did not know, of course, that the weapon he was feeling had once belonged to Mazeus, son of Hystomannus; or that his was the first hand to touch it since that fatal night, more than two thousand five hundred years before, when the *haboob* had overtaken Cambyses' army. But he remembered vaguely what Kadar had said about a lance, and realized that by an amazing chance he had stumbled on the same weapon. Still, he could do nothing about it now, for the caravan had nearly reached the hills, and he had to hurry to be in time to intercept it.

He reached the spot for which the caravan was obviously making, a clearly defined pass, almost like a dried-up water-course, and he was at once struck by the significance of the fact that if the caravan knew so exactly where to enter the hills, at least one of the party must have been there before. It looked rather as if the hills were on a regular caravan route, after all, and but for the incident of the spear he would have dismissed the possibility of their having arrived at the long-lost Oasis of Zenzura.

He had little time to ponder the matter now, however, for by this time the caravan was almost upon him, and he crouched behind a rock to watch it pass, hoping that by some word or sign the errand on which it was bound, or its leadership, would be revealed to him. Nor was he disappointed, for although the line of shrouded figures, some twenty in all, with two men riding side by side at the head, filed past without a sound, he learned two things. At first his discovery filled him with dismay, but this was soon replaced by fierce satisfaction.

He saw at once that the night riders were Tuareg. The veils they wore over the lower part of their faces told him that. There was nothing remarkable about the leaders, but the last seven riders in the line were each leading another camel which was heavily loaded. Not that this struck him as unusual. It was the last led camel of all that caused him to catch his breath, thrilling under the shock of his discovery. For he had seen it before. It was a light fawn in colour, with a peculiar white stocking on the near foreleg. When Kadar had bought the camels for the caravan Algy had been with him, and just such an animal had been amongst those he had bought. It seemed impossible that there could be two camels marked in such an unusual way. Then, in a flash, he understood everything. The Tuareg were those who had raided their caravan, murdered their drivers and stolen their stores. The tracks of the raiders had led in a southerly direction. The Tourer had been blown south by the *haboob*, which had no doubt delayed the caravan. Everything fitted perfectly.

This discovery threw Algy's brain into such a state of chaos that for a few moments he could not see the vital facts of the situation in their true perspective. They altered everything. But as he sat and wrestled with the problem, certain predominating factors emerged. In the first place, the raiders represented a new and hitherto unsuspected danger, one of which Biggles and the others would be unaware. If they were still alive it was not unlikely that they would encounter the caravan, with disastrous results. Again, when the raiders had left the scene of the massacre they had taken the petrol with them. They had also taken the stores, but these paled into insignificance beside the petrol, which was the one thing that could get them back to civilization. There was, he realized, a chance that the Tuareg had unburdened themselves of the petrol, but this seemed unlikely, for had the mere destruction of the spirit been their object they could have pierced the cans as they lay on the ground, and thus settled the business there and then. No, he decided; the obvious inference was that if they had taken the petrol in the first place they still had it with them, although what they proposed to do with it he could not imagine. He spent several seconds thinking about this, for it was the weakest link in his chain of deduction, but the solution baffled him. A little

later, when he did know, he realized that had he spent the rest of
his life thinking about it he would not have guessed the answer.

By this time the tail of the caravan had disappeared round a
bend in the pass, and he emerged from his hiding-place torn by
indecision. If only Biggles and the others had been there! Petrol
had arrived in a way that on the face of it seemed little short of
miraculous, although it was, in fact, due to a perfectly natural
sequence of events. What ought he to do? What would Biggles
do in such circumstances?

The trouble with Algy was that he wanted to do two things at
once—to be in two places at once. He wanted to rush back to the
machine to see if Biggles had returned, and he wanted to follow
the caravan, fearing that it might disappear in the hills. It must
be remembered that he had no idea of how far they stretched. In
the end he decided to follow the caravan, anyhow until it made
camp. With the camp marked down he would then dash back to
the machine and tell the others—assuming that they had
returned—what had happened. If they had not returned—
well, in that case he did not know what he would do. He would
have to decide whether to go in search of them and abandon the
petrol, or return to the caravan in the hope of making contact
with them later.

His feet making no sound on the sand, he set off up the path in
the tracks of the camels, scouting each corner carefully before
rounding it. It was nerve-trying work, for the pass was in deep
shadow, and the camels travelled so noiselessly that he was
terrified that they might stop and he would blunder into them.
Presently, however, the sides of the pass fell away so that it
became a shallow *wadi* into which the moon penetrated, and he
was able to see his quarry some distance ahead. Keeping in the
shadows on the edge of the valley, he hurried on after it. Would
it never halt? Hour after hour it went on until he began to regret
his decision to follow it. The thought of the long journey back
appalled him, but it was no use thinking of turning back now.
He had come so far that it would be galling to have to give up.
He had expected it to halt any minute, and he still expected it to,
but the night was far advanced when, to his unspeakable relief,

he saw the camels standing in a group in the centre of a small cup-shaped depression. Watching from a distance, he saw them 'couch' and saw the Arabs unloading them.

Again he was worried by indecision. Should he start back at once, or should he try to approach nearer? But for the petrol he would not have hesitated. He would have gone straight back. But the most vital question of all could still not be answered with certainty. Had the Tuareg got the petrol with them or had they discarded it? In the end he decided that he ought to find out, and with this object in view he crept forward.

The place was strewn with rocks of all shapes and sizes, so there was really very little risk of being seen, and as there was still sand underfoot there was little likelihood of his being heard. He also gathered confidence from the fact that the Arabs would not suspect that they were being watched in such a remote place, so it was extremely unlikely that they would post a guard or even keep a lookout.

Comforting himself with this thought, he advanced, and was soon as near as he dare approach. The Tuareg had lighted a small fire with the fuel they invariably carried with them, and around this they were sitting in a rough circle. Suddenly one of them laughed, and the sound was so unexpected that Algy stared in amazement. Somehow he could not imagine a Tuareg laughing. The mutter of their deep guttural voices reached him. They seemed to be in good spirits. He saw one reach forward and pick up what was unmistakably a two-gallon petrol can, and that told him what he was so anxious to learn. They still had the petrol with them. But what was the fellow doing with the can—with the petrol? Then, to his utter and complete astonishment, he saw the can being passed round. They were drinking from it!

When he recovered from his astonishment his first feeling, not unnaturally, was one of intense disappointment and mortification. Not because they were drinking the precious petrol. His common sense refused to believe that any one in his right mind drank petrol. Clearly, therefore they had thrown the petrol away, and were using the cans for the transport of water. So certain was he of this that he was about to retire, when one of the Arabs, after drinking from the can, spat deliberately into the fire. There was a shout of laughter as a tongue of flame spurted upward, curled in the air for a moment and then died down again. Algy's spirits soared with the flame, for it told him that, incredible though it appeared, the ignorant savages were actually drinking petrol.[1] Whether they drank it because they liked the taste of it, whether they really thought that it was a white man's beverage, or whether, knowing what it was, they drank it simply in order to intoxicate themselves, he neither knew nor cared. As far as he was concerned the only thing that mattered was that the petrol was there, and if the silly fools drank themselves into unconsciousness, so much the better. They would be a lot less formidable in that condition, anyway, he thought, not without satisfaction; and when, presently, one of them got up and staggered about—nearly falling into the fire— he knew beyond all doubt that what he hoped had come to pass. The petrol was there; not necessarily all of it, but there was at least some, and in their condition it was more precious than gold.

Another one stood up, a short man, dressed rather differently from the others in that he wore a *kafieh*, the normal Arab head-dress, which is a strip of linen bound around the crown by a piece of rope, or gold thread, according to rank. He watched him toss the *kafieh* aside as though he found it irritating, and for a moment the orange glow of the fire played on his face. Algy recognized him at once. It was Zarwan.

To say that he was astounded is to put it mildly. He was staggered. He had almost forgotten the man's existence, and to find him in such a place, at such a time, and with such companions, completely bewildered him, for it put the whole situation on a different footing.

This condition did not last long, however, and as soon as he had recovered his wits he began to back away. At all costs Biggles must know of this, he decided, and without

---

[1] *Drinking petrol is a very common practice with native races in many parts of the world.*

further delay.

Once in the shadow of the pass, he broke into a trot, a pace that he maintained until, just as the dawn was breaking, he arrived back at the machine. One glance was enough. They were not there. They were, it will be recalled, just bursting out of the tombs of the dead, pursued by the bats, but, of course, he knew nothing about that. He only knew that they were not there. Exhausted and sick at heart, he flung himself down to rest, and to think.

14
ALGY TO THE RESCUE

A DEATHLY hush settled over everything, yet still he sat there, no longer daring to hope, hardly daring to contemplate his plight; for thus does the unutterable silence of the desert corrode the will to live, even as the drifting sand wears away the rocks until they, too, become sand. After a time he lay down, and, later, must have dozed, for it was broad daylight when he returned to consciousness.

Springing to his feet, he looked about him wildly, but the scene was just the same. Nothing moved. The pleasant dawn wind had gone, and the silence was so intense that it worried his ear-drums. A dreadful feeling crept over him that he was alone in the world; that a calamity had befallen it, leaving him the only creature alive. He tried to dismiss the thought, knowing that madness lay that way, the fatal mental state which the French desert troops, the Foreign Legion, and the Bataillon d'Afrique call *le cafard*, but it persisted. In any case, he thought, it was no use waiting any longer. It would be better to follow the caravan while he still had his wits, in the hope that it would lead him to an oasis, or, at least, a water-hole. Anything was better than sitting by the silent machine. There was just a chance, too, if he followed the caravan, that he might find an opportunity to recover some of the petrol, even a little—enough to allow him a few minutes' flight. Ten minutes in the air would be more likely to reveal the others, dead or alive, than a month of searching on foot.

Thus decided, he slung a water-bottle over his shoulder, put a few biscuits in his pocket, and, picking up the rifle, set off towards the pass where the caravan had entered the hills. Had he known that the others, at that particular moment, were hurrying back from the oasis towards the *wadi*, this story would have had a different ending; but he did not, so he trudged along, forcing himself to keep going in spite of an insidious voice that whispered to him to give up, that his effort would be in vain.

The heat became torture as the sun climbed majestically towards its zenith, unmindful of the little figure that plodded wearily along the foot of the rocks, sometimes sinking down to escape the fierce rays whenever scant shade offered itself, not only to escape the glare, but to gain a brief respite from the burning sand.

It was his feet that worried Algy most. The sand was so hot that he appeared to be walking over a furnace, and the pain was almost unbearable. He did not know that even Arabs will refuse to step out in the open during the heat of the day, on account of the discomfort caused to the feet.

However, he reached the lance, and, dragging it from its resting-place, crawled into the cavity where, two thousand five hundred years before, Mazeus had crept in to die. And so he found him, the pathetic sun-bleached bones shown here and there through the joints of the ancient armour.

Algy did not stay long. The relic was too grim a reminder of what was likely to be his own fate; so he drank a little water and hurried on, using the lance as a staff, unconcerned with the importance of his find. He was concerned only with the present, not with the past.

The going was not quite so bad in the pass, for under the eastern wall there was still a little shade, and he made the most of it, striding along with dogged determination, but realizing more and more that he had been unwise to start such a journey in the heat of the day. Still, as he had started he might as well go on, he thought miserably.

It was twilight when he came to the place where the caravan had halted the previous night, for in spite of his determination he had found it necessary to halt and rest occasionally. With thoughtful eyes he surveyed the scene. All that remained was a dead fire and two empty petrol-cans. He was not surprised, for he had not supposed that the sun-parched depression was the caravan's final destination. The camel-tracks were plain enough in the sand, showing which way they had gone, and he was not a little concerned to note that they led away into the very heart of the hills. For a few minutes he regarded them wearily, sick at heart, realizing that he could not hope to overtake the caravan that day. He was, in fact, physically and mentally worn out, and as it was now nearly dark, he decided that his best plan would be to pass the night where he was.

Scooping a hole for his hip, and piling up the sand to form a pillow, he lay down, and so exhausted was he that, in spite of his discomfort and anxiety, he was soon asleep. Nor did he awake until the dawn wind fanned his brow.

Refreshed, he sat up, drank a little water, and then, picking up his things, set off once more on the trail of the caravan, little dreaming that Biggles and the others were, at that precise moment, turning their backs on the Tourer and starting off down the *wadi*.

The pleasant conditions of dawn were short-lived. In a little while the sun flamed up above the hill-tops, and the dreaded heat came again to torture him. Inevitably his stride shortened, but he struggled on, with the hoof-marks of the camels now dancing before his eyes.

The trail seemed interminable as hour after hour he dragged his protesting body through a shimmering nightmare-world of heat and desolation. Would it never end? More than once he was on the point of giving up, almost overwhelmed by a sense of hopeless futility. He felt that he had been marching for weeks instead of hours; he had no idea of how far he had travelled, for time and distance had become meaningless.

He was nearly at the end of his endurance, and he was swaying as he walked, when, rounding a heat-distorted mass of rock, he saw the thing he had begun by hoping to find, but had long since dismissed from his thoughts: an oasis. At first he could not believe it, so unreal did the green palms look after the colourless wilderness through which he had passed; but when at last he convinced himself that it was really there, he took a good drink of water and strode on with renewed vigour.

The oasis was, he judged, not more than two miles away, but in this, like Biggles, he was mistaken, for it took him nearly an hour to reach it. On his right rose a towering hill, but he paid little attention to it, being more concerned with the oasis and the village which he now saw behind it.

As he neared the motionless palms, he began to move with more caution, realizing that the caravan had probably halted in their shade. Dodging from cover to cover, he approached, and he soon saw that there was good ground for his suspicions. Camels were standing among the trees, but all seemed very quiet, so, with the stealth of a Red Indian on the war-path, he crept nearer.

Presently he saw the pool, and passed his tongue over his dry lips at the thought of burying his face in the cool water. But this was a pleasure in which he could not immediately indulge, for lying near the edge were two Tuareg, asleep, judging by their attitudes. Several camels browsed in the palms behind them, beside their loads, which included the petrol-cans.

For some minutes he watched the two Arabs, but when they did not move he decided to take a chance. Creeping round to the opposite side of the pool, he wormed his way forward until he could reach the water; then, unslinging his water-bottle, he held it under the surface until it was full.

Still the Arabs did not move, so, emboldened by his success, he crept nearer, and was about to plunge his face into the water when an incident occurred that caused an abrupt change in his plan. The water on the far side of the pool parted as a long black object broke the surface and surged towards the sleeping men. He saw at once that it was an enormous crocodile, and he sprang back into the trees in a panic, fearing that there might be more.

In that brief moment the dreadful thing had happened. The

crocodile, moving at a speed that he would not have imagined possible, dashed forward, and its huge jaws closed over the legs of the nearest Tuareg.

In a split second all was uproar and confusion. The doomed man let out a scream of terror, and clawed madly at the sand over which he was now being dragged towards the pool. He might as well have clutched at the air for all that it helped him. His companion seemed to lose his head. Aroused suddenly from a heavy sleep, at first he could only dash up and down shouting at the top of his voice; then, seeing that this was likely to be of no avail, he rushed into the trees and returned an instant later with a rifle. Hardly pausing to take aim, he blazed into the flying spray at the edge of the pool.

Whether the shot had any effect on either man or beast Algy did not wait to see, for, ricocheting off the water, it came near to hitting him, and he darted out of the line of fire. Vaguely he had wondered what had become of the rest of the caravan, and the crashing report answered the question for him, for, from the near distance—from the village, it seemed—came answering shouts. He waited for no more, but with the lance and water-bottle in one hand, and the rifle in the other, he made off as fast as his legs could carry him. Where he was going he did not know, for the palms obstructed his view. Not that he cared particularly; his one idea was to place himself as quickly as possible some distance from the pool, so that the other Tuareg, whom he could now hear running down the hill from the village, would not discover him. For a good ten minutes he ran, and then, hearing no sound of pursuit, he paused to recover his breath. A short distance away a tiny white object caught his eye, and he picked it up curiously, wondering what it could be. It was, he found, a piece of paper, but it was not that fact alone that made him drop his weapons and stare at it in dumb amazement. There was printing on it, and the words were in English. Reading them, he perceived that what he held was a fragment of one of the old newspapers that had been used to wrap up certain of their stores. The significance of it was not lost on him; he knew that the others must have been there, and that with food and water available they should still be alive.

Gone now as the old lethargy, and he looked eagerly to right and left in the hope of finding another clue. Seeing nothing of the kind, however, he turned his interest to his surroundings, and observed that he was on the edge of the oasis on the side nearest to the village. No one was in sight, and a babble of voices from the direction of the pool told him the reason: the Tuareg had forgathered there. Where was Biggles and the others? Where had they gone after leaving the oasis? With the Tuareg about, it seemed hardly likely that they could still be in it. Had they gone back to the machine, assuming that they knew the way, or had they gone up to the village? The latter seemed most likely; in any case, it seemed fairly certain that they would go and explore it before returning to the machine. His best plan, he decided, was to do the same thing. If he did not find them in the village then he would return to the original rendezvous.

Making a wide detour that took him some distance round the hill, to a position where he could not be seen from the pool, he began his arduous ascent, beating off the flies that swarmed around his head. He could see no sign of a gateway, but following the wall as the others had done, although some distance from the point where they had struck it, he found a place where the rampart had crumbled, and up this, not without difficulty, he made his way.

Clambering down over the falling stones on the inside of the wall, he found himself in a narrow deserted street, but there appeared to be an open space at the far end, for he could see white sunlight blazing down into it. Still using the lance as a staff, in which capacity he had found it very useful, and with the rifle under his left arm, he made his way quietly down the street, keeping a sharp watch for signs of the others, but little dreaming of the spectacle that awaited him at the end. Alert for danger, he peeped round the corner into the square.

He must have remained motionless, staring, for a good half minute, while his eyes conveyed to his brain the almost unbelievable truth; and it was only Kadar's voice, raving in delirium, that finally spurred him to action.

In the centre of the square, not more than a score of paces away, lay three figures which he recognized at once, although the grim details were not immediately apparent. Standing near them, with their backs towards him, were three Tuareg, rifles under their arms. A short distance away a small group of camels patiently awaited their owners' pleasure.

Algy realized that a few moments before all the Tuareg must have been there, but the diversion caused by the crocodile had sent most of them rushing down to the pool to see what was the matter; and, needless to say, he was more than thankful that it was so, for he had no delusions about the fighting qualities of the Tuareg, and the three who had evidently been left on guard over the prisoners were likely to prove a formidable nut to crack.

His opening move was not very successful. Leaning the lance against the wall in order to leave his hands free, he took aim at the nearest Tuareg, for he knew that the only arguments the desert nomads understood were bullets and cold steel, and any other method of approach would be mere foolishness. So he prepared forthwith to reduce the number of his opponents to two.

But there is much truth in old proverbs, and the one about 'many a slip 'twixt the cup and the lip' is no exception. In this case it was the lance that slipped, and even as his finger was tightening on the trigger, it slid down the wall and struck the ground with a crash.

The Tuareg, who by their very natures are always alert for danger, whirled round at the precise moment that Algy's rifle cracked, with the result that the bullet missed its mark. Dropping on to one knee, he jerked another cartridge into the breech, and by that time the Tuareg were half-way towards him. The rifle spat again, and this time there was no mistake; the leading Arab crashed forward into the dust. One of the others fired as he ran; the bullet smashed against the wall near Algy's face, and the sting of the soft lead, some of which splashed against his shoulder, nearly knocked him over. He fired again, and the second Arab went down, but he was only wounded, and was soon on his knees, still holding his rifle.

But Algy was now in evil case, for the last Tuareg was on him. Fortunately, as it happened, he was the man who had already discharged his weapon, but, whirling it round, he prepared to use the butt. Algy made a desperate attempt to get another cartridge into the breech, but his haste was his undoing, and, in attempting to close the bolt before the cartridge was in line, the weapon jammed. There was no time to clear it. Springing to his feet, he swung it above his head to protect himself from the other's flailing butt. He was only just in time. The big, old-fashioned weapon came down with a crash across his own, splintering to pieces under the impact and knocking him over backwards.

In an instant the Tuareg had whipped out a long, curved knife, and with his evil, pock-marked face grinning with savage delight, he leapt forward to drive the weapon home. Algy twisted like an eel as he endeavoured to thrust himself to one side, and his hand closed over the haft of the lance. Acting now under the sheer impulse of self-preservation, he jerked the weapon up just as the Tuareg flung himself on him. The point of Mazeus's lance never found a more fatal mark; it caught the Tuareg squarely in the throat and impaled him as cleanly as a butterfly is impaled upon a pin.

Exerting all his strength, Algy flung the weapon sideways, and the Tuareg with it, for he had seen that he was by no means out of danger. The fellow he had wounded had levelled his rifle, and he leapt aside as the weapon roared. The bullet whistled past his face, and the Arab, seeing that he had missed, drew his dagger.

Algy did not hesitate. He took out his automatic and deliberately shot the savage dead. For a moment he stood swaying while he recovered from the shock; then, snatching up the dagger that lay near his feet, he ran forward, cold with the fear that he might be too late. He reached Biggles first, and shuddered as he saw the broad, black line of ants hurrying towards him.

Biggles was far gone, but he managed to smile, and whisper 'Good boy.'

In four swift slashes Algy had cut him free. Unslinging the water-bottle, he thrust it into his hands. Then he cut the thongs that held the others, by the end of which time Biggles was sitting up, drinking.

Algy did not stay. For all he knew there were other Tuareg near at hand and, being a soldier, his first thought was the consolidation of their position. 'Look after the others,' he shouted at Biggles, and then dashed back to his fallen rifle. It took him a moment to clear the jam, and this done, he ran to the gateway, prepared to hold it until Biggles was able to take charge. To his relief he saw that the hill-side was clear, although two or three Arabs, no doubt alarmed by the shots, had run out from the trees and were staring up the track. Others joined them, and they began to run forward, so he dashed back to inform Biggles of the circumstances.

Biggles and Ginger, he was relieved to find, were already on their feet and helping Kadar, who was sitting up, although clearly in a bad way. Not that Biggles or Ginger were themselves normal; Biggles's lips were bleeding, and Ginger had a bad sun-blister on the side of his face; also he still seemed somewhat dazed. Kadar appeared to be suffering chiefly from shock; his eyes rolled and he rambled incoherently, although with each gulp of water he seemed to improve. They all suffered more or less from ant bites, but they were not serious, for the main body of the ants had not quite reached the spot.

'You were just about in time,' Biggles told Algy in a brief aside, while he brushed several ants from his person. 'Another five minutes and we were goners. What is happening down below?'

'The Tuareg are on their way back—to see what the shots were about, I suppose.'

'Somebody fired a shot down by the pool; it was that and somebody shouting that sent them rushing down there,' Biggles told him. 'Was that anything to do with you?'

'No. I'll tell you about it later on. What are we going to do—try to hold the gate?'

'I don't think so. It is as hot as Hades up there, and the place is

alive with poisonous snakes, anyway. I haven't had time to think
properly yet, but the first thing we must do is to make ourselves
scarce, and leave that swine Zarwan and his toughs wondering
where we have gone. Did you know he was here?'

'Yes, and they've still got the petrol with them. I'll tell you all
about it as soon as we get clear. The street I came down is the
best way for us to go, I think, because there is a breach in the
wall through which we can get clear of the town.' Algy spoke
rapidly, knowing that their position was still desperate.

'All right,' agreed Biggles. 'You get the others into it, while I
try to hold up the Tuareg. Grab a water-skin off one of those
camels and take any weapons that are likely to be useful.' With
that he took the rifle out of Algy's hands and hurried across to
the gateway.

15
CAPTURED

ALGY managed to get Ginger and Kadar into the shade of the
narrow street down which he had come, and the sight of the
lance seemed to bring Kadar round to normal more quickly
than the water had done.

'Where did that come from?' he gasped.

'I found it in the desert,' Algy told him, as he recovered the
weapon.

'It's Persian work,' cried Kadar. 'I hope you remember where
you found it.'

'We'll talk about that later on, if you don't mind,' suggested
Algy. 'We're not out of the wood yet—or rather, the village. The
Tuareg are on our track. Hark at that,' he went on, as Biggles's
rifle cracked twice in quick succession. 'He wouldn't use
ammunition at that rate if things weren't getting hot. Come on;
we must keep going.'

They reached the spot where the wall had broken down, and
there, a few minutes later, Biggles joined them.

'Where are we bound for?' he asked quickly. 'We've no time

to waste. Those black devils are crawling up the hill under cover of the rocks; they'll be at the gate in a minute or two.'

'From where they are they will not be able to see us if we go out this way,' declared Algy. 'We're too far round the corner. I vote that we evacuate the place and try to find a hide-up in that corn down below. That will at least give us time to get our breath and make some sort of plan. Zarwan is bound to think we are still in the village, and will probably spend some time looking for us.'

'That sounds a sensible idea to me,' agreed Biggles, 'although I am tempted to wait and try to get a shot at that murdering villain Zarwan. Still, that will come in time, no doubt. Perhaps we had better get down below. I am anxious to hear about this petrol.'

Without any further waste of time they made their way down over the fallen boulders of which the wall had been built and, hurrying on, at length came to rest in the welcome shade of a spreading fig-tree that stood at the junction of the belt of prickly pear and a wide expanse of maize.

'Now then,' said Biggles, sitting down at the foot of the tree. 'Cut out the details; what about the petrol?'

In a few words as possible, yet omitting nothing of importance, Algy told the others his story; of how he had seen the caravan coming out of the desert, and his subsequent discovery of the petrol. He also told them about that affair at the pool when the Tuareg had been seized by the crocodile.

'We all know about that gentleman,' declared Biggles grimly, referring, of course, to the crocodile. 'He jolly nearly got Ginger.'

'What on earth happened to you?' asked Algy. 'Why didn't you come back to the machine?'

'We got lost,' replied Biggles tersely. 'As a matter of fact, we did find our way back to the machine at the finish, only to discover that you weren't there. We couldn't stand the heat, so we decided to go back to the oasis which we had found—the one down below. We left a note for you pinned on the fuselage, saying that we had been back and had gone again, with a map showing you how the oasis could be found.'

'When was that?'

'This morning. We left the machine at dawn.'

'Ah! I haven't been back to the machine since then, so I didn't find the note. I spent last night in the desert.'

'I see,' nodded Biggles. 'We haven't time to discuss these things now; the one thing that really matters above everything else is the petrol. If we can get it, it answers all the questions in front of us. We should then be able to get away, and deal with Zarwan in our own time. By jove! I believe we could do it. How many Tuareg do you reckon there were altogether when you first saw them, Algy?'

'Twenty.'

'Very well. You got three. The croc. got one, and I just plugged one from the gate—that leaves fifteen, and there must be very nearly that number now storming up to the gate. If a guard has been left over the petrol and stores it can't be more than two or three men, and we should be a match for them.'

'But we couldn't carry all that petrol,' said Algy wonderingly.

'I know we couldn't, but with luck we might be able to hide it. If we could find a hole in the sand—and I seem to remember seeing several that would do—we could put the cans into it and cover them up. How we should get it again is something I can't answer, but while it exists there is always a chance that we might, which is more than can be said once it is drunk or destroyed. It might be a thousand years before any more petrol is brought here, and that is a bit too long for us to wait. I'd rather throw the cans into the pond, crocodile or no crocodile, than Zarwan should have it. He thinks we're still in the village, so, as I see it, this is an opportunity that may never occur again. It is a risky business, I know, but I am game to try it if any one else is.'

Algy and Ginger agreed promptly; and so, for that matter, did Kadar, but he was in no condition to fight, so Biggles told him to keep close behind them, carrying the water-supply.

Mustering their weapons, they found that they had the rifle, with six rounds of ammunition, Algy's automatic, a loaded Tuareg rifle, two daggers, and the lance. Biggles's, Ginger's, and

Kadar's automatics had, of course, been taken from them when they were captured.

These weapons were disposed as follows: Biggles took their own rifle and a dagger, Algy kept his automatic and the other dagger, while Ginger took the Tuareg rifle. Kadar, at his own request, was given the lance. This done, they set off in single file towards the oasis, taking care to keep under cover, and ten minutes saw them on the outer fringe of it but still some distance from the pool.

They now proceeded with as much speed as was compatible with the utmost caution, and a little while later Biggles called a halt while he went forward to reconnoitre. He was soon back at a run. 'Come on,' he cried exultantly. 'The coast is clear. I believe the whole lot of them have gone up to the village.'

'If they'll stay away long enough we might be able to grab the whole lot and get it back to the machine,' said Kadar eagerly, as they ran forward.

'They'd have to stay away the dickens of a long time,' returned Biggles. 'We should have to make several journeys. Our best plan is to hide the stuff and make sure of it; then, if they'll give us time, we could shift it farther away.'

The pool came into sight, and it looked as if Biggles was correct, for not a soul was there. In high spirits, they hurried round to the side where all the stores had been piled in one large dump; and, apart from the petrol, they saw many of the boxes that were their own property and had formed part of the load of their own ill-fated caravan.

There were several depressions in the sand, of various sizes, as is usual amongst sand dunes, and Biggles chose one near at hand, not far from the edge of the water; it was fairly deep, yet small in extent. Into this they at once began to pile the cans, Biggles putting them together in compact form while the others fetched them. He would, as he explained to Algy, have preferred a hole farther away, but the job would then have taken more time, and if the Tuareg returned before it was complete, then all their labour would be in vain.

It took them nearly half an hour to move all the cans, and

Biggles was about to tell Kadar to bring one or two boxes to top up, when, to everyone's dismay, Algy's automatic cracked. A moment later he burst out of the trees, pale with alarm.

'I couldn't help it!' he cried. 'The devil nearly got me.'

'What are you talking about?' snapped Biggles.

'An Arab. He must have been left on guard, but went to the edge of the trees to watch the village. I ran slap into him, and I had to shoot because——'

'Never mind why,' broke in Biggles crisply. 'The damage is done. It couldn't be helped, but I am afraid the report will bring the others back. All hands to cover up the cans. Quick's the word.'

In a moment they were all pushing and kicking at the sides of the depression, flinging the sand over the precious tins. But the task was still incomplete when a shout came from the direction of the village.

'Don't stop,' panted Biggles. 'At all costs we must finish this; we've got to make the sand level. Kadar, get where you can see the track, and tell us when you see them coming.'

Kadar ran obediently to the top of a knoll, while the others continued their work at frenzied speed, but almost at once Kadar called a warning.

'They're coming!' he shouted.

Biggles did not stop what he was doing until the task was complete. Then he smoothed the top over to remove all signs of the cache, knowing that in a few moments the sun would dry the fresh sand to the colour of that around it. Satisfied at last that it could not be improved, he ran up the knoll to where Kadar was standing. The others followed, and thus they were all in a position to witness a startling and utterly unexpected change in the situation.

The Tuareg were pouring down the hill, some of them having begun a sort of enveloping movement. But they were no longer the only people in sight. From both sides of the hill, from the cacti, from the corn fields, and anything else that offered cover, came a crowd of amazing figures. They observed no military formation, but they were clearly soldiers, for they all wore a similar costume, or uniform—if a suit of armour can be called a uniform—and were equipped with one of two weapons: either a long-handled, moon-bladed battle-axe or a short curved sword, and a round, knob-studded shield.

For a moment Biggles could only stare spellbound at this amazing array, but Kadar was dancing with excitement. 'It's Cambyses' army,' he cried over and over again.

'Rot!' broke in Biggles tersely. 'People don't live for two thousand years.'

'Well, they are wearing the same armour and carrying the same weapons,' explained Kadar, somewhat abashed.

'So they may be, but I should say they are a lot of Arabs who have found the remains of Cambyses' army——'

'Arabs!' cried Kadar. 'They're not Arabs. They're white.'

Biggles stared again and saw that it was true. 'Never mind what colour they are, we had better bolt for it; we can't face that mob,' he muttered, and turned to run, only to throw up his hands despairingly as he saw another crowd, spread out in the form of a crescent, advancing from the other side and effectually cutting off their retreat. It was a perfect ambuscade. 'Well, this looks like being the end of the performance,' he observed bitterly. 'The only bright spot seems to be that Zarwan will get it in the neck as well. Here come the Tuareg; I must say they don't lack for courage.'

If the tribesmen had aimed to cut off the Tuareg from the oasis, and it looked as if that had been their intention, their scheme just failed, for although some of the Tuareg had fallen, the survivors, fighting fiercely with rifle and dagger, managed to break through; but then, seeing that Zarwan was in full flight towards the oasis, they broke and followed him. Upon this, the tribesmen let out a wild yell and charged.

Biggles folded his arms. 'Did you ever see such a sight in your life?' he murmured.

'Are you going to try to stop them?' cried Algy.

Biggles laughed shortly. 'Don't be silly; it would need a machine-gun company to do that. There is just a remote chance that if we can make them understand that the Tuareg are our enemies as well as theirs they may let us go, but I wouldn't like to bet on it. Still, if we start killing them we shall certainly seal our fate, so we shall be better advised to do nothing. There is one thing I am going to give myself the satisfaction of doing though. Give me your pistol and take this rifle, Algy.' He thrust the weapon into Algy's hands, took the pistol, and then, as if changing his mind, he put it in his pocket and picked up a camel-wand—the yard-long cane used by all camel drivers.

Zarwan, green with terror under his brown skin, came bursting through the trees, imploring the airmen in broken English to protect him, although how he imagined that this could be done he did not say.

'Yes, I'll protect you, you murdering swine,' snarled Biggles, and before the others realized what he was going to do he had seized the abject half-caste by the back of the collar and began laying on the cane with all the power of his arm.

Two or three of the Tuareg dashed past, making for their camels; they took not the slightest notice of their leader's howls and screams. Nor did Biggles take any notice of the Tuareg, but continued laying on the cane, while the others watched the amazing spectacle, feeling that the villain was getting less than he deserved.

At last the camel-wand broke into halves; Biggles flung the pieces aside, and hurled the now sobbing half-caste from him. Then, with a curious expression on his face, as if he had suddenly remembered where he was, he looked about him. The others, following his example, saw that they stood in the centre of a ring of warriors, who had evidently stopped at the unusual exhibition they had discovered. A small party held three scowling Tuareg prisoners.

'Well,' said Biggles fatalistically, 'we shall soon know the verdict. Hello, look at this,' he went on quickly, as a tiny, monkey-like figure, waving a fly-switch made of the tail of some animal, came prancing through the ranks of the warriors. Suddenly it stopped dead and let out a series of piping shrieks in an unknown language.

Instantly, as if it was an order of some sort, the warriors closed in about the airmen, and holding them by the arms, started off up the hill towards the village.

'That's the creature we saw in the tombs, isn't it?' said Kadar.

Biggles nodded. 'Yes, I think it's the old lady herself,' he agreed.

16
A HOPELESS PROSPECT

'SURELY this crowd couldn't have been in the village when we were up there?' said Algy, as they marched along.

'It's all a mystery to me,' declared Biggles. 'How they all managed to keep themselves hidden until the crucial moment is more than I can imagine.'

'It is my opinion that they were not in the village at all, but in some place beyond it, and the old hag went and fetched them,' announced Kadar.

'That may be the answer,' agreed Biggles, glancing over his shoulder. 'All the same, they must have been watching us for some time; anyway, they seem to realize that we are two parties, or I don't think they would keep us apart. Zarwan and the three Tuareg are following along behind, and they are being handled pretty roughly.'

'I wonder what these people are going to do with us,' said Kadar plaintively. 'I am sure that this is an unknown tribe, and that they are the descendants of Cambyses' army. How else could they get their white skins? At least, if they are not white, they are nearly white. They are certainly not Arabs.'

'I don't care two hoots about the colour of their skins,' muttered Biggles. 'It is the way they are likely to behave that matters. They can be Persians, Chinese, Eskimos, Red Indians, or anything else, as far as I am concerned, so long as they don't try any funny tricks. They look a savage lot to me.'

'What else would you expect?' protested Kadar. 'If they are the descendants of people who came here thousands of years ago, and all that time have remained untouched by outside influences, it is only to be supposed that their habits will be the same as their forefathers', and they were—well, rather wild.'

'Well, we've found your missing oasis for you, so you won't mind my saying that the sooner I'm out of it the better I shall be pleased. In fact, I've got a feeling that before this business is over we shall be sorry that it didn't remain missing. Do you know anything about their language?'

'I couldn't speak it, but given time I might be able to write it. I shall try the experiment at the first opportunity.'

'All right; you go ahead with your note-book. By that time I hope I shall be on my way home,' answered Biggles.

They had now passed under the archway into the courtyard of the ants, but no halt was made. Instead, the procession proceeded down one of the streets on the near side and, after going for some distance, came to what looked like a moat, with sheer sides, some ten feet deep, cut out of the living rock. There was no water in it, but it was not empty. A drawbridge spanned it, and as they passed over they instinctively glanced down. A gasp of horror broke from Ginger's lips, and even Algy muttered something, for the entire bottom, as far as they could see, was a writhing tangle of snakes.

'Very pretty,' muttered Biggles in a hard voice. 'I fancy the object of that dyke is to keep the snakes on the right side of it, but quite a number fall in.'

'I shall never forget that sight as long as I live,' declared Algy. 'And I shall feel sick every time I think about it.'

'You'll have plenty of other things to think about in the near future, unless I'm mistaken,' Biggles told him grimly, as they were halted in front of a large, important-looking building with an iron-studded door—the first one they had seen. The door was opened, and they were urged inside.

After the glare outside they found it hard to see where they were, but their captors jostled them along, up a long winding flight of stairs, into a small room lighted by a single square window. The door slammed and they were alone.

'Well, at least we are together, and that's something to be thankful for,' muttered Biggles, as he crossed over to the window and looked out. 'Hello, I can see the oasis,' he went on. 'It looks as if we are in one of those high buildings perched on the wall; it must be a good seventy or eighty feet to the ground, which is a bit too far to drop, even if we could get through the window, which we can't, anyway, because it is too small.'

The room was absolutely destitute of furniture, so, thoroughly tired after their exhausting adventures, they squatted down on the dusty floor.

'We've been in some queer places in our time, but this trip has been about the limit,' snorted Ginger disgustedly. 'We've been out of the frying pan into the fire ever since we started.'

'We're in the fire now, at all events,' agreed Biggles.

'What are we going to do about it?' inquired Algy.

'If you can think of anything I should be grateful, for I'm dashed if I can,' answered Biggles.

'But this is most interesting,' began Kadar, but Biggles cut him short.

'For goodness' sake stop guessing who these people are and where they come from,' he told him. 'You can spend the rest of your life guessing after we get home. For the present, try to think of something more helpful.'

'But did you see their shields?' asked Kadar eagerly.

Biggles shook his head sadly. 'I saw their faces, and that was enough for me,' he muttered. 'Whatever they have in store for us, you can bet your sweet life that it is not pleasant; if it is, then they have an odd way of welcoming strangers.'

'It is doubtful if they ever had any before,' returned Kadar.

'Nor, if it is left to me, will they ever have any more,' Biggles told him shortly. 'Well, I suppose we can only wait and hope for the best.'

The atmosphere of the little room was heavy, and they were all thankful when the light began to fade and the sun to lose its heat. The short twilight passed, and night fell.

'This is getting pretty monotonous,' grumbled Algy, standing up and staring out of the window, the window being merely a square hole left in the structure. He tried to get his shoulders through it, but, as Biggles had said, it was too small. He next turned his attention to the sides of it, to see if there were any possibility of its being enlarged, but his efforts were interrupted by the arrival of three warriors, who brought with them some water, dates, and a soft substance that looked like crushed maize mixed with water. One carried a small torch of palm fibres bound together.

Kadar tried speaking to them in several languages, but the warriors, who they now saw had a definite Eastern cast of features, only shook their heads. Just as they were about to leave, one of them, with something approaching a smile, pointed to the window, whereupon Kadar showed him something that he had written in his note-book. The man smiled more broadly, took the pencil which Kadar held in his hand, and made a series of marks in the book underneath what he had written; then, without waiting to see if what he had written was understood, he went out with the others.

'They are certainly Persians,' declared Kadar, who had gone across to the window to study the marks in the uncertain light of the stars.

'Never mind what nationality they are, what does that fellow say?' inquired Biggles quickly. 'Can you read it?'

Kadar shook his head. 'No,' he said, 'but the characters of two words might be broadly interpreted to mean "sacrifice" and "crocodile".'

Biggles started. 'I wouldn't translate any more of it if I were you,' he answered grimly. 'Those two words, used together, have a rather disconcerting significance.'

Kadar shrugged his shoulders. 'I can't make anything out of the rest of it, anyway,' he said, 'but judging by the signs that fellow made, I think he meant us to watch something through the window.'

'He may have meant that we could watch a sacrifice to the crocodile by looking through the window,' suggested Ginger.

'Well, that would be better than taking part in the show ourselves,' murmured Biggles, and a moment or two later it seemed that Ginger's supposition was correct, for, with a banging of cymbals and loud chanting, a torchlight procession emerged from the entrance to the village, which could just be seen, and started to wind its way down the hill. In front of it danced the unmistakable figure of the old hag.

'By gosh! It looks like Zarwan!' cried Ginger. 'I can't be sure because he is struggling, and the others keep getting in the way.'

Biggles pushed him aside. 'I think you're right,' he said, staring down at the eerie scene. 'I am not, I hope, vindictive, but even if they are taking him to the crocodile, and that is what it looks like, I shan't break my heart about it. After all, he arranged something even worse than that for us. But why aren't the Tuareg there, I wonder; I can't see them anywhere.'

'They are probably holding them for slaves,' offered Kadar. 'It is the customary treatment for prisoners in the desert.'

'Ah! That may be it,' murmured Biggles, who was still gazing through the window.

By this time the procession had reached the oasis—by crowding round the window they could all see it—and there was no longer any doubt but that the pool was its objective. The actual water could not be seen, but the waving torches were clearly visible and marked the head of the column. The chanting became wild, hysterical screaming. Then, with the abruptness of a wireless-set or a gramophone suddenly turned off, silence fell. But this did not persist for very long; it was broken by a sound which every one in the room recognized at once, for they had all heard it before at one place or another. It was the coughing bellow of a crocodile.

Biggles turned away from the window, for apart from the torches little could be seen.

'I should say that human sacrifice to the crocodile is an ancient religious rite with these people, as it was with other desert tribes years ago,' observed Kadar quietly.

Biggles eyed him moodily. 'Whether it is a religious ceremony, or merely just fun and games, makes little difference to the poor devil flung into the pool,' he said thoughtfully. 'I ought to have shot that diabolical creature when I had the chance. Well, I've still got the pistol tucked into my armpit, so it may come to that yet. Before he gets his teeth into me that pretty little

pet of theirs is going to have his tonsils tickled by as many bullets
as I can plonk into them.'

As he finished speaking there arose a mighty shout from the
pool; it ended in a frenzied singing, and presently Algy
announced that the procession was starting back.

'Evidently the end of the first house,' remarked Biggles. 'It
now remains to be seen if the performance is held twice nightly.'

For an hour they waited in breathless expectation, but they
remained undisturbed. Silence had fallen, and at length Biggles
turned to the food, which remained on the floor where the
warriors had placed it.

'I've had better dinners than that put before me in my time,
but we might as well make the best of it,' he observed.

Conversation flagged as they proceeded to eat all that there
was to be eaten. This done, Biggles spent some time examining
the window, and afterwards the door. Finally he joined the
others where they were sitting on the ground with their backs
against the wall. 'With a hammer and cold-chisel, and a few
months to work in, we might make the window large enough to
get through. Then, if we had a hundred feet of rope, we might
get down,' he muttered sarcastically. 'But as we have none of
these things I suppose we might as well try to get some sleep.'

Nobody answered. Ginger, worn out, was already dozing.
Presently he slipped sideways so that his head rested on Biggles's
leg. Biggles did not move. He took out his last remaining piece of
cigarette from an inside pocket and puffed at it slowly while it
lasted. Outside, the silence of the desert night remained
unbroken.

17
CONDEMNED TO THE CROCODILE

THE dawn came, and one by one the prisoners stretched their
cramped limbs and sat up from the recumbent positions into
which they had fallen; that is, all except Biggles, who was still
sitting propped against the wall with his elbows on his knees and

his chin cupped in the palms of his hands. It was some time before any one spoke, for it seemed useless to talk of anything but their plight, and no one, it appeared, had any fresh observations to make on it. As Biggles had said, there was nothing they could do but wait.

Some time later they all looked up expectantly as, following a tramping of footsteps outside, the door was opened, and the same three warriors who had waited on them the previous evening brought in a further supply of the same unpalatable rations. They did not speak or make any signs; they simply set the food on the floor and went out again.

'How about trying to knock those fellows over the head the next time they come in?' suggested Algy.

'I have been thinking about the same thing,' answered Biggles. 'It is a difficult proposition. The trouble is, we don't know what they intend to do with us. For all we know, they may not intend to kill us, but if we set about these guards and manage to get out, and are afterwards taken again, we shall have pretty short shrift. Another thing that must be considered is that drawbridge we came over. I have a feeling that the moat goes completely round this part of the village, otherwise there would be no point in having a bridge. That bridge is normally kept up, or it would not have been necessary to lower it to let us come across. Again, if all the people we saw yesterday are still about, and we can only assume that they are, we couldn't hope to fight our way through them, let down the bridge, and get out. In any case, even if we were successful in doing that they would probably catch us again, since they must know every inch of the ground and are no doubt faster on their feet than we are. It's a long way back to the machine, and when all is said and done, it wouldn't be much good going back to it empty-handed. They would overtake us there, if not before. Then there is the question of petrol. Even if we were lucky enough to get hold of a few cans, as many as we could carry, and get them back to the machine, what use would they be to us? We've got to get right back across the desert or it would be better not to start. A forced landing half way, through shortage of fuel, would mean the end of us as certainly as any way these people could devise. It seems to me that there would be very little object in leaving the village for the hills, even if we could manage it, for we should simply be fugitives, and sooner or later they would be bound to recapture us—unless we died of thirst in the meantime.'

Algy nodded. 'Yes, it's the very dickens of a proposition, I must say,' he confessed. 'Yet this sitting here doing nothing is a bit nerve-trying.'

'Let us have some breakfast and forget about it,' suggested Biggles. 'Which will you have, Ginger, bacon and eggs, or a couple of nice grilled herrings? If you would prefer toast and marmalade, just say so.'

'I think I'll try a little porridge,' grinned Ginger, and Biggles passed him the crushed maize, which was contained in a beaten copper vessel. No eating utensils had been provided, however, so it was necessary to scoop up the mess with the fingers.

They all ate as much as they needed, and then settled in their original positions to pass the time.

The day seemed unending, for their captors did not reappear. However, all things come to an end, and at last the sun began to sink over the western hills.

'Suppose they try to repeat this crocodile stunt with us, what are you going to do?' Algy asked Biggles after a long silence.

'Just fight as hard as we can in the hope that they will club us over the head,' returned Biggles briefly.

Another silence fell, during which the sun set and a crescent moon appeared. Shortly afterwards a cymbal began beating not very far away, and presently footsteps were heard coming up the stairs outside.

'Here come the boys in the tin suits,' murmured Biggles, starting up. 'Now we shall soon know the worst, I fancy.'

Things turned out rather differently from what they had expected. For some reason or other, although they had not discussed it, the prisoners had taken it for granted that they would not be separated; that whatever fate was reserved for one would apply to all. This, up to a point, may have been correct, but it had not occurred to them that it might happen one at a time, so to speak. As it was, a large party of guards appeared; a smaller quantity of food and water was set upon the floor; but then two of the guards, instead of withdrawing, crossed the room, and, touching Biggles on the arms, made unmistakable signs that he was to follow them.

When he realized what was intended Algy sprang to his feet in a threatening attitude, as though he would have started the last fight then and there, rather than that they should be separated, but the point of a sword at his throat forced him back, impotent, against the wall.

'Don't give up hope,' Biggles told the others from the door. 'There is plenty of time for anything to happen. Watch the pool and you may see something.' He had no time to say more, for before he had finished speaking the escort was jostling him towards the door.

Now as he walked down the stairs he had one great fear, and that was that his hands would be tied together as a preliminary to the ceremony, if the crocodile sacrifice was, in fact, intended. This would make him utterly helpless, and he had decided in his mind that rather than allow it to happen he would produce the automatic, which he still carried under his arm, and make the best fight he could before he was killed, as would be bound to happen at the end.

However, to his infinite relief, no attempt was made to tie him, although this may have been due to some extent to his behaviour, for he obeyed instructions as meekly as a lamb. Or it may have been that the great crowd which surrounded him as soon as he was in the street made such a precaution, in the eyes of the warriors, quite unnecessary. Anyway, his hands were left free, and when the procession moved off he strolled along with them hands in his trousers' pockets as though he was merely out for an evening walk. In front gambolled the old hag. Behind her came torchbearers and then the cymbal beaters, the cymbals being, he now saw, two shields clashed together. More torchbearers and cymbal players fell in behind, while the rest, the spectators, brought up the rear.

In this fashion the procession advanced to the archway that

formed the entrance to the village, where the hag began singing in her high reedy voice, occasionally darting back to lash Biggles across his legs with her fly-switch. The chant was taken up by everybody except Biggles, and it swelled louder and louder as the column wound its way slowly down the hill towards the pool.

A queer smile played about the corners of Biggles's mouth as the sheet of placid water came into view, and he saw its ghastly inmate standing on the edge, with its forefeet resting on the dry sand. Doubtless it knew all about the procession and its purpose. having been fed in this way for generations.

Slowly the procession drew nearer; the singing rose to a pitch of fanatical frenzy, and the leaders of the cavalcade began to open out so that a sort of semi-circle was formed, with Biggles standing alone in front of it. Before him was the water, and on the edge the waiting crocodile, with saliva dripping from the corners of its gaping mouth.

The semi-circle now began to advance, very slowly, so that it would presently force the victim into the jaws of the waiting crocodile, but what Biggles had hoped for had come to pass, and he was now acting in a very surprising manner. So surprising, in fact, that the chanting of the simple tribesmen began to lose its volume, and presently died away altogether. It may have been that no prisoner had ever before behaved in such an ex- traordinary way. Biggles did not know, nor did he care, as he carried on with his acting.

Raising his right arm towards the moon, he began singing in his rather unmelodious baritone, and the song he sang—the first one that came into his head—was 'Rule, Britannia'. It is doubtful if it had ever before been sung under such peculiar conditions, or in a more remarkable place. This thought actually occurred to him, and, in spite of his predicament, as he sang he wondered what on earth the others would be thinking, knowing that they would be able to hear him; and as he sang he edged slowly along, with the mincing steps of a ballet dancer, towards the right.

The faces of the spectators registered only astonishment and wonder. It was obvious that not for one moment did it occur to them that the prisoner might be about to attempt to escape; and for this there was some justification, for a solid semi-circle of armed warriors, a dozen deep, hemmed him in on all sides. Indeed, there seemed to be not the remotest possibility of escape.

But Biggles had now reached the spot for which he had been making, and, still singing with extraordinary vehemence, accompanied from time to time by a dramatic wave of his right arm, he dropped to his knees and began scraping at the surface of the sand, while the crowd, by this time overcome by curiosity, pressed nearer to see what he was doing.

A gasp went up as he dragged a can of petrol to the surface, and for a moment beat a tatto upon it with the special key-opener that he had now taken from his pocket. He realized that the ignorant savages had not the remotest idea of what it was; nor was there any reason why they should, since it was unlikely that a can of petrol had ever before been within five hundred miles of the oasis. Judging by the hissing and muttering that went on, they took the whole thing as some sort of magical manifestation in which the moon played a part; at any rate, several of them glanced furtively towards it.

Six times Biggles repeated this performance, until six cans, three of them capless, stood on the sand beside him. The three with the caps intact he stood a little to one side, after which he scraped the sand back into the hole which he had made. Then, taking one of the open cans by the handle, he stood up, and with the other hand grasped it by the base.

There was a breathless hush while the crowd waited to see what was going to happen next.

Biggles did not keep his audience waiting. Raising the can high about his head, he swung it so that the spirit flew in all directions, but chiefly in front of the crowd. Naturally, quite a lot of it splashed on the feet of those in the front rank, and some may have gone on the people behind. Biggles did not care. Two cans he emptied thus, while the heavy stench of vapourizing petrol rose on the stagnant air. He was about to repeat the operation with the third can when some instinct of danger made him look round. To his horror he saw that the crocodile, evidently impatient, had come up out of the water, and was now rushing at him with open jaws.

The only thing he held in his hands which he could use as a weapon was the petrol-can, and this he flung straight into the creature's mouth, at the same time jumping back. He was only just in time. As it was, the crocodile's massive jaws came together, but instead of closing over the legs of its supposed victim, its yellow teeth sank into the thin metal tin as a fork goes into a ripe pear. The petrol at once gushed out through the holes, and apparently the beast did not like the taste of it, for it at once set up a hideious bellowing. This was answered by shouts from the crowd, and Biggles judged that the time had come for the grand finale of his performance.

The crocodile was standing about three yards away, shaking its great head as it strove in vain to rid itself of the unpalatable morsel. Very deliberately Biggles took his automatic from under his arm, and, taking careful aim, fired into the open jaws. A stream of sparks leapt from his hand to the crocodile's mouth.

Whatever he may have hoped for was far surpassed by what actually happened. Only those who have seen the contents of a two gallon petrol-can in flames can have any idea of what it is like. The crocodile was in the middle of one of its bellows; a sheet of flame shot out of its mouth so far that it actually scorched Biggles's legs. For a split second the reptile stood still, while sheets of flame spurted out of its mouth and poured back over its body where it had thrown the petrol. Then, with a frightful roar, it charged madly at the crowd.

Instantly all the loose petrol that Biggles had splashed about went up in a great sheet of flame, and the most appalling pandemonium ensued that it is possible to imagine. Flames were everywhere. The very air seemed to be on fire—as indeed it was, for it was saturated with petrol vapour. All those warriors who had been in the front rank rushed about screaming while they tried to extinguish their blazing legs, but they only flung the burning spirit on their companions who were behind. Into this incredible inferno, which reminded Biggles of nothing so much as an old print he had once seen of Hades, charged the crocodile, bellowing, blowing out streams of flame with each breath it took, and spraying blazing petrol over everything and everyone that crossed its path. It was, in very truth, the ancient conception of the dragon come to life.

Biggles himself was stunned. For a moment he could only stare, nearly as frightened as his wretched victims, while the reek of singeing hair filled his nostrils. His own eyebrows had gone, as had the front of his hair, but he did not realize it then. His legs were still smarting from the first blast of the crocodile's fiery breath.

The crowd had dispersed, although screaming fiery figures still tore wildly about among the palms; so, snatching up the three remaining cans of petrol, he tucked them under his left arm, and with his automatic ready for action in his right hand, he made off through the trees towards the hill that loomed darkly in the background, and the path that led to the tombs of the dead.

18

BIGGLES WINS THROUGH

It was the old hag who saw him first, as he dodged from tree to tree towards his objective. Most of the warriors who had not actually fled from the spot were far too concerned with themselves to worry about anything but their burns, but a few who had got away unscathed began to rally to the old woman's urgent cries.

Biggles cursed her inwardly, for she began to appear as his evil spirit. He had hoped that no one would see which way he went, for this would enable him to get a long start, but the mummy-like female saw to it that in this he did not succeed.

He passed the crocodile, still writhing feebly in a pool of dancing blue flames, and it was clear that the brute was near to death, from which he derived considerable satisfaction. Whatever happened now, he thought, he had at least escaped the fate of being torn to pieces by the monster; but sounds of pursuit now reached his ears, although a quick glance over his shoulder revealed nothing, owing to the heavy shadow in which that part of the valley lay. He reached the bottom of the hill and found the narrow path, but already he realized what a handicap his burden of three full petrol-cans was likely to prove. However, he clung to them, determined to retain them as long as possible.

The night was hot, and the heat thrown off by the sun-drenched rocks caused perspiration to pour down his face, for there was no sun to dry it off as there was during the daytime. On he struggled, with the sounds of pursuit drawing ever nearer; above them rose the old hag's screeching. He reached the limit of the shadow, and as he broke into the moonlit area there was a wild yell behind him. But he did not stop longer than was necessary to change over one of the petrol-cans, for the arm under which he had been holding them was becoming numb with the strain.

About three-quarters of the way to the entrance to the tombs he took another glance over his shoulder and saw that about a score of warriors were on his trail, led by the hag, who was some distance in front. These twenty men would be more than he could conveniently manage, should they succeed in overtaking him, he thought desperately; yet he could go no faster without discarding his precious burden, and this he was not yet prepared to do, so he struggled on, drawing his breath in great gasps as the path became steeper towards the summit.

Fifty yards short of the entrance to the cave he realized that he would not be able to reach it, for his pursuers were less than that distance behind and were now fast overtaking him, due to some extent to their natural physical hardihood, and partly to the fact that they were unburdened. For a few more paces he staggered on, and then he turned at bay.

His pursuers were now coming through a narrow causeway between two high rocks, at a point where the path sloped up very steeply, and although he regretted it, he decided that he would have to abandon one of his cans, if only to leave a hand free for the automatic. Nevertheless, it was not his intention merely to leave it behind. Quickly unscrewing the cap, he hurled the can straight down the path into the faces of the leading tribesmen. Down the path it went, bouncing over the rocks and discharging its contents in all directions. Then, taking out his matches, he struck one and tossed it into the track of his unusual missile.

A curtain of fire rushed along in the wake of the bouncing can, which had not yet quite reached the tribesmen. In the petrol-soaked air, the flames travelled as swiftly as a train of gunpowder, and overtook the can on the top of a bounce just in front of the warriors. For a moment, as it described a wide arc through the air, it presented an amazing spectacle, appearing as a comet dropping from the sky; then, with a roar, it exploded, shooting lines of fire in all directions like a bursting rocket.

Biggles waited for no more; hastily picking up the two remaining cans, he summoned all his strength and made a rush for the entrance to the cave, which he succeeded in reaching. For a moment he paused, staring down the hill behind him. His path was still marked by a line of curling blue flames, but of the tribesmen there was neither sight nor sound. Satisfied with his inspection, he started off along the cave.

Progress now became much slower, for several reasons, although the petrol cans were again the chief cause, for it was necessary to carry them both under one arm in order to leave the other free to hold a light. Again, he had very few pages left in his note-book, and it was essential that he should use them sparingly.

Unfortunately, his supply of matches was also running low, so he had to light one spill off another, and this resulted in a halt each time, while the petrol-cans were placed on the floor.

To make matters worse, he had an uneasy feeling that the hag, who he had good reason to suppose knew her way about the cave, might be following him, and although he did not fear her in the open, there was no knowing what devilment she might not practise in the eerie chamber. For this reason he often stopped to listen, but the only sound he heard was the occasional squeaking of a bat. Both matches and spills were exhausted before he reached the far end of the cave, having traversed the chamber of tombs without incident. With his last match, having no paper left, he lighted a strip of material torn from his shirt, but it burned badly, and in a short time went out, leaving him in the dark without further means of producing a light, so progress became both difficult and dangerous. Fortunately, as the cave was only a single passage, he had no cause to fear that he might become lost, so he continued on, feeling his way along the wall with his right hand, and holding the cans under the other arm.

He judged that it was nearly dawn by the time he approached the extremity of the passage, which he was able to identify by a rather sharp turning, and, remembering the scorpions, he dare not risk going on until it became light enough for him to see the exit. That last half-hour was perhaps the worst of all, for he could only sit still in the deathly silence knowing that without any means of making a light he was absolutely helpless should danger threaten. He derived some comfort from the automatic, which he again took out and held in his hand, but he did not need it, and at long last a vague grey light ahead told him that the new day was dawning.

In the interval of waiting, his thoughts had turned naturally to the precarious plight of the others. What would happen to them, after the appalling havoc he had caused at the pool, which included the death of the crocodile 'god', he dared hardly think. Still, it could not be otherwise, he reflected, for he certainly would not have helped them by allowing himself to be sacrificed. Nor did he know just what he was going to do when he reached the machine, assuming that he did. The petrol he carried, used economically, might keep the Tourer in the air for twenty minutes, not more. That would be time enough for him to fly the machine over to the oasis; but what then? The rest of the petrol was there, but would he be allowed to fill his tanks? It seemed hardly likely, unless the appearance of the strange monster out of the air terrorized the already shaken tribesmen. That was not too much to hope for, he decided, since it was reasonable to suppose that they had never before seen an aeroplane; anyway, therein lay his only chance, he thought, as he picked up the two cans and moved slowly towards the exit. With full tanks he might be able to help the others, but it was not easy to see how.

He was thankful to discover that there was no sign of the scorpions, so after a careful look round to make certain that all was clear, he went out, and started on the last lap of his journey.

A moment later he escaped death by an unpleasantly narrow margin when a boulder crashed down from the top of the precipice and buried itself, with a terrific thud, in the sand not half a dozen paces away from him. It so happened that it just touched a projecting piece of rock on the way down, and at the noise of the impact he turned in his tracks and threw a startled glance upwards. Seeing what was coming, he made a wild leap for safety, so that the missile, which he now saw was intended for him, missed its mark. Peering over the edge of the cliff was a tiny black head, and he knew at once to whom it belonged. The old woman, knowing that he had gone into the cave, and that he must ultimately emerge at one end or the other, had placed herself on the topmost part of the crag, from where she would be able to roll rocks down on him from whichever end he came out. So he reasoned as he proceeded to remove himself beyond the reach of further bombardment.

From a safe distance he turned and looked up, whereupon the old creature spat at him like an angry cat. Setting down the cans, he took out the automatic, but the hag evidently suspected its purpose, for she withdrew hurriedly; he watched the ridge for a minute or two, but when the head did not reappear he continued on his way, which by this time he knew quite well.

The sun was up by the time he reached the machine, which was still in the same position as it had been left, with the note he had written to Algy still pinned to the fuselage. There was some water inside the cabin, tepid, it is true, but he drank of it avidly, for his throat had become parched during the journey down the *wadi*. This done, he munched a few biscuits, and then set about preparing for what he suspected was likely to be his last flight.

There was not much to be done. The petrol he poured into the gravity tank, and then tossed the empty cans away. He removed the worst of the dust from the air intakes of the engines, and tested the controls, which he was relieved to find were in order.

Sitting in the cockpit, he put a new clip of ammunition in his pistol, and satisfied himself that it was working properly; he also filled a pocket with spare clips from the box in the cabin. Finally, having loaded it, he placed the large-bore signal pistol on the seat beside him, and with it a dozen or so rounds of emergency signal-flares, red, green, and white, which the machine carried as part of its normal equipment.

Satisfied that there was nothing more he could do in the machine, he went down the *wadi*, removing from his proposed line of take-off the boulders, large and small, that lay in the way. A last look down the *wadi* and he returned to the machine, closed the door, and started the engines. He did not waste petrol in testing them for revolutions, or in warming them up, for the sun had already done that. Opening the throttle, he raced down the valley, leaving a swirling cloud of sand to mark his passage.

19
A DREADFUL SENTENCE

GINGER never knew a more hopeless moment than when Biggles was led out of the room, for he never expected to see him again. The absence of his dominating personality and cheerful optimism made their own position seem so much worse; it was impossible to see how he could hope to escape the fate designed for him by their captors. Algy, naturally, felt the same, and squatted down on the floor with his back resting against the wall in an attitude of utter dejection. Kadar, now that the blow had fallen, accepted the situation with oriental fatalism.

'It is the will of God; it will be as He decides,' he murmured, shrugging his shoulders, revealing the religious side of his nature for the first time; it was obvious that he was prepared to let it go at that. From his point of view, to attempt to divert the inscrutable ways of God, or even to wish otherwise, was a sin not to be contemplated, and he made no secret of it.

Neither Algy nor Ginger was inclined to argue about it, but had it been possible to do anything they would certainly have done it, for their experience indicated that it was unreasonable to expect God to help any one who made no attempt to help himself. However, they did not discuss this difficult question, and as there was nothing they could do, they continued sitting on the floor in positions suggestive of acute misery.

'Has it struck any one,' asked Ginger presently, 'what an extraordinary thing it is that, after being isolated for perhaps thousands of years, these people should have two lots of visitors from the outside world almost within a day of each other?'

'I think that it is not so much a coincidence as it may appear to be at first glance,' answered Kadar. 'I have been turning the matter over in my mind, and it is my belief that one was a direct cause of the other. In other words, had we not come here, Zarwan would not have come here either.'

'You mean you think he deliberately came here after us?' asked Algy.

'More or less. Actually, I think his intention was, in the first place, to prevent us from reaching here. I do not think for a moment that he ever came here himself before this occasion. An Arab, or Arabs, perhaps from Siwah, stumbled upon this place, and if that was so, they would certainly return to it, for such delightful watering-places are rare in this part of the world. Either on the first occasion, or later, they made contact with the people who live here, or perhaps with the old hag, and opened a sort of trade, bartering their wares after the fashion of Arabs with such things as the local people could offer.'

'You are thinking of the jewels?' put in Ginger shrewdly.

'That is precisely what I am thinking of. We know that the old woman is aware of the existence of the tombs, because that is where we discovered her; she may even be in the habit of visiting them regularly; in fact, she might even live there. No one can say how long the dead ones have been in that cave, and if I know anything about it, and I am not without experience, I feel quite sure that nothing would induce the tribesmen to go into that deathchamber. There is another necropolis just like it at Siwah, but no native would go near it under any consideration. It is held to be haunted and not without reason. But that old ghoul of a creature, if she did not mind going into the place, as we have proved, would not be beyond taking rings, necklaces, and other jewellery from those who lie there. Even Arabs know the value of such things, and those who came here probably exchanged such articles as they had to offer for what the old woman found. They are secretive by nature, so they would not talk about it; but in due course the jewels would reach civilization, and it may have been that Zarwan was the first man of importance to see them. For all we know a regular traffic may have been going on; indeed, I think it is more than likely. Don't you see that that in itself would be a very good reason for Zarwan, when he heard of my plans, to try to prevent me from getting here? When he learned through his spies that I was trying to charter an aeroplane, he decided to adopt more drastic methods; as you yourselves saw, he was even prepared to commit murder rather than that I should reach you. When it was reported to him that you had agreed to fly me here, he set off immediately with the Arabs who knew where the place was in order to frustrate us. First, he ambushed the caravan, which he realized would leave us stranded. After that, no doubt he went on to the oasis which we had made our headquarters in the hope of finding us there. Had he succeeded, it is likely that we should now be drying in the sun. But, owing to unforeseen circumstances, which may have been very fortunate for us, we had already left, and that must have put Zarwan in a quandary. Where were we? Had we, after all, managed to reach the Lost Oasis? He decided to find out. Possibly he hoped, even if we were not here, to do a profitable trade with the inhabitants, whom he doubtless imagined would be ordinary Arabs, or Bedouins of some sort. If he thought that, then the reason why he kept the petrol is at once apparent; he intended to barter it as intoxicating liquor, to which all Arabs are prone, in return for jewels. Whether he fell out with the old woman, whether he tried to steal the jewels from her, or whether the old hag, alarmed by our intrusion, thought that he was trying to—how do you say?—double-cross her, we may never know. She went and fetched the tribe—unless, of course, some of them discovered us on their own account—with the result that we all know.'

Algy nodded approvingly when Kadar finished his rather long discourse. 'That all sounds reasonable to me,' he admitted. 'If the tribe treats visitors in this way it might well account for the fact that the oasis has remained undiscovered for so long. It would be interesting to know how many explorers have finished their travels in the crocodile's stomach.'

'I am convinced that these people are of Persian origin,' went on Kadar emphatically, lapsing into his old theme; but further conversation was checked by the noise of the procession as it emerged from the archway.

Ginger darted to the window. 'Great heavens!' he cried aghast. 'They're taking Biggles down to the pool. There he is, walking along just behind the front rank.'

Algy pushed him to one side in order to see. 'Yes, it's Biggles all right,' he muttered in tones of horror and despair. 'Why on earth doesn't he do something, I wonder? Surely he isn't just going to walk down to the pool and allow himself to be thrown in?'

'Not he,' declared Ginger. 'He's got some scheme in his mind, or he would not be strolling along as though he was going to somebody else's funeral instead of his own. I guessed he had something up his sleeve when he said "Watch the pool". That is where he will try to make a break. He'll give that crocodile a sore throat before it grabs him, I'll warrant.'

Nothing more was said for the moment. In breathless silence they all watched the torches approaching nearer and nearer to the dreaded pool; they could no longer see Biggles in person, but they could judge his position by the lights of the torchbearers. They heard the chanting rise to its highest pitch, and then die away suddenly.

'He's doing something,' muttered Ginger breathlessly. He was trembling with excitement.

Then arose in the still night air the most amazing sound ever heard in the Lost Oasis of Zenzura. There could be no mistake. It was Biggles singing 'Rule, Britannia'.

'Is he mad?' asked Kadar seriously, possibly thinking that the ordeal had driven Biggles out of his mind.

'Not so mad as some of those pig-faced Persians will be in a minute,' declared Ginger viciously. 'You wait till his gun starts popping.'

Then came a long delay, which was, of course, the period while Biggles was unearthing the petrol. But the watchers knew nothing about that; they had, in the stress of the moment, forgotten all about such things as petrol.

Suddenly there came a sound for which they had all been waiting—a single pistol-shot. But they were certainly not prepared for what followed, any more than the Persians were. The entire oasis in the region of the pool seemed to burst into flame, while into the night rose an outburst of yells and groans. Thereafter pandemonium broke loose.

'It's the petrol!' yelled Algy, beating on the window-sill with his fists in his excitement. 'It's the petrol! He's blown the whole perishing party up.'

'Attaboy! Attaboy! Set 'em alight!' screamed Kadar, lapsing suddenly and unexpectedly into American, which he must have picked up at some time or other from a western visitor.

'Gosh! I hope he hasn't blown himself up with it,' breathed Algy with a sudden change of tone, as the possibility of this occurred to him. Indeed, judging by the flames, it did not seem at all unlikely.

'The crocodile! Look at the crocodile!' cried Ginger tersely, as the beast charged through the trees, like a medieval dragon, breathing fire.

'Am I dreaming, or is this really happening?' asked Algy in a curious voice. 'It doesn't seem possible.'

'It doesn't, but it is,' declared Ginger enigmatically. 'I hope he's got away. I wish I knew.'

'Where the dickens will he go even if he manages to get clear?' demanded Algy. 'He said himself that there was nowhere——'

'Anywhere would be better than down that brute's throat,' declared Ginger. 'If only he has got clear, anything can happen. Look at what he has done already. No one would have given a fig for his chance as he walked down there surrounded by that mob, yet he has sprung a surprise that not even we thought of— Great goodness! What's that?'

'It is a volcano,' declared Kadar, while they all stared at the blazing can of petrol which Biggles had just flung down the hillside into the faces of his pursuers. 'It may be the end of the world,' he added thoughtfully.

'Not on your life it isn't,' said Algy crisply. 'It's petrol. He has got away and taken some petrol with him. You can see where he is. He has bolted up the hill and he has nearly reached the mouth of the cave. The crowd is after him, and he is bombing them with petrol-cans. Oh, lovely! Lovely! Frizzle, you blighters, frizzle!'

Nothing else, happened, for, as we know, Biggles had gone into the cave. Presently the watchers suspected it, and although they remained staring through the window, the excitement eased somewhat.

'Well, would you believe that?' said Ginger at last. 'I honestly believe he has got clean away.'

'And what is going to happen to him now?' asked Algy soberly.

'And what is going to happen to us?' muttered Kadar nervously.

'It isn't much use guessing,' opined Ginger. 'As Biggles himself would say, we shall have to wait and see, but I must say that it has put new life into me to know that he has got away. I never felt so absolutely hopeless in my life as when I saw him going down the hill.'

'Some of the people are coming back, judging by the sound of it,' observed Algy. 'I can hear them groaning. It also sounds as if some of them are cursing, and I don't wonder at it, for a lot of them must have got pretty badly burned.'

'So shall we be, I'm afraid, when they remember that we are up here,' murmured Kadar pessimistically.

'Biggles won't overlook that possibility,' declared Ginger confidently. 'He'll see us through. While he is at large anything can happen.'

'I should like to know what these Persian johnnies are thinking about the whole thing,' muttered Algy.

'They are probably having a council to decide what shall be done with us,' suggested Kadar. 'Having had a taste of our magic, as they will suppose Biggles's effort to be, they'll think very carefully before they try any more sacrifices.'

'They may take the view that if one of us can kill their god by producing fire out of the sand, what might three be able to do?' said Ginger hopefully.

'I hope you're right,' declared Algy fervently.

After that they fell silent, and the night wore on. None of them slept, for in their extreme peril repose was out of the question. Never to any of them had a night seemed so long. Once or twice, when one of them thought he heard a sound below, he went eagerly to the window and looked down, thinking perhaps Biggles had returned, but on each occasion the alarm proved false.

At last the sky began to grey with the approach of dawn, and Algy yawned. 'My goodness! I'd give something for a hot bath,' he muttered. 'Never in my life have I felt so filthy. Hark! Is that someone coming?' he concluded sharply.

A moment later footsteps could be heard coming up the stairs, accompanied by the low mutter of voices. The door was thrown open and several bearded warriors, evidently leaders of the tribe, stood on the threshold, regarding the prisoners with scowling faces. It was not difficult to guess the reason for their displeasure, for nearly all of them showed signs of the recent conflagration. One had a terrible blister on his cheek, and another had had most of his beard singed off. In their hands they carried strips of hide, evidently to be used as bonds, suggesting that they were not going to risk a repetition of Biggles's moonlight magic.

'I don't like the look of this,' said Algy quietly.

Before either of the others could answer, even if they had so wished, the tribesmen came into the room, and without any more ado proceeded to tie their prisoners hand and foot. Algy and Ginger, as soon as they realized what was intended, attempted to put up a fight, but against such hopeless odds their efforts were doomed to failure from the onset. They were thrown roughly to the ground, and held securely while the thongs were adjusted. This done, they were hauled to the door like a tailor's dummies being taken from a shop-window, and dragged down the stairs into the street, where a number of spear-armed warriors were waiting.

'Can you make a guess as to what they are going to do with us?' Ginger asked Kadar, for their heads were close together.

'No, but doubtless they have decided on an unpleasant way of killing us,' answered Kadar resignedly, and with that the assembly began to move off.

It was only with difficulty that they could see where they were being carried. Ginger went cold all over in spite of the heat as they crossed the drawbridge, for he had not forgotten the snakes underneath; but he breathed again as the procession moved on, and presently passed under the entrance arch into a world now flushed with the pink and gold of dawn. Presently the sun would mount above the hill-tops, and it would be baking hot, but Algy was doubting whether they would live long enough to feel its heat.

The procession passed along the side of the oasis, and as it reached the open space between the palms and the foot of the necropolis hill without showing signs of halting, Algy wondered where they could be going, for the leaders were still advancing towards the track that led to the tombs of the dead.

It was Kadar who told them the grim truth, and he had obtained the information in an unexpected manner. To his great surprise, a guttural voice near him whispered his name; turning his head with difficulty, he saw the Tuareg marching beside him with their arms bound securely to their sides, and he realized for the first time that the tribesmen evidently intended to dispose of all their prisoners at once. The faces of the Tuareg, gallant enough in battle, were a ghastly colour; their eyes rolled, and the teeth of one of them chattered in his head.

'What did you say?' Kadar asked the Tuareg who had spoken, in his own language, for he had not quite caught all the words.

'They are taking us to the tombs of the dead, to be buried

alive,' answered the Tuareg hoarsely, and Kadar passed the information on to the others.

Ginger looked up at the blue sky which presently he would see no more, for already the procession had reached the foot of the hill. As he stared upwards a small black object soared into view; at first he thought it was a vulture, but when, a moment later, he heard the deep hum of the Tourer's engines, he understood.

The tribesmen heard the noise too, and the procession stopped, while a nervous mutter ran down the line.

'It's Biggles!' yelled Algy.

20

BIGGLES STRIKES

AFTER taking off, Biggles had climbed swiftly to five thousand feet, and then, cutting his engines, began gliding towards the oasis, with his side window open, staring at the ground between the village and the foot of the hill.

In doing this he was following the plan he had decided to adopt. Not that he had much choice. He had enough petrol left in his tank for, roughly, five minutes' flying; at the end of that time he would have to come down wherever he was, and the only place that he could remember, apart from the *wadi*, where a landing might be made without disastrous results, was the open area between the palms and the foot of the necropolis hill. It so happened that his roving eyes had instinctively noted this piece of ground when they had walked across it, for it becomes second nature to most airmen to mark down a possible landing-ground when one is noticed. Biggles could not recall just what the surface of the ground was like, although he could not remember any serious obstructions; there were, he thought, a number of small pieces of loose rock, but none large enough to upset him. He did not relish the idea of landing there, but there was nowhere else. In any case, he could not get back to the *wadi* even if he had wished to—not that there would be any point in returning to the place which he had left only a few minutes before. The petrol-supply was near the pool, and since he could not hope to carry the petrol to the machine, the machine would have to be taken to the petrol, whatever the risk.

He had not expected to see any one there; he had hoped that after the débâcle of the previous night the place would be deserted, and a great wave of disappointment swept over him when he observed that, far from being the case, a column of tribesmen were actually on the march across it. From the altitude at which he was flying he could not, of course, distinguish individuals, and although he noticed vaguely that the tribesmen were carrying something, it did not occur to him that it might be Algy and the others. Not unnaturally, he imagined that they were still in the place where he had left them, and he cast several glances in that direction, wondering if they could see him, and if so, what they were thinking at the reappearance of the machine in the air.

His petrol was now nearly exhausted; willy-nilly, a landing would soon have to be made, so he resolved forthwith to fall back upon his last forlorn hope, which was that the machine would put the natives to flight and give him an opportunity of getting more petrol—at least some of it, if not all. Beyond that he did not think, for the hazards of the undertaking were such that further arrangements were uncalled for; time would come for that if he was successful.

He had dived many machines in his time, both in peace and war, but never before had he dived one so recklessly as he dived the Tourer, for on no previous occasion had the circumstances been so desperate. With the engines full on he pushed the joystick right forward and held it there with his right hand, while with his left he picked up the signalling pistol, the modern equivalent of the war-time Very pistol. Down went the nose of the Tourer, while the tail cocked high into the air behind it. The roar of the engines became a pulsating bellow; the wind screamed through the wires and struts, while the quivering needle of the air-speed indicator crept round the dial—200—300—350.

At just under four hundred miles an hour Biggles began to

ease the stick back, for he was getting low, and he had no desire either to dive into the ground or end matters by stripping the wings off his machine; in any case, he saw that further speed was unnecessary, for already the tribesmen were scattering like chips from a log under a woodcutter's axe. At a hundred feet, with the engines still running on full throttle, he levelled out, his eyes running swiftly over the scene below, on the lookout for a suitable mark at which to discharge the pistol. He chose his target, and a ball of crimson fire went screaming down into the middle of a group of warriors; and it was at that moment that Algy's white face caught his eye. So astounded was he that he stared at it for a full second, forgetting for the moment that an aeroplane travels far in that time. He snatched the stick back, and his wheels missed the palms by inches. The manoeuvre served this good purpose, however: it turned the retreat of the tribesmen into a panic-stricken rout. Some fled helter-skelter, flinging away their weapons; others flung themselves flat and covered their faces with their hands.

If Biggles had been prepared to 'shoot up' the district before seeing Algy and the others, their unexpected appearance put a new zest into his actions, and he treated the savages, did they but know it, to as fine an exhibition of crazy-flying as has ever been seen at a flying-display. Round and round he tore, diving and zooming, with sometimes his wheels and sometimes a wing-tip nearly scraping the ground. On the brief occasions when he flew level he reloaded the pistol, holding the joystick between his knees, and blazed red and green fire at the now widely scattered natives. Few were, in fact, still in sight, and these he chased until their actions became ludicrous. One dropped to his knees and raised his arms in an attitude of prayer.

Biggles was in the middle of a turn when his engines coughed, choked, and then cut out dead. Instantly the natives were forgotten as he concentrated absolutely on the tricky business of putting the machine down without damaging it. Never before had so much depended on a good landing, and he put all his skill into it. A gentle side-slip to the left brought him in line with the open area, with the nose of the machine pointing in the direction in which Algy and the others were lying. As he flattened out he wondered why they did not get up and run towards him, for his speed had not permitted him to see that they were tied; but now, as he skimmed low over them, he understood.

Slowly the machine sank nearer to the sand, while his eyes stared at the track along which he must now land. One boulder would be all that was necessary to seal their fate, but, as it happened, although there were several small pieces of rock which caused the machine to bump and wobble dangerously, there was nothing large enough to throw it over, and it ran to a standstill, with stationary propellers, in an unaccustomed silence.

The instant the machine stopped running Biggles was out, racing back to where the others were lying. Once he paused to snatch a sword from the hand of a warrior who had either been hit by one of his shots, or had died of fright; then he went on again, and, panting, presently dropped on his knees at Algy's side.

'Are you hurt?' was all he said, as he cut him free.

'No,' answered Algy.

'Then take this pistol and run for the petrol,' ordered Biggles. 'Don't stop for anything. If any one tries to get in your way, plug him. The petrol is our only chance.'

Algy ran off towards the trees, working his arms to restore the circulation.

Biggles cut Ginger's bonds, and told him to follow Algy. Then he freed Kadar, dragged him to his feet, and set off after the others. Not a soul attempted to stop them, and by the time he reached the *cache* the top cans were already uncovered. He snatched up two of them, and with a crisp 'Get 'em all out if you can manage it', he raced back to the machine.

It took him two or three minutes to empty the two cans into the gravity tank, but it was time well employed. Into the cabin he darted, and without bothering to close the door, he started the engines and taxied swiftly but carefully to the edge of the trees, where he switched off and jumped out.

'Take this and mount guard,' he told Kadar tersely, thrusting into his hands the signal-pistol, in which a cartridge remained. 'If you see any one coming, let drive. Ginger, get to the machine, and fill the tanks as we pass the cans to you. Take a couple with you.'

Perhaps never before in the history of aviation has an aeroplane been refuelled with such frantic haste. On one side of it a great pile of empty cans lay where they fell, as Ginger flung them aside after emptying them of their contents. Panting and staggering under the weight of the loads they carried, Biggles and Algy fed him with full ones, and not until only a few cans remained did he ease the pace.

'We are safe!' cried Biggles exultantly. 'We've done it! Keep your eyes skinned, Kadar. Don't let them surprise us.'

'I can see a few of them coming back in the distance,' called Kadar.

'Let us know if they get close,' replied Biggles, and went on with the work of refuelling until the last can had been emptied.

'Have we got enough to get us home, do you think?' panted Algy.

'I think so, but it's impossible to be absolutely certain,' answered Biggles. 'We've a long way to go. It's no use going merely to Semphis. It has got to be either Siwah or Dakhel. I fancy Siwah is our nearest contact-point with civilization, but not knowing just where we are, it's impossible to be sure. We can only take a course to the north-west, hoping to strike it. If we miss it we ought to be able to pick up a caravan, or a caravan trail, since we shall be in a district where people are moving about.'

When he had finished speaking Biggles took two spare water-bottles from the cabin and, running to the pool, filled them, a faint smile flitting across his face as he saw in daylight the scene of his adventure the previous night. Returning, he pointed out the dead, scorched body of the crocodile, still lying where he had last seen it. 'I warmed that beauty's tonsils for him, as I said I would,' he smiled. 'Hello, what's that—over there?' He pointed to a small dark object that lay at the foot of some rocks near the bottom of the hill.

'Great Scott! I believe it's the old hag!' cried Algy. 'Yes, by all that's wonderful, so it is. She must have tumbled down the rocks and broken her neck when you dived on the crowd just now—unless she died of fright.'

'Stay here and keep your eyes skinned, Ginger,' ordered Biggles. 'Yell if you see any one coming.'

'Ay, ay, sir,' answered Ginger cheerfully.

Biggles, with Algy beside him, hurried across to the body, and they saw that it was indeed the old hag. A glance told them that she was stone dead, and a jagged wound in her forehead, which looked as though it had been caused by a fall, showed how she had at last met her death. She was a dreadful looking creature, little more than a collection of bones covered by brown, wrinkled skin, and Biggles was about to turn away when Algy caught him by the arm.

'What are those things?' he asked, pointing to a little stream of what looked like semi-transparent marbles, some green and some red, that had evidently fallen out of a small goat-skin bag attached to the old woman's girdle.

Biggles picked one up, one of the red ones. 'Great heaven!' he whispered in an awed voice. 'I wouldn't swear to it, but I believe it's a ruby.'

'Look out, they're coming!' came Ginger's voice from the machine.

Biggles stooped swiftly, and jerking off the bag with a single tug, thrust it into his pocket, while Algy scooped up the loose stones. Then they turned and ran back to the others, hastened by shrill cries from the heart of the oasis, which suggested that the tribesmen were rallying there.

'All aboard,' cried Biggles, climbing into the cockpit. 'They'll change their minds about coming nearer, I fancy, when the engines open up.' He felt for the self-starter, and as the others scrambled aboard the powerful engines sprang to life.

Biggles taxied slowly to the extremity of the open area. Then, with his engines idling, he looked over his shoulder at Kadar. 'This Lost Oasis that you were so anxious to find,' he said, 'would you like to stay here and do a bit more exploring, or would you rather come home with us?'

Kadar smiled wanly. 'I think I've seen enough of it to last me for a little while,' he said.

'And I've seen enough of it to last me for the rest of my life,' Biggles told him definitely. 'Go steady with the water in there; there's a lot of sand between here and the place we are making for,' he added, and he eased the throttle forward.

The engines roared and the machine began to move forward; the tail lifted; the wheels bumped gently once or twice, and then the Tourer soared into the air.

Biggles glanced at Algy as he levelled out and swung the nose of the machine round towards the north-west. 'It's queer how things turn out, isn't it?' he mused. 'Twenty-four hours ago, what we are doing now seemed as unattainable as the moon. It just shows that you never know. All I ask now is that the gee-gees in the engines go on kicking until we get to the other side of this confounded sand.'

'What a treat it will be to get a bath,' murmured Algy, as he settled down in his seat for the long flight ahead.

'I'll believe that there are such things when I see one,' returned Biggles, as his eyes went to the compass and then down to the sterile landscape underneath. The *wadi* in which they had first landed was slipping away below, and he knew that whatever happened he would never see the Lost Oasis of Zenzura again.

21

MIRAGE!

FOR three long hours the machine roared on over the seemingly endless sand. To Ginger, sitting in one of the back seats, each passing hour, with nothing but dunes, and still more dunes, creeping up over the horizon, seemed more incredible than the last. It was hard to believe that such a place could exist on the face of a world that is assumed to be civilized and sophisticated. But here was nature as it always had been, and might be forever.

To Biggles the period was one of intense strain. Before he had experienced real thirst he had not been particularly concerned at the prospect of flying over long stretches of open desert, but now that he knew the horror of it he could only sit with his eyes fixed on the horizon, inwardly praying that some speck, some living thing, even if it were only an isolated palm, would come into view to break the eternal monotony of the yellow waste. No ocean crossing he had ever made, and he had made many, had filled him with so much dread.

From time to time his eyes dropped for an instant to the fast-sinking petrol-gauge, only to return again to the horizon, while he tried to keep the machine as steady as possible in the heat-rocked atmosphere through which it bored. He realized more clearly than ever before what a tangible thing the atmosphere was; over the rolling dunes, some of them many miles in length, the air seemed as fluid as water and as unstable as a storm-tossed ocean.

'Something ought to show up soon,' murmured Algy at last, holding his shirt away from his body for relief, for the heat in the little cabin was appalling.

'Yes,' was Biggles's only answer.

'How much juice have we got left?'

'With the gravity tank, I reckon about forty minutes.'

Algy said no more, but, like Biggles, concentrated on the horizon. Never did shipwrecked sailors watch for land with greater anxiety.

Twenty-five minutes went past; it seemed like an hour, and still there was no sign of a break in the sand.

'It begins to look as though the whole blessed earth has turned to sand,' muttered Algy.

Biggles said nothing, but switched over to the gravity tank as the main tank petered out.

'Land ho!' cried Ginger suddenly.

Biggles started. 'Where away?'

Ginger pointed due north.

It was difficult to see anything clearly on account of the quivering haze, for now that the sun had nearly reached its zenith the air rocked and shook like a jelly, but by focusing his eyes on the spot indicated Biggles could just make out a faint blue smudge.

'Mirage,' said Kadar, softly.

'I hope you are wrong,' muttered Biggles. 'If that is what it is, then we are out of luck, but I think I can make out what looks like the top of some palms.'

Kadar was standing up, bent forward, peering through the windscreen in his anxiety. 'I am afraid of it,' he said. 'The curse of the desert is that you cannot trust your eyes. They often show you things that are not there. The things are, of course, somewhere, but what appears to be just in front of you can be fifty miles away in any direction. It is an illusion, simply a reflection on the hot atmosphere.'

'Hey! Look at that!' cried Ginger, pointing to a line of huge, distorted camels, their supercilious faces held high, marching along below.

Algy gave a shout of joy. 'A caravan,' he said.

Kadar shook his head. 'It is a mirage. I have seen too many not to recognize one when I see it. Watch, and see what happens.'

As the machine roared on the camels seemed to grow enormous, until they towered up far into the sky, an un-believable spectacle. Then they began to fade into the haze. More and more indistinct they grew, until, when the Tourer roared over the spot where they had been, there was nothing as far as the eye could see but sand; no longer wind-blown dunes, but flat, gently undulating plain.

'See! They have gone,' said Kadar seriously. 'That is the usual way with a mirage. How many unfortunate people have seen visions of water, limpid streams, waving palms——'

'All right, don't make a song about it,' interrupted Biggles irritably. He was staring forward at the smudge, which had now become a dark, filmy green.

'I can see palms,' declared Algy.

'As likely as not you will see water presently,' returned Kadar quietly, 'but that does not mean that it is there. Do not think me pessimistic, but we must face facts, and a mirage is anything but a fact. It is pure hallucination.'

Biggles, still watching, saw the crest of a long line of palms appear; they seemed to grow rapidly larger, but at the same time there was something odd about them. Then he understood. They were upside-down, their fronds resting on the sand and their long straight boles pointing upwards to the sky.

Biggles blinked and shook his head. Then he looked again. 'Am I going crazy, or are my eyes going cock-eyed?' he snapped.

'Neither,' replied Kadar calmly. 'It is merely another trick of the mirage.'

'But do you mean to say that those things are not there?' demanded Algy incredulously.

'They are somewhere, or we should not see the reflections of them,' agreed Kadar, 'but they might be some distance away. They might even be below the sky-line. Still, it is comforting to know that we are at least in the region of an oasis, and a caravan; but, as I have warned you, one cannot rely on them being where they appear to be. Look! Look! Now perhaps you will believe me.'

While he had been speaking the palms had suddenly assumed colossal proportions. They seemed to fill half the sky, and were all the more terrifying on account of the fact that they were still upside-down. Then, suddenly, for no apparent reason, they became a vague blur, and soon, like a cloud of smoke on a windy day, finally disappeared altogether.

'Heavens, what a country to live in,' groaned Biggles. He still held on the same course, for there appeared to be no point in altering it.

'How much petrol have we left?' asked Ginger.

'I wish you wouldn't keep asking that,' answered Biggles coldly. 'Ten minutes at the outside.'

Nothing more was said while the seconds ticked past on the watch on the instrument-board, and the sky turned from dull blue to an intense steely grey.

'Is that another storm coming?' asked Ginger.

'If it is, we're sunk,' said Biggles curtly. He was feeling the strain.

'I do not think so; the sky plays all sorts of tricks in such heat as this,' Kadar told them. He was now the chief spokesman, for his experience of desert travel could not be ignored.

'How far is it to the horizon?' asked Biggles. 'I ask because we shall not get to it—anyway, not in this machine.'

'How far would you think?'

Biggles frowned. 'I'm dashed if I know,' he said. 'I am not sure whether I am looking at it or not, and that's a fact. In normal conditions I should say fifty miles, since there appears to be nothing in the way to interrupt the view. One can see as far as that on a fine day in England, sometimes farther.'

Kadar regarded the sky-line steadily for some seconds. 'It might be ten miles,' he said at last. 'It is certainly not more; it might be less.'

'But that sounds ridiculous,' argued Biggles.

'No doubt it does. In England you get fogs which restrict visibility. Here we get heat-haze which distorts everything hopelessly.'

'I'll take your word for it,' Biggles told him moodily.

'Look there!' shouted Ginger suddenly, pointing forward and downwards, and the others stared in surprise as a long line of camels, each animal accompanied by its own dense black shadow, appeared in a manner which could only be regarded as miraculous, so close were they.

'Where the dickens did they come from?' ejaculated Biggles. 'I could have sworn a moment ago that there wasn't a living thing in sight. I suppose it isn't another mirage?' he concluded doubtfully.

'Oh, no,' declared Kadar definitely. 'That is the real thing. There is no doubt about it. Look how clear-cut everything is. There must have been a change in atmospheric conditions. It was the reflection of this caravan that we saw just now; it has appeared out of the invisible haze I told you about. The drivers have seen us.'

This was obviously true, for the line of camels had halted, and white-robed figures could be seen staring upwards.

Biggles was now in a quandary, for if they went on without finding the oasis they might lose the caravan; on the other hand, if they went down it might be only to learn that the oasis they were trying to reach was not far away. But if the sand was soft, as seemed highly probable, they would not be able to get the machine off the ground again. Should he go down, or should he risk going on?

Kadar seemed to guess what was going on in his mind, for he urged him to continue. 'If the caravan was so close, it is likely that the oasis is close, too,' he said.

A moment later his assumption was confirmed in a startling manner. The atmosphere seemed suddenly to clarify, and there, only a few miles away, was an unmistakable oasis.

'Siwah!' cried Kadar delightedly. 'I recognize it. Look there are the ruins of Jupiter Ammon, the place Cambyses' army was trying to reach when it was overwhelmed. Is it not remarkable to think that for thousands of years the descendants of those same people have gone on living, while the temple their ancestors set out to plunder has been slowly falling into decay? They might have been a million miles away for all the hope they had of reaching it.'

Algy and Ginger looked with interest at the ancient ruins of such romantic association, but Biggles was more concerned with the present. He had already throttled back as far as he dared, to conserve his fast-diminishing supply of petrol, but he was still some distance away when, after the usual warning from the engines, it gave out, and he was compelled to put the Tourer into a glide. He had, however, nearly three thousand feet of altitude, and as the machine, with empty tanks, could glide for a mile to every thousand feet of height, he was able to reach the nearest palms with a hundred feet to spare. Choosing the smoothest area he could see, he glided down to land.

In this landing, apart from the care he exercised, he may have been lucky, for had he gone on a little farther he would have struck a patch of soft sand, and the machine might have somersaulted with serious, if not fatal, results. As it was, it ran for a little way over fairly hard gravel before reaching the sand, so that by the time it did reach it its speed was greatly reduced. The machine shuddered and the tail cocked high as the clogging sand embraced the wheels; but it also acted as a brake, and although the machine stopped dangerously quickly, it did not turn over.

Biggles sank up to the ankles as he jumped down, and when the others joined him he pointed to the wheels, buried for half their depth in fine dust. 'We are lucky we are where we are,' he said grimly. 'for we should never get off this without help. You have been to Siwah before, Kadar; do you think there will be any difficulty in getting labourers to drag the machine clear of this stuff?'

'I do not think so,' answered Kadar. 'Money will do most things even in the desert, as it does in civilized places.'

Hardly had he finished speaking when, with a shout, a party of horsemen appeared from the direction of the village, riding at breakneck speed.

'What's the idea, I wonder?' asked Biggles anxiously. 'Do they mean trouble?'

Kadar was watching the horsemen with a perplexed expression on his face. 'I trust not,' he said. 'I don't see why they should——' He broke off, peering forward with an expression of astonishment. 'Why—why—it's Sarapion,' he cried.

'*Who?*' inquired Biggles.

'Sarapion. He is one of our servants,' explained Kadar in great excitement, and rushing forward, he embraced a white-clad Egyptian who slid gracefully from his horse.

They spoke together for a little while, and then Kadar returned to the others, his face beaming. 'My father is here,' he said joyfully.

'Good! That should make things easier for us,' smiled Biggles. 'But he was soon on our track, wasn't he?'

'Yes, but it came about like this. One of the men with our caravan was mounted on a very fast camel, and he managed to escape the massacre. By good fortune and great endurance he reached Siwah, and from there sent a message to my father to tell him what had happened. My father, may heaven preserve him, went at once to the Governor and asked for his assistance, and I believe he is about to send aeroplanes in search of us.'

'They would have been a long time finding us at Zenzura, I am afraid,' murmured Biggles doubtfully.

'Yes, but that does not matter now. My father came on to Siwah at once in a small aeroplane which he was able to charter, in the hope of arranging for caravans to go and search for us in the desert. By offering a big reward he was able to do this, and several Arabs have already left. No doubt it was one of the search-parties that we saw just now.'

'This is all very comforting,' declared Biggles. 'What had we better do now?'

'We shall have to stay here for a little while, I am afraid, while a messenger goes back to Mersa Matruh aerodrome and arranges for petrol to be sent out to us—unless, of course, you prefer to go back on a camel.'

'Not for me, thank you,' replied Biggles quickly. 'I'd rather ride an aeroplane than a camel any day. How are they off for water here?'

'Oh, there is plenty of water. There are even some lakes.'

'Lead me to one,' murmured Biggles. 'Tell me when we get to it, because I may have forgotten what a lot of water in one piece looks like.'

22

FAREWELL TO THE DESERT

Two hours later, having bathed, shaved, and changed their clothes, they sat contentedly in a shady tent which had been pitched among the palms, telling Kadar's father the amazing story of their adventures.

The old man also had some news for them, which cleared up a lot of points, although certain of these were already suspected.

It appeared that the Society for the Preservation of Antiques, the organization of which Kadar had told them, had been on Zarwan's trail for some time, although the members had raised no objection to Kadar's trip because his genuine and impersonal motives were well known. Zarwan had, in some way, got wind of this and bolted from Egypt, which accounted for his sudden disappearance while the airmen were making their preparations. Active members of the society had gone both to Khargah and Siwah to await his return, so even if he had escaped his fate at the hands of the lost tribesmen, it was likely that he would have found death waiting for him in his own country. Moreover, the Egyptian police were on his track for supplying intoxicating liquor to natives, this having been his practice for some time past.

It was three weeks before the messenger who had been dispatched for the petrol returned with an ample supply. The airmen spent most of their time bathing in one of the lakes for which the celebrated oasis is justly famous—and there were no crocodiles—or resting in the shade of the palms. With their host they also visited the ancient ruins of the temple, and walked with awe over the stones that had been trodden by Alexander the Great and other men famous in history.

Kadar spent most of his time writing voluminous notes on his opionions and discoveries at the Lost Oasis, and these were in due course presented to an excited gathering of archaeologists in Alexandria, the city founded by Alexander the Great long before the birth of Christianity.

But at last, with its tanks filled, the Tourer stood at the end of a specially cleared runway, and they said goodbye to Kadar's father, who had decided to return by the more prosaic method which has been employed from time immemorial, that of a camel caravan.

One long day's flying saw the airmen back at Cairo, where they had a great reception and a civic ceremony, word of their discovery having preceded them. The jewels which they had found were, as Biggles had suspected, uncut gems of great value, and these were handed over to the authorities for disposal. Their sale realized a large sum, part of which was handed over to the explorers, and more than repaid them for the risks they had taken. Kadar, much to his delight, was also appointed an honorary curator of a well-known Egyptian museum where, as Biggles told him, he would be able to study antiquities to his heart's content without such attendant discomforts as thirst, scorpions, and crocodile sacrifices.

Sitting on the patio of the hotel where Kadar had first met them, Algy glanced suddenly at Biggles with a puzzled expression on his face but a twinkle in his eye.

'I seem to remember that when we first came here we were on our way to somewhere,' he murmured blandly.

'Quite right,' agreed Biggles. 'We were on our way to South Africa when Kadar came along with his bright idea for a joyride into the desert.'

'To a dinner of some sort, I think?'

'Quite correct,' agreed Biggles. 'If we started tomorrow morning we might still get there in time.'

Ginger yawned. 'Well, we seem to have seen all there is to see in Egypt, even things like oases which no one was quite sure existed. Sand is all right in small quantities, and it is even pleasant to look at by the seaside, but too much of it in one lump is apt to become monotonous. I, personally, am all for a change of scenery.'

'Yes, I feel that a nice green field or two would do our eyes no harm,' agreed Algy.

'Then if you'll be ready at the crack of dawn we'll tootle along southward,' Biggles told them, as he reached for the jug of iced lemon-squash that stood on the table.

BIGGLES
IN THE
ORIENT

THE WAY THE AIR FORCE SAYS IT

Airmen have always spoken a language of their own, and during the war a large number of words have been added to the vocabulary. Some of the older words and expressions have been discarded in favour of new ones. Again, it was inevitable that some of the apt terms used by American airmen should be approved and incorporated.

Official documents have also been responsible for changes. For example: the word aerodrome has given way to airfield; bandit, meaning an enemy aircraft, was originally an official code word.

Dialogue between airmen without the use of slang would therefore be unconvincing—at any rate to airmen. To readers outside the Service the meaning of these words might be obscure, and it is for them that the following glossary is intended; otherwise it would have been necessary to sprinkle pages with asterisks, indicating footnotes, throughout the book.

GLOSSARY OF TERMS

Air Commode: Air Commodore.
Scrambled eggs: Gold braid or oak leaves on the peak of the Service caps of Group Captains and above. Hence also Brass-hat.
A.O.C.: Air Officer Commanding.
Wimpey: Wellington bomber.
Gen.: Information.
Get weaving/Get cracking/Get mobile: Get going. Buck up.
Flap: Excitement. Something doing.
Ammo: Ammunition.
Gone for a Burton: Killed.
Freeze to the stick: To be pretrified with fear.
Perim.: The perimeter track, tarmac or concrete, that runs round the boundary of an airfield.
Browned off: Bored.
Jinked: To jink—to turn sharply.
Prang: To destroy, or damage.
Crumper: A bad crash.
A slice of cake: It's easy—an easy operation.
Blood wagon: Ambulance.
Zero: A type of Japanese fighter.
Ginning-up: To gin up—to take hard liquor.
Ropey: Not good. Doubtful. Unpleasant.
Buttoned up: Finished. Finally concluded.

OUTWARD BOUND

WITH the serene dignity of a monarch bestowing a favour, His Majesty's Flying-boat *Capricorn* kissed the turquoise water of the marine aircraft base at Calafrana, Malta, and in a surge of creamy foam came to rest by her mooring buoy, setting numerous smaller craft bobbing and curtsying in a gentle swell that was soon to die on the concrete slipways. Through the sparkling atmosphere of the Mediterranean dawn every detail of the rockbound coast stood revealed with a clarity unknown in northern isles.

In the cabin, Squadron Leader Bigglesworth, more commonly known to his friends (and, perhaps, his enemies) as 'Biggles', yawned as he stood up and reached for the haversack containing his small-kit that rested on the luggage rack above his seat.

'I've had a nice sleep,' he announced inconsequently, for the benefit of the several officers of his squadron who were pulling on shoes, fastening tunics, and the like, preparatory to disembarking.

It was the same little band of hard-hitting warriors that had fought under him during the Battle of Britain, in the Western Desert, and elsewhere, and more than one carried scars as perpetual souvenirs of these theatres of war. That none had been killed was, admittedly, a matter for wonder. There were some who ascribed this to astonishing good fortune; others, to leadership which combined caution with courage. Other reasons put forward were superb flying, straight shooting, and close co-operation—which is another way of saying that sort of comradeship which puts the team before self. The truth was probably to be found in a combination of all these attributes.

There were the three flight commanders: Algy Lacey, fair and freckled; Lord 'Bertie' Lissie, effeminate in face and manner, for ever polishing an eyeglass for no reason that anyone could discover; and Angus Mackail, twelve stone of brawn and brain, with heather in his brogue and an old regimental glengarry on his head. All wore the purple and white ribbon of the D.F.C.

The rest were flying officers; like the flight-lieutenants they were all long overdue for promotion, but as this would have meant leaving the squadron (wherein there was no establishment for senior ranks, and consequently no chance of advancement) they had forgone promotion to remain in the same mess. There was 'Ginger' Hebblethwaite, a waif who had attached himself to Biggles and Algy before the war, and who had almost forgotten the slum in which he had been born; 'Tex' O'Hara, a product of the wide open spaces of Texas, U.S.A.; 'Taffy' Hughes, whose paternal ancestor may have been one of those Welsh knifemen that helped the Black Prince to make a name for valour; 'Tug' Carrington, a Cockney and proud of it, handy with his 'dukes,' hating all aggressors (and Nazis in particular) with a passion that sometimes startled the others; Henry Harcourt, a thin, pale, thoughtful-eyed Oxford undergraduate, who really loathed war yet had learned how to fight; and 'Ferocity' Ferris, who, born in a back street of Liverpool, had got his commission, not by accident (as he sometimes said) but by sheer flying ability.

This strange assortment of humanity, which could only have been drawn together by the vortex of war, formed Number 666 (Fighter) Squadron, R.A.F. More usually it was referred to in places where airmen meet as 'Biggles' Squadron.' And this was the literal truth, for on the formation of the unit, to Biggles had been sent—with his knowledge, of course—pilots of peculiar temperament, men with only two things in common, utter fearlessness and a disinclination to submit to discipline—two traits that often go together. Nevertheless, by example, by the force of his own personality, and by a queer sort of discipline which appeared to be lax, but was, in fact, rigid, Biggles had moulded them into a team with a reputation that was as well known to the enemy as to the Air Ministry. The result was a third common factor—loyalty; loyalty to the service, to the team, and above all, to their leader.

'There's a cutter coming out, presumably to take us ashore,' observed Algy, from a seat that commanded a view of the port. 'Now we shall know what it's all about. I must confess to some curiosity as to the whys and wherefores of this sudden rush to Malta.'

'It isn't customary for an Air Commode to turn out to meet new arrivals,' remarked Ginger. 'There's an Air Commodore in the stern of that cutter—I can see his scrambled eggs from here.'

'Maybe it's a new regulation. Welcome to your new home, gentlemen, and all that sort of thing—if you see what I mean?' suggested Bertie, brightly.

A minute later the Air Commodore stepped aboard. He went straight to Biggles, who by this time was looking a trifle surprised at this unusual reception.

' 'Morning, Bigglesworth,' greeted the Air Commodore.

' 'Morning, sir,' answered Biggles.

'Everything all right?'

'Why not?' queried Biggles.

'Oh, I don't know,' returned the Air Commodore. 'The Higher Command seems to be particularly concerned about you. You'll find breakfast ready in the mess. Better not waste any time—you've only got an hour.'

The puzzled expression on Biggles' face deepened. 'An hour for what, sir?'

'To stretch your legs, I suppose.'

'But I don't quite understand,' murmured Biggles. 'I was ordered to bring my squadron here. Naturally, I assumed it was for duty on the island.'

'I don't know anything about that,' returned the Air Commodore. 'My orders—by signal received last night—were to give you breakfast and push you along to Alexandria. The aircraft leaves the water in an hour. My tender will take you ashore. You might as well leave your kit where it is.'

'Very good, sir.'

The Air Commodore walked forward to speak to the pilot.

'Well, stiffen me rigid!' exclaimed Ginger softly. 'What do you make of that?'

Biggles shrugged. 'I don't make anything of it. We've got our orders. Alex it is, apparently. Let's go ashore for a shower and a rasher of bacon.'

Eight hours later the *Capricorn* touched down in the sweeping bay of Alexandria. Biggles stood up and reached for his haversack.

'Just a minute,' said Ginger. 'There's another brass-hat in that cutter coming out from station headquarters.'

Biggles looked through the window. 'You're right,' he confirmed. 'It looks as though the Near East is littered with Air Commodores. Unless I'm mistaken that's Buster Brownlow. He's a good scout. He commanded Ten Group in the Battle of Britain.'

The Air Commodore came aboard.

'Hello, Biggles!' he greeted. 'Get cracking—you've only got an hour.'

Biggles started. 'What, *again?*'

The Air Commodore raised his eyebrows. 'What do you mean—again?'

Biggles laughed shortly. 'Well, last night, out of the blue, I got an order instructing me to hand over my equipment and take the squadron by road to Pembroke Dock, where the *Capricorn* was waiting to take us to Malta. We made our landfall at dawn, after a comfortable trip. The A.O.C., Malta, pushed us along here. Now you're telling us——'

'That you're not stopping. Quite right. There's a Wimpey on the tarmac waiting to take you to Baghdad, so you'd better get ashore.'

'Do you happen to know what this is all about?' questioned Biggles curiously.

'I know no more than you,' answered the Air Commodore, and returned to the motor-boat.

'Join the Air Force and see the world,' murmured Ferocity Ferris, with bitter sarcasm.

'That's it. The service is living up to its jolly old reputation, what?' remarked Bertie.

The sun was setting behind the golden domes of Khadamain,

the most conspicuous landmark in the ancient city of the Caliphs, when the Wellington rumbled to a standstill on the dusty surface of Hinaidi airfield, Baghdad.

Biggles stood up. 'Now maybe we shall get the gen on this circus,' he asserted.

The cabin door was opened and an officer wearing the badges of rank of a Group Captain looked in. 'Get weaving, you fellows,' he called breezily. 'A head wind has put you ten minutes behind schedule. You're moving off in fifty minutes. Leave you kit where it is and stride along to the mess for dinner.'

Biggles frowned. 'What is this—a joke?'

'Joke?' The Group Captain seemed surprised. 'Not as far as I know. What gave you that quaint idea?'

'Only that it's customary for officers to know where they're going,' answered Biggles. 'This morning we were in Malta.'

'Well, by tomorrow morning you'll be in India,' returned the Group Captain. 'My orders are to push you along to Karachi. Someone may tell you why when you get there. See you presently.'

Biggles looked over his shoulder at the officers who, with their kit, filled the cabin. 'You heard that?' he queried helplessly. 'We're on our way to India. The Air Ministry, having decided that we need a rest, is giving us a busman's holiday. If this goes on much longer we shall meet ourselves coming back.'

'I don't get it,' muttered Tex.

'Presumably none of us is supposed to get it,' replied Biggles. 'No doubt we shall though, eventually, if we keep on long enough.'

The stars were paling in the sky when, the following morning, the aircraft landed at Drigh Road airfield, Karachi.

'This, I should say, is it,' said Tug confidently.

'I wouldn't bet on it,' murmured Henry Harcourt, moodily.

The pilots stepped down. As they stretched their cramped limbs two jeeps came tearing across the sun-parched earth. After they had skidded to a stop a Wing Commander alighted.

''Morning Biggles,' he greeted. 'Get your fellows aboard and I'll run you to the mess. Coffee is waiting. You haven't long——'

'Okay, okay, I know,' broke in Biggles impatiently. 'We've only got an hour, then you're pushing us along to—where it it this time?'

'Dum Dum. Our best Liberator is waiting to take you. Say thank you.'

'Thank you my foot,' snapped Biggles. 'We've been careering round the globe for forty-eight hours. I'm getting dizzy.'

'I thought Dum Dum was a kind of bullet, look you,' grunted Taffy.

'So it is,' answered Biggles. 'It also happens to be an airfield about two miles from Calcutta, on the other side of India. They say that in the old days the first dum-dum bullets were made there. I could use some, right now. Let's go. Even if we're condemned to chase the rainbow we might as well eat.'

It was late in the afternoon when the Liberator landed its load of pilots at Calcutta. Biggles was first out, fully prepared to see a duty officer with a fresh movement order in his hand. Instead, his eyes fell on the last man he expected to see. It was Air Commodore Raymond, of Air Intelligence, who, as far as he knew, seldom left the Air Ministry.

'Hello,' greeted the Air Commodore with an apologetic smile.

Biggles shook his head sadly. 'I should have guessed it,' he said wearily. 'Was all this rushing from here to there really necessary?'

'You can decide that for yourself, after we've had a chat,' replied the Air Commodore seriously. 'Do you want a rest, or shall we get down to things right away?'

'Is the whole squadron included in that invitation?'

'No. I'd rather talk to you alone in the first place. You can tell your fellows about it later on—in fact, you'll have to. But the Air Office Commanding, India, and the G.O.C. land forces, are here, waiting to have a word with you. That'll give you an idea of the importance of the matter that caused you to be rushed out.'

'All right, sir. In that case we'd better get down to brass tacks right away. What about my officers?'

'They can go and get settled in their new quarters. Everything is arranged. You've got your own mess.'

'Then this really *is* the end of the trail?'

'I don't want to seem depressing, but it's likely to be the end of the trail in every sense of the word. We're up against it, Bigglesworth, and when *I* say that you can guess it's pretty bad.'

'So you send for me,' said Biggles plaintively. 'We were supposed to be due for a rest.'

'I didn't send for you,' denied the Air Commodore. 'The A.O.C. fixed that with the Ministry. Admittedly, I mentioned your name. See what comes of having a reputation. Matter of fact, I wasn't pleased myself at being hauled out here—I've been here three days.'

Biggles turned to speak to Algy. 'Take over,' he ordered. 'I'll join you later.'

Without speaking, the Air Commodore led the way to station headquarters, where, in an inner office, the two generals were waiting.

'Sorry to rush you about like this, Bigglesworth, but there were reasons,' explained the Air Officer, holding out his hand.

Biggles nodded. 'I've been in the service long enough to know that things don't happen without a reason, sir,' he said simply.

'We brought you out here as we did, for two reasons. The first was speed, and the second, security. The fewer people who know you are here, the better. The Japanese High Command knows all about you, so if they learned that you were on the way out they'd put two and two together.' A note of bitterness crept into the Air Marshal's voice. 'They might even have prevented your arrival. Of course they are bound to find out sooner or later, but by that time you'll be on the job—I hope. Take a pew.' The A.O.C. sat down, mopping perspiration from his forehead with a large handkerchief, for the air was heavy and hot. 'Raymond, I think you'd better tell the story,' he suggested.

WITH cigarettes lighted the four officers sat at a table that was entirely covered by a map of Eastern Asia.

'In this war of wars,' began the Air Commodore, looking at Biggles, 'from time to time one side or the other is suddenly confronted by a new weapon, or device, which, for a while at any rate, seems to defy counter measures. The result is a temporary advantage for the side employing the instrument. Hitler's magnetic and acoustic mines were typical examples. We have given *him* some hard nuts to crack, too. After a while, of course, the mystery is solved, but while it persists the Higher Command gets little sleep. Here, in our war against Japan, we have bumped into something that is not only lifting our casualties to an alarming degree, but is affecting the morale of pilots and air crews and, indirectly, the troops on the ground in the areas where we are unable to provide adequate air cover.'

'That's unusual,' murmured Biggles.

'Unusual but understandable, as I think you will presently agree,' resumed the Air Commodore. 'British fighting forces are rarely perturbed by odds against them, or any new method of waging war, provided they know what they are fighting against: but when a man is suddenly confronted by the unknown, by something that kills without revealing itself—well, he is to be pardoned if his nerves begin to suffer. As you know, as well as I do, in such circumstances weak characters try to find Dutch courage by ginning-up, drinking more liquor than they can carry; already we have had one or two bad cases. To put the matter bluntly, we have run into something very nasty, and to make matters worse, we haven't the remotest idea of what it is. Of course, the Oriental mind works on different lines from ours, but not even our Eastern experts can hazard a guess as to what is going on. And now, before we go any farther, I'll tell you what *is* going on.' The Air Commodore stubbed his cigarette.

'The trouble first occurred on our air route between India

and Chungking, in China,' he continued. 'You've probably heard something about that particular line of communication. When the Japs crashed into Burma, and put the Burma Road out of commission, we had to find a new way of getting war material to China. Our answer was a new life-line up the Himalayas to Tibet, and across the Tibetan plateau to China. At first coolies did the work, manhandling the stuff on their backs. But it was slow. To make a long story short we developed an air service, one that kept clear of the northern extremity of Burma, and possible Japanese interference. For a time all went well; then for some unaccountable reason, machines failed to get through. Not all of them. Occasionally one went through on schedule, and this only deepened the mystery. Perhaps I had better make that point clear. Naturally, when our machines first started to disappear, we assumed that the Japs had got wind of the route and had established an advanced base from which fighters could operate. And that may in fact be the case. But the astonishing thing is, pilots who *have* got through have invariably reported a clear run. They didn't see a single enemy machine the whole way. That's hard to explain. If the Japs know of the route, and are attacking it, it seems extraordinary that some machines should be allowed to pass unmolested. In a nutshell, our machines either got through untouched, or they didn't get through at all. There was nothing in between. What I am trying to make clear is, the machines that failed, disappeared utterly. There has not been a single case of a pilot fighting his way through. In the ordinary course of events one would expect machines to arrive at their destination badly shot up, to report that they had been attacked by enemy fighters. But that has not happened. As I say, once in a while a pilot makes an uneventful flight. The rest just vanish.'

'That certainly is odd,' murmured Biggles. 'What is the position on the route now?'

'Between ourselves, we are temporarily suspending oper-ations. We must. The surviving pilots are getting the jitters, and the commanding officer is jibbing at sending men to almost certain death. In the last few days a number of pilots have volunteered to rush through with some badly needed medical stores. None of them arrived. We can't go on like that.'

'But surely,' interposed Biggles, 'surely with radio a pilot could report the menace the moment it appeared? Whatever the trouble was, he would have warning of it, if only for a few seconds—time enough to flash a signal.'

The Air Commodore nodded. 'I was waiting for you to say that. You've put a finger on the most inexplicable part of the whole business. No such message has ever been received. In every case the radio has gone dead on us. We once sent a machine out with instructions to report to base every five minutes.'

'What happened?'

'The signals came through like clockwork for an hour. Then they just faded out.'

'Good Lord!' Biggles looked amazed. 'No wonder your pilots are getting jumpy. Tell me this. Does the interference apply to both ends of the route?'

'That's another astonishing thing. It doesn't. No machine has ever had the slightest difficulty in getting through from China to India. It's the India-China service that has been cracked up.'

'That certainly is a poser,' muttered Biggles, slowly. 'It doesn't seem to make sense. Have you tried operating at night?'

'We have,' asserted the Air Commodore. 'That was the first counter-measure we tried. It made no difference. Machines disappeared just as regularly as by day.'

Biggles shook his head. 'I don't wonder you're in a flap.'

'But just a minute,' went on the Air Commodore. 'There is worse to come. The same rot has now set in elsewhere, in the regular service squadrons. At the moment four stations are reporting abnormally high casualties without being able to offer the slightest explanation. In each case the casualty is a complete disappearance. The second place to suffer was right here, at Dum Dum. The third was Trichinoply, Madras, half-way down the coast, and the fourth, Ceylon, at the tip of the peninsula.'

'From which we may suppose that the Japs, perceiving that they are on a winner, are developing the thing, whatever it is,' put in Biggles grimly.

'Precisely,' interposed the Air Marshal dryly. 'I need hardly point out that if it goes on we soon shan't have any Air Force left in this part of the world. We're relying on you to get to the bottom of it.'

Biggles looked startled. 'But if your technical experts have failed, sir, what do you think I can do about it?'

The Air Marshal shrugged. 'I haven't the remotest idea. We're floored, stumped. Do what you can.'

'But that's all very well, sir,' protested Biggles. 'As far as I can see, to send my pilots out looking for nobody-knows-what, would merely be to send them for a Burton to no useful purpose.'

'You're our last hope, Bigglesworth,' said the Air Commodore, with something like despair in his voice. 'We can't just suspend air operations—we might as well pack up altogether as do that.'

'If you go on losing pilots and machines at the rate you are evidently losing them it will come to the same thing in the end.'

The Air Marshal stepped in again. 'See what you can do, Bigglesworth. You can have *carte blanche*, a freelance commission, have what equipment you like, do what you like, go where you like—*but this thing has got to be stopped*.'

Biggles tapped a cigarette on the back of his hand. 'Very well, sir. I don't mind going out myself, but it isn't going to be very nice to have to ask my boys to virtually commit suicide. They'll go if I tell them to go, but I'd like you to know how I feel about it. This business of watching one's officers go one by one——'

'That's just how four other station commanders are feeling at this very moment, Bigglesworth,' broke in the Air Commodore wearily.

Biggles pulled forward a scribbling-pad, and picked up a pencil. For a little while he made meaningless marks. Then he asked: 'What about altitude? Does that make any difference?'

'None,' answered the Air Commodore. 'In desperation we tried sending machines to their ceiling before leaving the airfield. They disappeared just the same.'

'I see. What is the longest period you have maintained radio contact with an aircraft that subsequently disappeared?'

'Four hours. That was on the Chungking run. It's a thousand miles.'

'No intermediate landing-ground?'

'None.'

'And what is the shortest period before you lost touch with a machine?'

'An hour.'

Biggles shrugged. 'The thing becomes uncanny. The time interval between one and four hours, translated to distance, is six or seven hundred miles. How can one even start looking for a thing that can strike over such an enormous area? You say that all the machines which disappeared, vanished into the blue. Am I to understand that not one of these crashes has ever been found?'

'That, unfortunately is so,' answered the Air Commodore. 'You've flown over the Himalayas, and the Burmese jungle, so you know what it's like. It would be easier to find a pin in a cornfield.'

'These crashes, then, always occur over enemy-occupied country?'

'Either that or over the sea. From here we operate over Burma. From Madras and Ceylon most of the flying is done over the Indian Ocean.'

'There has never been an unexplainable crash in India itself?'

'There have been one or two crashes—not more than one would expect in the ordinary course of flying routine. These crashes were, of course, examined—but you know what such a crash looks like?'

'No unusual features emerged at the courts of inquiry?'

'None. In each case the pilot was killed, so he couldn't tell us anything, even if there was something to tell. There was a crash on this aerodrome two days ago. The pilot tried hard to say something before he died—but there, that could happen anyway.'

'Had he been over enemy territory?'

'Yes.'

'What about the machine?'

'There was nothing wrong with it, as far as could be ascertained.'

'How long had this pilot been in the air?'

'About twenty minutes. He left a formation and turned back.'

'Why?'

'We don't know. There was nothing very remarkable about that. Machines occasionally turn back for one reason or another.'

'What I'm trying to get at is this,' explained Biggles. 'Has there ever been an instance of an aircraft, or a pilot, affected by the new weapon, crashing on our side of the lines?'

'Not as far as we know—unless the pilot I just mentioned was a case. That seems most unlikely though, as he was one of a formation of ten. Had he been attacked, surely the others would have been attacked, too.'

'Tell me about this particular show,' invited Biggles.

'It was the last big raid we attempted from this airfield,' replied the Air Commodore. 'The rot had already set in, you understand, so the pilots and air crews taking part were keyed up for trouble. Actually, there are four squadrons here, not counting yours; two bomber squadrons and two fighter. Incidentally, you have been posted here as a communication squadron. Two days ago, one of the bomber squadrons took off soon after dawn with every machine it could raise—ten Blenheims—for a raid on the enemy-occupied airfield at Akyab. The distance to the objective, by the direct route across the Bay of Bengal, is about four hundred miles. Actually, the raid was timed for dawn, but there was still some mist about so the take-off was postponed till it cleared.'

'And you say the pilots were aware of the mysterious weapon?'

'Yes. All personnel were very much on the alert.'

'Go on, sir.'

'About twenty minutes after the take-off one of the Blenheims was seen coming back. It was fairly low, gliding, in a manner which might be described as unsteady.'

'Which implies that the pilot was having trouble?'

'Yes—but then, had he not been in trouble he would not have left the formation.'

'Did he speak over the radio?'

'No.'

'So you have no idea what the trouble was?'

'Not the remotest. Shortly after passing over the boundary of the airfield the aircraft stalled, and crashed, with what result I have already told you. At the Court of Inquiry, which went into the evidence very carefully, it was decided that such an accident could occur quite apart from any secret weapon. In fact, it was that sort of accident that could occur, and does occur, regularly.'

'What was the name of this pilot?'

'Cratton.'

Biggles made a note. 'What happened to the rest of the formation?'

'The flight ended in disaster,' said the Air Commodore heavily. 'An hour after taking off, one of the nine remaining machines, before enemy opposition was encountered, without warning went into a spin and fell into the sea. Just before reaching the objective, in precisely the same conditions, another machine went down. One was shot down in combat over the target area. The six survivors dropped their bombs and turned for home. On the return journey four more went down at irregular intervals. Only two got back safely, both perfectly all right beyond being shaken by the tragedy of their comrades, and the strain of flying with the same fate impending.'

'There was absolutely nothing wrong with them physically?'

'Nothing.'

'And what about the machines?'

'They were all right, too.'

'And the surviving pilots could offer no explanation as to why the others went down?'

'None. The story was the same in every case. The stricken machine flew badly for a moment or two and then appeared to fall out of control. Sometimes the engines were cut, sometimes the machines hit the water with the motors running.'

Biggles lit a fresh cigarette. 'I understand what you mean about pilots becoming unnerved. Anyone would freeze to the stick with that sort of thing going on round him. As far as a solution to the mystery is concerned, inevitably one thinks of death rays, so called, which I believe have often been used in fiction, but never in fact. Scientists say that such a ray is not possible—but then, scientists are not always right.'

'You think there may be something in the death ray idea, then?' suggested the Air Marshal. 'We've considered it, of course.'

'Frankly, no,' replied Biggles. 'And I'll tell you why. If such a device was being used one would suppose that once they were within the sphere of influence all machines would be affected. In a daylight raid most aircraft keep a tight formation. I mean, if the thing could strike down one machine surely it would be able to strike down the others? We can hardly suppose that some machines are vulnerable while others are not. How was it that two came back? They were in all respects identical with those that fell. Then again, why the interval of time between the falling out of the last machines?'

The Air Marshal spoke. 'Our experts assert positively that the death ray is not yet a practical proposition, but there may be a beam device which could affect the electrical installation of an aero engine. For want of any other explanation we are inclined to accept that view.'

'I'm not,' returned Biggles bluntly.

'Why not?'

'In the first place, because the failure of its power unit doesn't necessarily cause an aircraft to go down out of control. The pilot would automatically put the machine into a glide, and while the machine was gliding he would have ample time to send out a signal. Then again, air crews wear parachutes. If the aircraft was vitally affected the men in it would bale out. To me it looks more as if machines are being sabotaged on the ground.'

'You can rule out sabotage,' said the Air Commodore. 'Those Blenheims were inspected and tested down to the last detail before they left the ground. With all this going on you can be quite sure that close watch is kept on equipment.'

Biggles thought for a moment. 'The one incontestable fact is that something is going wrong. If the trouble isn't caused in the air, then it must start on the ground. Against trouble in the air is the absence of anything like structural failure, which would certainly be spotted by the other machines in the formation. I still think it is extraordinary that none of these crews baled out, or tried to bale out.'

'It isn't always easy to abandon an aircraft that is falling out of control,' remarked the Air Commodore.

'And in the case of the Blenheims the Bay of Bengal was underneath, don't forget,' put in the Air Marshal. 'The bay is infested with sharks.'

'That may have been the reason,' agreed Biggles. 'For all we know, the crews of some of the machines that were lost on the China route *may* have baled out. Even if they got down alive, I imagine they'd find it impossible to get back on foot.'

There was another short silence. All eyes were on Biggle's face as he pondered the problem.

'Tell me,' he went on presently, 'was there any rule about the number of pilots in these lost machines? I mean, has disaster ever overtaken a machine with two pilots in the cabin?'

The Air Commodore answered. 'I'm not quite sure about that. Out here we have to be economical with pilots, so in most cases only one pilot was on board; but I believe there was one case—it was on the China run—when two pilots were lost together.'

Again silence fell. Biggles chewed a matchstalk reflectively. Outside, the brief tropic twilight was passing, but the sultry heat persisted. The Air Commodore switched on a light. A large white moth flew in through the open window and fluttered round the globe with a faint rustling sound as its wings beat with futile effort against the glass.

'Any more questions, Bigglesworth?' asked the Air Marshal anxiously.

Biggles looked up. 'No, sir.' He smiled wanly. 'You've given me plenty to think about. I'd like to sleep on it.'

'Then you'll—er—take the matter in hand?'

'I'll do my best with it, sir.'

'It's urgent—desperately urgent.'

'That's about the only aspect of this affair that's really obvious, sir,' answered Biggles. He got up. 'I'll go now and have a word with my officers. Between us we may get on the scent of the thing. If we do I'll report to the Air Commodore. I take it that no one on the station will be told the real reason why we have come here?'

'I'll see to that,' promised the Air Commodore. 'Even the station commander, Group Captain Boyle, supposes you to be an ordinary communication squadron, sent out here for special duty.'

'He's not likely to interfere with us?'

'No. I've told him that you will come directly under the Higher Command for orders. The presence here of the A.O.C. will confirm that.'

'Very good, sir. By the way, are you staying on here?'

'For the time being, at any rate,' answered Air Commodore Raymond. 'You can regard me as a sort of liaison officer between you and the Air Officer Commanding. Call on me for anything you need.'

Biggles saluted and withdrew. Deep in thought, and not a little worried, he made his way along the silent tarmac to the quarters that had been allocated to the squadron.

3

BIGGLES BRIEFS HIMSELF

THE buzz of conversation died abruptly as Biggles walked into the ante-room and closed the door behind him. Only the radio went on, unheeded, relaying music from London. A short, stoutish, olive-skinned, middle-aged man, dressed in white duck trousers and mess-jacket, wearing a beaming smile, was standing by a low table on which rested a brass tray bearing a coffee-pot and cups.

Biggles called to him. 'Hi!, you; that'll do,' he said curtly.

'Plenty coffee, sahib. You likee some, mebbe?' answered the steward.

'When I want anything I'll let you know,' returned Biggles. 'Pack up now.'

'Very good, sahib.' Still beaming, the steward picked up his tray and departed.

Biggles looked at Algy. 'Who's that?'

'Lal Din.'

'Who's he?'

'One of the waiters from the canteen. He's all right.'

'I don't doubt it,' replied Biggles. 'But in the East it's better not to talk in front of staff. They gossip.' He indicated the radio with a thumb. 'Turn that thing off, somebody.'

Angus complied.

'What's cooking, chief?' asked Tex eagerly.

'A dish with a nasty smell and a worse flavour,' replied Biggles quiety. 'Gather round, everybody, and I'll tell you about it. By the way, has anybody been out on the station?'

Several voices answered. 'I had a look round to see what machines we had on charge,' said Algy. 'Some of the others took a stroll to get their bearings.'

'In that case you may have heard something?' suggested Biggles.

'I didn't hear anything, but there's a sort of grey atmosphere in the central mess,' put in Ginger. 'There were only a few chaps there, but they looked at me as if I were something blown in off a dunghill.'

'I ran into Johnny Crisp on the perim,' said Algy. 'You remember him—he picked up two bars to his D.F.C. in Wilks' squadron? He's a flight-loot in 818 Squadron now. He told me a little. Ginger is right about the atmosphere. It's sort of—brittle, as if everyone was waiting for an unexploded bomb to go off. Johnny has aged ten years since I last saw him, a few months ago.'

Biggles nodded. 'I'm not surprised. I'll tell you why.'

He devoted the next twenty minutes to a résumé of the sinister story he had just gathered at headquarters. No one interrupted. All eyes were on his face. When he concluded, still no one spoke.

'Well, has nobody anything to say?' queried Biggles.

'What is there to say?' asked Ginger.

'Sure, I guess you're right, at that,' put in Tex, blowing a cloud of cigarette smoke at the ceiling. 'Looks like we've come a helluva long way to find trouble. So what?'

'Has anybody an idea about this thing?' demanded Biggles. No one answered.

'Stiffen the crows!' exclaimed Biggles. 'You are a bright lot. Do I have to do all the thinking?'

'What's the use of us trying to work it out if you can't?' murmured Tug.

'What do you think about it yourself, old boy?' asked Bertie.

'Frankly, I can't even begin to think,' admitted Biggles. 'We have one single fact to work on. Something is affecting our machines, or the pilots. We don't even know which. That's the first thing we've got to find out.'

'You tell us how, and we'll get right on with it,' asserted Ferocity.

'That would be easier if I knew what we were looking for,' went on Biggles. 'One thing is certain. We shan't find it by sitting here. We've got to go out—where the others went. That will mean . . . casualties. And that's putting it nicely. We aren't the only suicide squadron on the station, but that doesn't make it any easier from my point of view. I've never yet asked a man to do a show I wouldn't do myself, so I shall make a start. After that it will be a job for volunteers. If anyone would like to fall out, he may. Now's the time.'

Nobody moved.

Biggles glanced round. 'Okay, if that's how you feel about it,' he said softly. 'Now you know what's likely to happen, let's get down to it. I shall make a start in the morning by going up to Jangpur, the Indian terminus of the China run, to have a look round. I am planning to take an aircraft over the course.'

'You mean—go to Chungking?' cried Algy.

'Yes.'

'But that's daft, mon,' protested Angus. 'How can ye find a thing when ye dinna ken what ye're looking for?'

'Has anyone an alternative suggestion?'

There was a chorus of voices offering to go out, but Biggles silenced them with a gesture. 'Don't all talk at once, and don't let's have any argument about who is going out. You'll all get your turns. I shall do the first show. That's settled. If I don't come back Algy will take over. If he fades out, too, the others will carry on in order of seniority until the thing is found, or until there is no one left to look for it. That's all quite simple. What machines have we got, Algy?'

'A mixed bunch,' was the reply. 'It looks as if Raymond has got together anything he thought might be useful. There's a Wimpey, a Beaufighter, a Mosquito, three Hurricanes, three Spits and a Typhoon. If you've made up your mind to go out why not take the Beau, and have somebody else with you? Then, if anything went wrong, the second pilot could bring the aircraft home.'

'From what I understand, flying two pilots together is just an easy way of doubling the rate of casualties. Two go instead of one. Whether the new weapon affects the men or the machine, the whole outfit goes west.'

'That doesn't entirely fit in with what Johnny Crisp told me,' declared Algy.

'What did he tell you?'

'Well, it seems that some fellows are either extraordinarily lucky, or else they—or their machines—are unaffected by the new weapon.'

'What do you mean by that, precisely?'

'Johnny tells me that he has made eleven sorties since the trouble started and has never seen or heard anything to alarm him. But he has seen others go down, seen them dropping like shot birds all round him—that's how he put it. He told me that what with this ropey spectacle, and expecting his own turn to come every minute, he froze to the stick, with fright. Once he was the only one of five to return. Another chap, a pilot officer named Scrimshaw, has been out nine times, and has got away with it.'

Biggles regarded Algy with a mystified look in his eyes. 'That certainly is interesting,' he said slowly. 'What squadrons are these chaps in?'

'They're both in 818, flying Hurrybombers. There are only five of them left in the squadron, although they have had replacements several times. Some chaps went west on their first show.'

'I suppose it must be luck, but it seems queer,' muttered Biggles. 'There can't be anything unusual about their machines—they're all standardised.'

'They haven't always flown the same machines, anyway,' volunteered Algy.

'Then obviously we can't put their luck down to their equipment. Yet the fellows themselves must be flesh and blood, like other men. It *must* be luck. I don't see how it can be anything else.'

'If this new weapon is so hot, why haven't the Japs handed it on to their partners, the Nazis?' inquired Henry Harcourt.

'Ask me something easier,' returned Biggles. 'All the same, Henry, I think you've got something there. So far the trouble is localised in the East. One would suppose that the Japs would pass it on to the Nazis. All I can say is, God help us if they do.'

'Maybe the Japs don't trust the Nazis,' contributed Ferocity, practically. 'They may be windy of having the thing turned on them, if ever they fell out with their partners.'

'That may be the answer,' acknowledged Biggles.

'How about gas?' suggested Henry. 'Have you thought of that?'

'It passed through my mind,' averred Biggles. 'But there are several arguments against it. The first is, you can only get gas in quantity to a great height, by carrying it, or shooting it up, and nobody has seen any sort of vehicle or missile capable of doing that. Then again, what about formations? If a trail of gas *could* be laid across the sky, why are some pilots affected and not others? And how are we going to account for the irregular intervals of time between the machines falling out? I can't believe that the Japs could plant gas all over the place, at different altitudes, without being spotted. Finally, if gas were used, what is there to prevent the Japs themselves from flying into it, bearing in mind that the locality would not be constant? The wind, up-currents and sinkers, would blow the stuff all over the place. Still, we'll bear the possibility in mind.'

'It was just an idea,' murmured Henry.

'Let's get back to the question of action,' suggested Biggles. 'We've got to find this hidden horror before we can do anything about it, and no doubt some of us will do that. Plenty of others have found it,' he added significantly, 'but unfortunately they couldn't get the information home. In other words, without mincing matters, it seems that the man who finds the thing, dies. Our problem is to find it and live—or live long enough to pass back the secret. It means going out, and I shall make a start, beginning in the area where the thing struck first—that is, on the Jangpur-Chungking route. The rest of you will stay here till I get back. That's an order. On no account will anyone go into the air; nor will anyone refer to the fact, either here or anywhere else, that we have been sent out specially to hunt this thing down. At all times you will pretend that we are what we are supposed to be, a communication squadron scheduled for co-operation with forces inside India. You needn't be idle. Give the machines a thorough overhaul. I shall go up to Jangpur in the Typhoon. Algy, I'd like you to get a list of all persons outside Air Force personnel who work on the station, or have permits to visit the airfield for any purpose whatsoever. There are certain to be a lot of men of the country, coloured men; there always are on Indian stations. For the benefit of those of you who haven't been to India before, we don't use the expression *natives*. It's discourteous. Raymond probably has such a list already made. That would be the first thing he'd do, I imagine, in checking up for possible saboteurs. If anyone asks where I've gone you can say I'm doing a test flight—which will be true enough. Now let's get some sleep.'

4

BIGGLES MAKES A WAGER

THE following morning, the first glow of dawn saw Biggles in the air, in the Typhoon, heading north for Jangpur, the Indian terminus of the China route. He had not far to go—a trifle more than a hundred miles. As he landed and taxied to the wooden office buildings he noted a general absence of movement, an atmosphere of inactivity. The duty officer, a pilot officer, came to meet him. His manner was respectful, but listless, as if his interest in everything about him was perfunctory. He told Biggles that the station commander, Squadron Leader Frayle, was in his office.

And there Biggles found him, looking as though he had not been to bed for a week. His eyes were heavy from want of sleep; his hair was untidy and his chin unshaven. The desk was a litter of dirty cups, plates, and glasses.

Biggles did not appear to notice this. 'Good morning,' he greeted cheerfully. 'My name's Bigglesworth.'

The squadron leader's eyes brightened. 'So you're Biggles? I've heard of you. Take a seat. Can I get you anything?'

'No, thanks,' answered Biggles. 'At this hour of the morning I work better on an empty stomach.' He pulled up a chair and lit a cigarette.

'What in the name of all that's unholy brought you to this God-forsaken, sun-blistered dustbin?' inquired Frayle curiously.

'I'm told you've had a spot of trouble here,' replied Biggles. 'I've been sent out from home to try to iron it out.'

'Go ahead,' invited Frayle bitterly. 'The airfield's yours— and you're welcome to it. I've lost four officers and four machines in four days—the last four to go out, in fact. That should encourage you to keep your feet on something more solid than the floor of a fuselage. I've three officers left out of eighteen. Not bad going, eh?'

'I heard the position was pretty grey,' said Biggles

sympathetically.

'Grey! It's blacker than a black-out.' Frayle's voice took on a quality of bitter resentment. 'Grey, they call it. It's hell, that's what it is. Can you imagine what it's been like for me, to sit here day after day sending out lads who I know I shall never see again?'

'I can imagine it,' answered Biggles quietly.

'There's another one going this morning,' went on Frayle. 'I didn't order him to go. Not me. I've finished picking the roster with a pin to decide who was to be the next man to die. He just told me he was going. There's a load of medical stores urgently needed in Chungking. Tomorrow I shall be down to two pilots.'

'You haven't tried doing the run yourself?'

'No. As I feel that would suit me fine. My orders are to stay on the carpet. They say my job is on the station. Well, tomorrow I'm going, anyway, orders or no orders. I can't stand any more of this.'

'It's no use talking that way, Frayle,' said Biggles softly. 'You know you can't do that.'

'But I—I——' Frayle seemed to choke. He buried his face in his hands.

'Here, take it easy,' said Biggles gently. 'I know how you feel, but it's no use letting the thing get you down like this. Get a grip on yourself. Can't you see that by cracking up you're only helping the enemy? What about this lad—has he gone off yet?'

'No, they're loading up the machine.'

'Good. Stop him.'

Frayle looked up. 'But this stuff is supposed to go through.'

I know. Never mind. Stop him.'

'But what shall I tell headquarters?'

'You needn't tell them anything. I'll take the stuff.'

'*You'll* take it?'

'Yes.'

'You're out of your mind.'

Biggles smiled. 'You may be right, but I'll take this stuff to Chungking just the same. Send for the lad who was going. What's his name?'

'Bargent. He's a flying officer—a South African. You'll find him as amiable as a rhino that's been shot in the bottom with a charge of buckshot.'

'I'll have a word with him. You snatch a bath, treat your face to a razor blade, and have something to eat; you'll feel better. I'll fix things while you're doing it.'

Frayle gave the necessary order. Presently Bargent came.

'Now what's boiling?' he demanded in a hard voice.

'You're not doing this show,' said Biggles.

'And who says so?' questioned Bargent hotly.

'I say so,' replied Biggles evenly.

Bargent flung his cap on the floor, which was to Biggles a clear indication of the state of his nerves.

'And if you start throwing your weight about with me, my lad, I'll put you under close arrest,' promised Biggles, in a voice that made the flying officer stare at him.

'But I *want* to go, sir,' said Bargent, in a different tone of voice.

Biggles thought for a minute. 'All right. You can come with me if you like.'

'With you?'

'That's what I said.'

The South African laughed shortly. 'Okay. The machine is all ready.'

Biggles turned to Frayle. 'How many machines have you got left?'

'Two, able to do the run.'

'What are they?'

'Wimpeys.'

'And one's loaded?'

'Yes.'

'Did that arrangement appear in last night's orders?'

'Yes.'

'In the ordinary way the other machine would stand in a shed all day?'

'Yes.'

'Have you a duplicate set of these medical stores?'

'We've a hundred tons, all overdue for delivery.'

'Where are they?'

'In store.'

'Locked up?'

'Yes.'

'Who's your storekeeper?'

'Corporal Jones.'

'That's fine,' declared Biggles. 'I'm going to try being unorthodox. For a start we're going to unload this loaded machine, and take every package to pieces. Then we'll take the machine to pieces.'

'You're wasting your time.'

'What do you mean?' asked Biggles quickly.

'We've tried that a dozen times. You suspect sabotage? So did we. The first action I took was what you propose doing now, supposing that someone was sticking a time bomb in the load. We've never found such a thing, or anything like it.'

Biggles thought for a little while. 'H'm. I was bound to try that,' he asserted. 'But if you've already done it there doesn't seem to be much point in repeating it, so we'll proceed with the second part of the programme. I want you to go and tell Corporal Jones, privately, to prepare a second load. Tell him to keep it out of sight. Swear him to secrecy. In a minute or two I'll bring the spare machine over and we'll load it ourselves.'

'What shall I do with the first load? The machine is waiting to go.'

'For the time being leave it just as it is. Put a guard over it.'

'This all seems a waste of time to me, but I'm willing to try anything,' said Frayle heavily.

'Then go and talk to Jones. Tell him to get a move on. Then I'd advise you to have a clean up. You may be sick, but it does no good to advertise it.'

Frayle went off.

Biggles turned to Bargent. 'You don't fancy your chance of coming back from this trip, do you?'

'Not much. Do you?'

'Yes. I think we've quite a good chance.'

'What leads you to think you are any different from anyone

else?' Bargent couldn't keep sarcasm out of his voice.

'I didn't say I was different. But I've done quite a lot of flying, and I've never yet seen in the air anything capable of knocking a machine down without showing itself. I doubt very much if there is such a thing. So far, anything I've seen I've been able to dodge. It may sound like conceit, but I fancy my chance of going on doing that.'

'Would you like to bet on it?'

Biggles hesitated, but only for a moment. 'I don't go in much for betting, but I'd risk a hundred cigarettes.'

'I'll take that,' declared Bargent. 'Just what is the bet?'

'The bet is, by lunch-time I shall be in Chungking, and back again here for dinner tonight.'

'You hope,' muttered Bargent. 'I'd say you're on a loser.'

Biggles laughed. 'Well, you can't win, anyway.'

Bargent started. 'Why not?'

'If I lose—that is, if we don't get back—I doubt if I shall be in a position to pay you and you'll be in no case to collect your winnings. We shall both be somewhere either on the mountains or in the jungle between here and China.'

'I'm nuts. I never thought of that,' said Bargent, grinning, and then laughing aloud.

'That's better,' remarked Biggles. 'While you can keep a sense of humour you've got a chance. Come on, let's go and get the Wimpey.'

Ignoring the machine that had been detailed, with its little crowd of loaders, they walked over to the hanger in which the spare machine was parked. Biggles climbed into the cockpit. 'You stay where you are,' he told Bargent. 'Walk beside me when I taxi over to the store. If anyone tries to get within ten yards of this machine throw something at him. If you let anyone touch you, my lad, you're not getting into this aircraft. I'm standing to lose more than a hundred cigarettes on this jaunt and I'm not taking any chances. Understand?'

'Okay.'

Biggles started the engines and taxied slowly through the glaring sunlight to the store shed. On the way, some of the native porters that had been working on the other machine came hurrying across, but Bargent waved his arm, and yelled to them to keep away. He picked up and hurled a stone at one man who came after the others had stopped. He retreated.

Frayle, in a bath wrap, appeared at the storehouse door.

'Is the stuff ready?' shouted Biggles.

'Yes, it's all here.'

'Help us to get it on board. Tell Jones to punch on the nose anybody who tries to get near us.'

'You do have some quaint ideas,' said Frayle, as he complied.

'Maybe that's why I'm here,' murmured Biggles.

In ten minutes the big machine was loaded to capacity with bundles of British and American stores, labelled CHUNG-KING.

'What about something to eat before you go?' suggested Frayle.

'No, thanks,' refused Biggles.

'It's a long trip.'

'We can manage.'

'Not even a last drink?' queried Bargent.

'Not even a last drink,' decided Biggles firmly. 'I make a point of doing one thing at a time, and the thing at the moment is to get this pantechnicon to China. Get aboard. So long, Frayle. I'm aiming to be back for tea.'

'I'll have it ready,' promised Frayle.

'Put a guard on my Typhoon. Don't let anyone touch it.'

'Okay.'

Before Bargent had properly settled himself in his seat Biggles had opened the throttle, and the big machine was bellowing across the airfield.

'Have you made this trip before?' asked Biggles, as he throttled back to a steady cruising speed of just over two hundred miles an hour.

'Four times.'

'You must be lucky.'

'Maybe so. But I reckoned it couldn't go on. No sense in riding your luck too hard.'

'I suppose that's why you were trying it on again today?' said Biggles smoothly.

'Pah! It had got to come sooner or later, and after seeing the others go, I thought the sooner the better.'

'Desperate fellow,' murmured Biggles. 'Well, we shall see. Keep your eyes skinned.'

'I suppose you realise that we're flying without gunners in the turrets?' said Bargent suddenly. 'That's asking for trouble, isn't it?'

'I have a feeling that we shan't need guns on this trip.'

'Why not?'

'Put it this way. Guns couldn't save the other crews. If guns can't stop this rot what point was there in bringing gunners? In the event of things going wrong we should only push up the casualty list. My gosh! That's pretty rough country below.' Biggles was looking below and ahead at a terrible yet magnificent panorama of mountain peaks that stretched across the course from horizon to horizon.

'It's like that pretty well all the way to China,' asserted Bargent. 'Where it isn't mountains, it's what the books call untamed primeval forest. Anyone going down in it wouldn't have a hope. They say it's unexplored.'

'Let's hope we shan't have to explore it,' returned Biggles. 'Let me know if you see anything queer, in the air or on the ground.'

After that the two pilots fell silent. The Wellington droned on, devouring space at a steady two hundred and twenty miles an hour. Mountains, groups and ranges and isolated peaks, many crowned with eternal snow, rolled away below. Valleys and depressions were choked with the sombre, everlasting forest.

'It's about time we were bumping into something,' said Bargent once, after looking at the watch. 'We must be half-way.'

'Begins to look as if this trip is going to cost you a hundred cigarettes, my lad,' said Biggles slyly, with a sidelong glance at his companion.

'If I don't lose more than that I shan't grumble,' murmured Bargent.

Two hours later the airport of Chungking came into view.

'That's it,' confirmed Bargent. 'What's the programme when we get there?'

'We'll sling this stuff overboard and start straight back,' replied Biggles.

'We're not stopping for lunch?'

'We're not stopping for anything.'

Bargent shook his head. 'You certainly are a queer bird,' he muttered.

'So I've been told. But never mind the compliments. As soon as we're in, jump down and keep the crowd away from this machine. I don't want anybody to touch it. I'll push the stuff out. They can collect it after we've gone. I shall leave the motors running.'

'Okay.'

As soon as the Wellington was on the ground a crowd of Chinese surged towards it; but Bargent held them off, gesticulating furiously. Biggles was throwing the stores out.

A Chinese officer came forward, speaking English.

'That's close enough!' shouted Bargent. 'Here's your stuff. Some more will be coming through.'

'You in gleat hurry,' said the Chinaman, impassively.

'We've got to get back,' answered Bargent.

'No want any petrol?'

Bargent looked at Biggles.

'No!' shouted Biggles. 'We've got enough to see us home.'

'You no stay to eat?' questioned the Chinaman.

'Not today, thanks,' returned Bargent. 'I've got a date with a girl in Calcutta, and she'll jilt me if I'm not back on time.'

The Chinaman grinned. 'Me savvy.'

'Okay, Bargent!' shouted Biggles. 'Get aboard. We're on our way.'

The South African picked his way through the pile of bales that Biggles had thrown out of the aircraft, closed the door and resumed his seat. The engines roared, and the machine swung round, scattering the crowd, to face the open field. In another minute it was in the air again, India bound.

'Get those cigarettes ready,' said Biggles.

Bargent laughed. 'I'll help you smoke 'em.'

'Oh, no, you won't,' declared Biggles. 'I reckon I shall have won 'em.'

There was no incident of any sort on the home run. There was no flak; no aircraft of any type, friend or foe, was sighted. As they glided in to land Bargent swore that he had never felt better in his life.

Frayle, in uniform, greeted them. 'So you got back?' he cried in a voice of wonder.

'If you think this is a ghost plane, try walking into one of the airscrews,' invited Biggles. 'You'll find it hard enough, I'll warrant.'

'Well, that's a mystery,' said Frayle.

'Not quite so much of a mystery as it was,' returned Biggles.

'What are you going to do now?'

Biggles glanced at the sun, now low in the west. 'I want to get back to Dum Dum before dark, but I've just time for a snack.'

'You think it's safe to use the route now?'

'I didn't say that,' answered Biggles quickly. 'The Chinese now have a little to go on with, so you can afford to keep everything on the ground till you hear from me again. Yes, I know we got away with it this time, but that trick may not work again. By changing the planes at the last minute we slipped a fast one on the enemy. More than that I can't tell you for the moment. I want you and Bargent to keep your mouths shut tight about this show. If you talk it may cost you your lives. Keep the machines grounded. I'll be back. Now let's go and eat.'

An hour later, in the crimson glow of the Eastern sunset, Biggles landed at Dum Dum and walked quickly to the mess, to be met by an enthusiastic squadron.

'I say, old boy, that's marvellous—absolutely marvellous,' declared Bertie. 'Don't tell me you've been to China?'

'There and back,' answered Biggles. 'Let's get inside. I've got to talk to you chaps, and I don't mind admitting that I'd rather curl quietly in a corner and go to sleep. I seem to have done a lot of flying lately.'

'If you're tired, why not leave it until tomorrow?' suggested Algy.

'Because tomorrow morning I shall be just as busy—and so, perhaps, will you.'

'The point is, did you spot the secret weapon?' demanded Ginger.

'Not a sign of it,' returned Biggles, with a ghost of a smile. 'Serious, now, everybody. Lock the door, Ginger. Today I carried out what we might call an experiment,' he went on, when everyone had settled down. 'It leads, as most experiments do, to another. Tomorrow morning I'm going to do a sortie over Burma.'

'Alone?' queried Algy, looking askance.

'I hadn't thought of taking anyone,' admitted Biggles.

'At least take someone with you,' pressed Algy. 'There may be something in this double pilot idea.'

'It isn't that I'm trying to run the show single-handed,' asserted Biggles. 'It's just that I want to avoid casualties if it is possible. There's no point in using more men on a job than it calls for. One machine can do what I have in mind tomorrow morning. Why risk two?'

'Then why not take the Beau, or the Mosquito, and have someone with you for company?' suggested Algy.

'Yes, I might do that,' agreed Biggles.

There was a chorus of voices offering to go, but Biggles held up a hand. 'There's only one way to settle this, and that's by drawing lots,' he declared. 'That doesn't apply to flight commanders, though; they'll get their turns if I don't come back. Algy, write six names on slips of paper and put them in a hat.'

'Aren't you going to tell us what happened today?' queried Tex, while Algy was doing this.

'There's really nothing to tell,' answered Biggles. 'Nothing happened: that's a fact.'

Algy came forward with a hat in which lay six slips of paper, folded.

'Shake 'em up,' ordered Biggles.

Algy shook the hat.

Biggles closed his eyes and put out a hand. His fingers closed over a slip. He raised it. In dead silence he unfolded it and glanced at the name. He took it to Tug and smiled.

'You're it, Tug,' he announced.

'Whoopee! That's a corker,' cried Tug. 'That's the first time I've ever won a draw in my life.'

'Unless it's your lucky day it's likely to be the last,' joked Biggles grimly.

'I'll risk it,' flashed Tug, grinning. 'What time do we leave the carpet?'

'We'll decide that when we see what the weather is like,' returned Biggles.

'Do we wear brollies?'

Biggles shrugged. 'In this affair they don't seem to make much difference, but I suppose we might as well. Don't mention this sortie to a soul, neither in nor outside the mess. Should anyone ask what we are doing you can say we're browning off waiting for orders. That's all. Let's go in to dinner.'

5
SUICIDE PATROL

It was still dark, but with that faint luminosity in the sky that heralds the approach of the Eastern dawn, when Biggles was awakened by the sudden bellow of an aero engine. This is not an unusual sound on an airfield, and he turned over with the intention of snatching a final nap, supposing that the noise was created by a motor under test. But when a second, and then a third engine opened up, he sprang out of bed and strode to the window. In the eerie light of the false dawn he could just discern the silhouettes of what he thought were Hurricanes, moving slowly on the far side of the airfield. For a moment or two he stood gazing, sleep banished, a frown puckering his forehead; then he slipped a dressing-gown over his pyjamas and picked up the telephone.

Two minutes later Algy arrived, also in pyjamas. 'What's going on?' he asked tersely.

Biggles hung up the receiver. 'Take a look outside,' he invited. 'Those five survivors of 818 Squadron are going off on a bomb raid in the danger area. My God! They've got a nerve.'

Algy nodded. 'Yes, I remember now. Johhny Crisp told me last night that there was some talk of a final do-or-bust show in the hope of finding the thing that killed the others.'

'They'll do that, no doubt—or some of them will,' returned Biggles, in a hard voice.

'Johnny said they were going crazy, just sitting on the ground doing nothing. He, being the only remaining flight commander, will lead the sortie. Personally, I think he's right. You know how it is: when a fellow's nerves start slipping he has only one chance of saving himself—if he ever wants to fly again; and that's to get in the air.'

'Maybe. But these chaps are practically committing suicide, and they must know it.'

'Johnny, and the other fellow I told you about, Scrimshaw, have always got back,' reminded Algy.

'So far. But there's such a thing as pushing your luck too hard.' Biggles started. 'Just a minute! Yes, that's it. I'm going to hook on to this raid, to watch what happens. All the evidence we have up to now is hearsay.'

Algy's eyes opened wide. 'But——'

'Don't stand gibbering. Go and get Tug out of bed and tell him to meet me on the tarmac in five minutes.'

'What about breakfast?'

'There'll be more time for that when we get back.'

'You mean—if you get back,' said Algy, with gentle sarcasm.

'Okay.' He departed.

Five minutes later, when Biggles went outside, Tug was there, waiting, parachute slung over his shoulder. The rest of the squadron was there, too, grim-faced, silent. The five Hurricanes were just taking off, sending clouds of dust swirling across the parched airfield.

'Look at 'em,' said Biggles in a low voice. 'There they go.

That's guts for you. Come on, Tug; we'll catch 'em in the Mosquito.' It did not seem to strike him that he was doing the same thing. He glanced round the ring of anxious faces, and smiled the queer little smile they all knew so well. 'So long, chaps; keep your tails up.'

'I say, old boy, watch out what you're up to, and all that,' blurted Bertie.

'May I follow in a Spit?' cried Ginger huskily.

'No,' answered Biggles shortly.

'But——'

'You heard me. Come on, Tug. Let's get cracking, or we'll lose sight of those crazy Hurry-wallahs.'

In a few minutes the Mosquito, probably the best and fastest long-range medium bomber in the world, was in the air. It carried no bombs. Biggles was at the control column, with Tug sitting beside him instead of adopting the prone position which the special structure of this type of aircraft permits. Both wore the regulation parachutes. The five Hurricanes were mere specks in the fast-lightening sky, but the Mosquito began slowly to overhaul them.

Below, looking eastward, like an army of black snakes, was the pattern of waterways that comprise the delta of the river Ganges. Rivers, streams, and irrigation canals, lay asprawl a flat, monotonous terrain, cutting it into a vast archipelago before emptying themselves into the Bay of Bengal. Here and there a village nestled in a verdant bed of paddy-fields, or clung precariously to the fringe of one of the numerous masses of forest that had invaded the fertile land from the east. By the time these had given way to the more sombre green of the interminable Burmese jungle the sky was turning from lavender to blue, with the Mosquito about a mile astern and two thousand feet above the Hurricane formation.

'What's their objective—do you know?' queried Tug.

'Apparently there's a bridge over the Manipur River which the army is anxious to have pranged, to interrupt the Jap lines of communication.'

'Do you know where it is?'

'Not exactly, but it's somewhere north-west of Mandalay; you'll find it on the map.'

Tug unfolded the map on his knees and studied it closely for a minute. 'Okay, I've got it,' he remarked.

'We must be pretty close to enemy country, even if we're not actually over it,' said Biggles presently. 'Let me know at once if you see anything suspicious. You might get down and have a squint below, to see if you can spot any sign of ground activity.'

Tug dropped to the prone position and for a little while subjected the landscape to a searching scrutiny. Then he climbed back to his seat. 'Not a blessed thing,' he stated. 'All I can see are trees and rivers. No sign of any trenches, or anything like that, to mark the no-man's-land between our troops and the Japs.'

'What with jungle and camouflage I didn't expect to see much,' returned Biggles. His eyes were on the Hurricanes.

'Listen, Tug. We'd better have some sort of a plan. I'll watch the formation. You watch the sky. If you see anything, *anything*, let me know. Let me know, too, if you feel anything. If I see or feel anything unusual I'll let you know. It may sound silly, but if I start behaving in a manner that strikes you as odd, you take over and get back home straightaway.'

Tug grinned. 'Okay. Funny business, this waiting for something to go pop.'

'I don't think funny is the right word,' argued Biggles. 'I'd say it's dashed uncomfortable. We must be well over enemy country now, so something may happen any time. Hello—that tells us where we are.'

A few wisps of black smoke had appeared in the sky round the formation, which went on without altering course.

'That's ordinary flak,' declared Tug.

'Biggles had a good look at it before he answered. He even flew close to a patch, studied it suspiciously, and then dispersed it with his slipstream. 'I think you're right,' he agreed. 'Just ordinary flak.'

It soon died away and no more came up. A quarter of an hour passed without incident. The Hurricanes roared on with the

Mosquito keeping its distance.

'I'll bet those boys are wondering what this Mossy is doing, trailing 'em,' chuckled Tug. 'They seem to be all right so far.'

'So do we.'

'Maybe it'll turn out to be a false alarm after all.'

'Maybe.' Biggles was noncommittal. Not for a moment did he take his eyes off the Hurricanes.

Another twenty minutes passed and the formation began to lose height, at the same time opening out a little.

'What are they doing?' asked Tug.

'It's all right. That bridge over the river ahead must be the target. They're going down to prang it. Keep your eyes skinned for enemy aircraft—or anything else.'

Nothing happened—that is, nothing out of normal routine. The Mosquito held its altitude, circling wide, while the fighter-bombers went down and did their work. Pillars of white smoke leapt skyward in the target area. Biggles noted one direct hit and two near misses, and made a note in the log he was keeping. There was no flak, no enemy opposition of any sort. The Hurricanes, their work done, turned away, closing in again to the original formation, and headed for home, taking some altitude.

'Well, that's that,' mused Biggles. 'I didn't see anything unusual did you, Tug?'

'Not a thing,' muttered Tug. 'I don't get it.'

'One would have thought that if the Japs *could* have stopped them, they'd have done it on the way out, before the bombers reached their target,' said Biggles pensively. 'The thing gets more and more inexplicable. Keep a sharp look-out, we aren't home yet.'

'They're still flying pretty,' observed Tug after a glance at the Hurricanes.

'So are we if it comes to that,' answered Biggles, glancing at the watch on the instrument panel and making another note.

Fifteen minutes later he observed that one of the Hurricanes had moved slightly out of position, so that its opposite number had to swerve slightly to avoid collision. Biggles stiffened, staring, nerves tense, but aware that this might have been the result of a moment's carelessness on the part of the pilot. But when the same machine swerved, and began to sideslip, he uttered a warning cry.

'Look! There goes one of them!' he shouted. 'By heavens! Yes, he's going down!'

Tug did not answer. Both pilots watched while the Hurricane maintained its swerve, getting farther and farther away from the formation, which held on its course. At the same time the nose of the straying machine began to droop, until presently the aircraft was plunging earthward in a dive that became ever steeper.

'Pull out!' yelled Tug—uselessly. He began to mutter incoherently.

The Hurricane, still running on full throttle it seemed, roared on to a doom that was now only a matter of seconds.

'Why doesn't he bale out?' cried Tug in a strangled voice.

'No use, Tug. He's finished,' said Biggles through his teeth, and pushing the control column forward he tore down behind the stricken aircraft. A swift glance revealed the other four machines still in formation, but nose down, racing on the homeward course, which, in the circumstances, Biggles realised, was the wisest action they could take. Long before he could overtake the doomed aircraft it had crashed through the tree-tops and disappeared from sight like a stone dropping into opaque water.

Tug caught his breath at the moment of impact, and then cursed through bloodless lips. His face was pale and distorted with fury; his eyes glittered.

'No use swearing, Tug,' said Biggles evenly. 'That doesn't get anybody anywhere.'

He went on down and circled over the spot where the Hurricane had disappeared, revealed at short distance by fractured branches. Nothing could be seen. 'The crash hasn't taken fire, anyway,' he muttered, and then looked at his own instrument dials, in turn. 'We seem to be still okay,' he added. 'Do you feel all right Tug?'

'More or less—just savage, that's all,' growled Tug.

'Keep watch up topsides,' warned Biggles.

Still circling, without taking his eyes from the scene of the tragedy he climbed back up to two thousand feet.

'Listen Tug,' he said crisply. 'I'm going to bale out.'

'You're *what!*'

'I'm going down.'

'What's the use? The chap in that kite hadn't a hope.'

'I know that, but I'm going down to try to find out just what happened. Unless someone examines one of these crashes we may never know what causes them. This is my chance.'

'You'll get hung up in the trees.'

'That's a risk I shall have to take.'

'What about Japs? There may be some down there.'

'I've got a gun in my pocket.'

'But don't be crazy. How are you going to get home?'

'Walk if necessary.'

'But we must be a hundred miles from the nearest of our troops. I can't pick you up. There ain't an open patch as big as a handkerchief within seeing distance.' Tug spoke in a shrill, protesting voice.

'All right, don't get excited,' returned Biggles. 'There is one way you can collect me, when I've seen what I want to see. Take a look at that river, about a mile away to the left.'

'What about it?'

'I don't know how deep it is, but if it has any depth at all it should be possible to put down a seaplane or flying-boat on it. Now listen carefully. After I bale out I want you to return to base, going full bore. Tell Algy what has happened. Tell him to find Raymond and get him to requisition a marine aircraft of some sort from anywhere he likes. I believe the Calcutta Flying Club used to have some Moth seaplanes—but I'll leave that to Raymond. Whatever he gets, you come back in it and pick me up. And when I say you I mean *you*. Algy will probably want to come, but he's in charge at base and my orders are on no account is he to leave. This is tricky country, and having seen the spot you should recognize it again. It that clear so far?'

'Okay. Where do I pick you up, exactly?'

'I shall be waiting by the river, on this bank, as near as I can get to the larger of those two islands you can see. They stand in a straight reach of river so it ought to be all right for landing. That island is the mark. Take a good look at it before you go because there may be similar islands higher up or lower down the river.'

'Okay, skipper. Is there some way you can let me know if you get down all right?'

'I've got my petrol lighter. I'll make a smoke signal. If you see smoke you'll know I'm on the carpet. Take over now, and glide across the crash. There doesn't seem to be any wind to speak of.'

They changed places and Biggles opened the escape hatch.

Tug throttled back and began a run, at little more than stalling speed, towards the spot where the Hurricane had crashed.

'Keep her as she goes,' said Biggles. 'That's fine. See you later.' He disappeared into space.

Tug pushed the throttle open, and having brought the aircraft to even keel banked slightly to get a view below. The parachute was floating down almost directly over the objective. He watched it sink lower and lower until eventually it remained stationary on the tree-tops.

'My God! He's caught up!' he muttered through dry lips. He continued to circle, watching, and saw the fabric split as a broken branch poked through it. But he could not see Biggles. He could only suppose that he was suspended by the shrouds somewhere between the tree-tops and the ground. It was several minutes before a thin column of smoke drifted up.

Tug drew a deep breath of relief, and 'blipped' his engines as a signal that the smoke had been seen. He turned to the river. For a minute he cruised up and down making mental pictures of the island from all angles. Then, banking steeply, he raced away on a westward course.

6

RENDEZVOUS WITH DEATH

Tug's fear that Biggles' parachute would become caught up in the tree-tops was fully justified; it would only have been remarkable had it been otherwise. Biggles knew this, so he was not surprised when he found himself swinging in his harness below tangled shrouds and torn fabric some thirty feet above the fern-carpeted floor of the jungle. He was not unduly alarmed, being well satisfied that he himself had escaped injury. By pulling on a line to increase his swing he managed without any great difficulty to reach a bough. In five minutes he had slipped out of his harness and made a cautious descent to the ground, leaving the parachute in the trees, where, he realised, it was likely to remain. A party of monkeys, after chattering at the intrusion, swung quietly away.

Perspiring profusely in the stagnant atmosphere from his exertions he mopped his face with his handkerchief, and after listening for a little while for sounds that might indicate danger, he made the smoke fire as arranged. His petrol lighter, an old letter from his pocket, and some sere undergrowth, provided the means. He heard Tug's answering signal, but he did not move until a fast-receding drone told him that the Mosquito was homeward bound. The sound died away and silence fell—a strange, oppressive silence, after the vibrant roar which had for so long filled his ears. Bracing himself for his ordeal, for he had no delusions about the harrowing nature of the task before him, he made his way to the crash. He had not far to go.

The Hurricane was much in the condition he expected. Both wings had been torn off at their roots. One hung from a splintered bough a short distance from the wreck; the other, fractured in the middle and bent at right angles, lay near the fuselage. The blades of the airscrew had folded up and the boss had bored deep into the soft leaf-mould. The fuselage was the right way up, more or less intact. The only sound was a soft drip-drip-drip, as liquid escaped from radiator, tank, or a broken petrol lead. Moistening his lips he walked on to the cockpit.

The pilot, whom he did not know, a lad of about twenty with flaxen hair and blue eyes, was still in his seat. He was dead. No attempt had been made to use the parachute. A head wound, where his forehead had come into contact with the instrument panel at the moment of impact, was alone sufficient to have caused death, which must have been instantaneous.

Biggles lifted the limp body out, laid it on the ground and removed the identification disc. THOMAS GRAFTON MOORVEN, R.A.F., it read. He then took everything from the pockets— cigarette case, wallet, personal letters, some snapshots and some loose coins—and having made a little bundle of them in the handkerchief, put it on one side. This done, he paused again to mop his face, for the heat was stifling. It may have been the anger that surged through him, causing his fingers to tremble, that made the heat seem worse than it really was. Accustomed though he was to war, and death, there was something poignant about this particular tragedy that moved him strangely, making his eyes moist and bringing a lump into his throat. After months of training and eager anticipation the boy had travelled thousands of miles to meet his death without firing a shot. He had not even seen the enemy who had killed him, the weapon that had struck him down. Fully aware of the risks he was taking he had gone out willingly to seek the thing that had killed his comrades, only to meet the same fate, to die alone in the eternal solitude of a tropic forest. There would be no reward, no decoration for valour. Those at home would not even know how he died. This, thought Biggles, as he stood looking down on the waxen features, was not war. It was murder—and murder called for vengeance. His hand, he decided, would exact retribution, if the power were granted him. He drew a deep breath and set about the task for which he had descended.

First, he examined the body thoroughly, but could find no wound, no mark that might have caused death, apart from those that were obviously the direct result of the crash. There was no sign of burning, such as might have resulted from an electrical discharge of some sort. He examined the eyes closely, and noticed that the pupils were dilated. This struck him as unusual, but neither his technical or medical knowledge could help him to associate it with a cause of death. He made a mental note of it, however.

He next turned to the aircraft, starting with the wings. He did not expect to find anything there, for had they in some mysterious way been fractured in the air he would have seen it before the machine crashed. They told him nothing, so he turned to the fuselage, beginning with the motor, paying particular attention to the ignition system. All electrical equipment seemed to be in perfect order. From airscrew to rudder he subjected the machine to such an inspection as he had never before devoted to any aircraft; yet for all his efforts he found nothing, no clue that might remotely suggest a solution to the mystery. Again mopping his face, and brushing away the mosquitoes that were attacking him, he returned to the cockpit. He had already been over it. He went over it again, methodically, but found nothing except normal equipment. He took the map from its recess, unfolded it, studied it on both sides, even smelt it. He was turning away when a small object on the floor, under the seat, caught his eye. He picked it up. It was a slip of paper, pink paper of a sort that is called greaseproof, about three inches square. There was printing on one side: WITH THE COMPLIMENTS OF CHARNEYS, LTD., LONDON. NOT FOR SALE. SUPPLIED FOR THE USE OF H.M. FORCES ONLY. He raised the paper to his nostrils. It smelt faintly of mint. Smiling wanly he screwed the paper into a ball, tossed it aside and resumed his search.

Finally, reluctantly, he gave up, no wiser than when he began. There was nothing more he could do, he decided. Tug might return at any time now, so he had better be making his way towards the river.

One last problem, one that had been in the background of his mind all along, now demanded solution. The aircraft, of course, would have to be burnt, to prevent it from falling into the hands of the enemy. But what about the body? He had no implement with which to dig a grave. There seemed little point in carrying it to the river even if this were possible. The undergrowth was so thick that he alone, with both hands free, would find the operation difficult enough. Even if he succeeded in carrying the body to the river there would be the question of transport to the base. In any case it would involve prodigious labour and delay, which would jeopardise his life, and Tug's, for no reason outside sentiment. On the other hand he did not like the idea of leaving the body there to become the prey of creatures of the forest. He could think of only one method of disposing of it, and that was the way chosen by some of the greatest warriors of the past, the way of the Romans, the Vikings, the Indians. All reduced the bodies of their chiefs and warriors to ashes, burning their weapons, their war-horses, and their hounds with them. After all, many good airmen, including some of his best friends, had gone out that way, he reflected.

Having steeled himself for this last grim ceremony, he was moving forward when voices at no great distance brought him to an abrupt halt, in a listening attitude. There was no doubt about the voices; with them came a trampling and crashing of undergrowth. Very soon it was clear that those responsible for the disturbance were approaching.

Biggles drew back and found a perfect retreat among the giant fronds of a tree-fern. In doing this he was actuated by more than casual curiosity. It seemed possible, indeed it seemed likely, that the Hurricane had been seen to fall, in which case enemy troops would be sent out to locate it. There was just a chance that these men were part of the team that operated the secret weapon. If that were so they would be worth capturing for interrogation.

The voices and the crashing drew nearer. The men seemed to be in a carefree mood. Biggles could not speak a word of Japanese, but he was in no doubt as to the nationality of the newcomers. He took out his automatic examined it, and waited. The voices continued to approach.

In a few minutes a man burst from the undergrowth. He stopped when he saw the crash, and then let out a shrill cry. A second man joined him.

Biggles was disappointed. They were ordinary Japanese soldiers, infantrymen, dirty, with the usual twigs attached to their shoddy uniforms for camouflage purposes. Both carried rifles and were smoking cigarettes. No other sounds came from the forest so it was fairly certain that they were alone.

Their immediate reaction to the spectacle before them was not unnatural. They broke into an excited jabber as they walked on to the fuselage. When one of them pointed at the dead pilot and burst out laughing, after a momentary look of wonder Biggles frowned: friend or foe, to European eyes the sight was anything but funny. When one of them kicked the body every vestige of colour drained from his face. His lips came together in a hard line; his nostrils quivered. Still he did not move. But when one of the men, with what was evidently a remark intended to be jocular, bent down and inserted his cigarette between the dead pilot's lips, and then, shouting with laughter, stepped back to observe the effect. Biggles' pent-up anger could no longer he restrained.

'You scum,' he grated. The words were low, but distinct.

The two Japanese spun round as if a shot had been fired. They stared in goggle-eyed amazement, no longer laughing, but fearful, as though confronted by a ghost—the ghost of the body they had violated. Superstitious by nature, they may have believed that.

Biggles spoke again. 'You utter swine,' he breathed.

This spurred the Japanese to movement. With a curious cry one of them threw up his rifle. Biggles fired. The man twitched convulsively. Again Biggles' automatic roared. The man's legs crumped under him; the rifle fell from his hands and he slumped, choking. The second man started to run. Quite dispassionately, without moving from his position, Biggles took deliberate aim and fired. The Jap pitched forward on his face, but crying loudly started to get up. Biggles walked forward and with calculated precision fired two more shots at point-blank range. His lips were drawn back, showing his teeth. 'You unspeakable thug,' he rasped. The man lay still.

As the echoes of the shots died away a hush fell, sullen, hot, heavy. The only sound was the hum of innumerable mosquitoes. For a few seconds, breathing heavily, the smoking pistol in his hand, Biggles stood gazing at the man he had shot. Then he walked quickly to the dead pilot, snatched the cigarette from his lips and hurled it aside.

'Sorry about that, Tommy,' he said quietly. 'Sort of thing one doesn't expect,' he added, as if he were talking to himself.

Pocketing his pistol he picked up the body, placed it gently in the cockpit and closed the cover. Then, lighting a slip of paper he dropped it by a leaking petrol lead. Fire took hold, spreading rapidly. In a moment the forepart of the aircraft was wrapped in leaping flames.

As Biggles stepped back his eyes fell on the Japanese. 'We've no dogs, Tommy,' he murmured; 'these hell-hounds are a poor substitute, but they'll have to do.' Having confirmed that both were dead he dragged the bodies across the tail unit, which had not yet been reached by the flames, afterwards backing away quickly, for the ammunition belts were exploding their charges and bullets were flying. Picking up the handkerchief containing the dead pilot's belongings he walked to the edge of the clearing. There he turned and stiffened to attention. His right hand came up to the salute.

'So long, Tommy,' he said quietly. 'Good hunting.' Then, without a backward glance he strode away through the jungle in the direction of the river.

Behind him, to the roll of exploding ammunition, the smoke of the funeral pyre made a white column high against the blue of heaven. He realised that it might be seen by the enemy and bring them to the spot. He didn't care. He rather hoped it would. He was in the sort of mood when fighting would be a pleasure.

It took him the best part of an hour to reach the river, and he was dripping with sweat when the turgid water came into view. The only living things in sight were a small crocodile, lying on a mudflat, and a grey heron, perched on a dead limb overhanging the water. There was no sign of Tug. He was some distance above the island that he had chosen for the rendezvous, and it required another twenty minutes of labour, working along the river bank, to bring him in line with it. There was still no sign of Tug, so choosing the crest of a small escarpment for a seat, he lighted a cigarette and settled down to wait. There was nothing else to do. The mosquitoes were still with him. He brushed them away with a weary gesture and mopped his dripping face, which was still pale, and set in hard lines. The strain of the last two hours had been considerable.

He passed the next half-hour in silent meditation, smoking, pondering over the events of the morning, and the problem which they had done nothing to elucidate, before he heard the sound for which he was waiting—the drone of an aircraft. But because his ears were attuned to the nicer distinctions between aero engines, at first he was puzzled. Very soon, though, he solved the mystery. There were two engines, of different types. The main background of sound was provided by the deep roar of a high-performance motor, but against it, quite distinct, there was the busy chatter of a lighter type. It seemed unlikely that there could be two light planes in that particular theatre of war, so he was not surprised when a Gipsy Moth float-plane swung into view, tearing low up the river. Behind it, weaving in zigzags but definitely keeping it company, was a Hurricane.

Biggles smiled faintly as he stood up and waved. The ill-assorted pair needed no explanation. Tug had returned in a marine craft as arranged, and it had brought an escort. Biggles' immediate reaction was one of relief, not so much on his own account as because, in spite of the secret weapon, Tug had obviously managed to get home, and make the return trip. He had been gone a long time, and Biggles had just begun to fear that the nameless peril had claimed him.

Tug evidently saw him at once, for he cut his engine and put the machine straight down on the water. Without waiting for it to finish its run he came round in a swirl of creamy foam to that point of the river bank where Biggles was now waiting. Biggles waded out through two feet of water and six inches of mud to the aircraft, and climbed aboard.

'Good work, Tug,' he greeted. 'Have any trouble?'

Tug grinned. 'Not a trace. I saw a bunch of Zeros, high up, as I went home, but they didn't see me. Did you find anything?'

'No.'

'Who was it—Grainger, Larkin or Moorven?'

Biggles started. 'What do you mean?'

'All three failed to get back. The others say the hoodoo got 'em all.'

'The others? Do you mean that Johnny Crisp and Scrimshaw got back *again*?'

'They did. I left Johnny stamping and cursing on the airfield, and Scrimshaw roaring round in circles looking for somebody to shoot. Queer, ain't it?'

During this brief recital Biggles had remained still, half in and half out of the spare seat, staring at Tug's face. 'Queer! It's more than that. It's uncanny. It can't be luck. It *can't* be. But we'll talk about that when we get home. Who's in the Hurricane?'

'Angus.'

'Who told him he could come?'

'Algy.'

'Algy, eh? I like his nerve.'

Tug grinned again. 'Algy's in charge, don't forget, during your absence. Don't blame him. The whole bunch wanted to come and Algy had his work cut out to keep them on the carpet. They reckoned someone ought to come to keep an eye on me while I was keeping an eye open for you. In the end Algy agreed to let one of the flight commanders go. Angus and Bertie tossed for it. Bertie lost. I left him trying to rub a hole through his eyeglass.' While Tug had been speaking he had eased the throttle open a trifle and moved slowly to deeper water.

Biggles was looking up at the Hurricane. 'What the . . . ! What in thunder does Angus think he's doing?' he asked sharply.

Tug looked up and saw the fighter coming down in a shallow swerving dive as if it intended pancaking on the river. 'He's giving you the salute,' he said, slowly, in a voice that did not carry conviction.

Biggles did not answer at once. He stared, while the

Hurricane continued its downward swoop. 'You're wrong,' he forced through dry lips. 'Angus has bought it. Look out!'

The warning was no mere figure of speech, for the Hurricane was coming in dead in line with the Moth. Tug realised it, and shoved the throttle open with a lightning movement of his hand. 'Hang on!' he yelled, as the engine roared and the light plane shot forward. He was only just in time.

The Hurricane's port wing-tip missed the Moth by inches. It struck the water with a mighty splash that drenched the Moth with spray and set it rocking violently. It bounced and splashed again, this time to disappear except for a swinging rudder.

Tug tore to the spot. 'I told him not to come!' he cried wildly. Then again, 'I told him not to come. I told him——'

'Shut up,' snapped Biggles. 'Watch for me,' he added, and dived overboard.

When, a minute later, he reappeared, gasping, with Angus in his arms, Tug was out on a float, on his knees, waiting. He took Angus first, and then helped Biggles to get astride the float. The weight tipped the plane at a dangerous angle, and Tug leaned away to the other float to counteract the list. Angus was dead or unconscious—it was not clear which.

'Help me to get him into the spare seat,' ordered Biggles.

'How is he do you think?'

'I don't know, but he must be in a bad way. He's got a broken leg, if nothing worse. We can't do anything for him here. His only chance, if he is still alive, is hospital.'

'But this machine won't lift three—there's no room, anyway.'

'I know it,' answered Biggles curtly. 'You get him back. I'll wait. I shall be all right here. You ought to be back in a couple of hours if nothing goes wrong. Better 'phone Algy from the slipway to let him know what's happened—and tell him to keep everybody on the ground till I get back. That's an order.'

'Okay,' grunted Tug.

After some delay, and with no small difficulty, Angus' limp body was lifted into the spare seat. As Biggles had said, there was no question of doing anything for him on the spot.

'Run me close to the bank and I'll get off,' said Biggles. 'There are crocs. in this river.'

Tug taxied close to the bank and Biggles waded ashore.

'Okay, get cracking,' ordered Biggles.

Tug waved. The engine roared. The little plane swung round and raced away down the river. Biggles watched it until it was out of sight and then resumed his seat on the escarpment. Automatically he felt for his cigarette case. The cigarettes were, of course, soaking wet, so very carefully he laid them out on the rock to dry.

7
BIGGLES INVESTIGATES

BIGGLES waited, waited while the sun climbed over its zenith and began its downward journey. In the low ground through which the river wound its sluggish course, the air, heavy with the stench of rotting vegetation, was still. The heat was suffocating. The swampy banks of the river steamed, the slime at the water's edge erupting gaseous bubbles. Biggles sweated. Once, a flight of three Mitsubishi bombers droned overhead on a westerly course; a little later six Zero fighters, flying at a great height, passed over, heading in the same direction, towards India.

'They must know our machines are grounded, so they're getting cocky,' mused Biggles.

It was clear that if the secret weapon was still in operation the enemy planes were not affected, which proved that the thing was under control. and discounted anything in the nature of poison gas which, once released, would be uncontrollable, and would—unless the Japanese pilots wore respirators—affect both friend and foe alike. If a beam, or ray, were being used, it could not be a permanent installation, for this also would operate against all types of aircraft regardless of nationality. Had enemy planes been insulated against such a ray the insulating materials would have been discovered by technicians whose work it was to examine the enemy aircraft brought down on the British side of the lines. Not the least puzzling aspect of the new weapon was the distance over which it was effective—or so it would seem from the immense area in which British machines had been brought down. It suggested that the instrument was highly mobile, or else there was a number of them installed at points throughout the entire forest. Yet if this were so, why had the Hurricanes been allowed to reach their objective? Had it been possible to stop them, then they would most certainly have been stopped. The fact that the Hurricane formation had reached its objective that morning suggested that the weapon had its limitations. Thus mused Biggles, sweltering on his lonely rock.

It was getting on for three hours before Tug returned. Biggles was glad to see the Moth, for apart from the delay, and the wearisome nature of his vigil, the danger of flying in the area had been demonstrated.

'You've been a long time,' greeted Biggles.

'I had to snoop around a bit,' answered Tug. 'There are bandits about, poking their noses close to India—taking advantage of our machines being grounded, I suppose.'

'How's Angus?' asked Biggles anxiously, as he climbed aboard.

'He's alive, but that's about all. They took him to hospital. I didn't wait for details.'

'Did he recover consciousness?'

'No.'

'You spoke to Algy?'

'Yes. I 'phoned him.'

'What did he say?'

'Oh, he got a bit worked up—wanted to send the gang out, for escort. I told him what you said about staying put. He just made noises.'

'Where did you get this Moth, by the way?'

'Raymond fixed it. It was up a backwater the other side of Calcutta. Raymond lent me his car to get to it. It used to belong to an air taxi company. That's all I know. It flies all right—and that's all I care.'

'As we can't land at Dum Dum we shall have to go back to the place where you got it.'

'I reckon so.'

'Is Raymond's car still there?'

'No, we shall have to get a taxi.'

'Okay,' said Biggles as he settled himself in his seat. 'Better keep low: we don't want to run into a bunch of Zeros.'

The flight to Calcutta was uneventful. On several occasions enemy aircraft were seen, mostly flying high, but the Moth, skimming the tree-tops, escaped observation. By the time it had been moored, and a taxi found, and the trip made to Dum Dum, the sun was low in the western sky. Without stopping to wash or remove the mud from his clothes Biggles walked straight to the mess. The others were waiting.

His first question was, 'How's Angus?'

Algy answered. 'I've been to the hospital—just got back. They wouldn't let me see him—not that there would have been any point in it. He's still unconscious, and likely to remain so. He's badly smashed up—broken arm, broken leg, three ribs stove in and concussion. If he gets over it, it will be months before he's on his feet again. We can reckon him off the strength as far as this show's concerned.'

Biggles shook his head sadly. 'Poor old Angus. Tough luck. Still, it's something that he is still alive. I suppose it was expecting too much to hope that he might have come round. I wanted to talk to him. He might have been able to tell us something—what happened, and how he felt. As far as we know, he's the first victim of the new weapon who has survived, or who has got back.'

'Then you don't know what hit him?' said Bertie.

'I haven't the remotest idea,' admitted Biggles. 'The machine just dived into the drink as if the controls had jammed, or as if he had done it deliberately. That's how it struck me. What do you think, Tug? You saw it.'

'Same as you.'

The others were crowding round. 'You didn't see anything break?' queried Ginger.

'Not a thing,' answered Biggles. 'When the machine hit the water, as far as one could see, there was absolutely nothing wrong with it.'

'What about Moorven's crash?' asked Algy. 'Did you find anything there?'

'Nothing. I'll tell you all about it later, after I've had a bite and a clean up. I really only looked in to get the latest news about Angus. I shall be busy for a bit, making out a written report on Moorven's crash, handing over his effects, and so on. I also want to have a word with Johnny Crisp and Scrimshaw. There's something unnatural about the way they always get back. It can't be luck. There must be a reason, and if we can put a finger on it we shall be half-way towards getting this thing buttoned up.'

At this point Air Commodore Raymond came in. 'I heard you were back,' he announced. 'What happened?'

'Just a minute, sir,' protested Biggles. 'I haven't had anything to eat today yet, and blundering about in the jungle was a dirty business—as you can see. Give me a few minutes for a bath and a bite and I'll tell you all about it. Wait here—the others will want to hear the story, too. I'll be back.'

In rather less than half an hour he returned, his material needs satisfied. 'Let's sit down,' he suggested.

He then told his story. Narrated in his usual concise manner, it did not take long. 'The only satisfactory thing about the show,' he concluded, 'was sending those two stinking Japs for a Burton.'

'Then we still haven't got anywhere,' said the Air Commodore despondently.

'I wouldn't say that exactly,' argued Biggles. 'Certain broad aspects are beginning to emerge. When I've had time to think about them I may be able to get a line on the thing.'

'What are you going to do next?'

'It's dark, so there's nothing more we can do in the air. I'd like a word with Crisp and Scrimshaw. There's a bit of a mystery about the way they keep getting back. Of course, it may be luck, but if it isn't, then they, or their machines, must be immune from the thing that's causing the mischief. I'd also like to have a chat with the last man who touched Moorven's machine before he got into it.'

'I've already made inquiries about that,' said the Air Commodore. 'It was a sergeant named Gray. He went over all the machines just before they took off. He seems to be terribly cut up about the three machines going west—somehow feels that they were his responsibility.

'But that's silly.'

'That's what I told him.'

'What sort of chap is this sergeant?'

'He's a fellow of about thirty, with ten years' service. Exemplary record, and a first class all round fitter-rigger. Before the show, knowing what might happen, he went over every machine, and every engine.'

'I see. Well, we'll leave him till later. Let's get hold of Crisp and Scrimshaw.'

'Where shall we see them—in my office?'

Biggles thought for a moment. 'No. Let's make it informal. I can imagine how they feel. They'll be more likely to open up here than in your office. And I'd like to ask the questions, if you don't mind.'

'Very well,' assented the Air Commodore. 'Get one of your chaps to fetch them. He'll probably find them in the bar at the central mess.'

Biggles raised his eyebrows. 'Drinking?'

'Scrimshaw, who normally doesn't touch anything, is beginning to spend too much time in the bar. It's understandable. After all, these two have watched a squadron wiped out, and some of them have been together since the Battle of Britain.'

Biggles nodded to Ginger. 'Slip along and fetch them,' he ordered.

Ginger went. The others continued the debate for the next few minutes, when Ginger returned with the two officers.

'Sit down, chaps,' invited Biggles quietly. 'Pull up a couple of chairs.'

Crisp and Scrimshaw sat down. Biggles took a quick glance at them in turn as he offered cigarettes. They were both in the condition he expected, for he knew only too well the symptoms resulting from nerve strain, shock, and impotent anger. Scrimshaw's face was flushed and his eyes unnaturally bright. His manner was belligerent to the point of rudeness. He smoked his cigarette in quick short puffs, tapping it incessantly whether there was any ash on it or not. Crisp was pale but steady; his eyes were a little bloodshot in the corners. The fingers of the hand that took the cigarette shook; the forefinger was yellow with nicotine stain.

'We're trying to get to the bottom of this business,' began Biggles casually.

'Getting time somebody did something about it,' rapped out Scrimshaw.

'No one is likely to argue about that,' replied Biggles gently. 'All is being done that can be done. The Japs have slipped a fast one on us, and the only way we shall get it buttoned up is by keeping our heads. To let it get us on the floor would be playing into their hands.'

'I hear you went down and looked at Moorven?' snapped Scrimshaw.

Biggles looked up. 'Who told you that?'

'I don't know—I heard it.'

'Where did you hear it?'

'In the mess, I expect.'

Biggles glanced round. 'Have you fellows been talking?'

'I don't think anybody has spoken outside this mess,' said Algy. 'In fact, apart from my visit to the hospital I don't think anyone has been out.'

'I remember. It was Lal Din told me,' said Scrimshaw.

Biggles looked at Algy. 'Has Lal Din been here?'

'Yes.'

'When?'

'He served coffee after lunch.'

'I told you not to discuss this thing in front of the staff,' rasped Biggles.

There was an uncomfortable silence.

It was broken by Scrimshaw. 'Pah! What does it matter?'

Biggles ignored the question. 'Let's get on,' he resumed,

looking at Crisp and Scrimshaw. 'So far you two fellows have been lucky——'

He winced as Scrimshaw laughed—a harsh, jarring sound.

'Is that your idea of luck?' sneered Scrimshaw.

'All right. Let's say it wasn't luck,' said Biggles imperturbably. 'Let us say there may be a reason. If we are right in that assumption we soon ought to get the thing pranged.'

'Then you didn't find anything at Moorven's crash?' asked Crisp.

'I found a couple of Japs,' returned Biggles.

'What did you do with them?' demanded Scrimshaw.

'I shot them,' answered Biggles evenly.

Scrimshaw let out a yell. 'By thunder! I wish I'd been there. I'd have——'

'Maybe you'll get a chance to do even better later on,' interrupted Biggles curtly. 'I baled out over Moorven's crash today hoping to find out whether the new weapon strikes at the man or the machine. Unfortunately there was no indication. What I'm trying to find out now is, what you two fellows did that Moorven did not do. Conversely, what he did that you did not do. It may have been something that happened in the air or on the ground. I should have liked to put this same question to one of my flight commanders, who bought it this morning, but unfortunately he is not yet able to speak. Johnny, I want you to think very carefully and tell me everything you did from the moment you got up this morning.'

'Where's that going to get us?' demanded Scrimshaw, lighting a fresh cigarette from the one he already held.

'It may get us nowhere,' admitted Biggles. 'But let's look at it this way. Only one thing is quite certain. Either our machines are being attacked by something we can't see, or the pilots in them. I'm going to deal with both possibilities in turn. Right now I am working on the personal aspect. Go ahead, Johnny.'

'I got out of bed,' began Crisp. 'I took off my pyjamas and dressed.'

'Didn't you wash, or have a bath?'

'No.'

'Go on.'

'I then went over to the mess, where I stood by the big table and had some coffee and biscuits.'

'Was anyone else there?'

'Not when I got there. The others came in later.'

'And what did they do?'

'They joined me at the table.'

'And had coffee and biscuits?'

'Yes.'

'You're sure of that?'

'Scrimshaw's here, ask him.'

'That's right,' said Scrimshaw shortly. 'We all had coffee and biscuits. Nothing funny about that, was there?'

'Nothing at all,' agreed Biggles calmly. 'And this coffee all came out of the same pot?'

'Yes,' Crisp answered.

'What about the biscuits?'

'We all helped ourselves from the same plate.'

'And there was nobody else in the room all this time—I mean staff?'

'Nobody. The stuff is put out and anybody who wants can help himself. That's the usual arrangement.'

'Go on,' invited Biggles.

'The five of us then walked over to the machines together.'

'Didn't you smoke after finishing the coffee?'

'Sorry—yes. I forgot that. I had a packet of cigarettes in my pocket. Being finished first I had one, and passed the packet.'

'Then you all smoked cigarettes from the same packet?'

'What's all this?' snapped Scrimshaw. 'Are you trying to make out——'

'Take it easy,' interrupted Biggles. 'I'm not trying to make out anything. I'm asking for facts. Go ahead, Johnny.'

'That's all. We got into our machines and took off.'

'You didn't touch anything else?'

'No.'

'Did you speak to anyone?'

'Yes, I spoke to the sergeant—Sergeant Gray.'

'What about?'

Johnny looked uncomfortable. 'About the change-over.'

'What change-over?'

'Well, you see, I swopped planes with Moorven.'

'You *what?*'

'Changed planes.'

'Why?'

'Well, I reckoned perhaps somebody was tinkering with the machines, but for some reason or other mine was always left alone. We decided to change kites to see what happened. If I went west, and Moorven got back, it would begin to look as if there was some peculiarity about my machine that was saving me all the time. It was because of this I feel so rotten now. If poor old Moorven had stuck to his own machine he would have got back.'

'You mean—he *might* have got back,' said Biggles softly. 'I understand, Johnny. What you really did was to take a big chance of going west yourself. That was pretty noble of you. I'm glad you mentioned this because it rather goes to prove that the machine doesn't make any difference, and that's important. Sergeant Gray knew about this change?'

'Yes.'

Biggles turned to Scrimshaw. 'Did you speak to anybody?'

'Not a soul.'

'And in the air neither of you did anything beyond controlling the aircraft?'

Scrimshaw laughed mirthlessly. 'What else was there to do?'

Crisp nodded. 'That's right enough. What else could we do?'

'I don't know,' answered Biggles. 'That's what I'm trying to find out. You say you both did nothing, so that settles that. And neither of you at any time heard or felt the slightest thing, no noise, no jar, nothing unusual?'

'Nothing at all,' said Johnny.

'That goes for me too,' added Scrimshaw.

'Not even when Moorven fell out of position?' queried Biggles.

'No.'

'You saw him go, of course?'

'Yes, we both saw him go,' confirmed Johnny.

'Moorven didn't say anything over the radio?'

'Not a word.'

'Did you speak to him?'

'Yes. I called him, and asked him what he was doing.'

'Didn't he answer?'

'No.'

'And the others went down in similar circumstances?'

'Yes. Grainger fell out about ten minutes after Moorven went, but Larkin lasted nearly all the way home. He went down about five miles inside the Jap lines.'

'I see—thanks.' Biggles looked at the Air Commodore. 'Any questions you would like to ask?'

The Air Commodore shook his head. 'No. I think you've covered the ground pretty thoroughly. There's just one thing, though.' He looked at Crisp and Scrimshaw. 'What are you two fellows going to do? Your squadron is washed out for the time being. Would you like a spot of leave?'

'Not for me, sir,' answered Scrimshaw. 'Leave is the last thing I want.'

'And me,' added Johnny. 'We'll go on flying till we hit the deck or get to the bottom of this thing, one or the other.'

'It won't do either of you any good to go on living in an empty mess,' suggested the Air Commodore gently. 'Bigglesworth has today lost one of his flight commanders. Crisp, why don't you let me attach you, temporarily, to his squadron, to fill the gap? I'm sure he'd be glad to have you. And you, too, Scrimshaw. You'll work better if you have someone to talk things over with.'

'Yes, why not?' put in Biggles quickly.

The two pilots looked at each other.

'That suits me fine,' said Johnny. 'That is, if Scrim. will come over?'

'I'll come anywhere,' muttered Scrimshaw. 'It's all the same to me.'

'It may be, but it isn't all the same to me,' said Biggles coldly. 'The boys in this squadron have covered a lot of sky since the war started, and it wouldn't be fair to them to turn in more risks than they normally take. Frankly, Scrimshaw, we haven't much confidence in fellows who grab a bottle when things get sticky.'

Scrimshaw flushed scarlet. 'Who said——?'

'I said,' broke in Biggles without raising his voice. 'And what I say I mean. The sooner you understand that the better. Oh, I know how you feel. I've been through it myself, more than once. I was going through it when you wore safety-pins instead of buttons, but I got over it—if I hadn't I shouldn't be here now. If you go on ginning-up you'll be no use to yourself or anyone else. We needn't say any more about it—but think it over. Make a party with my fellows after dinner and take a trip round the town. They'll do anything you want to do, but they don't brood and they don't booze—those are the only two things we bar. We've too much to do. That's all for now.' Biggles got up.

8

DEATH MARCHES ON

As the officers dispersed, talking over the mystery quietly among themselves, Biggles turned to Air Commodore Raymond. 'I think I shall go along right away and have a word or two with Sergeant Gray, sir,' he announced. 'There's just time before dinner.'

'Do you mind if I come with you?' asked Johnny Crisp. 'It's partly my pigeon. Gray is in A Flight—my flight.'

'Come by all means—only too glad to have you along,' invited Biggles. 'He'll probably say more to you than to strangers. That'll be enough, though, we don't want a crowd.'

Biggles, the Air Commodore and Johnny, left the officers' quarters and walked along to the sergeants' mess, where they learned that Sergeant Gray was out.

'Any idea where he is?' Biggles asked the flight sergeant who had come to the door.

'I think I heard him say something about going down to the flight shed, sir,' returned the flight sergeant. 'He wanted to have another look at those two machines that got back this morning.'

'Thanks,' acknowledged Biggles. 'Maybe we'll find him there.'

'I hope he isn't going to let this thing prey on his mind,' remarked Johnny, as they walked on to the hangar in which the two surviving A Flight machines were parked. 'He's a good chap. He's been in the squadron pretty nearly since it was formed at Kenley, years ago.'

The hangar was in darkness. The Air Commodore switched on a torch. The beam fell on the two Hurricanes, but there was no one with them.

'Anyone about?' called Biggles.

There was no answer.

Biggles saw a narrow crack of light half-way down and on one side of the building. 'That must be him, in the flight office,' he observed.

They walked on to the door. Biggles opened it. He stopped. 'Take a look at this,' he murmured dryly.

Lying on the floor, breathing stertorously, was a sergeant.

'That's Gray,' said Johnny. 'Drunk as a lord, by the look of it.'

'You seem pretty sure of that,' challenged Biggles.

'He's done it before. The same thing happened last week. If I'd put him on a charge he'd have lost his stripes, and I hate doing that to a good airman. I made him promise he wouldn't do it again.'

'Does he make a habit of doing this sort of thing?' asked the Air Commodore.

'Not as far as I know,' replied Johnny. 'I think he's only taken to it lately. Pity.'

Biggles shook the sergeant by the shoulder. 'Come on, snap out of it.' he ordered peremptorily.

The sergeant did not move.

'Get up, Gray,' snapped Johnny irritably.

The sergeant lay still, snoring.

Biggles pummelled him, and in the end slapped his face.

The sergeant grunted, but did not move.

'He certainly has got a skinful,' muttered Johnny. 'He sort of went to pieces when I told him that Moorven and the others had gone west, but I didn't think he'd take it like this.' He shook the sergeant again.

'It's no use,' said Biggles quietly. 'We shan't get anything out of him in that state. There's only one thing that might bring him round. Slip over to the mess, Johnny, and get a jug of black coffee, hot.'

Johnny went off at a run.

While they were waiting, the Air Commodore spoke to Biggles. 'What do you really make of all this?'

'It's fantastic—that's the only word for it,' replied Biggles. 'What beats me is, the thing is so infernally inconsistent. Today, Tug made three trips well into enemy country and got away with it every time. Why? How? There must be an answer to that, if only we could hit on it. There were a lot of enemy machines about; I saw them; yet they weren't affected. They flew as if they had nothing to fear. Very queer. I have a feeling, not based on anything concrete, that——'

Johnny came in, slightly breathless from his run. 'There was no black coffee on tap, so I ordered some,' he announced. 'Lal Din says he will bring it over right away.' He looked at the sergeant. 'Silly fool, letting the flight down like this.'

A minute or two later the steward came in. His habitual smile broadened when his eyes fell on the sergeant.

'He cachum flenty whisky,' he chuckled. 'Here coffee, sahib. Velly stlong.'

Biggles took the coffee-pot, a small copper one, from the tray, and walked over to the sergeant. 'What part of the world do you come from, Lal Din?' he asked casually. 'You don't talk like a man of this country.'

'Me Burmese. I blong Mandalay,' was the answer.

'You don't look much like a Burman,' said Biggles without looking up, as he dropped on his knees beside the unconscious N.C.O.

'Father Burman, but he dead long time. Mother, she Chinese. Bling me up China fashion,' said Lal Din.

Biggles forced the N.C.O.'s teeth apart, not without difficulty, and poured coffee into his mouth.

The sergeant spluttered. Biggles looked over his shoulder at Lal Din, who was still standing just inside the door. 'What are you waiting for?' he asked sharply.

'I wait for coffee-pot, sahib. Canteen ploperty. Maybe someone else want coffee.'

'You can fetch it later on. We may be some time.'

'Velly good, sahib.' Lal Din went off.

'What's the matter with him? Don't you trust him?' asked the Air Commodore.

'In a show like this, the only people I trust are those I know,' answered Biggles, pouring more coffee into the sergeant's mouth.

Again the sergeant spluttered, chokingly. His head lolled from side to side. His eyes opened.

'Come on, Gray; pull yourself together,' rapped out Biggles tersely.

'Wash-washer matter?' gasped the sergeant.

'You're drunk,' said Johnny bitingly.

The sergeant was indignant. 'Thash a lie. Not drunk.'

Biggles gave him more coffee.

'He says he isn't drunk,' said Johnny, looking at Biggles and the Air Commodore in turn.

'Of course he does.' The Air Commodore laughed lugubriously. 'Did you ever know a drunken man admit that he was tight? I didn't.'

'If you tell him he's drunk he'll spend the rest of the night trying to prove that he isn't,' put in Biggles wearily.

The sergeant's eyes were clearing. 'Wash wrong?' he demanded in a dazed voice, and was then violently sick.

'Tight as an owl,' muttered Johnny. 'You won't get any sense out of him till he's slept it off.'

'I'm afraid you're right,' agreed Biggles sadly. 'What a nuisance.' He shook the sergeant again. 'Listen to me, Gray. Can you hear what I say?'

'Yes—shir.'

'That's better. We'll talk to you later.'

'Don't wanner talk—hic. Those yellow monkeys—killed my

officers. I wanner get at 'em. You hear me? I wanner——'

Biggles stood up. 'Yes, we know. You go to your bunk and sleep it off.'

'Schleep what off?' slurred the sergeant drowsily.

'You're all ginned-up,' put in Johnny, who was getting more and more angry. 'You promised me you wouldn't touch the stuff.'

'Drunk! Hark at him,' pleaded the sergeant. 'Says I'm drunk. I was never drunk—in my life—no shir.'

'We'll settle that argument later,' averred Biggles, arranging a packed parachute under the sergeant's head. 'Have a sleep. Here, you might as well finish the rest of the coffee.'

Without assistance the N.C.O. took the remainder of the coffee at a gulp. 'Thash berrer,' he declared sleepily 'I just wanner be alone,' he rambled on. 'I only came here to be alone. Sat here, chewing the thing over, thas all. I may be sick, but I ain't drunk—no shir.'

'Silly ass,' muttered Johnny.

'I wouldn't be too hard on him,' said Biggles as they went out. 'His nerves are probably in rags. You say he's been with the squadron a long time? Well, now he's seen the squadron washed out. He ought to be sent home for a rest.'

'I'll get him posted,' promised the Air Commodore.

They went to the mess and had dinner. Later, after listening to the news on the radio, they sat in a corner with Algy and Bertie discussing the mystery from all angles, without, however, coming any nearer to solving it. Biggles said little. Eventually he looked at his watch.

'Eleven o'clock,' he announced. 'I think I shall turn in, and leave Sergeant Gray until tomorrow.'

'I'll just walk down and make sure he's all right,' offered Johnny.

'Be as well,' agreed Biggles.

The Air Commodore got up. 'I'll be getting along, too,' he decided. 'See you in the morning.' He nodded to the others and departed.

Johnny went off. Biggles stood for a minute or two talking to

Algy and Ginger, who wanted to know if he had made any plans for the following day. He told them he wanted to do some more thinking before he decided on a definite programme.

He was walking along the path that led to the officers' sleeping quarters when an airman overtook him.

'Excuse me, sir, you're wanted on the 'phone,' said he.

'Which 'phone?' asked Biggles.

'The one in the hall, sir.'

Biggles turned back. 'Where have you just come from?' he asked.

'I was on duty in the kitchen, sir.'

'I see.' Biggles stepped into the hall and picked up the telephone.

'Is that you, Biggles?' said a voice. 'This is Johnny here. I'd like you to come down to the flight shed.'

'Something wrong?' queried Biggles.

'Yes, it's the sergeant.'

'Is he still there?'

'Yes.'

'Is something wrong with him?'

'Plenty,' said Johnny. 'He's dead.'

'Stay there,' said Biggles tersely. 'I'll be right down.'

Biggles ran to the shed. Johnny was there, alone, bending over the sergeant, who was lying on his back on the floor, the position in which they had left him. One glance at the open mouth and staring eyes was enough.

'He's a goner all right,' said Biggles in a hard voice. He shook his head. 'I don't get it. He was coming round fast when we left him. Well, there goes my hope of learning anything from him. I wonder why he died? You've had a look at him I suppose?'

'Of course. Can't find a thing. Not a wound, not a mark of any sort. Can't make it out. He must have passed out in a drunken stupor.'

'Well, there's nothing we can do except send for the doctor,' said Biggles.

'I wonder if he did himself in, in a fit of remorse?' suggested Johnny.

'I imagine it is very difficult to commit suicide without leaving some sign of it,' returned Biggles. 'Go and fetch the M.O.'

Johnny departed on his errand.

After gazing at the body for a moment or two Biggles looked round the little room, his eyes taking in everything. Nothing had been disturbed. The room appeared to be precisely as when he had last seen it. The coffee-pot and the tray were still there. He went to the pot and picked it up. It was empty. Thoughtfully, he put it down again. For a while he did not move from where he stood; then his eyes stopped on a tiny object that lay on the floor near the waste-paper basket. A quick step took him to it. Stooping, he picked it up. It was a round pellet of paper, pink. Slowly he unfolded it and found in his hand a slip of grease-proof paper, about three inches square. There was printing on one side. He read it: WITH THE COMPLIMENTS OF CHARNEYS, LTD., LONDON. NOT FOR SALE. SUPPLIED FOR THE USE OF H.M. FORCES ONLY. With a frown lining his forehead he raised the paper to his nostrils. His eyes switched to the dead N.C.O. He went over to him, and dropping on his knees, looked into the eyes.

There came a sound of quick footsteps and the M.O. entered, followed by Johnny. Ignoring Biggles the doctor went straight to the body. Silence settled in the death chamber while he examined it. After a while he stood up. 'I'll get him over to the mortuary,' he said.

'What do you make of it?' asked Biggles.

'I'd rather reserve my opinion till after the post-mortem examination,' replied the doctor.

'There'll be an autopsy?'

'Of course.' The doctor looked at Johnny. 'He was in your flight, wasn't he?'

'Yes.'

'Can you offer any explanation of this?'

'We found him here, drunk, about three hours ago,' answered Johnny. 'We left him in the same state. He was badly cut up about the casualties today.'

'Have you known him to get drunk before?'

'Yes. I had him on the mat for the same thing about a week

ago. But surely, Doc, booze doesn't *kill* a man?'

'In the East, in the sort of weather we've been having lately, it can induce heat stroke, which does. More often, though, the man runs amok. In that condition he often tries to commit suicide. You'd better go, now. I'm going to lock the door till the ambulance comes to collect the body.'

They went out. The M.O. locked the door.

'Where are you going now, Johnny?' asked Biggles.

'I think I shall push along to bed.'

'Me too,' said Biggles.

'Mind if I tell Scrimshaw about this?'

'Not in the least,' answered Biggles. 'I'll see you in the morning. Good night. Good night, Doc.'

Biggles walked on alone. He did not go straight to his quarter, but walked slowly to the sergeant's mess, where he sent for the mess secretary and the barman. He took them outside.

'Sergeant Gray has just been found dead,' he announced quietly. 'He looked as though he had been drinking. Did he have anything here before he went out?'

'I didn't see him at the bar,' said the mess secretary—a warrant officer.

'Yes, he came, but he didn't stay,' volunteered the barman. 'I served him with an iced lemonade—I think it was. I know it was a soft drink because someone pulled his leg about it. Then he said he was going down to the sheds. I recall that because the flight sergeant told him it didn't do any good to mope about.'

'Did Gray seem at all agitated or upset?'

'No, sir, I can't say that he did. I didn't take much notice of him, but from what I remember he was quieter than usual.'

'Thanks,' said Biggles. 'That's all I wanted to know.'

Deep in thought he turned away and went to his quarter. For a long time he sat on his bed, thinking, smoking cigarettes. Then he undressed and got between the sheets.

9

BIGGLES PLAYS FOX

THE following morning Biggles was up early. Before doing anything else he called the hospital on the telephone to inquire about Angus. He learned that his condition was the same; he was still unconscious.

Before he had finished dressing there was a tap on the door and Air Commodore Raymond came in. He looked worn with worry. 'I've just heard about Sergeant Gray,' he said in a tired voice. 'This is awful. What do you suggest we do?'

'For a start, sir, I'd advise you to ask the doctor to give you something to help you to sleep, or you'll be the next casualty.'

'How can I sleep with this horror hanging over my head?' said the Air Commodore. 'What do you make of this business of Gray?'

'I have an uncomfortable feeling that we're partly responsible for that,' returned Biggles, without looking round. He was washing out his shaving kit.

'What on earth do you mean?'

'We were too ready to take it for granted that he was drunk.'

'Wasn't he?'

'No. At least, I don't think so, unless he got the stuff outside somewhere. The indications are that he didn't leave the station.'

'How do you know that?'

'I made it my business to find out.'

'If he wasn't drunk, then what was the matter with him?'

'Why waste time guessing? The M.O. is holding an autopsy. Presumably it will be this morning, since it is customary here to bury people on the same day as they die. We shall soon know the truth—I hope.'

'There's a rumour about the station that it was suicide.'

Biggles flicked his tie angrily. 'How did *that* start? Rumour—rumour—rumour . . . always rumours. If people only knew the harm they do. I'd like to know who started this one.'

'You're not suggesting that it was started deliberately?'

'That wouldn't surprise me. Rumour is a weapon in this war.'

'You don't believe this one, evidently?'

'I prefer to keep an open mind until after the autopsy.'

'If he didn't die from natural causes then it must have been suicide.'

Biggles put on his tunic. 'It doesn't seem to have occurred to you that it might have been murder.'

'Murder!' The Air Commodore looked aghast.

'That's what I said.'

'But what possible motive could anyone have for murdering a harmless fellow like Gray?'

Biggles lit a cigarette. 'The same motive that cost Moorven and the others their lives.'

'I don't understand.'

'The man who was responsible for Moorven's death wanted Japan to win the war. It may be that the man who killed Gray— if Gray was, in fact, murdered—was actuated by the same desire.'

'But why Gray?'

'You seem to forget that Gray was A Flight fitter; that he was the last man to look over the three machines that were lost yesterday, and that we were waiting to interrogate him. If Gray could have talked he might have told us something, something that might have put us on the track of the secret weapon. If that were so, then there was ample motive for killing him.'

'I didn't think of that,' murmured Raymond.

'Don't breathe a word of it to anyone,' adjured Biggles. 'I mean that seriously and literally. It's only my opinion. Let's wait for the result of the autopsy before we start barking up what may turn out to be the wrong tree.'

'I shan't say anything,' said the Air Commodore heavily. 'I've another worry now.'

'What is it this time?'

'The rot has started at another station.'

Biggles turned sharply. 'Where?'

'Darwin, Australia. They lost five machines yesterday out of one formation—all down in the sea. It's clear that unless we can stop it, the thing will spread over the entire Pacific. We've got to work fast, Bigglesworth.'

'You flatter me,' returned Biggles curtly. 'The whole Intelligence branch has been working on this thing for weeks yet you expect me to produce results in twenty-four hours. Have a heart.' He finished dressing and picked up his cap.

'Where are you going now?' asked the Air Commodore despondently.

'To get some breakfast. It's a good thing to eat, sometimes.'

'And then?'

'I'm going to take out a patrol.'

'Good God, man! You can't do that!' objected the Air Commodore in a startled voice.

'Why not?'

'Because you're our one hope now. If anything happens to you——'

'It'll be worse for me than it will for you,' interposed Biggles dryly. 'The thing won't come to *us*. We've got to find it.'

'Are you taking the whole squadron out?'

'No.' Biggles smiled faintly. 'I'll leave some for tomorrow—in case.'

Algy came in. He saluted the Air Commodore and looked at Biggles. 'What's the programme?'

'I'll tell you over breakfast. I'll be across in a minute. Do something for me.'

'What is it?'

'I'm smoking too much. Walk along to the canteen and buy me a packet of chewing-gum.'

'Okay.'

'What am I going to tell Darwin?' asked the Air Commodore.

'I may be able to suggest something later in the day,' answered Biggles, putting his map in his pocket. 'Meantime, I'll push along.'

At the door they parted, the Air Commodore returning to headquarters and Biggles walking over to the dining-room, where he found the rest of the squadron, including the new members, Johnny and Scrimshaw, already gathered, drinking coffee and munching biscuits from a large plate. Before joining them he rang the bell.

Lal Din, smiling, obsequious, answered it.

'Listen, chaps, this is the programme for this morning,' announced Biggles. Then, noticing the steward, he said, 'Bring me a packet of cigarettes.'

'Yes, sahib.' Lal Din went out.

Biggles poured a cup of coffee, spread his map on the table and looked at it for a minute or two. 'We're going to do a sortie,' he went on. 'I shan't be going myself. I'm not sending the whole squadron—just two machines. Johnny and Ginger can go. One reason for that is I don't want a mixed formation. We'll use two Hurricanes. You, Johnny, will fly X M, which leaves X T for Ginger. The others, for the moment, will have to stay on the ground. This will be the course. After taking off the two machines will head east for an hour. That will take them into the area where the machines were lost yesterday, and not far from where Angus went down. They will then turn north for fifteen minutes, after which they will return home.' Biggles looked at Johnny and Ginger. 'Is that clear?'

They nodded.

'All right, then.' Biggles looked at his watch. 'You will leave the ground in twenty minutes. Finish your coffee. There's no immediate hurry.' He looked round. 'Where's that heathen with my cigarettes? Ah! There you are, Lal Din. Thanks.' Biggles took the cigarettes from the proferred tray and signed the chit.

The steward went out.

Biggles lit a cigarette and sipped his coffee. Then he beckoned to Algy and took him on one side. 'Did you get that chewing-gum?'

'Yes.' Algy produced the tiny package and handed it over.

Biggles glanced at it and dropped it in his pocket. 'I've got a job for you,' he said in a low voice. 'Don't say a word about it to anyone, either here or anywhere else. I want you to go first of all to the M.O. and ask him to give you something guaranteed to make a man sick. If he jibs, go to Raymond. But if you tell him it's for me I think he'll let you have it—he knows I'm on a special job. You will then borrow the reserve ambulance, and driving it yourself, take it to the practice landing-ground at Gayhar. That's a little place among the paddy-fields about six miles north of here. You'd better push off right away, because I want you to be at Gayhar inside an hour.'

Algy's eyes had opened wide while Biggles was giving these instructions, but he did not question them. 'Have you got a line on something?' he breathed.

'I think so,' answered Biggles softly. 'This is really an experiment to test a theory.'

'What am I to do at Gayhar?'

'Nothing. Just sit on the edge of the field and wait.'

'Wait for what?'

'For me. Push off now.'

Algy went out, and Biggles returned to the others who—probably to conceal their real feelings—were making joking remarks about the two pilots detailed for the patrol. He sat down and finished his coffee. Some minutes later he again looked at his watch.

'All right, you chaps, you'd better get along now. I'll walk down with you and see you off. The rest will stay here till I come back. I may need you.'

With Johnny and Ginger he walked towards the machines, which were being wheeled out on to the tarmac. 'What a grand day,' he remarked. 'I think I'll come with you, after all. I'll fly a Spit.'

'You will!' cried Ginger delightedly.

'Yes.'

'I'm glad you've changed your mind,' remarked Johnny.

'As a matter of fact I haven't,' returned Biggles evenly. 'I intended coming all along.'

Johnny stared. 'Then why didn't you say so?'

'Because I am getting nervous of letting too many people know my movements,' declared Biggles. 'I want you two fellows to remember what you're doing and keep your wits about you. The moment either of you feels anything happening to you, let me know—if you can.'

'You mean, when we get into enemy country?' queried Johnny.

'No. We're not going into enemy country. We're going to stop this side of the lines.'

Johnny pulled up dead. 'Then what's the idea of this sortie?'

'The idea is,' replied Biggles, 'if either of you falls out I'd rather it were where I can get at you.'

Johnny looked astonished. 'But what *can* happen, this side of the lines?'

'You may be surprised,' answered Biggles vaguely.

'But what about you?' put in Ginger. 'You talk as though something might happen to us, but not to you.'

'If my guess is right, I don't think it can,' answered Biggles. 'That's enough questions. We're not going far—only to Gayhar landing-field. When we get there we shall land, and just sit in our seats for a couple of hours, leaving the engines running. Conditions will then be the same as if we were up topsides, only our wheels will be on the carpet. I'm afraid it's going to be rather boring, but it may be worth it. Let's go.'

The three machines, two Hurricanes and a Spitfire, took off in formation, with Biggles heading due east for a time, as if they were bound for Burma. But as soon as he had satisfied himself that they were out of sight of the airfield he swung round, and in a few minutes had the flight circling over the practice landing-ground.

Ginger spoke over the radio. 'What's that blood-wagon doing down there?'

Biggles answered: 'I suppose somebody thinks it may be needed. That's enough talking.'

He continued circling for a little while and then went down. The three machines landed as they had taken off, and finished within a short distance of each other. And in that position they remained, the motors throttled back, the airscrews ticking over.

After an hour had passed Biggles got out and walked over to Ginger's machine. Having climbed up on the wing he asked, 'Are you still feeling all right?'

'Right as rain,' answered Ginger.

'Stay where you are,' ordered Biggles, and went over to Johnny.

'Are you still feeling all right?' he inquired.

'I'm getting a bit browned off, otherwise okay.'

'Stay where you are.'

Biggles returned to his Spitfire and resumed his seat in the cockpit.

Another hour—a long, weary hour—passed. Again Biggles got out and went over to Ginger. 'Still feeling all right?'

'Never felt better,' declared Ginger. 'This is a slow game, Biggles. How long is it going on?'

'Stay where you are,' commanded Biggles, and went on to the other Hurricane, increasing his pace when he noted that Johnny's head was sagging on his chest as if he were asleep. He jumped on a wing. 'Johnny!' he shouted.

Johnny did not answer.

Biggles touched him. Johnny lolled, limply.

Biggles moved fast. He switched off the engine and dashed back to Ginger. 'All right!' he shouted. 'Switch off. Johnny's bought it. Come over and help me to get him down.' Then, turning towards the ambulance he raised his arms above his head, beckoning. As soon as the vehicle started forward he ran back to Johnny's Hurricane, and with Ginger's help, got the unconscious pilot to the ground. By the time this had been accomplished Algy had brought the ambulance to the stop, and had joined the little party.

'Bear a hand, Algy. Let's get him into the blood-cart,' said Biggles tersely. He had turned a trifle pale.

They lifted Johnny on to one of the stretchers.

'Did you get that stuff from the doctor?' Biggles asked Algy.

'Yes. He says it would make an elephant heave its heart out.'

'Let's have it—quick.'

Algy handed him a bottle.

Biggles tore the cork out with his teeth and coaxed a little of the liquid the bottle contained between Johnny's pallid lips.

Johnny spluttered. He gasped. He retched. Then he was sick.

'Okay,' said Biggles softly. 'Keep that blanket over him to

keep him warm.'

Johnny was sick again. Panting, he opened his eyes. They were dull, with the pupils dilated. He was sick again.

'Pass the water, Algy,' ordered Biggles. He wiped Johnny's face and bathed the temples. 'There should be some smelling-salts in that first-aid cabinet,' he told Ginger.

Ginger brought the bottle.

Johnny gasped as the pungent fumes struck his nostrils, but they hastened his recovery.

'What—what was it?' he gasped.

'Take your time, old lad—you'll soon be okay,' said Biggles soothingly.

Johnny's eyes cleared, and he was soon able to sit up.

'Feel well enough to tell us what happened?' asked Biggles.

'Yes, I think so. My God! It was awful.'

'Lucky your wheels were on the floor, eh?'

'If they hadn't been—I should—have come a crumper. Is this—what got—the others?'

Biggles nodded. 'Tell us what happened.'

Johnny had another drink of water. 'Well, I just sat there for what seemed a long time,' he explained. 'Then I felt a queer sort of feeling coming over me. At first I thought it was the heat; then I realised it wasn't. But by that time I was too far gone to do anything about it. It was hell. Phew! Does my head rock! It feels as if there were a couple of pistons inside it.'

'That'll pass off,' said Biggles. 'Go on with the story.'

'I thought I was dying,' continued Johnny. 'Everything round me was all distorted. I had a feeling I was flying upside-down. The instruments were all heaped in a pile. I tried to move, to call you on the radio, but I couldn't. My bones had all gone to jelly. Then I couldn't make out what things were—they sort of flowed about into each other, as if they were liquid. They turned all colours.'

'But you were still conscious?'

'I can't say I knew what was happening. The pain in my head was terrible. It felt as if my brain had split into two parts. One part was mad, and the other part a sort of spectator. I couldn't

do anything—couldn't make a sound. That's the last I remember. I suppose I must have passed out. The thought of that
happening in the air makes my skin curl. What was it? Do you
know?'

'I think so,' answered Biggles. 'I fancy it was the piece of
chewing-gum you ate.'

Johnny stared at Biggles' face. 'Chewing-gum?' he ejaculated.
'What chewing-gum?'

Biggles' expression changed to one of questioning surprise.
'Didn't you find a packet of chewing-gum in the pocket of your
instrument panel, and put a piece in your mouth?'

'No. I hate the stuff, anyway.'

Biggles looked incredulous. 'Are you *sure*?'

A smile, faintly sarcastic, curled Johnny's lips. 'Dash it all! I
may look dumb, but I'm not so cheesed that I don't know when
I chew gum. I tell you, I never touch the stuff.'

Biggles bit his lip, looking really crestfallen. 'If that's the case
I'm on the wrong trail after all. I still don't understand it
though. Are you absolutely positive that there was no gum in
your cockpit?'

'Not today.'

'What do you mean by that exactly? Does it imply that you
have had some gum in your cockpit on other occasions?'

'There usually is a piece. It's a free issue, you know. Might
almost call it normal equipment.'

'You find it in the machine when you get in?'

'Yes.'

'Who puts it there?'

'Sergeant Gray used to. He sort of did the round before a
show.'

'But there was no gum in your machine today? Why not, I
wonder?'

'Probably because I told Gray yesterday morning that he was
wasting his time putting it in.'

Biggles looked at Ginger. 'Wasn't there any gum in your
machine, either?'

'No.'

An expression of baffled bewilderment came over Biggles' face. He shrugged his shoulders helplessly. 'This is a bone-shaker,' he said in a disappointed voice. 'Everything turned out just as I thought it would, except that I expected Ginger to be the one to crack up. I've gone wrong somewhere—or else the devils have been too smart for me. I would have bet my life that I was on the right track. I'd more or less proved it—as I thought—this morning. I offered you a piece of chewing-gum—Algy had got it for me from the canteen. You refused. I offered Scrimshaw a piece. He refused, too—told me he never touched the stuff. I was suspicious of chewing-gum, and when I discovered that neither you nor Scrimshaw touched the stuff it seemed to confirm my theory—that the stuff was phoney. I was convinced that you and Scrimshaw always got back because, by a lucky chance for you, neither of you chewed gum. By passing out this morning, Johnny, you've knocked my theory sideways.'

'What set you on this chewing-gum line of argument?' asked Ginger curiously.

Biggles took a small square of pink paper from his pocket and showed it to Johnny. 'This is the stuff the gum is packed in, isn't it? Really, I needn't ask you, because I bought a packet this morning.'

'That's right,' agreed Johnny.

'I found a piece of this paper in Moorven's machine. That told me he had been chewing gum in the cockpit. I paid no attention to it at the time—after all, there was nothing remarkable about it. But when, last night, I found a piece of the same paper in A Flight office, where Gray was lying apparently drunk, I began to think. When I learned from the sergeants' mess that Gray had had nothing to drink there, I thought still harder. I thought I was on the track. When, this morning, as I have said, I learned that you and Scrimshaw, the survivors of a squadron, never touched gum, my surmise began to look like a certainty. Now it looks as though the gum has nothing to do with it . . . but I still think there's something queer about it.'

'Since Gray is dead, he couldn't very well put gum into any of the machines this morning,' Algy pointed out.

'That's true enough,' admitted Biggles. 'And I'm afraid that settles the argument. There was no gum—yet Johnny passes out. Obviously, it wasn't gum that did the trick.' He sat down on the end of the stretcher and lit a cigarette.

'Well, there was certainly no gum in my machine,' declared Ginger. 'If there had been I should probably have nibbled a piece. I was getting pretty browned off, sitting there doing nothing.'

For a little while Biggles sat with his chin in his hand, deep in thought. Then he got up. 'Stay where you are,' he ordered. 'I'm just going to have a look round these machines.' He went off, climbing first into the cockpit of Johnny's machine, and then treating Ginger's in like manner. He was not long away. 'All right,' he said briskly when he returned. 'We may as well get back to Dum Dum. Don't mention this business to anyone, nor even speak of it among yourselves in the mess. I don't think you're quite fit to fly yet, Johnny, so you'd better trundle back in the blood-wagon. Do you feel well enough to drive it?'

'Yes, I'm all right now,' answered Johnny. In spite of his assurance he still looked somewhat shaken.

'Fine. Algy will fly your machine home. Let's go.'

Biggles walked over to his aircraft, and after waiting for Algy and Ginger to get into position, took off.

10

THE BLITZ THAT FAILED

WHEN Biggles landed at Dum Dum, and taxied in, he observed with mounting curiosity that the airfield was, to use the common Air Force expression, in a state of flap. Airmen were running about, orders were being shouted, and engines roared as aircraft were dispersed all round the perimeter of the airfield. Having stepped down, he was gazing with mild surprise at this spectacle, when Air Commodore Raymond, followed by Group Captain Boyle, the station commander, came hurrying to him.

'Thank heaven you're back,' began the Air Commodore in a

tense voice. 'You're the very man I want to see.'

'What the dickens is going on here?' asked Biggles.

'We're in for a pasting, I'm afraid—and Calcutta, too, no doubt,' asserted the Air Commodore, pulling a wry face. 'We've just had a signal from our forward observers to the effect that the biggest formation of Jap bombers seen in this part of the world is heading in this direction. Ninety-eight of 'em. We suppose they're taking advantage of the situation created by the secret weapon to have a really good smack at us. They know we are powerless to stop them.'

'You mean, they *think* we are,' returned Biggles grimly. 'How far away is this formation?'

'They'll be here in twenty minutes.'

'What are they?'

'Mitsubishi bombers.'

'Any escort?'

'No. They have good reason for thinking they don't need one.

'What are you doing about it?'

'We're sending up six fighters to intercept them.'

'Six! What do you suppose six machines are going to do against that mob? Why only six? There are more fighters than that on the station.'

'I know, but we daren't leave ourselves without a reserve. With this secret weapon operating I don't suppose we shall see any of our machines again.'

Biggles pointed at a pathetically small formation of Spitfires just talking off. 'Are those the six?'

'Yes.'

'Stop them. Call them back.'

'But——'

I know what I'm doing, sir. Recall them.'

The Air Commodore hesitated. 'But if Calcutta is bombed—'

'You'r going the right way to get it bombed,' broke in Biggles impatiently. 'Look, sir, we've no time to waste in argument or explanations. If you'll leave this operation to me I promise you won't regret it.'

'But think——'

'I've never let you down yet, have I?'

The Air Commodore decided. 'All right.' He turned to the Group Captain. 'Recall those machines.'

The Group Captain hurried off, and in a few seconds the flight could be seen returning. Algy and Ginger had landed. Biggles waved to them, beckoning urgently. Then he turned again to the Air Commodore. His voice was brittle.

'Will you let me handle this?'

'Yes, but if things go wrong——'

'I know—you'll be held responsible. I'm afraid that's a risk you'll have to take, sir. I know how many fighters I've got, but how many others are there available on the station? I'm including the two Hurricanes belonging to Crisp and Scrimshaw in my outfit.'

'Apart from those we've seven—all that are left of 910 Squadron.'

'As Crisp isn't back yet, that means we can put up fifteen, all told, if we include my Beaufighter.'

'But are you going to leave the airfield without a single fighter on it?' cried the Air Commodore aghast.

'What are fighters for it not to fight? They'll never have a better opportunity than this, nor is there ever likely to be a greater emergency.'

'But suppose none of them get back?'

'That'll be your worry—I shan't be here,' answered Biggles curtly.

Algy and Ginger came running up. 'What goes on?' asked Algy quickly.

'There's a big formation of Jap bombers on the way,' Biggles told him without emotion. 'We ought to be able to hit them a crack. Algy, I want you to get every fighter on the station lined up—including those Spits that are just landing—with the pilots on parade behind them. Jump to it. Ginger, turn out the squadron. It will line up with the rest. Make it snappy.'

'You're sure you know what you're doing, Bigglesworth?' asked the Air Commodore, in tones of acute anxiety.

'No, I'm not sure,' answered Biggles frankly. 'How can anyone be sure of anything in times like these? I'm hoping, that's all, but that doesn't mean I'm guessing. Sorry I haven't time to talk any more now. See you later.' He walked briskly to where the machines had been mustered in line, with their pilots in a group behind them. He beckoned to Algy. 'Keep those fellows together until I join you; I want a word with them. I shan't be long.'

'Okay.'

Biggles walked on to the end of the line of machines. In a few minutes he was back, facing the line of pilots, officers and sergeants, who were fidgeting at the delay.

'Listen, everyone,' he said loudly. 'You all know what's been going on here—I mean, this secret weapon scare. Forget it. If anyone goes for a Burton today it will be from some other cause. Here is your chance to get your own back for what the enemy has done to those messmates who are no longer with us. There are a hundred Japs for you to carve at, so you can help yourselves. There's no escort so it should be a slice of cake. Scrimshaw, last night you seemed to have a load of dirty water on your chest. Now you can get rid of it. My crowd will remember what happened to Angus yesterday.'

'Here comes Johnny Crisp,' said someone.

Looking round Biggles saw Johnny running like a hare across the field.

'Hey! What's going on?' yelled Johnny.

'There's a big Jap formation on the way,' Biggles told him.

'Gimme an aircraft—gimme an aircraft!' bleated Johnny deliriously.

Biggles smiled. 'Sure you're fit to fly?'

'Watch me; oh boy, just watch me!' cried Johnny hysterically.

'All right, take the Beaufighter.' Biggles turned back to the waiting pilots. 'That's all. Give these perishers everything you've got. We haven't far to go. I shall lead in the Typhoon. Let's get weaving.'

There was a rush for the machines.

Biggles started for his aircraft. Pointing eastward, he shouted to the Air Commodore, who was standing by, 'Get in your car and head up the road that way. You might be in time to see something worth watching.'

The Air Commodore waved understandingly, and ran towards his car.

Biggles climbed into his machine, settled himself in the seat and felt for the throttle. Engines roared, and the mixed formation moved forward, swiftly gaining speed, sending clouds of dust swirling high into the air behind it. Heading eastward, Biggles eased the control column back for altitude.

Five minutes later, at fifteen thousand feet and still climbing he saw the enemy formation, composed of Mitsubishi bombers as the Air Commodore had stated, strung out like a great dragon across the sky, at an estimated height of twelve thousand feet. He smiled mirthlessly as he altered course a trifle to intercept it. He spoke in the radio.

'Tally-ho, boys! Tally-ho! There they are. We've got 'em. Bertie, get me that leader. Ginger, Tug, stay up to pick off stragglers. Here we go!'

Biggles launched his attack from the starboard quarter, aiming at the neck of the dragon. He went down in a steep dive, with the rest opening out as they streamed down behind him. In an instant the air was being cut into sections by lines of tracer shells and bullets. He picked a Mitsubishi on the near side of the enemy formation, the pilot of which was showing signs of nervousness. Being nearest to the descending tornado he was edging away, forcing others inside the formation to swerve, and lose position in their efforts to avoid collision. To Biggles this was as old as war flying itself. There is usually one such machine in a big formation, and it becomes as much a menace to its own side as to its opponents.

Biggles planned to aggravate the trouble. He held his fire. Tracer flashed past him, but he paid no need to it, even if he saw it. But when bullets began splashing off his engine cowling he frowned, and pressed a foot gently on the rudder-bar, but without taking his eyes off the bomber he had marked down. He took it in his sights, and at three hundred yards jammed hard on the firing button. The Typhoon shuddered a little as the guns flamed, concentrating a cone of bullets on the Mitsubishi, which swerved wildly, causing others to do the same. The first result of this was not immediately apparent, for the Typhoon had roared over its target to zoom steeply on the other side.

Turning on the top of the zoom Biggles saw that the onset had achieved all that he had hoped of it. The dragon had cracked across the middle, and the formation was now in the shape of a dog's hind leg. Four bombers were going down in different directions and at different angles, one in flames, one smoking. Two others, one of which, Biggles thought, was the swerver, had their wings locked—the prelude to disaster. As he watched they broke apart, one, minus half a wing, to fall spinning. The crew of the other baled out. A Hurricane was also going down, leaving a plume of black smoke to mark its trail. The pilot scrambled out on the fuselage, to be swept off instantly into space by the tearing slipstream.

A look of puzzled astonishment came over Biggles' face as he made out another Hurricane boring along up the middle of the enemy formation blazing a berserk path with its guns. Such madness, far outside the range of recognised tactics, was at all events effective, and the enemy machines were thrown into confusion. But it was also suicidal. Biggles recognised Scrimshaw's machine.

'Scrimshaw, come out of that, you fool,' he snarled into the radio.

Whether Scrimshaw heard the order or not Biggles never knew. He may have tried to obey. At any rate, the Hurricane, all the time under the fire of a dozen enemy gun turrets, whirled round, and then zoomed high. For a moment it hung in a vertical position, its airscrew flashing; then its nose whipped down viciously, dead in line with a Jap. Without altering its course it plunged on, and struck the Mitsubishi just aft of the centre section. There was a blinding explosion, which must have been felt by every aircraft within half a mile. Several other bombers in the immediate vicinity were hurled aside as dead leaves are swept up by a gust of wind. Pieces of the machines that had collided flew far and wide.

'There goes Scrimshaw,' muttered Biggles to himself, as he raced down to plaster the disturbed bombers before their pilots could regain control. At the same time he tried to keep an eye on what was happening. 'Strewth! What a scramble,' he murmured.

The air was now so stiff with milling machines at various altitudes that it was impossible to watch the end of any one incident. It was not easy to avoid collision. The battle resolved itself into a number of fleeting, disjointed impressions. Machines, fighters and bombers, were everywhere, banking zooming, turning, diving, some unloading bombs. Through this fearful whirlpool bodies were falling, some suspended on parachutes, others dropping sheer. Black, oily smoke, formed ugly streaks against the blue. Only one thing was clear. The big formation had been broken into pieces. It was no longer a cohesive fighting unit. Here and there one or two of the bomber pilots had managed to keep together, and these were being harried by the fighters. Below, bombs were exploding everywhere among the paddy-fields. The smoke of crashed machines rose in mighty pillars. In one place a wood was on fire.

Biggles made no attempt to call off his pack. He realised that no order he could give could make things worse for the bombers. It had to be a fight to a finish. He grabbed a little more altitude to try to get a clearer picture of the entire combat, to see how things were going; at the same time he edged towards the west to cut off any bombers that might still be trying to get through. Ginger and Tug were there—Tug with his undercarriage wheels hanging at a lop-sided angle—circling, sometimes darting in, guns grunting, at bombers that were swerving about in an attempt to get clear of the general mêlée. It was now apparent, however, that although the bombers might have an alternative target, they had given up hope of reaching the original one. In his earphones Biggles could hear Japanese voices babbling hysterically. He called Ginger and Tug to him.

'Let's give 'em what we've got left!' he shouted, knowing that his ammunition, and probably that of the others, was getting low.

In that last wild onslaught he got one bomber for certain, in flames, and two probables. He had a narrow escape. He flinched instinctively as a shower of bombs, flung off by a machine far above him, went sailing past at a curiously oblique angle. A Japanese pilot nearly fell on him, too, as he hurtled earthward with his parachute still packed. Then a sudden reek of glycol told Biggles that his radiator had been damaged, so he turned to the west, calling repeatedly on all pilots to rally.

The surviving bombers were now specks in the sky, most of them heading eastward. The fighters, too, were scattered; on those that were near he focused his eyes, in an endeavour to identify them. He saw Johnny's Beaufighter, looking considerably the worse for wear, limping along on one engine. Other machines, Spitfires and Hurricanes, closed in. In a few minutes, strung out in a line across the sky, they were following.

Biggles' motor packed up just short of the airfield boundary, but he managed to scrape in. Jumping out he watched the Beaufighter circle twice with its undercarriage retracted, and guessed the trouble. Johnny couldn't get his wheels down. At the end of the third circuit, with the ambulance chasing it round, the Beaufighter made a pancake landing, to finish cocked up on its nose. Biggles smiled when he saw Johnny take a flying leap out of the cockpit and scuttle for a short distance before turning to look at the mess he had made. No one moves faster than an airman leaving an aircraft that is likely to burst into flames. Johnny got a lift on the ambulance, and the driver ran on to pick Biggles up.

'What a party—what a party!' yelled Johnny, who seemed wild with excitement. He appeared to be unaware that his nose was bleeding copiously, the result of his crash landing.

'I think we sort of discouraged them,' said Biggles, grinning.

As they travelled slowly towards the tarmac Biggles checked the machines coming in. He counted eleven. 'Eleven out of sixteen—not bad,' he remarked. Then he saw another machine, flying low, that he had overlooked. 'Twelve,' he corrected.

The station commander was waiting. 'How did it go?' he asked tersely, anxiously.

'We gave them a pasting all right,' answered Biggles. 'Those that are left won't come this way, I'll warrant. A lot of them unloaded their bombs over the fields, so presumably they'll go back home.'

'How many did you get?'

'I can't tell you that till we've checked up,' replied Biggles. 'We intercepted just this side of the lines, so confirmation ought to be easy, by counting the crashes. The troops on the ground must have had a grandstand view.'

'No trouble with the secret weapon?'

'None at all,' asserted Biggles. 'Excuse me a minute, sir,' he added quickly, 'I'm anxious to find out who's missing. I know Scrimshaw has gone, for one. He either collided with, or deliberately rammed, a Mitsubishi. Something of the sort was pretty certain to happen; he was out for blood.'

The pilots who had landed were now getting out of their machines—all except one. It turned out to be a sergeant pilot of 910 Squadron with a bullet through his shoulder. An ambulance rushed him to hospital.

A quick check revealed that the missing pilots were Ginger, Henry Harcourt, Scrimshaw, and a pilot officer of 910 Squadron. One or two of those that returned had received minor wounds. All the machines showed signs of punishment. Bertie had had a remarkable escape. A cannon shell entering through the side of the cockpit had torn the sole off his boot without touching the foot, and then remained transfixed near the root of the control column without exploding.

'Did anybody see what happened to Ginger?' asked Biggles sharply. 'I was with him just before the finish. He seemed all right then.'

'Nobody answered. Apparently nobody had seen Ginger go down.

'He may have baled out,' said Biggles. 'That goes for all of them—except Scrimshaw. He went for a Burton in a big way.'

'I'm not sure, but I fancy Henry got it in the first dive,' put in

Tex. 'I didn't see him after that, but I noticed a machine going down, and it looked like his.'

'Well, we shall have to wait,' Biggles turned to the Group Captain. 'Where's the Air Commodore?'

'He went off up the road and hasn't come back yet,' answered the Group Captain. 'Good show, you fellows. That's a load off my mind, I can tell you. I wonder why the Japs didn't use their secret weapon?'

'There was probably a reason,' remarked Biggles softly. 'This looks like the Air Commodore coming now. He's got someone with him. Who is it?'

'It's Henry,' said Algy, as the car drew nearer.

The car did not stop, but raced on to the medical hut.

'That means Henry's hurt,' observed Biggles. 'Phew! Is it hot, and am I dry! Let's go and get a drink.'

Before they reached the mess the Air Commodore joined them. He was smiling. 'Great show, Bigglesworth—absolutely terrific,' he complimented. 'I never saw such a scramble. At one moment I counted five Mitsubishis all falling at once.'

'What about Henry?' asked Biggles.

'Nothing very serious, but I'm afraid he'll be off your strength for a bit. One of the bullets that set his machine alight slashed his arm badly. He baled out, but hit a tree and damaged his leg. I fancy it's broken.'

Biggles lit a cigarette. 'Bad luck. Did you see anything of Ginger?'

'Oh, dear! Isn't he back? No, I didn't see him. That's not surprising, though. Machines were falling all over the sky. There is this about it though; if he baled out he'll be on our side of the lines.'

Biggles nodded. 'How many bombers do you reckon we got? We haven't checked up yet.'

'I counted twenty-three hit the ground, but there must be a lot of others that won't get back. I noticed several making off, shedding bits and pieces, and they've a long way to go over that forest to their nearest airfield. Funny there was no sign of the secret weapon.'

'Very odd,' agreed Biggles, smiling faintly. 'I'm going in for a drink—I'm as dry as an old boot. I want a word with you later, sir, but I shall have to see about combat reports first, while the thing is fresh in everyone's mind. You might send someone up to the lines to ask the troops if they saw where our machines fell. It's not much use looking for them from the air, with all that mess about, unless we have some definite information to go on. You'd better arrange for a party to go out and collect the loose Japs, too; I saw a lot of them bale out.'

'I'll do that,' promised the Air Commodore. 'See you presently.'

Followed by the others Biggles walked on to the mess.

II
BIGGLES SUMS UP

It was shortly after lunch when Air Commodore Raymond walked into the ante-room, to find the officers of 666 Squadron sitting about, or reclining, for it was the hottest time of the day and the heat was intense. Conversation still centred on the morning's big dog-fight, concerning which fresh details were being remembered and narrated, some humorous, some tragic.

'Any news of Ginger, sir?' asked Biggles, when the Air Commodore entered, and the others gathered round him.

'Not a word. By the way, have you heard how Mackail is getting on?'

'I rang up the hospital about half an hour ago,' returned Biggles. 'He's about the same—certainly no worse. I'm worried about Ginger at the moment.'

'All units near the line are being questioned,' stated the Air Commodore. 'So many machines came down in a small area that it's hard to trace any particular one. How many bombers do you reckon you got, now you've made a check?'

'We make it twenty-six certain, ten probables, and at least thirty damaged.'

The Air Commodore smiled. 'Your fellows are too modest. There are thirty-one down on our side alone; several others were observed to be losing height as they made for home.'

Biggles nodded. 'Good. If we don't hear something about Ginger pretty soon we'll take what machines are serviceable and try to locate his aircraft. Has the M.O. made his report yet about Sergeant Gray?'

'Yes.'

'What has he to say about him?'

'He's a bit puzzled, because the state of the body presents some unusual features; but he can't find anything to account for death, which he has ascribed to heart failure. The queer thing is, he says Gray had not been drinking.'

'I could have told him that,' murmured Biggles. 'No sign of poison?'

'None. Nor were there any signs of a self-inflicted wound.'

'There wouldn't be,' said Biggles grimly.

'Why not?'

'Because Gray was murdered.'

The Air Commodore stared. 'Are you serious?'

'This isn't exactly an occasion for mirth.'

'You speak as though you are certain Gray was murdered.'

'I'm convinced of it—now.'

'But who on earth would kill Gray?'

'We've already discussed this, you remember? Any enemy agent would kill him. He was killed to prevent him from talking. I think I know who did it, but I'd rather not mention names until I have proof. I hope to have that very soon.'

'You astound me,' said the Air Commodore, looking shaken. 'You haven't wasted your time.'

'I've none to waste—life is too short. Besides which, India in the hot season isn't my idea of heaven. I want to get this job tied up so that I can go home.'

'What about the secret weapon? From the way you behaved when you took off to intercept the Jap formation I gathered you had an idea about it.'

'I've more than an idea,' answered Biggles. 'I know what it is. Only it isn't a weapon. I'd call it a trick.'

The Air Commodore looked thunderstruck. 'Are you telling

me that—you have—actually got to the bottom of the thing?'

'Let us say almost. I'm far enough into it to see the bottom, anyway.'

'But this is wonderful!' cried the Air Commodore. 'I'll tell the Air Marshal that we've got the thing buttoned up.'

'I didn't say that,' disputed Biggles. 'Let's put it like this. When I tackled the job it seemed to me that there were two angles to it. The first was to find the thing, and learn how it did the mischief; the second was to put a stop to it. The first part has been done, but the second part is still very much in the air. We've got to be careful. If once the enemy realises that we've rumbled his game he'll slide away like a ghost on roller skates, maybe tò start again somewhere else with a variation of the racket. We've got to bait the hook and strike our fish before he realises that we're after him. As it is, I'm a bit worried that he'll smell a rat.'

'Why?'

'Because of what happened this morning. He'll know how many machines we put up, and how many came back. In other words, he'll know that for once his secret weapon went off at half-cock. True, he may think that was partly due to luck, or to the fact that it was a short show. That's what I'm hoping. But he *may* guess the truth. It is even possible that he saw me spike his guns, so to speak.'

'You actually did that?'

'On this very airfield—right in front of your eyes.'

The Air Commodore looked at Biggles suspiciously. 'Are you pulling my leg?'

'Have a heart, sir. What have I ever done to create the impression that I'm an irresponsible humorist?'

'Where is this weapon?'

'In my pocket. Would you like to see it?'

'I certainly would.'

In dead silence Biggles put his hand in his pocket and produced a small bar of chocolate. 'That's it.'

No one spoke. In an embarrassing silence the Air Commodore looked at the chocolate, then at Biggles, whose face was expressionless. 'Are you out of your mind?' he asked coldly.

'You would be, if you browsed for a little while on this particular sample of confectionery.'

Understanding began to dawn in the Air Commodore's eyes. A mutter of amazement came from the assembled officers.

The Air Commodore's eyes came to rest on Biggles' face. 'Would you mind explaining?'

'I'm going to tell you the whole story, so far as I know it,' returned Biggles. 'I think it is my duty to do so, although the tale is not yet complete. In this detective line of business it was the practice of that prince of sleuths, Sherlock Holmes, to keep his clues and what-nots under his hat until he had the whole thing nicely rounded off, and then explode the solution with a rousing bang under the startled noses of his baffled associates. That technique, I regret to observe, has been maintained by the more humble members of his profession who have followed him. I say I regret it because it's stupid, it's selfish, and for all practical reasons, pointless. Had Holmes been knocked down by a cab, or otherwise accidentally been sent for a Burton, his secret, the result of his investigations would have gone west with him, and the villains would have got away with it after all. In our case I'm not going to risk that happening. If the skunk who is operating on this airfield didn't mind killing Gray, he would, if he knew I was after him, be delighted to stick a knife in my ribs. In case that should happen you will be able to carry on, so here's the gen as far as I've got. It's a bit of a mouthful, but by the time I've finished you'll know exactly what's been happening and how things stand right now. Taffy, go over to that door and don't let anyone come near it. Tex—Ferocity, you take the windows and do the same thing. Sorry to be dramatic, but I'm not taking any chances of being overheard. The rest of you make yourselves comfortable. We've got the afternoon in front of us, and it's too hot to do anything, anyway. Moreover, I'm not quite ready for the next move. This is the story, so far.' Biggles sank into an easy chair and lit a cigarette.

'The first thing that struck me about this weapon was that the Japs had invented it,' he began. 'The Japanese don't invent things—at least, not mechanical devices. They're good at copying other people's. They'll copy anything—they even copied their language from China. It would be a strange thing, you must admit, if they had produced a mechanical device, like a death ray, for instance, that has baffled Western scientists. For this reason I worked on the assumption that the hidden death was not a mechanical instrument. The next outstanding feature was the peculiar inconstancy of this alleged weapon. The machines on the China run that did get through, got through without any interference. Why? If this weapon was as efficient as it appeared to be on one occasion, why should it fail utterly on the next? The locality of the aircraft, the weather conditions, in fact, all conditions, were precisely the same. Yet obviously something was different. What could it be? There was another factor, a curious one, but to me, significant. Only machines flying from west to east were lost. Machines flying from Chungking to India got through. Again, why? A ray, or beam, or any other weapon, would surely work the same whichever way the aircraft was travelling. One was forced to the conclusion that whatever was happening was the result of something that started on the ground, not in the air. Clearly, the thing did not start at Chungking. There was no intermediate landing-ground, so it looked as if the trouble was at Jangpur. And whatever was happening there was happening, broadly speaking, to the aircraft.

'Now, an aircraft in flight consists of three parts—the airframe, the motor, and the pilot. The failure of any of these must result in the failure of the whole. Therefore, should any one of these be affected the result would be the same—the machine would not get through. The question was, which was it? I resolved to tackle the three things separately, in turn. Frankly, I suspected that either the airframe, the engine, or the pilot, was being sabotaged—and in the end I was not far out. It was, I suppose a natural assumption—the first thing that would strike anybody. The problem was to find out *what* was being sabotaged, and how.

'I could think of no other way of testing this than by actual practice, so I decided to fly from Jangpur to Chungking. It was not what you'd call a fascinating experiment, because I like living as much as anybody, and I was staking my life against an opinion. I made the trip, taking Bargent, the original pilot, with me. Nothing happened. Why didn't anything happen? The answer, according to my line of surmise, wasn't hard to find. Nothing happened because until I climbed into the aircraft no one, except Frayle, the C.O., Bargent, and myself, knew that particular machine was going to make the run. I took precautions to make sure nobody knew. In any case, the decision was taken so suddenly that there could have been no time for anyone to interfere with the machine. Another aircraft had been detailed, and I'm pretty certain that had I flown it, it would not have got through. Anyhow, there was lesson number one. I had proved that an unexpected pilot flying an unexpected aircraft could get through. This was in accord with my theory, and the implication was obvious. A saboteur was at work at Jangpur, a man who was in a position to know which machine was next on the schedule to make the run. It seemed safe to assume that what was happening at Jangpur was also happening here. I didn't risk a second trip at Jangpur. Oh, no. It might not have come off a second time.' Biggles lit another cigarette.

'So for my second experiment I came here,' he continued. 'It confirmed my opinion. Officially, we are a communication squadron, so nobody—I mean the saboteur—would expect our Mosquito to suddenly take off and head for Burma. Again I got away with it—for that very reason. Angus' arrival on the scene was not in my programme. He came up the river on his own account. But mark this! I understand there was some discussion in the mess as to who was going to escort Tug. This must have been overheard by the saboteur, who had time to sabotage Angus' machine before it took off. All this was supporting my theory.'

'But Tug Carrington went back up the river,' reminded the Air Commodore. 'Why was his machine not tampered with?'

'For the very obvious reason that he did not take a machine from this station. He flew a seaplane, and had to go some distance to get it. The saboteur, even if he knew about it, would have no time to get to it.'

'Of course, I'd overlooked that,' said the Air Commodore.

'Sergeant Gray, poor fellow, unwittingly provided the next link in the chain,' resumed Biggles. 'And a startling one it was. I told you that when I landed in the forest beside Moorven's crash I found nothing. That was not strictly true. I did find something, but at the time it suggested no sinister purpose. In fact, I threw it away and thought no more of it. It was a little square of pink paper, bearing the name of a British confectionery manu-facturer. When I found just such a piece in A Flight shed, when Sergeant Gray was there, drunk, as we thought, I began to wonder. There was something else in that room that aroused my suspicions. It was a coffee-pot. On the occasion of my first visit I sent for coffee. Gray drank it all.

'When I went back, hours later, the coffee-pot was still warm. I could find only one explanation of that. Somebody had been to Gray with a fresh pot of coffee. Gray was hardly in a state to fetch it. Had he wanted it, it is far more likely that he would have gone across to the canteen. The person who took that coffee, took it because he wanted an excuse for going there, in case he was seen. He had good reason for caution. He went to kill Gray, for fear Gray would talk. Gray, had he lived, would have insisted that he was not drunk. He could have proved it. This would have led to the question, were the other cases of drunkenness on the station—there had been some, you know—really that, or were the men the victims of a mysterious malady? The saboteur did not want that sort of talk, we may be sure. With one thing and another I began to get a glimmering of the truth. You see, after Johnny told me that on the day Moorven was killed they had swopped planes, I suspected that it was the pilot, not the aircraft, that was being tampered with.

'Now let me come to my first flight of this morning. I set a trap. In the mess I briefed two machines and two pilots to go out over Burma—Ginger and Johnny. I said nothing about going myself, although I intended going.' Biggles paused to smile. 'I wanted the saboteur to work on the other two machines, but not on mine. Actually, there was very little risk, because I had not the slightest intention of letting Johnny and Ginger go anywhere near Burma, nor, for that matter, be in the air long enough for the secret weapon to work. We landed at Gayhar, and sat there on the ground with our engines running. Things did not pan out as I expected them to, and I don't mind admitting that I got a shock when Johnny passed out. I thought it would be Ginger. Bearing Sergeant Gray in mind I was prepared to find one of them in a state *resembling* drunkenness, but actually in a condition of coma, the result of being drugged.'

'Hey! I like that,' cried Johnny. 'How did you know we weren't going to be poisoned?'

Biggles laughed at Johnny's indignation. 'Had the stuff been poison it would not have been necessary to murder Sergeant Gray, would it? No, he would have died anyway. I was pretty sure that the stuff was a powerful narcotic rather than a poison. There were strong arguments against the use of poison, as I shall presently explain. I had worked it out, from the discovery of the pink paper, that the dope was being administered in chewing-gum, which would occasion no surprise if it were found in an aircraft. It would be a simple matter to get the stuff into machines briefed for flights over enemy country. Judge my chagrin and alarm when Johnny, after we brought him round, swore that he had not touched any chewing-gum. Nor, in fact, was there any in his machine. I was flabbergasted. It looked as if I was wrong. But when I inspected Johnny's machine, and found on the floor the wrapping of a bar of chocolate, I knew I was right. This wrapping-paper, I may say, bore the same name as that on the chewing-gum wrapping— Charneys, London. Only the method had been changed. Chocolate was now being used instead of gum. I found a piece of the same brand of chocolate in Ginger's machine; as it happened, he hadn't touched it. If he had, he would have passed out, too. If Johnny had had a grain of common sense he would have told me that he had eaten chocolate.'

'I like that,' protested Johnny vehemently. 'I'm not a thought reader. You were talking about chewing-gum.'

'It's all confectionery,' declared Biggles. 'The next question was, why had the saboteur suddenly switched from gum to chocolate? That puzzled me for a little while. Then I hit on what I think is a reasonable explanation. The saboteur had realised that Johnny always got back *because he didn't like chewing-gum*, so to get him he baited his machine with chocolate. And he got him. Had Johnny gone out over Burma in that machine he wouldn't be here now.'

'But what about your machine, old boy?' put in Bertie. 'Wasn't there any chocolate or chewing-gum in that?'

'No.'

'Why not?'

'Because, my poor chump, I gave no indication that I was going on the sortie. The only person who knew I was going, was me. I took good care of that. Supposing that I was staying on the ground, the dope merchant did not bait my machine. Only machines briefed for operations received that sort of attention, otherwise the wrong people might have got hold of the bait, with awkward consequences. That, of course, is what happened to Sergeant Gray. Johnny never touches gum. A week ago he came back with a piece of gum still in the pocket of the aircraft where it had been planted. Gray, looking over the machine, as he was bound to, found it. He chewed it, and passed out. Everyone thought he was drunk. He wasn't. He was doped. The same thing happened yesterday. I would wager that when Johnny came back from the sortie when Moorven and the others were lost, he had a piece of chewing-gum on board. Am I right, Johnny?'

'Now you mention it I recall seeing a packet.'

'Exactly. Gray found it. The same performance was repeated. Dash it, poor Gray almost *told* us what had happened. He said he had been sitting their *chewing* the thing over, but no one took him literally. He became unconscious. It was known that we were waiting for him to come round to ask him questions. That hadn't happened on the previous occasion. It was realised that he might mention the chewing-gum to us. So he was quietly murdered. We now know why Johnny and Scrimshaw always came back. Neither of them touched chewing-gum.'

'What a devilish scheme,' muttered the Air Commodore.

'But horribly effective,' returned Biggles. 'What has been happening is now plain enough. A pilot takes off. Sooner or later he discovers a piece of chewing-gum in the aircraft. He chews it. The narcotic takes effect. By the time it is too late for him to do anything about it. Johnny has told me how everything suddenly swam before his eyes. He lost the use of his limbs. The machine falls, crashes, and the pilot is killed. Very simple, but as I just said, effective. The mysterious interval of time between the falling out of the machines is now explained. Naturally, the time when a machine went down would depend on when the pilot found the dope. Yesterday, three pilots died like that. Moorven was the first to find the gum. He was the first to fall. After he had put a piece of the stuff in his mouth he dropped the wrapping-paper on the floor, where I found it.'

'Frightful,' muttered the Air Commodore.

Biggles went on: 'To some people, this putting stuff in the cockpit of an aircraft might seem a haphazard sort of scheme. Actually, it was more likely to succeed in its purpose than a bomb. One would notice a bomb—but not a piece of chewing-gum. The more you think about it the more devilishly cunning it appears. Nothing could look more natural than gum, nothing more harmless. Scores of pilots chew gum regularly when in the air; we've all done it and we've all left odd packets in our machines. On a long flight a fellow would be almost certain to find the stuff: and having found it, ninety-nine out of a hundred would sample a piece. Of course, there would be occasional exceptions, like Johnny and Scrimshaw. I'm sorry about Scrimshaw. In his fury he lost his head—practically threw his life away. Yet even the exceptions like Johnny and Scrimshaw wouldn't escape indefinitely. As we have seen, chocolate could be substituted for gum. It it turned out they didn't like chocolate, no doubt in course of time they would have been tempted with biscuits, popcorns, or acid drops. Sooner or later their turn would have come.'

'A grim thought,' put in the Air Commodore.

Biggles continued: 'The devilish scheme had one big snag. Once put into action, it could not be allowed to fail. Had the dope got into wrong hands people would have started falling about all over the airfield, and the game would have been up. There is no doubt that this did happen once or twice. When I first arrived I was told that there had been several cases of drunkenness. These men weren't drunk; like Gray, they were doped; but who was to guess it? But too much of that sort of thing would have led to questions. We can see why dope was used instead of poison. Had these men, who were supposed to be drunk, died, there would have been trouble. That would have meant an investigation and the scheme might have been discovered. The after-effects of a narcotic are not unlike those of alcohol—which is, in fact, a narcotic.'

'Do you know what drug they are using?' asked the Air Commodore.

'Not yet. It doesn't matter much, does it? The East is rotten with drugs—opium, hashish, bhang, charas, quat, and heaven only knows what else. The next problem is to find the devil who dishes out the stuff.'

At this point Taffy, who was still at the door, let out a yell. 'Here comes Ginger, look you!' he shouted. 'By Davy! Is he in a mess!'

A moment later Ginger appeared in the doorway. He was hatless, perspiring freely, mud-plastered from head to foot with a layer of grey dust over the mud. But he was smiling.

'What cheer, everybody,' he greeted, and then flopped on the nearest settee. 'Blimey! What a climate . . . what a country,' he murmured with intense feeling.

12

THE ORIENTAL TOUCH

GINGER was welcomed with boisterous enthusiasm.

'Where have you been all this time?' demanded Biggles, when the babble had abated.

'Walking, mostly,' was the weary reply. 'I've walked miles and miles and miles. Eventually I got a lift on a bullock cart to a road, where I was lucky enough to be picked up by a jeep on the way to Calcutta.'

'What happened to you?'

'Nothing astonishing.' Ginger made a gesture of chagrin. 'I blotted my copy book,' he confessed. 'I got a brace of bombers and went out for the hat trick. One of my little ambitions has always been to get three birds with one stone, so to speak. Unfortunately I hadn't much ammo left, so to make sure I went in close.' Ginger smiled lugubriously. 'I went too close. I thought the rear gunner was looking the other way, but he couldn't have been. As soon as I opened up he handed me a squirt that nearly knocked my engine off its bearers. I had to bale out.'

'Did you get *him*?' demanded Ferocity.

Ginger shook his head sadly. 'That's the irritating part of it. I don't know. I couldn't hang around long enough to see.'

There was a titter of mirth.

'I got down all right—in the middle of a thousand acre paddy-field. The rice was growing in mud. I never want to see rice again. That's all. What's going on here—a mother's meeting?'

'Not exactly,' returned Biggles. 'Go and have a clean up and you'll be in time for tea.'

'I suppose I might as well,' murmured Ginger, rising. 'What a life.'

After he had gone the debate was resumed.

'We must get on with this,' averred the Air Commodore. 'I'm anxious to hear the rest. When Ginger came in you were saying something about the enemy agent who has been, and presumably still is, working here. You had previously said you thought you knew who it was. Whom do you suspect?'

'The genial Lal Din.'

'That moon-faced steward!' The Air Commodore looked incredulous.

'Yes.'

'But he has no business near the machines.'

'He may have no business, but as he is so well known it is doubtful if anyone would comment if he was seen strolling round. From what Johnny tells me it seems—ironically enough—that the culprit handed the stuff to Sergeant Gray to put in the machines. Very cute. Gray, of course, had no idea what he was doing. Lal Din—or whoever it is—would probably pass it over with a remark to the effect that the stuff was a regulation issue, or a free issue, from the people at home. Such a statement would not be questioned. It becomes still plainer to see why Sergeant Gray had to be silenced. Had we been allowed to question him it would have emerged that the only thing that passed his lips was chewing-gum. He would have remembered where he got it, how it got into the plane, and who gave it to him.'

'If we keep watch, we ought to be able to catch the scoundrel red-handed,' suggested the Air Commodore.

'If we keep watch,' argued Biggles, 'we shall be more likely to start the whole station talking. One word, and our dope merchant will take fright. I'm pretty sure it's Lal Din. He's not what he says he is, anyway. He tries to make out he's a Burmese Chinaman, and he talks English like one—up to a point. But his accent is a bit *too* pronounced for a man who has lived his life in Burma, and has been in British service. I'd say he's got Jap blood in him. Anyway, I started working this morning on the assumption that Lal Din was an enemy agent. I made sure he was present when I briefed the flight in the mess, by ordering a packet of cigarettes. He stood by with them on his tray while I was giving my orders. So at any rate he knew, or thought he knew, which machines were going out. I deliberately gave him time to do his dirty work. The same sort of thing must have happened before. As a mess waiter Lal Din would hear talk, and perhaps see Daily Orders on the notice-board. He was in this mess when Angus asked Algy's permission to escort Tug, when Tug was coming to fetch me in the seaplane. Incidentally, it may interest you to know that nearly all the machines which took off this morning to intercept the Jap formation were planted with dope—including the Spitfires I asked you to recall. I went to each aircraft before the sortie and collected the stuff. That's what I meant when I said I'd spiked the secret weapon under your nose.'

'I wondered what you were doing, dashing from plane to plane,' put in the Air Commodore.

'Now you will understand, too, what I meant when I spoke of the saboteur smelling a rat. It would probably be easier to get the dope put in the aircraft than recover it from them when they came back. He's probably puzzled as to why so many of our machines *did* come back. He'll be still more puzzled if he ascertains that the doped confectionery was apparently eaten— or at any rate, discovers that it has disappeared. We must be careful that he does not learn the truth. It was for that reason that I did not take the rather obvious course of putting a guard on the machines after they returned. This saboteur, whoever he is, is as cunning as only an Oriental can be, and once he spotted that the machines were being watched, not only would he keep clear, but he might fade away altogether. There are other ways of discovering who he is. I prefer to give him enough rope to hang himself—and other people. Assuming that the operative on this airfield is Lal Din, it doesn't follow that he is the instigator of the scheme, or that he is working alone. It is more likely that there is a big organization behind him. Similar men are on the same job at Jangpur, Ceylon, and elsewhere. We don't know who they are. We must find out before we can hope to rope in the whole network. When we strike we've got to make a clean sweep and pull in the brains behind the show. We've got to find out how the dope is getting into the confectionery. We can be quite sure that it doesn't come out of England like that. Charneys, the manufacturers, are a big, old-established British firm, quite above suspicion. Clearly, someone is getting hold of the stuff at this end and putting the dope into it. Not all of it, of course; but a certain quantity which is kept handy for use as required. Someone has access to this stuff when it arrives from England. He must be found, otherwise, if it becomes known that the chewing-gum and chocolate racket has been rumbled, we may have all sorts of foodstuffs being doped. That would mean scrapping thousands of tons of perfectly good food which would become suspect.'

'Yes—er—quite so,' said the Air Commodore, in a queer voice.

Biggles looked at him questioningly. 'Is something the matter?'

'No.' Raymond smiled—a funny, twisted smile. 'You've shaken me to the marrow, that's all. Not so much by the nature of this thing as by the way you've rooted it out.'

'We haven't finished yet,' declared Biggles, shaking his head. 'We're only half-way. Before we make our next move there will have to be some careful planning. The first question to arise is, what are we going to do about the other stations that are affected? Of course, it would be the easiest thing in the world to get in touch with the commanders of those stations and tell them to order their pilots to lay off the confectionery. But if we did that it's a dead cert that the enemy would hear about it. A safer plan would be to keep all machines grounded—except in case of dire emergency—for the time being. If we aren't ready to strike in twenty-four hours then I'm afraid we shall have to let the other stations know what is causing the trouble. But give me a few hours before you do that.'

'It seems to me,' said the Air Commodore, 'that the first thing we've got to do is to establish beyond all doubt that Lal Din is our man.'

'And then what?'

'We'll arrest him and make him talk.'

'Suppose he doesn't talk? We shall have stumped ourselves. Remember, if he's what we think he is, he's our only link with the enemy organization.'

'But I'm thinking about the urgency of the matter,' returned the Air Commodore. 'If it turned out that he was our man, and could be made to tell us the name of his employer, we could strike immediately and clear the whole thing up.'

Biggles shook his head. 'It's risky. Of course, if it came off it would be fine, but if it failed we should be worse off than before.'

'I think it's worth taking a chance,' decided the Air Commodore. 'Could you devise a means of finding out right away if Lal Din is the culprit?'

'That should be easy,' replied Biggles. He shrugged. 'We'll try it if you like, but if it fails, don't blame me.'

'Try it,' advised the Air Commodore.

'All right,' agreed Biggles, without enthusiasm. 'Algy, go to the 'phone, ring up the central canteen, and ask the manager to send Lal Din over here with some cigarettes.'

Algy went to the 'phone.

'When Lal Din comes in, you fellows at the door and windows keep on your toes in case, when he realises that the game is up, he tries to make a break,' ordered Biggles.

Presently Lal Din came, beaming as usual. 'Cigarettes?' said he, looking round the room.

Biggles, from the easy chair in which he was seated, put up a hand. 'Over here.'

Still beaming, Lal Din approached, and handed over the cigarettes. He was turning away when Biggles called him back.

'By the way, Lal Din,' he said, 'do you like chocolate?'

The Oriental did not start. His walk seemed to freeze to a standstill. He looked back over his shoulder—still beaming.

Biggles tossed a bar of chocolate on a small table in front of him. 'Try that,' he suggested.

Lal Din did not move. His broad smile became fixed, the humour gone out of it. The atmosphere in the room was electric.

'What's the matter?' said Biggles evenly. 'Don't you like chocolate?'

Very slowly the steward reached out and picked up the bar. 'Me eat after work,' he said.

'Eat it now,' ordered Biggles. He spoke quietly, but there was an edge on his voice.

The steward did not move. His eyes were fixed on Biggles' face, as if he would read what was going on behind the impassive countenance.

'Eat it,' snapped Biggles.

Very slowly the steward looked round the circle of faces.

Then, like an automaton actuated by a hidden spring, he moved. He streaked to the far side of the room, and as he ran he drew from somewhere a small, narrow-bladed knife. In front of the fireplace he dropped on his knees.

Biggles was on his feet. 'Stop him!' he shouted.

But he was too late. With a calm, but swift deliberation that was horrible to watch, the steward drove the blade into his side, and dragged it across his stomach. Gasping, he fell forward on his face.

The breathless hush that followed was broken by Biggles. 'Call the ambulance, somebody,' he said bitterly. 'Let's get him out of this.' He looked at the Air Commodore. 'That settles any doubt about his nationality. Only a Jap would commit hara-kari. Well, there goes our link with the enemy organization. We might have guessed he'd do something like that when he saw the game was up—and he knew it was up the instant he saw that chocolate. That would tell him why the big blitz failed this morning, and why so many of us got back. He'd never dare to tell his boss that he'd failed. That would mean losing face, which is worse than death to a Jap. So he took a short cut to eternity. Pity, but there it is. One can't be right all the time.'

13
FRESH PLANS

THE ambulance came, and went, taking the body of the treacherous steward. Also the bloodstained hearth-rug.

'Yes, it's a pity about that,' said the Air Commodore uneasily. 'It was my fault. I should have left you alone.'

'We found out what we wanted to know and a fat lot of good it has done us,' replied Biggles moodily. 'But there, the damage is done, and it's no use moaning about it. We tried a scheme that might have saved us a lot of trouble. It didn't work. Now we must think of something else.'

'I'd better leave you to it,' murmured the Air Commodore

contritely. 'When I butt in I do more harm than good. You've done marvellously, Bigglesworth. Keep it going.' He went out.

Biggles dropped into a chair.

'That was a dirty business,' remarked Algy.

'It was really my fault. I should have insisted on playing the game my own way. Still, let's be charitable. Raymond is nearly out of his mind with worry; he must be desperately anxious to get the business buttoned up.'

'What are you going to do next?' asked Algy. 'Is there anything you can do?'

'Oh, yes,' answered Biggles readily. 'There are plenty of things; the question is, which is the best? We've no time to lose. As it is, I'm scared that the return of nearly all our machines this morning will have made the whole enemy organisation suspicious. Now, on top of that, comes this business of Lal Din slicing himself in halves. When his boss hears about that——'

'But will he?' interposed Algy.

'If he doesn't hear about it he'll soon know that Lal Din is no longer here; or if he is, that he is not on the job.'

'I don't see why he should know.'

'Of course he will. Look at it this way. What will be the reaction of the chief enemy agent in India to the wiping out of the big Jap formation this morning, followed by the return of nearly all our machines? The first thing he'll do is try to get in touch with Lal Din, the man on the spot, to demand an explanation.'

'Yes, I think that's a reasonable assumption,' agreed Algy.

'He will then discover that Lal Din isn't available, and you can bet your life it won't take him long to find out why. That's why we've got to move fast.' Biggles thought for a moment. 'I'll tell you what. Let's go to the canteen to find out if anyone has already been making inquiries about Lal Din. I think it's an angle worth watching. Did you get that list of personnel I wanted?'

'Yes.'

'Who's the manager of the canteen?'

Algy took a sheet of paper from his pocket and ran an eye over it. 'Ali Mansur,' he answered. 'He's an ex-Askari, a retired sergeant of the King's African Rifles—twenty-four years' service. Got the D.C.M. and the Long Service Medal.'

'That should put him above suspicion, anyway,' declared Biggles. 'Let's go and see him.'

They found the manager in his office. He was an elderly, dark-skinned, heavily moustached man, with a soldierly bearing, wearing his medal ribbons on the lapel of a spotless white jacket. He had not yet learned of the fate of his assistant, and after dwelling for a moment or two on the need for secrecy, Biggles told him the truth, which in any case could not long be concealed—that Lal Din was dead by his own hand.

'This man was a Japanese spy,' said Biggles. 'He could not face defeat. The chief Japanese secret agent will soon want an explanation of the decisive blow we struck this morning against the enemy bombers. What I am anxious to know, sergeant, is this. Has anyone been here making inquiries for Lal Din?'

'Not today, sahib,' replied the sergeant.

'You're sure of that?'

'If such a one had been here I should know of it.'

'Has Lal Din been out, or asked for time off?'

'No, sahib. He could not leave the station without my permission.'

'What exactly did you mean when you said, not today? Have inquiries been made for him on other occasions?'

'Yes, sahib.'

'By whom?'

'His brother, or a man calling himself a brother, comes to see him.'

'Have you seen this brother?'

'No, sahib.'

'How's that?'

'I rarely leave the station, and the brother has no permit to enter. So we have not met.'

'What happens, then?'

'The brother, or any stranger, must go to the main gate. There he speaks to the N.C.O. of the guard, asking for Lal Din.

The N.C.O. rings me on the telephone, and if it is possible I allow Lal Din to go to the gate. You must understand, though, that there were days when Lal Din took time off. Then, doubtless, he left the station, although where he went I do not know. I can only tell you of what happens when the brother comes asking for him when he is on duty.'

'This has sometimes happened?'

'Often, sahib.'

'But it has not happened today?'

'No, sahib.'

'Thank you, sergeant. You have told me just what I wanted to know.' Biggles turned to Algy. 'We're lucky. No one has been here yet, but in view of what happened in the air this morning I think someone *will* call. Of course, it may be that the chief saboteur is waiting for Lal Din to report to him with an explanation. When he doesn't show up someone will be sent to find out why. That may take time. I can't afford to wait. I've another line of approach up my sleeve, and I'd like to tackle it right away.' Biggles turned back to Sergeant Mansur. 'There is another matter I would like to discuss with you. Who gave Lal Din his job at this station?'

'I did, sahib. As mess caterer I employ my own staff—with the approval of the adjutant, of course.'

'How did you get in touch with Lal Din?'

'There was a vacancy, sahib, and he came to me on a recommendation.'

'From whom?'

'Messrs. Tahil and Larapindi.'

'Who are they?'

'Shippers' and merchants' agents, sahib. They represent many British firms in India. Much goods imported go through their hands. They have a big warehouse at the docks, in Calcutta, and offices in many Eastern towns.'

'Does this firm supply stuff to our canteen?'

'Yes, sahib.'

'Things like chocolate, chewing-gum . . . ?'

'Yes, among other things, sahib.'

'When is this stuff delivered, and how?'

'When we need supplies I ring up Tahil and Larapindi, and they send the goods up in one of their cars.'

'And what happens when the stuff gets here?'

'It is unloaded and put out for sale.'

'Who unloads it?'

'Sometimes I check it in, sahib; sometimes Lal Din, or one of the other assistants, might do it.'

'Anyway, the stuff is taken to the canteen and made available for the troops?'

'Yes, sahib.'

'And this firm recommended Lal Din?'

'Not the firm exactly, sahib. Mr. Larapindi rang me up on the telephone and asked me to find work for a very good man he knew.'

'I see,' said Biggles slowly. 'What sort of man is this Larapindi—have you seen him?'

'Many times, sahib. He is Eurasian, but of what precise nationalities I do not know. He is a small man, with a brown face, and wears very large spectacles.'

'I am told there has been a free issue of chocolate and chewing-gum. Is that so?'

'Yes, sahib.'

'How long has it been going on?'

'It is not a regular thing. We had the first case sent up not long ago. It came with other goods from Tahil and Larapindi.'

'Was this after Lal Din arrived?'

'Yes, sahib.'

'And he dished the stuff out?'

'Yes, sahib—he offered to do it.'

'Thank you, sergeant. You have been most helpful.' Biggles turned to Algy. 'This is worth following up,' he said quietly. 'I've half a mind to abandon my alternative scheme, which was to slip up to Jangpur to try to nab the fellow there who is doing what Lal Din was doing here. If I could get my hands on him I might make him speak.'

At this moment Air Commodore Raymond came hurrying

into the canteen. 'I've been looking everywhere for you,' he told Biggles.

'Now what's wrong, sir?' queried Biggles.

'The Higher Command says we simply must get this China route in full operation again. The Chinese doctors are having to perform operations on their wounded without anaesthetics. Not only are medical stores urgently needed, but several senior officials are waiting to go through. Now we know what caused the trouble I thought perhaps you could do something about it, if it isn't upsetting your plans.'

'No. As a matter of fact it fits in with my plans quite well,' returned Biggles. 'You can reckon that the route will be functioning again tomorrow. I'll slip up right away to see Frayle. All you have to do is send him some machines, and pilots to fly them.'

'And you don't think there will be any more risk?'

'I don't think so, sir—at any rate, not if my plan succeeds.'

'Then I can tell the A.O.C. that the route will be open with effect from tomorrow?'

'It will—unless you hear to the contrary from me or Algy.'

'Good.' The Air Commodore hurried away.

Biggles turned back to Algy and the sergeant. 'Now this is what I want you to do, Algy. You keep in touch with Sergeant Mansur. If anyone comes asking for Lal Din the sergeant will let you know. You will go to the gate and see the man. Tell him that Lal Din is sick. Don't let him suspect the truth. When the man goes off to report to his boss, as it seems pretty certain that he will, you'll follow him and watch where he goes. Make a note of the place and return here. I shall have to go to Jangpur, but I'll get back as quickly as I can. It may be late tonight or early tomorrow morning. If the route is to open tomorrow I've got to pick up the man who is putting the dope in the machines.'

'Why not tell the fellows up there straight out not to touch any confectionary they find in their machines?'

'Because in five minutes everyone on the station would know what was in the wind—including the spy. He'd escape, and warn his boss in Calcutta. No, I've got to catch him. We're not ready yet to broadcast the story. I'd better warn Frayle that I'm coming.'

Algy's eyes went round when he heard Biggles, on the telephone, tell Squadron Leader Frayle that he was coming up right away to take another load of medical supplies to Chungking. Biggles continued: 'I want you to start loading the machine at once—yes, in the ordinary way. I don't mind who knows about it. I shall take off as soon as it's ready. By the way, I may be staying at Jangpur for a day or two, so you might fix me up with a room and a bed.'

To this Frayle apparently agreed, for as Biggles hung up he said with a smile, 'That's okay.'

Said Algy: 'Are you really going to Chungking?'

'No fear. I've too much to do here. But I'd like the gent at Jangpur who hands out the dope to *think* I'm going.'

'Ah,' breathed Algy. 'I get it.'

'I'll be getting along,' decided Biggles. 'You watch things at this end. I hope I shan't be long away.'

In a few minutes, having ascertained that the radiator had been repaired, Biggles was in the air, in the Typhoon heading north on the short run to Jangpur. A haversack containing his small-kit went with him.

Squadron Leader Frayle and Flying Officer Bargent met him on the tarmac, Frayle to say that the transport plane was ready, and Bargent to ask if he could go as second pilot. Biggles refused, gently, but firmly. 'I have reasons of my own for making this trip alone,' he said. 'With luck you should be able to take a machine through yourself, tomorrow.' Turning to Frayle, Biggles asked, 'Did you fix me up with a room?' On receiving an assurance that the room was available he walked over to look at it, and leave his haversack.

Bargent had wandered off, so Biggles was able to speak privately to the station commander who, without asking questions, nevertheless made it clear that there was something about this projected trip that struck him as phoney.

Biggles decided to take him into his confidence. 'The facts, briefly, are these, Frayle,' he said quietly. 'This route has got to start functioning again tomorrow. There's nothing phoney about that. More pilots and machines are being sent up to you. Unfortunately you've got an enemy agent on the station. You can't operate while he's about, so I'm here to nab him. If I succeed, you should have no further trouble. That machine standing out there ticking over has been tampered with—or at least, I hope it has. I've given the saboteur plenty of time to do his dirty work. Now then: after I have taken off certain things will happen that may surprise you. My subsequent behaviour for example. But whatever happens I want you to carry on as though everything was normal. And see that you officers do, too. Don't let there be any discussion. Show no surprise, and leave me alone. That's all. I'll push along now.'

'It's your funeral,' murmured Frayle simply. He was too good an officer to argue.

Leaving his small-kit in his room, in mellow evening sunlight Biggles walked across to where the Wellington was waiting. There were several airmen and native porters standing about, watching with interest, but they said nothing. Appearing not to notice them Biggles climbed into his seat, tested his engines, waved the attendant mechanics away, and took off.

As soon as his wheels were off the ground he put the aircraft on a course that was practically due east, for Chungking, and when he had settled down he examined the contents of the locker. Conveniently placed, he found a packet of chewing-gum. Smiling grimly he put it in his pocket.

The aircraft roared on through the fading light. The time, by the watch in front of him, was a quarter to six.

14
THE TRAP

PRECISELY half an hour later, in the silvery light of a full moon, Biggles roared back to the airfield at Jangpur and landed. The return of the aircraft caused a minor sensation. Mechanics appeared, running, and there was some brisk conversation when the transport machine was identified. The few remaining officers on the station, mostly ground staff, but with Frayle and Bargent among them, came out to see what was going on. In the clear moonlight this did not take them long.

Biggles climbed out. He seemed to be not quite steady on his feet, and after swaying for a moment rested a hand on an airman's shoulder as if for support.

'What's the matter?' asked Frayle anxiously. 'Why did you come back?'

'Engine—giving trouble,' answered Biggles in a dull voice. 'Getting a—lot of—vibration—starboard side. Thought I'd better—turn back . . . not risk—forced landing.'

'I should think so,' agreed Frayle, looking at Biggles with a curious expression on his face. 'Are you feeling all right—yourself, I mean?'

'No. Feel sort of—queer,' replied Biggles, holding his head in a dazed sort of way. 'Must have got—touch of sun. Twinge of fever—maybe.' He staggered and nearly fell.

The audience of airmen and native porters whispered among themselves. There was a titter of laughter when a voice was heard to say, 'Tight as an owl.'

'I think you'd better go to your room and lie down,' suggested Frayle.

'Yes,' muttered Biggles thickly. 'Best thing—I think. Head's sort of swimming. Must be—fever. Seems to be getting—worse.'

Frayle made a signal and the ambulance came out to meet the party. Biggles allowed the station commander to help him into it.

'Shall I send the M.O. along to see you?' offered Frayle.

'No, thanks. I'll be—all right. Go—sleep.'

'As you like,' returned Frayle.

The ambulance took Biggles to the sleeping accommodation that had been prepared for him—a small room in the station commander's bungalow, which was an extension of the officer's quarters. Most of the officers went back to the mess, but Frayle and Bargent, having removed Biggles' tunic, helped him on to the bed and took off his shoes. He appeared to fall asleep immediately.

Said Bargent, looking down at the recumbent figure: 'I've got a nasty feeling there's something fishy about this. If I hadn't done a trip with him I'd swear he was three sheets in the wind.'

'He half prepared me for something unusual,' replied Frayle. 'He said that whatever happened I was not to worry him, but leave him alone. I don't like leaving a fellow in this condition, but I suppose we shall have to.' They went out, leaving the electric light on.

As soon as they had gone Biggles raised himself on an elbow, listened intently for a minute, and then got off the bed. Moving quickly he switched out the light, locked the door, drew the curtains aside and arranged the window so that it could be opened easily. For a little while he stood surveying the airfield, a clear view of which the window commanded, while pale blue moonlight flooded the little room. Leaving the window he took out his automatic, examined it, and put it in a side pocket of the slacks he still wore. The time, he noted, was twenty minutes to seven. Then, apparently satisfied, he settled himself on the bed in a sleeping position facing the window, and half closed his eyes.

Time passed. For a while there were occasional sounds outside—footsteps of airmen going on or off duty, and voices as they talked or called to each other. But as the night wore on these sounds died away and silence fell. After a short interval the orderly officer could be heard making his first round. More time passed. Once, far away, a dog or a jackal yelped. A cock crowed in a distant native village, apparently misled by the brilliant moonlight into thinking that dawn was at hand. Biggles did not move a muscle. Only his chest rose and fell with his deep breathing. The difficulty, he found, was to do this without actually falling asleep, for he was beginning to feel the strain of working at high pressure, and he was really tired. His eyes, half closed, were on the window. Not for a moment did they leave it.

He lost count of time, but he estimated roughly that it was about nine-thirty when he saw that for which he had so long waited. There was no sound, but a shadow moved slowly across the square of moonlight framed by the window. It paused for a moment in passing, then went on. Within a minute it was back, stationary, close by the window. All this Biggles saw quite clearly through half-closed eyes. Moonlight flashed on the glass of the window as inch by inch it was opened. Still there was no noise, and as the man crept into the room Biggles marvelled that anyone could move with such a complete absence of sound. Standing close against the window, the visitor made no more noise than the vague shadow he appeared to be. Biggles could not make out any detail. Beyond the fact that the visitor was a native, naked except for a loin-cloth, carrying in his left hand a strip of rag, he could see nothing of him.

Like a black wraith the marauder appeared to float towards the bed. Again he stopped and listened, before bending over the prone form on the bed as if to examine it. His breathing was just audible. Then, taking the strip of rag in both hands he pressed it firmly over Biggles' lips and nostrils.

As the rag touched his face Biggles' hands shot up and seized his assailant by the throat. With a convulsive jerk the native broke free, and Biggles knew that he had made a mistake; for the brown throat was slimy with oil, and his fingers could not maintain their grip. The man streaked like a panther to the window. Launching himself from the bed Biggles got him by the legs: but they, too, had been oiled, and although the man fell, he was free again before Biggles could take advantage of the fall. The body slid through his hands like an eel. In a flash the man was on his feet. Biggles, too, was getting up. He caught the gleam of steel and flung himself sideways, but a sharp pain in the upper part of his left arm told him that the knife had found a billet. After the first stab there was no more pain; only a feeling of nausea.

By this time his assailant had turned, and had again reached the window. Biggles, by this time aware of the futility of trying to hold the body, grabbed at the loin-cloth, and tried to drag the man back into the room. But either the stuff was rotten, or in two pieces, for the part he had seized came away in his hand, with the result that he went over backwards. By the time he had recovered himself, although he was still on the floor, the native was half-way across the sill, a black silhouette against the moonlight. It was obvious that in another second he would be gone.

Now, Biggles' plan had been to catch the man alive, for which

reason he had so far refrained from using his pistol; but seeing
that the man was about to escape, and aware that if he
succeeded in this it would be fatal to his plans, he snatched out
his pistol. There was no time to take aim. He fired from the hip.
The weapon roared. The flash momentarily blinded him, so
that he could not see whether he had hit his man or not. Vaguely
conscious of hot blood running down his arm he scrambled to his
feet and dashed to the window. One glance told him all he
needed to know. A dark figure lay asprawl on the brown earth.
Panting, for the last few minutes had been strenuous, Biggles
backed to the bed and sat down heavily, to recover his breath
and his composure.

Outside, voices shouted. Footsteps approached, running,
both inside and outside the bungalow. A fist banged on the door.
Before Biggles could answer, or get to it, it was forced open with
a crash. Someone blundered into the room. The light was
switched on. Frayle, in pyjamas, stood there.

'What happened?' he asked sharply. 'Who fired that shot?'

'I did,' replied Biggles laconically.

'Good God, man! You're wounded.' Frayle's eyes were on the
bloodstained sleeve of Biggles' shirt.

'It's only a scratch,' returned Biggles. 'Give me a drink—
water will do.'

Frayle obliged.

'Thanks.' Biggles drank, and drew a deep breath. 'That's
better. Send for the M.O., Frayle, to have a look at that fellow
outside. Tell him to bring his needle and cotton—my arm may
need a stitch.'

Bargent entered through the window. 'I say!' he exclaimed, in
a perturbed voice, 'You've killed the fellow.'

'I'm sorry about that—in a way,' replied Biggles. 'I wanted
him alive. Who is he—do you know?'

'Of course I know. It's Kong Po, our *dhobi-wallah.*'[1]

'What was his nationality?'

---

[1] *Dhobi-wallah.* Indian military term for laundryman. From Hindustani
dhob—washing.

'We always supposed he was a sort of Chinese.'

Frayle spoke: 'He's Chinese according to his station identity card.'

'Alter it to Japanese,' cried Biggles.

Presently the M.O. came in. 'There's nothing I can do for that fellow outside—he's dead,' he announced. 'What about your arm?' He looked at the wound. 'Narrow, but rather deep,' he went on. 'You'd better have a stitch in it.'

'Go ahead,' invited Biggles. 'Don't be long; I've got to get back to Dum Dum. Give me a cigarette, Frayle.'

'Before you go, perhaps you won't mind telling me why you came here to bump off my *dhobi*?' Frayle's voice was soft with sarcasm.

'I didn't come here to shoot him,' replied Biggles evenly. 'I came here to get him, but he knifed me and I daren't let him get away. Too much was at stake.'

'Why did you want him?'

'Because,' answered Biggles, flinching as the M.O.'s needle pricked his skin, 'he was you own pet secret weapon. He came to this room to strangle me. I thought he would come. I hoped he would. One of our airmen at Dum Dum, a sergeant named Gray, was murdered in precisely the same circumstances and for the same reason. I planned for a repetition of the incident, and it came off. Your precious Kong Po was afraid I might put two and two together, and talk about it, when I came round from what he supposed was a stupor brought on by a drug.'

'But I don't understand,' said Frayle impatiently. 'How does this hook up with the secret weapon?'

'I'll tell you in plain language,' decided Biggles. 'Keep the story to yourself though, for the time being. There isn't a secret weapon—or not the sort you probably have in mind. The enemy has planted agents on certain of our airfields. With so many mixed breeds of Orientals about that wasn't difficult. The master-brain behind the racket had enough influence to get these men jobs. In our case, at Dum Dum, the spy was a mess waiter. The real work of these men was simple. All they had to do was arrange for a small supply of chocolate or chewing-gum to be put in each operational aircraft just before it took off. These sweeties were not the sort you'd give a baby to suck. They had been treated with a powerful narcotic. It needs little imagination to visualize what happened in the aircraft. During the course of the flight the pilot finds the confectionery and has a bite, with the result that he loses the use of his limbs and his brain, and crashes. It was always on the boards, however, that the stuff might fall into the hands of someone other than the man for whom it was intended. The sergeant I mentioned just now got hold of a piece. During the night, while he was still under the influence of the drug, he was murdered to prevent him from talking. I didn't know how it was done, but I do now. Strangulation was the method employed; I imagine it isn't hard to strangle an unconscious man without leaving a mark. This evening I set a trap. I took off but returned, ostensibly with engine trouble. There was dope in the machine. When I landed I acted as though I had fallen for it. Some of your fellows thought I was drunk. Only the spy, who was pretty certain to investigate, would know the truth—or what he thought was the truth. That I had been drugged. It was up to him to see that I didn't come round, so he came to do me in. I was waiting, with the result that he got it, not me. That's all. Now he's out of the way there won't be any more doped confectionery in your machines, so with effect from tomorrow the route will operate in the normal way. But to be on the safe side—you needn't say why—you can issue a secret order to your pilots forbidding them to touch any sort of food while in the air. In any case, I'm aiming to clean up the whole gang in the next few hours. Meanwhile, for obvious reasons, you will say nothing of this to anyone. Should someone come here inquiring for Kong Po— and that may happen—just say that he has met with an accident and is not available.'

'Well, stiffen my benders!' muttered Bargent. 'I never heard such a tale in my life.'

'The East is the home of strange stories,' returned Biggles dryly, as he tried moving his arm, which the M.O. had now finished bandaging.

'What beats me is, how you got on the trail of the thing,' said Frayle, in a voice of wonder. 'It was so simple, yet so subtle——'

'The Oriental mind works on those lines. I've been in the East before,' murmured Biggles as he stood up. 'I'll just have a look round this *dhobi-wallah's* bedroom and then get back to Dum Dum.

As Frayle led the way to the room Biggles asked: 'How did you come to employ this man—Kong Po?'

'A fellow in Calcutta rang me up and asked me if I had a vacancy for a good man. He said Kong Po had worked for him, so he could recommend him. The chap was out of work and he wanted to help him. So I took Kong Po on.'

'You knew this man who rang you up, I presume? I mean, he wasn't just a stranger?'

'Oh, no. I've met him several times. As a matter of fact he's a wealthy merchant who has often made presents to the mess. I wish there were more about like him.'

A ghost of a smile hovered for a moment round Biggles' lips. 'Was his name by any chance Larapindi?'

Frayle started. 'Yes. What on earth made you say that?'

'Only that he has showed an interest in Dum Dum, too,' replied Biggles casually.

The room turned out to be a tiny cubicle near the kitchens. A systematic search revealed only one item of interest—a small cardboard box containing several loose bars of chocolate, wrapped, and packets of chewing-gum. The box bore in large type the usual confectionery manufacturer's announcements, under the heading: CHARNEYS GOLD MEDAL CHOCOLATES. LONDON, AGENCIES AT CALCUTTA, CAPE TOWN, SINGAPORE AND SYDNEY.

'Very interesting,' murmured Biggles. 'As the stuff is loose we may assume that the box is merely a receptacle for the present contents which, I imagine, have been doctored. I doubt if the man had any hand in the preparation of the dope; the chocolate and gum would be issued to him in this form, ready for use. Better burn the stuff, Frayle, to prevent accidents.'

A corporal medical orderly came in. In his hand he carried a

packet of notes, brand new. 'I thought you'd better take charge
of this, sir,' he said, speaking to his station commander. 'I found
it tied up in Kong Po's loin-cloth. There must be close on a
thousand rupees—a lot of money for a man like that to have
about him.'

'Too much for an honest *dhobi-wallah*,' said Biggles softly. 'I'll
take charge of that, Frayle, if you don't mind; I have an idea it
will tell us something. Well, there doesn't seem to be anything
else; I think I'll be getting along.'

'Sure you feel fit enough to fly?' queried the M.O.

'I'm all right, thanks,' answered Biggles. 'Arm's getting a bit
stiff, that's all—but I don't fly with my left hand.'

In twenty minutes he was back at Dum Dum. The time was
just after ten o'clock. He went straight to Air Commodore
Raymond's quarter. The Air Commodore was there, writing a
report.

'I thought it would ease your mind to know that the
Chungking run is okay now, sir,' reported Biggles. 'The regular
service will be resumed in the morning. Things are moving fast,
and may move faster before dawn. While I'm talking to my
chaps I want you to do something for me.'

'Certainly.'

Biggles took from his pocket the notes that had been found on
the dead *dhobi-wallah*. 'From the condition these are in it seems
likely that they were issued recently,' he surmised. 'I want you to
find out which bank issued these notes, and to whom.'

The Air Commodore looked dubious. 'At this hour? People
will have knocked off work.'

'Then tell them to knock on again,' requested Biggles. 'This
business won't wait. You ought to be able to get the information
on the 'phone.'

'I'll try,' promised the Air Commodore. 'I take it you've got
the enemy agent at Jangpur ear-marked?'

Biggles was at the door. He looked over his shoulder, smiling
grimly. 'I ear-marked him all right—with a forty-five pistol
slug. See you later.'

He went on to the mess. Algy and the rest were there waiting.

Some were dozing, but there was a quick, expectant stir, when Biggles entered. He spoke to Bertie.

'Get some coffee and see that it's strong. I'm dog tired, but we're going to be busy for a bit. You might scrounge some sandwiches or biscuits at the same time.' He turned to Algy. 'Did you have any luck?'

'It worked out as you expected,' replied Algy. 'A man calling himself Lal Din's brother rolled up, asking for him. I told him Lal Din was sick. He went off and I followed him.'

'Good. Where did he go?'

'To the docks, to the warehouse of Tahil and Larapindi. I hung around for some time but he didn't come out, although there seemed to be a fair amount of activity.'

'There'll be more, presently,' promised Biggles. 'I fancy that warehouse is the target for tonight. I'm just waiting for confirmation. I shall be glad when this show is over; I'm missing my beauty sleep. Ah—here's the coffee.'

'What happened at Jangpur?' asked Ginger. 'The others have told me what happened here.'

Biggles gave a brief account of the events at Jangpur. He had just finished when the Air Commodore came in.

'I got the information you wanted,' he announced. 'I'm afraid you'll be disappointed; the money seems to have been issued in the ordinary course of business.'

'It would be,' muttered Biggles cynically.

'It's part of a pay-roll issued by the Peninsular and Oriental Bank, to—just a minute.' The Air Commodore fumbled with a slip of paper.

'Tahil and Larapindi?' suggested Biggles.

The Air Commodore stared. 'That's right. How the deuce did you guess that?'

'I wasn't guessing,' returned Biggles. 'Thanks, sir. You can go to bed now. I may have some good news for you in the morning.'

'Are you going out?'

'We are.'

'Can I come?'

Biggles shook his head. 'You'd be better advised to keep out of the way. What 666 Squadron is going to do, or may have to do, tonight, is entirely unofficial. There's no place for an Air Commodore.'

'All right. I'll leave you to it.' The Air Commodore looked at Biggles suspiciously. 'Be careful.' He went out.

'Are we really going down to this warehouse place?' asked Tug.

'Probably. It depends. I have a call to make first.'

'But I say, old boy, it's a bit late for making calls, isn't it?' queried Bertie.

'Not too late, I hope.'

'Say! Suppose there's nobody at the warehouse?' put in Tex. 'How shall we get in?'

'It was never my intention to ring the front-door bell,' said Biggles. His manner became brisk. 'Algy, see about transport. Better get a light truck, one we can all get in. And in case there's an argument you'd better all bring guns. On the other hand, there may be nothing for you to do. We shall see. Ginger, you're about the best fitter in the party. Put a few tools in a bag in case we have to do a spot of housebreaking. Which reminds me; I think it would be a good idea if everyone wore tennis shoes, or something with a sole that won't make a noise.'

'Where do we go first?' asked Algy.

Biggles went to the telephone directory, looked up a number and made a note. 'I want you to drive me first to Mimosa Lodge, Razlet Avenue. If I remember, that's one of those wide streets in the European quarter east of the Maidan. I'll guide you.'

'What are you going to do there?' asked Algy.

'I'm only going to make a call.'

'On whom?'

'A gentleman by the name of Larapindi,' answered Biggles.

15

BIGGLES MAKES A CALL

ALGY drove the car, a light, covered, service lorry, to Calcutta. Biggles sat on one side of him, with Ginger on his left.

On the short drive in Biggles said: 'I can't tell you exactly what I'm going to do because I'm not sure myself. The business has reached that touchy stage when anything can happen. I'm a bit scared of the plan I have in mind, but our hands are being forced. We've got to move fast, before the enemy learns what has happened to his operatives at Dum Dum and Jangpur. I'm pretty sure this fellow Larapindi is in the racket, and if he's not actually the head man, he's pretty high up. The broad idea, if I find Larapindi at home, is: first, to allay his suspicions, if they are aroused; and secondly, to get him to do something that will give us the necessary evidence to hang him.'

'Couldn't we get the police to raid his premises, both his home and the warehouse?' suggested Algy.

'We could, and that is what the police would probably do if they knew what we know. But I don't think it would do the slightest good. It's ten to one they wouldn't find anything. Spies aren't such fools as to leave incriminating evidence lying about when they know the police are on the job. Police actions are governed by regulations. They have to announce their intentions by knocking at the door. If we asked for a police raid the chances are we should do more harm than good, by exposing our hand for nothing. I've always taken the view that when one is dealing with tricksters the best plan is to play tricky. So I'm going to try unorthodox tactics. If I slip up there will be an awful stink—a question asked in Parliament perhaps. We shall get a rap over the knuckles, and perhaps lose some seniority.'

'That should worry us,' remarked Algy sarcastically.

'We'll stop the car a little distance from the house,' went on Biggles. 'Here's the Maidan. I believe that's the Avenue Razlet, over there. Pull up against the kerb when I give the word.'

In view of the lateness of the hour—it was nearly eleven

o'clock—there were few pedestrians about, and very little traffic. The night was fine and hot. The Hugli River wound like a monstrous black snake through the resting city.

'You'll do,' said Biggles sharply. As the car pulled up he continued: 'Tell the boys to keep quiet while I'm away. If I'm not back in an hour you'll know something's gone wrong, so you'd better come looking for me. If you do, remember that unless my suspicions are all cock-eye, this Larapindi is as cunning as a jackal and as deadly as a cobra. Sit fast and keep your eyes on the house. I may be some time.'

Biggles walked on up the avenue. A policeman directed him to Mimosa Lodge, a magnificent house standing in its own spacious garden. A fine pair of wrought iron gates gave access to a short drive that ended at a sweeping flight of steps. The gates were not locked, and in a minute Biggles was pressing the bell.

The door was opened, as he expected it to be, by a coloured servant, quiet, efficient, in spotless white. The man looked a trifle surprised when he saw the visitor, but in reply to Biggles' inquiry said that Mr. Larapindi was at home. Biggles presented his card, and was then asked to wait in a hall, the furnishings of which were so fine, so rare and so costly as to give him a twinge of uneasiness. The house appeared to be the residence of a millionaire rather than that of an enemy spy. While the servant had gone to deliver his card his eyes roamed from one object of Oriental art to another, with rising misgivings. Then he realised that as a partner in the great firm of Tahil and Larapindi, the man whom he had come to see probably was a millionaire several times over.

The servant, walking with soft, easy steps, returned. 'This way, sahib,' said he.

Biggles followed him through a sumptuously furnished library to a door at the far end. On this the servant knocked before opening it. 'Enter, sahib,' he invited, with a little bow. 'Mr. Larapindi awaits you.'

As Biggles accepted the invitation he took in the scene at a glance. The room, not a large one, was fitted out in a manner that was something between a private sitting-room and a study.

Again the furnishings were impressive. Pieces of priceless Oriental porcelain, objects in carved ivory and exquisite work in precious metals, occupied the shelves. Behind a large lacquer writing-desk the owner was standing to greet his visitor. He was a small man immaculately dressed in European clothes. His skin was darker than Biggles thought to see. Having been told that the man was a Eurasian, he expected rather the pale olive tint peculiar to that type. Large gold-rimmed spectacles, slightly tinted, almost concealed his eyes.

'Please to be seated, sir,' said Larapindi, in faultless if rather suave English, at the same time indicating a heavily-carved chair that had already been pulled towards the desk in readiness. Having seen his visitor seated he himself sat down behind the desk.

'Thank you,' said Biggles.

'You wish to see me?' went on Larapindi smoothly. 'I do not think we have met before?'

Biggles smiled awkwardly. 'No. This is hardly the time to call, I'm afraid, but when I have explained the reason I hope you'll forgive me. It happened that in passing your house I re-membered, or it may have been that your house reminded me, of something my canteen manager once told me. But before I go any further I should explain that I am the temporary Mess President at Dum Dum airfield. Some time ago, Sergeant Mansur, our canteen manager, informed me that you had been good enough to recommend a man for work in the canteen. His name is Lal Din—or perhaps you don't remember him?'

'I recall him perfectly well,' said Larapindi, in an expression-less voice. He pushed towards Biggles a massive gold cigarette box. 'Please to have a cigarette, sir.'

'Thank you.' Biggles accepted the cigarette. 'This man Lal Din has turned out to be a most excellent steward—always cheerful, willing and obliging. We shall miss him.'

Larapindi's chin dropped a trifle so that he could survey his guest over his large glasses. 'Do you mean, he has—gone?'

'Not exactly,' returned Biggles. 'But the day before yesterday he complained of not feeling well. Yesterday he was obviously very ill, so I sent the Medical Officer to see him. It turns out that the poor fellow has smallpox.'

Larapindi drew a deep breath. 'Oh, dear! That is very sad.'

Biggles thought he caught a suspicion of relief, or it may have been understanding, in the way the words were spoken.

'Of course, it hardly needs me to tell you what an outbreak of infectious disease means on a station like Dum Dum,' he went on. 'Lal Din, poor chap, has been put in an isolation ward, and there, I'm afraid, he'll remain for some time. Which brings me to my point. We're going to miss him. Tomorrow morning I shall have to see about getting a new steward. In the ordinary way I should have advertised for a man, but this evening I had to come into the city, and in passing your house it struck me suddenly that your first recommendation had turned out so successfully you might know of another fellow. I don't expect you to produce another Lal Din off-hand, so to speak; but you might know of someone who could take up his duties right away. We shall be short-handed without Lal Din, and the sooner I have someone to replace him the better. In the ordinary way that might take two or three days. Now you know the reason I hope you will pardon me for breaking in on you at so late an hour.'

Larapindi made a deprecatory gesture. 'Do not speak of it,' he protested. 'Call on me at any time. If I can be of service the honour will be mine. It happens that you have called at a most fortunate moment. Only today my business manager came to me telling me of a man who has applied to us for work, a most excellent man. I should be glad to employ him myself, but I shall account it an honour if you will allow me to send him to you. I forget his name for the moment, but he is a Burmese from Rangoon, one of those unfortunate creatures who had to fly to India before the invasion of these hateful Japanese. He has been a house servant, and has had experience as a waiter. When would you like me to send him to you?'

'First thing in the morning,' requested Biggles. 'The sooner he takes up his duties the sooner will the pressure on our overworked staff be relieved.'

'I shall see that he is there,' promised Larapindi.

'Thank you. That is really most kind of you,' said Biggles gratefully. 'By the way, on my last tour of duty in India I believe I once had the pleasure of meeting Mr. Tahil, the senior partner of your firm. I trust he is in good health?'

'Alas, no,' sighed Larapindi sadly. 'Evidently you did not hear of his tragic accident?'

'Why, what happened?' asked Biggles, who was genuinely surprised, and not a little interested.

'Poor Mr. Tahil died from snake-bite,' exclaimed Larapindi. 'It happened on a golf links, of all places. His ball fell in the rough. Stooping to pick it up he accidentally touched a *krait*[1] that must have been lying beside the ball. Unfortunately, we were some way from the clubhouse. I ran all the way, but it was no use. Before a doctor could arrive with serum he was dead. It was a lamentable affair, and caused something of a sensation in Calcutta, because Mr. Tahil was a noted philanthropist, besides being a good servant of the government.'

Biggles' eyes were on Larapindi's face. 'What a terrible shock it must have been to you. I take it you were playing together?'

'We were. It was indeed a shock. I've hardly recovered from it.'

'And a blow, too, I imagine,' murmured Biggles sympathetically. 'I mean, his death must have thrown a lot of extra work on your shoulders, since it would leave you in complete charge of the business.'

Larapindi shrugged. 'These things happen; we must face them. I am doing my best to carry on single-handed.'

Biggles shook his head. 'I am very sorry to learn of this.'

Now, during the latter part of the conversation his eyes had lifted to a framed photograph that hung on the wall behind his host. Actually, there were several such photographs, most of them portraying the various offices of the firm of Tahil and Larapindi throughout the Orient. But one photograph in particular claimed his attention, for it was a picture of an

[1] *Krait.* A small but extremely venomous Indian snake. Its bite is usually fatal in a few minutes.

aircraft, a civil marine aircraft—or to be more precise, a Gull. It was moored on a river, off the end of the slipway, with a private hangar bearing the name of the firm in the background. The aircraft, which carried the Indian registration letters VT-XQL, also bore on its nose the name of the firm.

'Pardon my curiosity, Mr. Larapindi,' said Biggles, 'but the photograph behind you arouses my professional interest. I see your firm operates its own aircraft?'

'It did, until the war put an end to private enterprise,' answered Larapindi, swinging round in his chair to glance at the photograph. 'We try to be progressive, you know. Our interests in the East are so widespread that the adoption of the aeroplane as a means of transport was almost automatic. We bought a machine, a Gull, and established a repair and maintenance depot a few miles higher up the river. It would have been developed had not the war put an end to our plans—only temporarily, I hope.'

'Of course,' said Biggles quietly. 'No doubt you had to ground the machine when the war started.'

'Yes, the government asked us to, and, naturally, we were only too anxious to oblige. We shall need pilots when the war is over, so if ever you abandon the service as a career I hope you will come to see me, to our mutual benefit.'

'I'll bear it in mind,' promised Biggles. 'But I must be on my way. I'm glad to have had this opportunity of meeting you.' He got up.

'I hope we shall meet again, sir,' said Larapindi, also rising.

'I'm sure we shall,' replied Biggles evenly. 'Meanwhile, I shall expect your man first thing in the morning.'

'He will be there.'

Larapindi saw his guest to the door, where they parted.

Biggles returned to the lorry.

'How did you get on?' asked Algy.

'I got what I went for,' answered Biggles. 'Now listen, everbody. I've told Larapindi that Lal Din is down with smallpox, and asked him to send us a man to replace him. He has promised to send one along first thing in the morning. That means he's got to get busy, tonight, finding a man, giving him instructions, and supplying him with a stock of doped confectionery. I doubt if he'll risk talking over the telephone. Unless I've missed my mark he'll attend to the business in person. We'll watch from here. If he goes out, we'll follow.'

Hardly had he finished speaking when a man, in the attire of an Indian servant, appeared at the iron gates, and walked briskly down the avenue.

'What about him?' asked Ginger.

'He's probably part of the organization, but we've got to go for bigger game,' answered Biggles. 'That chap has been sent out on an errand—probably to fetch the fellow Larapindi has in mind to replace Lal Din. We're all right. Either the man will be brought here, in which case we shall know it, or he will be taken somewhere else. If he is taken somewhere else, Larapindi will have to go out to see him. Ah! What's this?'

A servant had appeared at the gates and opened them wide. A minute later an expensive touring car crept through. The gates were closed. The car cruised away down the avenue.

'After him,' ordered Biggles crisply. 'Keep the car in sight, but don't get too close.'

'What about the Tahil part of the partnership?' asked Algy, as they followed the car. 'Aren't you interested in him?'

'Tahil is dead,' answered Biggles slowly. 'He was bitten by a snake while playing golf with Larapindi. Since it must have suited Larapindi remarkably well to be left alone in charge of the business, I have a feeling that there were two snakes on the links that morning. But let's discuss that presently.'

Five minutes later it was clear that the car was heading for the dock area.

'It looks as if he's going to the warehouse,' said Algy. 'This is the direction, anyway.'

This surmise turned out to be correct. The car stopped before the main entrance of the establishment of Tahil and Larapindi. The lorry had also stopped, some distance away, but close enough for Biggles to see Larapindi alight and enter the building. The car was driven back a little way, revealing that it had a chauffeur in charge, to be parked in a narrow turning, one side of which was entirely occupied by the warehouse.

'It looks as though he's going to be some time, otherwise the car would have waited at the front entrance,' remarked Biggles. 'It's a bigger building than I expected,' he added, taking stock of the warehouse and its position. Not that much could be seen. The building, a vast square pile, stood alone, separated from similar warehouses which lined that side of the road by narrow streets. It fronted the main road. The rear part, which seemed to be much older than the front, which was obviously modern, overlooked the broad, turgid, Hugli River.

'When I saw it in daylight, the place gave me the impression of being a very old building with a new front stuck on it,' said Algy. 'It's pretty ramshackle at the back.'

'Most warehouses are, or those I've seen,' answered Biggles. 'Hello, here's another car stopping. It's a taxi.'

The taxi pulled up at the front entrance, deposited two passengers and drove on.

'We're doing fine,' murmured Biggles. 'One of those fellows is Larapindi's servant, the one we saw leave the house. The other must be the man he went to fetch—the man Larapindi is going to send along to replace Lal Din. Brought him in a taxi, eh? Must be in a hurry. This is how I hoped it would pan out. If I'm right, Larapindi is going to give that fellow his instructions. Instructions wouldn't be much use without the dope, so it must be kept here. This is where we take a hand. Listen everybody. Algy and Ginger will come with me. We've got to get into that building somehow. Bertie, you'll take charge of the rest of the party. Leave someone here to look after the lorry. Post the others round the building to see that no one gets out. If you hear shots, or anything that sounds like a row, break in and lend a hand.'

'Why not wait for this new assistant to come out and grab him with the goods on him?' suggested Johnny Crisp.

'I'm not interested in him,' answered Biggles. 'The man I want is Larapindi, and we've got to catch him handling the dope, or he'll slip through our fingers like a wet fish. Come on, Algy. Come on, Ginger—bring your bag.'

In a minute they were on the pavement, at a corner of the big warehouse. Biggles set off down a side turning, looking at the windows. 'We've got to get in without making a noise,' he said quietly. He continued walking until they had nearly reached the river, and then pulled up by a door, a side entrance to the building. As a matter of course he turned the handle, to find, as he expected, that the door was locked. He turned to Ginger. 'What have you got in that bag?'

'I've got a hacksaw, a file, some tyre levers, a drill——'

'Good. The drill ought to do the trick,' interrupted Biggles. 'Make a hole near the handle, and cut out a piece of wood big enough to get a hand through. The key will probably be in the lock on the inside.'

This conjecture proved to be correct, but ten minutes were occupied in cutting the hole. Ginger did the work while Biggles and Algy kept watch. As it happened no one passed through the little street, so the work was not interrupted. As soon as the hole had been made Biggles inserted a hand, and with an exclamation of satisfaction brought out the key. He inserted it in the lock on the outside. As the door swung open, the warm, aromatic aroma of mixed Indian merchandise, tea, spices, jute, oilseeds and grain, poured out to greet them. Without a sound they stepped inside. Biggles closed the door. There was a faint snick as he switched on his torch. Its beam stabbed the darkness.

16

THE GREEN IDOL

Not until he was inside the building did Biggles realise fully the size of it, and the problem this presented. It was apparent, however, that they were in that part devoted to the storage of merchandise, and by the character of it, the export department. Cases of tea, sacks of grain, bales and boxes stacked in orderly arry from floor to ceiling, with narrow corridors between to permit the passage of those whose business it was to handle these goods. To Biggles, it seemed unlikely that Larapindi would conduct his affairs in that section of the building; it was almost certain that he would be somewhere in the administration department, and with the object of finding this he set off, moving quietly but quickly along a corridor that ran parallel with the narrow street outside, in the direction of the front entrance. Algy and Ginger followed close behind. The reek of the goods was not unpleasant, but it was almost overpowering in its pungency.

After a little while, however, this smell began perceptibly to change, and the reason was soon evident. There was a break in the ranks of merchandise, and on the far side of the passage thus made the type of produce changed abruptly. Here, now, were wood and cardboard boxes bearing the names of British and United States manufacturers; clearly, the import department. Once Biggles stopped, and without speaking pointed to a large notice stencilled on one of the cases. The words were: CHARNEYS, LONDON. CONFECTIONERY. STOW AWAY FROM ENGINES.

Biggles continued to walk forward, and presently perceived that he was nearing his first objective—the administrative block. The merchandise ended, to give way to numerous passages, with wood-partitioned offices, some large, some small, bearing the names of wholesale and retail departments and the names of their managers. Biggles' progress became slower and more cautious.

So far not a sound of any sort had broken the tomb-like silence of the warehouse; but now, passing an unpretentious stairway there came from somewhere in the distance, high above, no louder than the rustle of dry leaves, a murmur of voices. Biggles hesitated for a moment and then went on. He did not go far, being brought to a halt when the passage ended at swing doors, panelled with panes of frosted glass, through which came a feeble but steady light. Switching out his torch, and laying a finger on his lips for silence, he made a stealthy reconnaissance. Then, with infinite care, he allowed the door to sink back into place and turned to the others.

'It's the main hall,' he breathed. 'There's a man on duty inside the front door. We can't go any farther this way without being seen. We shall have to go back.' He retreated as far as the narrow stairway, and after listening for a little while to the distant sound of talking began a discreet ascent.

The staircase, after making two right-angle turns, ended in a corridor on the first floor, lighted by a single electric bulb. The corridor extended for some distance on either side, with doors at frequent intervals. All were shut. It was now possible to distinguish a single voice, a voice of authority it seemed, speaking rapidly. It still came from above. Biggles explored, and half a dozen paces along the corridor found another staircase leading upwards. It was precisely the same as the first, and for practical purposes a continuation of it. It mounted to the second floor, to another corridor identical with that of the floor below. The voice still came from above. Another advance took Biggles and his companions to the third floor. Still the voice came from higher up. It was now fairly clear, but after listening for a moment Biggles shrugged his shoulders. He could not identify the language, much less make out what was being said.

Farther upward progress was now barred by a door on which a single word had been painted in white letters in several languages. One of the languages was English. The word was PRIVATE. Biggles tried the door. It opened readily, revealing another staircase. But this one was different. On the floors below the boards had been left bare; here hey were covered by a thick red carpet. After a slight inclination of his head Biggles went on up to the next floor, into an atmosphere altogether different from those below. Gone, now, was any impression of a warehouse or business office. The appointments were those of a luxury hotel, or a suite in a block of expensive flats. The staircase ended in what might best be described as an outer hall of some size, richly furnished and carpeted. Around this hall, opposite the intruders as they stood at the head of the staircase, were four doors. One stood ajar. The room to which it gave entrance was lighted, but it was not from here that the voices came. It was the room next to it.

Biggles looked at the others with a puzzled expression on his face. He did not speak, but by a gesture indicated what he was thinking. Indeed, something was now explained that had puzzled Ginger all the way up the stairs—the loudness of the voice inside the room. It did not speak in an ordinary conversational tone, but was pitched high as though it were reading aloud to an audience. No explanation of this being forthcoming, after a little grimace to indicate his lack of understanding, Biggles crossed the hall to the open door, and without touching it, peeped in. A faint click of the tongue, denoting surprise, brought the others to his side. Very slowly he pushed the door wide open so that the whole interior of the room could be seen. Strictly speaking it was not a room. It was a laboratory.

After a swift survey of the scene Biggles paid no attention to the scientific apparatus that stood about, or the rows of jars and bottles that occupied the numerous shelves. He went straight to a bench on which had been accumulated an assortment of objects, a curious assortment—curious because they were not what one would expect to find in a laboratory. Most conspicuous were two cardboard boxes, bearing in bold type a name, and certain announcements, which to Biggles were becoming familiar. The name was Charneys. Both boxes had been broken open and part of their contents strewn on the bench. In one case it was chewing-gum; in the other, chocolate. Near these was a pile of loose wrapping-papers, some pink, some brown, that had obviously been torn carelessly from the products named on the boxes. The contents of the wrapping-papers, however, were not there. Close at hand, in two separate boxes, were identical wrapping-papers, but these were brand new. There were only two other objects on the bench, but they were significant. One was a small glass jar half filled with an oily, colourless liquid, and the other, a case across which lay a hypodermic syringe.

It needed less time to observe these things than to describe them, and after a long penetrating stare Biggles said softly: 'This is it. We're in the dope shop. Larapindi didn't lose any time preparing samples for the new man to distribute at Dum Dum. This little collection tells the whole story. He takes the stuff as it arrives from England, unwraps as much as he needs, gives each sample a shot of dope with the needle, and rewraps it in a new paper. He can't inject much dope into a solid bar of chocolate, but no doubt one drop would be ample to knock out anyone not used to the stuff. I knew a fellow who once chewed a piece of charas—the dope that's most popular in India. To be on the safe side he nibbled a piece only half the size of an orange pip, but he went out as if he'd been hit on the head with a rolling-pin. We may assume that the stuff in that bottle is highly concentrated. I'd like to make Larapindi drink the lot. That's him talking in the next room; I recognise his voice, although what he has to shout about I don't know. We've enough evidence here to hang him, so let's see what he has to say about it. There may be some slight argument when he sees us, so have your guns handy. Algy, you stay here and don't let anybody touch this stuff. I'd like Raymond to see it just as it is. Come on, Ginger.' As he finished speaking Biggles took his automatic from his pocket and slipped it into his right sleeve, so that it was held there by his fingers.

Leaving Algy by the bench, followed by Ginger he returned to the hall and walked on to the door through which the voice still came. 'He seems to have a lot to say,' he murmured. 'I shall try to open the door—assuming it isn't locked—without being seen, but I don't think there's much hope of that. I've no idea of how he'll behave when he sees us, but you'd better be ready to move fast. Hold your hat—here we go.'

Biggles' fingers closed firmly over the handle of the door. Very slowly he turned it. The door moved. A slit of light appeared between door and frame. He released the handle: but instead of the door remaining open only a few inches, as he intended, it continued the opening movement—slowly, but quite definitely.

The result was inevitable. The movement was seen. But before that happened Biggles was granted three seconds' grace to absorb the picture presented to his gaze. It was enough, although what he saw was not what he expected. Far from it. He had thought, indeed, he had convinced himself—unwisely, as he later confessed—that there would be not more than three persons in the room; Larapindi, the steward who was to replace Lal Din, and perhaps the servant who had fetched him. Instead, there were not fewer than seven or eight people present. He did not count them. There was no time for that. Not that it mattered much. These men were seated round a large mahogany table, so that the proceedings had the appearance of a board meeting; a strange one, perhaps, because the centre of the table was occupied by a green stone idol. Larapindi was standing at the head of the table, unfortunately for Biggles, at the far end, because in that position he was facing the door. The heads of his disciples, or assistants, or agents, or whatever they were, were bowed in the direction of the idol in reverent adoration.

Now, had this been all, Biggles might have been embarrassed, for he would have been the last man to interrupt a devotional ritual, whatever religion was involved. But it was not all. In front of each man, looking absurdly out of place on account of its blatantly European character, was a little heap of packets Biggles had come to know so well; packets of chewing-gum and chocolate. This told him all he needed to know. The fact that several agents, instead of one, were being instructed in their duties, and that these agents were obviously being bound to their murderous tasks by a religious ceremony, made no difference to the broad situation. He had, as he had planned, caught the plotters red-handed. That was the dominating factor. Whether he and Ginger would be able to apprehend so many was another matter. They had at least the advantage of surprise.

Larapindi was the first to observe the open door. He must have seen Biggles at the same time. His voice broke off abruptly. And thus, for a long second, the scene remained, immobile, frozen, as it were, like a screen play suddenly arrested. Then, as if wondering at the sudden cessation of sound, the bowed heads were raised. The agents looked at their chief. They saw his fixed expression and noted the direction of his stare. With one accord they turned.

Biggles' gun slid into his hand and came up like the head of a striking cobra. 'Don't move, anybody,' he snapped. He would have avoided bloodshed had it been possible.

It was not. Perhaps the agents did not understand. Be that as it may, the words broke the spell. The order was ignored.

Movement returned, and it returned with a rush. With a unanimous gasp of alarm, and a crashing of over-turning chairs, the agents sprang to their feet in panic. In doing this they came between Biggles and Larapindi, who was not slow to seize the opportunity this human cover provided. He sprang to the wall, and on the instant the room was plunged into darkness.

Three streams of orange sparks leapt across the room. They started at the muzzle of Biggles' gun and ended at the spot where he had last seen Larapindi. Loud cries of fear accompanied the reports. There were answering shots from different points of the room, to be followed instantly by the thump of falling bodies. A little light entered through the open door from the hall, but it was not sufficient to enable Biggles to see clearly what was happening, except that all was in confusion. Men were staggering about, colliding with each other and falling over the chairs. It was a situation for which he was not prepared, and one that seemed to defy immediate remedy. He had no desire to perpetrate a massacre. Realising that he could serve no useful purpose by remaining inside the room, and that there was a chance of his being knocked down in the mêlée, he backed to the hall. It seemed to be the wisest course, particularly as he had only to keep the door covered from the outside to prevent anyone from escaping. On the spur of the moment he assumed this; and it was no doubt a natural assumption; but in the event it turned out to be another mistake. He took up a position in the lighted hall on one side of the door, few paces from it, and shouted at Ginger to take up a similar position on the other side.

'Plug anybody who tries to get away,' he ordered grimly.

'What a mess,' muttered Ginger in a disgusted voice, as he obeyed. He side-stepped briskly as a little brown man darted out, blazing wildly with a small automatic.

Biggles fired and the man went down. 'I'm afraid we've started something,' he said, with a worried frown, as from somewhere in the lower regions there came a crashing and banging, with a few sporadic shots.

'That must be our crowd breaking in—they've heard the rumpus,' opined Ginger. 'Why not lock the door, and keep

Larapindi and the rest until the police come to collect them?' he suggested, indicating the room, from which now came an excited muttering.

'That's an idea,' agreed Biggles. He went to the door, and having taken the key from the far side, slammed it. He turned the key.

While this brief operation was in progress other things were happening. Algy put his head round the laboratory door and demanded to be told what was going on. Biggles gave him a brief idea of what had happened, and ordered him to remain where he was. Voices were shouting somewhere below. Feet thumped on stairs.

'Bigglesworth! Where are you?' called one voice.

'That sounds like Raymond,' said Ginger. 'What's he doing here?'

'He must have followed us—like an old hound that won't be left out of the hunt,' answered Biggles, smiling. 'Perhaps it's as well. I'll hand this mess over to him.'

Tug, gun in hand, appeared at the head of the stairs. There was blood on his face and on the front of his tunic. 'Have you got 'em?' he asked excitedly.

'Not exactly,' replied Biggles. 'What have you been up to?'

'I met a bloke on the stairs,' explained Tug. 'He tried to stop me coming up. We had a row about it and he got the worst of it.'

Air Commodore Raymond, panting heavily, was the next to arrive. 'What on earth are you doing here?' he demanded.

'I might ask you that,' returned Biggles curtly. 'I told you to keep out of it, so that——'

'I know. So that if things went wrong you could shoulder the blame. I'm not having that. I brought you out, so if anyone is going to get a rap it will be me.'

'It may come to that,' declared Biggles. 'Larapindi is a big bug in this part of the world, and he may be able to pull enough strings to cause serious trouble in India. But we can talk about that later. Larapindi is the boss of the local spy ring—I've got all the evidence I need to prove that. He's in that room with some of his gang.'

'Then let's have him out,' said the Air Commodore bluntly.

'Okay,' agreed Biggles. 'But someone's liable to get hurt. I wanted to avoid that. I'm by no means sure of the nationality of some of these fellows, and we don't want to have a political issue made out of it. Still . . .' He went to the door, turned the key, and pushing the door open, stepped inside. 'Come out of that,' he ordered. 'The place is surrounded. You can't get away.'

There was a brief pause. Then, one by one, four men came out.

'These men may be dressed like Hindus, but if they aren't Japs I'll eat my buttons,' swore the Air Commondore.

'Where are the rest?' said Biggles. The beam of his torch cut a wedge into the darkness of the room. He ran in and switched on the light. Three men were lying on the floor. Larapindi was not among them. Biggles' eyes flashed round the room. There was only one possible hiding-place—a large safe that stood open. He went to it and looked inside, but the man he sought was not there.

'He's got away,' he rasped. 'There must be a secret way out of this room—probably a lift. It's no use looking for it now.' He turned to the Air Commodore. 'I'll leave you to take care of things here, sir. Algy's in the next room with some things you ought to see. Tug, you stay here with Ginger and give the Air Commodore a hand to clean up the mess. He'll need some help.'

Biggles made for the stairs.

17
THE END OF THE TRAIL

BIGGLES went down the stairs three at a time, not a little annoyed at the turn the affair had taken—annoyed with himself, that is, for not having taken more direct action in the room upstairs. He should, he thought, have foreseen the possibility of the move Larapindi had made; for should the chief enemy agent escape, the coup he had planned would have to be accounted a failure. There was a chance that Larapindi might still be somewhere in the building, and if that were so, by posting the rest of the squadron to cover the exits, his escape might be frustrated.

He nearly fell over a body that lay at the foot of the second-floor staircase—presumably the man Tug had shot on his way up. Biggles turned his torch on him, and caught his breath sharply when it revealed a Japanese Air Force tunic. It was not until later, though, that he grasped the full significance of this. At the moment he was simply astonished that an enemy airman should wear uniform in such a place and at such a time. Without giving the matter serious thought, it flashed into his mind that the Japanese might possibly be one of those who had baled out in the combat, and had made his way under cover of dark to the warehouse, knowing that Larapindi would provide him with a hiding-place. The man still clutched in his hand a Japanese general service pattern revolver.

Biggles ran on down to the main hall. The first thing he saw was a man in native dress—the hall porter, he thought—lying on his back on the floor. A knife lay beside him. Taffy Hughes, as pale as death, sat in a chair, one foot in a pool of blood, with Johnny Crisp, on his knees, twisting a tourniquet round his leg.

'What's happened here?' asked Biggles sharply.

Johnny answered: 'Taffy and I bust the door in when the shooting started. Taffy was first. This guy'—Johnny indicated the man on the floor—'stuck a knife in him.'

'Look after him,' ordered Biggles. 'Have you seen a man go out through this door?'

'No one has gone out this way,' replied Johnny.

'Where are the others?'

'Outside, I suppose. Only Tug followed us in, and he went on up the stairs.'

Biggles went out into the street. The lorry was there, with Ferocity, alone, in charge.

'Have you seen a man come out of the building?' asked Biggles tersely.

'Not a soul,' returned Ferocity.

'Where's Bertie and Tex?'

'They went down the side street to grab Larapindi's car.'

'Okay. Stand by,' commanded Biggles. 'Taffy's been knifed, but Johnny is with him. If it turns out that Taffy is badly hurt you'll have to run him back to hospital. If not, wait for the others.'

Biggles ran on down the side street. Larapindi's car was still there. Tex, gun in hand, was standing beside it. The native driver cowered against the wall with his hands up.

'Have you seen anybody come out, Tex?' asked Biggles.

'Sure,' answered Tex. 'A little feller in European clothes shot out of a side door. When we shouted to him to stop he had a crack at us and then bolted towards the river. Bertie went after him.'

Biggles raced on down the street. It ended abruptly at the river, but to the right there was a long wharf, flanking the rear of the warehouse. 'Bertie! Where are you?' he shouted.

The answer was two pistol shots in quick succession. The reports came from the far end of the wharf, which was occupied by cranes, conveyors, trollies and similar dock equipment. Biggles ran towards the sound. More shots guided him as he ran. Then came another sound, one that spurred him to a sprint. It was the throbbing hum of a powerful motor-boat. He came upon Bertie taking long distance shots at a long low craft that was tearing the surface off the water as it headed upstream.

'The blighter's got away,' muttered Bertie. 'Sorry, old boy.'

'Was he a little fellow in European clothes, wearing spectacles?'

'Yes. I lost sight of him in all this clutter. Next thing I saw was the boat.'

'Are there any more boats?' asked Biggles.

'I haven't seen any. I shouldn't think there are two like that.' Bertie pointed to the fast disappearing speedboat. 'Let's follow in the car,' he suggested. 'The blighter's got to come ashore somewhere, sooner or later.'

Biggles clicked his fingers. 'My gosh!' he muttered, aghast. 'I've just remembered something. I'll bet I know where he's making for. He's got an aircraft up the river. He's going to pull out.' Biggles went on quickly. 'We've still a chance. Bertie, go into the main hall and call Dum Dum on the 'phone; tell them to bring a Spit out and have it started up. I shall be there in five minutes.'

Without waiting to see if Bertie followed Biggles raced back to Larapindi's car. 'Look out! I want this car,' he told Tex in a brittle voice. 'Take your prisoner inside and hand him over to Johnny. Tell Johnny to call an ambulance from the airfield to pick up Taffy. Then join Ferocity in the lorry and try to overtake a motor-boat that's heading up-stream. Larapindi's in it. He's got a hangar somewhere up the river, with a machine in it. Try to stop him from getting away. If the hangar is this side of the river you may have a chance.'

Biggles was moving as he spoke, and by the time he had finished he was in the driving seat. The car shot forward, and in another minute was racing along the road to Dum Dum.

In the short drive that followed Biggles took risks which in the ordinary way he would have considered unjustifiable. The driver of a belated bullock cart, which he missed by inches in avoiding a careless pedestrian, would doubtless have agreed with him. But everything depended on speed. He reached the airfield without mishap, and after skidding to a standstill at the main gate to announce his identity, went straight on across the landing-field to where a Spitfire was standing, its engine idling.

'Is she all right, flight-sergeant?' he shouted to the N.C.O. in charge, as he jumped out.

'Okay, sir,' was the answer.

Biggles climbed into the cockpit. An instant later the engine roared and the Spitfire moved forward. In five seconds it was in the air, swinging round in a wide turn towards Calcutta. The river came into view. Biggles eased the control column forward. On reaching the river he turned steeply, and roared up-stream with the floor of his fuselage not more than fifty feet above the water. He noted several cars outside the warehouse as he flashed past. Ahead, all he could see was that the placid surface of the river had been disturbed. There was no sign of the motor-boat. He tore on for three or four minutes, annihilating distance. Before him the moon gleamed on the broad face of the water. He had always realised the futility of trying to make any sort of search in the dock area, which stretches for miles, but he hoped that somewhere above it, where there was less congestion of vessels, he would see either the motor-boat, or the aircraft. He saw neither. Doubts assailed him. It was only assumption that Larapindi would try to effect his escape by air. The enemy agent had asserted that the Gull was grounded for the duration; and so, undoubtedly, it had been—officially, Biggles reflected. But that would not prevent Larapindi from keeping it in an airworthy condition if he thought there was a chance that he might need it.

Biggles zoomed. Banking gently, his eyes probed the deep blue void through which he moved. He began to circle, extending his range with each turn. There was no sign of the aircraft he sought. Moodily he began to wonder if he had been wise in rushing into the air; and he was still wondering, torn by indecision, when during a turn he saw two bright sparks of light on the ground, winking at him. He took the lights to be the headlamps of a car, on the far bank of the river. With quickening interest he realised that this might be a signal to him, bearing in mind that the lorry would be able to judge his position by the sound of his motor.

Making for the lights he nearly collided with the Gull, and thereby had what must have been one of the narrowest escapes of his career. He did not know it was the Gull. He barely saw it. He was concentrating his attention on the winking headlights, trying to make out if the flashes formed a signal in Morse, when the thing happened. To say that a shadow appeared in the darkness would convey only a poor impression of the actual event. When two high-performance aircraft are approaching each other head-on, even in broad daylight, from the moment they become visible to each other, to the moment of contact, is a very short time indeed. At night the time factor is lessened, in ratio with reduced visibility. The black shape of the Gull did undoubtedly approach, but from the time it came into sight, to the moment of passing, was a split second. Biggles hardly saw it. Rather did he become aware of it. He acted without conscious thought. It was one of those occasions, and there are many in every pilot's career, when there is literally no time for thought. Life depends on perfect co-ordination of brain and limb. The two things, actuated by an impulse which is akin to instinct, must operate simultaneously, or all is lost. Biggles' right hand and foot jerked. The Spitfire reacted convulsively, like a horse startled from sleep. The two shadows seemed to merge. Then they flashed past each other. The danger was averted. Again Biggles moved. His nerves were rigid from shock, the sensation as when we say our heart stands still; but he moved. The control column was back in his thigh, and the Spitfire had whirled round almost in its own length. Then for the first time he really saw the Gull, and recognised it.

The rest was comparatively easy. Glancing down to see where he was he observed that by an ironic twist of fate the Gull was just passing over the eastern boundary of the airfield, from which the enemy agents had sent so many British pilots to their deaths. He waited for a moment and then fired a short burst past the Gull's cabin. He assumed that the civil machine would be unarmed, and he resolved to give the pilot a chance to land should he prefer surrender to death, although it would probably come to the same thing in the end. He did not think his enemy would accept the invitation. And he was right. The Gull jinked, and then, to Biggles' surprise, someone in the cabin opened fire on him with a machine-gun, presumably a mobile weapon. He hesitated no longer. Swinging round to the off-side quarter of the fugitive he closed in, took careful aim, and fired. Tracer flashed across the intervening distance. The apex of the cone of fire struck the Gull full amidships; the machine appeared first to crumple, and then break across the cabin. Pieces broke off and whirled away astern. The nose of the stricken machine dropped. It dived. The motor was cut, but still it dived, in an ever-steepening swoop earthward. With expressionless face Biggles watched it strike the edge of a paddy-field. He circled twice and then turned away, not feeling inclined to risk a night landing near the wreck, although the country was open. In any case, he knew that there was nothing he could do for whoever might be in the machine. So he cruised back to the airfield and landed, taxi-ing on to the ambulance station.

'I've just shot an enemy machine down, not far from the road, about two miles east of the airfield,' he announced. 'I fancy there are casualties. I'll come with you.'

'I thought I heard shooting sir,' answered the driver, as Biggles got in beside him.

There were two bodies in the wreck. One was Larapindi. The other, obviously the pilot, was unknown to him. The ambulance returned to the airfield and the bodies were taken to the mortuary. Biggles went back to Larapindi's car, which still stood where he had abandoned it, and drove quietly back to the warehouse.

Things were different from when he had left. A line of police cars occupied the kerb outside the main entrance, from which he gathered that the Air Commodore had considered it advisable to call for assistance. He found a little crowd in the hall; it included most of the members of the squadron, and the Air Commodore. His arrival caused a stir.

'What about Larapindi?' asked the Air Commodore urgently, anxiously.

'He won't give any more trouble,' answered Biggles.

'Where is he?'

Biggles took out his cigarette case. 'What's left of him is in the station mortuary,' he replied.

'How did that happen?'

'He'd got an aircraft parked up the river, apparently with a tame pilot standing by. He must have kept the machine there for just such an emergency.'

'We've found five Japanese airmen here so far, hiding in different parts of the building,' put in the Air Commodore. 'This must have been a rendezvous for enemy pilots who were forced down on our side of the lines. It seems that that was another of Larapindi's activities. The search is still going on. I take it you shot him down?'

'I had to, or he'd have got away. He was heading east. That's all there was to it. What's happened here?'

'Nothing very exciting, since you left. We're still cleaning up. We've taken everybody into custody. That stuff in the laboratory was interesting, but not so interesting as the contents of Larapindi's safe. You caught him on one foot, so to speak; otherwise, if he had had time, no doubt he would have destroyed everything. As it is, we've got particulars of the dope operatives on the other stations, to say nothing of other agents, and where they are working. They are being rounded up. By dawn the whole organization should be wiped out.'

'Was Larapindi a Jap?' asked Biggles.

'I haven't been able to get to the bottom of that yet,' answered the Air Commodore. 'He was a Fascist, anyway. He was a wealthy man, but that wasn't enough. He wanted power, which is an obsession with a certain type. I found a document in the safe, a sort of agreement, promising him a high political position in India should the country be taken by Japan. He played for a big stake, and lost.'

Biggles nodded. 'Have you found any indication as to whether this dope business was his own idea, or whether he was put up to it by Japan?'

'We don't know yet. We may never know—not that it's important.'

'What's the position of the firm?' queried Biggles.

'Oh, it was genuine enough, originally, there's no doubt of that,' asserted the Air Commodore. 'Larapindi was the crook. With Tahil out of the way it provided a wonderful background for espionage. The firm has agents and branches everywhere, and the top floor of this warehouse must have been an ideal meeting-place for enemy agents. Tahil died from snake-bite, you know.'

'So Larapindi told me. I should say Larapindi was the snake that bit him.'

'Old Tahil was a good fellow. It must have suited Larapindi to have him out of the way. Young Tahil, the old man's son, is at Oxford. I imagine he'll come back and take over the firm. Well, you've done a good job, Bigglesworth. I'll see that you get credit for it.'

'You mean, you'll see that the squadron gets credit for it,' corrected Biggles.

The Air Commodore smiled. 'Of course—that's what I meant. I suppose you'd like to get back to England now? If you go right away I'm afraid you'll have to leave Mackail and Harcourt here.'

'How are they? Have you heard lately?'

'Yes, I rang up the hospital this evening. Harcourt is doing fine—he wasn't seriously hurt. Mackail has come round, and the M.O. says he'll recover, but it will be some time before he flies again.'

'Good. What about Taffy? The last I saw of him he was sitting here bleeding like a pig. One of Larapindi's men had knifed him.'

'It's nothing serious,' stated the Air Commodore. 'In fact, Crisp, who went back with him in the ambulance, tells me that the M.O., after putting a stitch or two in him, has let him go to his own quarters.'

'Bertie and Tex saw Larapindi take off,' put in Ginger, who was one of those standing by, listening to the conversation. 'They went with Ferocity in the lorry. They couldn't do anything to stop him because they were on the wrong side of the river.'

'Absolutely,' declared Bertie. 'All I could do was wink my jolly old headlights at you, to show you where we were.'

Biggles smiled. 'I saw them; and I was so interested in them that I nearly flew into Larapindi. If he was more scared than I was he must have died from shock. I shall have a nightmare tonight—the thought of collision always did give me the jitters.' He yawned. 'Which reminds me, a spot of sleep wouldn't do any of us any harm. Let's get back. I want to have a little wager with Tug.'

'What is it?' asked Algy.

Biggles laughed. 'I'm going to bet him that the hole in my arm is deeper than the one in his leg. Come on. Let's go, before the Air Commodore thinks of another tangle for us to straighten out.'

BIGGLES

DEFIES THE
SWASTIKA

I

AN UNPLEASANT AWAKENING

SQUADRON-LEADER JAMES BIGGLESWORTH, D.S.O., better known in flying circles as 'Biggles', was awakened by the early morning sun streaming through the open window of his room in the Hotel Kapital, in Oslo. As he stretched out his hand towards the bedside bell, to let the chambermaid know that he was ready for his coffee, he became vaguely aware that instead of the usual bustle in the street below there was a peculiar silence, as if it were Sunday. It struck him that he might be mistaken in the day, and that it was Sunday after all; but this thought was instantly dismissed by the absence of church-bell chimes. He reached out for the morning paper, which the hall porter, without wakening him, had on previous days put on his bedside table, only to frown with surprise and disapproval when he found that it was not there.

Looking back, he could never understand why this sequence of events did not suggest the truth to him. Perhaps he was not fully awake; or it may have been that his mind was filled with other things. Be that as it may, no suspicion of the real state of affairs occurred to him. He was in no immediate hurry to get up, for he had nothing in particular to do, so he lay still, basking in the early spring sunshine, thinking over the peculiar nature of the mission that had brought him to Norway, and wondering if it was time for him to get into touch with Colonel Raymond, of the British Intelligence Service, with a view to asking if he could now return to France.

When, some two months earlier, Colonel Raymond had broached the project to him, Biggles had listened without enthusiasm, for he was quite content to be where he was. At that time he was in France, commanding a special squadron which included amongst its pilots his two best friends, Flight-Lieutenant the Hon. Algy Lacey and Flying-Officer 'Ginger' Hebblethwaite; and one of the reasons why he received Colonel

Raymond's proposal with disfavour was that the acceptance of it meant leaving them, and going alone to Norway.

The mission which Colonel Raymond asked him to undertake was, on the face of it, neither difficult nor dangerous. Briefly, it was this. According to reports received from their secret agents, the British authorities were of the opinion that the Nazi government contemplated an invasion of Scandinavia, and in the event of this taking place, British troops would at once be sent to the assistance of the country attacked. But this was only the major issue. If troops were sent, then they would have to be supported by aircraft, and Colonel Raymond's department was anxious to ascertain what air bases would be available. This did not mean established civil or military aerodromes, particulars of which were already known, but tracts of land which might, in emergency, be converted into aerodromes. Failing that, which lakes or fiords were the most suitable for marine aircraft? Such technical information as this could only be obtained by a practical pilot, and Biggles was asked to undertake the work. There were, however, minor difficulties, one of which was the political aspect. For example, if it became known that a British pilot was carrying out survey flights over Norway it might lead to unpleasant repercussions, and in order to avoid such a possibility a scheme had been evolved.

Biggles—assuming that he accepted the task—would proceed to Norway as a Norwegian subject who had for many years resided in Canada. This would account for his being able to speak English fluently, and at the same time explain his imperfect Norwegian. As a matter of fact, Biggles knew no Norwegian at all, and his first job would be to pick up the language as quickly as possible. For the rest, he would be provided with papers pronouncing him to be Sven Hendrik, born in Oslo. On arriving in Norway he would join a flying club and buy a light aeroplane in which he would make cross-country flights, ostensibly for sport, but in reality to collect the information required. Should the threatened invasion actually occur, all he would have to do would be to get into his machine and fly back to England forthwith.

It all sounded so very simple that it found no favour in Biggles's eyes, and he said as much, pointing out that it was a job any pilot could do. But Colonel Raymond, with shrewd foresight, did not agree. He admitted that while all went well the mission was unlikely to present any difficulty, but should unforeseen circumstances arise—well, it would save him a lot of anxiety if someone of ability and experience was on the job. It would not last very long—perhaps two or three months. If he, Biggles, would undertake it, Algy Lacey could command the squadron in France until he returned.

In the end Biggles had agreed to go, for as the matter was put to him he could not very well refuse, particularly as Colonel Raymond asked him to go as a personal favour. So he said goodbye to Algy and Ginger and in due course arrived in Norway. He would, of course, have taken his two comrades with him had this been possible, but Colonel Raymond vetoed it on the grounds that three strangers might attract suspicion where one would not.

For nearly two months he had been in Norway, making long survey flights in his little 'Moth' when the weather permitted, and swotting hard at the Norwegian language on every possible occasion. To live in a country is the best and quickest way of learning its language, and after seven weeks of concentrated effort Biggles was able to carry on a normal conversation in Norwegian. Also, by flying over it, he had got to know the country very well; indeed, there were few physical features that he had not seen, including the rugged coast-line. He had sent his reports home with many photographs, so it was reasonable to suppose that he might be recalled at any moment. Indeed, it was in anticipation of this that he had left his room at the flying club, which was a small private landing-ground near the village of Boda, and voted himself three days' holiday in Oslo to see the sights. Oslo was only thirty miles from Boda. He apprehended no danger in leaving his base, for nothing of note had happened the whole time he had been in Norway, and as far as he could see nothing was likely to happen. In fact, in his heart he was beginning to suspect that the British Intelligence Service had been mistaken in thinking that the Germans were contemplating an attack on Norway.

He looked at his watch. It was now nearly eight o'clock, and still his coffee had not arrived. This was curious, for the chambermaid was usually prompt, and he was in the act of reaching again for the bell when a sound reached his ears that brought a puzzled frown to his forehead. However, still without alarm, he flung off the bedclothes and was on his way to the window when the door of the room burst open and the chambermaid appeared. She seemed to be in a state bordering on hysteria.

'What's the matter?' asked Biggles shortly.

The woman nearly choked in her excitement and dismay. With a quivering finger she pointed to the window. 'The Germans,' she gasped. 'The Germans are here!'

Biggles experienced an unpleasant shock, for he realized that the woman was speaking the truth. Two swift strides took him to the window. One glance was enough. A double file of Nazi troops were marching up the street. A few civilians stood on the pavement watching with expressions that revealed what they felt, but otherwise the street was comparatively deserted.

Biggles bustled the woman out of the room. He had often found it necessary to dress quickly, but never before had he got into his clothes with such speed as he did now. And all the time his brain was racing as he strove to form a plan, to make some provision for the alarming contingency that had arisen; in other words, to escape with all possible speed from the trap in which he found himself.

Where the Nazi troops had come from so miraculously, and apparently without opposition, he could not imagine. At last, he assumed that there had been no opposition, or he could not have failed to hear the firing. The thing was inexplicable. The Nazis, incontestably, were in control of the city, and that was sufficient reason for him to evacuate it with all possible speed. Curiously enough he did not expect any great difficulty in achieving this, for was he not, to all intents and purposes, a harmless Norwegian citizen? Even the Nazis, he reasoned, would hardly massacre the entire civil population in cold blood, nor would they prevent people from going about their normal business.

Before he had finished dressing Biggles had decided on his line of action. It was the obvious one. He would charter a taxi and drive straight to the aerodrome. Once there it would not take him long to get his machine out of its hangar and into the air; and once in the air, only engine failure would prevent him from reaching England. Fortunately, from sheer habit, he had seen his tanks filled before he left the aerodrome. So, broadly speaking, his flight—in both senses of the word—seemed a fairly simple matter. His luggage didn't matter; there was nothing incriminating in it, and nothing that was irreplaceable, so he was quite prepared to abandon it. His only thought was to get to the aerodrome.

He took a quick glance at himself in the full-length mirror and decided that there was no reason why anyone should suspect that he was anything but what he pretended to be—a Norwegian subject. His grey flannel suit he had actually bought in Oslo on his arrival in the country. His nationality papers were in order, and he had plenty of ready money, so it seemed that he had little to worry about. Humming nonchalantly, he went down the stairs into the hall, and there he received his first shock. It was a rude one.

Four German troopers, under an *unteroffizier*, were there. They saw him at the same moment that he saw them, and as to retire would obviously invite suspicion he kept on his way. He was brought to a halt by the point of a bayonet. The *unteroffizier* addressed him harshly.

'Who are you?' he barked.

Biggles affected an expression of surprise. 'My name's Hendrik,' he answered at once. 'Why do you ask? What is happening here?'

'Norway is now under the control of the Third Reich,' answered the German. 'Return to your room and remain there until further notice.'

Biggles looked at the hotel manager. Slumped in his desk, he was as white as death. He seemed stunned. 'It is correct,' he said in a low voice.

Biggles shrugged his shoulders. 'Very well,' he said, and walked back up the stairs.

But this state of affairs did not suit him. Far from it. The last thing he intended doing was to sit passively in his room, so as soon as he was on the first floor he hurried to the end of the corridor and looked out of the window. It overlooked a courtyard—full of Germans. Plainly, there was no escape that way. He tried the windows of several unoccupied rooms, and finally found one overlooking a narrow side street. The only people in it were a small group of women, talking excitedly. They were, of course, Norwegians, so having nothing to fear from them, he opened the window wide, climbed over the sill, and, after hanging to the full extent of his arms, dropped lightly to the pavement. Another moment and he was walking briskly down the street towards a garage which he had previously noted. But alas for his hopes! A squad of Germans had already taken possession of the building, so Biggles walked on without pausing.

He was now somewhat at a loss, for although he had been in Oslo twice before, he was by no means sure of his way. He reached the main street to find it full of marching Germans, with Norwegians standing about watching them helplessly. What upset him, however, was the complete absence of motor traffic, and he realized with something like dismay that the invaders must have at once put a ban on mechanical transport. This was disturbing to say the least of it, but it did not affect his determination to get to the aerodrome. Nevertheless, he knew it was no use thinking of walking; it would take too long. He perceived that if the Germans had stopped motor traffic they would also have stopped private flying—or they would as soon as they reached the aerodrome. Thus, his only chance of getting away lay in reaching the aerodrome before the German troops took over—as they certainly would.

He was standing at the edge of the kerb wondering which way to go when an errand-boy dismounted from a bicycle not far away, and, leaving the machine leaning against a lamp-post, disappeared into a shop. Covertly watching the people around him to see if his movements were observed, Biggles walked quickly to the cycle. Nobody took the slightest notice of him; they were all far too interested in the Germans. In a moment he had straddled the machine and was pedalling a somewhat erratic course down the street—erratic because it was many years since he had ridden a bicycle. Moreover, the only bicycles he had ridden were the rather heavy old-fashioned type which had upright frames, whereas his present mount was a light roadster with ram's-horn handlebars that swept nearly to the ground. He felt awkward on it, clumsy, and could only hope that he did not look as conspicuous as he felt.

Even so, it was entirely the German's fault that he collided with him. He—Biggles—was just turning into the broad highway which he knew ran past the aerodrome when the Nazi, a corporal, stepped right in front of him. Biggles did his best to stop, but he couldn't find the brake, and the result was that the handlebars caught the German under the seat of his pants and knocked him flying into the gutter.

Biggles stopped at once, for he knew that to go on was to court disaster. The corporal, white with fury—for several of the spectators had laughed at his discomfiture—strode swiftly back to where Biggles was standing.

'Fool!' he snarled, kicking the bicycle out of the way and striking Biggles across the face with his open palm.

By what effort Biggles controlled himself he did not know. He clenched his fists and his jaws clamped together, but he stood still, suffering in impotent silence, for around him were a dozen or more fully armed soldiers. But even now the corporal was not satisfied. He lifted his heavy field boot to kick. Biggles stiffened, and his eyes glinted dangerously, for to stand still and be kicked by a German corporal was more than he was prepared to endure. How the matter would have ended had there not been an interruption is a matter for conjecture, but at that moment a Storm-trooper officer on a swastika-bedecked motor-cycle pulled up alongside and spoke crisply to the corporal, demanding to know why he wasn't getting on with his job. Without waiting for the corporal to answer he fired out a string of orders.

The corporal saluted, mustered his men, and marched them behind the officer to the corner of the street, a distance of perhaps forty paces, where the officer proceeded to post the men as sentries.

Biggles looked at his bicycle. The front wheel was buckled and the tire was flat. Obviously, it would take him no farther. There was not another vehicle in sight—except the Nazi-flagged motor-cycle, resting on its stand as the officer had left it.

It did not take Biggles long to make up his mind what to do. He knew now that once the German net had closed around the city he would be caught in it, and would probably remain in it until the end of the war—if nothing worse happened to him. His only chance of escape lay in reaching the aerodrome immediately. In an hour, two hours at most, it would be too late. The motor-cycle offered a chance, a chance that might never present itself again. Biggles had spent most of his life taking chances, and he did not hesitate to take this one.

There was a gasp of horror from the spectators as he swung a leg over the saddle. His heel slammed down the self-starter. There was a yell from the Germans as the engine sprang to life, but he did not waste valuable time looking back. In a moment he was tearing down the street, crouching low over the handlebars to minimize the risk of being hit by the shots which he presumed would follow.

2

ALARMING DEVELOPMENTS

ACTUALLY, only two or three shots were fired, and they whistled harmlessly past, before Biggles came to a side street into which he lost no time turning. Then he steadied his pace, for he did not want another collision, nor did he wish to attract attention to himself by riding at a dangerous speed. A hundred yards farther on he took a turning which brought him back to the main road. Several parties of German troops were stationed at various turnings and cross-roads, and although they sometimes looked at him curiously as he swept past, they made no attempt to stop him. He realized that he, a civilian, must have cut a strange figure on a swastika-flagged motor-cycle, but the Nazi emblem acted as a passport, and he was content to let the flags remain.

In five minutes he was through the suburbs of the city and on the open road, doing sixty miles an hour, determined that no one should overtake him before he reached the aerodrome. If there was a pursuit, and he fully expected that there would be one, he saw no sign of it, and when, twenty-five minutes later, he swept into the straight piece of road that led to the aerodrome, he imagined that his escape was assured. He could have shouted with glee as he turned into the short drive that ended at the club-house. He did, in fact, purse his lips to whistle, but the sound died away before it was formed; for outside the club-house was a group of men. One or two were civilians; the rest were in uniform—the grey uniform of the German Air Force.

Shaken though he was by shock, Biggles realized what had happened, and a glance towards the hangers confirmed it. A dozen machines were parked in line—but they were not club aeroplanes. They were Messerschmitts, sleek monoplanes bearing the familiar Latin cross, and the swastika of the German Air Force.

The German pilots, laughing, suddenly spread across the road, raising their arms in salute; and, as Biggles jammed on his brakes and stopped, they crowded round him. One of them, a captain, stepped forward, and Biggles steeled himself for the worst. To his utter and complete amazement the German clapped him on the back with every sign of friendliness.

'Welcome!' he cried.

Biggles's brain seemed to go numb, for not by any stretch of the imagination could he make out what was happening. Far from treating him like an enemy, the Germans seemed pleased to see him. He couldn't understand it at all, and he began seriously to wonder if, after all, the whole thing was not an evil dream. Then, dimly, he began to see daylight—or he thought he did. It was the motor-cycle—or rather, the swastika flags on it.

The Germans took him for one of themselves.

But the next remark made by the German captain dispelled this delusion. He took Biggles by the arm in the most friendly manner, although his friendliness had an oily quality which Biggles found it hard to stomach.

'Why didn't you tell us you were one of us?' he said slyly, nudging Biggles with roguish familiarity.

Something in the man's voice made Biggles look at him more closely; and then, for the first time, he recognized him. Doubtless it was the uniform that had so altered him that he had not recognized him at first. He was one of the members of the flying club.

Biggles's brain raced to keep pace with the situation. 'But wouldn't that have been risky?' he said vaguely, in order to gain time. 'I thought you were a Norwegian.'

'So I am,' was the staggering reply, 'but I've always admired the Nazis—and it was made worth my while to play on their side. There were three of us here in the swim, but none of us guessed that you were in it, too.'

At last Biggles understood. Three of the members of the flying club were in German pay, and now that he had arrived on a Nazi motor-cycle they assumed, not unnaturally, that he, too, was in Nazi employ. The knowledge shook him to the very core. Spying was something he could understand; there had always been, and always would be, spies. It was one of the oldest professions in the world, and was, after all, a part of the unpleasant business of war. But what he could not understand, and what he could not forgive, was a man playing traitor to his own country. Yet there were three such men here, men who were far worse than spies; they were renegades, traitors in the most despicable sense.

Biggles swallowed something in his throat and forced a sickly smile. 'I wasn't taking any chances,' he said in German. 'As a matter of fact,' he continued, as he saw a new loophole of escape, 'I'm not officially in the German service—yet. I heard a whisper that some of you were, so I bided my time; but as soon as I saw the troops land this morning I borrowed this motor-bike and headed for the aerodrome in the hope of being able to do something.'

'You'll be able to do something,' the other assured him. 'We shall need all the pilots we can get, and having seen something of your flying I can recommend you. Ever flown a Messerschmitt?'

'No.'

'You will, and you'll like it. It's a lovely machine. The trouble will be finding somebody to fight.'

'You don't expect much opposition then?'

The other scoffed. 'None at all. The only military machines in the country are obsolete types.'

'But suppose the British send some machines out?' queried Biggles.

The other laughed scornfully. 'We'll deal with them when they come,' he boasted.

'By the way, is my machine still here?' asked Biggles in a voice he strove to keep steady. He had no wish to find himself in the German Air Force.

'Yes, but you won't be allowed to fly it. All machines are grounded—the Commandant's orders.'

Biggles nodded. 'Of course—very wise,' he agreed. 'Well, here I am. What ought I to do next?'

'You'll have to wait here until the Commandant arrives, then I'll introduce you to him. No doubt he'll be glad to have you in the service, particularly as you know the country. Here he comes now.'

The man, whose name Biggles now remembered was Kristen, nodded towards a big car that came speeding up the road, a swastika flag fluttering on its bonnet.

Biggles's astute brain had now got the whole situation fairly well straightened out. Kristen, and two other members of the club, had actually got the aerodrome ready for German occupation. A number of Messerschmitts, flown by regular German officers, had already landed. The new Commandant of the station was just arriving to take charge of operations. He, Biggles, was assumed to be of Nazi persuasion, and might, if he played his cards properly, actually be admitted into the German

Air Force as a renegade Norwegian. The prospect nauseated him, but he felt that if it offered a chance of escape he would be foolish not to take it. There might even be some satisfaction in beating the Germans at their own underhand game. In any case, he knew that if ever it was learned that he was British he was likely to have a bad time. Should the Germans learn his real name, and the Nazi Intelligence Service hear of his capture, then things would look very black indeed, for they had his record and had good cause to hate him.

The assembled pilots clicked their heels as the Commandant's car came to a stop and he alighted.

'Hauptmann Baron von Leffers,' whispered Kristen.

There was some delay while the Commandant spoke to the officers, some of whom got into their machines and took off. Von Leffers watched them go and then beckoned to Kristen.

'Good,' he said, 'you have done well. Presently you will be given one of our machines, but before that I want to go over with you the list of all machines and accessories that you have here. You have it prepared?'

'Yes, Herr Kommandant.'

The Baron looked at Biggles. 'Who is this?'

'He is one of us, but as yet his appointment has not been confirmed.'

'So? How is that?'

Kristen explained that Biggles had not been very long in the country, and had been flying his own machine. He was, he asserted with more confidence than Biggles's statement warranted, entirely in sympathy with the Nazis, and would like to fly for them.

'You have your own plane?' queried the Commandant.

Biggles bowed German fashion. '*Ja, Herr Kommandant.*'

The Baron smiled dryly. 'You must have plenty of money?'

Biggles shrugged. 'I had some, but I have spent most of it. Flying is an expensive pastime.'

'It won't cost you anything now,' returned the Baron. 'I'm afraid we shall have to take your machine. You will be paid for it, of course—after the war.'

'Quite so, Herr Kommandant.'

'And you would like to fly one of our fighters?'

'Yes, Herr Kommandant.'

'Have you any experience of fighter machines?'

'Yes. I was a test pilot for a while in America.'

In making this statement Biggles was telling the truth; for once, in America, he had tested some machines for the British Government with a view to purchase.

'We will see about it,' the Baron promised curtly, and, beckoning to Kristen, walked away.

Biggles was left alone. He was not sorry, for he wanted time to think. He was far from pleased with the situation, but he realized that it might have been worse—a lot worse. He was at least still free, and he only wanted to find himself alone in an aeroplane— to make a bee-line for home. It was for this reason, of course, that he had agreed to the suggestion of his flying a German fighter, for a Messerschmitt would suit him just as well as his own machine—better, in fact, since it was both faster and had a longer range. In any case, to dispute the suggestion would at once have made him an object of suspicion. The immediate future was still obscure, but he was prepared to match his wits against those of the Germans.

His chief fear was that he would be followed from Oslo by the fellow whose motor-cycle he had taken, and be recognized. And it was for this reason that his first action was to put the machine in a shed out of sight. Then, with the idea of escaping forthwith if it were possible, he made his way to the hanger in which his machine was kept, but a glance showed him that this was now out of the question. The hangar was full of Germans; what was even worse, they had already dismantled all the light aeroplanes to make room for the fighters, and were stacking the components against the end wall. Perceiving that nothing was to be gained by remaining there, particularly as several of the Germans were glancing at him suspiciously, he made his way to what had once been the club-house, but was now the officers' quarters.

As he strolled across, a curious smile played for a moment round the corners of his mouth. His Norwegian 'holiday' seemed to be shaping into something very different.

Presently he encountered Kristen, who, for some reason not altogether apparent, seemed to have taken him under his wing. It appeared that Kristen was one of those fussy, busy people who get satisfaction out of making other people's arrangements for them. Perhaps it flatters their vanity. Anyway, up to a point this suited Biggles quite well, and he played up to the man's weakness. At the moment, no doubt on account of the Nazi invasion and the part he had played in it, Kristen was looking very pleased with himself.

'Have you finished with the Commandant?' inquired Biggles, adopting a meek, almost humble, air. He spoke in German.

'It is useful that you speak German so well.'

Biggles nodded.

'Yes, I've given the Commandant all the information about the place,' went on Kristen. 'Of course, it's unlikely that such a little aerodrome will get as much limelight as the big air bases, but we shall make our mark—you watch it.'

'Yes, I shall certainly watch it,' said Biggles seriously, and he meant it.

'By the way, I've brought you this.' Kristen held out a red armlet bearing a black swastika, within a white circle.

'What's that for?' inquired Biggles.

'To wear. You won't be able to get a uniform until tomorrow, perhaps not for a day or two; in the meanwhile the Commandant says you are to wear this. It will show that you are not an ordinary civilian and may save you trouble with the guards.'

'Thanks.' Biggles took the armlet and fastened it on his sleeve.

'We may as well go and have a bite to eat,' suggested Kristen.

'Good idea,' agreed Biggles, and they walked together to the officers' mess. He smiled as they went in, for it had been the club dining-room. In a few hours it had been converted into a Nazi military depot. More than once, as he ate the food set before him, Biggles smiled faintly as he wondered what his comrades would think could they see him, swastika on sleeve, calmly eating in a German mess.

Later in the day the Commandant sent for him, and after a

close interrogation, in which Biggles's statements were supported by his Norwegian papers of nationality, he was admitted into the German Air Force on probation with the rank of *Leutnant*. No uniform was yet available, but the Baron promised to procure one for him in the near future. In the meantime Biggles was to wear the swastika armlet.

Biggles didn't like this; nor did he, in fact, like the whole arrangement, but since refusal to accept the conditions would unquestionably jeopardize his freedom, if not his life, he thought it expedient to accept. He promised himself that it would not be for long.

Indeed, within five minutes of leaving the Commandant's office he was making new plans for flight. He still hoped that it might turn out to be a simple business after all. Heavy gunfire could be heard in the distance, and machines, chiefly Messerschmitts, were constantly coming and going; so he found Kristen and asked him frankly if he could make a flight. The not unnatural retort to this request was, 'Why so soon? What was the hurry?' Biggles answered reasonably enough, that as he was now in the Air Force but had never flown a Messerschmitt, it was time he put in a bit of practice.

To his disappointment his request was refused, not on account of any suspicion on Kristen's part—that was obvious—but because no machines were available for such a purpose. They were all in use.

So Biggles had to make the best of it. He nodded and walked away. His time, he though, would come. He was rather at a loss to know what to do next, but this, as it turned out, was decided for him—and in no uncertain manner. Rounding a corner of the officers' quarters he came face to face with the officer whose motor-cycle he had borrowed. He had just stepped out of a large touring car in which sat three men wearing the uniform of the dreaded Gestapo.

3

ACROSS THE FRONTIER

COMING face to face as they did they recognized each other instantly, and never did Biggle's presence of mind stand in greater stead. Before the man could speak, and while his brows were still darkening with anger, Biggles clapped him on the shoulder, laughing at the same time.

'So there you are,' he said cheerfully. 'I was hoping you'd come along. I'm dreadfully sorry for what happened this morning, but I was in the dickens of a mess—and in a hurry. I should have been at the aerodrome the moment our troops arrived, but the fool woman at my hotel forgot to wake me. You were all busy, so rather than worry you I tried to get to the aerodrome by myself. As you saw, I borrowed a bicycle. Then, after the accident, knowing that you'd have no difficulty in getting another machine, I borrowed yours and dashed along here. I would have seen to it that you got it back, of course.'

While he had been speaking, out of the corner of his eye Biggles saw Kristen coming towards him. He now looked at him and cried, 'That's right, isn't it?'

'What is?' asked Kristen, hastening his steps.

'My machine was here.' Biggles didn't say *what* machine.

'Yes, that's right.'

Biggles turned to the Gestapo agent. 'There you are.'

In the face of this evidence the German accepted the explanation, but not with very good grace.

'You'd no right to take my machine,' he growled.

'I admit that,' agreed Biggles readily. 'But don't make a fuss about it, there's a good fellow, or it may lead to trouble for all of us.'

'Where is my motor-cycle now?'

'Here. I put it in the shed for safety. I've reported to the Commandant, so I can now take it back to Oslo if you like.'

'It doesn't matter,' was the gruff reply. 'I've borrowed a car from one of these miserable Norwegians—he won't want it again. The car suits me better than the motor-cycle. Still, you'd better take it back to Oslo some time.'

'Where shall I find you?'

'Leave it in the garage of the Nordic Hotel.'

'Certainly,' Biggles promised. 'Have a glass of beer while you're here? I feel I owe you a drink.'

'No, I haven't time now. I must get back. Naturally, I had to find out who it was who made off with my machine.'

'Of course.'

The German went back to his car, and Biggles drew a deep breath of relief. It had been an awkward moment. Kristen was still standing there, but he announced that he was on his way to the hangars, where he had a job to do.

Biggles gave the fellow a dark look as he departed. True, he had been of service to him, but not willingly. Had he known the truth it would have been a different story. As far as Biggles was concerned the man was worse than a spy; he was a traitor, and that was something he could not forgive.

He decided to go over to see if the motor-cycle was still where he had left it. It was, and as he gazed at it a fresh scheme took shape in his mind. It did not make so much appeal to him as his original plan for getting out of the country. But the motor-cycle was, after all, a fast vehicle, and it was not so far to the Swedish frontier. Sweden was still a neutral country, and if he could get across the frontier into it there was no reason why he should not assume his real nationality, and tell the truth—that he was a fugitive from the Nazi invasion of Norway. He would report to the nearest British Consul, who could, no doubt, make arrangements for his immediate return home. Thinking it over, Biggles decided that it was a reasonable plan, and decided to put it into operation forthwith.

The sun was now far down in the west, and he reckoned that he had only about half an hour of daylight left; but this did not bother him; indeed, he decided that darkness would probably suit his purpose better than broad daylight. He examined the petrol tank and found that it was nearly full, so as there was nothing to delay him he wheeled the machine out and started the engine. Several Germans were about, but none took any notice of him, and in a few minutes he was cruising down the main road.

It was an anxious journey, for he realized that every man was his enemy. The Norwegians, seeing his Nazi armlet, would hate the sight of him. Any German, were the truth known, would shoot him on sight. Nazis of all ranks were everywhere—in cars, on motor-cycles, in armoured cars, and even light tanks; and Biggles was aghast as, for the first time, he saw how widespread the German movement was. It was obvious that far more Germans had landed than he had at first supposed. He wondered vaguely what the Allies were doing about it all, but of course he had no means of knowing.

The traffic grew more congested as he neared the frontier, chiefly with refugees trying to escape from the country—going anywhere to evade the Nazis. German soldiers and storm troopers were turning them back, and from observations made by the people Biggles learned that many of these same Nazis had been living in the country as ordinary citizens, and were known to them. In other words, they had been planted in the country before the invasion actually occurred. Thus Biggles learned of the treachery that enabled the Nazis to effect the landing. Still, his armlet and the swastika-beflagged motor-cycle served their purpose, and took him anywhere he wanted to go. Indeed, on more than one occasion Nazi troops held up the traffic to let him pass.

By this time he had got to within a few miles of the frontier, and the traffic began to thin out. The Germans were fewer, from which he judged that he had about reached the limit of their operations. The calm manner in which the peasants were walking home from the fields suggested that they had not yet heard that their country had been invaded.

As twilight closed in and darkness fell, Biggles stopped. A signpost told him that the frontier was only a mile ahead. He contemplated the motor-cycle, and knew that it would not do to try to get into Sweden on such a machine. Already alarmed by what had happened to Norway, the Swedes would not want anything German in their country. He decided that he would have to abandon the machine, but he hardly liked to leave it by the road-side, where it would certainly attract attention, so he turned down a lane and lifted it bodily into the bottom of a deep ditch, near a coppice, covering it with any rubbish he could find so that it would not be noticed by a passer-by. He took off his armlet and pushed it under the saddle.

This done, he made a cautious survey of the landscape, as far as it was possible in the darkness, and then set off at a brisk walk for the frontier. He now had only one fear. Would the Swedes allow a Norwegian to enter the country? For that is what his passport proved him to be—Sven Hendrik, a Norwegian subject. The photograph on the passport, and the particulars it registered, were, of course, correct; only the name was false; but the Swedes, in their natural anxiety, might refuse to allow him to enter the country. Had he possessed any British papers this difficulty would not have arisen; but he had none—it would have been far too dangerous to carry such papers on his person.

As he expected, the frontier barrier was down, but he marched boldly up to it and took his place at the end of a short queue of people who were waiting to get through. All were pedestrians, for vehicles had been stopped and confiscated farther back. He had no difficulty in passing the Norwegian guards. His difficulty would be at the next barrier—the entrance to Sweden—a few paces ahead.

In the queue everyone was talking at once, talking to anybody, as always happens when danger is a common enemy. There were even two or three English people there. Actually Biggles found himself next to an American tourist—who had chosen a bad moment to visit Norway. He was bewailing the folly that had brought him from his own country, and cursed with hearty sincerity everybody responsible for the upheaval.

Slowly the queue shuffled towards the Swedish police and soldiers, who had come to reinforce the frontier guards. Some people were allowed through, but others were turned back. The man in front of Biggles was an elderly Norwegian, and Biggles waited with tense interest to see what would happen to him. He soon learned.

'Nationality?' snapped the passport officer.

'Norwegian.'

'Sorry, but you can't come through here.'

'But I must.' The man's voice was desperate.

'Why must you?'

The man poured out a score of reasons.

'Sorry, but we can't take in any more Norwegian refugees. Only foreigners passing through the country on their way home can be admitted, and they won't be allowed to stay in Sweden without a good reason.'

The man pleaded, but in vain. Sobbing, he was turned away.

Biggles had already realized that if he gave his nationality as Norwegian he, too, would be stopped, so he switched his plan abruptly.

'Nationality?' questioned the officer.

'British.'

'Where are your papers?'

'Sorry, but I haven't any.'

The officer frowned. 'Why haven't you a passport?'

'I was in my hotel in Oslo when the Germans rushed in and seized everything,' answered Biggles readily, and this was no less than the truth. 'In the circumstances you can hardly blame me for not stopping to argue over my luggage. I reckoned I was lucky to get away at all.'

The officer bit his lip thoughtfully. 'So you've absolutely nothing to prove you identity?'

'Nothing, but I'm sure the British Consul will vouch for me if only you will let me see him.'

'Hm——'

The officer was obviously in a quandary. It was clear that he didn't want to refuse admission to an Englishman; indeed, he had no reason to refuse; but, on the other hand, he didn't want to admit an enemy. If he admitted a man without papers he would be taking a serious risk.

Biggles saw the man hesitating and pressed his case. 'I've plenty of money on me,' he announced. 'You can take charge of it so you won't be put to any expense on my account. All I ask is that you take me, under guard if you like, to the nearest British Consul, and allow him to vouch for me. After all, if he accepts responsibility for me you won't have anything to worry about.'

This was so obviously true that it carried the point. The officer drew a deep breath. 'All right,' he agreed, and beckoned to two policemen. 'Escort this traveller to Rodas,' he ordered. 'If the British Consul there will take responsibility for him you can get a receipt and leave him. Otherwise, bring him back here.'

Biggles almost gasped his relief as he passed through the narrow gate. He was more or less under arrest, but that did not worry him. He was free, free from the Nazis, and therefore free from worry. His one thought now was to get back to France. If there was one anxiety that lingered in his mind, then it was fear that Sweden, too, might be invaded before he could get out of the country.

He was put in a car and taken to Rodas, less than half an hour's journey, and thence to the British Vice-Consulate. The Vice-Consul was still in his office, so Biggles introduced himself without loss of time, asking to be taken under protection.

Biggles stood in front of the two Swedes, so they did not see him drop an eyelid meaningly. The Vice-Consul did, however, and, realizing that there was more in the case than appeared on the surface, asked the guards to wait outside. He said he would take responsibility.

As soon as they were out of the door Biggles confessed everything. 'Believe me, I'm glad to be out of that,' he concluded feelingly.

The Vice-Consul was interested, as he had every reason to be, for queer things were happening in Scandinavia. Over a cigarette and a cup of coffee Biggles told the whole story, quietly and concisely, holding nothing back, as a sick man might explain his symptoms to a doctor.

'My word! You were certainly lucky to get out,' said the Vice-Consul when he had finished. 'I expect you want to get straight back home?'

'You bet I do!' returned Biggles. 'The sooner I let Colonel

Raymond know where I am the better.'

The Vice-Consul looked up sharply. 'Would you like to speak to him?'

'Speak to him? How?' Biggles was amazed.

'On the telephone.'

'Can you get through to London?'

'Of course. Sweden isn't at war—at least, not yet.'

Biggles was delighted. 'Why, that's fine.'

'I'll get Raymond for you,' the Vice-Consul promised.

He was as good as his word, but there was a long delay before Biggles found himself speaking to the Colonel. In a few words he told him what had happened, describing how he had narrowly escaped serving as a traitor Norwegian in the Nazi Air Force. Even before he had finished a doubt crept into his mind, a doubt as to whether he was wise in telling the Colonel this now. It would have been better to wait until he got home. The Colonel might ask him . . . .

The Colonel *did* ask him. Biggles knew instantly what was coming from the sudden change in Colonel Raymond's voice.

'You know what I'm going to ask you to do?' said the Colonel.

Biggles hesitated. 'I've got a pretty good idea,' he said slowly. 'You want me to go back into Norway.'

'Yes. Fate or fortune has put an astounding opportunity your way. It's a chance that we ought not to lose. With you behind the German lines in Norway, serving as an officer in the Air Force, we should learn every move——'

'Oh, no,' interrupted Biggles curtly. 'I'm a pilot. I've had quite enough of Secret Service work.'

The Colonel made a longish speech in which he dwelt on the extraordinary opportunity that pure chance had put in Biggles's way, and the wonderful service he could render his country by going back.

'Of course,' he concluded sadly. 'I can't *order* you to go. But, frankly, you're not the man I take you to be if you let this golden opportunity slip.'

'But I'm not a professional spy,' protested Biggles vigorously.

'My dear Bigglesworth, you yourself have seen what Germany is doing in Norway. There's black treachery for you, if you like. We've got to fight the enemy with his own weapons, if only for the sake of the Norwegians.'

Thus spoke the Colonel. It was a subtle argument that he put forward, put in such a way that Biggles could hardly refuse.

'All right,' he said at last, wearily. 'How am I going to get into touch with you when I have something to report?'

'Leave that to me,' said the Colonel quickly. 'I can't tell you now. Arrangements will have to be made, but you'll get further instructions in due course. Get back to the aerodrome and learn all you can about the enemy's movements.'

'Just one request,' put in Biggles. 'I feel very much on my own up here; if you could get Lacey and Hebblethwaite somewhere handy, somewhere where I could reach them in emergency, I'd be grateful. As you know, we always work as a team, and I need a little moral support, anyway. If they hear nothing they'll be worried to death about me.'

'I'll get them within striking distance of you at once,' promised the Colonel without hesitation. 'As a matter of fact, knowing things were warming up, I brought them home from France yesterday, since when they've been waiting on the East Coast ready to slip across in case you needed help. They can be over in a couple of hours.'

'But how can I make contact with them?'

'I shall have to think about that, but I'll arrange something immediately, don't worry. Good luck. I mustn't hold the line any longer.' The Colonel rang off.

The Vice-Consul heard Biggles's end of the conversation, of course. He shrugged his shoulders sympathetically.

'Bad luck, old man,' he said quietly. 'But you must admit that Colonel Raymond is right. It is on such chances as this that wars are sometimes won or lost. How do you propose getting back into Norway?'

'I think the easiest way would be for you to refuse to accept responsibility for me,' suggested Biggles readily. 'In that case the Swedes will soon hand me back across the frontier.'

The Vice-Consul nodded and pressed the bell. The two

policemen came back into the room.

'I have had a conversation with this—er—applicant,' said the Vice-Consul coolly. 'He may be telling the truth, but he has no means of proving it, so in your interests as well as mine I'd rather not accept responsibility.'

'You'll leave him with us to deal with, then?' said the senior of the two police.

'Yes, I'm afraid no other course is open to me.'

The officer tapped Biggles on the arm. 'Come,' he said.

Obediently, Biggles followed.

Half an hour later he was gently but firmly shown across the frontier back into Norway. He made no demur. It would have been a waste of time even if he had wanted to stay in Sweden. For a while he walked slowly down the road, but as soon as he was out of sight of the frontier post he quickened his steps and made his way to where he had left the motor-cycle. It was still there, so he dragged it out and recovered his swastika armlet from under the saddle. Deep in thought, he started the engine. Reaching the main road, he turned away from the frontier and headed back towards Boda, back towards the enemy.

He had no difficulty in getting back—his swastika flags saw to that. As he dismounted near the club-house Kristen hurried towards him.

'Hello,' he said curiously. 'Where have you been?'

'Only for a ride,' answered Biggles casually. 'Why?'

'Baron von Leffers has been asking for you.'

Biggles nodded. 'I'll report to him at once,' he said quietly.

4
CROSS-EXAMINED

BIGGLES found von Leffers in his office. He was not alone. Two other men were there. One was the man whose motor-cycle he had got; the other was an elderly, hard-faced civilian whose pugnacious jaw, gimlet eyes, and arrogant bearing bespoke an official of importance. His grey hair had been cropped so short that he appeared to be completely bald. Biggles guessed to what department he belonged before he was introduced.

Baron von Leffers stared at Biggles stonily. 'Leutnant Hendrik, this is Oberleutnant Ernst von Hymann,' he said curtly, waving a hand towards the stranger. 'He is a senior officer of the Gestapo. He wishes to speak to you. You have kept him waiting.'

'I'm very sorry, sir, but I didn't know he was here,' returned Biggles contritely.

To his infinite relief the Commandant did not ask where he had been. He left it to the Gestapo officer to continue the conversation.

Von Hymann invited Biggles to be seated, and then stood up, his legs apart, to face him squarely. In some strange way he reminded Biggles of a mangy bulldog. When he spoke his voice was brittle.

'Leutnant Hendrik,' he began, 'earlier today when you were interviewed by the Commandant of this aerodrome you gave him certain particulars of your flying career. Among other things you said that you had been a pilot in America, and more lately in Canada. Is that correct?'

'Quite correct, sir.'

'As you may have heard,' continued von Hymann, 'we make a point of checking up on every statement made by aliens. You, as a Norwegian, come into that category.'

'But——'

'We shall get on faster if you leave me to ask the questions.'

Biggles bowed.

'You further stated that when you were in Canada you were employed as an air pilot.'

'Correct.'

'And you were once employed by a firm called Arctic Airways, located at Fort Beaver?'

'Quite right.'

Von Hymann crouched like a wild beast about to spring.

'We have been unable to confirm that you ever had any connexion with Arctic Airways.'

Biggles remained calm. 'To whom did you go for your information?'

'Our agents in Canada have been through the official records. We also have newspaper reports of the scandal in which the company was involved.'

'You mean the stealing of the Moose Creek gold?'

Von Hymann relaxed slightly. 'Well, you do at least know something about it,' he conceded. 'Yes, that was what I meant.'

Biggles had, of course, flown for Arctic Airways, so he knew all about the incident, as well as the company's affairs. But it had been under his own name, so he could understand why the German agents in Canada had failed to find any particulars of a pilot named Hendrik. However, since he, Biggles, knew all about the company, and all that he had said concerning it was true, he was not unduly alarmed by the cross-examination to which he was being subjected. But then he did not know what it was leading up to.

Von Hymann continued: 'In the reports concerning Arctic Airways we can find no record of a pilot by the name of Hendrik.'

'That's quite likely,' remarked Biggles coolly. 'It is unlikely that any record would be kept. Pilots were always coming and going. I imagine that the only ones whose names were noted in the files were those mentioned in the newspapers in connexion with the gold robbery.'

'Can you name the pilots chiefly concerned?'

The atmosphere in the room was now tense, and Biggles perceived what was coming. He had just been asked a leading question, for if it were true that he had flown for Arctic Airways he would—or should—be able to name the pilots.

'Certainly,' he replied easily. 'Arctic Airways was run by a fellow named Wilkinson, an Englishman who established a base aerodrome at Fort Beaver. The trouble started when a fellow named McBain tried to grab the aerodrome, bringing with him two pilots and two German transport planes. His pilots were both ex-crooks. One was named Sarton and the other Feroni.'

Von Hymann nodded. 'What about Wilkinson's pilots?'

Biggles thought for a moment. 'There was a chap named Graves—he was killed, I remember. Then there was Lacey, and—oh yes, a lad named Hebblethwaite—or some such name.'

'Anybody else?'

Biggles saw the trap clearly now, but his expression did not change.

'Yes, there was another fellow—a fellow with a curious name—Tigglesworth—or was it Nigglesworth?'

'Was it Bigglesworth?'

Biggles started. 'That's right—funny name.'

'You must have seen something of him?'

Biggles's pulses were beginning to beat faster. He didn't like the trend of the conversation, but he still hoped there was nothing serious behind it. One slip, though, and he was lost. An expression of anxiety on his face would be noted at once by the cold eyes that were fixed on his in unwavering intensity.

'Oh, yes, I often saw Bigglesworth,' he admitted.

'Would you know him again if you saw him?'

'I should think so. Of course, this Arctic Airways business happened some time ago, but if he hasn't grown a beard or anything like that, I think I should know him at once.'

'Could you describe him?'

'More or less. He was a slim fellow with fair hair—rather sharp features. As a matter of fact, he was about my build.'

Von Hymann glanced at a paper that he held in his hand. 'He must have been very much like you.'

Biggles smiled. 'Nobody has ever mistaken me for him,' he observed lightly. 'Why all this about Bigglesworth—do you know him?'

Von Hymann ignored the question. Instead, he asked another.

'Do you know what became of him subsequently?'

Biggles shrugged. 'How should I? I believe he went back to England, but I wouldn't swear to it.'

The German's manner became grim. 'I'll tell you what he did. He returned to England and set up as a freelance pilot, and while he did a certain amount of casual work, in reality he was the British Intelligence Service's chief flying agent.'

Biggles made a grimace. 'I shouldn't have thought that was much in his line—he always struck me as being a nervous sort of fellow.'

'It seems that it was very much in his line. Not long ago he was in Finland. We now have reason to believe that he has transferred his unwelcome attentions to Norway.'

'You mean—he is actually in Norway?'

'This morning he was seen in Oslo by one of our agents.'

'Why didn't you pick him up?'

'Unfortunately the agent lost him in the crowd—the fool.'

Biggles nodded. 'Pity. But what has all this got to do with me?' he asked.

'I will tell you. The man who saw Bigglesworth has dashed back to Berlin to get further particulars about him from Hauptmann von Stalhein, who has had more to do with him than anyone else. In the meantime, he is the only man on my staff who could recognize Bigglesworth if he saw him, so I want you to go into Oslo and see if you can find him. 'We've rounded up a lot of suspects; if he isn't among them you had better search the hotels and the streets until you find him.'

'I don't care much for this sort of thing. I really wanted to do some flying,' protested Biggles as cautiously as he dared.

'There will be time for that later. At the moment you are under my orders. Go to Oslo at once. You can stay at an hotel. If you see Bigglesworth, don't let him out of your sight. Call the first soldiers you see and have him arrested. You had better take that armlet off and put it in your pocket for the time being, so as not to attract attention to yourself.'

'Very well, sir. But if I don't wear an armlet will the soldiers accept my orders? Isn't there a risk of being taken into custody myself?'

'I was prepared for that.' Von Hymann took a small, square card from his pocket. It was printed in red and black, and bore the number 2001. 'That is a pass, signed by myself,' continued the German. 'It will take you anywhere without question. While

you are working for me you will not use your name; use your
official number.'

Biggles noted the number and put the Gestapo pass in his
pocket. 'Suppose I want to get into touch with you, sir?'

'My headquarters are at the Hotel Port, on the waterfront.'

'If I don't find Bigglesworth at once, how long do you want
me to go on looking for him?'

'Until you hear from me again.'

'Very good, sir. I'll attend to it, but—if I may be allowed to
say so—I hope you won't keep me on the job too long. As a pilot,
naturally, I'm anxious to get into the air, in which respect I
should be useful, for I know the country pretty well. Moreover,
as you know, I have had experience of flying over similar
country and in similar weather conditions in northern Canada.'

'I'll bear it in mind,' returned von Hymann crisply. He
turned to the Commandant. 'Have you any questions for
Hendrik?'

'No.'

'That's all then.'

Biggles risked a last question, for the information would be
valuable to him if he could get it. 'What is the name of your man
who knows Bigglesworth?' he inquired. 'I ask because it might
be a good thing if we met some time, and compared notes.'

'Brandt.'

'Thank you, sir,' Biggles saluted and departed.

As he closed the door behind him he drew a deep breath and
moistened his lips with his tongue, for they had gone dry during
the strain of the interview. For a moment he stood still, getting
his nerves under control. They had not failed him during the
difficult cross-examination, but the inevitable reaction, now
that the immediate danger had passed, left him slightly weak. At
the same time he endeavoured to adjust his ideas to meet the
new situation.

'Suffering rattlesnakes! Where am I getting to?' he murmured, a ghost of a smile softening his face. 'First I'm sworn into
the German Air Force; now, of all things, I'm a full-blown
Gestapo agent. I've done some queer jobs in my life, but this is

the first time I've had to look for myself.' Then his face hardened again, for he realized that that might well be a more difficult, and more dangerous, task than it sounded.

He went to the dining-room and had a quiet bite of supper. Then he found Kristen, with whom he was anxious to keep in touch, for he made a point of neglecting nothing and nobody who might be of service to him. Without divulging his mission he told Kristen that he had got to go into Oslo on temporary duty, and would probably stay at the Hotel Kapital. Kristen was curious, but knowing who von Hymann was, asked no questions concerning Biggles's task.

'How are you going to get to Oslo?' he inquired.

'I've got a motor-bike; I will use that,' returned Biggles.

An hour later he was in Oslo, parking the motor-cycle in the hotel garage. The manager was still there, and recognized him. He said that the room Biggles had previously used was still available, and as this suited Biggles he decided to take it. At the foot of the stairs he was stopped by two men who stepped out of the shadows.

'Who are you?' asked one of them curtly.

Biggles showed his Gestapo pass, and the power of it was instantly apparent, for not only did the two men withdraw hastily, but they apologized for troubling him—a rare concession for Nazis.

Biggles continued on up the stairs, deep in thought. He was most worried by the knowledge that in the same city as himself there had been a man who knew him by sight. True, from what von Hymann had said, the man was now in Germany. But how long would it be before he returned? Obviously, not long. Moreover, he had gone to see von Stalhein, Biggles's arch-enemy, the man of all men whom he had the greatest cause to fear. The report that he, Biggles, was in Norway would probably be quite sufficient to bring von Stalhein to Oslo at top speed. In an aeroplane he could make the journey in two or three hours. He might even now be on his way to Norway. Indeed, for all Biggles knew, he might already be in Oslo; it all depended on how long Brandt had been gone, and the precise hour of his departure was something Biggles did not know. He knew the man's name, and that was something; but he didn't even know him by sight.

Worn out by the day's exertions and anxieties, Biggles flung himself on his bed just as he was to rest. He wanted to sleep, but his racing brain made it impossible. From far to the north came the low roar of bursting bombs; he could feel the thud and vibrations of the explosions; and as the window-panes rattled his face hardened with anger.

'Well, I'm here, and if I can put a spoke in the wheel of the savages who drop bombs on helpless civilians I certainly will,' he mused grimly.

The suspense of not knowing what was happening, or if Brandt had returned, became intolerable, and, unable to rest, he got up and looked at his watch. It was not yet eleven o'clock. Perhaps he would sleep better if . . .

In a moment he had made up his mind. He would find out if Brandt had returned. If he had, then he would be in a better position to know how to act. On the other hand, if Brandt was still in Germany, then he could at least reckon on a few hours' grace. How could he obtain the information? Obviously, there was only one way, one place, and that was at Gestapo headquarters at the Hotel Port. By going there he might be putting his head into a noose, but anything was better than this gnawing anxiety, which would certainly impair his usefulness to Colonel Raymond.

He put on his hat and went out. The same two men were in the hall, but they only nodded to him. There were few people in the streets, and no taxis, so he had to walk to his objective—not that that mattered, for it was only a short distance away. German troops were everywhere, particularly near the water-front, where stores and guns were being unloaded. Biggles surveyed them with eyes trained by long experience; he noted particularly the number of guns and their calibres, the types of vehicles, and the quantities of other stores. He was stopped twice by plain-clothes men and questioned, from which he was able to gather an idea of the precautions being taken to prevent useful information from reaching the Norwegian troops, who—so he learned from snatches of conversation between passers-by—were putting up a spirited resistance farther north. However, in each case the production of his Gestapo pass acted like magic, and he went on to the Hotel Port.

Two storm-troopers were on duty outside the main entrance. They stopped him, of course, and asked his business.

Biggles smiled and showed his ever-ready pass. 'Perhaps you can help me, and save me worrying people while they are busy—as I see they are,' he said. 'Do either of you know Herr Brandt by sight?'

One of the men said he did.

'Is he back yet, do you know?'

'Yes,' answered the man unhesitatingly. 'He came in about half an hour ago. He came by 'plane—there it is.' He pointed to a civil flying-boat that rested on the placid water, slightly apart from a number of military marine aircraft.

'Was he alone?' queried Biggles.

'No, there was another man with him.'

'You don't know his name?'

'No.'

'Was he by any chance a thin man, with sharp features, wearing a monocle?'

'Yes, that's right,' agreed the man.

'I see,' said Biggles casually.

'You can go in if you want to speak to them,' invited the trooper.

Brandt and von Stalhein were the very last two people on earth Biggles wanted to see at that moment, but he did not say so.

'They're probably tired after their journey,' he remarked, yawning. 'I'm tired myself. I'll call again in the morning. Phew! What a day it's been.'

The storm-trooper grinned. 'You're right there.'

'What's happening, d'you know?'

'They say we've got most of the country except Narvik. There's a rumour that British troops are being landed there.'

This was welcome information, and Biggles made a note of it. He chatted for a few minutes, learning where the Norwegians were resisting the German advance, and picking up scraps of news about the German forces, concerning which the two storm-troopers were quite ready to boast.

All the while he was talking he was standing in a position from which he could see through the glass-panelled doors into the vestibule beyond. And it was a good thing that he did so, for, suddenly, from the foot of the stairs, appeared two men. One he did not know, but the other was his old enemy, Erich von Stalhein of the German Secret Service. Both were dressed as if they were going out.

Biggles tarried no longer. 'Well, I'll get along and see about some sleep,' he announced. 'It looks as if we shall have a busy day again tomorrow. Good-night.'

He walked away, but turning into a lane between two warehouses, watched the door of the hotel. He had not long to wait. A few minutes later von Stalhein and the other man— whom he presumed was Brandt—came out, and walked briskly along the waterfront. From his retreat Biggles watched them pass within ten yards of him. They were talking animatedly, but in tones too low for him to catch what they said. As soon as they had got some distance ahead he followed them.

At first he was glad that they took a direction which suited him, for it was the direction of his own hotel. It did not occur to him that they were actually going to the hotel until, from the opposite pavement, they walked straight across to the entrance and disappeared through the swing doors.

Now Biggles, having stayed in it, knew the hotel well. He knew all the entrances—there were three, including a luggage entrance. Walking past the front door he saw the two Germans in the hall talking to the hotel manager, so hastening his steps, he hurried to a side entrance which he knew also led to the hall. But he did not go right in, for he wanted to know what the Germans were saying. He opened the door quietly and took a few paces along a corridor until he could hear their voices.

The trend of the conversation was much what he expected.

Brandt was describing 'Bigglesworth', and asking the hotel manager if he knew anything of him. The manager replied, of course, in the negative. He declared that the only person in the hotel who fitted the description was a Norwegian named Hendrik, who, at the moment was out. On receipt of this information the two Germans announced that they would wait for him to come back, and made themselves comfortable on a settee.

As there was no further point in remaining, Biggles returned to the street. He found a café still open, and sat at a side table over a cup of coffee to ponder his position, which he felt was getting desperate. Brandt and von Stalhein were now looking for Hendrik, all because the quick-witted Brandt had unfortunately caught a glimpse of him. Still, this did not necessarily mean that either he or von Stalhein now believed Hendrik to be Bigglesworth, but the very fact that they were anxious to interview Hendrik proved that they were suspicious. Once they saw him the game would be up, so if he remained in Oslo it was certain that sooner or later they would find him.

For a little while he could not make up his mind what to do for the best. There were moments when he felt inclined to devote his entire energy to getting out of the country, for which Colonel Raymond could hardly blame him, for when he had agreed to remain the position had been altogether different. At that time he had been simply a renegade Norwegian, and in no immediate danger. He was not suspected of being Bigglesworth, and von Stalhein had not been in the country. Yet, on the other hand, he felt that with his Gestapo pass in his pocket, never before had he been in such an admirable position to gather information, information that might well be of vital importance to the Allies. In short, he felt that it would be insane to remain, yet despicable to run away—even if he could. But he would certainly have to get out of Oslo. That, of course, would make von Hymann suspicious, and perhaps start a hue and cry. What excuse could he give for leaving the city?

Sitting there alone in a quiet corner he worked out a plan; a plan which, if successful, might answer a lot of questions for him.

The weakness of it lay in his abandoning—at least for the time being—the aerodrome at Boda, for it was clear from what Colonel Raymond had said that he was going to get in touch with him there, presumably by means of a secret agent. In the end Biggles decided that this could not be avoided. He got up, paid his bill, and went along to the garage at the corner of the street. It was, of course, owned by a Norwegian, so the wretched man was in no case to resist German demands. Biggles said he was a member of the Gestapo and demanded a car.

The proprietor raised no objection. He pointed to an Opel saloon. 'Will that do?'

'Yes. Are the tanks full?'

'Yes.'

Without another word Biggles got in the car and drove slowly out of the city. He was stopped several times, but his pass always carried him through. Reaching the suburbs, he pulled up outside a telephone call box and rang up the Hotel Port, giving his number and asking for Oberleutnant von Hymann.

He was told that von Hymann had been in, but had gone out again.

Having ascertained that he was speaking to a Gestapo operator, Biggles then asked if he could leave a message, and was told that he might.

'Take it down,' he ordered. 'My number is 2001. Say I have located Bigglesworth. He has left the city in a car, heading northward. At the garage where he got the car he asked how far it was to Narvik, so that is presumably where he is bound for. I'm following him, and am not far behind. I'll report again at the first opportunity. Got that?'

The operator read over the message.

'That's right,' confirmed Biggles, and hung up. He went back to the car. For a minute or two he studied the map which he always kept in his pocket; then he drove on, heading northward, whence came the sounds of battle.

5

UNEXPECTED ALLIES

In acting as he did, Biggles was actuated first and foremost by the obvious necessity for getting out of Oslo; also he wanted time to think, to muster the many features and various aspects of his position. And this, presently, he did, having turned into a by-road for the purpose. He stopped the car so that he could concentrate on the problem.

Slowly the situation clarified itself into a number of issues, all governed by the outstanding fact that not only was it known to the Gestapo that Major Bigglesworth was in Norway, but von Stalhein was also in Norway for the purpose of finding him. Von Stalhein and Brandt knew him by sight, so it would be merely foolish to hope that he could continue to move about the country without being spotted. To carry out espionage work in such conditions would impose a strain not lightly to be borne, a strain that would certainly impair his activities as well as his efficiency. He felt that if Colonel Raymond knew this, he could hardly fail to ask him to leave the country. The trouble was that he had no means of getting into touch with the Colonel except by again crossing the frontier into Sweden. Yet, apart from the obvious risks involved in such a procedure, such a course would be letting Colonel Raymond down, for the Colonel, acting under the assumption that he was in Norway, might be making all sorts of plans, the success of which depended on his being at Boda. Raymond was even then taking steps to get into touch with him at the aerodrome, and would expect him to be there. If the secret agent arrived at the aerodrome and failed to find him, the consequences might be tragic. All of which meant that he ought to return to the aerodrome. But now, apart from Oslo, the aerodrome was the most dangerous place in the country. Von Stalhein and Brandt were interested in Hendrik, whose failure to return to the hotel would only deepen their suspicions. They would continue their search vigorously, and it could only be a question of time before they—or someone—discovered that a

Norwegian named Hendrik had joined the Nazi Air Force at Boda. Von Stalhein's agile brain would instantly perceive what had happened, and that would be the end.

A further point not to be overlooked was this. He was supposed to be acting under von Hymann's orders, and while his telephone message might be sufficient to allay suspicion for the time being, unless he showed up pretty soon, or reported again, von Hymann, too, would start wondering what had happened to Hendrik.

Now in introducing the town of Narvik into his message to von Hymann Biggles was prompted by one reason only. From scraps of conversation overheard he had gathered that a British force was landing there. British troops might be landing at other places as well for all he knew, but owing to the suddenness of the German attack the whole country was in a state of confusion. Nobody seemed to know what was happening.

At the back of Biggles's mind, when he had rung up to speak to von Hymann, was a vague idea of getting 'Bigglesworth' out of the country. That is to say, if he could lead von Hymann to believe that Bigglesworth had fled the country, via the British-held port of Narvik—a not unreasonable possibility—then the hue and cry would die down. Von Stalhein would be informed and would probably return to Germany. Brandt might go, too, leaving Biggles to do his work in a less unhealthy atmosphere. So, if this could be brought about, it would be a useful stroke of work. But could it? Obviously, it was not going to be easy to get to Narvik, or anywhere else for that matter, for not only were more and more German troops arriving in the country, but the Norwegians themselves were mobilizing and putting up a stiff resistance. So it seemed that he would have to pose as a Gestapo agent when talking to the Germans, and as a Norwegian when intercepted by Norwegians. He would have to adopt a dual personality. He still had a Norwegian passport as well as his Gestapo ticket, so he could use either as circumstances demanded, and as he was still in civilian clothes he felt that this ought to be possible.

There was one final point that worried him. In Oslo he had

picked up information which the British authorities would be glad to have, but this information would be of no value unless he could pass it on immediately, for the position was changing every few hours. Could he reach the British forces? He did not know, but he could try. If he succeeded in getting into the town of Narvik he would get a message through to von Hymann from there, to the effect that Bigglesworth had escaped. At the same time he would ask permission to return to Boda, and stay there until he got Colonel Raymond's permission to leave the country. He was anxious, desperately anxious, to get out, not so much on account of the danger of his task as his dislike for the work he was doing. Spying as a profession made no appeal to him, although more than once he had been forced to do it. In the present case only a sequence of unforeseen circumstances had combined to thrust him, against his will, into the unenviable position in which he now found himself. He much preferred the straightforward life of a fighting pilot, which, really, was what he was.

He looked again at his map, noted the shortest way to his objective, started the car, and set off on his long journey.

Biggles covered fifty miles in fair time, although, as was inevitable, he was stopped several times by German patrols, but on the production of his pass he was allowed to proceed. Once he found himself near some brisk fighting and took refuge in a peasant's cottage—posing, of course, as a Norwegian. The peasant told him of a detour by which he could avoid the battle, and he lost no time in taking it. Now, having passed the extremity of the German forces, he started to run into Norwegian patrols, who also stopped him. But when he showed his Norwegian passport, and said that he was on his way to Narvik to offer his services to the British, no obstacle was put in his path. The noise of war died away behind him, but progress was slow on account of the state of the road, particularly in the passes where the snow was still deep. Naturally, the farther north he got the more arctic the conditions became, and once he was compelled to wait for a snowstorm to blow itself out before he could go on. He was desperately tired, but matters were too urgent for him to rest—at least, for the time being.

On and on he drove into the darkness of the night. He passed a signpost pointing to Trondheim, away to the west. There was firing there, too, but who was responsible for it he did not know, for he was still unaware that Germans had landed at several places on the coast. Leaving Trondheim far behind, and reaching a village called Stol, he halted. He was so weary that he was beginning to sway in his seat. To proceed farther in his present state would be to court disaster by accident, so he went to the inn. The landlord and his wife were still up; several villagers were there too, all discussing the calamity that had befallen their country. Biggles introduced himself—as Hendrik, of course—said that he was on government service and was on his way to Narvik. He was worn out, so could he have a bed for the rest of the night?

The kindly souls assured him that he might, but would he please tell them what was happening in Oslo? They had a wireless set, but they knew it was in German hands and they were anxious to know the truth. Biggles told them as much as he thought was good for them. Afterwards he fell on his bed and slept the sleep of exhaustion.

As soon as it was daylight he had a good breakfast and continued his journey. The scenery had always been wild, but now it grew rugged in the extreme, far more savage than it had seemed from the air. On all sides towered mountains, gaunt, still white with snow. The lower slopes bristled with countless conifers. For the most part the road ran through valley or gorge, but not infrequently if followed a cornice round the mountain side so that sheer cliff rose on the one hand and a fathomless void dropped away on the other. The surface of the road got worse and worse.

But Biggles was not concerned with these details. He was concerned only with reaching his objective, which had become a sort of mania. Once, from an eminence, he caught a distant view of the sea far away to the left, and he knew that he was now in the narrow northern end of Norway. Shortly afterwards the road struck a fiord, one of the many deep-thrusting arms of the sea for which Norway is famous, and thereafter it more or less followed the coast. He breathed a sigh of relief when, from the top of the hill, he saw a town in the distance that he knew could only be the port for which he was bound.

He might not have seen the sailors had not one of them deliberately exposed himself, making strange signals. Biggles stopped at once. As the man drew near—he was little more than a lad—Biggles saw that he wore the uniform of an officer of the British Mercantile Marine. It was dirty and torn.

The man came nearer. 'Me British sailor,' he said, pointing to the braid on his sleeve. Then he pointed to his mouth. 'Me hungry—no food,' he continued.

That he was telling the truth was obvious, for his face was pinched and pale. It was apparent that he assumed Biggles to be a Norwegian, and therefore a friend.

Said Biggles, coolly, 'What on earth are you doing here?'

The sailor started violently. 'Great Scott! Are you a Britisher?' he asked joyfully.

Biggles did not answer the question. 'What are you doing here?' he repeated.

'We were torpedoed off the coast—the trawler *Seagoer*.'

'We?'

'Yes. Me and some of the ship's company managed to swim ashore. That was two days ago. We've been on the run ever since—without a bite of food.'

'How many of you are there?'

'In my party—seven.'

'Why didn't you go to Narvik?'

The sailor stared. 'To Narvik? That's the last place we're likely to go to—unless we're caught and taken there.'

Biggles sensed a disturbing implication in the statement. 'Why, what's wrong with Narvik?' he asked quickly.

'The Germans have got it.'

Biggles was speechless while this staggering piece of information sank in. 'But—but I thought the British had landed there?'

The sailor laughed harshly. 'There was talk of them landing there, but they're not there yet, you can take that from me. The fiord is stiff with Jerry destroyers. They've got the town.'

Biggle's scheme crashed to the ground. 'What are you trying to do?' he asked.

'Find someone to hide us until our fellows arrive, or else find a ship to pick us up. That's why we're sticking near the coast.'

'Do the Germans know you're ashore?'

'Unfortunately, yes. They've been chasing us.'

'Where are the rest of you?'

The sailor jerked his thumb over his shoulder. 'Hiding in a little dell.'

Instinctively Biggles glanced in the direction indicated, and as he did so a movement caught his eye. He looked again and saw that he had not been mistaken. A German soldier was creeping towards them, taking cover between the rocks. Others were there too, to left and right. Quickly Biggles looked behind him and saw more Germans advancing stealthily through the trees that cloaked the side of the hill.

'What's wrong?' asked the sailor sharply, taking alarm from the expression on Biggles's face.

'I'm afraid you're out of luck, old man,' returned Biggles quietly. 'We're surrounded. Are you armed?'

'We haven't a weapon between us.'

'Then you'd be wise to give yourselves up. There's no sense in throwing your lives away uselessly.'

'You're talking about us. What are you going to do?' asked the sailor suspiciously.

Biggles could already see a plan by which the incident might be turned to good account, but it depended largely on the courage and fortitude of the sailor. He drew his automatic.

'What the——' began the sailor aghast, but Biggles cut him short.

'Answer my questions quickly,' he said. 'I'm a British spy, and I'm going to put my life in your hands. I've got to get back to England with vital information. Got that?'

'Yes,' gasped the sailor.

'What's your name?'

'Evans—Bill Evans.'

'It's in your power to help me—and the country. Will you do it? You'll be taken prisoner, anyway, so it won't make things any worse for you.'

'What do you want me to do?'

'First, put up your hands. That will lead the Jerries to think I've captured you.'

The sailor raised his hands.

Biggles went on quickly, for he could see the Germans fast closing in:

'They think I'm a German agent,' he said. 'After you're taken I shall come to question you. I shall ask you if you had anyone else with your party. At first you will refuse to answer, but under pressure you'll admit that a Britisher named Bigglesworth attached himself to you. When I ask what's become of him you'll say he left you—stole a dinghy and rowed out to a steamer. Got the name right?'

'Bigglesworth.'

'That's it. Actually, I'm Bigglesworth, and I've got to make it look as if I've escaped out of the country—understand?'

'Yes.'

'Fine. That's all. Act as you never acted before. Remember, however tough your plight may seem, mine is a lot worse. One slip and it's a firing party for me.'

'By gosh! You've sure got a nerve,' muttered the sailor admiringly. 'I won't let you down.'

'Thanks, pal. If you get back home and I don't, find Colonel Raymond of British Intelligence and tell him that you saw me, and that I did my best. Prime your friends about Bigglesworth, but don't tell them more than you need, and on no account let them know it's me. Simply tell them to remember that Bigglesworth got away on a ship—a slim fellow with fair hair. Now take me to the others.'

Still with his hands up, Biggles walked close behind him with the pistol raised, the sailor marched stiffly to the dell. The others sprang up in dismay when they appeared.

'Hands up, everybody,' ordered Biggles curtly. 'March out into the open in single file.'

'Do what you're told, boys,' said Evans tersely.

Slowly the weary sailors raised their hands, and at the expression on their faces Biggles nearly weakened. He would have much preferred to fight side by side with them.

'Out you go,' he said shortly.

At that moment the German troops sprang up and ran forward. An officer was at their head.

Biggles received him with a cold smile. 'You've arrived at a useful moment,' he said harshly, showing his Gestapo pass. 'I saw these fellows skulking among the rocks so I went after them. You'd better get them in a safe place.' As he spoke he took out his armlet and replaced it on his sleeve.

The German officer, who was quite young, was all politeness. 'Leave them to me,' he answered. 'Forgive me for saying so, but you shouldn't have risked your life as you did. These fellows are a desperate lot and they might have attacked you. We've been following them for some time, to round them up.'

'No harm done,' returned Biggles briefly. 'I must get on, so I'll leave you to finish the job.' With a curt nod he got back into his car and drove on into town.

Even before he reached it he saw that what the sailor had told him was only too true. German troops were everywhere, and five destroyers lay in the fiord. There was also a number of flying-boats and seaplanes.

He went straight to General Headquarters and asked to see the officer in charge of operations. He had to wait a few minutes; then two senior naval officers came out and he was shown in.

A colonel, with his adjutant at his elbow, received him coldly but politely. From their manner Biggles judged that they had little love for the Gestapo, but feared them too much to be anything but civil. He showed his pass.

'I'm looking for an English spy named Bigglesworth,' he said without wasting words. 'He bolted from Oslo, heading north. We have good reason to think that he was coming here. Have you any English prisoners?'

'Yes, we have a few.' The Colonel looked at his adjutant.

'Eighteen, sir, I think.'

'Have they been examined?' inquired Biggles.

'Of course.'

'Is Bigglesworth among them?'

'He may be, but if he is he didn't give that name,' answered the adjutant.

'I'd better see them,' said Biggles curtly.

The adjutant took him to a small schoolroom which was being used as a prison camp. Several sentries were on guard. The prisoners were paraded. They stood in a line, coldly hostile, defiant, in spite of the state they were in, for they all looked as if they had been through a bad time. There were one or two Air Force uniforms, but most of them were sailors. One, a leathery-faced old salt, cursed Hitler and everything German in a steady stream of invective.

Biggles glanced at him. 'Shut up!' he snapped, 'or I'll give you something to shout about, *Schweinehund*.' He walked slowly along the line.

Now all this, of course, was merely play-acting, part of the scheme that had now crystallized in his mind. He would certainly not see the man he professed to be looking for, nor did he expect to recognize anyone; so he merely glanced at the faces as, with the adjutant and an armed soldier following, he walked slowly down the line. But when he came to the seventh man he stopped dead.

It was Algy.

6

THE NAVY ARRIVES

How Biggles kept control of himself at that ghastly moment he never knew. For two palpitating seconds he stood stock still, while he felt the blood draining from his face. Then he walked on, looking for Ginger, who he felt must be there too. But of Ginger there was no sign, so he walked back along the line to Algy, feeling that he ought to make some excuse for stopping in front of him.

'Haven't I seen you somewhere before?' he asked harshly.

Algy didn't move a muscle. Actually, he had got over his shock at seeing Biggles, for he saw him immediately he entered the room—long before Biggles saw him.

'You may have seen my picture in the papers,' sneered Algy. 'I won the world championship at snakes and ladders—up one minute and down the next.'

There was a titter along the line.

Biggles spluttered with rage, German fashion. 'Silence!' he bellowed. Then he turned on his heel and walked away. 'He isn't here,' he told the adjutant. 'Let us go back to the Colonel—I must speak to him again.'

They returned to headquarters.

'Did you find your man?' inquired the Colonel.

'No,' answered Biggles shortly. 'There'll be trouble if he gets away. He's a dangerous man. I must ring my chief in Oslo.' He broke off and glanced over his shoulder as from outside the door came the sound of quick footsteps. 'What's happening?' he asked.

The door opened. An N.C.O. came into the room and saluted. 'Seven more prisoners, sir,' he announced.

'Good,' said Biggles sharply. 'My man may be among them. Bring them in here—you don't mind, Colonel? I only want to see their faces.'

'Bring them in.'

The seven prisoners, the seven sailors whom Biggles had encountered on the hillside, were marched in. Every face was expressionless.

Biggles scrutinized each man in turn. 'Who is the senior officer?' he snapped.

'I am,' growled Evans.

'Were there any more of you?'

Evans did not answer.

'Answer me!'

Still the sailor maintained a stubborn silence.

Biggles's jaw set in true Prussian fashion. 'I think you forget where you are,' he grated. 'I hope it will not be necessary for me to remind you. Were there ever more than seven in your party?'

Evans hesitated. 'There was one more, but he left us.'

'Why?'

'To get back to England, I suppose. He found a dinghy, and without waiting for us, rowed out to a steamer. But he wasn't really one of our party.'

'What do you mean?'

'As we walked down the coast we met him coming up. He said he had escaped from Oslo.'

Biggles affected a start. 'Oslo! What was his name?'

'He told me his name was Bigglesworth. He seemed in a mighty hurry to get home. That's all I know about him.'

Biggles turned a grim face to the Colonel, who was watching the scene with intense interest.

'You heard that?' he said in a low voice. 'That was my man without a doubt. He must have left the road and gone down to the rocks; that was how I came to miss him. It looks as if he's got clean away. I'm afraid there will be trouble about this. I trust, sir, that you will confirm that I did everything possible in the time at my disposal? The man had gone before I got here. I'd better ring up my headquarters at once. As you are the senior officer here perhaps you would be good enough to speak to my chief?' Biggles glanced at the escort. 'All right; I shan't want these prisoners again.'

As they filed away Biggles's eyes met those of Evans and flashed his thanks.

The Colonel had already picked up the telephone. He handed it to Biggles, who put a call through to Gestapo headquarters, at the Hotel Port, Oslo. When the operator spoke he asked for Oberleutnant von Hymann, and in a moment he was speaking to him.

'This is 2001, speaking from General Headquarters, Narvik,' he said. 'I have to report that I tracked Bigglesworth to here, but he had left in a steamer before my arrival. I obtained this information from a party of British prisoners with whom Bigglesworth had for a short time been keeping company. One moment, sir, the Commanding Officer will speak to you. I am telephoning from his office.' Biggles handed the instrument to the Colonel.

There followed a long conversation in which the Colonel confirmed in detail all that Biggles had said, and added details of how the information had been obtained, remarking that he had been a witness of it. He asserted that everything possible had been done to apprehend the wanted man, but as he had left the country before steps could be taken to arrest him no fault could be attached to anyone. The conversation was concluded and the Colonel hung up the instrument. He turned to Biggles. 'Oberleutnant von Hymann says that you are to return to Boda at once,' he said.

'Very good, sir.' Biggles saluted and withdrew.

His plan had succeeded to the fullest possible extent, and but for one fly in the ointment he would have been elated. It was Algy.

What Algy was doing in Narvik, and how he had come to be taken prisoner, Biggles, of course, had no means of knowing; nor dare he risk arousing suspicion by making inquiries; but from the fact that he was in R.A.F. uniform Biggles could only conclude that, in accordance with his request to Colonel Raymond, Algy had been sent to Norway in an aeroplane with a view of getting into touch with him. If that were so, what had happened to Ginger? It seemed certain that they would start together. One fact was significant, and Biggles did not overlook it. Algy had come to Narvik, and that at once suggested that Narvik was to be the scene of British operations, otherwise he would not be so foolish as to land in territory held by the enemy. Again, if he, Algy, had come to Narvik, then there was good reason to suppose that something was in the wind, that some plan had been evolved to bring Biggles to the same place, in order that they could make contact. But it was a problem no amount of reasoning could answer; the facts could only be obtained from Algy himself. The point paramount in Biggles's mind was that von Hymann had ordered him to return to Boda, and to Boda he would have to go or lay himself open to dangerous questioning when he next saw the Gestapo chief. Yet he could not contemplate departing from Narvik leaving Algy a prisoner in German hands.

He was still standing near the wharf pondering this difficult problem when a German flying-boat appeared round a bend in the fiord, flying very low and at terrific speed. It was obvious that the pilot's mission was an urgent one. With professional interest Biggles watched the machine land and taxi quickly to the wharf where the other machines were moored. Even before the aircraft had stopped moving the pilot had scrambled out, shouting something in a voice that was hoarse with excitement. Instantly all was confusion.

Biggles hurried forward. 'What is it?' he asked a soldier, for he had not caught the pilot's words.

'British destroyers are coming up the fiord—five of them,' shouted the soldier as he dashed towards headquarters.

Biggles's pulses began to race. Things were going to happen in Narvik, that was certain. What part was he to play?

His first thought was not for himself nor for Algy; it was for the destroyers. Was the Commander of the flotilla aware that six German destroyers lay in the fiord? If so, did he know where they were? They were not all in the open water. Some were hidden behind promontories of rock, where their presence would not be suspected. The British destroyers might be steaming into a trap, and if so his first duty ought to be to warn them, regardless of anything else.

These were the thoughts that flashed through Biggles's mind in that tense moment, and it did not take him long to reach a decision. The Dornier flying-boat from which the German had landed was still floating on the water where its pilot had left it. Nobody was bothering about it, which was hardly surprising, for everyone was much too engrossed in other affairs. Sailors were rushing back to their ships. Pilots were running to their moorings; some were already taxi-ing higher up the fiord to get out of the way of the storm which they guessed was coming. Anti-aircraft gunners were hurring to their posts. Troops were taking up positions, mounting machine-guns at points overlooking the fiord.

Biggles walked calmly down to the Dornier. A German pilot getting into a nearby machine had time to notice him, possibly because he was in civilian clothes.

'What are you going to do?' he shouted.

'Have a look at these *Englander*', answered Biggles promptly.

'Can you fly?'

Biggles laughed. 'Watch me! I've just brought a message from Oslo.'

The German had no further time to waste on idle curiosity, so he turned away. Biggles got into the Dornier and started the engine. Then, sitting quietly in his seat, he tore a page out of his notebook and wrote a message. On another sheet he made a rough sketch-map of the inner fiord, showing where the German destroyers were waiting. This done, he put both pages in his silver cigarette case and slipped it back in his pocket. A quick glance round revealed that the position ashore remained unaltered, so he eased open the throttle and surged towards the open water. Another moment and his keel was cutting a line of white foam across it. As soon as he was in the air he turned, and, flying low, raced down the fiord.

He saw the British destroyers at once, for they were only about three miles away, steaming at high speed. They saw him, too— or the anti-aircraft gunners did, for instantly the air round him was filled with smoke, lacerated with flame and hurtling metal. With white face and set lips he swerved, dived and zoomed, anything to spoil the gunners' aim; but he still held on towards the ships.

His plan was to drop the cigarette case, with its message, on the deck of the leading destroyer, but such was the inferno that had broken out around him that he felt it was attempting the impossible. Apart from the archie, he knew it was no use trying to achieve his object by dropping the case while travelling in the opposite direction to the destroyers, for he would pass over them in a split second; his only chance was to overshoot them, turn, and then, travelling as slowly as possible, drop the message while going in the same direction.

For the next two minutes he became a machine, a part of the

aircraft. His brain concentrated on one thought only, but it was not easy. Shells burst in front of him, beside him, above and below him, causing the Dornier to rock like a leaf in a gale. It quivered and shuddered as pieces of flying metal ripped through the wings and fuselage. Pieces of fabric streamed aft, and he fully expected the machine to break up at any moment. He had never known an aircraft to stand up to such punishment.

He had a brief respite after he had dashed past the ships, for he was flying nearly on the water, and the gunners had not had time to turn their weapons.

Steeling himself for the ordeal that lay before him he banked vertically and started back, using the smoke thrown out by the destroyers as a screen as far as this was possible. The acrid fumes stung his eyes and made him cough as they bit into his lungs, but he gritted his teeth and held on, telling himself that it could only last another minute; then, one way or another, it would be over.

In a sort of lazy dream he counted the destroyers as he flashed over them, for his objective was the leader. One—two—three—four—the stern of the fifth came into view. With savage determination he jammed the joystick forward and dived into the very muzzles of the guns. His arm, with the cigarette case clutched in his hand, projected over the side. His fingers jerked open. The silver case flashed down. He saw it hit the deck, bounce, and slide to a standstill. Then he was past. But not unscathed. His port wing was wobbling and his engine was back-firing furiously. Black, oily smoke spurted out of it. Hot oil drove against the windscreen, blinding him. The stench of petrol vapour struck his nostrils, and he pushed the joystick forward, tilting his nose towards the water. The engine coughed, and stopped. Leaning over the side, he saw that he was almost on the water; he jerked the joystick back, but he was a fraction of a second too late. The hull struck the placid surface of the fiord with a crash, and the machine bounced high. For a moment it hung in the air, wallowing like a wounded seagull, then it stalled. There was another crash as it struck the water. The Dornier at once began to sink as water poured through a score of holes.

Half dazed, Biggles scrambled out of the cockpit on to the back of the splinter-riddled hull. But in his heart he felt that his case was hopeless, for the leading destroyer was within a hundred yards, bearing straight down on him at a speed that would drive the knife-like bows through the flimsy aircraft like an axe. There was nothing he could do except hang on with one hand and wave with the other, although it seemed futile.

As it happened, it was not. The destroyer altered her course a fraction, revealing a party of sailors crowding near the rail. The vessel was, of course, too close to stop, even if the Commander had wished to do so—which in the circumstances was hardly likely. But a rope coiled out. Well and truly thrown, it fell across the fuselage, now half submerged by the bow-wave. Half smothered with spray, Biggles grabbed the line and gave it two quick turns round his waist. He had no time to do more. The next instant he had been whipped off his perch and was being dragged through the water. But he clung to the rope with both hands, for he felt it was likely to cut him in halves unless something was soon done to relieve the strain.

. What happened after that he didn't know. He never did know. All he knew was that he opened his eyes to find himself gasping like a stranded fish on the deck of the destroyer. Several sailors were looking at him curiously. Then an officer hurried forward and bent over him.

'Thanks,' he said. 'We got the case—and your message. But who the devil are you?'

Biggles saw that the officer was staring at his swastika armlet, which for the moment he had completely forgotten. 'Oh that,' he laughed weakly. 'Don't take any notice of that. I'm a British agent. Take me to you skipper at once.'

Half supported by two sailors, for his legs were a bit groggy, he was taken to the bridge, where he was at once the cynosure of all eyes.

He looked at the captain. 'You got my message?'

'Yes—but—who——'

Biggles broke in, and in a few crisp sentences told him who he was, what he had done, and why he had done it. Naturally, he was able to go into more details than had been possible in the written message, with regard to the disposition of the enemy forces. 'If you shoot at the shore batteries, try not to hit the schoolhouse—it's full of British prisoners,' he concluded. 'Phew, I've had a hot five minutes.'

'Hot!' The captain permitted himself to smile. 'I'd call it something worse than that. It's likely to be hot on this ship, too, when we get round the next bend. You'd better get below.'

Biggles tried hard to think. Had it not been for Algy he would have been quite content to remain where he was, but he felt that somehow he ought to get back to the schoolhouse. Algy had come out to help him, so he could not leave him now.

'I've got to get back on shore,' he said at last.

The captain stared. Then he shrugged his shoulders. 'Well, you know your job,' he said simply. 'All I can say is I'd rather have my job than yours. I'm much obliged for the information. I'll remember it. By the way, what's your name?'

'Bigglesworth—Squadron Leader, R.A.F. If you get home safely you might notify Colonel Raymond of M.I.5. that you saw me. I won't waste any more of your time. I fancy the balloon is about to go up. So long and good luck.'

Biggles left the bridge. He was determined to get ashore, but how this was to be done was not easy to see unless he swam for it, and the shore was nearly a quarter of a mile away. Normally he would be quite able to swim that distance, but he doubted his ability to do it in ice water, fully dressed; yet he could not discard his clothes. Still, he saw that he had just a chance. The Narvik fiord, like most fiords, was not straight; not only did it bend like a dog's leg, but there were places where cliffs jutted far out into the water. They had already passed one or two; another was just ahead, and Biggles saw that the captain had for some tactical reason altered his course to pass very close to it. Much as he disliked the idea, he decided that if the destroyer passed within a hundred yards of the rock he would go overboard. Beckoning to a chief petty officer who was standing near, he made him aware of his intention in order that it might not be thought that a man had accidentally fallen overboard. Then, standing tense, he waited for the crucial moment.

The rocky promontory, beyond which lay the town of Narvik, seemed to float nearer as the destroyer raced towards it. Beyond lay the enemy ships. Within a minute the battle would start. To his great satisfaction Biggles saw that the captain had edged even nearer to the rock than he had dared to hope. The intervening distance was not more than sixty yards or so. The time had come: it was now or never. Bracing himself, he took a running dive to get as far from the vessel as possible in order to clear the churning screws.

By the time he had come to the surface the destroyer's guns were roaring. The enemy ships had also opened fire and shells were dropping into the water. With his eyes on the rock, he put every ounce of strength he possessed into his stroke, and reached the point with greater ease than he had expected. Dragging himself ashore, he paused for a moment to wring as much water as possible out of his clothes, and then ran towards the town.

As he had hoped, he found everything in the wildest confusion, which was hardly to be wondered at, for until the German pilot reported their presence in the fiord, the arrival of the destroyers on the scene had not been expected. On the fiord itself a terrible battle was raging between eleven destroyers. Several German store-ships were also firing and shore batteries added to the din. Nobody took the slightest notice of Biggles as he dashed towards the schoolhouse; indeed, very few people, either soldiers or civilians, were in sight. No doubt the troops were all at their stations, and the civilians had taken cover. The din was indescribable.

At the schoolhouse Biggles found a curious state of affairs. Only two elderly German soldiers remained on guard, and they were trying vainly to quieten the prisoners, who were cheering hysterically.

He went straight to the guards. 'Are the doors locked?' he asked tersely, indicating the schoolhouse.

'Yes.'

'Then I'll take charge here.' Biggles showed his Gestapo pass. It was wet, but that didn't matter. 'Give me the keys. You've got to get down to the shore,' he added. 'The British are going to land marines.'

The two soldiers did not question the order. There was no reason why they should, for it seemed highly probable that a landing would be attempted. Indeed, Biggles really hoped that a landing would be made. He watched the two Germans out of sight and then unlocked the school door. He was greeted with cheers, but by holding up his hands he managed to quell the clamour.

'You'll have to bolt for it,' he said. 'I can't do anything more for you. You'll have to take your chance. Get as far down the fiord as you can and hide. If our destroyers withdraw signal to them, and there is a chance that they may pick you up. That's all.'

The prisoners wasted no time. With the exception of Algy they made for the door.

'What had I better do?' asked Algy.

'You go with them.'

'And leave you here?'

Yes, but only for the time being. I shall follow you,' said Biggles tersely. 'Believe me, I've had about enough of this. But it wouldn't do for us to be seen together. Where's Ginger?'

'He's somewhere off the coast in an aircraft carrier—at least, he ought to be. That's where I left him.'

'I see. We can't stop to talk now. You get along. I'll try to rejoin you outside the town. If the Boche see us together they'll guess what has happened. Cheerio—see you later.'

Algy dashed off after the sailors.

Biggles watched him go. He was by no means happy over the state of affairs. He would have much preferred to remain with Algy, but the reasons he had given for not doing so were genuine. If he was seen with the escapees the Germans would realize at once that he was not what he pretended to be. It was better that he should go alone. Later, perhaps, he would be able to join the fugitives and get away with them. He wished now that he had asked Algy a few questions about his movements, and about Ginger. The trouble was, the situation really demanded serious thought, but there had been little or no time to think. Things had happened—and were still happening—so fast that there was no time for lucid reasoning. Shells were now dropping into the town. Several buildings were alight and small parties of Germans were dashing about. A mighty cloud of smoke hung over everything, making it impossible to see what was happening on the fiord. Yet he felt he ought to know, for unless he knew who had won the battle he would not be able to judge if there was any chance of being picked up by one of the destroyers. Then, of course, there was always a chance that the British sailors would attack the town and capture it, in which case it would be safe for him to remain where he was. On the other hand, if the British destroyers were beaten off he would find himself isolated with the Germans. When things settled down there would be inquiries. The prisoners would be remembered, and if he were found going down the fiord it would look suspicious. In the end he decided that before doing anything else he would find out what was happening.

He went straight to the German headquarters, and was not questioned until he accidentally ran into the Commandant.

The Colonel frowned. 'I thought you had orders to get back to Boda?' he queried sharply.

'Quite right, sir,' returned Biggles evenly. 'Believe me, I wish I was on my way.'

'Why aren't you?'

'I started back in a 'plane, but by a bit of bad luck we were shot down by British anti-aircraft guns. We crashed in the fiord and I had to swim ashore. What is happening here?'

'The British are sinking our ships.'

'Will they try to land, do you think?'

'No. I've just heard that they're going back down the fiord.'

At that moment a German pilot in Air Force uniform came running up. He saluted the Colonel.

'I'm getting away now, sir,' he said.

'Good.' The Commandant started. 'Just a minute. Have you got room for a passenger?'

'Certainly.'

The Colonel turned to Biggles. 'Here's your chance,' he declared. 'Schaffer is flying down to Oslo immediately. You can go with him and go on to Boda afterwards; you might not get another chance.'

'I can drop him at Boda if he likes,' offered Schaffer. 'I shall pass over the aerodrome on my way to Oslo.'

This didn't suit Biggles at all. He didn't want to go back down south, either to Boda or anywhere else. Now that he had learned that the British destroyers were going back down the fiord he wanted to rejoin Algy, get aboard one of them, and go back to England. But he daren't refuse the offer. All he could do was make excuses in.the hope that Schaffer would go without him.

'I'm soaked to the skin,' he protested. 'I can't fly in these wet clothes—I shall be frozen stiff.'

'Don't worry about that,' put in Schaffer quickly, with irritating generosity. 'I can lend you some kit. My suitcase is in the machine; you can change in the cabin.'

'That's right,' cried the Commandant. 'You'd better obey your orders.'

Biggles saluted. 'Very good, sir.'

He followed Schaffer down to the wharf, to where a big flying-boat floated.

'You can't land me at Boda in a flying-boat,' Biggles pointed out.

Schaffer smiled condescendingly. 'She's an amphibian.'

'Ah! I understand.' A new hope sprang into Biggles's mind. Schaffer was unaware that he was a pilot, so he might overpower him in the air and take charge of the machine. If he could succeed in doing this he might fly straight on to England.

He followed Schaffer into the flying-boat, and his hopes instantly collapsed. There were already three German officers in it.

Schaffer pulled a suitcase off the rack. 'Here you are,' he said cheerfully. 'You'll find a spare uniform inside.' Then he went through to the cockpit.

In five minutes the flying-boat was in the air, heading south. Astern, from the fiord, a great pillar of smoke was rising.

7

WHAT HAPPENED AT STAVANGER

It was late in the afternoon when Schaffer landed Biggles at Boda. He was still wearing the German's spare uniform, for his suit was not yet dry. He arranged with Schaffer that he would send the uniform on when his own things were dry, although as the German was by no means certain of his movements he would have to let Biggles know where to send them.

As soon as Biggles was on the ground, carrying his wet things in Schaffer's suitcase, the German pilot took off again, leaving Biggles standing on the aerodrome, now a scene of considerable activity.

Alert for danger, Biggles walked towards the officers' quarters. His position was, he knew, perilous in the extreme, but he couldn't remain standing on the aerodrome. What he feared was that he might run into Brandt, the man who knew him by sight. If von Stalhein happened to be with him, as seemed probable, then all deception would be at an end. All Biggles could do was mark down a Messerschmitt not far away, this offering the only possible means of escape if the worst came to the worst. To complicate matters, he would have to let von Hymann know that he was back, otherwise the Gestapo chief would start looking for him. He would learn that Schaffer had flown him back to Boda from Narvik, so should he, Biggles, fail to report, it would look most suspicious.

He dumped the suitcase in the room that had been allotted to him, and subjecting everyone he met to the closest scrutiny, he began making his way towards the station headquarters. In doing so he met Kristen, who greeted him cordially but with surprise.

'Hullo!' he cried. 'Where the deuce have you been?'

Biggles smiled ruefully. 'Don't talk about it,' he said sadly. 'I had to go to Narvik on a special job. I was just starting for home, by air, when a flotilla of British destroyers arrived and we were shot down. We fell into the fiord, but I managed to swim ashore.

Himmel! Was it cold!'

Kristen laughed. 'All in a day's work. Where are you bound for now?'

It struck Biggles as odd that Kristen did not mention his uniform. He wondered why.

I'm just going to station headquarters to report,' he answered. 'By the way, how do you like my uniform?'

'It fits badly. Also, I didn't know you had been promoted to *Oberleutnant.*'

'It isn't mine,' laughed Biggles. 'I got wet through, so these things were lent me by a fellow named Schaffer—the chap who flew me back here.'

'I see. Some uniforms have now arrived here, so I thought, naturally, that you'd been and got yourself one. You can get one as soon as you like, but don't be too long, or you may find them all gone. See you later.'

Biggles went on to headquarters and reported to the Commandant, Baron von Leffers. He asked permission to use the telephone.

'Yes, you'd better report to von Hymann right away,' returned the Commandant sourly. 'There have been a lot of inquiries for you. Two fellows were here yesterday asking where you were.'

'What were their names?' inquired Biggles casually.

'Brandt and von Stalhein—a fellow in the Secret Service.'

Biggles nodded. 'I was expecting them,' he announced calmly, and put a call through to the Hotel Port.

In a minute he was speaking to von Hymann. Wasting no words, he reported that he was back at Boda, and was going on to report with more detail what had happened at Narvik when von Hymann stopped him.

'We know all about that,' said the Gestapo chief. 'After you left I had a long talk with the Commander of the Narvik garrison, and he told me how Bigglesworth had got away—as he had learnt it from the British prisoners. Von Stalhein was very upset. He seems to hate this fellow Bigglesworth like poison, and he, too, had a long talk with Narvik. Pity this fellow Bigglesworth didn't remain with the party you captured, then we should have got him. Still, it's no use crying over spilt milk.'

Biggles's muscles tightened as his chief went on: 'Van Stalhein is here with me now. He says that this Bigglesworth is a tricky customer, so he wants all the particulars from you that he can get. He's coming along to see you.'

'When?'

There was a brief delay, presumably while the chief spoke to von Stalhein.

'Now,' answered von Hymann. 'He says he'll come along right away. He'll be with you in less than an hour.'

It was the answer Biggles dreaded. 'Very good, sir.' Trying not to let his face reveal what he felt, he hung up the receiver.

'Everything all right?' inquired the Baron coldly.

'Right as rain,' returned Biggles.

Dusk was closing in as he left the office and started walking back towards his quarters. He had got to move quickly, that was certain. He had got to get away before von Stalhein arrived— but how? He felt that he was in a net, a net that was slowly but surely closing round him, and he could not even find respite, much less a way of escape.

So engrossed was he with his thoughts that he saw no one near him. He was hardly conscious of the light touch that fell on his arm. Something—it felt like a slip of paper—was pushed into his hand. Then the man was gone, faded into the shadows. Biggles caught no more than a glimpse of a grey uniform. He glanced around swiftly and then walked on slowly; and as he walked he unfolded the slip of paper. There was a message on it, printed in small block letters. It read:

> 'What is happening at Stavanger Airport? Particulars of planes and anti-aircraft defences urgently wanted. Also particulars of damage done. Get your report to Fiord 21, where messenger awaits you. If you are unable to land there, put message in a bottle and drop in fiord. R.'

Biggles memorized the message; then he put the slip in his mouth and chewed it to pulp. He could have laughed had his position not been so desperate. As if he hadn't got enough on his mind already! Now, in the middle of all his worries, was a message from Colonel Raymond, asking him to undertake a mission which bristled with difficulties. There was this about it though, he thought on reflection. His position was already so alarming that it could hardly be worse. Colonel Raymond, as promised, had got in touch with him. The man who had delivered the message, obviously a secret agent, must know him by sight—but (Biggles reasoned) he could have learned to recognize him from a photograph.

It gave him strength to know he was not alone within the enemy lines. Other men were doing the same thing. The fellow who had so cleverly slipped the paper into his hand was one of them. It was cleverly done because he had not even seen the man's face. He would not recognize him if he saw him, so he could not betray him, either by accident or intentionally. They were all playing a dreadful game in which no one took a risk that could be avoided. He tore the chewed-up message to pieces and threw the pieces away.

Reaching the officers' mess, he stood still for a moment staring into the gathering gloom, trying to get his racing thoughts into some sort of order. Colonel Raymond's message was clear enough. He wanted him to go to Stavanger. Obviously he could not remain at Boda once von Stalhein had arrived on the scene, and since he had got to go somewhere, Stavanger suited him as well as anywhere. But after that he would not be able to return to Boda. Von Stalhein would be furious, not to say suspicious, when he arrived and found that the man whom he had come to see had gone off without leaving a message. What would von Stalhein do then? Biggles wondered. Most likely he would return to Oslo and voice his suspicions to von Hymann, who would start a hue and cry for him. Still, there was no way of preventing that. He couldn't let Colonel Raymond down. He would do his best to obtain the required information, and get it to Fiord 21. He knew the fiord well. Indeed, the number 21 was the one he had himself given it. It was one of the fiords he had marked down during his survey flights, and as it was a possible landing-place he had given particulars of it in the reports he had sent home. No doubt the Colonel had used the number, instead of the fiord's proper name, in order to convince him that the message was genuine. Further, should the message fall into wrong hands the recipient would not know to which fiord the number 21 referred. As far as Stavanger Airport was concerned, there was only one way he could get to it, and that was by air. The only aircraft available was a Messerschmitt—there were now several standing on the aerodrome. It meant flying in the dark, but he didn't mind that. The greatest danger would come when he tried to take the plane. However, he could but try.

Biggles went round to the back of the canteen, found a small empty bottle with a well-fitting cork and put it in his pocket. It was all the equipment he needed. He then returned to the aerodrome and reconnoitred the part where the planes were standing. Most of those which had been operating during the day had now returned, and were parked at intervals along the edge of the aerodrome—an anti-bombing precaution which suggested that a raid was feared. However, Biggles was not concerned with that. All he wanted was a machine, and as few people were about there did not appear to be any great difficulty in getting one. There might be an alarm when he took off, but by that time he would be in the air, so it wouldn't matter.

Unhurriedly, and without being accosted, he walked over to the nearest Messerschmitt and laid his hand on the engine cowling. It was still warm. A glance around revealed no sign of danger, so he climbed into the cockpit. Still no alarm was raised. He examined the instrument board carefully, and perceiving that the controls were of orthodox design, he decided to start. He had no flying kit, but that did not worry him; the journey, not more than a hundred miles, was too short for him to get really cold.

He wasted no more time. The engine spluttered as it sprang to life, and in another minute the machine was racing across the turf. He had taken off in the direction of his destination, so he could keep straight on towards the western coast, keeping low so that his identification markings could be seen easily if he were challenged. He was, many times. Searchlights leapt up along his line of flight, only to fade again as the operators found him and identified the aircraft for one of their own.

In less than half an hour he was gliding down through a perfect maze of searchlight beams that surrounded the airport of Stavanger. He made a mental note of the number of them, for they formed an important part of anti-aircraft equipment, about which Colonel Raymond was anxious to have particulars. Some of the beams followed him down, so as soon as the machine had finished its run he taxied straight on to the aerodrome buildings. A working-party under an N.C.O. ran out to meet him and to guide him in.

'I thought single-seaters were not to fly after dark unless there was a raid?' said the N.C.O.

This was evidently a new order, and Biggles knew nothing of it. 'Quite right,' he said smoothly. 'It happens, though, that the order does not apply to the special communication squadron to which I belong. I have a message for the Commandant.'

'Couldn't it have been telephoned, or radioed?' queried the N.C.O., who was evidently of an inquisitive nature.

'So that the enemy could pick it up, too?' sneered Biggles sarcastically. 'Not likely. Where is the Commandant's office?'

The N.C.O. pointed. 'Over there.'

'Thanks.'

Biggles walked on, leaving the working-party to continue its duties. He had no intention of seeking an interview with the Commandant. There was no reason why he should. He thought he could learn all there was to know about the place without asking pointed questions, either of the Commandant or anyone else. Which, in fact, he did. He went into the canteen, and, lingering over a coffee, listened to the conversation going on around him. After that he walked round outside, noting everything of interest—the number of machines, types, position of guns, etc. Only one man, a police corporal, challenged him, but the Gestapo pass worked as usual and the corporal said no more. Finally, Biggles returned to the canteen and, sitting quietly in a corner as though writing a letter, committed all the information he had gathered to writing. He was well aware of the danger of doing this, for should he for any reason be searched it would provide conclusive evidence against him. When it was done he returned to the aerodrome, and in the darkness inserted the paper into the bottle, afterwards corking it tightly.

Now all this had occupied more than an hour, and Biggles was just moving towards his machine with a view of going straight on to Fiord 21 when he became aware of a commotion. There was nothing definite about it; it took the form of a slightly increased activity. A messenger ran along the concrete apron in front of the hangars, shouting to another man. Small parties began to collect, talking excitedly. One such group stood near his machine. He walked quickly towards it but kept in the background.

'What's going on?' he asked a simple-looking soldier who stood near by.

'They say this machine was stolen from Boda,' was the startling reply.

'Stolen?'

'All I know is, a friend of mine in the orderly room told me that a message has just come through by telephone from Boda saying that someone had made off with the machine. They gave the number of it, and it has just been discovered that this is it. They're looking for the pilot who brought it here.'

Biggles did not doubt for one moment the truth of this alarming information. Nor did he waste time asking who was looking for the pilot. Obviously it would be fatal for him to go near the machine now. He would have to borrow another. Having reached that decision, he was turning away when there was a general stir. The searchlights switched on again, sweeping the heavens, whence came the noise of a gliding plane. A silver spark gleamed against the sky, and a minute or two later the machine, a two-seater, glided in and landed. As soon as it was on the ground it taxied quickly to where the Messerschmitt stood. A man jumped down, and Biggles had no need to look twice to see who it was. It was Erich von Stalhein. The German walked quickly towards the Commandant's office.

'It's getting time I was moving on,' Biggles told himself, and turned quickly towards the machines that lined the boundary of the aerodrome. In doing so he came face to face with a man whom he had no wish to see at that moment. It was the N.C.O. in charge of the working-party, the man who had accosted him on landing.

'Here! They're looking for you!' cried the N.C.O. sharply.

'Looking for me?' queried Biggles foolishly. 'Who's looking for me?'

'Everybody. You'd better come with me to the office and see the Commandant.'

Had the man been alone, Biggles might have been tempted to make a break for it, but during the conversation several soldiers and airmen had gathered round until he and the N.C.O. were in the centre of a circle. Nevertheless, he had not the slightest intention of walking unprotestingly to his doom—for that was what the Commandant's office amounted to now that von Stalhein was there. What he would have done had things remained normal will never be known. For once, he was at a loss to know how to act for the best. And while he stood there staring at the N.C.O., trying to make up his mind, he heard a distant sound that set his pulses racing. It was the choking *whoof-whoof-whoof* of anti-aircraft gunfire, and it was drawing rapidly nearer.

'D'you know who I am?' Biggles asked the N.C.O., simply to gain time.

'Who are you?'

Biggles produced his Gestapo pass.

The corporal's manner changed; he became more respectful, but he did not retract. 'All the same, sir, I think you'd better report to the Commandant,' he insisted. 'There seems to be some trouble over your——'

The N.C.O. broke off, staring at the sky, while the soldiers and airmen dispersed like mist on a summer morning; for, from overhead, there came a sudden burst of aero engines. Apparently the machine, or machines, had been gliding. Almost simultaneously with the roar of the engines came an even more sinister sound. It was a shrill whine, increasing swiftly in volume until it sounded like the whistle of an express train.

The N.C.O. knew what it was. So did Biggles, for once heard there is no mistaking the sound of falling bombs. No longer concerned with Biggles, the N.C.O. ran for his life. Biggles, too, bolted, for he had an idea of what was going to happen to the aerodrome. From one point of view the British bombers had done him a good turn, but he had no desire to be blown to pieces by their bombs. He started to follow the N.C.O. and his men, assuming that they would know the nearest way to cover, but before he could overtake them the first bombs were bursting. The searchlights were raking the sky. Anti-aircraft guns roared. Bombs thundered. In short, pandemonium broke loose.

Biggles flung himself flat, his hands over his ears to prevent himself from being deafened. Bombs were falling all around. Some fell on the buildings and set fire to them, and in the lurid glare he could get a rough idea of the damage that was being done. The first wave of bombers passed, but he could hear more coming, and then, suddenly, he knew what they were doing. Apart from destroying the aerodrome buildings, they were churning the aerodrome itself into a sea of craters, thus putting it out of action.

Biggles caught his breath as he realized what this implied. If the bombers were going to make it impossible for machines to land, then they would also make it impossible for machines to take off, in which case he would be stranded at Stavangar—with von Stalhein. He perceived that if ever he was to get away it would have to be now, before any further damage was caused. Already it would be a risky business taking off, for if he got a machine and struck a crater while travelling at high speed, he would certainly break some bones. Furthermore, some of the machines were ablaze, and it seemed likely that they would set fire to the rest.

In a flash Biggles was on his feet, racing towards a machine which had so far escaped damage. He could hear another salvo of bombs coming down; guns flashed and lines of tracer bullets streaked through the air. The noise was deafening. With one thing and another, he felt that he had suddenly gone mad in the middle of an inferno. There was this about it though, he thought, as he tore towards the machine: everyone would be too busy doing something, or taking cover, to pay any attention to him, even if he were seen.

Panting for breath, he reached the machine he had selected, and he laughed aloud when he recognized it for the one in which von Stalhein had arrived. Then he flung himself flat again as another lot of bombs rained down.

'Go to it, boys!' he yelled, giving way to a fierce exultation as the bombs exploded. While the last report was still ringing in his ears he clambered into the machine.

In all his long flying career, with its many breathless incidents, he had never made a more fantastic take-off. Fantastic only half describes it. It was, he felt, the act of a madman—but then it would have been lunacy to remain.

To start with, it was neither light nor dark. It was both. Pitch darkness alternated with vivid flashes of blinding orange light as bombs exploded and guns flashed—not that it would have made much difference had the light been constant, for the aerodrome was now blackened in a pall of smoke. As if this were not enough, several bombs had fallen on the landing field, leaving yawning craters.

For a moment, with his hand on the throttle, he blinked in a sort of daze through the windscreen, trying to make out something, anything, as long as it would give him a line to fly on, and help to keep him straight.[1] But there was nothing—nothing but smoke. Again, the noise was indescribable, and sufficient in itself to prevent coherent thought.

In sheer desperation Biggles jerked the throttle open, and in a moment was tearing blindly through the turmoil. There then followed twenty seconds of such strain that his nerves seemed to be stretched like elastic; but at the end of that brief period of time—which, in fact, seemed longer than the bare figure suggests—he could tell by the 'feel' of the controls that the

---

[1] *In taking off a pilot chooses a mark, usually on the boundary of the aerodrome, to prevent swerving.*

machine was ready to lift. He eased the joystick back. Instantly the cessation of vibration, caused by the wheels running over the ground, told him that he was air-borne. He could still see nothing, but as he climbed the smoke thinned, and a vague misty world began to take shape around him.

The first substantial object that he saw was another machine coming straight towards him, and only by a spasmodic jerk of the controls did he avoid a head-on collision. As the other machine flashed past he made out the dim silhouette of a Blenheim. Dry-lipped with strain, he held the stick forward for a moment or two and then zoomed high into a blue-black world torn by jabbing flame and hurtling metal. Below, the aerodrome was an inferno. The risk of collision with the British bombers or of flying into the bombs that were raining down was still imminent, but he could do no more than hold on a steady course and hope for the best. Another anxious minute passed, each second of it reducing the risk, and then his taut nerves began to relax.

'Holy smoke! What a picnic,' he gasped, and then swung round to the north towards Fiord 21. He could see the sea below him now and the deeply indented coastline, so his immediate mission became nothing more difficult than straightforward flying, or so he thought.

His destination lay about fifty miles away, and he had covered half that distance in a few minutes when he detected a faint reek of petrol. He was unable to see anything, so he could only feel about with his hand, and in doing so he made the disconcerting discovery that the floor of his cockpit was wet with petrol. He guessed what had happened. Either while the machine had been standing on the ground, or after it was in the air, it had been hit by a piece of shrapnel, and the tank had been holed. There was nothing he could do about it, of course, except switch on the instrument-board light and look at the petrol gauge. One glance told him the worst. The tank was practically empty. He at once looked at his altimeter, which told him that he had climbed to four thousand feet. That gave him a chance. If only the engine would hold out for another five minutes he would be within gliding distance of the fiord.

It did—nearly. He could see the fiord in the distance, for he had flown over the district several times for the purpose of making his reports, and had it not been for this he would have been in a worse case than he was. He was still by no means certain that he would reach the fiord, but he could only hold on in an endeavour to do so. He switched off the ignition, for the engine was back-firing, and anyway it could serve no useful purpose. In dead silence he glided on towards the fiord, losing height slowly but steadily. And as he glided he made up his mind what he would do when he reached the water. Not that there was really any choice, for the aircraft was a land machine, without any adaptations for landing on water. This at once meant that he would have to 'pancake' on the surface of the fiord, for a landing on the jagged rocks that surrounded it was out of the question. Still, he thought that with judgement, and a little luck, the machine would remain afloat until—until what? He wondered. Someone would be there waiting for him—or at any rate for the bottled message. It seemed unlikely that Colonel Raymond would order a message to be dropped into the fiord unless he was positive that someone would be there to collect it. Indeed, his message said that someone would be there. In that case he, Biggles, would be picked up. If there was no one there, then he would have to swim ashore, and with the possibility of this in view he decided to pancake as near the rocks as possible.

And this is what he did. Skimming the towering cliffs that bordered the fiord with only a few feet to spare, Biggles turned up the long narrow stretch of water, losing height, and keeping as near to the cliffs as he dared. He knew that a short distance ahead this cliff had partly collapsed in a mighty landslide, and this, if he could reach it, would provide the easiest place to get ashore.

As soon as the landslide came into view he side-slipped steeply to lose height. Ten feet above the surface of the black water he flattened out, and as the controls began to go 'sloppy', telling him that the machine was about to fall out of his hands, he kicked the rudder hard to bring the nose towards the sloping mass of boulders that thrust outward like a promontory and ended at the water's edge.

He was well satisfied with his landing. There was a terrific splash as the aircraft flopped bodily on to the water, but it floated, and surged forward to within a few yards of the rocks. By climbing along the wing he would be able to jump ashore, which pleased him immensely, for he fully expected a ducking, and the idea of spending the rest of the night in wet clothes was not pleasant to think about. He was kneeling on the centre section preparatory to climbing along the wing to the shore when a voice spoke.

'D'you always land like that?' asked someone, evenly in English.

Biggles nearly fell into the water. His hand flew to his gun, and half drew it. Then he stopped dead, staring. Slowly he pushed the pistol back into his pocket.

'Christopher Columbus!' he gasped. 'Ginger! How in the name of all that's miraculous did *you* get here?'

Ginger stood on a rock with his hands thrust deep into his trousers' pockets. 'I shouldn't call it a miracle,' he answered calmly. 'Raymond sent me along to meet you. Mind you don't slip—the water's colder than the tip of an Eskimo's nose.'

8

EXPLANATIONS AND DECISIONS

BIGGLES scrambled ashore. He was just in time to escape a ducking, for the aircraft was sinking fast.

'How long have you been here?' he asked.

'Since last night.'

'Great Scott! You must be hungry.'

'Not me,' grinned Ginger. 'For all I knew it might have been a week before you turned up, so I brought some grub along.'

'Lead me to it,' returned Biggles promptly. 'I need some nourishment. We can talk as we eat—and there seems to be a lot to say. I assume you've got a machine here?'

'Of course.'

'Thank goodness for that. After we've eaten we'll push off home—and I don't mind telling you I shall be mighty glad to get out of this.'

Ginger looked up sharply. 'Home?'

'Of course—why not?'

'But what about Algy?'

'What about him?'

'He's gone to Boda.'

Biggles swayed. Then he sank down on a rock. For a moment or two he was speechless. 'Gone to Boda?' he managed to get out. 'What in heaven's name for?'

'To find you.'

Biggles shook his head sadly. 'Get the grub,' he said wearily. 'It's time we got this straightened out.'

Ginger led the way to a tiny cove where, under an overhanging cliff, a seaplane rested on the water. From behind a rock he produced a heavy bag. 'Help yourself,' he said, dropping the bag in front of Biggles. 'There's bread, cheese, sardines, and a flask of cold tea. That's all I could manage.'

'That'll suit me,' Biggles assured him. 'Now let's try to untangle things. I'll start. I got a message from Raymond asking me to get information about Stavanger and bring it here. I was told if necessary to drop the information in a bottle. Instead, I dropped myself—I'll tell you why presently. The bottle is still in my pocket. I've got the information and we've got to get it to Raymond. That's all I have to say except that the last time I saw Algy he was a prisoner at Narvik. I helped him to get away—at least, I hoped he'd got away.'

Ginger nodded. 'That's right, he did.'

'Before we go any farther, d'you reckon this is a safe spot?' inquired Biggles.

'I should say not; but nowhere in Norway is safe, and this is as good as anywhere. We can't be seen, except, of course, by a vessel coming up the fiord, and only then in daylight.'

'Good. Now tell me about Algy.'

'Well, what happened was this,' explained Ginger. 'To start

with, Colonel Raymond brought us back home from France; he told us what you'd been doing and how you were fixed. I may say we were both pretty fed up about it, but that didn't cut any ice. Naturally, we felt that we ought to be helping, but it wasn't easy to see what we could do, or how we could get into touch with you. Raymond soon fixed things up though. He said a British force was on its way to Norway, but he wasn't allowed to tell us where the landings would be made. The force would be supported by the Navy, and machines of the Fleet Air Arm, which would operate chiefly from aircraft carriers. Raymond was able to arrange for us to fly out to a carrier; he told us to keep an eye on Narvik, as if possible he would get a message through to you asking you to fly up to Narvik Fiord. If you could then make a smoke signal we might be able to pick you up. I must say it seemed a pretty wild hope, but it was all Raymond could do.'

'I didn't get any message asking me to go to Narvik,' put in Biggles.

'We suspected that—in fact, we knew it, because the agent sent a signal back to Raymond to say that you'd left Boda. At least, he couldn't find you there. Obviously if the fellow couldn't get into touch with you he couldn't give you the message.'

'True enough,' agreed Biggles.

'Well, we joined the carrier off the coast of Norway,' continued Ginger. 'We were flown out, but being super-numeraries we couldn't get machines of our own; consequently we could only get trips in other fellows' machines. I did a trip, but saw nothing. Mind you, we were still hoping that the agent would find you and send you up. Algy then went off straight away as a gunner in a Shark. It got its engine shot up and was forced to land on the fiord. That's how he came to be taken prisoner. Naturally, I didn't know anything about it at the time. All I knew was that the Shark failed to return, and I reckoned poor old Algy was a goner. Dash my wig if he didn't turn up with a tale that I found pretty hard to swallow.'

'You mean—he got back to the carrier?'

'Yes, he was picked up by a destroyer. He told me a fantastic tale about being taken prisoner, and with some other fellows being shoved into the schoolhouse at Narvik. Then who should blow along, as large as life, but you, acting as though you'd bought the whole outfit. You inspected the prisoners and went off again. Shortly afterwards our destroyers barged into the fiord and had a crack at the enemy. Upon this you came back and set the prisoners free. Algy said he kept with the crowd, expecting you to follow, but he didn't see you again. He didn't know what your game was, so when our destroyers steamed out, and the party had a chance of being picked up, he went aboard with the rest. There were three fellows off the carrier among the prisoners, so the destroyer dumped them back on board. That's how Algy got back, and how I learnt all about this.'

'What happened next?'

'Well, we didn't know what to do for the best, and we were still scratching our heads when Raymond got another message through to us. He said his man was still trying to make contact with you at Boda, because he felt certain that you'd return there sooner or later. If the agent did make contact with you he was to ask you to go to Stavanger and collect information, and then come on here, to Fiord 21. Raymond suggested that we should get an aircraft and come down here to wait for you. If you turned up we were to fly you home.'

'That sounds as if Raymond has given me permission to leave the country.'

'That's pretty obvious.'

'But how did Algy——'

'Just a minute—I'm coming to that. There was a snag, and it was this. There was no great difficulty in our flying down here, but we didn't know, and had no means of finding out, if you'd got the message asking you to come here. If you *hadn't* got the message, then we might have sat here for the duration waiting for you. The result was that Algy, who knew you must be in a pretty tight spot and anxious to get away, got one of his bright ideas. It was that he should go to Boda to find you, and so make certain of getting you here.'

'But how the dickens did he propose getting to Boda?'

'His idea was to get one of the fellows on the carrier to fly him over, at night. He would step out with his parachute.'

Biggles stared aghast. 'But he must have been crazy!'

Ginger shrugged his shoulders. 'He always was, wasn't he?'

'And d'you mean to tell me that's what he did?'

'That, chief, is what he did.'

'But surely not in his own uniform?'

'More or less. He'd picked up a German greatcoat from somewhere, and he simply wore that over his uniform. The last I saw of him he was getting into the machine, bound for Boda. I was to come here and wait, and here I am.'

'And you don't know what's happened to Algy?'

'Absolutely nothing. I haven't heard a word since he took off. Of course, I hoped you'd arrive together.'

Biggles squatted on the rock with his chin in the palms of his hands. 'Well, this is a pretty kettle of fish, I must say,' he muttered. 'Here am I, at last able to get out, only to find that Algy has got himself stuck inside.'

'When he finds you're not at Boda he may be able to grab a machine and fly here.'

Biggles snorted. 'Suffering crocodiles! Is he daft enough to think that the Boche leave their machines lying about for anybody to pick up?'

'You seem to have managed it.'

'That's different. I'm an officer in the German Air Force. If that isn't enough I'm also a member of the Gestapo, with a special pass, signed by the chief, in my pocket. It wasn't hard for me to move about, although it was a bit risky because von Stalhein is in Norway looking for me. By a bit of bad luck it was learned that I was in Norway.'

Biggles gave a brief account of his adventures. 'So you see,' he concluded, 'it was a lot easier for me to get a machine than it will be for Algy. If he's in Boda, then I reckon he's stuck there.'

Ginger stared moodily at the sombre surface of the fiord. 'In that case the question is, what are we going to do about it?'

Biggles thought for a moment. 'The most important thing of all is to get this information about Stavanger back to Colonel Raymond,' he decided. 'We can't allow personal matters to

interfere with our Service jobs. You'd better take this information back. Raymond is expecting it.'

'What about you?'

'I shall have to stay here to see if Algy turns up. If he does,
we'll both be here when you return, so you'll be able to pick us
both up. You can leave the food here with me. What's the time?'
Biggles looked at his watch. 'It's nearly midnight—let's see—
it's nearly four hundred and fifty miles across the ditch—call it
three hours. If you spend an hour with Raymond—no, I'm
afraid you couldn't get back here before daylight.'

'What's the matter with coming back after daylight?'

Biggles shook his head. 'Too risky. There are too many eyes
along the coast right now. It would be much safer to slip in after
dark. You could cut your engine well out to sea and glide in.'

'But that would mean you'd be here all day tomorrow.'

'That can't be prevented.'

'What about Algy?—I'm worried about him.'

'Let's leave it like this,' suggested Biggles. 'You get the
information home—I've got it written out. You can also tell the
Colonel what I've told you. I'll wait here for Algy; otherwise, if
he came back and found no one here, he'd wonder what had
happened. When you come back bring a spare parachute. If
Algy hasn't turned up then you'll have to fly me over to Boda.
I'll drop off and look for him. You could then fly back here and
wait.'

'Okay,' agreed Ginger. 'But I'm bound to say it sounds a
sticky business to me,' he added glumly.

'All war is a sticky business,' Biggles reminded him. 'Get off
now and concentrate on getting home. That should give you
plenty to think about without worrying about me.'

Ginger cast off the mooring rope that held his machine close
against the rocks and climbed into the cockpit. Biggles, putting
his hands on a float, pushed the machine clear. For a few
moments a brooding hush reigned, a hush broken only by the
gentle lap of the dark water. Then the engine shattered the
silence. The aircraft surged down the fiord and disappeared into
the gloom.

Biggles put the food behind a rock and settled down to wait. From far away came the deep rumble of guns, but in the little fiord all was quite. Nothing moved.

9
BACK AT BODA

ALGY did not come.

All through the long night hours Biggles waited, listening, hoping, for he had no wish to return to Boda. Several times he sat up, alert, as he heard the purr of aircraft. But they were only patrols—British or German, he knew not which—exploring the starlit heavens. Each time the sound died away he sank back again to wait. There was nothing he could do.

Dawn came, and with it still more aircraft, always flying very high. Only one, a German reconnaissance 'plane, came low over the silent fiord. Biggles took cover, and presently, apparently satisfied that the fiord was deserted, the German passed on. Occasionally Biggles ate a little of the food from the bag, but he ate mechanically and without relish, for he was too concerned with the state of affairs. The day wore on. The sun went down. Purple twilight, ever darkening, hung for a little while over the silent waters, and then gave way to night. Stars appeared, twinkling. Biggles munched a biscuit thoughtfully.

It was about half-past nine that he heard the sound for which he had been waiting, the musical hum of a gliding 'plane, and presently he saw its dark silhouette dropping slowly towards the water. There was a surging splash as it struck the surface and forged on towards the promontory formed by the landslide. Slowly it came to rest, and Ginger's head appeared. He gave a low whistle.

Biggles answered and, reaching out, caught a float to steady the machine.

'Everything all right?' inquired Ginger.

'Yes, nothing's happened here.'

'Did Algy come?'

'No.'

'Then it looks as if he's in a jam.'

'I'm afraid so. How did you get on? Any trouble?'

'Nothing to speak of. I ran into a Hun over the North Sea, but I managed to lose him. I saw Raymond and told him how things stood here. He was in favour of your flying straight back home.'

'But what about Algy?'

'He said he'd try to arrange for one of his agents in the country to pick him up and get him across the frontier into Sweden.'

Biggles shook his head. 'That won't do. Raymond ought to know we don't work like that. While Algy's inside the country I'm not going to leave it.'

'As a matter of fact, I think Raymond knew you'd take that attitude, and merely made his suggestion to let you know that if you wanted to come home he wouldn't object. What are you going to do?'

'It's no use my sitting here any longer. I doubt if Algy will come now. I shall have to go to Boda to fetch him. You've got a brolly?'[1]

'Yes.'

'Then you can take me over to Boda right away.'

Ginger, who by this time had come ashore, looked glum. 'I don't like it,' he muttered. 'It would be safer for you to go and sit on the edge of a volcano than go to Boda. What are you going to say when they ask you why you pinched that Messerschmitt?'

'They don't know definitely that it was me.'

'They'll assume it was, I bet. They are certain to ask you about it.'

'I shall have the answers ready.'

'What about von Stalhein? I know you last saw him at Stavanger, but he may have gone back to Boda.'

Biggles shrugged his shoulders. 'That's a risk I shall have to take. I'll keep my eyes open.'

'You haven't forgotten that von Stalhein knows Algy? If he spotted him and has had him arrested, he'll be waiting for you to

---

[1] *Parachute.*

arrive. He knows by now that if he finds one of us it's only a question of time before the others turn up. I——'

'It's no use raising objections,' broke in Biggles impatiently. 'Whether he's got Algy or not, I'm going over to look for him. I've still got my Gestapo pass. After I drop off you come back here and wait; but if anyone spots you you'd better see about saving yourself.'

Ginger nodded.

'Then let's get away.'

Biggles donned the parachute, adjusted the harness, and took his place in the spare seat.

'You know better than I do where the aerodrome is, so keep me on my course if I look like going astray,' said Ginger as he got into the cockpit. 'I expect we shall get a good plastering from archie.'

'Head out to sea first and get plenty of height,' advised Biggles. 'Switch off your engine when I tell you, and glide.'

'Will the aerodrome be blacked out?'

'I expect so, but I know too well where it is to have any difficulty in finding it. Go ahead.'

In a few minutes they were in the air, standing out to sea, climbing steadily for height. Not until they were at fifteen thousand feet did Ginger turn and head back towards the questing searchlight beams that marked the positions of enemy forces. These positions were avoided as far as possible, but more than once a beam leapt up and passed close enough to the machine to reflect on it a ghostly radiance. On such occasions Ginger throttled back and employed such ruses as Biggles had taught him.

'You're getting a little too far north,' Biggles said once, and that was the only remark he made until they were nearing their objective, when he gave more detailed instructions. They were now at twenty thousand feet.

'Hold her as she is and you'll pass right over the aerodrome,' he said finally. 'As soon as you feel me go off get back to the fiord. After that you'll have to use your discretion. Well, here we go.'

'S'long, chief,' called Ginger huskily.

'S'long, laddie.' The machine rocked as Biggles dived overboard.

Ginger instinctively looked down, but he could see nothing except the inevitable searchlight beams that were still seeking him. It was with a heavy heart that he turned towards the coast.

Biggles was still falling through the war-stricken sky. He had deliberately delayed pulling the rip-cord for several seconds, but when he did so, and the fabric ballooned out above him, he gazed down at the darkened earth beneath. He could see the aerodrome now, and was satisfied that his jump had been well timed; he would touch down not more than a few hundred yards to the east of it.

He fell when he landed, but he was on his feet in a moment. He could still hear the drone of Ginger's machine fading away to the west, otherwise all was silent. Working quickly, he folded the parachute into a ball and looked round for a place to hide it. There appeared to be only one, and that was a ditch. There was water in the bottom of it, and into this he thrust the parachute and trod on it. This done, he made his way towards the aerodrome, aware that he was taking the most appalling risk he had ever willingly undertaken, a risk compared with which his original task was as nothing. If von Stalhein had returned to Boda, then he was virtually committing suicide.

Nobody challenged him as he walked towards his quarters, for this, he decided, might be the safest place for him until he had made certain inquiries that he had in mind, inquiries concerning Algy and von Stalhein. Near the officers' mess he met a German whom he knew slightly, and he was about to accost him when Kristen appeared. Kristen stopped dead when he saw Biggles.

'Where have you come from?' he demanded in an amazed voice.

'What do you mean—where have I come from?' returned Biggles.

'Where were you all day yesterday?'

'I've been doing a job for the Gestapo—I thought I told you that?'

'Yes, you did, but—well, I thought—people have been looking for you.'

'People? For me? Why?' Biggles feigned bland surprise.

'But wasn't it you who took the machine from here, the Messerschmitt, and made off with it?'

'Machine? What on earth are you talking about?'

'Somebody took a Messerschmitt from here without permission, and as you couldn't be found it was thought that you had taken it. A fellow named von Stalhein was here looking for you. Then word came that the missing machine had landed at Stavanger, so he went on there.'

'Then I'd better have a word with him—that is, if he is back here,' said Biggles calmly. 'D'you happen to know if he came back?'

'He may have done, but I haven't seen him.'

'Then I'll ring up my chief in Oslo and find out.'

Biggles moved on towards the orderly room, but stopped suddenly. 'By the way, what is this rumour I hear about an English spy being captured here?'

Kristen shook his head. 'I haven't heard anything about it. What did you hear?'

'Only that a strange Englishman had been found prowling about the aerodrome.'

'Well, I've heard nothing of it.'

Biggles nodded. 'Evidently it was only a rumour—see you later.' He walked on, well satisfied with his inquiries.

While it was by no means certain, he thought, it rather looked as if von Stalhein had not come back to Boda; and it was hardly likely that Algy had been captured without Kristen hearing something about it. It might be assumed, then, that Algy was still at large, and since his mission was to find Biggles, it was reasonable to suppose that he would be near the aerodrome—if not actually on it. Where could he be?

Biggles tried to put himself in Algy's place, asking himself how he would have acted had the position been reversed. The most reasonable supposition, he concluded, was that Algy would not actually be on the aerodrome, where he would be open to question, but was more likely to be hiding near the boundary, watching and waiting for a chance to speak to him. In the circumstances Biggles thought he might take a walk round the aerodrome boundary, whistling a tune known to both of them; then, if Algy were near, he would reveal himself. But there was something he would have to do first, and that was to endeavour to allay suspicions concerning himself. The best way of doing that might be to ring up the Hotel Port and speak to von Hymann. He could tell him that he had been looking for von Stalhein.

With this object in view he made his way to the squadron office, where, finding the adjutant in charge, he asked permission to use the telephone for the purpose of getting into touch with von Hymann at the Hotel Port. Permission was given, but not until he had been subjected to a further difficult cross-examination, for it seemed that the adjutant was also under the impression that it was he who had taken the Messerschmitt. However, Biggles satisfied him by referring vaguely to his Gestapo duties, and put the call through to von Hymann.

It was answered by von Stalhein. He announced his name.

Even before his crisp 'Hullo' had faded from the wire Biggles knew that he had made a blunder. Not so much a blunder, perhaps, as an error of judgement. He felt that he should have thought of the possibility of von Stalhein answering the telephone, since, after the bombing of Stavanger, Oslo was the most likely place for him to go to; and in Oslo he would certainly make for Gestapo headquarters.

Biggles realized this now, but up to that moment the possibility had not dawned on him. However, he did not lose his head. He could not afford to do so, for the adjutant was watching him curiously. And for this same reason he dare not dissemble by giving a fictitious name. All he dare do was alter his tone of voice, for unless he did so von Stalhein would recognize it at once. He might do so, anyway.

'This is number 2001,' said Biggles; 'I wish to speak to Oberleutnant von Hymann.'

'Von Hymann is not here. I am answering for him,' returned

von Stalhein curtly. 'What did you say your number was?'

'2001.'

There was a brief pause. Then, 'What is your name?' asked von Stalhein.

'My orders were to use a number only, sir.'

'I am now asking you for your name. What is it?'

'Hendrik—Leutnant Hendrik.' Biggles could almost see von Stalhein's face at the other end of the line.

There was another short pause. 'What game d'you think you're playing? You know I've been looking for you?'

'So I understand, sir, but it seems that we have just missed each other. I was given a job to do by Oberleutnant von Hymann.'

'Where are you speaking from now?'

'From Boda.'

Another pause. 'Indeed! Well, I want to see you, to get details of your adventure in Narvik.'

'You mean about the English spy, Bigglesworth?'

'Yes.' Von Stalhein's voice was little more than a whisper.

'Would you like me to proceed farther with the——'

'No,' interrupted von Stalhein sharply. 'Remain where you are.'

'I'll come to Oslo and report to you if you wish,' offered Biggles, to gain time.

'No, I'd rather come out to Boda. On no account leave the aerodrome until I arrive.'

'Can I expect you—tonight?'

There was yet another pause. 'No, I'm too busy here to leave just now. I'll be along in the morning,' said von Stalhein casually.

'Then I'll wait for you here. Goodnight, sir.'

Biggles hung up, thinking fast. He knew that both he and von Stalhein had been bluffing. No doubt the German had been as taken aback by the call as he had been to hear him answer it. Both had fenced—neither of them could very well do anything else.

'I gather you're not very popular at the moment,' said

the German.

Biggles grimaced. 'It isn't my fault. I wasn't attached to the Gestapo from choice. I'm a pilot. Frankly, the sooner I've finished with this Gestapo business and get on regular flying work the better I shall be pleased.'

The adjutant seemed inclined to be sympathetic. Like most German soldiers he had no love for the Gestapo. 'I'll see what I can do about it,' he promised. 'Meanwhile don't leave the aerodrome.'

'Of course not,' agreed Biggles, and went out.

But he did not go far. He had a suspicion. Whether von Stalhein had recognized his voice or not he did not know, but in any case he would be very, very anxious to see this elusive Norwegian named Hendrik—too anxious to wait until the morning. Biggles knew von Stalhein too well to suppose that he would delay his visit for several hours—time for him to get away. No! It was quite possible that von Stalhein had said that he would not be along that night in order to lull him into a false sense of security. It was far more likely that he would start for Boda forthwith in a fast car.

A minute later Biggles heard the sound he expected to hear. It was the shrill jangle of the telephone. Standing close to the door he heard the adjutant pick up the instrument and answer it. Without straining his ears he could hear the adjutant's end of the conversation.

'You mean Hendrik, sir?' he was saying. 'Yes, he's still on the aerodrome.'

Biggles smiled grimly.

'Did you say arrest him?' continued the adjutant in a surprised voice. 'Of course, sir, if you say so. What is the charge? Leave it until you come—very well, sir. I'll have Hendrik watched, and if he attempts to leave the aerodrome I'll have him arrested immediately. You'll be along in—half an hour. Very good, sir.' There was a clang as the adjutant hung up the receiver.

Biggles waited for no more. With the adjutant about to detail men to watch him, and von Stalhein due to arrive in half an hour, he felt that Boda, from being unhealthy, had become malignant. He walked briskly away into the moonlight, realizing that he was now virtually a fugitive, yet forbidden by his code of honour even to attempt to escape while Algy was there looking for him. Where was Algy?

In sheer desperation Biggles began walking along the boundary of the aerodrome, whistling quietly, aware that now people on the aerodrome were looking for him the very minutes of his freedom were numbered. He broke into a run, and finally, in sheer desperation, called Algy by name. But there was no reply. Sick at heart, he hurried on and completed a circuit of the aerodrome. Looking at his watch he saw that half an hour had elapsed since von Stalhein had rung up. The moon was now high, making it dangerous for him to move about.

Despondent, and hardly knowing what to do next, he made his way to the hangars, taking care to keep within their deepest shadows. Watching, he saw a car coming up the private drive that led from the main road to the clubhouse. Outside the orderly room, which was less than a hundred yards from where he stood, it stopped. A slim figure alighted and moved quickly. It was von Stalhein.

Biggles watched him for a moment with a peculiar smile on his face; then he walked quickly towards the main road. He felt that whatever Algy's predicament might be, no useful purpose could be served by remaining where he was. He could not stay at Boda. If he did, capture was inevitable, and once that happened all hope of helping Algy—or himself for that matter—would be gone. While he remained at large there was still a chance—not a very bright one, admittedly, but a slim chance is better than none at all.

Now in order to reach the main road it was necessary for him to walk across the open moonlit area traversed by the drive. There were no trees, no bushes, nothing to offer cover, for these, as is customary near aerodromes, had been removed to prevent them from becoming obstructions to the movement of aircraft. He had only gone a few yards when there was a shout behind him. Looking back he saw Kristen, running, followed by a car—

von Stalhein's car.

Kristen shouted. 'Hi! Stop! They want you in the office.'

'You're telling me,' muttered Biggles grimly.

He could, he thought, outrun Kristen, but there could be no escape from the car, which had now increased its speed and was fast overtaking him. Seeing that flight could no longer avail him, he drew his pistol and waited. He was in no mood to face von Stalhein's triumph.

As the car drew level a head appeared at the window, and he saw that the driver wore a German uniform greatcoat.

'Can I give you a lift?' said a calm voice, in English.

For a split second Biggles stood transfixed, his lips parted, his expression almost one of idiocy. Then he gulped and flung himself into the car.

The driver was Algy.

'Where would you like to go, sir?' he inquired whimsically, after the manner of a taxi-driver.

'Anywhere,' gasped Biggles, 'but get going and make it fast.'

'Certainly, sir.' Algy swung into the main road and pressed the accelerator flat.

10

ON THE RUN

FOR perhaps a minute neither Biggles nor Algy spoke. As a matter of fact it took Biggles that time to recover from the shock. Then, 'Where the dickens did you spring from?' he inquired.

'Oh, I was just hanging around, you know, in case I was wanted,' returned Algy lightly.

'Where did you get that uniform?'

'It's only a greatcoat. I borrowed it from the souvenir chest of the ship I was in.'

'Oh, yes—I remember now; Ginger told me about it,' nodded Biggles. 'Where did you get this car?'

'It was standing outside station headquarters.'

'You know to whom it belongs?'

'Too true I do. I saw von Stalhein get out.'

Biggles laughed hysterically. 'Strewth! Last night I pinched his plane; now we've got his car. We shall have to drop him a line and thank him for providing us with transport.'

'As a matter of fact,' continued Algy, 'I was hanging around near headquarters hoping to see you—which I did. I saw you break cover and make for the road, and it was obvious that you were in a tight spot. Von Stalhein's car was standing where he had left it, so, knowing how you hate walking, I thought I might as well bring it along.'

'Thanks, laddie,' said Biggles seriously. 'You were just about in time. Things were getting hot—too jolly hot.'

Algy grinned. 'So I gathered. But isn't it time we decided where to go?'

'Ginger's waiting for us in the fiord,' declared Biggles. 'We ought to try to get to him, but I'm afraid we should never get there in this car. Von Stalhein will get on the phone and warn his patrols to be on the lookout for us. Of course, it would take a bit of time to warn everybody, so there's a chance that we might reach Oslo. If we go on at this rate we ought to do it in twenty minutes, and that will hardly be long enough for von Stalhein's crowd to get barricades up. Make for Oslo.'

'And then what?'

'Let's wait until we get there before we decide that. We may have to leave the car and hide, and hiding will be easier in a city than in open country. We'll make for the harbour. There were some flying-boats there the last time I saw the place. For your information, I'm a member of the Gestapo; I mention that because I've got a pass in my pocket which may help us.'

'Will it still work, do you think?' queried Algy. 'Won't von Stalhein take steps to have the bearer arrested?'

'Unquestionably; but with the country in this state it will take a bit of time to notify every German in Norway. Speed now is everything.'

'So you've seen Ginger? What had he got to talk about?'

'He gave me the low-down on everything. Afterwards I sent him to England with some information, and when he came back he brought me over to Boda. He should be back at the fiord now. Unfortunately I got there too late to stop you coming to look for me. Incidentally, in the information I sent back to Raymond I told him about Boda, and suggested that our bombers came over and knocked the place about a bit. That was one of the reasons why I was in a hurry to get out of it.'

'This may be our boys coming now,' put in Algy, peering upwards through the windscreen.

Looking through the window, Biggles saw that the sky was ablaze with searchlights. At a terrific height specks of flame marked the bursts of anti-aircraft gunfire.

'By Jingo! You're right! Those are out fellows,'. declared Biggles. 'They've come at a good moment. When they start dropping their loads on the aerodrome the people there will have something else to think of besides telephoning to Oslo about us.'

'I hope a bomb lands right in von Stalhein's lap,' muttered Algy vindictively.

'That would be a pity,' protested Biggles reproachfully. 'It would take half the interest out of life.'

'It would make life a thundering sight easier,' snorted Algy. 'I'm all for a quiet life, and this is not my idea of it.'

'By gosh! Look at that archie!' broke in Biggles. 'There's a chance that when von Stalhein tried to get through to Oslo he found all the wires engaged, giving air-raid warnings. Hullo! There goes the first crump,' he went on quickly as the flash of an exploding bomb lit up the sky.

'Shall we stop and watch the raid?' suggested Algy.

'Not on your life. I was caught in one at Stavanger last night, and that will last me for a long time. Let's push on to Oslo.'

As they sped down the road Biggles gave Algy a brief account of his adventures since he last saw him at Narvik, and Algy described his, although having talked to Ginger, there was little Biggles did not know.

By the time these notes had been exchanged they were running through the suburbs of Oslo. They were stopped only once, at a cross-roads, but the Gestapo pass worked as usual.

Whether von Stalhein had been unable to get through to Oslo on the telephone, or whether his conversation, or the subsequent arrangements, had been upset by the raid, they did not know, but it was evident that the patrol knew nothing about the car being taken. As far as the occupants were concerned, as both were—or appeared to be—in German uniforms, there was nothing in their appearance to arouse suspicion.

Biggles guided Algy to the port, and thence to the lane from which he had watched von Stalhein and Brandt emerge from Gestapo headquarters.

'This will do,' he said. 'Stop here. It's unlikely that anyone will touch the car. Let's walk.'

They got out of the car, closing the doors, and stood for a moment while they made a quick reconnaissance. Everything seemed quiet. There were a few soldiers about, and two storm-troopers were as usual on duty outside the Hotel Port. Biggles pointed out the building to Algy and told him what it was.

'Never mind about that—where are these 'planes you spoke about?' demanded Algy impatiently. 'I'm getting nervous.'

Biggles's eyes explored the harbour, but not a single machine could he see.

'They're gone,' he said simply.

'What!'

'I'm afraid it's true. The last time I was here there were at least a dozen machines on the water. If it comes to that, there were also far more vessels here then than there are now. Where the dickens have they all gone? Something must have happened. Just a minute—you wait here. I'm going to find out what's going on.'

'How?'

'By walking across to those troops and asking them—or listening to their conversation. I'll also have a good look at the harbour and make sure that there isn't a machine available.' Biggles walked away.

He was gone about ten minutes.

'Here, don't leave me like that again,' protested Algy when he returned. 'I can't speak German like you can, and if I'd been questioned by anybody I should have been sunk. Well, did you find out anything?'

'Yes. It seems that we've landed an expeditionary force—in fact, two or three as far as I can make out. The nearest is just south of Bergen. Another landing has been made at Trondheim.'

'How does that help us?'

'It doesn't, unless we can get to one of those places. But it's worth knowing.'

'Did you find a machine, that's what I want to know?'

'No.'

'So what? We can't stay here. We've got to get some place, and before daylight, too. I'm nearly asleep on my feet, anyway.'

Biggles thought for a moment. 'The question is, dare we use the car?'

'It's risky.'

'There's no doubt about that, but we shan't get far on foot—even when we've decided where to go.'

'How far away is Bergen?'

'The best part of a hundred and fifty miles, but I gather that the landing has been made somewhere south of the actual town, so the distance may not be more than a hundred and twenty or a hundred and thirty miles.'

'That's a long way. How far is it to Ginger—to Fiord 21?'

'About thirty miles farther on to the north. Our nearest point of contact with our people is Bergen. We might try getting through that way. If we can't, we'll go on to Fiord 21. We shall have to go on there sooner or later, anyway, to make contact with Ginger and let him know that we've got clear of Boda; but since Bergen is nearer, we might borrow an aircraft or get someone to run up to the fiord with a message for Ginger.'

'Yes, that sounds the best plan,' agreed Algy.

Biggles nudged him. 'Just a minute. Don't speak while this fellow is going by.'

The man to whom Biggles had referred was in civilian clothes, and Algy assumed, not unnaturally, that he was a Norwegian. With bent head, as if deep in thought, he was walking quickly along the pavement. Not until he drew level with the car did he raise his head and look Biggles in the face.

Recognition was mutual and instantaneous. It was Brandt, the existence of whom Biggles had almost forgotten. He was, no doubt, on his way to his headquarters at the Hotel Port.

The German opened his mouth to shout, but the only sound that passed his lips was a grunt. Biggles's left fist shot out and took him in the pit of the stomach; then, as his head jerked forward, Biggles's right flashed up in a vicious hook to the jaw. Brandt went over backwards; his head came into violent contact with the wall at the back of the pavement, and he lay still. The whole incident occurred in two seconds.

Biggles looked swiftly up and down the lane, then at Algy. 'This fellow knows me,' he said by way of explanation, for Algy, who had, of course, been unaware of this, had stared at the proceedings with amazement. 'We daren't leave him here,' went on Biggles tersely. 'Help me to get him in the back of the car.'

Not without difficulty, for Brandt was a heavy man, they bundled the limp body into the rear seat, from where it slid in a heap to the floor.

'You get in the back and take care of him,' ordered Biggles. 'I'll drive. I know my way about better than you do.'

As he spoke Biggles got swiftly into the driving-seat. Algy jumped in behind. The doors slammed. The car shot out into the road and cruised up the main street.

'Where are you going?' asked Algy.

'We'll stick to our plan and make for Bergen. If we can't make contact with the British force there we'll push on to Fiord 21. I'd go right on to the fiord if I was certain we could get there, but now these landings have been made there's no knowing what we shall run into.'

'What are we going to do with this fellow? Are you going to take him with us all the way?'

'Not on your life. We'll dump him at some lonely place from which it will take him a long time to get into touch with Oslo.'

Biggles drove on into the night, heading north. For twenty

miles he travelled at cruising speed, careful not to attract attention to himself by fast driving; then, reaching a wild stretch of country, he stopped.

'We'll leave Brandt here,' he said quietly.

The German was now semi-conscious. That is to say his eyes were open, but he seemed dazed—as doubtless he was, for the blow he had received on the head was a severe one.

'Gestapo policy would be to bump him off, and so remove all risk of his setting the country on to us,' murmured Algy reflectively.

'Probably you're right, but Gestapo policy isn't ours,' returned Biggles briefly. 'Let's get on.'

Leaving Brandt half sitting, half reclining, against a rock where he would be seen by the first passer-by when daylight came, they re-entered the car and continued their journey.

'We must be getting pretty close to Bergen,' remarked Algy after a long interval of silence.

'It can't be more than ten miles,' replied Biggles.

'If our fellows landed here, then there must be Germans here too,' said Algy thoughtfully. 'Hasn't it struck you as odd that there's no sound of a battle?'

'Yes, there's something funny about that,' agreed Biggles. 'However, we're likely to run into Boche troops at any moment. If we do I'll ask them what's happening.'

Before long they reached the German forces. There was no need to seek them. The car was stopped by a patrol.

Biggles got out, his pass in his hand. 'It's all right,' he said casually. 'We've got orders to keep watch for suspicious characters. What's happening here?'

The German he addressed, a sergeant, did not question his presence there, or his authority. 'It's all over,' he startled Biggles by stating.

'All over—what do you mean?'

'The British have gone.'

'Gone?' Biggles was flabbergasted.

'Yes—we kicked them back into the sea.'

Biggles laughed, but there was little humour in his voice.

'Good work,' he said. 'Well, we'll get on. By the way, we're patrolling the coast northward; will there be any difficulty about getting through?'

'If you keep straight on there may be,' replied the sergeant. 'There are barricades across the road and troops are moving. But if you take the next turning to the right it will take you right out of the battle zone.'

'And it I turn left again farther on will that bring me back to the coast?' Biggles had taken out his map and was looking at in the light of a headlamp.

'Yes, you could do that,' agreed the sergeant.

'Then we'll try it,' declared Biggles, folding the map and putting it back into his pocket. He got into the car and drove on.

'Phew! That was a bit of a bone-shaker,' said Algy in a strained voice. 'I wonder what made our fellows withdraw?'

'It's no use guessing,' returned Biggles briefly. 'We've got to get to Fiord 21 now, or we shall be in a mess. We've got to get there before daylight, too. There is this about it, we're not likely to run into any opposition so far north. You try to get a spot of sleep. Later on you can relieve me at the wheel and I'll have a nap. The worst of these jobs is, one doesn't get time to eat or sleep.'

'Good thing we've had a bit of practice at it,' observed Algy, smiling weakly. He snuggled back in his seat and closed his eyes.

Biggles drove on. He was tired to the point of exhaustion, and it was only by keeping a fierce hold on himself that he prevented himself from falling asleep over the wheel. He seemed to have been driving for an eternity. At last, as the grey of dawn stained the eastern sky, realizing that his endurance was at an end, he stopped the car and nudged Algy, who awoke with a start.

'Take the wheel,' said Biggles. 'I'm about played out.'

They exchanged seats, and Biggles sank back with a weary sigh.

It seemed that he had no sooner closed his eyes than he was being violently shaken.

'Brace yourself,' said Algy tersely. 'We're there—or as near as we can get to the fiord by staying on the road. What had I better do with the car?'

'Anything you like—we shan't need it again,' muttered Biggles. 'Perhaps you'd better drive into that gully just ahead. Nobody's likely to see it there, and it won't give rise to inquiries should the Boche come along.'

Algy obediently drove the car off the road into a narrow gorge, the sides of which were thick with stunted firs. They got out at once, closed the doors and returned to the road. By the time they reached it pink dawn had lighted the wild landscape, enabling them to see for a considerable distance, but to their relief no one was in sight. Some distance to the left lay the sea; nearer, a jagged ridge marked the crest of the cliff that hemmed in the fiord.

'Thank goodness,' ejaculated Biggles. 'If Ginger hasn't got into trouble we're as good as home.'

Walking briskly, they soon reached the ridge. Throwing themselves flat, for it was a nasty drop into the fiord, they looked down. Neither spoke, although Algy hissed through his teeth.

Ginger's machine was not there. But the fiord was not abandoned. On its placid surface floated a squadron of Dornier flying-boats.

11

COMPLICATIONS

Biggles was the first to break the silence. He lay still, staring down into the fiord.

'It looks as if I was not the only one who realized that this fiord would make a useful operating base,' he said bitterly.

'You're dead right there,' agreed Algy, gazing down into the fiord, which presented a scene of lively animation. In addition to the flying-boats there were two store-ships, from which were being unloaded war materials of many descriptions. A large green and brown camouflaged tent had already been erected on the one spot available, and into this the stores were being carried by several men. A little group of pilots sat on the rocks near the machines, smoking.

'What do you suppose became of Ginger?' asked Algy, after he had gazed at the scene for a few minutes.

'We can only guess,' returned Biggles slowly. 'If he was here when this crowd arrived they might have sunk him before he could get off the water. Not necessarily, of course. He would certainly hear them coming, and by acting quickly might have got clear. On the other hand, if he came back and found this lot here, obviously he wouldn't land. From the fact that I can't see any trace of his machine, or any quantity of oil on the water, I'm inclined to think he got away. In that case, knowing that we intended coming here, he'd stick around. There need be no doubt about that.'

'Then where is he now?'

'He might be sitting in another fiord not far away, or he might have gone off to get a load of bombs to knock the daylights out of these Dorniers.'

'The question is, what are we going to do about it?'

Biggles smiled faintly. 'Laddie, there are times when you ask the most difficult questions. I'm dashed if I know what to do for the best, and that's a fact. Personally, I should like to curl up and have a nice long sleep, but this doesn't seem to be either the time or the place for a nap. We're not out here on a pleasure cruise; we're here primarily to gather information about the enemy. If, incidentally, we can make life hard for him, then it's up to us to do it. We ought to let our people know that these Dorniers are sitting here. They've got some scheme on, no doubt. By watching them we may learn what it is. In any case, we daren't go away, because if we do we shall certainly lose touch with Ginger. Sooner or later he'll come back, and our only chance of making contact with him is to remain here. Give me a minute to think.'

Biggles was still squatting among the rocks that lined the rim of the fiord, concentrating hard, when from out of the west came the roar of aero engines.

'There they are,' hissed Algy, pointing to a line of tiny black specks that had emerged from the thin mist that hung over the sea. 'They look as if they're coming straight to this spot.'

By this time Biggles was on his knees, stiff with excitement. 'You're right,' he rapped out. 'They're our boys, too, if I know the sweet song of Merlin engines. By gosh! I've got it. Ginger has fetched them to bomb the place. Keep your head down. This is going to be a warm spot in a minute.'

As they drew near, the machines, which it was now possible to identify as Skuas of the Fleet Air Arm, dived steeply. The Germans, of course, had seen them coming, and everything below was in a state of something like panic. Some of the pilots were getting into their machines. Mechanics ran for cover, or hastily mounted machine-guns. Engines burst into life. Smoke poured from the funnels of the store-ships, but, generally speaking, the Germans had no time to establish an adequate defence.

Lying on the rocks, Biggles and Algy watched the raid with bated breath. In line ahead, the British machines, flying low, swept up the fiord, and as they passed over the German camp a cloud of bombs went down. Spouts of water leapt high into the air, while echoes flung back the thunder of the explosions. After the first salvo the watchers could see nothing, for the fiord was filled with smoke, above which circled the Skuas, dropping the remainder of their bombs, or, when these were exhausted, firing into the rising cloud of smoke with their machine-guns.

Biggles, watching the machines, had no difficulty in picking out Ginger's seaplane, for it kept a little apart from the rest.

'There he is,' he told Algy. 'We've got to attract his attention. He'll be on the watch for us.'

He sprang to his feet, but before he could do anything in the way of making a signal the smoke, rising from the fiord as from the crater of a volcano, hid everything from view.

'Confound the smoke,' snarled Biggles. 'It's going to jigger us. For all we know Ginger may have already spotted us. If he has he'll land on the fiord—or at the entrance to it. I'll tell you what. You stay here in case the smoke clears, in which case he'd be more likely to see you up here than down below. I'll go down to the water to see if he has landed. If he has I'll dash back here and let you know.'

Biggles made for the landslide which, as far as he knew, was the only way down into the fiord. The smoke was still rising, so visibility improved as he went down, and by the time he reached the water level he could see for some distance. He noted that one of the store-ships was in flames; the other appeared to have run aground. At least five of the Dorniers had been wrecked; two had been beached, and the remaining two were taxi-ing at high speed towards the open sea. But he was not concerned with these things at the moment, for Ginger was just landing. As soon as it was on the water the seaplane swung round and roared towards the place where Biggles stood.

Ginger, white with excitement, stood up in the cockpit and yelled, 'Where's Algy?'

'He's waiting on top!' shouted Biggles. 'We weren't sure if you'd spotted us. Stand fast—I'll fetch him.'

Without wasting words, Biggles set off back up the landslide, little guessing what he was to find at the top.

Algy had followed his instructions to the letter; that is, he had remained on the edge of the cliff overlooking the fiord. And, lying there, he distinctly heard Ginger hail Biggles—and, in fact, heard the brief conversation that passed between them. Yet, knowing the danger of departing from a fixed plan, he dared not leave the spot, for the smoke was thick around him, and there was a risk that if he started down the landslide he might pass Biggles without seeing him. If that happened then Biggles would arrive at the top only to wonder what had become of him. What he did was to fling his German greatcoat aside, for it impeded his movements more than a little; at the same time he stood up ready to make a dash towards Biggles the moment he saw him. He heard someone coming, and he thought, not unnaturally, that it was Biggles, although it struck him that there was a lot of noise being made by one person. Then, before he could move, out of the smoke burst a crowd of Germans—a few officers and the rest mechanics. One of the officers was still carrying a sub-machine gun, with which, presumably, he had been firing at the raiders. The instant he saw Algy he covered him.

The whole thing was so unexpected, and had happened so suddenly, that Algy had no time to do anything. Indeed, at that moment he wouldn't have given a fig for his life, for the Germans were wild with excitement, and seemed likely to fire at him anyway. At point blank range they could hardly miss. In the circumstances, self-preservation came first, and Algy probably did the wisest thing he could do. He put his hands up.

Panting, the Germans closed in around him.

'So we got one of you,' said the officer who carried the machine-gun, in fair English.

Algy nodded ruefully. His brain was still in a whirl.

The officer smiled. He appeared to bear Algy no particular animosity. 'Hot work, eh?' he said, as one pilot to another.

'Very hot,' agreed Algy bitterly, wondering what was going to happen next.

At that moment Biggles appeared over the rim of the fiord, not ten yards away. He stopped dead when he saw the crowd, but then came on again. He saw at a glance what had happened—that somehow Algy had got mixed up with fugitives from the raid.

'Hullo, what's all this?' he asked in a queer voice.

'We got one of them,' answered the officer who had spoken to Algy. Then a puzzled expression leapt to his face. 'Where have you come from?' he inquired. 'You weren't one of us.'

As we know, Biggles was in German uniform, but as the officer had remarked, he was not one of the squadron that had been raided. Obviously it was no use trying to pretend that he was.

'I was just flying into the fiord when the British arrived,' he announced calmly. 'There wasn't room to turn. Then the bombs burst and in the smoke I couldn't see a thing. I managed to get down, only to crash against the rocks and sink my machine. After that I did what you evidently did—saw about getting out of the way until the British had gone.'

The German officer laughed. He seemed to be a cheerful sort of fellow. It was obvious that no suspicion of the true state of affairs had entered his mind. Indeed, there was no reason why it should.

'Well, here we are,' he said. 'The British didn't waste any time in finding us and smoking us out.'

Biggles got off this dangerous subject. 'What are you going to do with this prisoner?' he asked—speaking, of course, in German.

'We shall have to take him with us. We can't do anything else.'

'And where are you going—I'm a stranger in these parts myself.'

'So am I,' confessed the officer readily. 'It looks as if we shall have to walk, and try to find a telephone to get in touch with headquarters. I'm afraid there will be trouble about this. We'd got an important assignment.'

'In that case I'll come with you,' said Biggles wearily.

Meanwhile, Ginger, standing in his cockpit down on the fiord, could not understand why Biggles and Algy did not come. Naturally, he expected them down immediately, but when the minutes passed and they still had not come, he realized that something had gone wrong; but what it was he could not imagine. Presently, as the smoke began to clear, a rifle cracked and the bullet zipped through his fuselage. A moment later another whistled unpleasantly close to his head, and looking across the water he saw that the sailors on the store-ship which had run aground were shooting at him. Obviously he could not remain where he was, for he would soon be under the fire of every German who had survived the raid. All he could do was to open the throttle and take off, hoping that from the air he would be able to locate the others and somehow pick them up.

He soon saw them; he also saw the Germans and guessed pretty well what had happened. There was nothing he could do, and when the Germans opened fire on him with rifles and a machine-gun he lost no time in removing himself from such a dangerous position. The other British machines had already disappeared out to sea. For a little while, from a distance, he watched the party walking inland along the edge of the cliff.

Then, feeling utterly helpless, he turned away and headed north.

Biggles and Algy watched him go—without comment, of course, for their attitude towards each other was that of captor and captured. Algy strode along with a mechanic on either side of him. Biggles stayed with the officers. Some were glum; others were cheerful, and, where Algy was concerned, inclined to be sympathetic. They were well able to appreciate his position.

They came to a farmhouse where they stopped, drank milk, and made a frugal meal. The Norwegian to whom it belonged was in no case to refuse what was asked of him. After a short rest they went on to the main road—the same road over which Biggles had passed earlier in the day. And while they were standing on it, undecided which way to go, a motor-cyclist storm-trooper came tearing along. He stopped and dismounted when he saw the party, and was soon told what had happened.

'I shall have to let headquarters know about this,' he declared. 'I'm on the trail of two British spies, and they may have had something to do with the raid. You'd better keep your eyes open for them.'

He actually made this request to Biggles, who promised that if the spies fell into his hands they would have short shrift.

As the motor-cyclist went on Biggles wondered why he had addressed him, and saw for the first time that he was the senior officer of the party, in that he was an Oberleutnant—or wore the uniform of one—whereas the others were only Leutnants. He determined forthwith to take advantage of this, and from that moment more or less placed himself in command of the party.

'I'm by no means sure that we did right in leaving the fiord,' he told the other officers. 'I don't know about you, but I'm by no means clear as to what has happened there. Headquarters may send new machines up, so I'm wondering if, instead of wandering about the country like this, out of touch with everybody, it wouldn't be better for us to go back there.'

What Biggles really wanted was time to think, to form a definite plan. At present he had none, and the appearance of the motor-cyclist made it only too clear that they could not continue for long to move about the country without being arrested. Moreover, the farther they got from the fiord, the farther they were getting away from Ginger, their only contact with home, and their only means of escape. He noted that from time to time squadrons of German planes passed high overhead, all heading northward, and he asked the Germans if they knew the meaning of this.

The senior Leutnant smiled knowingly. 'Haven't you heard?' he said softly.

His manner was so mysterious that Biggles was intrigued. At the same time he was conscious of a disturbing uneasiness.

'No, I haven't heard anything,' he said.

'Then you were not on the same job as us, that's certain.' The Leutnant hesitated, but then went on, confidentially. 'Keep this to yourself,' he whispered, 'but the British North Sea Fleet is sailing into a lovely trap.'

Biggles did not move a muscle. 'How?' he asked.

'Well, to start with, they are going to land troops at Narvik— our Intelligence people know that for a fact. To cover the landing the British Fleet will use, as a base, Westfiord, which is handy. Our spies watched them survey the place for that purpose, and they're heading straight for it now. But what they don't know is this. Since they were there we have been busy. We've stuffed the fiord with magnetic mines until it is as full of them as a pudding is of plums. When the ships sail in there'll be one big bang, and that will be the end of them. Meanwhile, the British troops won't know this. They'll attempt to land at Narvik and then our planes will shoot them to bits. Our machines are concentrating up there now for that purpose.'

Biggles felt a cold hand settle over his heart. He moistened his lips. 'You're quite certain about this fiord, Westfiord, being full of mines?'

'I ought to be,' grinned the German. 'My squadron put them there. That's what we've been doing.'

Biggles smiled—but only with his lips. There was no humour in his eyes, for this staggering piece of news and its deadly significance altered all his ideas. The trap sounded such a likely one, and was so typically Nazi in its conception, that he did not doubt the authenticity of it for a moment.

Algy was standing close enough to hear what had been said but his expression did not change. His eyes met those of Biggles only for a moment, but they held a question.

As far as they were concerned, from that moment escape became of secondary importance. The only thing that mattered was getting a warning to the ships of the Royal Navy engaged in the enterprise, and to the commander of the troops bound for Narvik.

Said Biggles to the Leutnant: 'I believe two of your machines escaped when the raid started. D'you think they'll come back?'

'They're almost certain to, if only to see what has happened,' returned the German without hesitation.

'In that case,' observed Biggles quietly, 'I think we'd better get back there. The machines would at least enable us to get into touch with headquarters.'

'I think you're right there,' agreed the other. 'What about the prisoner?'

Biggles shrugged his shoulders, as if the matter was a minor one. 'It looks as if we shall have to keep him with us—for the time being, at any rate.'

'He may get in the way,' demurred the Leutnant. 'Remember, he's a pilot, so it won't do to let him get near an aircraft.'

Biggles nodded. The last thing he wanted was to be parted from Algy. 'Trondheim is the nearest depot,' he pointed out. 'And that's nearly forty miles away,' he added. 'The only thing we can do with the prisoner for the moment is to keep him with us. If a machine comes into the fiord we may be able to get rid of him then, either by flying him up to Trondheim, or by sending him to Oslo.'

'Yes, that seems to be the best plan,' agreed the Leutnant.

They set off back towards the fiord.

12

DESPERATE MEASURES

It was past midday when they got back to the fiord, to find that it had more or less settled down. There was a fair amount of wreckage floating on the water. One of the store-ships had burnt itself out; the other was still aground, in spite of the efforts of the survivors of both crews to get her off. A little party of airmen, apparently odd members of the squadron that had dispersed when the raid occurred, were sitting or standing about the spot where the store-tent had stood. Biggles noted that, as so often happens, the sailors and the airmen, members of the two services, kept apart from each other, as if they were acting under separate orders—as no doubt they were. Those airmen who had remained at the fiord greeted the return of the others with cheers.

From the top of the landslide, which was the easiest way down to the water, Biggles surveyed the fiord. 'No aircraft have arrived yet,' he observed.

The Leutnant declared that it could only be a matter of time before something, or somebody, arrived, for news of the raid must by then have reached either Trondheim or Oslo, perhaps both. It was a reasonable assumption, and the party made its way to the others on the rocky beach, where the raid was discussed. Algy, under guard, sat a little apart from the others. Biggles, of course, mixed freely with the Germans.

This state of affairs lasted for about an hour, during which time Biggles racked his brains in vain to find a way out of the curious position in which he and Algy now found themselves. Things might, he thought, have been worse. At least he had his liberty, and had it not been for the disquieting information about the trap which had been prepared for the British fleet he would have been content to wait quietly until something turned up. He still felt that his best chance of getting away lay in remaining at the fiord, because Ginger knew that they must be there, or in the vicinity. So there seemed no point in leaving.

Even if he, Biggles, and Algy could get clear, they would only wander about the country without a definite objective. True, there was the car which they had concealed, but he felt that by this time it would be a dangerous vehicle to take on the road. Whether or not word had gone out for that particular car to be apprehended, it would certainly be stopped by every patrol, and with so few roads it would be impossible to get far without encountering patrols. Indeed, Biggles had a shrewd suspicion that a proper hue and cry had been started for them. Brandt, whom they had left by the roadside, and who by now must have been picked up, would probably see to that.

It was, then, with relief that after they had been back in the fiord about an hour Biggles saw a flying-boat approaching. It was a Dornier, and was recognized immediately by the members of the squadron for one of their own. Biggles caught Algy's eye and winked, for this was what he had been waiting for. He resolved that this was the machine that should carry them to safety. There was no other way.

The Dornier landed and taxied up to the beach, where it was made fast by one of the airmen who had walked forward to meet it. The pilot came ashore to be greeted with a volley of questions.

'Where have you been?' asked one of the German officers.

'I dashed down to Oslo to report the raid,' was the reply. 'They sent me back with orders that we are to stand fast here until help is sent. I suppose they will send us new machines.'

Biggles was staring at the pilot in alternate alarm and satisfaction, for it was none other than Schaffer, the officer whom he had first met at Narvik, and who had afterwards flown him to Boda; in fact, it was Schaffer's uniform that he was still wearing. And at that moment, looking round, Schaffer saw him. An extraordinary expression at once crossed his face.

'Hullo, what are you doing here?' he said, moving forward slowly at the same time.

Biggles forced a smile. 'I deserve all you must have thought of me for not returning your uniform,' he said in tones of self-reproach. 'As you see, I'm still wearing it, but to tell the truth I've been so rushed since I last saw you that I haven't had time to see about getting it back to you.'

Schaffer still gazed at Biggles with a peculiar expression on his face. A struggle seemed to be going on inside him.

As for Biggles, he could well imagine what Schaffer was thinking. It is a far cry from being merely suspicious to making a direct accusation; but that Schaffer was suspicious was obvious; or, if not actually suspicious, he felt that there was something odd going on. What Biggles did not know, and perhaps it was as well for his peace of mind that he did not, was the extent of the hue and cry that had been started for him. He did not know that every German agent and every patrol in Norway was looking for him; and this being so, strange rumours were afoot, rumours that had reached the ears of nearly every German in the country, including Schaffer. Unaware of this, although he dimly suspected something of the sort, Biggles did not take it into account. He saw Schaffer hesitating, and had a good idea of what was in his mind. He knew that the German was wondering if he ought to cross-examine him there and then, and perhaps accuse him of being a spy, or wait until he could get through to Oslo and leave this task to those whose specific duty it was to attend to such things.

What Schaffer actually did was to walk a short distance away, taking the other officers with him. These he engaged in earnest conversation, and from covert glances thrown in his direction Biggles knew that he was the object of the discussion. It was quite apparent that even if nothing worse happened, from that moment he was a marked man, and the first false move he made would be quite enough to fan smouldering suspicion into the flame of direct action. He glanced at the machine riding on the water, and then at Algy, wondering if he ought to risk all on a sudden dash for liberty. It was one of those difficult decisions upon which so much might depend. At the finish he decided against the plan, chiefly because there were so many Germans about that to hope for success was to hope for something in the nature of a miracle.

He made a swift survey of the weaknesses in his position, for they were plain enough to see. When Schaffer compared notes with the others—and that was undoubtedly what he was doing at that moment—they would perceive that there was something very odd in the manner in which he had appeared, from nowhere, so to speak. And the same with Algy. Up to now it had been assumed automatically that he was one of the British raiding party, and had been shot down. But what had happened to his machine? No one had seen it fall. There was no crash to mark the spot. Biggles felt that once the Germans started thinking on these lines, and they could hardly fail to do so, his freedom would not last long.

He was not told what the result of the conference was. He was able to form an idea of it, however, when, a few minutes later, he noticed that two of the airmen, armed with rifles, were never far away from him. And when a little while later Schaffer came over and told him, with a nonchalance that was obviously affected, that he was flying to Oslo, and invited him to go with him, Biggles understood the general scheme. Schaffer was not prepared to run the risk of arresting one who might in fact turn out to be a member of the dreaded Gestapo; instead, he would get him to Oslo and put the onus of responsibility for this on someone else.

Biggles answered at once that he would be glad to go. He could not very well do otherwise. Nor dared he hesitate, knowing how thin was the hair on which his freedom depended.

'In that case we'll take off right away,' said Schaffer.

As these words were spoken Biggles saw Algy being taken along the beach towards the supply-ship, which, for want of something better adapted for the purpose, was evidently to be his temporary prison. It was not a very desirable one, for from remarks let drop by the airmen Biggles knew that it was loaded with petrol and ammunition. Indeed, he could see some of the oil drums which had been put ashore to lighten the ship, evidently in the hope that it would float off the rock on which it was aground at the next high tide.

Biggles told Schaffer that he had no kit to collect, so he was ready to move off. He still had a card up his sleeve, and it was this. Schaffer did not know that he was a pilot. The fact that he wore a pilot's uniform meant nothing—at least, as far as the German was concerned, for he knew that it was his own. Biggles hoped, therefore, that he would be able to overpower Schaffer in the air and seize the machine. His chief fear was that other officers might be in it—more than he could deal with.

Great was his relief when, a minute or two later, Schaffer beckoned to him and led the way towards the aircraft, for it was clear that the others were remaining in the fiord.

'Where would you like to sit?' inquired Schaffer.

Not for a moment did Biggles abandon his original pose of quiet assurance. 'Well, I'm a bit nervous of these things, you know,' he said, simulating slight embarrassment. 'If it's all the same to you I'd like to sit beside you.' He had noted that there was side-by-side seating in the Dornier, but only one set of controls.

Schaffer agreed so readily that Biggles became more and more convinced that the last thing the German expected was that he might be attacked in the air. Indeed, if, as he supposed, Biggles was a mere land-lubber, then he had nothing to fear on that score, for no one but a lunatic—or, of course, another pilot—would interfere with a man at the controls of an aircraft.

They took their places. The machine was cast off, and Schaffer taxied out to the middle of the fiord to take off.

'There's a chance that we may run into hostile aircraft,' he announced. 'If we do just sit tight and leave things to me.'

'You bet I will,' promised Biggles. 'I'm afraid I shouldn't be much use.'

Schaffer opened the throttle. The flying-boat sped across the water and rose like a bird into the air. For a little while the pilot held the machine straight, climbing steeply for altitude, and then banked round in the direction of his destination.

Biggles knew that it was not much more than half an hour's flight, so he had no time to lose. No sooner were they out of sight of the fiord than he opened the proceedings by very gently taking Schaffer's revolver from its holster. He had a pistol of his own in his pocket, but he felt that if he disarmed the German as a first precaution it would make his task easier.

He was in the act of putting the revolver into his own pocket when Schaffer happened to glance round. He saw at once what was happening. Fear and anger leapt into his eyes.

'What are you——' he began, but Biggles cut him short.

'I'm sorry, Schaffer,' he said curtly. 'I must ask you to let me have this machine. I should be sorry to have to hurt you, so I hope you'll be reasonable about it.'

Schaffer had turned as white as a sheet. His eyes blazed.

'Then I was right,' he hissed. 'You are a spy.'

'It would be futile to deny it,' admitted Biggles, 'but if I am it is by force of circumstances and not as a result of any desire on my part. Actually, like you, I am a pilot. I was caught in Oslo when the war started and I've been trying to get home ever since. I am now going. Please vacate your seat.'

'I will not,' snarled Schaffer, and abandoning the controls, he flung himself at Biggles in such a fury that Biggles was taken by surprise. Before he could prevent it Schaffer's left hand had caught him by the throat, forcing him back into his seat.

Biggles deliberately kicked the joystick, and then, hooking his leg round it, dragged it back. The machine plunged, and then reared up like a frightened horse. Instinctively the German spun round to right the aircraft, which was in danger of falling into a spin, but Biggles now caught him by the arms, and thrusting his knee in the small of his back, flung him back into the cabin. He then made a dive for the controls to prevent the machine from stalling.

Schaffer went at him again. He appeared to have gone mad.

'Look out, you fool!' yelled Biggles. 'You'll kill us both.'

Schaffer's reply was to hook an arm round his neck.

Now if there is one thing a man cannot do it is fly an aeroplane and fight at the same time. The controls of a modern high-performance aircraft are extremely sensitive, and a movement of an inch of the joystick or rudder is sufficient to throw a machine out of level flight. To any violent movement of the controls an aircraft responds instantly.

In his efforts to free himself Biggles was compelled to release the controls, with the result that the machine was left to its own devices. His aim now was to break clear from the clinch in which Schaffer held him in order to get his hand into his pocket for his pistol. Schaffer knew this, and hung on like grim death. Locked in fierce embrace, they surged up and down the cabin. Still locked, they fell, and rolled towards the tail. Their weight caused the nose to rise, with the result that the machine stalled, and then plunged earthward like a stone. Torn apart by the rush through space, both antagonists were flung against the instrument board. Through the windscreen Biggles saw the rock-bound coast leaping towards them, and realized that if something were not done instantly to check the fall, they were both doomed.

'Wait!' he yelled, and grabbing the joystick, eased the machine out to level flight. It finished only a few hundred feet above the cliffs.

Schaffer, panting with rage and exertion, fingers hooked ready to resume the struggle, waited.

But Biggles had had enough of this sort of fighting. One more bout like the last, now that they had no height to spare, would be the end. Satisfied that the machine was trimmed to fly straight, he whipped out the revolver—which Schaffer appeared to have forgotten—and covered the German.

'One move and I shall have to shoot,' he threatened. 'Believe me, I don't want to have to do that, Schaffer, but if it is to be one or the other of us, it isn't going to be me.'

Schaffer made no answer, so Biggles, still watching him, got more securely into the pilot's seat. He flew with one hand on the control column. The other held the revolver.

'I'm going to land,' he said, snatching a glance at the sea, which looked calm enough for that operation. 'We'll finish the argument in more stable conditions.'

He cut the throttle and began gliding towards the water. After the roar of the engine the silence was uncanny. A more fantastic tableau it would be hard to imagine, and Schaffer evidently realized it, for a peculiar smile crept over his face.

'You English bring your nerve with you,' he conceded.

'No use leaving it at home,' returned Biggles lightly.

Another silence fell, broken only by the whine of wind over the wings.

The flying-boat was still a hundred feet above the water when into the silence burst the vicious clatter of machine-guns. A stream of bullets struck the hull. Glass flew from the instrument board, and splinters of three-ply from the fuselage.

Biggles steepened his dive. It was all he could do, for to examine the sky to locate the attacker would be to invite fresh trouble from Schaffer.

The German, however, was not prepared to submit so tamely. With a mutter of fury he flung open a small chest, of the purpose of which Biggles had been unaware, and dragged out a machine-gun.

Biggles acted with the speed of light. He jerked the throttle open and flung the machine into a vertical bank. Schaffer went over backwards, the gun crashing out of his hands. Biggles left the controls, snatched it up, and then jumped back into his seat. He was only just in time, for the machine, now within fifty feet of the water, was wobbling on the verge of another stall.

Schaffer, who seemed to be slightly dazed by his fall, staggered to his feet as the keel kissed the water. It was a bad landing, not surprising in the circumstances, but Biggles didn't mind. He was only concerned with getting the machine down. The flying-boat surged on to a standstill, while from outside came the roar of an aero-engine.

Looking through a side window, Biggles saw that he had come to rest within fifty yards of the shore, which at that point took the form of a cliff, fringed at the foot by a strip of sand. Opening the throttle a little, he turned the machine nearer to it.

'Can you swim?' he asked Schaffer grimly.

'Yes.'

'Then get going—it isn't far.'

Schaffer hesitated, but another burst of fire, which struck the machine aft, seemed to decide him.

'I shall be interested to watch the outcome of the argument between you and your countryman,' he said bitingly. 'We shall meet again.'

'Perhaps,' smiled Biggles. 'If we do I hope it will be after the war. Look me up at the Aero Club, and I'll stand you a dinner in return for the use of your uniform.'

Schaffer nodded curtly and jumped into the water.

Seeing that it only came up to his armpits, Biggles flicked the throttle away towards more open water. From time to time above the roar of his engine he could still hear the harsh tattoo of machine-guns. He was soon in a position to take off, but before doing so he looked out to ascertain the nature of the machine that was attacking him. He knew, of course, that it must be a British machine, and assumed that it was either a patrolling formation of the Fleet Air Arm, or a lone scout. Curiously enough, the truth never occurred to him.

He gasped when he saw the machine overhead, for he recognized it at once. It was Ginger's seaplane.

13

FRESH PLANS

To say that Biggles was shaken would be to put it mildly, yet on second thoughts he perceived that the fact that Ginger was in the other machine made little or no difference to the situation. He could not hope to be recognized at the distance which separated the aircraft even if he showed himself, and Ginger would naturally take him for an enemy. His problem was how to get away, for he could not engage in a fight with a British plane.

With his heart in his mouth, he proceeded to take off, for while he was doing so he was at a big disadvantage. However, as soon as he was off the water he held the machine down and looked back to see what Ginger was doing. He was not surprised to see him swooping down on his tail. And that was not all Biggles saw. High up behind Ginger's machine was a line of black specks, specks that grew larger even as he watched them. There was no need to look twice to see what was happening; it was all too plain. Ginger, intent only on his quarry, had allowed himself to be surprised by a German patrol, and it was obvious from the way he was flying that he was still blissfully unaware of it.

Biggles groaned. He felt that the situation was beyond him. It had been bad enough before the Boche machines appeared, but now it was so complicated that he almost abandoned hope of finding a solution. It came to this. By some means or other he had to prevent himself from being shot down by Ginger; at the same time he had to warn Ginger of what was happening behind his tail. To achieve this difficult object the only thing he could do, he decided, was to place himself between the seaplane and the German formation; then in looking at him Ginger would—or should—see his danger. After that he would have to rely on his own resources.

Things did not pan out as he had planned, however. He could see that he would fail, even before the worst happened, for by the time he had zoomed high preparatory to getting behind the seaplane, the German machines had closed in and had launched their attack.

Ginger at once half rolled, a manoeuvre which told Biggles that he had perceived his danger. The rest was more or less a foregone conclusion, for the newcomers were Messerschmitt 110's, and there were eight of them. Ginger, abandoning the Dornier, now did his best to get away, but the seaplane was outclassed, as well as outnumbered.

Sick at heart, Biggles landed to watch the end of the affair, for there was nothing he could do. White-faced, he threw open the cockpit cover and stared up at the circling machines. It could hardly be called a combat. Time and time again the Messerschmitts darted in at their prey, their guns spurting flame, and the great wonder to Biggles was that Ginger could hang on for so long. But the end came at last. A Messerschmitt came down on the tail of the luckless seaplane. Ginger swung round and pulled up his nose to meet it, but the next instant black smoke was pouring from his engine. The seaplane at once went into a steep slide-slip towards the sea, but while it was still two thousand feet above it flames licked out through the smoke. Ginger appeared. For a moment he stood poised on the fuselage.

Then he jumped clear.

For a thousand feet he dropped like a stone, slowly turning over and over as he fell. Then a white ribbon flashed above him. It grew longer, and then his fall was checked as the parachute blossomed out.

A great gasp of relief burst from Biggles's lips as he dropped back into his seat. He pushed the throttle open, and in a moment was taxi-ing at dangerous speed towards the area where he judged Ginger would fall. There was a splash of foam as Ginger struck the sea.

Biggles reached the spot within a minute, but all he could see was the parachute fabric spreading out like an enormous jellyfish on the surface of the water. It was the work of a moment to cut the throttle, reach over the side and seize the shrouds. He seemed to be hauling for an eternity before Ginger appeared, puffing and blowing like a grampus.

Biggles never forgot the expression on Ginger's face as he dragged him into the machine and relieved him of the parachute, allowing it to fall back into the sea. Ginger collapsed in a heap on the floor of the cockpit. He was too far gone to speak. He could only gasp and get rid of vast quantities of sea water.

For a moment Biggles let him lie there. He wanted to get rid of the Messerschmitts, which were still circling round like a pack of hungry wolves. It was not a difficult matter. He merely climbed up on his centre-section and waved his arms, a signal which he hoped would be construed by the Germans as thanks for saving him, and at the same time to convey to them that their assistance was no longer needed. Apparently the Messerschmitt pilots read the signal that way, for they at once reformed in formation and sped away to the south. Happening to glance towards the shore, a bare half mile away, Biggles saw a solitary figure standing on the edge of the cliff that frowned down on the strip of beach. He knew it could only be Schaffer, who must have chosen this grand-stand to watch the end of the affair.

Biggles waved a friendly greeting.

Schaffer waved back, and disappeared over the brow of a hill.

'Who the deuce are you waving to—Algy?' panted Ginger, dragging himself into a sitting position and wringing the water out of his hair.

'No—a friend of mine,' replied Biggles. 'A German named Schaffer. Not a bad chap when you get to know him. This is his uniform I'm wearing; and, incidentally, this is his machine. He'll have a tale to tell when he gets home.'

'By thunder! He's not the only one!' declared Ginger weakly, but with heavy sarcasm. 'So it was you I was trying to shoot down,' he added.

'Yes. Of course, you would have to choose me.'

'I was in the right mood to shoot down anybody,' declared Ginger.

'Are you hurt?'

'No, but I'm wet and I'm cold, to say nothing of being tired and hungry,' announced Ginger. 'What about going home? I'm fed up with this. For the love of Mike, what's going on here, anyway? Where's Algy?'

'The Boche have got him. He's a prisoner in a store-ship in the fiord.'

'I thought I'd cleared that bunch out,' swore Ginger furiously.

'You didn't do so badly,' grinned Biggles. 'One of the ships ran aground. The Boche have gone back there now, but they've no aircraft—at least, they hadn't any when I left. This was the only one, so I borrowed it. Schaffer decided to take me down to Oslo to find out just who I was; at least, that was the intention, but on the way down we had a little dispute as to who should do the flying—and I won.'

'So what?' demanded Ginger.

'There are two things we've got to do, and there's no time to be lost.'

'Is that all?' sneered Ginger. 'The last time I saw you there was only one thing to do, which was to get Algy out of Boda. Now there are two things. At the rate we're going there will soon be three.'

'I shouldn't be surprised,' sighed Biggles.

'Well, what are these things we've got to do?' demanded Ginger.

'First, get a message to the Admiralty. Second, get Algy out of the clutches of the Nazis.'

'Okay, go ahead,' invited Ginger. 'I can't think any more.'

'I'm afraid you'll have to try,' returned Biggles seriously, and described the trap into which the British fleet was steaming.

'What d'you suggest?' queried Ginger.

'We've got to move fast,' Biggles told him. 'Schaffer is ashore, and while he's got some way to go I expect he'll make for the fiord. We shall have to part company again. You put me ashore somewhere near the fiord, and then go on and warn the fleet about the trap. I'll try to get hold of Algy.'

'How am I going to get near the fleet in this swastika-painted kite? They'll shoot me to bits as soon as I show up.'

'That's a little problem you'll have to work out for yourself,' declared Biggles. 'But I think your best plan would be to locate the fleet, and then land on the water somewhere ahead, with your prop stopped. They won't shoot at you if they think you're disabled, and they'll certainly pick you up. Tell the skipper about the trap and ask him to send word to the troop transports.'

'Good enough,' agreed Ginger. 'Where shall I put you ashore?'

'Fly along the coast for about twenty miles; then anywhere will do.'

'And what are you going to do? I mean, how shall I get in touch with you again?'

'I shall make for the fiord and try to make contact with Algy. You'll have to come back and pick us up. You should have no difficulty in getting hold of a machine—you might even go on using this one. If I get Algy away we shall stick to the coast. You'll have to try to spot us; there's no other way. We'll make a smoke signal if we can. Now get going, or it will be dark, and then you'll have a job to find our ships.'

The sun was in fact sinking fast towards the horizon as Ginger took off and headed north, keeping close to the coastline. After a flight of ten minutes he landed again, near the entrance to a tiny fiord, into which he taxied.

'This will do fine,' announced Biggles.

'Suppose someone sees you go ashore?' queried Ginger.

'It won't matter, since I'm landing from a German machine, and in a German uniform,' Biggles pointed out, as Ginger taxied to a natural wharf so that Biggles could land dry-shod.

Biggles clambered up on the rocks. 'So long,' he called. 'Don't forget that everything depends on you now.'

Ginger waved. 'I'll get through,' he promised, and turned towards the open sea.

Biggles watched him take off, and then, making his way to the top of the cliff, he turned towards Fiord 21.

Ginger headed north-west, scanning the ever widening area of sea that became visible as he climbed higher and higher. It may seem strange that it had not occurred to him that he might be unable to find the ships he sought, but then it must be remembered that he was aware of their objective, and assumed that they would be steaming straight towards it; moreover, prior to his making contact with Biggles, his ship had actually been operating with the fleet, so he knew where it was at that time.

It was not until he had been flying for nearly an hour, by which time sea and sky had merged in a mysterious twilight, that doubts began to assail him, doubts that sharpened quickly to alarm as his petrol gauge fell back and neither ship nor 'plane broke the loneliness that surrounded him. In something like a panic he climbed higher in ever increasing circles. He could still see the rim of the sun, a slip of glowing gold, but he knew that it was invisible to those at sea level where purple shadows, fast darkening to sullen indigo, were obliterating the gently heaving water. With sinking heart he flew on, nursing his engine until the inevitable happened. It back-fired as the petrol supply dried up; then it stopped altogether, and he had no alternative but to drop his nose and begin a long glide towards the sea. When, finally, he was compelled to land, he was in the grip of a despair such as he had seldom known. It was aggravated by a sense of impotence. He felt that he had let Biggles down; that he had let everyone down. Too late he realized that the last thing the fleet would do was to sail directly towards its objective.

There was absolutely nothing he could do except climb on to the centre-section and stare dumbly into the leaden darkness that surrounded him. Except for a gentle slap of wavelets against the hull of his machine, silence reigned. Fortunately for him the sea was calm, but he had no guarantee that it would remain so, and he was well aware that should the wind freshen, bringing with it a heavy sea, then his frail craft, with no means of maintaining headway, would quickly break up. Not that he thought very much about this; he was far too concerned over the failure of his mission.

How long he sat there he had no idea; he lost all count of time; but he reckoned that it was approaching midnight when he heard a distant sound that set the blood coursing through his veins. The sound was faint, but there was no mistaking it; it was the dull methodical beat of a heavy engine, but whether it was made by a British ship or a German Ginger had no means of knowing. The sound grew louder as the minutes passed, implying that the vessel was approaching, but as it showed no lights he was as yet unable to see it. He was showing no lights, either; nor, for that matter, had he any to show; so he was well aware that unless the vessel passed within hailing distance he would not be seen. The question that now arose, and he felt that it was a vital one, was this. Should he hail, or should he not? It he did, and the vessel turned out to be British, then all would be well; on the other hand, if it proved to be a German, then the worst would have happened. He decided to take the risk, for since there were more British craft than German on the North sea, he felt that the odds were in his favour.

A squat, bulky ship took shape in the darkness, not more than a cable's length away. Evidently the look-out did not see him, for it ploughed straight on without altering course, chugging into the darkness of the night on its unknown mission. Drawing a deep breath, and cupping his hands round his mouth, he let out a hail.

It was answered immediately.

'Ahoy there! Who are you?' came a voice—in English.

Ginger fairly gasped with relief. 'Friend!' he yelled back. 'I'm in an aircraft, on the water. I've run out of fuel.'

'Stand by while we come about,' sang the unseen sailor.

A bell rang and the black hull slowed down, churning the water as it swung in a wide curve. In a few minutes it was alongside, and Ginger could just see a knot of figures near the rail discussing him in low tones. He heard someone say, 'Blimey! Look out, it's a Jerry bus.' Whereupon he called out that the machine was, in fact, a German 'plane in which he had been trying to escape, but had landed on account of fuel shortage.

No doubt his voice did much to prove his assertion, and he was soon taken aboard what turned out to be a British armed trawler, under the command of a naval officer. The aircraft having been taken in tow, Ginger was led to a cabin, where he explained his plight to two keen-faced officers, one of whom was the captain. To them, hardly pausing for breath, he poured out his story, laying particular emphasis on the trap that had been laid in Westfiord for the British fleet. He also described the base which the Germans had established in Fiord 21, and mentioned the store-ship that was still there.

When he had finished he was given some refreshment while the naval officers withdrew to confer. 'Whatever you do you must stop the fleet,' he told them desperately. 'I suppose you've got wireless?'

'We have, but we're under sailing orders,' replied the captain. 'What's more, we're only supposed to use our radio in case of dire emergency. It's dangerous. The enemy can pick a message up as well as our people, don't forget.'

'But you've got a code.'

'Yes, we have,' admitted the naval officer, who seemed to be rather worried.

And that is all Ginger was told. The officers departed and a steward brought into the cabin a square meal, which pleased Ginger not a little, for he felt that he could now safely leave things to the Navy. Somehow or other they would do what was required. What he himself was going to do he did not know. Engrossed in his meal, and thinking of the present rather than of the future, he had not even considered this aspect when he was flung across the cabin by a fearful explosion which took him completely unawares. Instantly all the lights went out.

As he picked himself up he heard shouts on the deck above, and other noises which convinced him in a vague sort of way—for he was took shaken for lucid thought—that the ship had blown up. His meal forgotten, he made his way—not without difficulty for the trawler had taken on a heavy list—to the deck. He realized that some sailors near him were lowering a boat, but the darkness was such that he could see nothing distinctly; nor could he make out what was happening. The trawler lurched again, and almost before he was aware of his danger water was swirling round his legs. A sailor hurried past him shouting, 'Swim for it, boys!'

Ginger would have asked him what had happened, but before he could do so the man had disappeared into the darkness. He moved forward, only to fall over that turned out to be a pile of lifebelts. Not knowing the ship, he had no idea where he was. There was no confusion; occasionally he saw forms in the gloom, but beyond the fact that the trawler was sinking he could not get a grasp on the situation. All he could see fairly clearly were the upper works of the vessel; they were leaning over at an angle so acute that they made him feel giddy. The doomed vessel lurched again, causing a great hissing of steam, and he realized that if he were to avoid being sucked down in the vortex, the sailor's advice to 'swim for it' was not to be ignored. Sliding across the deck, he jumped blindly into the sea, and as soon as he came to the surface he started swimming as fast as he could to place as great a distance as possible between him and the vessel. He could still see nothing, but there were shouts in the darkness around him. They sounded strangely unreal.

Whether he swam into the submarine, or whether it rose up under him, he never knew. He was suddenly aware of a black bulk right beside him, and, instinctively, he tried to climb on to it; but his clawing fingers could get no grip on the smooth metal. After that the whole thing became a nightmare. He didn't know what was happening and he didn't much care. The fact was that exhaustion and shock had reduced him to a state of semi-consciousness. In a dreamy sort of way he was aware of hands clutching at his jacket, and dragging him up. What happened after that he did not know.

14
TRAPPED!

AFTER he had watched Ginger out of sight Biggles made his way cautiously to the fiord. It took him some time to reach it, and if he had entertained any doubts about its still being occupied they were dispelled even before he reached the rim. Judging from numerous voices, and a certain amount of hammering, it sounded as if salvage work was in progress.

From the edge of the cliff, which by this time he knew well, he looked down; but all was shrouded in darkness, and except for a cluster of lights near the stranded store-ship, whence came the noise of hammering, he could see nothing. It was towards this ship that Algy had been led, so he assumed—and hoped—that he would be in it. All his plans for rescue depended on that one fact. If Algy was not there, then he would not know where to look for him; but if he had been confined in the ship, then one factor was in his favour. He had not failed to note that the airmen and the sailors went about their work almost unmindful of each other, so there seemed a reasonable chance that, although the German airmen had been informed by Schaffer of his suspicions concerning Biggles's real identity, the sailors knew nothing about it. After all, he thought, as far as the officers of the air squadron were concerned, he, Biggles, was by this time safely lodged in Oslo; and there appeared to be no reason why they should discuss the matter with the sailors. If that were so, then the sailors would know nothing about him. They would not know him by sight even if they saw him, and they certainly would not be prepared for an attempt to rescue their prisoner.

Biggles made his way down the landslide without any great difficulty, but took no chances and moved with extreme caution.

Having reached the water-level, he then had to make his way along it to the rock on which the ship was beached. Fortunately it lay between him and the airmen's camp, so he was saved the difficult business of getting through that. Looking along the beach, he could just make out the silhouette of a Dornier flying-boat riding at anchor a few yards from the shore, and he noted its position carefully.

What concerned him now was the fact that the ship lay a short distance out—perhaps thirty or forty yards. In order that the sailors could get to and fro, an improvised gangway, consisting of a number of planks, had been erected. This gangway was in constant use, and on the face of it, it appeared to be out of the question to get on board without coming face to face with some of the sailors. Admittedly, he was wearing a German officer's uniform, so there was a chance that the seamen would take no notice of him. Even if he were questioned, he thought, he might be able to bluff his way through. Nevertheless, this involved a certain amount of risk which would be better avoided if it were possible. After considering the problem for a little while he decided he would only use the gangway if he could find no other means of getting on board.

Moving nearer, he was delighted but not altogether surprised to see on the water, close to the narrow strip of beach, a small collapsible canoe, of the sort used by the marine branch of the German Air Force; that is to say, it was of the pneumatic type, to be inflated when required. Such boats were standard equipment in all German sea-going aircraft. Evidently it had been required for some purpose, presumably to enable the sailors to get to and from the ship without using the gangway—or else to enable them to examine the far side of the ship from water-level. Biggles felt that if he could secure this useful craft without being observed it would serve his purpose admirably.

The fact that it was dark simplified his task; and that the sailors were too concerned with their respective duties to notice what others were doing, was another factor in his favour. So, taking every opportunity when the coast was clear, he worked his way along the beach, drawing ever closer to his objective, until at last he slipped quietly into the frail craft and pushed himself clear. Any noise that he made, and it was negligible, was drowned in the hammering that was still going on. Picking up the paddle, he worked his way round to the far side of the ship— that is, the side farthest from the shore, and from which, of course, he could not be seen from the beach. Here he felt comparatively safe, and he experienced that thrill of satisfaction which comes when a difficult job has been well begun.

The next step was to discover, if possible, the cabin in which Algy was confined. That it would be fitted with a porthole he felt sure, but even so there was no indication of the side of the ship it would be on. He had simply gone to the far side first because it presented less danger than the near side. If he could locate Algy, then he would have to go aboard to seek him, trusting in his uniform, or the Gestapo pass, to carry him through if he were questioned.

He spent nearly half an hour working up and down the side of the vessel, trying each porthole in turn, peeping into those that were open and tapping on the glass of those which were not. But it was all in vain, and finally he was compelled reluctantly to conclude that Algy must be on the other side of the ship; either that or in a central hold unprovided with any direct communication with the outer air. It was clear that no further progress could be made unless he actually went on board the ship, and this he now determined to do. A rope ladder hung conveniently—too conveniently he afterwards realized—from the rail, and up this he now proceeded. As his eyes drew level with the deck he looked around. Not a soul was about. In a moment he had swung a leg over the bulwarks and was aboard. A ventilator offered a handy hiding-place, but he had not taken more than two paces towards it when a voice spoke.

'Welcome on board, Major Bigglesworth,' it said mockingly.

Biggles spun round. And that was all he could do, for menacing him from half a dozen places were as many weapons. He could not distinguish the features of the man who had spoken, but he recognized the voice only too well; it was that of von Stalhein.

The German stepped forward. 'We were expecting you,' he said suavely.

'And just why were you expecting me?' inquired Biggles.

Von Stalhein laughed softly. 'With Lacey here, a prisoner, it was obviously only a question of time before you arrived.'

Biggles perceived the truth of this assertion, and bit his lip in vexation.

'I was so sure that you'd come,' continued von Stalhein pleasantly, 'that I arranged for a boat to be convenient, and for a rope ladder to enable you to get aboard. So you see, Major Bigglesworth, we can do a little planning—as well as you.'

'You've been so slow about it this time that I'd almost forgotten it,' rejoined Biggles smoothly. 'I'll be more careful on future occasions.'

'It is unlikely that there will be any future occasions,' said von Stalhein softly.

'I seem to have heard you say that before, too,' Biggles told him.

'Quite right,' admitted the German frankly, 'but we all learn from experience—or we should. As far as you are concerned, I'm afraid the opportunity has passed. Hitherto it has always been a source of irritation to me that at least one of you was at large, even although I held the other two; but at last, as was bound to happen sooner or later, I have you all in the net together. You cannot imagine the satisfaction that it gives me.'

Biggles did not understand. He knew, of course, that Algy was a prisoner, but von Stalhein spoke as if he held Ginger, too, and that, surely, was impossible. He suspected a trap, and was careful to be non-committal in his reply. 'Congratulations,' was all he said.

'Ah, I see there is a doubt in your mind,' continued von Stalhein imperturbably. 'A doubt about our young friend with the difficult name—Hebblethwaite. You will be sorry to learn that he has had a piece of bad luck.'

'Really?' Biggles was still taking no chances of giving information away.

'Yes,' went on the other, fitting a cigarette into a long holder.

'He had the misfortune to fall into the sea, where he would certainly have drowned had it not been for the timely arrival of one of our submarines, which rescued him. The commander of the submarine that picked him up signalled to his base for instructions, so, naturally, as the boat was not far away, I asked for him to be brought here. Presently you will all be together, when you will be able to compare notes, and ascertain, perhaps, how and where your plan went wrong.'

Biggles did not know whether to believe him or not, but it was not like the German to lie over such a matter; there appeared to be no point in it; moreover, there was a ring of confidence in his voice that made the statement sound like the truth. Biggles realized that such a state of affairs as the one von Stalhein had described might easily have come to pass.

'You certainly seem to hold all the cards,' he conceded. 'What are you going to do about it?'

Von Stalhein ignored the question. 'How would you like to have a chat with Lacey?' he suggested.

'Thanks.'

'I am sorry Hebblethwaite is not here yet, but his arrival cannot be delayed long. When he comes I'll send him down to join you. I'm sure he will be overjoyed to see you again, even though, of course, the reunion will be for a short time only. I am very busy at the moment, as you will readily believe, but I can give you until the morning to write any messages that you may wish to send home. Colonel Raymond, for example, will doubtless be anxious to hear how it all came about—unless he is too overwhelmed by the disaster which by that time will have overtaken the British naval forces operating on the Norwegian coast. With your admirable knack of learning things, no doubt you have heard about the little surprise we have in store.'

'Mind your scheme doesn't go off in your hand and burn your fingers,' warned Biggles coolly. 'The ships aren't in the fiord yet.'

He spoke mockingly, but his heart was sick, for if what von Stalhein had said was indeed true, and there seemed little reason to doubt it, then he could not imagine how the fleet could escape.

Von Stalhein went on. 'After your recent feverish activities—carried out, I must confess, with your customary initiative and zeal—you must be weary. Come below and join Lacey. Oh, we'd better have that pistol of yours, if you don't mind.'

Biggles had no alternative but to hand over the weapon. To attempt to use it at this juncture would have been suicidal, for he was still covered by half a dozen weapons at point-blank range. Having handed it over, he proceeded with an escort down the companion-way.

As he had already begun to suspect, the cabin in which Algy was confined turned out to be in the middle of the ship. Light was admitted during the day through a heavy glass skylight in the deck immediately overhead. An armed sentry was on duty outside the door.

Von Stalhein opened it and went in. The cabin was lighted by a single unprotected electric-light globe. 'A friend of yours to see you,' he said, with just a trace of cold humour in his voice.

Algy was sitting on a bunk, but he jumped up when he saw Biggles. 'Hullo! I expected you'd be along,' he said cheerfully.

Von Stalhein screwed his monocle into his eye. 'This is a picture I've always wanted to see,' he remarked softly. 'Well, I shall have to leave you now. Make the most of your time. The fiord will be abandoned first thing in the morning, but as our accommodation is limited you will not be coming with us.'

'Quite so,' answered Biggles calmly.

'Your young friend will be joining you shortly,' promised von Stalhein, and went out.

The door was bolted on the outside, and the sentry resumed his pacing up and down.

Biggles seated himself on the bunk. 'So here we are,' he murmured.

'How did it happen?' asked Algy—referring, of course, to Biggles's capture.

'I was trying to get to you, but unfortunately von Stalhein anticipated the move and was waiting for me. I should have come anyway, of course.'

'I was afraid of that,' said Algy sadly. 'I suppose he told you about Ginger being captured?'

Biggles nodded.

'D'you think it's true?'

'I'm afraid it is. I don't see what purpose he could have in lying to us.'

'How did they get hold of him, I wonder?'

'We got together during the day,' explained Biggles. 'You saw me take off with Schaffer? As soon as we were in the air I grabbed the machine. Ginger was hanging about outside the fiord, and in trying to shoot us down got shot down himself. I picked him up, and then came ashore while he went off in the machine to look for the fleet. Presumably he was shot down, or ran out of petrol; anyway, he must have found himself on the water, and was picked up by a U-boat. It's this business of the fleet that upsets me more than anything.'

'He might have got through to it.'

Biggles shook his head. 'I doubt it. If he did, it's unlikely that he would have been captured.'

'He might have delivered the message and then started back to pick us up, hoping that we'd got away.'

There's just a chance of that,' agreed Biggles, 'but somehow it doesn't strike me as being the answer. If he was picked up by a U-boat, then he must have been in the water, and had all been well he wouldn't have been in that position.'

Algy shook his head. 'I still think he might have been prowling about the coast looking for us, and ran into trouble.'

'It's no use guessing,' declared Biggles. 'No doubt he'll tell us how it happened when he arrives—not that it matters very much now. Von Stalhein has got us in a nasty jam, and it would be foolish to deny it. Still, it isn't the first time.'

'I gather from what he told me that he intends to—er—dispose of us in the morning.'

'That, I imagine, is his idea,' returned Biggles. 'But it isn't mine. Morning is a long way off. Let's have a look round to see if there's any way out of this den.'

'There isn't—I've looked,' returned Algy promptly.

'Jack Shepherd once asserted, and on more than one occasion proved, that neither bolts nor bars will hold a man if he is determined to get out. There's always a way—if you can find it. Let's try.'

They made a complete survey of the cabin, and were soon forced to admit that escape appeared to be a hopeless proposition. There were only two exits. One was the door, which was bolted and guarded by a sentry. The other was the skylight in the deck, which they had no means of reaching; in any case it seemed to be fastened from the outside. For the rest, a glance was enough to reveal the futility of trying to make any impression on the heavy, hard-wood timbers of which the ship was built. It would have been difficult enough with proper tools, and they had nothing remotely resembling a cutting instrument. Nor was there a fitment of any sort that could be removed and used as a weapon. There was a bunk at one end of the cabin, but like everything else it was stoutly built and offered no solution to the problem. There was a mattress in it, together with a rather dirty sheet and an old brown blanket. Biggles looked at them reflectively for a moment or two and then turned back to Algy.

'I agree with you in this respect,' he said. 'There's only one way out of this room, and that's the way we came in—through the door.'

'It's not likely to be opened.'

'On the contrary, it will be opened when Ginger arrives.'

'Yes, but he'll have an escort of at least two or three armed men with him. We're hardly in a case to take them on with our bare fists.'

'By the time they arrive we ought to have something better than bare fists,' asserted Biggles. 'After all, we have this advantage. We know that the worst that can happen is that we shall be shot, and as we shall be shot in any case if we don't get away, we've nothing to lose if we fail.'

'Really, they've absolutely no right to shoot us,' protested Algy.

'What von Stalhein has a right to do, and what he does, are two entirely different things,' returned Biggles smiling. 'If he needs an excuse for treating me as a spy, he's got one in this Boche uniform I'm wearing. But we're wasting time. I'm going to see about getting out.'

'What, now?'

'Certainly. There's only one sentry on duty. We'll tackle him first.'

Biggles took up a position immediately under the electric lightbulb. 'Switch off the light,' he ordered. 'I don't want to electrocute myself.'

Algy crossed to the switch and turned off the light. He heard the sound of a jump, followed by a splintering noise. 'What on earth are you doing?' he muttered.

'It's all right, I've got what I wanted,' answered Biggles. 'It's the electric flex.' As he spoke he removed the bulb from the end.

'What are you going to do with that wire?'

'I'll show you. What I want you to do now is lie here, just inside the door, and groan. When the sentry comes in he's bound to look at you—enough light will come in from the corridor for him to see you. I shall then proceed to throttle him with the noose I'm making in this flex. All right, go ahead with the groaning; I'm ready and we've no time to waste.'

Algy did as he was told, and his groans echoed pitifully in the little cabin. Biggles waited until he heard the sentry's footsteps approaching and then hammered on the door.

The sentry stopped. 'What is it?' he demanded.

'My friend is ill—I think he's dying,' answered Biggles, and Algy's groans seemed to confirm his statement.

A key scraped in the lock, and the German looked in, bayonet at the ready. It was obvious from his attitude that he was taking no risks. 'What's happened to the light?' he asked, glancing up.

'It went out,' replied Biggles vaguely.

The sentry looked at Biggles, who was standing in a passive, dejected attitude, and then took a pace nearer to Algy, who was curled up on the floor, still groaning. He leaned towards him. 'What's the matter with you?' he asked gruffly.

Biggles jumped like a cat, slipped the noose over the man's head, and in a single jerk pulled it taut round his bare throat, cutting short the cry that rose to his lips. The rifle clattered to the floor as instinctively he clutched with both hands at the wire which was throttling him.

'Shut the door,' snapped Biggles.

Algy jumped to the door and closed it.

Biggles forced the sentry to the floor. 'Keep still or I'll choke you,' he snarled. Then to Algy. 'Get that sheet. Tear it into strips and tie him while I hold him.'

The sentry made no resistance. Indeed, as he was already nearly dead, he was in no condition to do so.

'Buck up,' urged Biggles. 'I don't want to kill the wretched fellow.'

For a minute or two, after he had loosened the wire, he really thought he had killed him, for the man's eyes were projecting and his tongue hanging out. His body was limp. However, by applying artificial respiration they restored him, after which Biggles relieved him of his jacket and trousers. This done, he was securely bound and gagged, and lifted into the bunk. The blanket was spread over him.

'Why all this performance?' queried Algy. 'There's nothing to prevent us making a bolt for it, is there?'

'You seem to have forgotten Ginger,' Biggles reminded him. 'We can't go without him. From now on I'm the sentry.' As he spoke Biggles threw off his officer's uniform and put on that of the soldier. 'You stay here and keep an eye on Fritz,' he ordered. 'I'm going outside.'

'I get it,' answered Algy, as Biggles picked up the rifle and went out into the corridor.

'All clear,' he whispered; then he locked the door and took up the sentry's duties.

It was clear that everything now depended upon Ginger's early arrival, for should this be delayed a dozen contingencies might arise to betray the plot. The sentry might be relieved; von Stalhein might come and recognition follow; the N.C.O. in charge of the guard might come along and perceive that the sentry was not the man he had posted. Still it did not occur to Biggles to leave the boat without Ginger. The minutes ticked by.

All seemed quiet. The men who had been working outside had evidently been dismissed.

15

THE LAST ROUND

I⊤ was a good half-hour before Biggles heard with satisfaction the sound that he had so anxiously awaited; it was the tramp of feet coming up the gangway. There was a challenge; it was answered; the footsteps came on again, now on the deck, towards the head of the companion-way. Biggles walked up and down past the cabin door.

A minute later there appeared at the end of the corridor a procession consisting of four persons. First came a naval officer, in oilskins, a belt on the outside carrying a revolver-holster. He was followed by two seamen, also in oilskins, carrying rifles. Between them, looking very forlorn, marched Ginger. He did not even glance up as the party came to a halt in front of the door where Biggles awaited it.

Biggles saluted, unlocked the door, and threw it wide open. The party went on inside. All eyes were on Algy, for enough light entered from the corridor for him to be seen. Biggles brought up the rear.

As soon as he was across the threshold he dropped the point of his bayonet until it was pointing at the officer's back. 'The first man who moves or makes a sound dies,' he said quietly, but distinctly.

Every head, including Ginger's, turned.

Biggles stood like a statue just inside the doorway. His eyes met those of the officer. 'One sound and it will be your last,' he said coldly. 'We're desperate men. Algy, take his revolver. Ginger, collect the rifles.'

None of the Germans made a sound, nor did they protest; they seemed stunned, which was hardly surprising. Such movements as they made were slow, and they were disarmed almost before they realized what was happening.

Biggles now came inside and closed the door. 'Take their oilskins and caps, then tie them up,' he ordered. 'Use the rest of the sheet, and the flex.'

As soon as this had been done he took the blanket, cut it into three pieces with his bayonet, and tied them over the prisoners' heads. 'They'll do,' he said shortly. 'Let's go. We've no time to talk now, but there's one thing I must know.' He turned to Ginger. 'Did you get that message through to the fleet?'

Ginger started. He seemed to be in a dream. 'No, I didn't,' he confessed. 'I looked for it until I ran out of petrol, then——'

'Never mind the rest,' cut in Biggles. 'That's all I want to know. We've got to get that message through somehow. There's still time, but there's only one way. A hundred yards along the beach there's a Dornier flying-boat. We've got to get to it. If there's trouble on the way and I drop out, don't wait for me. Go on to the machine. One of us at least ought to reach it. The fleet must come first. Let's get into these oilskins and caps; in the dark we ought to pass for the escort returning ashore having delivered the prisoner. We'll try to bluff our way through. If that fails we shall have to fight.'

He put on the officer's oilskins and cap. As the others followed suit with the remaining garments he looked them over critically. 'You'll do,' he announced. 'Let's march off.'

With Biggles at the head, the little party marched along the corridor to the companion-way. A dozen steps took them to the deck. Biggles did not stop, but went straight on to the gangway where a guard stood on duty. The night was cloudy, with rain threatening, so it was not until he was almost within touching distance of the guard that he saw, just beyond, near the stern, in the dim glow of a partly obscured lamp, two other men. One he recognized instantly by his figure; it was von Stalhein. The other appeared to be the captain. Biggles distinctly heard von Stalhein say, 'I must go below now; I want a few words with this new prisoner.'

Biggles did not alter his pace. The man on duty stiffened to attention as he passed, but said nothing. They went on down the narrow gangway to the rocks, which were deserted. Here Biggles paused for a moment to get his bearings, and it was while they stood thus, in the silence, that he heard von Stalhein speak to the man at the head of the gangway.

Said he, in the harsh peremptory tones which German officers employ when addressing subordinates, 'Did somebody go ashore just then?'

'Yes, sir,' answered the man. 'It was the guard that brought the prisoner aboard.'

Von Stalhein uttered an exclamation of annoyance. 'I wanted to speak to that officer,' he snapped, presumably to the captain. Footsteps moved swiftly towards the companion-way.

'We've got to get a move on,' said Biggles softly. 'He's going below. In three minutes he'll discover that his birds have flown. We'll make for the aircraft. Keep close, and don't make any noise unless it becomes necessary.'

They walked quickly along the beach to the point where the air squadron was stationed. Biggles hoped that no sentry would have been posted actually on the beach, but in this he was disappointed. A figure loomed up in the darkness.

'Halt! Who goes there?' rapped out a voice.

A split second later, before Biggles could reply, there was a shout from the boat, now some seventy or eighty yards away. 'Stop those men!' roared a voice.

The sentry took a pace nearer. 'Who are you?' he asked suspiciously, for he had, of course, heard the shout.

'Here's my warrant,' answered Biggles casually, taking a pace nearer as though to show a pass. At the last moment he moved like lightning. Grabbing the sentry's rifle with his left hand, he brought the butt of his revolver down on his head.

The sentry collapsed like a wet blanket.

By this time there was a commotion on the boat; von Stalhein's voice, shrill with anger, could be heard above the others.

'Run for it,' said Biggles tersely, and sprinted along the beach until he was opposite the Dornier, which was anchored a few yards out.

He discovered the reason why it was so close as soon as he

plunged into the water, for the beach shelved quickly, and he was wet to the waist by the time he reached the cabin door. Without waiting to see how the others fared, he ran forward and hauled up the anchor. By the time this was done the others were aboard, the flying-boat rocking with the abruptness of their entry.

'Algy, you take the centre gun-turret,' he ordered curtly. 'If there's no machine-gun, use your rifle, but don't start shooting until we're rushed. Ginger, stand by me and watch the shore. Tell me what happens. Use your rifle when you have to.' With that Biggles dropped into the pilot's seat, switched on the petrol and ignition, and felt for the starter.

'There's a crowd coming along the beach; I can hear them, but I can't see them yet,' said Ginger in the manner of a radio commentator. 'I can hear von Stalhein telling people to rush the machine,' he went on. 'The flying personnel are turning out. They're manning the searchlight.'

'Keep them back,' ordered Biggles, and the starter whirred. But the engine was cold and nothing happened. He tried again. Still nothing happened.

Ginger's rifle spat, and the single report was followed by the crash of a machine-gun somewhere close at hand. In the middle of the pandemonium that followed the engine came to life. Simultaneously several shots were fired at the machine. Ginger staggered back and flopped down, grabbing his shoulder. His rifle clattered to the floor. 'They've got me,' he muttered. 'Go on, it's only my shoulder.'

Algy's gun was playing a vicious tattoo on the crowd rushing towards the aircraft, but it was drowned in the roar of the engine, as Biggles opened the throttle. The Dornier surged forward across the smooth surface of the fiord.

'We're away,' cried Ginger weakly, pressing his hand on his wound.

But Biggles was not so sure. He couldn't see a thing. To make matters worse, the searchlight suddenly came on, and the beam, sweeping low across the water, came to rest on the flying-boat, dazzling him. Actually, it was this light that gave him his position, for he knew where it was stationed. The difficulty was, it was only possible to take off straight down the centre of the fiord, and if he veered to either side he was likely to collide with the cliffs that hemmed it in. Knowing the position of the searchlight, he swung the aircraft round until it was facing what he thought—and hoped—was the right direction, and pushed the throttle wide open. He dared not delay any longer, for shots were now striking the machine, and he knew that it only needed one in a vital place to put it out of action.

Bending forward to peer through the windscreen into the blackness ahead, he held the joystick forward, and waited. The stick tightened as the machine gathered flying speed. He gave it another few seconds to be on the safe side and then took it off the water.

Algy's gun ceased firing and presently he appeared.

'Have a look at Ginger,' ordered Biggles. 'He's been hit. There ought to be a first-aid outfit on board.'

Algy disappeared into the cabin, and presently came back with the outfit. 'I've got it,' he called. 'Incidentally, I see we've got a load of bombs on board.'

'Have we though?' A curious smile crossed Biggles's face as he said the words. He looked down. Now at two thousand feet, just below the clouds, the coast-line and the outlines of the fiord could easily be traced. He could not actually see the boat from which they had just escaped, but he knew roughly where it was, and he swung round in a wide curve to fly back over it. Two or three other searchlights had now joined the first, and their beams criss-crossed the sky in search of him. Flecks of flame showed where archie was bursting, but the fire was not intense and caused him little concern. A glance over his shoulder revealed Algy attending to Ginger. Then he went on with his eyes on the target. His hand moved to the bomb release and the load of high explosive went hurtling down, to burst with a glare that lit up the sky like lightning. It was, of course, impossible to ascertain what damage had been done, but satisfied with his parting shot, Biggles turned towards the west, and soon the coast was a dark shadow behind him.

He was now faced by two problems, although they were to a great extent linked together. The first was how to warn the fleet of its danger, and the second, how to get home in a German machine without being shot down by British anti-aircraft defences. He felt that if he could solve one, the other might solve itself. That is to say, if he could make contact with the fleet, or any British patrol vessel fitted with wireless, the warning would be flashed out, and they, at the same time, would be picked up. The trouble was, he had no idea of the position of the fleet. Thinking it over, he saw that an alternative would be to fly straight on home. It would come to the same thing in the end, for a radio message would soon stop the fleet. After some consideration he decided that an attempt to locate the fleet might end, as Ginger's flight had ended, in running out of petrol before the object was achieved; he resolved, therefore, to go straight on towards England. If he passed a patrol ship on the way, well and good. He would try to land near it and get the skipper to send the all-important warning.

Algy, having got Ginger comfortable, joined Biggles in the cockpit.

'How is he?' asked Biggles.

'Not bad. The bullet got him just under the collar-bone and went right through. He'll be all right after a day or two in hospital. How are we going to get on the carpet without being shot to bits by our own people?'

'I've just been thinking about the same thing,' answered Biggles. 'If there was a torch on board we could signal in Morse.'

Algy made a search, but came back to say that he couldn't find one. 'There are a couple of parachutes, some flares, and some parachute-flares,' he announced. 'If you can get over the coast I wouldn't mind going down on a parachute to arrange for a landing. I could at least stop the guns——'

'No use,' broke in Biggles. 'Apart from the risk of being shot down while crossing the coast, it would take too long.'

'Then how about landing on the water if it isn't too rough?' suggested Algy.

'And find ourselves in the middle of the main minefield? It

runs right down the coast, you know. Not for me. Our best chance, I think, is to risk everything and go right on—unless we spot a ship on the way.'

'If we do it will shoot at us.'

'In that case we'll pretend to be hit and land on the water. Then we should be picked up. Let's have a look at the water for a start. Get ready to drop a parachute flare.'

Biggles took the Dornier down a few hundred feet, and in the light of a parachute-flare saw that the sea was comparatively calm; but it seemed that the flare was seen by other eyes, too, for almost at once, no great distance away, a searchlight stabbed the sky. Biggles didn't wait for the archie which he knew would follow. Blipping his engine to attract attention, he went straight on down and landed on the water, where, a few minutes later, the searchlight picked up the machine.

'We should look silly if that vessel turned out to be a Hun,' remarked Algy.

'The chances of a German ship being in the North Sea are so small that we needn't consider them,' Biggles told him confidently.

His confidence in the Navy keeping the sea clear of enemy shipping was justified a few minutes later when the slim outline of a British destroyer loomed up in the gloom. Naturally it carried no lights. The airmen were already hailing it, yelling that they were British, to prevent a mistake that might end in tragedy.

'Who are you?' came a voice, amplified by a megaphone.

'British prisoners escaping in a German 'plane,' roared Biggles. 'Please pick us up.'

Further explanations at that stage were unnecessary, but the destroyer was taking no risks, and its guns were trained on the aircraft as it came alongside.

In five minutes the three friends were aboard her, talking to her commander in his cabin. Ginger, with his arm in a sling, looking rather pale, was present, for he had insisted on making light of his wound.

'My name's Bigglesworth,' announced Biggles without preamble. 'I'm a Squadron Leader in the R.A.F. These are two of my officers. We've just come from Norway.'

The skipper started. 'Why, I've heard of you,' he declared. 'Aren't you the fellows who got the message through to the fleet, warning it to keep out of Westfiord?'

Biggles stared. 'Then the fleet's all right?'

'You bet it is.'

Biggles sank down in a chair and wiped imaginary perspiration from his brow. 'Phew! That's a relief,' he muttered. 'But how did it happen—I mean, how did the fleet get the message?'

'I don't know the details,' answered the captain. 'All I know is that one of our Intelligence blokes—a fellow named Bigglesworth, so it was said—got into touch with the skipper of a trawler. The skipper sent a signal to the Admiralty, and the Admiralty issued fresh orders to the fleet. That's all there was to it.'

'But the trawler was sunk by a torpedo,' burst out Ginger.

'That's right—but that happened afterwards. The skipper had already been in touch with the Admiralty. Shortly afterwards another signal came through from this same trawler, this time an SOS, to say that they had been torpedoed and were sinking. One of our destroyers hurried along and picked up most of the survivors. Apparently some time was spent looking for the fellow who had brought the message about the trap that had been laid for the fleet, but he couldn't be found.'

'For a very good reason,' put in Ginger, smiling. 'He had already been picked up by the U-boat. It was me.' He looked at Biggles. 'So that's how it happened.'

'That's it,' continued the skipper. 'I'll put you ashore as soon as I can. Meanwhile, is there anything you want?'

'Plenty,' returned Biggles promptly. 'Among other things a bath, a square meal, a comfortable bunk and home.'

'If that's all, I think we can supply the lot,' grinned the naval officer. 'We're going back to port to refit—in fact, we're setting a course for home right now. Come below and I'll fix you up with the rest.'

'Lead on,' invited Biggles.

Five hours later, without misadventure, the destroyer

steamed slowly into an east coast port. The comrades, washed and refreshed by a short sleep, watched the landing-jetty creep nearer.

'Do you see what I see?' murmured Ginger.

'I think so,' replied Biggles. 'You mean Colonel Raymond? I expected that he'd be here. I got the skipper to send a signal saying that we were aboard.'

As the destroyer was made fast Colonel Raymond came briskly across the gangway. 'Welcome home,' he said cheerfully. 'Between ourselves, I was just beginning to wonder if you ever would get home,' he confessed.

'You didn't wonder about that as much as we did, I'll warrant,' remarked Biggles grimly. 'If you've come here to say that something, somewhere, is waiting to be done, then I'll tell you right away that you've come to the wrong place.'

'Oh dear! I'm sorry to hear that,' announced the Colonel in a pained voice.

Biggles looked at him suspiciously. 'Then you *had* got something on your mind?'

'Yes. As a matter of fact, I had a little idea,' admitted the Colonel. 'I've got my car here, and I thought perhaps a bite of dinner at the Savoy——'

Biggles caught him by the arm. 'That's different,' he declared emphatically. 'If that's the next mission, let's get right along. When you hear what we've got to tell you I think you'll agree that we've earned it.'

BIGGLES

IN THE
JUNGLE

I
BIGGLES MEETS AN OLD FRIEND

WITH its altimeter registering six thousand feet, a travel-stained amphibian aircraft nosed steadily southward under a Central American sky of azure blue. To port lay the deep green of the Atlantic Ocean, rolling away and away to the infinite distance. To starboard, the primeval forest sprawled like a great stain, filling the landscape until at last it merged into the purple haze of the far horizon. Immediately below the aircraft a white, irregular line of surf marked the juncture of land and sea.

There were three passengers in the machine. At the controls was Squadron Leader Bigglesworth, D.S.O., better known as 'Biggles'. In the spare seat beside him, regarding the vast panorama with dispassionate familiarity, was his protégé, 'Ginger' Hebblethwaite. Behind, plotting a compass course, sat their mutual friend and comrade, Captain the Honourable 'Algy' Lacey. He completed his calculation and came forward.

'I make us out to be off the coast of British Honduras,' he announced.

Biggles smiled faintly. 'You're a bit late in the day, old boy. Unless I'm mistaken, that's Belize, the capital of the colony, just ahead of us.'

'Are you going down?' asked Algy.

'We shall have to,' answered Biggles. 'That confounded head wind which we ran into this morning was outside my calculations; it lost us so much time that we shall have to fill up with fuel and oil before we go on. This is no place for a forced landing.'

'You mean—you'll go down at Belize?'

'Yes. There's a Pan-American Airways maintenance station there. They're a decent crowd. They'll let us have some juice.'

'Do you know anybody there?'

'I don't know the Pan-American staff, but I know a fellow in the Government House—that is, if he's still there; a chap named

Carruthers. I did him a good turn some years ago, when he was British Vice-Consul at La Paz, in Bolivia, on the other side of the continent. We might look him up. If he's still here no doubt he will be glad to repay an old debt by offering us hospitality. He'll probably be glad to see us in any case; I don't suppose he gets many visitors at an off-the-map place like Belize.'

As he spoke Biggles retarded the throttle and allowed the aircraft to lose height in a steady glide that carried it on towards a little town that nestled on the edge of the sea, backed by the sombre forest. He was in no hurry, for—for once—the party was on a pleasure cruise, with no particular object in view beyond seeing something of the world, in fair weather, as an alternative to remaining in London through a dull winter.

Ginger had been largely responsible for the trip. Bored by a spell of inactivity, he had threatened to go off alone, taking the aircraft, an amphibian named *Wanderer*, if the others refused to bestir themselves. Biggles, always tolerant, had proposed a trip to Central America to examine the possibilities of an air service between British possessions on the mainland and the West Indies. This project, he declared, need not necessarily be definitely pursued. It provided an object for the flight, as opposed to aimless wandering.

So far the trip had been uneventful. The adventures which in his heart Ginger had hoped they might encounter had failed to materialise. He was getting slightly bored, and made no secret of it. As a form of relaxation on the ground he had decided to collect butterflies, the beauty of which at some of their ports of call had entranced him, with the result that he was taking a new interest in entomology.

Biggles glanced at him. 'Do you know anything about Honduras?' he asked.

Ginger shook his head. 'No. I once saw the name on a postage stamp, otherwise I shouldn't have known that the place existed. Is there anything remarkable about it?'

'No, I can't say there is,' replied Biggles reflectively. 'It's much the same as the rest of Central America. Outside the capital I imagine it's a pretty wild spot. I'm told there's some fine timber there—some of the best mahogany comes from Honduras. The most interesting thing about it from our point of view, having done a bit of aerial exploring, is the Unknown River.'

'Unknown River?' But that doesn't make sense,' protested Ginger. 'Either there is a river or there isn't. If there is—well, it must be known. If there isn't, why worry about it?'

'Nobody's worrying about it as far as I know,' returned Biggles. 'The mouth of the river is known, but from what I can make out the upper reaches have never been explored. It's supposed to rise somewhere in Guatemala, which backs on to Honduras.'

'Why hasn't it been explored?'

'Presumably because nobody has had the energy, or the money, or any reason to do so.'

'Then why are people concerned about it?'

'Because the river crops up from time to time in the newspapers in connection with the lost Carmichael treasure. There was a talk on the radio about it not long ago.'

Ginger started and sat up. 'Treasure! Why didn't you say that at first? That sounds more my mark. Tell me about it.'

Biggles smiled sadly. 'I was afraid you'd get excited if I mentioned the treasure. Don't get any wild ideas—I'm not going off on a treasure-hunt.'

'Of course not,' agreed Ginger airily. 'Still, there's no harm in my knowing about it, is there?'

'I suppose not,' assented Biggles. 'It's an old tale, not much more than a legend. This country is stiff with legends about treasures. Speaking from memory, this particular yarn started away back in 1860, or thereabouts, when a fellow named Carmichael, travelling up-country, saved the lives of two Indians. In return they promised to show him the spot where Montezuma hid his treasure from the Spaniards. They went, and found a ruined city. Carmichael cut a cross—or made a mark—on a temple, or the ruins of a temple, under which the Indians said the gold was buried; then he came back for help. When he returned he couldn't find the temple—or the city, for that matter. Nobody ever has found it, although they've discovered quite a number of other old cities. The fact is, there are so many of these old cities now swallowed up by the jungle that they can't work out which is the right one. Anyway, most people in Central America have heard of the Carmichael treasure. Several attempts have been made to locate it, but all people find are the traces of a vast and very ancient civilisation—that's all.'

A thoughtful look came into Ginger's eyes. 'While we're on the spot we might collect what facts there are available,' he suggested hopefully.

'To what purpose?' inquired Biggles coldly.

'Well—I mean—of course, I'm not suggesting a definite trip, or anything like that; but if we happened to be near the place——'

'If I have my way we shan't be near it,' declared Biggles. 'All you'd be likely to find in that jungle would be Indians, mosquitoes, leeches, ticks, snakes, and a few other horrors. If you didn't find them they'd find you. Tropical forests may sound great fun, but they can be very, very uncomfortable. Believe me, I know.'

'Does no one ever go into this forest?'

'Oh yes. Rubber collectors and chicle-hunters—mostly natives.'

'Chicle? What's that?'

'The stuff they make chewing-gum out of—at least, chicle is the base. Like rubber, it's the sap of a tree. Chicle is the colony's most important export.'

Ginger shook his head. 'Sounds a sticky business to me.'

And there the conversation ended, for Biggles had to concentrate his attention on putting the aircraft on the water. This he did on an open stretch marked by buoys and a wind-stocking pole, which, as he expected, turned out to be an emergency landing-ground for the big Pan-American Clippers that operated up and down the coast from the United States to Argentina. The local superintendent was helpful, giving them a mooring and promising to fill the tanks. Well satisfied with this arrangement, the airmen went into town to have a meal, seek accommodation for the night, and, if he was still in the colony, call on Carruthers.

As it happened, they met him just leaving his office, and after greetings had been exchanged, and introductions effected, he insisted on their making their home in his roomy bungalow while they were there.

Ginger, although he did not comment on it, was rather disappointed in the size of the town, considering that it was the capital of a British colony. He realised that there was nothing remarkable in meeting Carruthers as they did, for the administration of the colony was carried on by a small staff. Normally, it turned out, Carruthers was senior Resident Magistrate, but at the moment, the Governor being away on leave, he was acting for him. He was a fair, good-looking young man in the late twenties, with keen blue eyes and a closely clipped moustache. His manner was debonair, but behind it was an alert, authoritative bearing.

'You know, Carruthers,' observed Biggles, as they sat over their after-dinner coffee, 'you've aged a good deal since I last saw you.'

'Do you wonder?' Carruthers' tone was rather bitter.

'You mean—it's the climate?'

'Not entirely, although it's certainly enervating. To turn your hair grey, you should try keeping order in thousands of miles of jungle with a handful of men. That's what I'm up against all the time. I know it sounds easy, and you may think I haven't much to do, but believe me, my hands are full.'

'How does the jungle make so much work for you?' put in Algy.

'It isn't the jungle; it's the people in it.'

'Hostile Indians?'

'There are plenty of those, of course, but left alone they wouldn't give us much trouble; but lately they've been playing Old Harry with the up-river stations, and with chicle-collectors and other travellers from the coast. Something seems to have happened. It's almost as if the Indians are organised. In fact, the coastal natives say that is the case, but it's hard to find out just what is going on. There is wild talk—rumour, of course—about a fellow who calls himself King of the Forest, or some equally fantastic title; but what his game is, if he really exists, I haven't yet been able to discover. It's practically impossible to separate rumour from fact. All the same, if half the rumours I hear are true, then there are brains behind the scheme. I'm responsible for the country, so it gets me worried. If anything goes wrong, I have to take the blame.'

'But as long as this so-called King of the Forest doesn't interfere with you, what does it matter?' queried Biggles.

'But he is beginning to interfere with me—or somebody is, although I'm still in the dark. For instance, as you probably know, chicle is an important commodity here. It's collected by natives. They are jibbing at going up the river, consequently the stuff isn't coming in as it should. Yet the amazing thing is, there are indications that Honduras chicle is still reaching the U.S.A. in quantities as large as usual. Where is it coming from? Who's collecting it? On top of all this I get an inquiry from the Home Office about three white men who are supposed to have disappeared into the interior. I haven't all the facts yet, but apparently they were on a crazy treasure-hunt.'

'Then there is a treasure?' put in Ginger quickly.

Carruthers shrugged his shoulders. 'I suppose there must be some foundation for the rumour. It was alleged to have been seen years ago by a fellow named Carmichael. Beyond that I know no more than you do about it. How these three white men got into the interior without official permission, or why they should go without first reporting to me, so that in the event of trouble I should know roughly where they were, I don't understand. They were last heard of on the Unknown River. With two of them I'm not particularly concerned, but the other, a young fellow, happens to have a wealthy and anxious father in the United States, and he's kicking up a nice row because I can't find his son.

'If this fellow who calls himself King of the Forest really exists, and if these Americans have fallen foul of him, they may have had their throats cut. So you see, with one thing and another, I'm having a pretty worrying job. It takes my small staff all its time to handle the ordinary business of the country, without wandering about the jungle looking for lost Americans, chicle-collectors, and self-appointed kings. There is talk of the American archaeological survey people coming back here to resume their work. If they do they may be murdered. Yet if I refuse to grant permission there'll be a scream from the Foreign Office.'

'What do these people want to do?' inquired Biggles curiously.

'Go on with their survey work—delving into the old ruins that exist in the jungle. As a matter of fact, they've made some very interesting discoveries on the sites of two ancient cities called Tikal and Uaxactun. They now want to locate some more sites which they feel sure exist. It shouldn't be hard, because most of these old cities are marked by pyramids like those of Egypt. They're enormous, and although they are buried in the jungle, the tops are often higher than the highest trees.'

'Obviously, what you'll have to do is ascertain if this King of the Forest fellow really exists,' declared Biggles. 'If he does you'll have to arrest him. You won't have any peace until you do.'

Carruthers laughed bitterly. 'Arrest him? How? Who is going to find him, for a start?'

'There's no indication of where he hangs out?'

'None. The natives tell a ridiculous story about a secret town in the forest, which doesn't strike me as being likely.'

'Still, if that were true, it shouldn't be hard to find.'

'You might look for years without finding it.'

'In a search from ground level, I agree. I was thinking of reconnaissance from the air.'

'That would be an entirely different matter,' asserted Carruthers. 'Unfortunately, I don't happen to have an Air Force. I can't get a new launch, much less a plane.'

Biggles smiled. 'I have one,' he reminded. 'You can borrow it with pleasure.'

'Thanks, but who's going to fly it? I'm not a pilot—nor do I know of one in this part of the world.'

Biggles took a cigarette and tapped it thoughtfully on the back of his hand. 'We're not in a hurry,' he said pointedly. 'We might find time to have a look round for you—if the idea makes any appeal. There seems to be plenty to look for—pyramids, ruined cities, lost Americans, the king's secret town—treasure— we ought to be able to find *something*. If we did spot anything we could pin-point the place on the map and let you know. That would be a help.'

'A help! I should jolly well think it would,' declared Carruthers. 'Do you seriously mean you'd do this?'

'Why not? We're doing nothing in particular. We might as well do something useful. In any case, although I hadn't mentioned it to the others, I was contemplating a survey flight up the Unknown River, just as a matter of curiosity.'

'That would be an important piece of work even if you found nothing else,' remarked Carruthers. 'I'd really be most grateful if you'd do this.'

'Then you can consider it settled,' affirmed Biggles.

'Fine. You have official sanction for the undertaking. When do you propose to start?'

Biggles shrugged his shoulders. 'It doesn't really matter. As far as I'm concerned I could start tomorrow. If the others aren't too tired——'

'I'm not tired,' put in Ginger quickly. 'This promises to be interesting. I always did like looking for things.'

'Very well. If it's all right with you, Algy, we'll start in the morning,' concluded Biggles.

An hour later, to the serenade of bull-frogs croaking in a nearby swamp, Ginger went to bed, to sleep and to dream of kings and lost Americans fighting for a treasure on the summit of a pyramid.

2

AN UNEXPECTED ENCOUNTER

As the first rays of the tropic sun splashed the eastern sky with gleaming gold and turquoise, the thin miasma of mist which hung over the silent lake began to rise, revealing a number of things that floated on its placid surface—a giant water-lily with thick, circular leaves, each as large as a table; over the snow-white blossom a humming-bird, a living ruby with an emerald breast, hung motionless on whirring wings, its three-inch bill probing the nectary for honey; a log, with two protuberances at one end—or what appeared to be a log, although it had a curious trick of submerging and reappearing in another place. There was also an aircraft, an amphibian, which bore on its nose the single word *Wanderer*.

The aircraft rocked gently, so that ripples lapped its sides, as Ginger's head appeared above the central hatchway, to be followed a moment later by the barrel of a rifle. For a brief moment the silence persisted, then it was shattered by a gunshot. The 'log' jerked spasmodically, lashing the water to creamy foam before it disappeared. At the sound of the shot a flock of green parrots rose screaming from the nearby forest. Ginger drew himself up level with the hull, regarding intently the spot where the alligator had disappeared.

'Did you get him?' called Biggles from inside the machine.

'I don't think so, but I tickled him up a bit,' returned Ginger. 'It was the same big brute that was nosing round in the night.'

Silence returned as Ginger settled himself down on the hull and regarded the forest with keen, interested eyes. They travelled slowly up the mighty trunks of the trees that disappeared out of sight into a canopy of foliage high above; lianas wound round every bole and hung from every bough, passing from tree to tree like a fantastic network of cables. Below, in many places, the ground was strewn with the petals of flowers that bloomed far overhead. Climbing ferns and orchids, too, clung to the trees, sending down aerial roots that added to the tangle. Near the water magnificent tree-ferns flung out feathery fans twenty feet or more in width. Through the maze thus formed swept butterflies, the huge, metallic-blue *Morphos*, and yellow, swallow-tailed *Papilios*. A toucan, with a monstrous red-and-black beak nearly half as big as its body, sat on a branch, but flapped away heavily at the approach of a troop of spider-monkeys.

On the morning following the conversation with Carruthers the *Wanderer* had proceeded up the Unknown River, sometimes flying and sometimes taxi-ing. Three nights had been spent on the river itself before the lake on which the *Wanderer* now rested had been discovered—a smooth sheet of water that nestled in the jungle a hundred miles from the coast, and the same distance, therefore, from anything in the nature of civilization. It had been decided that the lake would make a good base from which to explore the surrounding country. So far nothing had occurred to interrupt the tranquillity of the cruise, for the *Wanderer* was well equipped with stores and such accessories as were likely to be required.

Ginger called down the hatchway, 'Are you fellows getting up?'

'Coming now,' answered Biggles.

Ginger grunted, for he was anxious to be off; he could not go ashore because the aircraft was moored some distance from the bank in order to avoid the mosquitoes and other insect pests which were all too plentiful. However, in a few minutes Biggles appeared, and the *Wanderer* was soon surging across the surface of the lake to take off on another survey flight. So far they had not seen any of the pyramids of which Carruthers had spoken, although according to Biggles's reckoning they were in the region of the two ancient cities, Tikal and Uaxactun, where the American Archaeological Society had carried out its excavations.

From the air, the scene presented was one of strange monotony. On all sides, as far as the eye could see, stretched the primeval forest, an undulating expanse of green in various hues reaching to the horizon. In one direction only was it broken. Far away to the west the sun glinted on another lake, which Biggles supposed to be in Guatemala. Not that there was anything to mark the boundary. As in the case of most countries in tropical America, the frontier was assumed to be somewhere in the forest, but it was not possible to say precisely where. The *Wanderer* roared on, climbing steadily.

Presently there was a slight change in the scene, and it became possible to make out areas of open savannah, or rolling meadow-land, although these were often broken by groups of trees and outcrops of rock. Biggles explained to the others that it was generally thought that these areas had originally been cleared by nations that had dwelt there in the past; the jungle, however, was steadily advancing over them again, so that they were fast being swallowed up by the forest.

It was Ginger who first spotted the apex of a pyramid. He caught Biggles by the arm and pointed. 'Take a look at that!' he cried.

Biggles cut the throttle and flew lower, so that there was no longer any doubt as to what it was. Near it, two other pyramids, not so high, could just be made out, peeping over the top of the green ocean.

'I should say that's Tikal,' observed Biggles.

'I vote we have a look at it from the ground,' suggested Ginger.

Biggles, surveying the panorama, noticed a lake nearer to the pyramids than the one they had left, but even so it was some distance away, and he shook his head doubtfully. Flying towards it, however, he came upon another and hitherto unsuspected sheet of water. It was much smaller, and not exactly a lake in the true sense of the word. It appeared rather to be a fairly extensive depression in the ground that had been flooded by a river—probably a tributary of the Unknown River. A stream flowed into it at one end, and out at the other.

'What about that stretch of water?' suggested Ginger. 'We ought to be able to get down on it.'

Biggles looked dubious. 'It's large enough,' he admitted. 'What I'm afraid of is obstructions. Trees are always falling into these rivers, particularly during the rainy season. If there happens to be any floating about in the middle of the lake, and we hit one of them, we shall be in a mess. We don't know how deep the water it, either. Not that all these hard-wood trees float; if the water is shallow, and there are any lying on the bottom, we shall tear the keel off the boat.'

'It looks deep to me,' remarked Ginger encouragingly. 'Try that patch where there are no water-lilies.'

By this time Biggles was within a few feet of the water, leaning over the side eyeing it critically. 'All right,' he agreed, as he zoomed up to avoid the trees at the far end of the lake. 'We'll try it.'

Banking steeply, he turned and came back at landing speed. Very slowly, the aircraft sank towards the stretch to which Ginger had referred. There were no visible obstructions. The *Wanderer's* keel slashed the surface of the water, and then sank down with a surging rush that sent ripples racing towards the shore. The machine ran quickly to a standstill.

'Fine!' cried Ginger. 'Let's get nearer to the beach—at least, there seems to be a bit of sand over there.' He pointed.

Biggles taxied towards it, and brought the *Wanderer* to a standstill with her keel scraping gently on a shelving strip of sandy gravel. 'Well, here we are,' he announced.

Ginger was about to wade ashore when Biggles caught him by the arm. 'Just a minute,' he said tersely, staring fixedly at a certain spot.

'What is it?' asked Algy quickly, sensing danger from Biggles's tone of voice.

'Can you see what I see—or am I mistaken?' said Biggles quietly. 'Just on the edge of the timber, under that spray of crimson orchids.'

The others stared.

'Great heavens, it's a man!' breathed Algy.

'Get your guns,' ordered Biggles curtly, and, revolver in hand, he stepped down into the shallow water.

The man was lying half in and half out of the forest, his head towards the lake, with one arm outflung as though he had fallen while making a desperate effort to get to the water. That he was a native, or a coloured man, was by this time apparent. He wore only a ragged remnant of shirt and a pair of blue dungaree trousers, also in rags.

'He must be dead,' muttered Ginger as they approached.

'I don't think so,' returned Biggles quickly. 'If he was dead— or if he'd been dead more than an hour or two—he'd be half eaten by this time. There's a hungry army always on the prowl in the forest, looking for meat—and in the water, too, if it comes to that.'

Biggles dropped on his knees beside the man and turned him on to his back. He was unconscious. 'He's lost a lot of blood,' he continued, pointing to an ugly stain on the man's trousers. 'Let's see what caused the damage.' Taking his knife he cut a slit in the garment so that the wound was exposed. 'That's a gunshot wound,' he said crisply. 'How the dickens did it happen, I wonder? It looks as if there are other people in the forest besides us.'

'What on earth would the fellow be doing in a place like this, anyway?' put in Algy.

'I should say he's a chicle-collector—or else a rubber-tapper,' answered Biggles. 'As I told you, chicle is still collected wild in the forest.' He glanced up at Algy. 'Get the brandy flask and the medicine chest; we shall have to do what we can for the poor wretch.'

He cleaned the wound—a flesh wound in the thigh—and dressed it, while the others, with brandy and water, did what they could to restore consciousness. It did not take them long. The man opened his eyes. Instantly, with a gasp of terror, he tried to get to his feet, but they held him down.

'I wonder what language he speaks,' said Ginger.

'If he comes from Belize he'll probably speak English,' replied Biggles. 'If that fails I'll try Spanish'. He said a few words, and as soon as he saw that the man understood he told him that he had nothing to fear.

Together, they got him into a more comfortable position. Ginger, watching closely, noted that the man was older than he had at first supposed; he judged him to be not less than fifty years of age. He had a pleasant if rather wild countenance, and his skin was so dark that he appeared to have both Indian and negro in his ancestry.

Presently the man sat up and regarded his benefactors with incredulous eyes.

'What's your name?' asked Biggles.

The man uttered an unpronounceable word.

Biggles smiled. 'That's all right,' he told the others. 'We'll call him Dusky for short. What are you doing here, and who shot you?' he continued, again addressing the wounded man.

Before Dusky could answer there was a swift footfall near at hand. It brought the comrades round swiftly to face an enormous man who had just emerged from the forest. No one, perhaps not even he himself, could have guessed his nationality; his skin was more white than brown, but it was apparent that he was a half-caste of some sort. Well over six feet in height, and broad in proportion, with a gun over his arm he looked an ugly customer. The only garments he wore were a dirty shirt, open at the throat, and a ragged cotton suit. Nothing more. The lower part of his face was concealed in a tangle of black beard. His eyes were bloodshot and had an unpleasant glint in them. So much the comrades saw in their first appraising glance.

Biggles faced him squarely. Pointing at the wounded man, he said, 'Do you know anything about this?'

The stranger took a pace forward, his eyes, heavy with suspicion, darting from one to the other. 'What you doing here?' he demanded harshly.

'We might ask you the same question,' returned Biggles coolly. 'Did you shoot this chap?'

For a moment the man did not answer. He glanced at Dusky, scowling, and then looked up again at those who confronted him. For a moment he regarded them reflectively, malevolently.

'What do you here?' he questioned harshly, addressing Biggles.

'Why—have you bought the place or something?'

The scowl grew deeper. 'You git out—*pronto*.'

Biggles looked surprised. 'Are you presuming to tell us where we can go?'

'You git out, or mebbe you don't git out no more,' snarled the man.

Biggles appeared to consider the order. Actually, he was wondering if there was any point in staying. It was not as though they had any reason for remaining there.

'What you come here for, huh?' went on the man suspiciously.

'Believe it or not, we're just a picnic party.'

The sarcastic leer with which this remark was received made it clear that it was not believed.

'One lake is as good as another to us,' continued Biggles. 'If you feel that this one is your particular property, we'll pull out. In any case we should have done so, because we shall have to take this man'—Biggles indicated Dusky—'to Belize. His wound needs treatment.'

The other started. 'No, you don't,' he grated.

'But I said we do,' returned Biggles calmly.

The man made a significant movement with his gun.

'I shouldn't try that if I were you,' Biggles told him evenly. Then, turning to the others, he said, 'Get aboard. You know what to do.'

Algy nodded, and touched Ginger on the arm. They returned to the aircraft.

Ignoring the stranger, Biggles turned to Dusky. 'Do you feel able to walk, or shall I carry you?'

'I can walk, boss.' Dusky got stiffly to his feet, standing on one leg.

The man took a quick pace forward as if he would prevent his departure, but stopped when Biggles turned on him with a crisp, 'Stand back! Take a look at the boat.'

The man glanced swiftly at the aircraft, over the side of which now projected a light machine-gun of the type known as the 'Tommy' gun. For a moment he hesitated, his lips drawn back, showing discoloured teeth; then, turning on his heel, he strode into the forest. An instant later the shrill blast of a whistle rent the air.

'He fetch de others,' said Dusky in a panic.

'Get into the boat,' snapped Biggles, and taking cover behind a tree, he watched the forest, whence now came answering cries. Not until Dusky had been hauled into the *Wanderer* did he abandon his position and follow him. He was only just in time, for barely had he joined the others when a gang of men, as unsavoury a crowd as could have been imagined, appeared in the gloomy recesses of the forest, running towards the spot. A shot rang out, and a bullet struck the machine somewhere near the tail.

'Get her off,' he told Algy, who was already in the pilot's seat. 'If we get mixed up in a brawl somebody's liable to be hurt, and then we may find ourselves in the wrong with the authorities.'

'Shall I give 'em a burst—just to let 'em know that the gun isn't a dummy?' suggested Ginger tentatively.

'No—we may need our ammunition,' answered Biggles.

The last word was drowned in the roar of the engines as Algy started them. The *Wanderer* surged across the water and rose gracefully into the air.

The last they saw of the lake was a crowd of men on the beach they had just left. One, standing in front of the others, was shaking his fist.

'I should be sorry to run into that gang after this,' declared Ginger.

'I should have been sorry to run into them at any time,' returned Biggles curtly.

'Where shall I make for?' called Algy.

'Go back to the lake—the one we started from this morning,' ordered Biggles. 'I want to have a word or two with Dusky before we decide what we're going to do.'

3
DUSKY TELLS HIS STORY AND
GINGER LEARNS A LESSON

IT did not take them long to get back to the lake, for on a straight course it was not more than forty miles from the scene of their encounter. As soon as the *Wanderer* was safely down preparations were made for a meal, for it was lunch-time, and in any case it was obvious that Dusky was in a famished condition. Little was said until everyone was satisfied, although it was some time before Dusky stated that he had had enough. Ginger made coffee over the spirit lamp while Biggles examined Dusky's wound and dressed it again more carefully.

'It's nothing serious,' he announced. 'The bullet went right through, so we haven't got to extract it. Luckily it missed the bone. The flesh looks clean enough, so it should heal in a few days.'

In making this statement Biggles did not allow for the astonishing recuperative ability of a healthy native, and the wound actually healed at a speed that amazed him. Dusky, possibly because he was accustomed to pain and discomfort, treated it as a mere scratch.

As soon as they were settled Biggles asked Dusky to tell them just how he had come by his wound. Scenting a mystery, he wanted to know about the whole affair.

'Yes, massa, I tell you plenty,' answered Dusky eagerly.

'All right; make a start by telling us what you were doing in the forest and how that big stiff go hold of you.'

'You mean Bogat.'

'It that his name?'

'*Si señor*—Cristoval Bogat.' Dusky spoke English with a soft negro accent, curiously broken by odd words of Spanish, a method of speech common enough in Central America.

'I'se chicle-collector, massa,' he went on. 'Me and my brudders we buy canoe and work for ourselves; take de chicle down de ribber to Belize. One time we do well, den we git scared

because chicle-collectors who go up ribber don't come back no
more. Den, we ain't go no more money, we make one more trip.
We run into dees Bogat men. Dey shoot at us. Dey kill my
brudders and capture me, and say me work for dem. Dey make
me slabe.'

Biggles frowned. 'Slave? Do you mean that seriously?'

'Sure I do, massa.'

'But slavery was done away with long ago.'

Dusky shook his head sadly. 'Not up *dis* ribber, massa.'

'Which river are you talking about?'

'De Unknown Ribber.'

'But we're on a lake.'

'Dat so, but de ribber run fro de forest not far away.'

Biggles nodded. 'I see. Do the authorities know about this
slave racket?'

Dusky shrugged his shoulders. 'Mebbe. De black trash along
Belize talk plenty about it. Mebbe Gov'ment can't do nuthin.'

'Who is this fellow Bogat?'

'He sorta right-hand man for de King of de Forest.'

Biggles wrinkled his forehead. 'King of the Forest? Great
Scott! That's an ambitious title. Who is this precious monarch?'

'Ah dunno, boss. Nobody knows for sure. Some say he black
man who kill Gov'ment man in Belize and run away; udders say
he white man. Dey call him de Tiger. He mighty big boss, and
eberyone mighty afraid of him. He boss tousands of Indians and
all sorts of men. Dey say he got town up de ribber.' Dusky
paused.

'Go ahead,' invited Biggles; 'this is getting interesting. Tell us
all you know.'

Dusky scratched his short, curly hair. 'Der ain't much ter tell,
massa.'

'Tell us what happened to you.'

'Dey capture me and set me to work wid gang ob chicle-
collectors. Some gangs dey tap de rubber.'

'I get it. And the Tiger gets it all, eh?'

'Sure he does, massa.'

'What does he do with it?'

'Ah dunno fo' sure, but dey say it goes out ob de country de udder way, up de ribber and across de mountains.'

'That's a pretty state of affairs. The stuff is collected in British territory and then smuggled out of the country, presumably so that the Tiger doesn't have to pay duty on it. Go on, Dusky.'

'I work fer a year, mebbe more; I dunno. We slaves all sick wid bad food, and when we can't work dey beat us wid whips. Bogat, he's worse dan de debbil himself. Den one day two white men come. Dey ask ter go see de Tiger. Bogat take dem. Presently dey all together drinking like brudders. After that we don't collect chicle no longer. We made ter go for de forest to big old spooky city, and dere we dig.'

'What for?'

Dusky shook his head. 'Nobody knows—nobody 'cept de Tiger and de white men. But we reckon dey dig fer gold. Fust we dig under de old temple——'

'Did you find anything?' put in Ginger quickly.

'Not much. Some silber mugs. Den we go on digging udder places.'

'Why did they shoot you?' asked Biggles.

'Becos I run away. I can't stand dem whips no longer, so one night me and some frens, we run, think mebbe we get back ter Belize. Bogat and his gang shot at us—mebbe dey t'ink if we get back to Belize we say what's going on. De udders all get killed or else caught. I get shot too, but I run till I can't run no longer.'

'And these friends of yours who were shot—were they all chicle-hunters from Belize?'

'Sure dey were.'

Biggles looked at the others. 'This is a nice thing,' he muttered savagely. 'These fellows were British subjects—or at least under British protection. It seems to me that it's high time this self-appointed King of the Forest was shot out of his throne. It must be the fellow Carruthers told us about. I think the thing now is to go down the river and let Carruthers know about this. He may prefer to decide what we ought to do. There is this about it: we now have a useful ally in Dusky, who probably knows his way about this particular stretch of forest.'

'The only thing against us going back to the coast is that, as there has been trouble, Carruthers may not want us to come back. He seems to regard all travellers in his province as his responsibility,' observed Algy cautiously.

'I'll tell you how we could get over that,' declared Ginger. 'We needn't all go down the river. If two of us stay here the machine would have to come back to pick us up.'

'That's an idea,' agreed Biggles. 'Algy, suppose you run down to Belize and have a word with Carruthers? The rest of us will stay here. Tell him what we have learned and ask his advice. You could slip down today and come back tomorrow. There's no desperate hurry.'

'Okay, if you think that's a wise plan.'

'I can't think of anything better. Come on, let's get some stores ashore and make camp. Ginger will have a chance to collect more butterflies while we're waiting.'

Thus it was agreed, and shortly afterwards Biggles and Ginger, standing in front of a green canvas tent which they had erected, watched Algy in the *Wanderer* take off and head towards the coast. After it was out of sight they spent some time making the camp ship-shape, stacking the stores and fixing up their hammocks and mosquito nets. Dusky rested quietly in the shade on a waterproof sheet, on a small area of ground which he had burnt to drive away insect pests.

When this task was completed, and there was nothing more they could do, Ginger took his butterfly-net and announced his intention of collecting some specimens. To his surprise, and somewhat to his indignation, Dusky protested, stating with sincere earnestness that this was a most dangerous thing to do. In response to Ginger's demand to be informed in what way it was dangerous, he declared that not only were there many pests, chiefly insect and reptile, in the forest, but there was also great danger of becoming lost. This Ginger found difficult to believe. As far as the pests were concerned, although he did not say so, he held the opinion that these were exaggerated. So far he had seen none except a few mosquitoes. He knew, of course, that such creatures as ticks and leeches abounded, but he felt that these were more likely to prove a source of annoyance than constitute any real danger to a well-dressed traveller.

Biggles did not forbid him to go, but he warned him to be careful. Ginger readily gave his promise to take no risks, and said that in any event he would not go far from camp. He carried a revolver in his hip pocket, and this, he asserted, would enable him to take care of himself. With his butterfly-net under his arm and a killing-jar in his haversack, he set off into the forest.

At first he did not attempt to capture any butterflies, although he saw several, for he was too fascinated by his surroundings. In particular, the humming-birds of many species, all of brilliant colour, occupied his attention. Other birds were less common, although screaming macaws, in gorgeous liveries of yellow, blue and scarlet, occasionally flew overhead. There were also a number of toucans and tanagers, conspicuous in their black plumage with a fiery red blotch above the tail. Occasionally, too, he saw monkeys, but more often was only aware of their presence by the howling they set up as he approached.

At one place, near a pool, he saw numerous butterflies, large blue *Morphos*, and others. Some were drinking; others circled above the pool like a fountain of flowers. He also noted a great variety of wasps, beetles, bees and bugs such as he had never seen before.

He decided that he would endeavour to take some of the butterflies that were hovering over the pool, but he found it difficult to approach from the side on which he stood. Generally speaking, the forest was fairly open, except of course for the festoons of lianas, but between him and the pool there was a screen composed of a lovely creeping plant, with pink and rose coloured blossoms. It grew so thickly as to be impassable.

When just before he had given his word that he would be careful not to lose his way, he had had every intention of observing it to the letter. Not even when he tried to reach the pool did he relax his vigilance, for he turned often to study the trees behind him so that he would recognize them again on his way back. Still taking note of his path, he started to make a detour in order to reach the pool from the far side. In doing this he came to a smaller pool, set in a sylvan glen of breath-taking beauty, and as there were as many butterflies here as round the larger pool, he decided that it would serve his purpose just as well. Forthwith he got busy, and had no difficulty in capturing as many butterflies as he could accommodate. He often took several with one sweep of his net, and afterwards spent some time sorting them out and admiring them. At length, having decided that he had enough, he set about the return journey, observing that he had been rather longer than he intended, for it was beginning to get dark.

It was now—as he afterwards realised—that he made his initial mistake. Some little distance away he saw the curtain of pink creepers that had prevented him from going straight to the larger pool, and thinking to cut off a corner, he went straight towards it. It was not until he reached the flowers, and saw no pool, that he realised that he had been mistaken in assuming that the flowers were those which he had originally seen. However, he was not in the least dismayed, for he could see the curtain of creepers a short distance ahead. Or he thought he could. It was not until he had reached them, and failed to find the pool, that he realised that these groups of creepers were common in the forest.

It now began to rain, and the big drops added to his discomfiture. Giving way to a sense of annoyance, he struck off in the direction in which he felt certain his outward trail lay; and indeed he may have been right; but if so, then he crossed the trail without seeing it. In another five minutes he knew that he was lost. To make matters worse, the foliage overhead was so thick that little light penetrated through it at the best of times; now, already, it was nearly dark. However, he did not lose his head. He did what in the circumstances was the wisest thing he could do. He stood still, and drawing his revolver, fired three shots in quick succession into the air. These were answered almost at once, and he drew a quick breath of relief to know that he was still within earshot of the camp. He started walking in the direction from which the answering shots had come, and this was, of course, his second mistake, although it was a natural one to make. When some minutes had passed, and he still did not meet Biggles, a doubt came into his mind, and he fired again—a single shot. It was answered by the report of a rifle, but it sounded a great distance away. In fact, it sounded farther off than it really was, for he had not yet learned that noises, and even shots, do not carry far in the density of the forest.

After another interval he fired again, but this time there was no reply. It was now quite dark. Angry with himself for behaving, as he thought, like a greenhorn, he decided to make a fire, and with this object in view he incautiously broke off a piece of dead wood from a branch near at hand. A cry of pain broke from his lips, and he dropped the branch as if it had been red hot, for a numbing sensation in the palm of his hand told him that he had been stung. In the darkness he could feel something crawling up his arm. With a shudder of horror he dashed it off. At the same moment another burning pain stung his neck, and he realised that he must have shaken one of the creatures— wasp, ant, he knew not what—off one of the upper branches.

For a minute or two he stood still, getting himself in hand, well aware that at all costs he must not give way to panic. With a soft swish something brushed his face as it flew past, and he broke into a perspiration of fear. The rain stopped, and strange rustlings could be heard in the undergrowth. Once there was a coughing grunt not far away, a sinister sound which could only have been made by a large animal or reptile. Perhaps his greatest horror was that he would accidentally step on one of the snakes with which the jungle abounded.

For how long he groped about in the darkness he did not know, but what with the pain from the many stings he received from insects and pricks from thorns, he became convinced that he would lose his reason long before dawn. Already he was on the border of delirium, and it was in sheer desperation that he fired his last shot.

To his amazement and joy, it was answered by a shout no great distance away, and presently he saw the glow of a torch coming towards him. It was held by Biggles. Dusky, hobbling on two sticks, accompanied him. He stood still until they joined him, after which Dusky led the way back to camp.

Ginger thought little about his butterflies when he got back, for although he had been in the jungle only a few hours he had been stung all over, and had been pricked by countless thorns. Leeches were clinging to his legs, although these were easily removed. Weak and haggard from strain, he allowed Biggles to put some liniment on his wounds, and then retired to his hammock.

Biggles did not reproach him. 'I think you'd be wise to follow Dusky's advice in future,' was all he said.

'Don't worry, that was as much of the forest as I want—at any rate for the time being,' declared Ginger bitterly.

'Twenty-four hours of that is about as much as any man can stand,' Biggles told him seriously. 'And now I think we'd better turn in.'

4

A VISITOR AND A MYSTERY

It was shortly before noon the following day that the drone of the *Wanderer's* engines announced the return of Algy. He landed, and taxi-ing up to the camp, shouted, 'I've brought a visitor!'

Biggles stared, and saw a man in white ducks sitting next to him. 'Great Scott!' he ejaculated for Ginger's benefit, 'it's Carruthers.'

The acting-Governor came ashore with Algy, bringing with him a tall, emaciated-looking man whose skin, yellow from recurrent bouts of fever, seemed to be drawn tightly over the bones. He carried a portfolio.

Carruthers greeted the others warmly, and introduced the tall man as Marcel Chorro, his head clerk.

'So you've run into trouble?' he queried.

'It doesn't seem to surprise you,' returned Biggles.

Carruthers shrugged his shoulders. 'Why should it? I've already told you that most people do, sooner or later, in this part of the world. If it isn't one thing it's another. But I must admit that you weren't long bumping into it.'

'I assume that Lacey has told you what has happened?' asked Biggles.

'Yes.'

'Good. Then let's sit down and discuss the matter. I'm anxious to hear your views. Ginger, you might bring something to drink.'

'Okay, chief.'

The party was soon arranged, and Carruthers opened the conversation.

'I think the first point to settle,' he began, 'is how you fellows feel about this affair. I mean, do you want to stay here or do you want to continue your pleasure cruise?'

'I've got an open mind about it,' confessed Biggles. 'Frankly, what we do depends largely on your advice. What do you want us to do? You know the country; moreover, you're in a position of authority, so we certainly shouldn't run counter to your orders. How do you feel about things?'

Carruthers sipped his drink, and lit a cigarette before he replied. 'It's a bit difficult,' he admitted. 'As I told you, we had heard rumours of the existence of this man who calls himself King of the Forest. There has also been talk of his assistant Bogat; but as for who they are, you know as much as I do. I knew nothing about this slave traffic, or about these excavations that are being carried on. Nor did I know of the coming of the other two white men. I can't imagine who they are.'

'They aren't by any chance the survivors of the American party?' suggested Biggles.

'I should hardly think so. Why should they join up with brigands?'

'I take it you'd put a stop to this king business if you could?' questioned Biggles.

'Of course. Really, we ought to stop it.'

'Then why don't you?'

Carruthers raised his hands, palm upwards, indicating the forest on either side. 'My dear fellow, do you realise how far the jungle extends? You could drop an army in it, and then spend

the rest of your life looking for it without finding it. You'd
certainly need an army to do any good, and that's something we
haven't got here. Think what it would cost to send even a small
body of men, with the necessary stores and equipment, on such a
job.'

'I'm afraid I can't agree with you,' returned Biggles imperturbably. 'If I had the handling of this situation I shouldn't
think in terms of armies. Half of the men would be in hospital
most of the time, anyway. This is a job for a small, mobile unit.'

Carruthers looked up sharply. 'You mean—like your party?'

'Put it that way if you like.'

Carruthers rubbed his chin. 'Perhaps you're right,' he
admitted. 'All the same, it's quite obvious that you don't know
what you're up against. What would you do? How would you
start?'

'Clearly, the first thing would be to locate the headquarters of
this gang, and then ascertain just what they're doing. If they're
breaking the law—and there doesn't seem to be much doubt
about that—then the next step would be either to take them into
custody or drive them out of their retreat.'

'How?'

'You're going rather too fast. It would necessarily depend
upon circumstances. There must be a way of doing it, though. I
say that because I have yet to be faced by a problem for which
there is no solution.'

Carruthers grimaced. 'It would be a dangerous business.'

'What's that got to do with it?'

The acting-Governor stared hard at Biggles. 'By Jingo! I like
you,' he declared. 'I'm afraid we poor blighters who get stuck in
the tropics get a bit slack. Seriously, would you, if I gave you the
necessary authority, have a look round for me, and make some
suggestions as to how we can put an end to this racket?'

'I should think so,' returned Biggles slowly. 'What do you
mean by authority?'

'I could swear you in as special constables, but'—Carruthers
laughed awkwardly—'you realise that I've no funds to meet this
sort of thing? You would only get constable's pay—three bob a

day. All the same, if the affair was brought to a successful conclusion no doubt the finance people at home would refund your out-of-pocket expenses.'

'From a financial point of view I shouldn't call that an opportunity to be jumped at,' said Biggles, smiling. 'The Tiger must be robbing the State of thousands of pounds a year. If I apprehended him and secured a conviction I should expect a bonus.'

Carruthers laughed. 'Of course, if you did secure a conviction these fellows would get a pretty heavy sentence; they would have their money taken off them, in which case there might be funds to meet your case. Suppose you leave that to me?'

'Certainly. That's good enough,' agreed Biggles readily. 'I had to raise the point because we're not exactly millionaires. We should have to have a free hand, of course, so that we could go about the thing in our own way.'

'Naturally.'

'All right.' Biggles looked at the others. 'That's seems to be all there is to say. We'll see what we can do.'

'Splendid,' declared Carruthers. 'I'll leave the affair in your hands. And now, if that's all, I'd better be getting back to my office. I've plenty to do with the Governor away.'

'In that case we'll have a bite, and then I'll fly you back,' answered Biggles. 'It was good of you to come up here.'

'Not at all. On the contrary, I'm obliged to you for your help. Is there anything I can do for you?'

'Yes, there is,' returned Biggles promptly. 'One of my difficulties is going to be petrol. You see, we reckoned to cruise about always keeping within easy reach of Belize, where we could refuel. My machine has got a pretty useful range, but I've always got to keep enough petrol in the tanks to get back to Belize. That is to say, if I find myself far from Belize I shan't have much margin for cruising, and running up and down to the coast would be an expensive business. Could you send some petrol up to us? It you could send it up the river the boatmen could make a dump somewhere handy.'

'I see your point,' answered Carruthers. 'That can be

arranged. In fact, I can send you some right away. There's a small supply at one of our posts not far down the river, for the use of the government launch. I'll send it up by express paddlers. The main supply can follow. Meanwhile I'll get a message through to our nearest river post for the emergency petrol to be brought up to you. Keep an eye on the river. If you see the canoe coming it might be a good idea to land near it and tell the men where you want the stuff put.'

'That's a sound scheme,' agreed Biggles. 'It will save us a lot of trouble. I take it we can rely on this emergency supply coming? We should be in a mess if our tanks ran low and the stuff didn't arrive.'

'Don't worry. I'll see to it,' promised Carruthers.

'That's good enough for me,' declared Biggles.

And that was the end of the interview. After lunch Biggles flew the acting-Governor back to Belize, where he spent the night, leaving the others in charge of the camp.

He was in the cockpit early the following morning, anxious to get back to discuss ways and means of starting on their new project. Both for safety and simplicity he followed the river—for safety because it offered the only possible means of getting down should engine trouble develop, and for simplicity in that it marked an unmistakable course, and so enabled him to fly yet give his mind to other matters. Fortunately—as it transpired— he cruised along quietly, and there was never an occasion when he found it necessary to turn sharply, or otherwise put a strain on the aircraft. Not that there was anything unusual about this, for Biggles, like the majority of experienced pilots, never, in any circumstances, performed useless stunts.

He was about fifty miles short of his destination, and was on the point of leaving the river for the lake, when he noticed the loose turnbuckle. Just why he noticed it would be hard to say, except that it becomes an instinctive habit for a pilot to keep an eye on everything around him, even though there may not appear to be any immediate necessity for it. His roving eyes, passing over the turnbuckle which braced the flying wires between the starboard wings, stopped suddenly and remained fixed. A second later his left hand slid to the throttle and eased it back; at the same time he moved the joystick forward slightly so that the *Wanderer* began a slow glide towards the river, at this point about a hundred yards wide.

Although to anyone but a pilot it might have appeared a small thing, what he had noticed was this. The turnbuckle should have been screwed up so that none—or not more than one or two—of the threads on the cross-bracing wire were visible. At least six threads could now be seen, and as there were only eight or nine in all, it meant that the entire strain was being carried by two or three threads; even an ordinary strain on the wings might therefore be sufficient to pull the wire clean out of the buckle—which takes the form of a longish, rather fat piece of metal; and since the wings are held in place by these particular wires, should the wires break, or pull out of the turnbuckle, there would be nothing to prevent the wings from tearing off—that is, if one excludes the small fishplates which fasten the roots of the wings to the fuselage.[1]

Now, the turnbuckle concerned was on the starboard side. What made Biggles look at the turnbuckle on the port side he did not know; but he did, and to his alarm, and unspeakable amazement, he saw that the same thing had happened there. His face was pale as he brought the machine down as gently as he could, and a breath of relief broke from his lips as it settled safely on the water. It made him feel slightly weak to realise that the whole time he had been in the air a 'bump' might have been sufficient to take his wings off. Once on the water the strain was taken off the wires, and he sat still for a little while regarding the turnbuckles with brooding eyes. When he had first noticed the starboard one he had assumed, not unnaturally, that it had worked loose of its own accord; that it was one of those accidents

[1] *The cross bracing wires between the wings of a biplane are called respectively 'flying-wires' and 'landing-wires'. Flying-wires keep the wings of the plane down while the machine is in flight; landing-wires hold them up when the machine is at rest. Naturally, when a machine is in flight, the strain on the wings is upward, and the flying-wires hold them down. When the machine is at rest, the strain, imposed simply by gravity, is downward, and it is the landing-wires that hold them up.*

which can occur to any mechanical device. It should not, of course, be allowed to happen, and since the *Wanderer* was examined every day, it was not easy to see how it could happen. It would have been remarkable enough if only one turnbuckle had worked loose, but that two should become unscrewed at the same time by accident was incredible. In short, such a coincidence was enough to tax the imagination to breaking point.

Biggles's face was grim as he climbed out on the starboard wing and made the necessary adjustment. The turnbuckle was quite loose, and held the wire by only two threads. It was the same on the other side. Vibration alone might have been sufficient to give the turnbuckles the final twist that must have caused him to crash. Satisfied that they were now in order, he took off and flew over to the lake, where he found everything as he had left it. Algy and Ginger were there, waiting for him.

He taxied to the bank, switched off, and tossing the mooring rope ashore joined the others.

'Ginger, it was your turn yesterday to look over the machine,' he said quietly. 'You didn't forget by any chance, did you?'

Ginger looked hurt. 'Of course I didn't,' he retorted hotly. 'What made you ask?'

'Only that coming along this morning I happened to notice that the turnbuckles on both flying wires were loose—nearly off, in fact. I had to land on the river and fix them.'

There was dead silence for a moment.

'Did you say on *both* wires?' Algy burst out.

'I did.'

'Then somebody must have unscrewed them,' declared Algy, with such emphasis that he made it clear at once that he was not prepared to accept coincidence as an explanation.

'Yes, I think that's the only answer,' agreed Biggles.

'It couldn't have been done here, that's certain,' put in Ginger.

'I agree. That means it could only have been done in Belize.'

'You didn't put a guard over your machine last night?' queried Algy.

'No. Why should I? What possible reason had I for thinking that it might be interfered with? I shall take jolly good care it doesn't happen again, though.'

'Somebody must have deliberately tried to crash the machine.'

'He tried to do more than that. He tried to kill me at the same time.'

'But who on earth in Belize could have done such a thing?'

Biggles smiled faintly. 'That's something we may find out presently,' he said. 'The only possible enemies we can have in this part of the world are those connected with the Tiger, or his pal Bogat; it would seem therefore that the Tiger has friends in Belize.'

'That's the only solution,' murmured Ginger. 'The Tiger's ramifications evidently extend to the coast. Well, forewarned is forearmed, they say; we shall have to keep our eyes open.'

'We certainly shall,' agreed Biggles warmly. 'But come on, we may as well have a bite of lunch; it's too late to start anything today, so we'll get all set for an early move tomorrow. How's Dusky getting along?'

'Fine, he's hopping about already,' Ginger answered.

'Did you tell him that we're going to try to put a spoke in the wheel of the Tiger?'

'Yes.'

'What did he say?'

'He's flat out to help us,' declared Ginger. 'He hasn't forgotten that Bogat murdered his brothers.'

'Good. I think he's going to be useful,' returned Biggles. 'Now let's have a bite then talk things over.'

5
THE ENEMY STRIKES

THE upshot of the debate, in which Dusky took part, was this. They would turn in early, and, leaving the lake at dawn, proceed under Dusky's directions to that area in which the headquarters of the Tiger was assumed to be. Whether Dusky would recognise landmarks from the air remained to be seen; on the ground, at any rate, he appeared to have no doubt as to the general direction. Pending this survey, nothing could, of course, be done. As far as they themselves were concerned, the present camp would serve for the time being; if, later, a suitable base could be found nearer to the enemy, then they would move to it. Nothing further could be arranged immediately. This decided, they spent a little while preparing the camp for a more extended stay, clearing the bushes and piling them on the forest side of the tent. At nightfall, with the *Wanderer* moored close in, they got into their hammocks, closed the very necessary mosquito curtains, and went to sleep. There was a short discussion as to whether or not they should take turns to keep guard, but in the end they voted against it, a matter in which they were guided by Dusky, who said that as they were not in the region of savages there was no need for this precaution.

It was therefore with surprise that Ginger awoke some time later—what hour it was he did not know—to find Dusky in quiet conversation with Biggles. He realised that it was the sound of their voices that had awakened him.

Seeing that he was awake, Biggles said, 'Dusky swears that there is somebody moving about in the forest.'

'Does he mean that he's actually heard somebody?'

'Not exactly. I gather that there have been sounds made by night creatures that indicate that human beings are on the move. He believes that they are coming in this direction.'

'But nobody could possibly know that we are here.'

'That's what I've told him. All the same, he insists that he's right. You'd better wake Algy.'

'Perhaps it's a party of chicle-hunters—nothing to do with us?'

Dusky shook his head. 'Not *chicleros*,' he announced definitely. 'Dey not march at night—too mighty scared.'

'We should be foolish not to heed what Dusky says,' declared Biggles, starting to put on his clothes. 'Wake Algy, and both of you get dressed. We'll go outside the tent and listen. Bring your guns.' He himself picked up a rifle and slipped a cartridge into the breech.

Gathered outside the tent, they stood near the edge of the forest, listening intently. A crescent moon hung low in the sky, throwing a broad band of silver across the placid surface of the lake, but within the jungle profound darkness reigned. The air was heavy with heat and the tang of rotting vegetation; vague rustlings betrayed the presence of the invisible army of insects that dwelt in it.

For some minutes the silence continued; then a curious sound came from the forest; it was as though a branch was being violently shaken.

'What on earth was that?' muttered Biggles.

'De monkeys. Dey shake de branches when mens go underneath,' breathed Dusky, slightly hoarse with nervousness.

Biggles looked at the others. 'This is a funny business,' he said quietly. 'It's hard to know what to do for the best. Dusky is convinced that somebody is about, but that doesn't necessarily mean that we're being stalked. On the other hand, it may be Bogat's men—whether they're looking for us or not.'

'They couldn't possibly know we're here,' put in Algy.

'No, but they might guess it. They probably know of the existence of this lake, in which case they might have decided to investigate on the off-chance of finding us here. We're in no case to withstand a serious attack.'

'What's the time?' asked Algy suddenly.

Biggles glanced at his watch. 'Nearly five.'

'It will start to get light in an hour.'

Again, out of the forest, came the sinister rustling of branches. A monkey barked, and then broke off abruptly.

Biggles shook his head. 'I don't like this. I think we'd better start getting ready for a quick move. You two put the stores back in the machine. Don't make a noise about it. I'll walk a few yards into the forest with Dusky. If I shout an alarm, start the engine.'

Twenty minutes passed without further development, except that by the end of that time everything portable had been put on board. Algy and Ginger returned to the edge of the forest where presently Biggles joined them.

'Dusky was right,' he said softly; 'I can hear them now, distinctly.'

'We've got everything on board except the tent,' announced Algy.

'Good—stand fast.'

'Where's Dusky?'

'In the forest, scouting.'

Hardly had the words left Biggles's lips when Dusky returned; he was shaking with excitement. 'Dey come, massa,' he panted.

'We'd better play safe until we see how many of them there are,' decided Biggles promptly 'Into the machine, everybody. Algy, get ready for a snappy take-off; Ginger, you man the gun, but don't use it until I give the word. Get going.'

Not until the others were aboard and the machine cast off did Biggles leave the bank. As he climbed into the aircraft he pushed it a few yards from the shore, leaving it in such a way that the nose faced open water.

'Absolute quiet now,' he ordered.

Silence settled again over the scene. The *Wanderer*, plainly visible from the bank, floated motionless, like a great bird asleep. Algy was in the pilot's seat with his hand on the starter, but Biggles and Ginger crouched by the gun, only their eyes showing above the top of the fuselage. The silence was uncanny, and Ginger found it hard to believe that human beings were abroad in the forest, creeping towards the site of the camp. Then he saw an indistinct shadow flit along the fringe of the forest a little way higher up, and he knew that Dusky's woodcraft had not been at fault.

'Here they come,' he breathed.

Another figure appeared, another, and another, until at last there were at least a dozen shadowy forms creeping towards the tent. Ginger made out the massive form of Bogat, and nudged Biggles; an answering nudge told him that his signal was understood.

With infinite stealth and patience the outlaws closed in on the tent. Then Bogat, gun at the ready, took the lead and advanced to the flap. He threw it open, and at the same time leapt back. 'Come out!' he shouted. The rest raised their guns, covering the entrance.

There was a brief, palpitating interval, then Bogat barked again. 'Come out! You can't get away.' He naturally assumed the airmen to be in the tent, for after a first penetrating stare at it, he ignored the aircraft.

'Don't move, Bogat; I've got you covered,' snapped Biggles. 'Do you want something?'

There was a unanimous gasp from the assembled men. Bogat swung round. He half raised his gun, and then, evidently thinking better of it, lowered it.

'I said, do you want something?' repeated Biggles. 'If you do it's waiting—a hundred rounds of nickel-coated lead. If you don't want anything, clear out of my camp.'

Bogat ducked like lightning, and at the same time fired his gun from the hip.

Ginger's gun spat. He swore afterwards that he didn't consciously pull the trigger; he declared that the shock of Bogat's shot caused his finger automatically to jerk the trigger. Above the uproar that instantly broke out Biggles's voice could be heard yelling to Algy to start up. The engines came to life, and the blast of air flung back by the propellers sent a cloud of fallen leaves whirling into the faces of the outlaws; it also struck the tent and laid it flat. The *Wanderer* surged forward across the water, with Ginger firing spasmodic bursts at the flashes that stabbed the darkness along the edge of the forest. Two or three bullets struck the machine, but as far as could be judged they did no damage. It was impossible to see if any casualties had been inflicted on the enemy. The *Wanderer*, gathering speed, rose into the air.

'Where to?' shouted Algy.

'Make for the river,' Biggles told him.

The stars were paling in the sky, but it was still dark. However, this did not worry Biggles, who knew that dawn would have broken by the time they reached the river, so that there would be no difficulty in choosing a landing place.

'We've lost the tent,' remarked Ginger angrily.

'But for Dusky we might have lost our lives, and that would have been a far more serious matter,' declared Biggles. 'We can always get another tent. I must say that I don't like being hounded about by these dagos, but it was a case of discretion being the better part of valour. Our turn will come. From now on it's open war.'

Nothing more was said. The *Wanderer* cruised on over the tree-tops. The rim of the sun crept up over the horizon and bathed them in a pink glow. The river appeared, winding like a gigantic snake through the jungle. Biggles took the joystick, and in a little while the aircraft was once more at rest, moored near the bank. The bullet-holes were quickly examined, and it was confirmed that nothing vital had been touched.

'Well, let's have some breakfast,' suggested Biggles. 'Then we'll move off.'

'Move off—where to?' asked Algy.

'To have a look round. What has happened need make no difference to our programme. Bogat has declared war on us, so we know just how we stand.'

An hour later the machine was in the air again, heading north-west, following from a considerable height the course of the Unknown River. For the purpose of exploration Biggles would rather have flown lower, but this he dare not risk, for the nearer they flew to the source of the river the narrower it became, and places suitable for landing were fewer and farther between.

For a long time they saw only the same monotonous ocean of jungle, with the jagged peaks of a mountain group cutting into the blue sky far to the north. Dusky stated that the base of these mountains was generally regarded as the boundary between Honduras and Guatemala.

'We may as well have a look at them for all there is to see here,' announced Biggles. 'I'm beginning to wonder even if there is a city in the forest, whether we should notice it. These confounded trees hide everything. If we can't see anything from the air we might as well pack up. I'm not tackling the job on foot, not for Carruthers or anyone else. When I look at the forest from up here I begin to realize what we're up against. The mountains, at any rate, will be a change of scenery.'

Cruising at three miles a minute, instead of—as Dusky assured them—three miles a day, which could be reckoned as normal progress on foot, they reached the mountains in about a quarter of an hour, and from the altimeter it was possible to form a rough estimate of the height. It was necessary to fly at nearly six thousand feet to clear the highest peaks. The jungle persisted for some distance up the slopes, but for the most part the tops were clear of timber, and alternated between stark rock and, in the valleys, grassy savannah. Biggles remarked two or three places where it ought to be possible to land, although without having first examined the ground there would be a certain amount of risk involved.

It was Ginger who spotted the ruined city, although at first he did not recognize it as such. Gazing down on an unexpected plateau, he saw, on the very lip of the steep descent on the southern side, a jumble of rocks of such curious formation that he commented on it.

'That's a queer-looking collection of rocks,' he observed casually. 'Look how square they are. They might almost be houses.'

Biggles stared down at the spot indicated, and as he did so a strange expression came over his face. He pushed open the side window and looked again. 'You're dead right,' he said slowly. 'I'm by no means sure that they're *not* houses.'

'What!' cried Ginger incredulously. 'Let's go down and have a look.'

Biggles cut the throttle, and pushing the joystick forward, began to circle lower. Presently the *Wanderer* was flying at not more than a hundred feet above the plateau, and the matter was no longer in doubt. Apart from the shape of what Ginger had taken to be rocks, the regular manner in which they were laid out convinced them all that the work could have been done only by the hand of man.

'By gosh!' Let's land somewhere. We must have a look at this,' declared Ginger excitedly.

Biggles's eyes were still on the city, around which it was now possible to make out the remains of a wall. 'It's deserted,' he said. 'If anyone was there, he would certainly come out to have a look at us.'

As he spoke Biggles studied the savannah beyond the town where it formed the plateau. It was too narrow to be an ideal landing-place, but there was plenty of length, and he decided that with care a landing might be made. He lowered the wheels, made a cautious approach, and settled down to a safe if somewhat bumpy landing.

Ginger was first out. 'Come on!' he shouted, starting off towards the ruins. 'I shouldn't wonder if the place is littered with gold.'

'I should,' returned Biggles drily.

Leaving the machine where it had finished its run, they walked briskly to the ruins, for the buildings were no more than that, although it was obvious that at one time the place had been a town of importance. Certain buildings larger than the rest marked the sites of what had once been temples or palaces. The whole place, situated as it was on the edge of a chasm overlooking the southern forest, was in the nature of an eagle's eyrie.

Ginger's dream of gold was soon dispelled. With the exception of numerous broken potsherds, and a bronze hammer which Algy found, the houses—or as many as they visited— were empty.

'I'm afraid we're a few hundred years too late,' smiled Biggles. 'This place was either abandoned, or sacked, centuries ago. Still, it's an interesting discovery, and archaeologists concerned with ancient American civilisations will be tickled to death when they hear about it.' He pointed to an obelisk that stood in an open square, carved on its four sides. 'That's called a stele,' he remarked. 'There are any number of them in the forest. That weird-looking carving you can see is writing, but no one has yet learned how to read it. Mind you, I'm only speaking from what

I've learned in books.'

'You don't think this is one of those old cities where excavations have been going on?' inquired Algy.

'Definitely not, otherwise there would be trenches and other signs,' answered Biggles. 'This is a new discovery.'

'What I should like to know,' put in Ginger, 'is how on earth the people who lived here got up and down from the forest—or did they spend their lives here?'

'Even if they spent their lives up here, as they may have done after they were driven out of the forest by the people who conquered them, there must have been some way of getting up,' replied Biggles. 'If we look around we may find it.'

It did not take them long to. Walking round the ruined wall, they came to an opening with the remains of an old gate, from which descended a staircase so fantastic that for a little while they could only stare at it with eyes round with wonder. It was partly natural and partly artificial. That is to say, a remarkable feat of Nature had been helped by the hand of man. It was fairly clear what had happened. At some period in the remote past, when the cliff—indeed, the whole mountain—was being formed, the rock, then in a plastic state, had settled down, leaving a narrow projecting cornice running transversely right across the face of the cliff, from top to bottom. The face of the cliff was not smooth, but in the form of gigantic folds, yet the cornice followed each fold faithfully. There were places where it disappeared from sight behind mighty shoulders of rock.

In its original form the cornice had no doubt been extremely rough, and of a width varying from two to six feet, and in that state a mountain goat might well have hesitated to descend by it. Then had come man, presumably one of the extinct nations of America. At any rate, men had worked at the cornice, cutting steps where they were required, so rendering the descent possible; but even so, the path was not one to be taken by a traveller subject to dizziness.

'Jacob's Ladder,' murmured Ginger.

Biggles nodded. 'It certainly is a remarkable piece of work. I should say that it can't be less than five or six miles from the top to the bottom, following the path, and therefore taking into account the irregular face of the cliff. I remember reading in a book about Bolivia about just such a path on the eastern slope of the Andes. An amusing tale was told of an engineer being paid an enormous salary to superintend a gold mine at the bottom of the staircase; but when he got to it, and saw where he had to go, he not only chucked up the job but declared that he wouldn't go down the path for all the gold in South America.'

'I don't blame him,' remarked Algy feelingly. 'I'd hate to go down this one.'

'Oh, I don't know; it isn't as bad as all that,' returned Biggles. 'After all, some of the corniche roads in the Alps are pretty grim, and people who live in the mountain villages have to go up and down them constantly.'

'It must have been a colossal task, cutting those steps,' put in Ginger.

'The ancients apparently liked colossal tasks,' replied Biggles. 'What about the pyramids of Egypt, and the Great Wall of China? This is nothing compared with them.'

At this juncture, Dusky, who had so far remained silent, interrupted with the surprising statement that he had seen the bottom of the stairway. Interrogation elicited the information that while he had been working for Bogat, clearing undergrowth from the ruins in the jungle near the foot of a cliff, he had come upon just such a flight of steps leading upwards. Asked by Biggles if he had revealed this discovery to Bogat, he said no, the reason being that, although he did not know where the steps led, he thought they might one day provide a means of escape. He had made the discovery about six months ago, as near as he could judge.

'Well, I must say it seems highly improbable that there can be two such stairways,' remarked Biggles. 'In that case, if we followed these steps we should come out either in, or very near, the excavations where the Tiger and the two white men are working. When you think about it, that is not altogether surprising; in fact, it seems quite a natural thing that there should be a town at the foot of these steps as well as at the top.'

'The question that seems to arise in that case is, has the Tiger discovered the staircase since the time Dusky was working at the bottom?' put in Algy.

'I should say not,' answered Biggles without hesitation. 'If the Tiger had discovered the steps he would most certainly have come up here, and even if he didn't start excavating—as seems probable—he would surely have left some traces of his visit— old tins, or ashes of the fires where he did his cooking.'

'Yes, that's reasonable,' agreed Algy. 'What it comes to, then, is this. If Dusky's supposition is correct, we have discovered a way down into the Tiger's camp.'

'That's it,' nodded Biggles.

'What are we going to do?' queried Ginger eagerly. 'I'm all in favour of doing a bit of exploring up here on our own account.'

'We might have time to do that later on, but at the moment, since our stores are not unlimited, I think we owe it to Carruthers to stick to our job.'

'You mean—go down the steps and try to get hold of the Tiger?'

'What else?'

Ginger looked at the stairway and drew back, shuddering. 'Strewth! I'm not so keen on that. I don't mind looking down from a plane, but to crawl down that dizzy path, with all that way to fall if we miss a step, doesn't strike me as a jaunt to be undertaken lightly.'

'Oh, that's all right,' replied Biggles calmly. 'All the same, I'm not entirely happy at the idea of all of us going. Somebody ought to stay to look after the machine. Apart from that, if we got in a jam going down we should all be in the same boat, whereas if somebody stayed behind he might be able to help the others.'

'That's sound reasoning,' murmured Algy.

'I'll tell you what: let's compromise,' decided Biggles. 'Algy, you and Dusky stay up here to keep an eye on things. Ginger and I will do a bit of exploring. If we find it's easy going all the way down we'll come back and let you know; on the other hand, if we find we can't get down, we shall have to come back anyway.'

'Good enough,' agreed Algy. 'When are you going?'

'Right away. There's no need to wait until tomorrow.'

'What about kit?'

'We'll take a tin of bully and some biscuits, a water-bottle and our rifles. That ought to be enough—for the first trip at any rate.'

This being agreed, the party returned to the machine, where the necessary kit was obtained and a meal taken. They then returned to Jacob's Ladder. Biggles, with his rifle slung on his left shoulder, started down. Ginger, after a deep breath, followed.

6
DOWN THE UNKNOWN TRAIL

FOR the first hundred steps Ginger's head swam to such an extent that he felt sick and dizzy; more than once he had to halt and lean weakly against the sheer wall of the cliff that rose up on the right-hand side of the path, hardly daring to look at the frightful void that fell away on his left. In places the cliff was more than sheer; owing to faults in the rock, the path had been dug so far into it that the wall overhung the steps. There were places, too, where the path projected over the abyss in the manner of a cornice, so that one false step would mean a drop of four thousand feet or more to the forest. A slight heat haze hung over the tree-tops, making them look farther away than they really were; it also gave the forest an atmosphere of mystery, and created an impression of looking down upon another world. Thus, thought Ginger, might a man feel descending to Earth from another planet.

Biggles appeared to be little troubled by the terrifying drop. He strode on, rifle on his shoulder, whistling softly, and stopping only to warn Ginger of bad places, places where the wind and rain had worn the steps away so that no more than a smooth, narrow projection remained.

However, one becomes accustomed to anything, and after the first hundred yards Ginger began to breathe more freely. Once, while Biggles was waiting for him, he remarked, 'What would happen if we met somebody coming the other way? I should hate to try to pass anybody.'

Biggles laughed softly. 'I don't think we shall meet anyone on this path,' he observed lightly. 'Save your breath; we shall need it coming back.'

They went on. Condors appeared, stiff-winged, looking as big as gliders; they circled slowly, their heads turned always to face the invaders of their domain. Ginger eyed them nervously.

'We should be in a mess if they decided to attack us,' he said anxiously.

'So would they,' answered Biggles briefly, tapping his rifle.

Rounding the shoulder of rock that up to now concealed what lay beyond, they stopped for a moment to admire the stupendous view that unfolded before them; it seemed that the very world was at their feet. The path, after cutting into a colossal gorge, reappeared again on the far side, five hundred feet below; a mere thread it looked, winding down and down interminably. For the first time Ginger appreciated the full length of it.

'I shouldn't think the people who lived up top were ever invaded,' he opined. 'Why, a couple of men could hold this path against an army.'

'Easily,' agreed Biggles. 'I'd rather be the man at the top than one of the fellows coming up.'

After that, for an hour they walked on with hardly a word. The heat flung down by the sun, and radiated by the rock, always intense, became worse as they descended. As Ginger remarked, it was like going down into a furnace.

They were nearing the bottom—at least, they were more than three-quarters of the way down—when the steps ended abruptly in a veritable chaos of rock. At first Ginger thought they had reached the foot of the stairway, but Biggles pointed out that this was not so, and investigation soon proved his theory, which was that in the remote past a landslide had fallen across the path, carrying a section of it away.

'If we can find a way across this mass of detritus we ought to strike the steps again on the other side,' he declared. 'We know that the steps go right down to the forest, because Dusky saw them there.'

'Yes, of course,' answered Ginger.

'All the same, anyone coming up the steps, encountering this pile of debris, might well think that they had come to the end of the stairway,' resumed Biggles. 'Unless they persevered, and forced a way across the landslide, they would not know that the steps continued and went right on up to the top. Let's push on. Be careful where you're putting your feet, because some of this stuff doesn't look any too safe. If we started a movement the whole lot might slide again. Come on—this seems to be the easiest way.'

Biggles proceeded, choosing his path carefully, with Ginger following close behind. From his point of view there was now at least one advantage: there was no longer the precipice to fear, for the route Biggles had chosen traversed the landslide.

And so they came upon the village. It was entirely un-expected, for there had been absolutely nothing to indicate its presence. Reaching the bottom of a steep incline, across a confused jumble of mighty boulders, they found themselves confronted by a drop of some thirty or forty feet into a pleasant valley which the giant forest trees had failed to cross. That is to say, the valley marked the top limit of the big timber. Trees could be seen on the far side, and these, presumably, went right on down to the forest proper. There were no trees on the side where they stood regarding the scene. Nor were there any big trees in the valley, which was carpeted with verdant grasses and flowering shrubs. Up the centre of it ran a wide track, ending at a modern village. Actually, it appeared to be something more than a village, although they used the term for want of a better one. In the centre of a fairly extensive group of ramshackle buildings stood a fine bungalow, well built of heavy timber. At the back of it, and evidently a part of the premises, was a range of outbuildings roofed with corrugated iron. Radiating from this centre were rows of small houses. From a courtyard between the bungalow and the outbuildings smoke was rising lazily into the air from an outside cooking stove. A woman, conspicuous with a scarlet handkerchief tied round her head, did something at the fire and then disappeared into the house. Apart from some mules grazing higher up the valley, which appeared to end abruptly, there was no other sign of life.

As soon as Biggles and Ginger came in sight of this utterly unexpected feature they stopped, and after a few seconds' incredulous contemplation of it, sat down abruptly.

'Great Scott!' Biggles muttered. 'What the deuce is all this?'

Ginger, squatting beside him, answered, 'Don't ask me.'

Biggles regarded the village thoughtfully. 'There's only one answer,' he said slowly. 'The Tiger would never tolerate a second gang in the same area, so this must be part of his organisation. If that is so—and I'm convinced I'm right—then this might even be his secret retreat: the place Dusky spoke about. The fact that there are women—or at least one woman—here, proves fairly conclusively that this is a permanent settlement. The big house proves it, too, if it comes to that.'

'So what?' inquired Ginger. 'We should be taking a chance if we tried to cross that valley. There must be others here besides that woman we saw. We should be spotted for a certainty.'

'We may not have to cross the valley,' answered Biggles. 'I have a feeling that this is our objective.'

Ginger started. 'What do you mean—our objective?'

'Well, we were only going to the bottom of the stairway in order to locate the Tiger's headquarters. There was no other purpose in our going down. That bungalow, unless I am mistaken, is the palace of the King of the Forest, so there is no need for us to go any farther.'

'What are you going to do—go back and let Algy know what we've found?'

'I don't think so—not for the moment, anyway. We should only have to come down again.'

'If Carruthers and his police were here we could raid the place,' murmured Ginger.

'Quite, but they don't happen to be here. In any case, there wouldn't be much purpose in raiding the place if the Tiger wasn't here. He's the man we want—he and Bogat. Unless they are captured the racket would still go on.'

Ginger shrugged his shoulders. 'Well, you're the boss. What's the plan—or haven't you got one?'

'There's only one thing we can do, as far as I can see,' replied Biggles, 'and that's have a look round the village while we're here, while the place is comparatively deserted. We may not get another such chance. Don't forget that so far we have no actual proof of what the Tiger is doing—that is, proof that would carry weight in a court of law. It wouldn't be any use just talking vaguely about the Tiger being a crook, a slave-driver, a chicle thief, without evidence to prove it. This may be our chance to get such evidence. I'm going down into the village.'

Ginger stared aghast. 'Going down! You must be crazy.'

'We shan't collect any evidence sitting here.'

'We could watch them, though, and spot what was going on.'

'Even so, I can't see that we should learn more than we already know. We must get some concrete proof to secure a conviction. All the same, if we could capture the Tiger, or Bogat, and get back to the coast, we might hold him until we'd obtained the proof we need. Perhaps some of the slaves would give evidence. But we shan't get any of these things sitting here. I'm going down.'

'What do you want me to do? Shall I come with you, or stay here?'

Biggles thought for a moment. 'I think you'd better come with me,' he decided. 'I may need a witness if I find anything—otherwise I should only have my unsubstantiated word.'

'Suppose things go wrong? Algy won't know what's happened to us.'

'We can easily get over that.'

Taking his notebook from his pocket, Biggles tore out a page and scribbled a brief message to the effect that a village was in the valley just ahead, and they were going down into it. Returning to the stairway, he put the message under a stone in a conspicuous place, and built a little cairn beside it so that it could not be missed by anyone coming down. This done, they returned to the valley, and after hunting about for a little while found a way down into it.

'Keep this place in your mind's eye,' said Biggles quietly, surveying the spot where they had descended. 'We may have to come back this way—in a hurry. Try to get a mental photograph of the silhouette of the rocks, in case we have to find it in the dark.'

This did not take long, after which Biggles turned towards the village.

'I think our best policy is to go straight up to the house,' he surprised Ginger by saying. 'In fact, I don't see that we can do anything else. There's no real cover, so even if we tried stalking tactics it is almost certain that we should be seen; and if we were spotted skulking like a couple of thieves, there would probably be an outcry. I think this is a case of bluff. All the same, we needn't expose ourselves unnecessarily; we'll just stroll along, and if nobody sees our faces we may get away with it.'

'You know best,' agreed Ginger, 'but it seems a risky business to me. I never was one for jumping into a lion's den without first making sure that the lion wasn't at home.'

Biggles smiled, and walked on towards the village, the nearest buildings of which were not more than a hundred yards away.

They had covered about half the distance when Biggles touched Ginger on the arm, and with an inclination of his head indicated something that he had seen. The boundaries of the valley were now apparent. Hemmed in by cliffs, sometimes high, and, in a few places, fairly low, such as at the spot where they had entered it, there was only one proper entrance. This was a narrow pass at the southern end of the track, a mere defile through the rock wall, presumably where those who lived in the village descended to the forest some four hundred feet below. At this natural gateway two men were on guard; at least, they were armed with rifles. Smoking, they lounged against the wall of the pass.

'If that is the only entrance to the valley, those fellows will wonder how the deuce we got in,' said Biggles softly. 'There is this about it, though; the people in the village—if there are any—knowing that men are on guard at the entrance, might suppose that we are here on business. My word,' he went on, glancing round, 'what a spot for a hide-out. Carruthers was right. An army might have wandered about in the forest for years without even suspecting that this place was here. It would need an army to capture it, too, against a score of determined men.'

'There's one thing that puzzles me,' remarked Ginger. 'Dusky said he found the foot of the stairway. Anyway, he saw a stairway, so we must assume that it was the terminus of the path we came down. Yet, judging by the way he mentioned it—he was actually clearing the jungle, you remember?—it seems that those steps weren't used, which means there must be another way up. In fact, the Tiger may still not know that Dusky's stairway exists.'

'By jove! I didn't think of that,' returned Biggles quickly. 'You're dead right. Whether they have known about the stairway all along, or discovered it since Dusky was there, it seems unlikely that it is used. There is probably an easier way down. It doesn't matter at the moment, but we'll bear it in mind.'

By this time they had reached the village, still without seeing anyone apart from the two men on duty. A drowsy silence broken only by the hum of insects hung on the air. Biggles avoided the main street, a dusty track often interrupted by outcrops of rock, which wound a crooked course between the houses—most of them little better than hovels—and kept to the rear of the buildings, moving steadily towards the big bungalow. As they neared it they came suddenly upon a woman; she was on her knees, grinding maize; she looked surprised when she saw the strangers, but said nothing, and after they had passed they could hear her going on with her monotonous task.

'It would be a joke, wouldn't it, if this isn't the place we're looking for, after all?' murmured Ginger. 'It might turn out to be a perfectly legitimate village.'

'People don't post guards at the entrance to a perfectly legitimate village,' Biggles reminded him. 'Moreover, if this place was above-board, there would surely be some attempt at cultivation; and there would be no need for *chicleros* to sweat up and down four hundred feet of rock every time they went to work. All right—here we are; keep quiet now.'

They had reached the entrance to the yard that gave access to the outbuildings of the big house, the back door of which also opened into it. The fire which they had seen from the rocks was still burning; above it was suspended an iron cauldron from which arose an appetizing aroma.

'We'll try the outbuildings first,' said Biggles quietly, and walked over to them; but if he hoped to see what they contained he was disappointed, for they were locked, every one of them, and there were six in all, large and small. But from the far one they were granted a view of something which hitherto had been hidden by a corner of the house. It was a garden, a walled-in area, an unsuspected Eden. Grapes hung in purple clusters from an overhead trellis; scarlet tomatoes gleamed among the golden stalks of Indian corn; huge yellow gourds lay about among vines that wandered through flowers of brilliant colours. A bush loaded with great blue plums made Ginger's mouth water. This pleasant scene was enhanced by a pigeon-cote, where several birds were preening themselves. Into this unsuspected paradise Biggles led the way. Ginger made for the plums, but Biggles dragged him back into a shady arbour where a tiny fountain bubbled.

'Don't be an ass,' he muttered; 'we're on thin ice here. Don't you realise that we're in the king's garden? Stand fast.'

Peering through the creepers that covered the arbour, Ginger saw that they were now at the side of the house. A long, low window overlooked the garden. Near it was a door. It was open.

'We're doing well. Let's have a look inside,' murmured Biggles, and went on to the door, which gave access to the garden, but obviously was not the main entrance to the house. After a cautious peep inside Biggles took a pace over the threshold, Ginger at his elbow. He whistled softly as he looked round.

'And I should say this is the king's parlour,' he whispered.

The room was magnificently, if ostentatiously, furnished as

something between a lounge and an office. An old, beautifully carved Spanish sideboard was disfigured by a lot of cheap, modern bric-à-brac. Bottles and glasses stood on a brass-topped table. A modern roll-top desk, littered with account-books and papers, stood near the far wall; but the piece that fascinated Ginger most was a fine, leather-covered chest. In strange contrast, near it stood an American steel safe. A second door led into the interior of the house. A strange foreign odour hung in the sultry air.

So much the visitors saw at a glance. After listening intently for a moment, Biggles walked over to the desk, where he began to scan the papers, but without disturbing them. He opened a ledger, and whistled softly as his eyes ran down the items.

'This is all we wanted to know,' he breathed. 'This is the Tiger's sanctum all right, and these are his accounts. There's enough documentary evidence here to hang him twice over. He's evidently a gentleman of some taste, too. Hullo, what's this?'

As he spoke Biggles picked up a tiny slip of flimsy paper that was lying on the desk, held in place by a cartridge used as a paper-weight. As he picked up the paper and read what was written on it his brow creased with anger and astonishment; he stared at it for so long that Ginger's curiosity could not be restrained.

'What is it?' he demanded.

'You might well ask,' replied Biggles through his teeth. 'It explains a lot of things. Take a look at that.' He passed the paper.

Ginger read the message, his lips forming the words:

'Keep watch for three Britishers in airplane. They are government spies sent to get you, acting for Carruthers. Names are Bigglesworth, Lacey and Hebblethwaite. They have been sworn in as police, and have got one of your peons, the man Bogat shot. They will use him as evidence.

'M.C.'

'Did you note the initials?' inquired Biggles.

'Yes. Who on earth——'

'M.C. stands for Marcel Chorro—who else? He's the only man besides Carruthers who knows what we're doing. Evidently he is one of the Tiger's spies. My goodness! No wonder Carruthers found it hard to get evidence. Chorro must have been the swine who loosened my turnbuckles—yes, by gosh! Now we know how Bogat knew we were camping at the lake. He marched straight through the forest to attack us.'

'But how the dickens could Chorro have got a message through in the time?' gasped Ginger. 'The fastest canoe on the river couldn't get here much inside a week.'

'You saw the pigeon-cote outside, didn't you? Notice the thin paper used for the message.'

Ginger caught his breath. 'So *that's* it. Chorro and the Tiger run a pigeon post.'

'Undoubtedly. Come on, we've seen enough. It's no use tempting providence—we'll get back to Algy right away.'

Biggles started towards the door, but recoiled in horror. With staring eyes he clutched Ginger by the arm and held him back.

Ginger, following the direction of Biggles's eyes, felt his blood turn to ice. For some minutes he had been aware that the strange aroma had been getting more noticeable, now he saw the reason.

Emerging slowly from the chest that he had so much admired was a snake, but such a snake as not even a nightmare could have produced. As thick as a man's thigh, coil after coil was gliding sinuously out of the chest as though it would never end. Already fifteen feet of rippling horror lay stretched across the room, cutting them off from the door and the window.

7
IN THE CLAWS OF THE TIGER

How long Ginger stood staring at the snake he did not know. He seemed to lose all count of time; he forgot where he was, and what he was doing. He was conscious of one thing only—the snake. Its little black eyes, glinting like crystals when the light caught them, fascinated him. After the first gasp of horror not a sound left his lips.

Pulling himself together with a mighty effort, he looked at Biggles, and saw that he, too, was at a loss to know what to do. He stared at the snake, then at the door, then back at the reptile. Once he braced himself as if he contemplated taking a flying leap; then he cocked his rifle and tried in vain to draw a bead on the swaying head.

'Go on—shoot,' urged Ginger, in something very near a panic.

'I daren't risk it,' muttered Biggles. 'That head is a small mark for a rifle, and if I miss, the shot will raise the place. If I only wounded the beast goodness knows what would happen.'

Curiously enough, the snake—which Biggles thought was a python—made no attempt to attack them; it lay across the floor, watching them in an almost human manner; it was as if it knew they were intruders, and had determined to prevent them from escaping. Every time they moved, it raised its head, hissing venomously, causing them to retire.

Torn by doubt and indecision, Biggles was still trying to think of a way out of their quandary when from outside came the sound of voices, followed a moment later by the trampling of footsteps; and almost before he was fully alive to their danger the inner door was thrown open and a man came in to the room. He took one pace only and then stopped dead, staring at the spectacle that confronted him. Then his hand flashed to a holster that was strapped to his hip, and came up holding a revolver.

At first Ginger thought he was going to shoot the snake, but it was soon clear that this was not his intention, for he took not the slightest notice of the creature, although it had turned towards him and was now rubbing its sinuous body against his leg. Not until then did Ginger realise that the reptile was a pet, and not a wild creature that had invaded the house from the forest.

The newcomer, who was clearly the owner of the house, even if he were not the reputed King of the Forest, was a striking figure, but certainly not a pleasing one. He was a half-caste, the black predominating, of about fifty years of age; he was of medium height, but of massive, though corpulent, proportions. His arms and shoulders might have been those of a gorilla, but as an example of physique he was spoilt by a paunch of a stomach which, like his face, was flabby from over-eating or self-indulgence, or both. His cheeks were puffy, but his chin was pugnacious. His eyes were small and dark; they were never still, but flashed suspiciously this way and that. His hair was long and luxuriant, but had a unmistakable negroid twist in it. An enormous black moustache drooped from his upper lip. He was dressed—or rather, over-dressed—in a uniform so elaborate, so heavy with gold braid, and of colours so brilliant that not even a cinema commissionaire would have dared to wear it. The general effect was that of a comic-opera brigand; but, looking at the coarse face, Biggles judged him to be a man of considerable mental and physical strength, vain, crafty, and unscrupulous; a man who would be brutal for the sheer pleasure of it, but who, at a pinch, might turn out to be a coward.

The newcomer broke the silence by calling out in a loud voice, 'Marita! Who are these men?' He spoke in Spanish.

A woman, evidently Marita, she who had tended the fire, appeared in the background. In the same language she answered, nervously, that she did not know the men. She had never seen them before—which was true enough.

The man came farther into the room. He spoke in a soft, sibilant voice to the snake, which writhed out of sight under the desk. Then he eyed Biggles suspiciously.

'What language you speak, eh?' he asked, talking now in English with an American accent, from which it may be concluded that he assumed the airmen to be either British or American.

'We speak English,' answered Biggles.

'What you come here for, huh? rasped the half-cast. Then, before Biggles could answer, understanding flashed into his eyes. They switched to the desk, and Biggles knew that he had remembered the note from Chorro.

'Am I right in supposing that I'm speaking to the King of the

Forest?' inquired Biggles calmly.

The half-caste's eyes narrowed. 'I am the king,' he said harshly. 'Where is the other man?'

'What other man?'

'There are three of you. Where is he?'

'What are you talking about?' demanded Biggles, although he knew well enough what was meant.

'Which of you is Bigglesworth?'

Biggles realised that it was useless to pretend. The Tiger knew they were in the district; he was also aware that the chances of any other white men being there were so remote as to be ignored.

'I'm Bigglesworth,' answered Biggles quietly.

An ugly smile spread slowly over the Tiger's face. He put a small silver whistle to his lips and blew a shrill signal. Instantly men came running. With them were two white men whom Biggles guessed were those to whom Dusky had referred. The first was tall and cadaverous; he could only be called white by courtesy, for jaundice had set its mark on his face, leaving it an unhealthy yellow. The same unpleasant tint was discernible in the whites of his eyes, which were pale grey and set under shaggy brows. His mouth was large, with thin lips; nor was his appearance improved by ears that stuck out nearly at right angles from his head. His companion was a weedy-looking individual of nondescript type. Lank, hay-coloured hair co-vered his head; a moustache of the same tint straggled across his upper lip, stained in the middle with nicotine. An untidy, hand-made cigarette was even then in his mouth.

The Tiger called them in and indicated the prisoners with a theatrical wave of his arm. 'The cops got here before us—that saves us the trouble of going to fetch them.' Then a look of doubt returned to his eyes. 'Where's the other one?' he purred.

'Oh, he's about,' returned Biggles evenly.

'Where is he?'

'Look around, maybe you'll find him . . . maybe not.'

The Tiger changed the subject. 'How did you get here? Who brought you?'

Biggles smiled faintly. 'We brought ourselves.'

'That's a lie,' snarled the Tiger, crouching as though to spring, and Biggles began to understand how he had got his doubtful nickname. 'Somebody showed you the way in—who was it? I'll tear the hide off him.'

'Sorry,' said Biggles, 'but that's a pleasure you will be denied, for the simple reason that no such person exists.'

'How did you get past the guards?' The Tiger seemed to be genuinely worried by the fact that strangers had penetrated into his retreat.

'Oh, they were looking the other way,' returned Biggles truthfully.

The expression on the Tiger's face boded no good for the sentries, but Biggles was not concerned about their fate.

'Take them away,' snapped the Tiger.

Several men, a rag-tag but nevertheless picturesque set of ruffians, stepped forward and disarmed the prisoners. They offered no resistance, knowing it to be useless.

'What shall we do with them, your Majesty?' fawned the man who appeared to be in charge.

Biggles smiled at the words 'your Majesty.' It seemed that the title of King was actually enjoyed by the Tiger among his subjects.

The Tiger considered the prisoners reflectively; then a smile crept over his face. 'Put them next to Juanita; she must be getting hungry,' he ordered. 'When we get the other we will lift the bar and leave them together. All right; take them away.'

Rough hands were laid on the prisoners. Biggles did not protest, perceiving that with the man with whom they had to deal it would be a waste of time. No doubt he had already been responsible for the death of scores of wretched slaves, so another murder, more or less, would not affect his conscience. In any case it was obvious that he thought himself safe in his secret retreat.

As they were marched towards the outbuildings, Ginger wondered who Juanita was, although that she was something unpleasant he had no doubt whatever. He was soon to learn. A door was opened, and they were pushed inside a shed. The door slammed, and a heavy bar crashed in place.

After the dazzling sunshine outside it seemed to be pitch black within, but as his eyes grew accustomed to the darkness Ginger began to make out some of the features of their prison. The first thing he saw was Biggles standing beside him, also peering about; next, a row of stout vertical bamboo bars that separated them from another compartment. This second stall had another barred wall, or part of a wall, beyond which was open air. It needed no second glance to see that it was, in fact, a cage. Perhaps a better description would be to call the whole place a cage, divided by bars into two compartments. They were in one part. But what was in the other? Ginger looked for the occupant—for he knew that there must be one—but in vain. If proof that they were not alone were needed, a menagerie-like stench of wild beast provided it. Then he saw a small hole at the back of the next compartment, and he looked no farther; he knew that the beast, whatever it was, was inside, in its lair.

Biggles put a hand on the partition, and shook it. 'This is the bar the Tiger meant when he spoke about lifting it,' he remarked. 'Juanita is on the other side. Apparently, when feeding time comes, the partition is raised from the outside, leaving us all together.'

8
ALGY EXPLORES

ALGY spent some time loafing about the ruined village, but as the day wore on, and Biggles and Ginger did not return, he became conscious of an uneasiness which presently turned to anxiety, and he took up a position at the top of the steps from which he could keep a look-out. Dusky said nothing, but knew well enough what was in his mind.

The day faded under a canopy of crimson glory; night fell, and still there was no sign of the explorers. Their failure to return put Algy in a quandary. He had been asked to remain on the plateau to look after the machine, and he was aware of the danger of leaving his post without letting the others know; all the same, he could not dispel the feeling that something had gone . wrong. Ought he to go down Jacob's Ladder and investigate? There seemed to be little point in remaining where he was, for it was hard to see what could happen to the machine, which was still standing, an incongruous object, near the ruins. Again, he reasoned, if he met Biggles and Ginger coming up the path he could always come back with them. In the end he decided that if they had not returned by the time the moon rose he would go in search of them.

He was in some doubt what to do about Dusky, but thought it would be better if he remained behind; the old man, however, when the project was broached, had his own opinion on this, and declared that nothing would induce him to remain in a place which, without any doubt, was haunted by the ghosts of the past.

To this Algy had to submit, and as the silver moon crept up over the distant horizon he set off down the staircase, carring his rifle, with Dusky following close behind.

By daylight the others had found it a difficult and dangerous journey, but in the uncertain moonlight Algy found the descent an unnerving ordeal. However, he did not hurry, but adopting the principle of slow but sure, moved cautiously down the cornice, hardly looking at the terrible void that fell away on his left. He still hoped to meet the others coming up, but there was no sign of life; no sound broke the heavy silence. He and Dusky might have been the only people on earth.

It was Dusky who, in the first light of the false dawn, spotted the cairn that marked the message which Biggles had left against just such an emergency. Algy picked up the paper, read it, and made Dusky acquainted with its contents.

'They may be all right, but it's strange they should stay away so long,' he said. 'The only thing we can do is go on to the valley . and try to locate them.'

They had no difficulty in finding it, and making their way down the rocks, paused to consider the situation, for there was no indication as to which direction they should take; to march straight into the village struck Algy as being a dangerous undertaking, one that might do more harm than good.

Then, as they stood there, in the pitch blackness that precedes the true dawn, they became aware of a curious, not to say alarming, sound. It was a low snarling, punctuated from time to time by a crash, as if a heavy body was being flung against an obstruction. Having listened for a while, Algy asked Dusky what he thought it could be.

The old man answered at once that the snarling could only be caused by a wild beast. He thought it was in a cage, trying to free itself, and he offered to confirm this. Algy assenting to the proposal, he crept away into the darkness.

Not for a moment did it occur to Algy that the sound had any direct connection with Biggles and Ginger. There was no reason why it should. He had no objection to Dusky going off scouting, although for his part he preferred to remain where he was until it became light enough for him to get a better idea of his surroundings.

Pink dawn was beginning to flush the eastern sky when Dusky returned. He said no word, but beckoned urgently. Algy knew that the old man had discovered something, and without a question followed him. Descending to the foot of the rocks, they went on for some distance, keeping clear of the village, and after a while it became obvious that Dusky was making his way towards some outbuildings. As they drew nearer the snarling became louder, and it was clear that the beast, whatever it was, was in one of them. Then, in an interval of silence, came a low mutter of voices, and Algy thought he recognised Ginger's. He now took the lead, and went forward quickly.

Ten yards from the nearest building he stopped, listened for a moment, and then called sharply, 'Biggles—is that you?'

The answer came instantly. 'Yes, we're in here.'

Algy went forward again, and after a minute or two grasped the situation. He found that the building was, in fact, a cage divided into two compartments. In one of them was a black panther. As he came up it was tearing with its claws at the far

side of its cage, but as soon as it saw him it turned its attention to
him with a rush that made him take a quick pace backwards.
However, when he saw that the bars held firmly he moved
nearer, and dimly, for it was not yet properly light, made out
Biggles and Ginger in the background. Without waiting for
explanations he cocked the rifle and took aim at the beast.

Biggles uttered a sharp cry. 'Don't shoot!'

'Why not?' demanded Algy, lowering the weapon.

'The shot will bring a crowd here,' Biggles told him tersely.
'Try to find a way of getting us out. It doesn't matter about the
animal.'

Algy soon saw the wisdom of this, but a quick reconnaissance
revealed that escape was not going to be easy. There was a door
to the compartment in which the others were confined, but it
was heavily built, and locked, and without the key he was
helpless. He passed this information on to Biggles, and then
explored farther. The door of the animal's cage was, he
discovered, operated from above, as was also the partition, the
raising of which would throw the two compartments into one.

'I'd better shoot the brute,' he told Biggles desperately. 'I
could then lift the dividing bars, and by opening the door of the
cage, let you out.'

'All right—go ahead,' agreed Biggles. 'As soon as we're out
we'll make a dash for the stairway.'

Algy raised his rifle, but before he could fire a cry of alarm
from Dusky brought him round facing the village. There was no
need to look farther. A dozen men, mostly natives, but with
some white men among them, were racing towards the spot.
One fired a revolver as he ran.

Seeing that it was now too late to put his plan into operation,
Algy's first thought was to take cover and try to hold the crowd
at bay. Dusky was already on his way to the rear of the
buildings, and he followed him, but even as he ran he got an idea
that speeded him on.

'Help me up!' he shouted to Dusky, and using the old man's
back as a vaulting horse, he scrambled on the roof of the
building. Shouts from the oncoming crowd told him that he had

been seen, but he gave no heed. Dropping the rifle, he seized the lever which operated the door of the animal's cage, and dragged it back. The door swung open. The panther was not slow to take advantage of the opportunity to escape, and shot out into the open, a streak of black, snarling fury. For a moment it crouched, as if uncertain which way to go; then it saw the crowd, which had stopped at its appearance, and the matter was no longer in doubt. It hated the men on sight, and went towards them like an arrow. The crowd fled, scattering.

Algy would dearly have loved to watch the rest, but there was no time. He raised the partition, and a moment later had the satisfaction of seeing Biggles and Ginger bolt out through the door by which the panther had vacated its prison.

'The stairway!' shouted Biggles. 'Make for the stairway.'

Algy snatched up his rifle, dropped to the ground, and in another second all four were in flight towards the rocks. A volley of shots made them look round, and they were just in time to see the panther fall. It had overtaken one of the white men and pulled him down, but the King of the Forest, with a courage worthy of a better cause, emptied his revolver into the animal's sleek flank.

'Keep going!' shouted Biggles. 'If we can reach the stairway we can hold them.'

Shouts told them that the Tiger was rallying his men to resume the pursuit, and they waited for no more. A few shots were fired as they scrambled up the rocks, but the shooting was wild and the bullets did no harm.

'Good,' panted Biggles as they reached the top. 'Take cover, everybody. Algy, lend me that rifle.'

Crouching behind a rock, he took quick aim and fired at the Tiger. But the run had unsteadied him, and the shot missed. However, it made their pursuers dive for cover. Not that they remained still. They spread out fanwise, and Biggles knew that no good purpose could be served by remaining where they were.

'We'll go on up and get back to the machine,' he decided.

In single file they began the long ascent, Biggles, still carrying the rifle, bringing up the rear. He knew, of course, that they would be followed, and was sorry in a way that it had been necessary to reveal the continuation of the staircase, of which, he felt sure, the Tiger was in ignorance.

For half an hour nothing happened, and they toiled on, naturally finding the ascent more arduous than the descent. Then, round a shoulder of rock far below them, appeared the Tiger and his men, also in single file, for the steps were not wide enough to permit the passage of two people abreast. Biggles knew that they, too, must have been seen. He did not shoot, for the range was considerable, and the mounting sun was already causing the air to quiver, making accurate shooting impossible. However, he kept an eye on their pursuers, and presently saw five men, natives, forge rapidly ahead.

'The Tiger has sent some Indians forward,' he told the others. 'They may be used to this sort of thing, and no doubt the Tiger hopes they'll overtake us. There's nothing to worry about at the moment; if they get too close we'll give them something that should discourage them. Keep going; we're still some way from the top.'

For an hour they stuck doggedly to their task, which as time went on, strained their resources to the utmost. The heat became intense, and they were all breathing heavily, although they were still far from the top.

'I think it will pay us to take a breather,' announced Biggles presently. 'We shall never stand this pace right to the top.' He halted at a bend. 'This will suit us,' he continued, looking back.

Three hundred yards beyond them was another bend, beyond which it was not possible to see.

'The first man who pokes his nose round that corner is going to meet a piece of lead coming the other way,' announced Biggles, adjusting his sights, and holding the rifle at the ready.

Squatting on the steps, they recovered their breath. All were thirsty, but there was no water to be had, so no one commented on it. Ten minutes passed, and Biggles was just standing up preparatory to giving the order to march, when, at the lower bend, an Indian appeared. From the abrupt manner in which he stopped it was apparent that he was aware of his danger; but he did not withdraw; he said something to those behind him, the sound being clearly audible in the still air.

Biggles's rifle cracked, and the Indian vacated his position with alacrity, although whether he had been hit or not the comrades could not tell.

'That'll give them something to think about, anyway,' observed Biggles, giving the order to march.

Twice during the next hour he halted and surveyed the winding track behind them. There were places where it was possible to see for a considerable distance, but there was no sign of the Indians.

'I don't understand it,' he muttered, frowning. 'I can hardly think that they've gone back. However, as long as they don't interfere with us I don't care what they do.'

They went on, and shortly before midday reached the top of the steps.

'The machine is still all right, anyway,' remarked Ginger, noting that it was standing as they had left it.

'We'll go across and have something to eat,' declared Biggles.

Hardly had the words left his lips when a rifle cracked, surprisingly close, and a bullet whistled over his shoulder to smack against the rock behind him. So astonished was he that he looked around in amazement, trying to make out the direction from which the shot had come, but there was nothing to indicate it. As, realising his danger, he dashed for cover, there came another shot.

'Where are they coming from?' exclaimed Algy, in tones of surprise and alarm.

'I don't know, but I suspect those Indians know more about this place than we do,' answered Biggles, peering cautiously at the surrounding rocks. 'Somehow they must have got level with us by another route. If we aren't careful they may outflank us. I think we'd better make a dash for the machine and find a healthier parking place.'

'You mean—take off?' queried Ginger.

'Yes.'

'Where are you going to make for?'

'The river—there's nowhere else we can go. Besides, we don't want to get too far away. We'll find a quiet anchorage and think things over. When I give the word, run flat out for the machine. We'll open out a bit, so as not to offer a compact target. Ready? Go!'

Jumping up, they all ran towards the machine, but the moment they left cover several shots were fired, which revealed that more than one rifle was being used. However, none of the shots came very close, which struck Biggles as odd until he saw a piece of fabric ripped off the hull of the aircraft.

'They're shooting at the machine!' he shouted. 'The rest of you get in and start up, while I hold them off.'

They were now within a score of paces of the *Wanderer*. Choosing a shallow depression, Biggles threw himself into it and opened a brisk fire on the spot from where the shots were coming. Puffs of smoke gave the enemies' position away, and he saw that in some way the Indians had reached the high rocks beyond the village, where they had taken cover. He emptied the magazine of his rifle and then dashed to the machine, the engines of which had now been started. As he jumped into the cabin there was a cry of dismay from Ginger.

'They've got the tank!' he shouted. 'The petrol is pouring out.'

Glancing at the main tank, Biggles saw that this was indeed the case. A lucky shot had struck the tank a glancing blow low down, making a jagged hole, through which petrol was pouring at a rate that must empty the tank in a few minutes. The danger was instantly apparent, for without petrol they would be stranded; the aircraft would be useless, and their only means of getting away would be on foot, down the stairway.

For a moment Biggles tried to plug the hole with his handkerchief; but the spirit still trickled through, and he knew that it could only delay the inevitable end. To make matters worse, shots were still striking the machine, and it could only be a matter of seconds before one of them was hit. He dashed to the cockpit. They had, he saw, just a chance of getting away. If he could only get the machine off the ground, and over the rim of the plateau before the tank emptied itself, they might be able to glide to the river even though the engines were dead.

Algy saw Biggles coming, and guessing what he had in mind, vacated the seat. Biggles flung himself into it, and with a sweep of his hand knocked the throttle wide open. The engines roared. The machine began to move forward. He held the joystick and waited, knowing that it was going to be a matter of seconds. If the engines would continue running for another half minute all might yet be well. If they failed—well, it was better not to think of that.

The machine, now with its tail up, raced on towards the rim of the plateau. Biggles eased the stick back gently, and it lifted. One engine missed fire, roared again, and then, just as the aircraft soared out over the blue forest far below, both died away altogether. The propellers stopped. An uncanny silence fell. But the machine was in the air, gliding towards the nearest loop of the distant river.

9
NEW PERILS

Had Biggles been asked if he thought the machine, now without motive power, would reach the river, and had he answered truthfully, he would have said 'no'; but he knew that it would be a near thing. He had about five thousand feet of height, and some five miles to go, which would normally be within the gliding range of a modern aeroplane. But the *Wanderer* was heavily loaded, and that made a lot of difference. Again, it was not gliding towards an aerodrome where he could be sure of a landing-ground free from obstructions. That part of the river towards which he was gliding—and this, of course, was the nearest part—was new to him, and even if he reached it, there was always a possibility of it turning out to be a death-trap, by reason of dead trees floating on the surface, or sandbanks, or even the giant water-lilies that flourished in many places. However, he had no alternative but to go on, hoping for the best.

The others were well aware of the gravity of the situation, but since they could do nothing about it either, they sat still, watching the grey ribbon of water grow ever more distinct.

Some minutes passed, the aircraft gliding sluggishly at little more than stalling speed. The altimeter now registered two thousand feet, and the river was still a good two miles away.

'You ought to just about do it,' Algy told Biggles calmly.

'Just about,' answered Biggles, smiling faintly.

The machine glided on, the air moaning softly over its wings. Nobody moved. Nobody spoke.

Ginger watched the river with a sort of helpless fascination. It seemed to float towards them, a narrow lane bordered by a spreading ocean of tree-tops. It was clear that the final issue would be a matter of inches.

Algy afterwards swore that he heard the topmost branches of the trees scrape against the keel as the aircraft just crept over them, to glide down on the water; but that was probably an exaggeration. Ginger sagged a little lower in his seat with relief as the immediate danger passed; provided that there were no obstacles floating on the river all would now be well. Actually there were obstructions, as Biggles afterwards found out, but partly by luck, and partly by skilful flying, he avoided them, and the *Wanderer* sent swarms of crocodiles scurrying as it surged to a standstill on a long, open reach.

Biggles sat back. 'Well, so far so good,' he announced. 'It's time we had a bite to eat. Ginger, get some grub out of the box.'

'Wouldn't it be better to make her fast to the bank first?' suggested Algy.

'It probably would—but how are we going to get to the bank?' returned Biggles.

Algy frowned as he realised the significance of Biggles's question. With the engine out of action they were as helpless as if they had been afloat on a raft without a paddle.

'I don't think we need worry about that,' resumed Biggles. 'We shall drift ashore presently, probably at a bend. As a matter of fact, it suits us to drift downstream, because sooner or later we ought to meet the petrol canoes coming up, and until we repair the tank, and get some juice into it, we're helpless.'

'And then what are you going to do?' inquired Ginger.

Biggles shrugged his shoulders. 'I don't know,' he confessed. 'It's a grim business, but we have at least discovered the Tiger's headquarters, and that's something. I feel inclined to go down to the coast and tell Carruthers about it, and leave it to him to decide on our next move. However, we'll go into that when we've had something to eat.'

Squatting on boxes in the little cabin, they made a substantial meal, leaving the *Wanderer* to choose its own course, and in this way perhaps half an hour passed.

It was Dusky who, not without alarm suddenly called attention to the increased speed of the machine, which could be judged by the rate at which the forest trees on either side were gliding past. At Dusky's shout, the comrades broke off their conversation and climbed out on the hull.

One glance at the river ahead was enough to warn them of their peril, and Biggles could have kicked himself for not taking the possibility into account. Perhaps a quarter of a mile downstream the river plunged between two rocky hills; they were not very high, but they were quite sufficient to force the water into a torrent that boiled and foamed as it flung itself against boulders that had fallen from either side. Already the *Wanderer* was prancing like a nervous horse as it felt the surge of the current, turning slowly, sometimes floating broadside on in the middle of the river. Biggles looked swiftly at either bank in turn, but the nearest was a good fifty yards away, and this might as well have been a mile for all the hope there was of reaching it.

'If she hits one of those rocks she'll crumple like an eggshell!' shouted Algy, steadying himself as the machine gathered speed.

'I suppose it's no use trying to hook the bottom with an anchor?' suggested Ginger.

'No use at all,' answered Biggles promptly. 'Nothing will hold her now. Grab a spare spar, both of you, and try to fend her off when we come to the rocks. It's our only chance—but for heaven's sake don't fall overboard.'

So saying, he snatched up a spare strut and crawled forward

until he was lying spreadeagled across the bows. His expression was hard as he looked at the rapids ahead, for there did not appear to be the slightest chance of the *Wanderer* surviving the ordeal that was now inevitable—at any rate, not unless the nose of the machine could be kept straight.

None of them could really say exactly what happened during the next ten minutes. The period was just a confused memory of foaming water and blinding spray. The *Wanderer* bucked and jumped like a live creature, yet somehow, between them, they managed to keep her fairly straight. The greatest mystery was that none of them fell overboard as they thrust with desperate energy at the rocks which seemed to leap up in their path. Then, suddenly, it was all over, and the machine floated smoothly on another stretch of tranquil water.

Biggles crawled back from his hazardous position on the bows, wringing the water from his hair and inspecting the palms of his hands, which had been blistered by the strut. The others were in much the same state, and they sank wearily down to recover their breath and their composure.

'In future we'd better keep an eye on where we're going,' muttered Ginger bitterly, gazing ahead as they rounded a bend. His expression became fixed as he stared. Then, with a hoarse cry, he struggled to his feet. 'Look out, there's another lot ahead!' he yelled.

Biggles took one look in the direction in which Ginger was staring. Then he snatched up the end of the mooring-rope and dived overboard. Holding the line in his teeth, he struck out for the bank.

Had he not struck shallow water so that he could get his feet on the bottom sooner than he expected, it is unlikely that he would have reached it, for the *Wanderer* was already gathering speed as the river swept on towards the next lot of rapids. But having got his feet planted firmly on a shelving sandbank, he flung his full weight on the rope, and so caused the lightly floating aircraft to swing round near the bank lower down, close enough for Algy and Ginger to seize branches of over-hanging trees, and hang on until the machine could be brought to a safe mooring.

'Who suggested this crazy picnic?' muttered Biggles sarcastically, as, dripping, he climbed aboard.

'I did,' grinned Ginger.

'Then perhaps you'll think of a way out of the mess we're in,' returned Biggles. 'There are rapids below us and rapids above us and our tank is dry. We look like staying here for some time. You might get the tank mended for a start—in case we need it again.'

'Okay,' agreed Ginger, and went to work. 'What are you going to do?' he inquired.

'Walk down the bank to the next lot of rapids, to see how bad they are,' answered Biggles. 'We've got to make contact with the petrol which Carruthers promised to send before we can do anything. Come on, Algy. You'd better come too, Dusky, in case we need your advice.'

Leaving Ginger alone, the others made their way, not without difficulty, down the river-bank, disturbing more than one alligator that lay basking in the stagnant heat. Presently it was possible to ascertain that the rapids stretched for nearly half a mile; they were worse than the first, and Biggles at once dismissed all idea of attempting to shoot them in the aircraft. Beyond the rapids the river resumed its even course, winding placidly through the tropical vegetation. They followed it for some time, but as there appeared to be no change, they were about to start on the return journey when Dusky halted, sniffing like a dog.

'What is it?' asked Biggles quickly.

Dusky's big, child-like eyes opened wide as he whispered nervously that he could smell fire.

Biggles could not understand how this could be, for it seemed impossible that the green jungle, damp in the steaming heat, could take fire; but he followed Dusky, who was now creeping forward silently, every muscle tense, peering into the verdure ahead. After a little while he stopped, and, beckoning to the others, pointed.

Biggles, following the outstretched finger, saw that a little way in front, near the river-bank, the undergrowth had been cut and trampled down, obviously by human agency. In the centre of this area a fire still smouldered. Near it was a brown object, which presently he perceived was a human foot protruding from the debris. Flies swarmed in the still air.

'I'm afraid that fellow's dead, whoever he is,' murmured Algy in a low voice.

'Sure massa, he dead,' agreed Dusky.

Biggles went forward, and a moment later stood looking down at the dead body of a native; he wore blue dungaree trousers, and was clearly one of the more or less civilised natives of the coast. Biggles was still staring at the ugly scene, wondering what it portended, when a groan made him start, and a brief search revealed another native near the edge of the water. This one was not dead, but was obviously dying. Biggles knelt beside him and discovered a gunshot wound in his chest.

'Ask him who he is,' he told Dusky.

Dusky knelt beside the wounded man and spoke quickly in a language the others did not understand. The stranger answered weakly, and thereafter followed a disjointed conversation which went on for some minutes—in fact, until the wounded man expired.

Dusky stood up and turned a startled face to his companions. 'Dese men bring de petrol in one big canoe,' he announced. 'Dey get as far as dis and make camp; den Bogat's men come and dey all killed.'

'But where is the canoe, and the petrol?' asked Biggles in a tense voice.

Dusky pointed to the river, not far from the bank. 'De canoe sink dere,' he said. 'When Bogat's men rush de camp de paddlers try to get away, but bullets hit canoe and it sink.'

'When did this happen?'

'Last night, massa.'

Biggles turned to Algy and shrugged his shoulders helplessly. 'This is bad,' he said quietly. 'The petrol was our only chance of getting away.'

'But how on earth did the Tiger know that petrol was coming up the river?' demanded Algy.

Biggles laughed bitterly. 'Have you forgotten Chorro, Carruthers' assistant? He'd know all about it. As soon as Carruthers got back and ordered the petrol to be brought up to us, Chorro would naturally send the Tiger a message by pigeon post.'

Algy nodded. 'Of course; that explains it; I'd forgotten that skunk Chorro.'

'It looks as if we've only one chance,' went on Biggles. 'If the water isn't deep we might be able to save some of the petrol cans. Some would probably be punctured by bullets, but not all; if we can recover enough juice to get back to the coast, that's all that matters.' He turned to Dusky. 'How far out was the canoe when it was sunk?'

Dusky picked up a piece of rotten wood and tossed it on the water about twenty yards from the bank.

Biggles started removing his clothes. 'I'll take a dive and try to locate it,' he said.

Dusky shook his head vigorously. 'Not yet,' he protested. 'Maybe alligator, maybe piranhas.'

'Piranhas?' queried Algy.

'Man-eating fish,' explained Biggles. 'They're not very big, but they're the most voracious creatures in the world. They swim about in shoals. They've been known to make a skeleton of a man in five minutes.'

'Charming little creatures,' sneered Algy. 'What are we going to do about it?'

Biggles thought for a moment. 'We can't get the machine down here, so we'd better make a raft, and work from that. We might be able to locate the canoe by dragging the bottom with our anchor. What do you think, Dusky?'

'Yes, make raft,' agreed the old man.

'Then let's go back to the machine and get some tools,' suggested Biggles. 'It shouldn't be a big job.'

'Suppose Bogat's crowd is still hanging about?'

'I hadn't overlooked that possibility,' replied Biggles. 'We shall have to risk it. Come on, let's get back to the machine.'

They went back up the stream, and were relieved to find everything as they had left it. Ginger had just finished repairing the tank with a piece of sheet metal. They told him of their discovery and what they proposed to do, and in a few minutes the necessary equipment for making a raft had been brought ashore—as well as weapons.

'I don't like the idea of leaving the machine,' muttered Algy.

'Nor do I, but we can't help it,' returned Biggles. 'If we work fast we ought to get the raft finished by nightfall, ready to start diving operations tomorrow as soon as it gets light. Let's go.'

They marched back to the site of the burnt-out camp, and after burying the unfortunate natives, set about collecting timber suitable for their purpose, in which respect they were guided by Dusky, who knew which wood was light and easy to handle. Some, although Ginger could hardly believe this until he had proved it, was so hard that it turned the edge of an axe.

The sun was sinking in the west by the time the task was finished, and a rough but serviceable raft, moored to a tree, floated against the bank, ready for the morning. Biggles decided that it was too late to start diving operations that day, so picking up the tools, they made their way back towards the *Wanderer*.

They had not gone very far when, with squeals and grunts, a party of small, hairy pigs came tearing madly down the river-bank. Ginger's first impression was that the animals intended to attack them, but the peccaries—for as such Dusky identified them—rushed past with scarcely a glance. Nevertheless Dusky eyed them apprehensively, and as they disappeared down the river he held up his hand for silence, at the same time adopting a listening attitude.

In the sultry silence Ginger was aware of vague rustlings in the undergrowth around them, and, exploring with his eyes, soon located the cause. Small creatures, the presence of which had been unsuspected, were leaving their nests in the rotting vegetation and climbing rapidly up the trunks of the trees. He saw a white bloated centipede, a foot long, its numerous ribs rippling horribly under its loathsome skin, a tarantula, a hairy spider as big as his hand, went up a nearby tree in a series of rushes, seeming to watch the men suspiciously every time it halted. This sinister activity gave Ginger an unpleasant feeling of alarm, but he said nothing. He was looking at Dusky askance when, from a distance, came a curious sound, a murmur, like the movement of wind-blown leaves in autumn.

Dusky muttered something and hurried forward, and there was a nervousness in his manner that confirmed Ginger's sensation of impending danger.

'What is it?' he asked anxiously.

'De ants are coming,' answered Dusky.

At the same time he broke into a run, and it was with relief that Ginger saw the *Wanderer* just ahead of them, for by this time the clamour around them had increased alarmingly. Insects and reptiles of many sorts were climbing trees or plunging through the undergrowth; monkeys howled as they swung themselves from branch to branch; birds screeched as they flew overhead. It was an unnecessary commotion about a few ants—or so it seemed to Ginger; but then he had not seen the ants.

It was not until they were within fifty yards of the machine that he saw them, and even then it was a little while before he realised that the wide black column which rolled like molten tar towards them just above the place where the machine was moored was, in fact, a mass of ants. Some, in the manner of an advance guard, were well out in front, and he saw that they were fully an inch and a half long. Nothing stopped the advance of the insects as they ran forward, surmounting with frantic speed every obstacle that lay across their path. The noise made by the main body, the movement of countless millions of tiny legs over the vegetation, was a harsh, terrifying hiss, that induced in Ginger a feeling of utter helplessness. This, he thought, was an enemy against which nothing could avail.

There was a wild rush for the *Wanderer*, and they reached it perhaps ten yards ahead of the insect army. Ginger gave an involuntary cry as a stinging pain, like a red-hot needle, shot into his leg; but he did not stop—he was much too frightened. He literally fell into the machine.

Biggles was the last to come aboard. The mooring-rope was already black with ants, so he cut it, allowing it to fall into the water. The machine at once began to drift with the current, so he ran forward, and dropping the anchor, managed to get it fast in weeds, or mud. At any rate, further progress was checked, for the current near the shore was not strong.

Ginger pulled up the leg of his trousers and saw a scarlet patch of inflammation where the ant had bitten him.

'Get some iodine on that,' Biggles told him crisply, and he lost no time in complying, for the pain was acute.

Having done so he joined the others on the deck, from where, in silence and in safety, they watched the incredible procession on the bank. Ginger could not have imagined such a spectacle. The ground was black. Every leaf, every twig, was in motion, as if a sticky fluid was flowing over it. It was little wonder that he stared aghast, not knowing what to say.

'I've seen armies of foraging ants before, but never anything like this,' remarked Biggles. 'They clean up everything as they go. Heaven help the creature, man, beast or insect, that falls in their path.'

'How far do they stretch?' asked Ginger, for as yet he could not see the end of the procession.

Biggles asked Dusky, who announced that the column might extend for a mile, perhaps farther. He had seen the same thing many times, and assured them that if the ants were unmolested they would soon pass on.

The comrades sat on the deck and watched until it was dark, but it was some time later before the volume of sound began to diminish. They then retired to the cabin, where Biggles switched on a light and produced some tins of food.

'We may as well eat, and then get some sleep,' he suggested. 'We've got to make an early start tomorrow.'

Ginger went to sleep, to dream of ants. The forest had taken on a new horror.

10

SWIFT DEVELOPMENTS

GINGER was awakened in the morning by a wild shout from Biggles, a shout that brought him, still half dazed with sleep, to the deck. It was just beginning to get light, and it did not take him long to see what was amiss. The water, which normally was black, was now streaked with yellow, and was swirling past at a speed sufficient to cause the *Wanderer* to drag her anchor. There was, as far as he could see, no reason for this, and he said so.

'It must be raining higher up the river,' declared Biggles. 'The water is rising fast. We shall have to tie up to the bank—the anchor won't hold.'

By this time they were all on deck, and between them the machine was soon made fast to a tree-stump. Biggles stared for a minute at the sky, and then at the river.

'We've no time to lose if we're going to get that petrol,' he said urgently. 'Apart from the current, with all this mud coming down we soon shan't be able to see a thing under the water. Algy, you stay here and look after things. Ginger, Dusky come with me.' So saying, Biggles picked up a length of line, jumped ashore, and set off down the river-bank at a run, Ginger and Dusky following behind. Ginger noted that there was little, if anything, to mark the passage of the ants.

It did not take them long to reach the raft, where the water was only just becoming discoloured. Biggles carried a large piece of loose rock on board, and pushed off; then using the rock as an anchor, he brought the raft to a stop over the spot where the canoe had sunk—or as near to it as he could judge. Throwing off his jacket, and holding a spare piece of line, he prepared to dive.

'Here! What about the alligators?' cried Ginger in alarm.

'I shall have to risk it,' answered Biggles curtly. 'We've got to get some petrol, or we're sunk. Dusky, you keep your eyes open for danger.' With this Biggles disappeared under the water.

He had to make three dives before he located the sunken canoe. After this there was a short delay while the raft was moored directly over it. Then the work was fairly straight-forward, and had it not been for the rising water, and the discoloration, it would probably have been possible to salve every petrol-can, for Biggles had only to tie the line to a handle while the others hauled it up. As it was, by the time seven cans had been recovered the river was in full spate, and the raft straining at its moorings in a manner which told them that their position was already perilous. With some difficulty they got the raft, with its precious load, to the bank, after which began the work of transporting the cans to the aircraft. By the time this was done the river was a swirling flood, bringing down with it debris of all sorts.

'It's getting worse,' announced Algy, with a worried frown, as they poured the petrol into the tank. 'We shall never hold the machine here in this, and if she gets into the rapids she's a gonner.'

'We'll go down the river to the coast and report to Car-ruthers,' declared Biggles. 'It's no use going on with our job while that rat Chorro is at large, advising the Tiger of all our movements. We've got just about enough petrol to do it. Get those empty cans ashore, and stand by to cast off.' So saying, Biggles went through to the cockpit.

Algy went forward to cast off the mooring-rope, but seeing that he was having difficulty with it, for the *Wanderer* was pulling hard, Ginger went to his help. At the same time Dusky started throwing the empty cans on the bank. In view of what happened, these details are important. Actually, just what did happen, or how it happened, none of them knew—beyond the fact that the line suddenly snapped. Ginger made a despairing grab at it, slipped, clutched at Algy, and dragged him overboard with him. The *Wanderer*, breaking free, bucked, and Dusky, caught in the act of throwing, also went overboard. All three managed to reach the bank, while the *Wanderer* went careering downstream. From the bank, Algy, Ginger and Dusky stared at it with horror-stricken eyes, too stunned to speak, helpless to do anything.

Ginger felt certain that the machine would be wrecked in the rapids. Not for a moment did he doubt it. And it was not until he heard the *Wanderer's* engines come to life that he realised that Biggles still had a chance. He could no longer see the machine, for overhanging trees, and a bend in the river, hid it from view. But when, presently, the aircraft appeared in the air above them, and he knew that Biggles had succeeded in getting off, he sat down limply, weak from shock.

Algy looked at the machine, and then at the river.

'He'll never dare to land again,' he announced.

'He'd be a fool to try,' declared Ginger. 'At least, not until the flood had subsided,' he added.

They watched the *Wanderer* circle twice; then, as it passed low over them, something white fluttered down, and they made haste to collect it. It was an empty tin; in it was a slip of paper on which Biggles had written, 'Wait. Going to coast.'

'That's the wisest thing he could do—go down and fill the tank, and let Carruthers know about Chorro,' remarked Ginger. 'We shan't take any harm here for a few hours.'

'I hope you realise that we've no food, and that we haven't a weapon between us except Dusky's knife,' muttered Algy.

'In that case we shall have to manage without,' returned Ginger.

'Food—me find,' put in Dusky confidently, indicating the forest with a sweep of his arm.

'You mean you can find food in the forest?' asked Algy hopefully.

'Sure, boss, I find.'

'What sort of food?'

'Honey—roots—fruit, maybe.'

'Good. In that case we might as well start looking for lunch.'

'You stay—I find,' answered Dusky. 'Plenty fever in forest. I go now.'

'All right, if that's how you want it,' agreed Algy.

Dusky disappeared into the gloomy aisles of the jungle.

For some time Algy and Ginger sat on a log gazing moodily at the broad surface of the river. There was little else they could do, for they dare not risk leaving the spot, in case Dusky should return and wonder what had become of them. It did not occur to either of them that they were in any danger. Perhaps they felt that in such a case Dusky would have warned them, although later they agreed that they were both to blame for what happened—but then it was too late.

They did not even see where the natives came from. There was a sudden rush, and before they realised what was happening they were both on their backs, held down by a score or more of savage-looking Indians armed with spears and clubs, bows and arrows. It all happened in a moment of time. Still dazed by the suddenness of the attack they were dragged to their feet and marched away into the forest, menaced fiercely by the spears of their captors. They could do nothing but submit.

In this manner they covered some five miles, as near as they could judge, straight into the heart of the forest before the party halted in an open space on the bank of a narrow stream on which several canoes floated. A few primitive huts comprised the native village. Into one of these they were thrown, and a sentry was placed on guard at the entrance.

Inside, the light was so dim that they could see nothing distinctly, and Ginger was about to throw himself down to rest, for the long march through the oven-like atmosphere had reduced him to a state of exhaustion, when, to his utter amazement, a voice addressed him in English.

'Say, who are you?' inquired the voice, with a strong American drawl.

'Who on earth are *you*?' gasped Ginger when he had recovered sufficiently from his surprise to speak.

'Eddie Rockwell's the name,' came the reply.

'What the dickens are you doing here?' demanded Algy.

'Guess that's what I should ask you.'

Algy thought for a moment or two. 'We're explorers,' he announced, somewhat vaguely. 'We've got a plane, but our chief has gone to the coast for petrol. While he was away this mob set on us and brought us here. That's all. What about you?'

'My tale is as near yours as makes no difference,' answered Eddie quietly.

As their eyes became accustomed to the gloom the comrades saw that he was a young man in the early twenties, but in a sad state of emaciation. His clothes were filthy, and hung on him in rags.

'Having more money than sense, I was fool enough to allow myself to be persuaded to start on a treasure-hunt,' continued Eddie. 'My father told me that the whole thing was a racket, and I reckon he was about right—but of course I wouldn't believe it.'

'A treasure-hunt?' queried Ginger.

'I saw an advertisement in a paper that a couple of guys knew where a treasure was waiting to be picked up. The map they had looked genuine enough, and I fell for it. I financed the expedition, and everything was swell until we got here. Then my two crooked partners just beat it with the stores and left me stranded. If you've tried getting about in this cursed jungle, you'll know what I was up against. However, I did what I could. I blundered about till I struck a stream, and then started down it, figuring that sooner or later, if I could hold out, I'd come to the sea. Instead, I bumped into a bunch of Indians and they brought me here. I didn't care much, because I was pretty well all in. I'd been staggering about without grub for a fortnight, and the Indians did at least give me something to eat. They brought me here, and here I've been ever since. That's all there is to it.'

An idea struck Ginger. He realised that these must be the three Americans about whom Carruthers was so concerned. 'You've been here for some time, haven't you?' he asked.

'Sure.'

'How long?'

'Say, ask me something easier. Weeks, mebbe months.'

'These partners of yours,' resumed Ginger. 'Was one of them a tall, thin, jaundiced-looking bloke, with pale grey eyes and a big mouth, and the other a weedy-looking rat with hay-coloured hair and a wisp of moustache, stained with nicotine?'

Eddie uttered an exclamation of surprise. 'Say, that's them,' he answered quickly. 'I reckon you must have seen them?'

'You bet we have,' said Ginger bitterly, and then told their own story with more detail, including the events which had brought them into contact with the two white men in Tiger's secret village. He also mentioned that the disappearance of the party had caused the authorities some trouble.

'Say, now, what d'you know about that!' exclaimed Eddie when he had finished. 'Joe Warner and Silas Schmitt—they were my two precious partners—told me that there was a guy hereabouts who was boss of the whole works, but I didn't realise that he was such a big noise as you make out.'

'Your partners did, evidently,' put in Algy. 'They must have known that it was impossible for you to operate here without barging into him or his crowd, so it looks to me as if, having got you to finance them to the spot, they changed sides and left you in the lurch, knowing that you would never be able to get to the coast.'

'That's how it looks to me,' agreed Eddie. 'Can you talk the lingo these natives use?'

'Not a word.'

'What do you reckon they'll do with us?'

Algy shook his head. 'I've no idea, but judging from their behaviour so far it won't be anything pleasant.'

'Then you reckon we haven't a chance of getting away?'

'I wouldn't say that. Our chief is down the river, but he'll come back. Moreover, we've got a native servant about somewhere. It just happened that he was out of camp when the attack occurred, but when he gets back he'll guess what has happened, and he ought to be able to trail us. So, on the whole, things may not be as bad as they look.'

Eddie seemed to take encouragement from Algy's optimism. The conversation lapsed, Algy peering through one of the many flaws in the side of the hut in an endeavour to see what was going on outside. It seemed that the natives who had captured them were celebrating the event, with considerable noise.

He was still watching when, without warning, a volley of shots rang out from the edge of the jungle. Several Indians fell. More shots followed. There were wild shouts, and the assembled

Actually there was nothing to show what had happened—not until, in the long grass, he found a broken arrow. Even then he hoped that the arrow might be an old one that had lain there for a long time; but when he looked at the fracture, and saw that it was recent, he knew it was no use deceiving himself. Indians had been to the camp; this was so obvious that he no longer marvelled at the absence of Algy and Ginger. He spent some time hunting about in the bushes, dreading what he might find, and breathed a sigh of relief when his fears proved groundless. 'They're prisoners,' he told himself, and that was bad enough.

For once he was at a loss to know what to do for the best. He dismissed all thought of the Tiger. He was concerned only with Algy and Ginger, and, to a less extent, Dusky, whom he had left with them. Naturally, they would have to be rescued, but how he was to set about this in the jungle he could not imagine. No project that he could remember had seemed so hopeless.

Not for a moment did he relax his vigilance, for he realised that what had happened to the others might also happen to him. He lit a cigarette and tried to reconstruct the scene, and in so doing came up on the trail leading into the forest. This was a clue which he had not expected, for knowing that the Indians did most of their travelling by canoe, he had assumed that the attack had come from the river.

Now that he had something tangible to go on, he returned to the *Wanderer*, moored the aircraft securely to the bank and made it less conspicuous by throwing reeds and palm fronds over the wings. This done, he went to the cabin, selected a heavy Express rifle from the armoury, filled a cartridge-belt with ammunition and the pockets of his jacket with biscuits. Then, after a final glance round, he set off along the trail, which could be followed without difficulty.

He had not gone far when he was brought to an abrupt halt by a hoarsely whispered 'Massa.' He recognised the voice at once, but even so, his nerves tingled with shock.

'Dusky!' he called tersely. 'Where are you?'

Dusky dropped out of a tree and hurried to him.

'What happened?' asked Biggles shortly, wondering how

the old man had escaped.

This Dusky soon explained. In mournful tones he related how he had gone into the forest to find food, a quest which—fortunately for him, as it happened—had taken him into a tree. The tree was at no great distance from the camp, and the sound of the assault had reached his ears. From his hiding-place he had watched Algy and Ginger being led away into the jungle. He apologised for not going to their rescue, but pointed out that, as the only weapon he had was a knife, he was in no position to take on a crowd of Indians. This Biggles did not dispute. Indeed, when Dusky explained that he had remained in hiding, waiting for him to come back so that he could tell him what had happened, he congratulated him on his common sense.

'I suppose you've no idea where the Indians have gone?' asked Biggles.

Dusky shook his head, saying that he did not know the district, but gave it as a matter of opinion that the Indian village would not be far away.

'In that case we shall have to try to find it,' Biggles told him.

Dusky agreed, but without enthusiasm.

They continued on down the trail, Dusky now leading the way and stopping from time to time to listen. This went on for an hour, by which time, although they did not know it, they were getting near the village.

The first intimation of this came when shouts and yells reached their ears, sounds which Dusky interpreted correctly, as the Indian way of making jubilation over the capture of the white men.

They now proceeded with more caution, and were peering forward through the undergrowth hoping to catch sight of the village when a volley of shots sent them diving for cover. The shots, however, did not come their way, which puzzled Biggles more than a little. Dusky went up a tree like a squirrel, to return in a few moments with the unwelcome news that Bogat and his gang had attacked the Indians, scattered them, and taken over their prisoners. He also announced that there was another white man with Algy and Ginger.

Biggles wasted no time in futile guessing as to who this could be. He was too concerned about Algy and Ginger. He thought swiftly, undecided how to act.

'How many men has Bogat got with him?' he asked Dusky.

Dusky opened and closed his hands, twice.

'Twenty, eh?' muttered Biggles.

To attack twenty men single-handed—for Dusky could hardly be counted on—would be, he saw, a rash undertaking. With the advantage of surprise in his favour he might shoot two or three of them, but in the ensuing battle, even if he escaped, Algy and Ginger would be certain to get hurt. He perceived, too, that if he failed in an attempt at rescue now, the odds against him in future would be worse, for once his presence was revealed strict guard would be kept. Taking all the factors into consideration, he decided that it would be better to wait for a more favourable opportunity. Perhaps a chance would come after dark.

At this point Dusky, who had again ascended a tree, returned to say that Bogat and his men, with their prisoners, were moving off through the forest. This at once upset Biggles's plans, for he had assumed that Bogat would remain in the village for a while. To attack him while he was on the march was obviously out of the question, so he took the only course that remained open, which was to allow Bogat's party to go on and follow as close behind as was reasonably safe.

He told Dusky his plan, and the old man agreed, so after waiting for a little while to give Bogat a start, they once more took up the trail.

Biggles of course had not the remotest idea of where they were going, nor even if they were travelling north or south, for the green jungle hemmed them in on both sides, and overhead. Nor, for a long time, did Dusky know; but eventually the trail crossed another which he recognised as one he had used when collecting chicle for the Tiger.

'I reckon Bogat go to de Tiger's village,' he announced.

'But that's up in the mountains,' Biggles pointed out.

Dusky nodded. 'Sure. By-um-by we come to old ruins at

bottom of steps. Maybe Bogat stop dere; maybe he go up steps to de king.'

'You're sure you know where we are?'

'Yes, I'se sure, massa.'

'How far is it from here to the foot of the steps?'

'Half an hour's march—maybe a little more, or less.'

'If we're as close as that, then there must be a risk of our running into some of Bogat's Indians, chicle-collectors, or labourers.'

'Tha's right, massa.'

'In that case we'd better stay here and do a bit of thinking. Let's find a place where we can hide until it gets dark.'

Dusky turned aside from the trail and soon found a sheltered retreat.

Here they remained until the light, always dim beneath the towering tree-tops, turned to the gloom of evening. They saw no one, and heard nothing except the natural sounds of the forest. Once, a panther, as black as midnight, slunk past with twitching tail; it saw them, and its baleful yellow eyes glowed, but it made no attempt to attack them, and Biggles was relieved to see it pass on.

Dusky shivered. 'Dat's de debbil,' he muttered nervously.

'Forget it, Dusky. Devil or no devil, I warrant that he'd find an expanding bullet from this rifle a nasty pill to take.'

'He put a spell on you, den you can't shoot.'

'He won't put any spell on me, I'll promise you,' returned Biggles lightly.

'I reckon you don't believe in spells, massa?'

'No, I don't,' answered Biggles shortly.

'Den you watch out dem big snakes dey call anaconda don't get you. Why, everyone knows dey bewitch folds.' Dusky shivered again.

'I've heard that tale before, but I should have to see it before I believed it,' murmured Biggles cynically.

'Maybe if you stay in de forest long enough, you see,' whispered Dusky knowingly.

Biggles did not pursue the subject, and nothing more was

said for some time.

'You know, massa,' said Dusky after a long silence, 'I reckon de gang don't work down here no longer. You remember I said about de gang working at de bottom of de steps?'

'What makes you think they've gone?'

'Cos I don't hear nothing. Dem boys would sure be hollerin'.'

'Hollering? Why?'

'When Bogat's men crack dere whips on dere backs.'

'I see. How can we make sure? Shall I go and have a scout round?'

'Not you, massa,' said Dusky quickly. 'I go. I don't make no noise. You stay right here. I find out what's going on.'

'You're sure you'll be able to find me again?'

'Sure, massa. Dere's a wide stretch of savannah just ahead—I go dat way.'

'All right,' Biggles agreed, somewhat reluctantly, and Dusky glided away, to be quickly lost in the shadows of the primeval forest.

An hour passed, so Biggles judged, and he began to get worried, for it was now quite dark, and he was by no means certain—in spite of Dusky's assurance—that the old man would be able to find him again.

As time went on and there was still no sign of him, Biggles became definitely concerned. He stood up and whistled softly, but there was no reply. Something—he could not see what—slithered away in the undergrowth.

Staring in the direction which Dusky had taken Biggles became aware of an eerie blue glow, but taking a few paces forward, he soon solved the mystery. It was moonlight shimmering on a thin mist that had formed in an open glade, evidently the savannah to which Dusky had referred. He was about to turn back to the rendezvous, for he had no intention of leaving it, when a movement on the edge of the blue light caught his eye. It was, he saw from the shape of the object, a human being. Moving quickly but quietly to the edge of the clearing, he saw, as he hoped, that it was Dusky; but what the old man was doing he could not imagine. His movements were peculiar. With his arms held out in front of him, and his head thrown back, he was walking slowly across the savannah, step by step, towards the middle of it, in the uncertain manner of a person walking in his sleep.

As Biggles watched this strange scene he became aware of a queer musty smell that reminded him vaguely of something, but he could not remember what it was. At the same time he was assailed by a sensation of impending danger far stronger than anything he had ever before experienced. It was so acute that he could feel his nerves tingle, and presently beads of perspiration began to form on his forehead. This was something new to him, but his response was irritation rather than fear—perhaps because he could not see anything to cause alarm. Alert for the first sign of danger, walking softly, he moved forward on a line that would intercept Dusky somewhere about the middle of the savannah.

He could still see nothing to account for it, but as he advanced his sensations approached more nearly to real fear than he could ever recall. The only object that he could see, apart from the surrounding vegetation, was what appeared to be a black mound rising above the rough grass, and it was towards this that Dusky was stepping with slow, mechanical strides. A sudden suspicion darted into Biggles's brain, and he increased his pace, and even as he did so the mound moved. Something in the centre of it rose up sinuously, and remained poised. It was the head of a snake, but of such a size that Biggles's jaw dropped in sheer amazement.

For a moment he could only stare, thunderstruck, while the great flat head began to sway, slowly, with hideous grace, Then Biggles understood, and, with knowledge, power returned to his limbs.

'Dusky!' he shouted hoarsely.

But he might have remained silent for all the notice the old man took.

'Dusky!' he shouted again. 'Stop!'

The old man continued to walk forward, arms outstretched, as though to embrace a friend.

A cry of horror broke from Biggles's lips, and he dashed forward. At a distance of ten paces from the mound, which he saw was coil after coil of snake, he halted, and raising his rifle, tried to take aim. Perspiration was pouring down his face. The stench was now overpowering. The mist caused the target to dance before his eyes, yet he knew that it would be worse than useless to fire blindly into the body of the creature. It must be the head or nothing.

To make sure, there was only one thing to do, and he did it. He ran in close, took deliberate aim at the squat head now turning towards him, and fired.

In the silent forest the crash of the explosion sounded like the crack of doom. It was followed, first, by a wild scream from Dusky, who fell flat on his face, and, secondly, by a series of furious smashing thuds, as if a tornado was flinging down the mighty trees. The mound was no longer there; instead, the centre of the clearing was occupied by seemingly endless coils which, with insensate fury, threshed and looped over and among the rank grass. The end of one such loop caught Biggles in the back and sent him spinning, but he was up again in an instant; waiting only to recover the rifle, which had been knocked out of his hands, he caught Dusky by the scruff of the neck and dragged him like an empty sack towards the edge of the jungle. Behind him, the crashing and thumping continued with unabated fury, and he recalled vaguely having read somewhere that even if it is decapitated, the anaconda, the great snake of the Central American forests, may take twenty-four hours to die.

Dusky began to howl, so Biggles stopped and dragged him to his feet. 'Shut up,' he snapped. 'You're not hurt.'

'Oh, massa, oh, massa, I thought dat ole snake had got me,' moaned Dusky.

'Come on, let's get out of this,' growled Biggles, who, to his disgust, was more unnerved than he would have cared to admit.

Dusky, with many a nervous backward glance, followed him obediently back to the rendezvous.

'What made you go blundering towards the snake as if you

were crazy?' inquired Biggles, half angrily, half curiously.

'I didn't see no snake, massa,' answered Dusky weakly.

'Then how did you know it was there?'

'I dunno, massa. I just knew, that's all.'

'So you went up to it? What were you going to do—play with it?' sneered Biggles.

'I just couldn't help going,' protested Dusky. 'De snake called me, and I went. I told you dem ole snakes bewitch folks.'

'Well, that one won't do any more bewitching,' replied Biggles crisply. He knew it was useless to argue with the old man, for nothing would shake his inherent conviction that he had been bewitched. Indeed, Biggles, to his annoyance, had an uneasy feeling that there might be something in the superstition after all, for he himself had been conscious of a sensation for which he could not account.

He could still hear the dying monster flinging itself about in the savannah, but he knew there was nothing more to be feared from it.

'Come on, Dusky, pull yourself together,' he exclaimed. 'I've blown the snake's head off, so it can't hurt you now. I only hope that my shot was not heard by Bogat or the Tiger. Are you feeling better?'

Dusky drew a deep breath, 'Yes, massa,' he said shakily, 'I'se better now. But dat ole snake——'

'Forget about it,' snapped Biggles.

'Yes, massa.'

'Were you on your way back?'

'Yes, massa.'

'Then you've been to the bottom of the steps?' What did you discover?'

'Just like I said, massa—dey's gone.'

'Gone? What do you mean?'

Dusky explained that he had been right up to the foot of the stairway, to the spot where, at the time of his escape, he had been forced to dig with the gang working among the ruins. These diggings were now abandoned except for one old man who had been left in charge of a store-shed. This old fellow was well known to Dusky; he was one of the forced labourers, and consequently had no love for his taskmasters. For this reason Dusky had not hesitated to reveal himself; but except for the fact that everyone, including the newly captured white men, had gone to some distant place far up the stairway to dig in some fresh ruins, he knew nothing.

'If he said distant place, it rather looks as if they've gone right up to the top—to the plateau where we landed the machine,' said Biggles thoughtfully. 'There are some ruins up there, as we know. Had they only gone to the valley where the king's house is situated, he would have said so.'

Dusky agreed.

'Then we shall have to go up there, too,' announced Biggles.

'We get captured fo' sure,' muttered Dusky dubiously.

'I can't see any alternative,' continued Biggles. 'We can't just sit here and do nothing—they might be up there for months.'

'How about de airplane?' suggested Dusky.

'That's no use. We couldn't land on the plateau without being seen or heard. No, Dusky, I'm afraid it means going up on foot, but you needn't come if you don't want to.'

'I don't want to, but I'll come,' offered the old man courageously.

Biggles thought for a moment. 'I'll tell you what, though. I shall be pretty conspicuous in these clothes. If I could make myself look a bit more like one of the workmen I might be taken for a slave if we are seen. Is there any chance of getting an old pair of blue pantaloons, like those you wear?'

Dusky thought he could get a pair at the store-shed.

'That old man won't betray us, I hope?'

'No, sah,' declared Dusky emphatically. 'He like the rest, be glad if you killed de Tiger so dey can all go back to de coast. He'll help us. I make your face brown with berries, den you look like a no-good Indian.'

Biggles smiled in the darkness. 'That's a good idea. Let's start. There will be less chance of our being seen if we travel by night. Can you find your way to the store-shed? I can't see a blessed thing.'

'You foller me, massa; I show you,' said Dusky simply.

They set off. Dusky was never at fault, but the darkness was such that progress was necessarily slow, and it was some time before they reached the foot of the steps, where, in the store-shed, the old watchman crouched over a smouldering fire. He made no difficulty about finding a pair of ragged pantaloons, and this was the only garment Biggles put on. Really, in the steamy heat of the jungle, he was glad of an excuse to discard his own clothes, which the watchman hid under a pile of stones. Without guessing how much was to depend on them, Biggles transferred his cigarettes and matches to the pocket of his new trousers.

He was in some doubt about the rifle, for it was obvious that he could not carry it without it being seen. In the end he decided to take it, even if it became necessary to hide it somewhere later on. His automatic he strapped to his thigh, under his trousers. Meanwhile, Dusky and the old watchman, taking a torch, had gone into the forest, and presently returned with a load of red berries. These were boiled in an iron pot, and after the liquid had cooled Biggles more or less gave himself a bath in it. Fortunately, he could not see himself, or he might have been alarmed at the change, for instead of being white he was now the colour of coffee.

Thanking the watchman, and promising him deliverance from servitude in the near future, Biggles and Dusky set off on their long climb up Jacob's Ladder.

They came first to the valley in which the village was situated; but all was silent, so they wasted no time there. Continuing on up the steps, they found themselves just below the summit about two hours before dawn—as near as Biggles could judge.

Here he turned off into a narrow ravine, for he was tired to the point of exhaustion. Dusky appeared to suffer no such incon-venience, and offered to keep watch while he, Biggles, had a short sleep, an offer that Biggles accepted, and ordered Dusky to wake him at the first streak of dawn.

He appeared to have done no more than close his eyes when Dusky was shaking him by the shoulder. Before dropping off to sleep he had made his plan, and this he now put into execution.

'You're going to stay here,' he told Dusky. 'You can take charge of the biscuits and the rifle and wait until I come back. If I'm not back within forty-eight hours you can reckon that I've been caught, in which case try to make your way to the coast and let Mr. Carruthers know what's happened. All being well, I shall be back here, with the others, before very long. Keep under cover.'

With this parting injunction, Biggles went back to the steps, and after a cautious reconnaissance moved on towards the top. He now proceeded with the greatest care; and it was as well that he did, for while he was still a hundred feet from the top he was mortified to see a man sitting on a rock, a rifle on his arm, obviously doing duty as sentry. To pass him without being seen was clearly impossible, so Biggles, after exploring the cliff on his left for the best place, scaled it, and went on through a chaos of rocks towards the plateau. Guided now by distant shouts, and the occasional crack of a whip, he worked his way forward, and presently, as he hoped, found himself in a position overlooking the plateau.

To his right, perhaps a hundred yards away, sat the sentry at the head of the stairway. With this man he was not particularly concerned—at any rate, for the time being. Immediately in front, and slightly below, lay the ruined village. Here a gang of men was working with picks and shovels, or carrying away baskets of earth. Altogether, there were about forty workmen, and Biggles had no difficulty in picking out Algy, Ginger and the stranger. They were working close together. Watching the gang were six guards, standing in pairs. They carried rifles. Another man, an enormous Indian, walked amongst the labourers swishing a vicious-looking whip. Not far away, in the shade of a ruined house, squatted the Tiger and his two white companions. Close behind them stood two natives in tawdry uniforms; they also carried rifles, and were evidently a sort of bodyguard. Beyond, shimmering in the heat of the morning sun, the plateau lay deserted.

For some time Biggles lay still, surveying the scene thoughtfully. A big patch of grotesque prickly pear attracted his attention, and he saw that if he moved along a little to the left he could use this as a screen to cover an advance into the village. Once among the houses, it should, he thought, be possible to get right up to the gang of workmen, and so make contact with Algy and Ginger—which was his main object. Beyond that he had no definite plan.

Like a scouting Indian he backed down from his elevated position and began working his way towards the prickly pear.

12

GINGER GETS SOME SHOCKS

WHEN Algy, Ginger and Eddie had been marched off through the forest by Bogat they did not know where they were being taken, but, naturally, they could make a good guess. Unless Bogat had some scheme of his own, it seemed probable that they would be taken to the Tiger. This suspicion was practically confirmed when they reached the foot of the stairway. Two hours later, utterly worn out, and in considerable discomfort from insect bites and scratches, they were standing before the King of the Forest, who eyed them with undisguised satisfaction.

In his heart, Ginger expected nothing less than a death sentence, but that was because he did not realise the value of labour in the tropics, particularly white labour, which is always better than native work. It was, therefore, with relief that the received the news that they were to be put in the slave-gang. Algy, being older, perceived that this was, in fact, little better than a death sentence; that without proper food, clothes and medical treatment, they were unlikely to survive long in a climate which sapped the vitality even of the natives. However, he agreed with Ginger's optimistic observation that while they were alive there was hope; for, after all, Biggles was still at large. Whether or not he would ever learn what had happened to them was another matter. They were not to know that Dusky had been a witness of the attack.

They were in evil case by the time they reached the plateau, for they had been given only a little maize bread and water, barely enough to support life. The stench of the stone building, little better than a cattle-pen, into which on arrival they were herded with the other slaves, all Indians or half-castes, nearly made Ginger sick. Life under such conditions would, he thought, soon become intolerable.

Tired as they were, sleep was out of the question, and they squatted miserably in a corner, waiting for daylight. At dawn the door was opened by a man who carried a heavy whip; behind him were six other men carrying rifles. A quantity of food, in the nature of swill, was poured into a trough; upon this the slaves threw themselves like animals, eating ravenously with their hands, scooping up the foul mixture in cupped palms. The three white men took no part in this performance.

A few minutes only were allowed for this meal, after which the gang was formed into line and made to march past a shed from which picks and shovels were issued. Thus equipped, they went to what had once been the main street of the village, where a shallow trench had been opened. The gang-boss cracked his whip and the slaves started work, deepening and extending the trench.

'What do you suppose we're doing?' asked Ginger, getting into the trench behind Algy.

'Probably laying the telephone,' returned Algy sarcastically.

'Ha, ha,' sneered Ginger. 'Very funny.'

The gang-boss advanced, brandishing his whip. 'No talking,' he snarled.

Ginger drove his pick viciously into the sun-baked earth, and thereafter for a while work proceeded in silence.

'Here comes the Tiger,' murmured Algy presently.

'I'll tear the stripes off his hide one day,' grated Eddie. 'They can't do this to me.'

'It seems as though they're doing it,' grunted Algy.

Ginger went on working. There was no alternative, for he had no wish to feel the whip across his shoulders.

A few minutes later, standing up to wipe the perspiration out of his eyes, he noticed something. It was nothing spectacular. He had already realised, from the nature of the ground, which consisted largely of broken paving-stones, that the trench was crossing the foundations of what must have been a large building. One or two of the supporting columns, although they had been broken off short, were still standing; one such column was only a few paces away on his right, and without any particular interest his eyes came to rest on it. They were at once attracted to a mark—or rather, two marks. At first he gazed at them without conscious thought; then, suddenly, his eyes cleared as he made out that the marks were initials.

There were two sets, one above the other. The lower ones had almost been obliterated by the hand of time, after the manner of an old tombstone, but it was still possible to read the incised scratches. They were the letters E.C., and were followed by the date, 1860. There was no need for him to look closely at the date of the initials above to see that they were comparatively recent. The letters were L.R., and the date 1937. A suspicion, dim as yet, darted into Ginger's mind. He threw a quick glance at the gang-boss to make sure that he was not being watched, and then leaned forward to confirm that his reading of the lower initials had been correct. In doing this he put his hands on the end of a stone slab in such a way that his weight fell on it. Instantly it began to turn as though on a pivot, and he flung himself back with a gasp of fear, for he had a nasty sensation that he had nearly fallen into an old well. Another quick glance revealed the gang-boss walking towards him, so he went to work with a will, aware that he was slightly breathless.

The lash swished through the air, but without actually touching him. It was a warning, and he took it—at least, while the boss was within hearing. Then he spoke to Algy, who was working just in front of him.

'Algy,' he whispered, 'you remember Biggles talking about a treasure supposed to have been discovered in these parts by a fellow named Carmichael?'

'Yes.'

'What was his Christian name, do you remember?'

would be anxious to escape. Apart from that, he would be an extra man on his side.

'Listen,' he said. 'We shall have to make a dash for it. There's no other way that I can see. We've got two useful factors on our side. The first is surprise—you can see from the way the guards are standing that the last thing they imagine is that they will be attacked. The second factor is my automatic. I'm afraid I shall have to use it. This is no time for niceties. This is what I'm going to do, and what I want you to do.'

Here Biggles had to pause and make a pretence of scraping earth from the bottom of the trench while the gang-boss went past. As soon as the man was out of ear-shot he continued:

'The next time those two nearest guards come this way I shall jump out of the trench and cover them with my gun to make them drop their rifles. If they refuse, I shall shoot. Either way, you'll grab the rifles and open fire on the other guards along the line. Don't get flustered. Be sure of hitting your man. In this way we ought to put four of them out of action before the others guess what's happening. If I know anything about it, when we start shooting they'll run.'

'What about the Tiger?' asked Ginger.

'Never mind about him for the moment. Having got the weapons, we'll fight a rearguard action to the top of Jacob's Ladder. If we can reach it, the rest should be easy. It that all clear?'

The others, including Eddie, announced that it was.

'Then stand by,' whispered Biggles tersely. 'The guards are coming this way. Remember, speed is the thing.'

The two guards to whom Biggles had referred, both half-castes, were walking slowly along the line of workmen. Strolling would perhaps be a better word. Hand-made cigarettes hung from their lips. One carried his rifle carelessly in the crook of his arm; the other held his weapon at the trail; and it was clear from their careless manner that they did not expect trouble. Thus does familiarity breed contempt, and Biggles judged correctly when he guessed that the men had performed their task every day for so long that they no longer apprehended danger. They sauntered along, smoking and chatting, throwing an occasional glance at the labourers. Biggles stooped a little lower in the trench, gripped his automatic firmly, finger on trigger, and waited.

He waited until they drew level. Then with a quick movement he stepped out in front of them, the pistol held low down on his hip.

'Drop those guns,' he rasped.

Never was surprise more utter and complete. The behaviour of the guards was almost comical. First they looked at Biggles's face, then at the pistol, then back at his face, while their expressions changed from incredulity to fear. Neither spoke. One of them dropped his rifle; or rather, it seemed to fall from his nerveless hands. The other made a quick movement as though he intended shooting. Biggles did not wait to confirm this. His pistol cracked, and the shot shattered the man's arm. The rifle fell, and he fled, screaming. This, the opening operation, occupied perhaps three seconds, and as it concluded Algy and Ginger played their parts. In a moment they had snatched up the fallen rifles and opened fire on the two guards next along the line. One spun round and fell flat. The other made a leap for the trench, but stumbled and fell before he reached it, the rifle flying from his hand.

'Come on,' snapped Biggles, and sprinted towards the spot.

The four white men had almost reached the second pair of rifles before the full realisation of what was happening penetrated into the minds of the other people on the plateau—the Tiger, his two white conspirators, his bodyguard, the two remaining guards, and the slaves. An indescribable babble, like the murmur of a wave breaking on shingle, rose into the still air. Then, abruptly, it was punctuated by shots from several directions. Some of them came near the fugitives, but none of them was hit. Biggles saw a workman drop.

While Eddie picked up the two rifles he looked round and saw that the situation had changed but little. The two remaining guards had run for some distance; then, taking cover, they had started firing. The Tiger was shooting with a revolver and shouting orders at the same time, and the uproar he created was hardly calculated to encourage his bodyguard to take careful aim. They were shooting, but with more speed than accuracy. The two renegade white men were firing their revolvers, but the range was too long for accurate shooting.

'All right,' said Biggles crisply. 'Let 'em have it.'

Four rifles spat in the direction of the Tiger's party. One of the bodyguard fell; all the rest dived for cover, and disappeared behind the house.

'Start moving towards the stairway,' ordered Biggles. 'I'll cover you.'

He knelt down and opened a steady fire on the building behind which the Tiger and his party had taken refuge, while under his protective fire the others hurried towards Jacob's Ladder.

So far Biggles's plan had worked without a hitch, and it seemed as if the stairway would be reached without difficulty, and without serious danger. But, unfortunately, the man who had been on guard at the head of the steps, and who had disappeared at the first shots, now came back, and kneeling behind a boulder, opened a dangerous fire.

Biggles had assumed, naturally, that the man had bolted, but hearing the shots he looked round quickly and realised what had happened. He did not waste time wondering why the man had returned; he was concerned only with the danger he represented.

Biggles dashed on after the others. 'We shall have to work round that chap,' he said curtly. 'Algy, come with me. We'll go to the left. The others go to the right. We'll get him from the flank.'

But before this manoeuvre could be made, a new factor arose, one that instantly made Biggles's scheme impracticable. He realised why the guard, who had bolted down the steps, had returned. He had not come back alone. At the top of Jacob's Ladder now appeared Bogat, and behind him nearly a score of armed men. They took in the situation at a glance, and spreading out, taking cover behind rocks, effectually blocked the steps.

Biggles perceived that Bogat and his gang must have been actually coming up the steps all the time. It was unfortunate, but it couldn't be prevented. In any case, he was not to know it. It was one of those unexpected mischances that can upset the best-laid plan. To advance in the face of a score of rifles was obviously a hopeless proposition; nor could they remain where they were. In the circumstances he gave the only reasonable order, which was to retire.

'Get back to the village!' he shouted. 'We'll find cover in one of the buildings while we think things over. Keep together. Don't waste ammunition. Run for it.'

Dodging among the boulders, for shots were now whistling, they made a quick but orderly retirement to the buildings. It was fortunate that they had not far to go. Biggles selected a group of stone houses near the spot where, a few minutes before, they had been working.

'This will do,' he decided, and dived through the doorway to temporary safety. The others followed him.

'Anyone hurt?' he inquired.

Eddie had been slightly wounded in the forearm, that was all; he made light of it, and tore a strip off his shirt for a bandage.

'Sorry, chaps,' said Biggles apologetically. 'The show came unstuck. Bad luck we chose the moment that Bogat and his toughs were coming up the steps. Not being able to see through solid rock, I wasn't to know that. Still, I think we ought to be able to hold them off this place for some time—at any rate, long enough to enable us to work out a new plan. Keep watch through the windows, but don't show yourselves. Phew! Isn't it hot.'

Eddie drew his sleeve across his forehead. 'You're telling me.'

13

STRANGE EVENTS

FOR some time they kept careful watch, but saw nothing of the Tiger or his associates. Sounds told them that the labourers had been herded back into their pen.

'What's going on, I wonder?' muttered Ginger at last.

Biggles answered. 'I should say that the Tiger, knowing we are on the plateau, has posted a strong guard at the head of the stairway. We are, he supposes, in a trap, and he has only to close the mouth of it to keep us in. Why should he hurry? He knows that we can't stay here indefinitely without food and water. No doubt he's watching the place from a distance. Then again, he may not be sure which house we are actually in, and doesn't feel like taking the risk of being shot in order to find out.'

'Did you come up the stairway?' asked Ginger.

'Not exactly,' returned Biggles. 'I came nearly to the top, but seeing a fellow on guard, made a detour and came in over the escarpment behind the village—at the back of those prickly pears.'

'Couldn't we get out that way?'

Biggles thought for a moment. 'Possibly. We could, of course, if no guards were posted, but I can't think that the Tiger would be such a fool as to shut the front door and forget to lock the back door—so to speak. The way I came must have been the way the Indians came when they chased us up the steps after we had escaped from the black panther. One thing is certain: it would be silly to try to get out of here in broad daylight. We'll wait for dark.'

It seemed a long wait—as indeed it was. Silence settled over the plateau. The sun struck down with bars of white heat. The only sound was the languid buzz of insects.

The shadows were lengthening when Ginger suddenly re-called the pivoting flagstone; he could see it from where he stood on guard at a window, not a score of paces away. In the rush of events following Biggles's arrival he had forgotten all about it.

'Here, Biggles,' he said, 'I've just remembered something.' In a few words he told the others of his curious discovery.

'Sounds interesting,' was Biggles's comment.

'You mean, the treasure might be in there?' put in Eddie. Biggles had by this time learned who Eddie was, and how he came to be with the party.

'It might be, but, to tell the truth, I wasn't thinking about that,' answered Biggles. 'It would be useful, of course, to locate the treasure, although I don't think we're in a position to clutter ourselves up with it at the moment. Our job is to get out. What I was thinking was that under Ginger's slab there might be a tunnel leading to another part of the plateau. At any rate, if there is a cave or something there it ought to be worth exploring.'

'Now?' queried Ginger.

'No. We'll wait till it gets properly dark.'

'There's no need for us all to go,' remarked Ginger. 'I know just where the thing is. I could explore, and then come back and let you know what's inside—if there is an inside.'

'That's a good idea,' agreed Biggles. And so it was decided.

Night came. The moon had not yet risen, but the sky was clear, and the stars gave as much light as was necessary for the reconnaissance.

'I'm afraid it's going to be a bit difficult, if there is a cave, or something, to get an idea of it without a light,' Ginger pointed out. 'I've no matches. All our things were taken away from us.'

'I've got some,' Biggles told him, remembering those which, with his cigarettes, he had put in his pocket. 'Take them, but go easy with them, and don't strike any in the open.'

Ginger took the box, and slipping through an opening that had once been a window, crept stealthily along a wall towards his objective, while the others covered his advance with their rifles. Hearing nothing, seeing no sign of life, pausing sometimes to listen, Ginger kept close against the wall until he reached the trench, which gave him all the cover he needed for the rest of his journey to the stone. Actually, there were several paving-stones, and in spite of his confidence, in the deceptive half-light he was some minutes finding the right one. It was an exciting moment when he felt it give under his weight, for, of course, he had not the remotest idea of what was underneath.

The stone moved slowly but easily; when the pressure was removed it swung back into place, and for this reason he was in some doubt as to how to proceed. He didn't like the idea of descending into the unknown without being quite certain that he would be able to get back. A closer examination revealed that the stone turned on a central pivot; for a primitive contrivance it was a beautiful piece of precision work, but before entering the void Ginger made sure of his exit by the simple expedient of fixing a loose piece of stone so that the slab could not entirely close. Then, rather breathless, he groped inside with his hands. He was not surprised when they encountered a step, also of stone.

If there was one, he reasoned, there should be more. And in this he was correct; but it was not until he was well inside that he risked lighting a match. He held his breath while it flared up, for he had no idea of what lay before him. He was prepared for anything.

Actually, the result of his first survey, while the match lasted, was rather disappointing. As far as he could see, a flight of well-cut steps led down, perfectly straight, to a room, a chamber so large that he could not see the extremities of it. There was no furniture. The walls appeared to be bare. He went on to the bottom of the steps and lit another match.

In its light everything was exposed to view, and it merely confirmed his first impression. He was in a large oblong room, the walls, floor and ceiling of which were of grey stone. At one end, the end farthest from the entrance, three broad, shallow steps led up to a dais, in the manner of an altar, on which squatted a hideous idol. It appeared to have been carved out of the living rock. Ginger went over to it, and by the light of the third match looked at it again. The image leered down at him, and he felt suddenly cold. For how many hundreds of years, perhaps thousands, it had been there, leering in the darkness, he did not know, but the effect of extreme antiquity affected him strangely. He struck yet another match, but there was nothing more to be seen. There was no door or passage leading to another room. If the treasure was in here, he thought, then they had been forestalled. It was certainly not there now, although it seemed likely that it had been there as late as 1937, or the explorer Roberts would not have carved his initials on the column.

It was a disappointing anti-climax, and feeling rather gloomy about the whole business, Ginger groped his way back up to the exit, from where, with due precautions, he returned to the house and told the others the result of his investigation.

'There's something funny about this,' declared Biggles quietly. 'Unless he was a first-class liar, Carmichael saw the treasure. So apparently did Roberts. Where has it gone? It seems very unlikely that anyone could have been on the plateau recently without the Tiger knowing about it, unless the explorers came as we did, by air, for they would have to come up Jacob's Ladder. Obviously, the Tiger didn't find the treasure, or he wouldn't be looking for it now—at least, I assume he's looking for it. I can't think what else he'd be looking for.'

'Just a minute,' put in Eddie. 'There was some writing in the corner of the map. I imagine Roberts wrote it.'

'What happened to this man Roberts?' asked Biggles curiously. 'Why did he dispose of the map? Why didn't he take the treasure?'

'His Indian porters deserted him. In fact, they tried to poison him.'

'So he couldn't carry the stuff?'

'That's right. It took him all his time to get back.'

'But why didn't he return afterwards?'

'He died.'

'How did these crooked partners of yours get hold of the map?'

'They bought it off Roberts' widow—so they said.'

'And this writing you just mentioned?'

'It was a list of instructions. I can't remember the words exactly, but there was something about a hinged stone—

presumably the one Ginger discovered.'

'Roberts definitely saw the treasure—with his own eyes?'

'Oh yes. He brought a gold cup home with him.'

'Did you see it?'

'No. His widow sold it after he died.'

'Hm.' Biggles was silent for a moment. 'I should like to have a look at this place,' he announced.

'So should I,' said Eddie.

'Then let's all go,' suggested Biggles. 'We shall be no worse off there than we are here—in fact, it might turn out to be a better hiding-place. If we could get hold of some food and water we could lie low there for week if necessary, in which case the Tiger might think we had in some way got off the plateau. Let's go. We can always come back if we don't like it. No noise. We'll go across one at a time. If we bump into trouble, rally here. Ginger, you know the way, so you'd better go first.'

Ginger, employing the same tactics as before, returned to the underground chamber. The others followed in turn, Biggles bringing up the rear. Everything remained quiet—from Biggles's point of view, suspiciously quiet. In spite of what he had said about the Tiger holding them in a trap by simply putting a guard on the stairway, he thought it was odd that no attempt had been made to dislodge them from the block of buildings in which they had sought refuge. Still, he did not overlook the fact that four desperate white men, armed with rifles, made a formidable force to capture or shoot down by sheer frontal attack.

Before going down through the trap-door Biggles made a short excursion to collect some tufts of dried grass; then, after a final survey of the scene, he followed the others into the chamber and allowed the slab to sink slowly into place. As soon as he was inside he twisted the dried grass into a wisp—it could hardly be called a torch—and taking the matches from Ginger, set light to it. The grass blazed up brightly so that everything could be seen. Not that there was much to see.

Nobody spoke while the fire was alight. Biggles still had a little more grass, but as there seemed to be no point in burning it, he held it in reserve.

'Well, that's that,' he murmured, sitting on the bottom step. 'Did anyone notice anything interesting, or worth exploring?'

The others admitted that they had seen nothing worth mentioning.

'This is a funny business,' resumed Biggles. 'I still don't understand what became of the treasure.'

'I wish I had the map,' remarked Eddie. 'There may have been something on it that I have forgotten. If there was, and the Tiger ever finds this place, he'll know just what to do.'

'Well, there doesn't seem to be much *we* can do,' returned Biggles.

Ginger started groping his way round the walls, knocking on the stones with his knuckles. 'They sound solid enough,' he observed.

'Lumps of stone, weighing half a ton apiece, would sound solid, even if there was a cavity behind,' Biggles pointed out.

'What are we going to do?' asked Algy. 'I can't see any point in staying here.'

'There's not much point in going back to the house, if it comes to that,' answered Biggles. 'I don't want to be depressing, but I don't think we're in any shape to stay either here or in the house for more than another day. We might manage without food for a bit, but we can't do without water. I'm afraid that sooner or later we've got to risk breaking through the cordon, either by rushing the steps, or trying to get out over the rocks, the way I came in. I'll tell you what. I'll go and have a scout round.'

'That sounds pretty dangerous to me,' muttered Eddie dubiously.

Biggles laughed mirthlessly. 'Whatever we do is likely to be dangerous. I'll go and make sure that the escarpment is guarded. Either way, I'll come back. If it isn't guarded we'll try to slip out.'

'Why not all go?' suggested Ginger.

'Because four people are more likely to be seen than one, and the chances of making a noise become multiplied by four. No, this is a one-man job. I don't suppose I shall be very long. Here,

Algy, you take the matches; you may need them.'

Biggles groped his way up the steps. There was a faint gleam of star-spangled sky as he went through the exit; then it was blotted out as the stone sank into place. Silence fell.

For a long time nobody spoke in the chamber. There seemed to be nothing to say—or it may have been that they were all listening intently for the first sign of Biggles's return. In such conditions it is practically impossible to judge time correctly, but when Biggles had been gone for what Ginger thought must be nearly an hour, he commented on it.

'He's a long time,' he said anxiously, almost irritably.

'I was thinking the same thing,' admitted Algy. 'If——'

Whatever he was going to say remained unsaid, for at that moment the silence was shattered by a deafening explosion. The chamber shuddered to the force of it. A moment later came the crash and spatter of debris raining down on the roof. It sounded like a roll of distant thunder.

Ginger flung himself flat, feeling sure that the whole place was about to collapse. This was purely instinctive, for he was beyond lucid thought. So were the others. The explosion would have been bad enough had it been expected, but coming as it did without warning, it was shattering. It took Ginger several seconds to convince himself that he had not been hurt. He was the first to speak.

'Are you fellows all right?' he asked in a strained voice.

The others answered that they were.

'What on earth was that?' continued Ginger.

'I don't know, but I'm going to find out,' replied Algy, groping his way up the steps.

Some time passed, but he did not speak again, although the others could hear him making strange noises. He seemed to be grunting with exertion.

'What's wrong?' asked Eddie.

'Plenty,' came Algy's voice in the darkness. 'Either some rocks have fallen on the slab or else the explosion has jammed it. It won't move.'

'You mean—we're shut in?' demanded Ginger.

'That's just what I do mean,' answered Algy, rather unsteadily.

Ginger squatted down on the stone floor. 'Not so good,' he remarked.

'What are you grumbling about? You wanted adventure,' Algy pointed out coldly. 'Now you're getting it. I hope you're enjoying it—but I'm dashed if I am.'

14
BIGGLES MAKES A CAPTURE

THE first thing Biggles noticed when he left the underground chamber was that the moon was rising over the edge of the plateau. He had no time to weigh up the advantages and disadvantages of this, for as, lying flat, he began to worm his way towards the trench, he distinctly saw a dark shadow flit silently away from the side of the house which they had recently evacuated. An instant later a low mutter of voices reached his ears, but precisely where the sound came from he could not determine. The conversation was soon followed by the sound of retreating footsteps. That something was going on seemed certain, but there was no indication of what it was. Fearing that he may have been seen, he lay still for a little while, trusting to his ears to advise him of danger; but when nothing happened he felt that it was time he continued his reconnaissance.

With eyes and ears alert for danger, he reached the nearest house, and taking advantage of the deepest shadows, went on towards the ridge of rock which he could see silhouetted against the sky beyond the village. He reached the outlying boulders without incident, and there paused to survey the skyline for any movement that would reveal the position of sentries. His vigilance was rewarded when he saw the glow of a lighted cigarette. It was stationary. This at once fixed the position of at least one sentry, and Biggles was about to move forward on a course that would avoid him when a faint smell, borne on a slant of air, reached his nostrils and brought him to an abrupt halt. It was vaguely familiar, but it took him a second or two to identify it as the reek of smouldering saltpetre. Instantly realising the significance of it, he half rose up and looked behind him, hoped to discover the source of it. The next moment a column of flame shot into the air; simultaneously came the roar of an explosion, the blast of which flung him headlong. Knowing what to expect, he lay still with his hands over his head while clods of earth and pieces of rock rattled down around him and the acrid tang of dynamite filled the air.

As soon as the noise had subsided he looked back at the spot where the explosion had occurred, and saw, as he already suspected, that it was the block of houses in one of which they had first taken cover. The buildings were now a heap of ruins. It was easy enough to see what had happened. The enemy, fearing to make a frontal attack, had entered one of the rear houses and destroyed the whole block with a charge of dynamite.

Naturally, Biggles's first reaction to this unexpected event was one of thankfulness that they had left the house, otherwise they must have all been killed. That the enemy assumed this to be the case was made apparent by the way they now advanced, with much laughing and talking, from several directions. The sentries on the escarpment left their posts and joined their companions at the scene of the supposed triumph. In a few minutes the shattered houses were surrounded by groups of figures, some of which, Biggles saw with misgiving, were very near the underground chamber.

He waited to see what they would do, for upon this now depended his own actions. He was not particularly concerned about the others, although he guessed that the explosion must have given them a nasty shock. Being underground, they would be safe. He was not to know that falling masonry had piled itself on the entrance slab, making the opening of it from the inside impossible. His one fear was that Algy and Ginger would emerge in order to see what had happened, and so betray the secret hiding-place—as, indeed, might easily have happened had it been possible for them to get out. Biggles was relieved when nothing of the sort happened.

The question now arose in his mind, would a search be made at once for the bodies which were supposed to be under the ruins, or would the Tiger wait for daylight? The answer was provided when the Tiger began shouting orders, and the crowd started to disperse. As far as Biggles could gather, the Tiger had merely dismissed his men without giving any hint of his future plans. A number of figures, presumably the Tiger's personal party, remained near the ruins, and had it not been for this Biggles would probably have returned to the chamber forthwith. He did, in fact, wait for some time with this object in view, but when the Tiger showed no signs of leaving, he decided that it would be a good moment, an opportunity that might not occur again, to make contact with Dusky, who, if he did not soon show up, would presently be leaving the ravine. So Biggles decided that he would go down to him, tell him what had happened, recover his Express rifle and some biscuits, and then, if the Tiger had gone, return to the chamber. He thought it ought to be possible to do this before daylight.

His mind made up, he struck off towards the clump of prickly pear in order to leave the plateau as near as possible to the spot by which he had entered it. He was not so optimistic as to hope that he would be able to find his track through the chaos of rock, but he had a pretty good idea of the general direction of the ravine, and once he reached it there should be no great difficulty in finding Dusky.

Actually, he was some time finding the ravine, for it was not an easy matter to keep a straight course through the bewildering jumble of boulders; and when he did strike it he saw that he was above the point where he had left it. This did not worry him, however, and he started making his way towards the place where he imagined Dusky would be. When he reached it the old man was not there. He whistled softly, but there was no reply. Rather worried, he continued on towards the stairway, no great distance.

Had not he seen the moonlight glint on the barrel of the rifle there might have been an accident, for he realised suddenly that the rifle was covering him.

cautiously towards the building, saw what he had not previously noticed. The French window was open, probably on account of the heat.

Quietly, but without loss of time, taking his rifle with him, Biggles moved forward until he could see into the room. Two men were there, seated at a table with a bottle between them. One was Bogat and the other Chorro.

Biggles's first feeling was one of surprise; the second, disappointment; the third, mystification. Where was the Tiger? Bogat was still wearing his hat, as if he had only just arrived. Could Dusky have made a mistake?

While Biggles was still pondering the question Bogat spoke, and his first words explained the situation.

'No, the king is busy up top,' he said. 'When he heard that you'd arrived he sent me down instead to hear what you have to say. If you'd rather see him, or if it's something important, I'll take you up top.'

Biggles understood. In the darkness Dusky had been mistaken. The man he had seen come down the steps was not the Tiger, but Bogat. Chorro had arrived from the coast, and the Tiger had sent Bogat down to get in touch with him.

Biggles was annoyed, for had he known the truth he would not have come down; but now that he was here, with the two men practically at his mercy, he felt that it would be a pity not to take advantage of the situation. He could not very well blame Dusky for the mistake; the old man had acted for the best. Still, the new state of affairs called for an adjustment of plan.

Biggles withdrew a little into the darkness to think the matter over. It would, he thought, be an easy matter to capture the Tiger's two right-hand men, but what was he to do with them? It did not take him long to see that there was only one thing he could do with them, and that was take them to the coast. This would mean leaving the others for longer than he originally intended. Still, if he went back up the steps and rejoined them now it was not easy to see what he could do single-handed. On the other hand, if he went to the coast and explained matters to Carruthers, the acting-Governor might lend him some extra men. He should be able to get back some time the next day. If Algy and the others remained where they were they should be safe.

So Biggles reasoned as he stood in the shadow of the palace, confronted, for the third time within a few hours, with a decision not easy to make. Successive unexpected events had made his original plan a thing of the past. However, he felt that by securing Bogat and Chorro and taking them to the coast he would have achieved the first step forward in his declared intention of breaking up the Tiger's gang.

With the rifle in the crook of his arm ready for instant use, Biggles strolled into the room.

'Good evening, gentlemen,' he said evenly. 'Keep quite still. It should hardly be necessary for me to warn you that if either of you make a sound I shall have to employ your own methods to discourage you. Keep your hands on the table.'

The two men stared. Neither moved. Neither spoke. In the first place, at least, their obedience was probably due to shock. While they were still staring Biggles walked behind each in turn and removed his weapons.

'Now,' he continued, 'we're going for a walk. On your feet. Keep going. I shall be close behind you.'

When they reached the spot where Dusky was waiting, Biggles gave him Bogat's rifle and ordered him to lead the way down to the forest, the first part of the journey to the *Wanderer*.

It was now bright moonlight, but so much had happened that Biggles had only a hazy idea of the time. He was anxious to reach the foot of the steps before dawn, because there was less chance of meeting anybody on the way.

As a matter of fact it was earlier than he thought, and he found it necessary to wait for some time at the bottom of the steps, for he dare not risk losing his two dangerous prisoners in the darkness of the forest, where, of course, the moonlight did not penetrate. As soon as there was sufficient light to see he gave the order to continue the march, Dusky still leading the way and he himself bringing up the rear. So far the two prisoners had been passive, but Biggles felt certain that Bogat, at least, would make an attempt to escape. Once he got off the trail into the forest he would be safe from pursuit, and Biggles repeated his warning as to what would happen if either prisoner attempted it. They trudged on in silence. It was broad daylight by the time they reached the river.

Now all this time Biggles had the advantage of knowing where they were going, whereas the prisoners did not. They hoped, no doubt, that camp would presently be made, in which case an opportunity for making a dash into the jungle might present itself. But as soon as the aircraft came into view—for in spite of Biggles's rough camouflage, it could be seen from a little distance—the manner of both prisoners changed. They must have realised that unless they did something quickly their minutes of opportunity were numbered. Once in the machine, and in the air, there could be no escape.

Not for an instant did Biggles relax his vigilance, for he knew that this was the crucial moment. He was in fact ready for almost anything; yet in spite of that he was not ready for what did happen.

When they were only a score of paces from the machine Dusky suddenly pulled up dead. For a moment or two he stood rigid, leaning slightly forward, his big nostrils twitching like a dog that catches the scent of its quarry. Then he turned his head slowly and looked at Biggles. His eyes were round with fear.

Even when he moved his lips, and opened them to speak, Biggles still had no idea of what the old man was going to say; but he sensed danger, and his muscles tightened as instinctively he braced himself. And as they all stood there, motionless, like a screen picture suddenly arrested in motion, the silence was broken by a curious sound, a sort of sharp *phut*.

Bogat started convulsively. Very slowly, as if it dreaded what it might find, his hand crept up to a face that had turned ashen, to where a tiny dart, not much larger than a darning needle, protruded. As his fingers touched it a wild scream burst from his lips, and he staggered back against a tree.

Chorro took one terrified look at him, and with the whimpering cry of a wounded dog, regardless of Biggles's order to stop, rushed into the forest.

Biggles raised his rifle, but he did not shoot. There was no need. For hardly had Chorro left the trail when there was a fierce crashing in the undergrowth, a crashing above which rose shrieks of terror. They ended abruptly.

Now all this had happened in less time than it takes to tell. Biggles knew, without Dusky's hoarse advice, that they had been ambushed by Indians, probably the same tribe that Bogat had so mercilessly attacked. He could do nothing for his prisoners. Chorro had disappeared, and it was not hard to guess his fate. Bogat was now on the ground, writhing and twisting in convulsions as the venom on the dart took effect.

Dusky panicked—which was hardly surprising. He fled back along the trail. Biggles followed, now concerned only with escape. He wondered vaguely whether it would be better to go back to the steps, or to try to reach the aircraft, although how this was to be done was not apparent. As he ran, wild shouts behind sent the parrots squawking into the air.

Dusky turned away from the trail like a hunted rabbit. Biggles followed blindly, not so much because he had any faith in his leadership—at least, in the present circumstances—as because he did not want to lose him. Presently he found himself splashing through mud, and saw the tall reeds that fringed the river just ahead. Dusky made for a tree on which the limbs grew low. Flinging aside his rifle, he went up it like a monkey. Biggles went after him, but kept his rifle, looping it over his shoulder by the sling to leave his hands free for climbing.

He thought Dusky would never stop going up, and for some absurd reason the memory of Jack and the Beanstalk flashed into his mind. The ground was about a hundred feet below when Dusky suddenly disappeared and Biggles, still following, found himself in a strange new world. They had arrived, so to speak, in a new jungle, a jungle with a fairly level floor from which sprang orchids and ferns, with great growths of moss and lichen.

Now Biggles had heard of these different 'layers' of forest, raised one above the other, but this was the first time he had ever seen one, and he looked about with interest. It was easy to see how they were formed. Branches fell, but instead of falling to the ground, they were caught by the branches below them. Across these in turn fell other branches, twigs and leaves, to form eventually a substantial carpet. On this carpet seeds fell from the flowering tree-tops. Others were dropped by birds. These took root and flourished for a time; then, dying, the seedlings collapsed, to give extra thickness to the mat of rotting debris. Over a period of centuries this mat became as firm as the solid earth far beneath, and supported a flora and fauna of its own. Here among the green tree-tops dwelt birds, and rats, and other small creatures.

Biggles was recalled from his contemplation of this pleasant scene by Dusky, who whispered, 'We hide here.'

Biggles nodded. He was in no mood to argue. All the same, he began to regret that he had left the others. He wondered what they were doing. Could he have seen them he would have been a good deal more disturbed in his mind than he was.

15
DESPERATE DIVERSIONS

IF Biggles supposed that Algy, Ginger and Eddie were sitting quietly in the underground chamber waiting for him to come back—and there was no reason why he should think other-wise—he would have been wrong. Very wrong. Things had happened. Several things.

They began soon after Algy's discovery that, as a result of the explosion, the stone over the exit had jammed. At least, that is what they thought. As a matter of fact, a block of masonry had fallen on it. Masonry had fallen all over the place. Comparatively speaking, this particular piece was not heavy, but it was of sufficient weight to upset the finely adjusted mechanism of the pivot and so prevent the slab from being tilted open from the inside. Those below it did not know this. As Algy remarked, 'The thing has stuck.' They were not at first unduly perturbed, for they assumed that Biggles would return and do something about it. But when presently the sound of many footsteps could be heard overhead, Algy began to get worried. This was, of course, when the Tiger and his men gathered round the scene of the explosion.

Conversing in low tones, the comrades tried to visualise the scene outside, and as a result of their combined imaginations they arrived fairly near to the truth.

'They've either brought up a cannon and shelled the place, or else blown it up with a stick of dynamite,' declared Algy.

'I only hope they didn't get Biggles at the same time,' muttered Ginger.

'He'd been gone a fair while,' Algy pointed out. 'He should have got clear.'

'We shall have to wait until he comes back.'

'We should have done that in any case,' reminded Algy.

Time passed, a long time, and still Biggles did not return. There were no longer any sounds outside.

'Surely it's time he was back?' murmured Ginger. 'This is awful, sitting here doing nothing.'

'I'm afraid you're right,' agreed Algy. 'If everything had gone according to plan he should have been back by now. It begins to look as if something went wrong.'

'What can we do about it?'

'Nothing. At least, I can't think of anything. Have you any ideas, Eddie?'

Eddie answered that he had not. 'I must have been nuts to set out on this jaunt with a pair of cheap crooks,' he added disgustedly—which made it clear how he felt about the whole business.

'How about striking a match and having a look at the slab?' he suggested presently. 'Perhaps we shall be able to see what's happened.' They had of course been sitting in the dark.

'Yes, we might do that,' agreed Algy. 'But we shall have to go steady with the matches—there aren't many left.'

'Why is it nobody seems to have any matches when they are really needed?' remarked Eddie bitterly.

'I'll see it never happens to me again,' declared Ginger.

'Before I set out on another trip I'm going to have a special belt made, one to go under my shirt. It will have little pockets all round it. In them I shall carry everything I've always wanted when I haven't had them—a box of matches, and an electric torch, a penknife with all sorts of gadgets in it, chocolates, string——'

'A few bombs and a Tommy gun,' sneered Algy. 'Pity you didn't think of it earlier. Stop romancing. Let's get down to brass tacks. I'm going to strike a match, so get ready to have a look round.'

As he spoke he struck the match. It flared up, dazzling them. As their eyes grew accustomed to the light they examined the slab eagerly, but there was nothing to indicate the cause of the trouble. Just as the flame was expiring a wild yell from Eddie nearly made Ginger fall off the step. The match went out.

'What's wrong? What are you yelling about?' snapped Algy.

'It's gone!'

'Gone? Who's gone? I mean, what's gone?'

'The idol.'

'You're crazy! Where could it go?'

'I tell you it's gone,' insisted Eddie. 'I happened to glance that way. It's no longer there.'

'Strike another match, Algy,' put in Ginger nervously. 'I don't like the idea of an image prowling about.'

In his haste Algy dropped all the matches, and several seconds passed—much to Ginger's irritation—before they could be collected.

'For the love of Mike get a move on,' he growled.

Another match flared, and they all stared in the direction of the image. One glance was enough. Eddie was right. It was no longer there.

With one accord, prompted by mutual curiosity, they started walking towards the place where it had been, but before they were half-way the match went out. Still, they had seen enough to give them an idea of what had happened.

'Strike another match,' urged Ginger.

'We can't go on striking matches at this rate,' protested Algy.

'Wait a minute. I'll tear a strip off my shirt,' offered Ginger. There came a noise of tearing material. 'All right, go ahead,' he resumed. 'I hope the stuff will burn.'

Another match blazed, and Ginger lighted the piece of material that he now held in his hands. 'That's better,' he said, as it flared up.

It was now possible to see precisely what had happened. The explosion had evidently been more severe than they had supposed, for there were several cracks in the walls and ceiling. With these they were not concerned. Their attention was riveted on a more interesting development. At first they could not understand what had become of the idol, but as they drew near they saw that the shock of concussion had caused it to tilt forward, revealing a square aperture behind it, a hole into which the base of the idol had previously fitted.

In order to reach this opening Algy had to climb on the back of the idol, but as soon as he touched it it swung still lower in a manner that explained how it operated. The idol was, in fact, a door, hinged at the bottom by a balancing device similar to the one that worked the slab above. So perfectly poised was the idol that the slightest pressure was sufficient to move it, but what hidden spring actuated it could not be discovered. With such precision did the ponderous stone with the carved face fit into the recess behind it, that, had not the explosion exposed the secret, it would not have been suspected.

'This is getting interesting,' murmured Algy.

'You bet it is,' declared Ginger enthusiastically. 'Go ahead. Let's see what's inside.'

'You've got the light, go ahead yourself,' invited Algy.

'Say, why argue? Let's all go,' put in Eddie. And in a moment they were all standing in the dark doorway, Ginger holding up the piece of burning stuff in order to throw a light as far as possible.

As a means of illumination the strip of shirt left much to be desired, but in its smoky yellow glow they saw three broad steps that led down into another chamber, a long, low room with what appeared to be heaps of debris piled at intervals on the floor. There was only one piece of furniture—a curiously carved chair.

'There doesn't seem to be anything to get worked up about,' observed Ginger in a disappointed voice, as they advanced slowly down the steps.

As Ginger trod on the bottom step it seemed to give under his weight, and he fell back with a cry of alarm. The light went out. Simultaneously, the chamber echoed to a dull, hollow boom.

Algy needed no invitation to relight the piece of rag. At first glance there appeared to be no change in the scene, and it was Eddie, who happened to glance behind him, who called attention to what had occurred. The entrance had disappeared. The idol had swung back into place.

'When I was a kid,' announced Eddie sadly, 'my Ma always swore that my inquisitiveness would be the death of me. I guess she was right. Unless we can find the gadget that tips old frosty-face, I reckon we're here for keeps.'

'Let's have a look before we try to find it,' suggested Algy. 'You may not have noticed it, but that idol fits into its socket like a piston into a cylinder. So does the outside slab. In that case, how does it happen that the air in here is so fresh? Look at the light. You don't suppose it would burn like that if the chamber wasn't ventilated somehow?'

'You're right,' agreed Ginger, sinking into the chair.

In an instant he was on his back, for the chair had collapsed in a cloud of dust. It did not break; it just crumbled, like tinder.

'That chair must have been standing there an awful long time,' said Eddie slowly.

Ginger, sneezing, sat on a pile of debris. It sank a little under his weight, and gave a soft metallic clink. A curious expression came over his face as he picked up a handful of the stuff. He said no word, but turning an amazed face to the others, allowed the pieces to drop one by one from his hand. They fell with a dull clink.

'For the love of Mike,' breathed Eddie. 'It's metal.'

Ginger laughed hysterically. 'Feel the weight of it,' he cried. 'It's gold!'

In a moment they were all on their knees examining their find, and soon established that the objects were not coins, but an extraordinary collection of small carved objects, trinkets, flowers, ears of corn, and the like. Digging into the pile, Algy pulled out a drinking-mug made in the form of a potato.

'It's the treasure all right,' he said in a strained voice, just as the light burnt out. 'Unfortunately, it's no earthly use to us at the moment, but it's nice to know it's here. Rip another strip off your shirt,' he ordered. 'Let's see about getting out of this trap.'

Ginger obliged, and by mutual consent they returned to the steps, from where they made a close examination of the back of the idol. They tried coaxing it open, and failing in this, they tried force. But it was no use. They could see the cracks that marked the dimensions of the opening clearly enough, but nothing they could do would widen them.

'We're wasting our time,' said Eddie in a melancholy voice.

'Don't you believe it,' returned Ginger. 'The old priests, or whoever made this dugout, wouldn't fix the thing without making some way of opening it from the inside. There's a trick in it. All we've got to do is to discover it.'

'If they were cute enough to make a trap like this you can bet your sweet life the trick won't be easy to solve,' said Eddie. 'Only those in the secret could get in and out.'

'What I should like to know,' remarked Algy, 'is where the fresh air is coming from. It can't percolate through solid stone.'

'You're dead right,' affirmed Eddie. 'There must be a hole, or a feed-pipe somewhere. And I'll tell you something else. Even if there is a hole the air couldn't get in if we were below the level of the ground.'

'What are you talking about?' demanded Ginger. 'Of course we're below the level of the ground. We came downstairs.'

'Unless the guys who built this hide-out installed a mechanical air-conditioning plant, which I'm not prepared to believe, then I say the air is coming in from some point below us,' declared Eddie.

'I think you're right,' agreed Algy thoughtfully. 'If we can find the hole we shall know more about it.'

Abandoning the sealed doorway, they set about exploring the chamber, starting with the walls; but everywhere the massive stones of which the chamber was composed fitted so perfectly that the task seemed hopeless. Eddie turned his attention to the floor, dropping on his knees to examine it more closely.

'You've got to remember that the ancients were clever engineers, but even so, their work was limited to simple mechanics,' he remarked. 'They had a primitive idea of hydraulics and levers, so——' The voice broke off abruptly. It was followed by a soft thud.

Algy looked round. So did Ginger. Then they stared at each other.

'Hi! Eddie!' shouted Ginger.

There was no answer.

Ginger turned wondering eyes to Algy. 'He's—he's gone!' he gasped.

'D'you think I'm blind?' sneered Algy with bitter sarcasm, which revealed the state of his nerves. 'Where was he when he disappeared?'

Ginger shook his head. 'I don't know. I was looking at the wall.'

'All right. Let's not get excited. There's dust on the floor. When we find the place where it has been disturbed we shall know where he was when he did the disappearing act.'

'I hope he isn't hurt,' muttered Ginger.

'He's probably groping about on the wrong side of one of these slabs, trying to get back,' asserted Algy, taking the light from Ginger's hand and starting to explore the flagstones which formed the floor. ·

'This is the place,' he announced presently. 'Apart from the dust, the cracks round this slab are wider than the others.'

'Perhaps it tilts, like the one up top,' suggested Ginger.

'That must be the answer, otherwise Eddie couldn't very well have fallen through,' replied Algy. 'Yes, that's it,' he went on quickly. 'The dust on this slab has disappeared. It probably fell into the hole, or whatever there is underneath, when Eddie went through. We're getting warm. I expect it's a case of applying weight to one particular spot. The most likely place would be near the edge, just here—Hi!'

Ginger grabbed Algy by the legs as the stone tilted suddenly and he started to slide. He nearly went in head first, and probably would have done had not Ginger dragged him back. As they struggled clear the stone swung back into place.

'Why did you let the hole close up again?' asked Ginger in a disappointed voice.

'Don't worry about that. We know the trick now,' answered Algy breathlessly. 'I don't want to land on my skull. We'll take this slowly; and as the trap closes automatically we'd better jam it open with something, otherwise it may close behind us and prevent us from getting back.'

Ginger went to one of the heaps of treasure and returned with what looked like a wand, or sceptre. 'This ought to do,' he said.

'Fine,' agreed Algy. 'Slip it in the crack when the stone moves. As soon as the crack is wide enough we'll drop a match in to see how deep the hole is underneath—if there is a hole.'

By the light of the match they ascertained that there was a drop, but only of about six feet; and the first thing they saw was Eddie lying crumpled up at the bottom, evidently unconscious.

Algy dropped down to him. There was no other way. Originally there had been a wooden ladder, but it now lay mouldering in a heap of dust. While Algy was examining Eddie, Ginger observed that the newly discovered cavity bore no likeness to the room they were in. It was more like an artificial cave, with the sides left rough. He also remarked a definite draught of air, refreshingly cool.

'How is he?' he called from above.

'He's got a nasty bruise on the forehead. He must have landed on his head; the blow knocked him out, but I don't think it's serious.'

'Is that a room or a tunnel you're in?'

Algy held up the match and looked round. 'It's a tunnel,' he said. 'You'd better come down. Jam the flags open so that we can get back if necessary.'

Ginger dropped into the cave. 'I say! A disturbing thought

has just occurred to me,' he remarked.

'What is it?'

'If Biggles comes back and finds no one in the chamber he'll wonder what on earth has become of us.'

Algy clicked his tongue. 'I'm afraid he'll have to wonder,' he muttered wearily.

16

CARRUTHERS TAKES A HAND

THEIR fears in this respect, however, had they but known it, were groundless. Biggles was miles away, sitting in a sylvan paradise between earth and heaven, wondering what to do next. Dusky, being a man of the country, was concerned only with the immediate danger—the Indians, who could be heard laughing and shouting some distance away.

'I'm glad they chose Bogat for a target, and not me,' remarked Biggles.

'Dey know Bogat. Dey want him for a long time. Dey take you for an Indian.'

Biggles thought that this was probably the correct explanation. Not being a hypocrite, he made no pretence of being sorry for the brutal Bogat, or the treacherous Chorro, who had got no more than their deserts. An idea struck him.

'Is this carpet firm enough to walk on?' he inquired.

'Sure, massa.'

'There's no risk of falling through?'

'No risk,' declared Dusky confidently. 'This stuff thirty or forty feet thick, maybe more.'

'In that case we ought to be able to work our way along so as to get above the aeroplane. The river will serve as a guide.'

Dusky shook his head. 'If we walk, dem old parrots will set up a squawking and tell the Indians where we are. Better if we wait. Presently de Indians go.'

'Won't they smash the machine?'

'Dey too afraid to go near it,' said Dusky definitely. 'Dey tink, maybe, it's a new god.'

Biggles was not so sure of this, but he was content to rely on Dusky's judgement. After all, he reflected, the old man had spent most of his life among the Indians, and should know their habits.

'Did you know the Indians were there?' asked Biggles, while they were waiting. He remembered that Dusky had stopped before the Indians had revealed their presence.

'Sure, massa.'

'How did you know?'

'I smelled dem,' explained Dusky simply.

Biggles nodded. He was prepared to believe anything.

That Dusky had judged the situation correctly was presently proved when the Indians passed along the trail, in single file and in silence. As soon as they had disappeared into the dim corridors of the forest Dusky announced that it was safe to move. He did not descend straight to the ground, but kept to the tree-tops, picking his way carefully, with Biggles following. They were soon escorted by parrots and monkeys, which, coming close, but taking care to keep out of reach, set up a hideous clamour. Evidently they resented the intrusion into their domain, and left the invaders in no doubt as to their disapproval.

In several places there were holes in the floor, usually near the trunks of trees, such as the one through which they had made an entrance, and Dusky took care to keep well away from them. Eventually, however, he selected one, and stamping with his feet to make sure that he was on a branch, worked his way towards the hole. He pointed, and Biggles, to his infinite relief, saw the *Wanderer* almost immediately below. There was no sign of any damage.

Getting down to the ground was tricky and hot work, and Biggles was not a little relieved to stand once more on terra firma. Watching the undergrowth closely, and with his rifle at the ready, he hurried to the machine, which, to his great satisfaction, appeared to be precisely as he had left it. Leaving Dusky on guard, he tore off the flimsy camouflage and prepared to cast off.

'Okay, Dusky, come aboard,' he said in a tired voice, for strain, exertion, lack of sleep, and the humid atmosphere were beginning to tell. He was weary, hungry and thirsty, not to say dirty.

'Which way we go, massa?' asked Dusky anxiously.

'I'm just wondering,' returned Biggles frankly, for now that the moment for departure had come he found himself in doubt. Two courses were open. The others, he knew, would be anxious about him, and he had an uncomfortable feeling that he had left them in the lurch. He had not stuck to his plan—not that this was entirely his fault. Algy and Ginger would no doubt agree that he had done the right thing when they knew what had happened, but in the meantime they would be worried. Nevertheless, it was not easy to see how he could rejoin them— anyway, until night fell. But apart from this he felt that the wisest course would be to go down the river and tell Carruthers what had happened. He might be able to make a suggestion. If not, Biggles reasoned, he would have to come back and carry on the war single-handed.

'We're going down the river,' he told Dusky abruptly, as he made up his mind.

He started the engines and took off with a vague feeling of surprise that at last something was going according to order. He half expected the engines to break down. Indeed, on the journey to the coast he listened to their note with as much anxiety as he could ever remember, for if they let him down now he hardly dared think what the fate of the others would be.

The engines did not let him down, and he offered up a silent prayer of thankfulness when the sea came into view. In twenty minutes, leaving Dusky in charge of the aircraft, he was in the presence of the acting-Governor.

Carruthers looked him up and down with real concern.

'I say, old man, you are in a mess,' he said sympathetically. 'You need a bath, a——'

Biggles broke in. 'I know. There are a lot of things I need, but I haven't time to attend to them now. Things have been happening—they're still happening, and I've got to get a move on. My friends don't know I'm here—but I'd better give you a rough idea of what has happened. While I'm doing that you might get me a spot of something to eat.'

Carruthers sent his servant for a drink and some sandwiches, and these Biggles consumed as he told his story as concisely as possible.

'By Jingo! You have been having a time,' exclaimed the acting-Governor when Biggles had finished. 'What do you want me to do?'

'To tell the truth, I don't know,' confessed Biggles. 'I thought you might be able to make a suggestion. After all, we're working under you, and apart from personal considerations, I don't want to do the wrong thing.'

'We've got to rescue your friends and this American, and, if possible, arrest the Tiger.'

'That's it,' agreed Biggles. 'We'll grab these two crooks Warren and Schmitt at the same time. They deserve hanging for abandoning young Rockwell in the jungle. The trouble is, I can't be in two places at once. I rarely ask for assistance, but this seems to be a case where a little help would be worth a deal of sympathy.'

'That's what I was thinking,' murmured Carruthers, his lips parting in a faint smile.

'Do you really mean that?' asked Biggles sharply.

'I might snatch a couple of days off to help you to clean up. If I could, what would you suggest?'

'Now you're talking,' said Biggles eagerly. 'You see, I can't be at both ends of that infernal stairway at the same time. The Tiger has got a guard posted at the top, to keep us trapped up there—at least, that's what he thinks. If we had some men at the bottom of the steps we could keep *him* trapped. Otherwise even if we landed an army on the plateau, he'd simply bolt down the steps and disappear into the forest. How many men can you spare?'

'Ten or a dozen—native police, of course. They're good fellows.'

'Got a machine-gun?'

'I could get one.'

Biggles thought quickly. 'Two good men under a reliable N.C.O., with a machine-gun, could hold the bottom of the stairway against an army. Three or four others arriving suddenly on the plateau, with another machine-gun, should be enough to stampede the Tiger's half-baked gang. Remember, I've already got three men up there. Let me see, by unloading most of my stores, at a pinch I could transport ten people up the river, including myself. Ten should be enough. We could land at the place where I just took off and unload Dusky, an N.C.O. and two men, with a machine-gun. Dusky would act as guide. He could show them where to place the gun so that it would cover the steps. Are you seriously thinking of coming?'

'Certainly.'

'Good. Very well. You and I, and four others, would take off again and land on the plateau, and make a rush for this underground chamber I told you about. The idea of that would be to let my friends out. We should then have a force of nine men, which should be plenty. When the Tiger sees you he'll guess the game's up and bolt for the steps. His gang will follow him. We shall then have the whole bunch between two fires, and unless he's a lunatic he'll surrender. Believe me, that stairway is no place to fight a defensive action.'

Carruthers nodded. 'That sounds a good plan. When shall we start?'

'The sooner the better. How soon could you be ready?'

'In an hour.'

'Fine. I'll refuel, have a bath, and meet you at the river in an hour from now. That will be one o'clock. If all goes well we ought to be back up the river by five—just nice time. There will be an hour or two of daylight left.'

'That suits me,' agreed Carruthers.

An hour later the heavily loaded aircraft, after a long run, took off and headed back up the river. Carruthers, with a service rifle across his knees, occupied the spare seat next to Biggles. Behind, packed in the cabin, was the little force of fighting men, all of whom were making their first trip in the air.

Biggles did not trouble about height—not that he could have gone very high with such a full load even if he had wanted to. Generally speaking, he followed the river, so that he would be able to land his human freight safely should the emergency arise.

After some time the first landing-place, the bend where Bogat and Chorro had met their deaths, came into view, and Biggles set the *Wanderer* down gently on the water. Here four men were disembarked—Dusky, a sergeant, and two policemen. In addition to their small arms, they carried a Vickers machine-gun. They knew just what to do, for their part in the operation had been explained to them before the start. Under Dusky's guidance they were to proceed to the foot of the stairway and take up a position covering it. Anyone attempting to come down was to be arrested.

Biggles watched them file up the forest trail, and then, with an easier load, took off and headed for the plateau.

He tried to visualise what would happen when he landed. As he worked it out, the Tiger and his white associates would suppose that he was alone, in which case their mistake might cost them dear. Actually, he was not particularly concerned whether the Tiger fought or fled. His immediate concern was to get to the underground chamber and relieve Algy, Ginger and Eddie from their tiresome ordeal.

By air it was only a short distance to the plateau. Biggles did not waste time circling, for he knew there were no obstructions to be cleared. Lowering his wheels, he made for the spot he had chosen on the previous occasion.

'Tell your fellows to be ready to bundle out smartly as soon as the machine stops,' he told Carruthers. 'We're likely to come under fire right away, so get the machine-gun in action as quickly as possible. I don't think the Tiger will face it.'

'Leave it to me,' rejoined Carruthers quietly.

As he glided down to land Biggles could see men running from the village and many faces staring upward. It appeared as if the arrival of the machine had caused something like consternation. At the distance, however, he could not distinguish the Tiger.

The wheels touched; the machine rocked a little, and then ran on to a safe if bumpy landing. Kicking on hard rudder, and at the same time giving the engines a burst of throttle, Biggles guided the machine towards an outcrop of rock which he thought would make good cover. As soon as the *Wanderer* stopped he switched off, and grabbing his rifle jumped down. The others poured out behind him. Shots were already flicking up the dust, so the men, under Carruthers' leadership, made a dive for the rocks and there assembled the machine-gun.

About a dozen of the Tiger's men, led by the Tiger himself, were by this time sprinting towards the aircraft; but as the machine-gun started its devastating chatter they acted as Biggles expected they would. They turned and fled, leaving two of their number on the ground. Biggles picked off another man and then jumped to his feet.

'Come on! Let's get after them,' he said crisply.

But now things took a surprising turn, a turn for which Biggles thought he should have been prepared, but as a matter of fact the possibility had not occurred to him. The labourers, who were really nothing less than slaves, were working in the trench. Biggles had noticed them before he landed, but they did not come into his calculations. It seemed, now, as if they suddenly realised that deliverance was at hand. They were nearly all natives from the coast, and perhaps they recognised Carruthers' spotless white uniform. Be that as it may, with one accord, and with a wild yell, they leapt out of the trench and attacked their masters, using as weapons the tools they held in their hands. Biggles saw the gang-boss go down under a rain of blows from picks and shovels. The survivors of this onset, the Tiger among them, bolted for the steps, pursued by a yelling crowd. Some, in their desperate haste to escape, threw away their rifles.

'What on earth is happening?' cried Carruthers.

'It looks as if the Tiger's slaves have decided to take a hand,' answered Biggles grimly.

They could do nothing to prevent the massacre that followed, for they were still a good two hundred yards away, and the slaves were between them and the fugitives. Biggles ran on.

followed by the others, hoping to save life if it were possible, and anxious to get to the chamber.

Just before he reached it he saw a fearful sight. Five or six brawny natives, fleeter of foot than the rest, overtook the two white men, Warren and Schmitt, at the head of the stairway. The hunted men screamed as hands fell on them and pulled them down. Carruthers, seeing what was likely to happen, shouted, but he might as well have saved his breath. For a moment there was a knot of struggling figures. Then they separated, and the two white men, clutching at the air, swung out over the awful void. Then they disappeared from sight, their screams growing fainter as they plunged to destruction.

Biggles left the rest to Carruthers. Feeling a trifle sick, he dashed to the chamber, and saw, for the first time, the effect of the explosion. He realised at once that the others must have been trapped.

He beckoned to some of the ex-labourers who were standing about talking in excited groups and made them clear the masonry. As soon as the slab was exposed he opened it.

'Hullo there!' he called cheerfully.

There was no answer.

Biggles felt his heart miss a beat. He went down the first few steps and struck a match, holding the light above his head. His fears were at once confirmed. The chamber was empty. And there he stood, flabbergasted, until the match burnt his fingers.

'Hullo!' he shouted again, in a voice that had suddenly become hoarse.

But there was no reply.

Slowly, hardly able to believe his eyes, he made his way back up the steps to the fresh air.

Carruthers appeared. 'What's the matter?' he asked quickly, noting the expression on Biggles's face.

'They're gone,' said Biggles in a dazed voice.

'Gone?' echoed Carruthers incredulously. 'Where could they have gone?'

Biggles shrugged his shoulders helplessly. 'Don't ask me,' he said bitterly. 'I'm no magician.'

BIGGLES might well have wondered what had become of Algy, Ginger and Eddie; and, as the idol had swung back into place, he might have searched for a long time without finding them. The earth had—as near as may be—opened and swallowed them up.

Eddie was a long time recovering from his fall, for only on the screen do people who have been stunned by a blow on the head recover in a few seconds. Algy and Ginger could do little to help him. They had not even any water. All they could do was squat beside him, rubbing his hands and fanning his face, at the same time debating whether they should try to carry him down the cave which they could see stretched for some distance—how far they did not know. It appeared to plunge down towards the centre of the earth.

They lost all count of time; indeed, they did not even know whether it was day or night when Eddie, after a few weak groans, eventually opened his eyes. Once consciousness returned he made fairly good progress, and presently was well enough to ask what had happened. He himself had no recollection beyond groping about on the floor looking for a trap-door.

'You found it,' Algy told him with humorous sarcasm. 'Having found it, you dived through and landed on your head.'

Eddie struggled into a sitting position. 'Where are we?'

'Ask me something easier,' returned Algy wearily. 'Still, if you're well enough to get on your feet we'll try to find out. It's no use going back, so we may as well go forward.'

Now, all this time Ginger had kept a small fire going by tearing pieces off his shirt, with the result that there was very little of the garment left.

Eddie got up, rather unsteadily, while Ginger recklessly tore the remaining piece of shirt into strips to provide illumination. With this improvised torch he led the way, the others following,

Eddie leaning on Algy's arm.

For some time nothing happened. The cave, a rough, narrow tunnel just high enough to enable them to stand upright, took a winding course downward at a steep angle. It seemed to go on interminably, but then suddenly opened out into a tremendous cavity in the earth, not unlike a cathedral. Enormous stalactites, like rows of organ-pipes, dropped from the roof to meet spiky stalagmites that sprang upwards from the floor. From all around came the faint drip, drip, drip, of water, an eerie sound in such a place.

'Now what have we struck?' asked Ginger in an awed voice, looking round. He took a pace forward, but backed hastily.

'What's wrong?' asked Algy.

'The floor's soft.'

'What do you mean—soft?'

'What I say. It feels like mud. It won't bear my weight.'

Algy stepped forward and tested it. 'You're right,' he said slowly. 'We seem to have struck a confounded bog.'

'It looks as if we shan't be able to get any farther.'

'Just a minute,' put in Eddie. 'Of course, there's always a chance that the bog has only been formed in recent years, but if it was always here, then surely there must be a way across, otherwise there would be no point in making the cave.'

'That's a reasonable argument,' agreed Algy. 'All the same I can't see any bridge.' He began exploring the mud with his feet. 'Just a minute, what have we here?' he cried. 'It feels like a lump of rock just under the surface.'

Ginger tried it. 'That's what it is,' he said, standing on it. Groping with his foot, he found another. 'That's it,' he went on. 'There are stepping-stones, but either they've sunk or the mud has risen and covered them. Let's see if we can get across.'

'Gosh! I don't think much of this,' muttered Algy as he followed. 'What about you, Eddie?' Can you manage?'

'Yes, I reckon so,' answered Eddie, holding on to the wall for support. He drew his hand away sharply. 'It's all right,' he went on quickly. 'It's only water. It's collected in a sort of basin in the rock. There must be a flaw, a fissure, in the rock, that lets the rain water in from above.'

'Water!' gasped Ginger. 'Let's have a drink. My throat's like dust.'

In a moment they were all drinking greedily out of their cupped hands.

'That's better,' exclaimed Ginger, rinsing his grimy face.

'You're sure right,' agreed Eddie. 'I feel a heap better for that.'

They now proceeded again, Ginger, carrying the flame, leading the way. Several times a false step got him into difficulties. Once he stepped off the path and sank up to the waist in slime. Algy had hard work to pull him out, while all around the disturbed area of mud quaked and threw up huge noisome bubbles.

'Phew! What a stink,' muttered Ginger disgustedly. 'We ought to have brought masks,' he added, trying to make light of the incident.

A moment later Eddie exclaimed, 'You're right at that.'

'About what?'

'Gas masks. My head's beginning to swim. There's sulphur in this gas. Push on, but don't fall in again, or you'll send up more gas.'

Ginger needed no second invitation, and it was with a shout of relief that he saw the stepping-stones ahead protruding above the mud. Once they could see them, progress became faster, and it was not long before they arrived at what appeared to be a continuation of the cave, although it was now much larger.

Ginger turned, and holding up the flame in such a way that it burned more brightly, took a last look at the subterranean mere.

'I say, you fellows, what's that?' he asked in a startled voice. 'I mean—that shadow—over there. It seems to be coming towards us.'

The others turned and looked, and saw, as Ginger had remarked, that a broad dark shadow was moving across the morass towards them. The strange thing about it was that it did not maintain an even rate of progress. It seemed to dart forward a little way, then pause, then come on again.

'Say! I don't like the look of that,' said Eddie. 'What could cause a shadow in here?'

'That isn't a shadow,' answered Algy in a hushed whisper. It's something—alive. I believe it's thousands of insects of some sort. Yes, by gosh, that's it. Just look at 'em. They look like whacking great water-spiders. What do they call those big spiders? Tarantulas. Their bite is poisonous.' He ended on a shrill note.

The others did not wait to confirm this. With one accord they turned about and fled up the cave.

After going a little way Ginger looked over his shoulder. 'Look out!' he yelled. 'They're coming!'

They blundered on. There was no longer any question of going back.

'The next time you want to go adventuring, my lad, you'll go alone,' panted Algy once, viciously.

It was more by luck than judgement that Ginger spotted the opening—or at least one opening, for there may have been others. They were not even thinking of one, for the cave still went downwards. Ginger happened to look up a side turning, and noticed a ghostly grey glow. He pulled up short.

'What's that?' he shouted.

The others stopped and looked. For a moment silence reigned.

'It's daylight!' yelled Algy.

There was a rush for the spot. Algy reached it first, and gave a cry of disappointment when he saw that the light came through a narrow crack only a few inches wide, although it was a yard or more long. A mouse might have got through it, but nothing larger. Beyond, showing as a strip of blue silk, was the sky. It was obvious that the crack was merely a flaw in the rock, due, no doubt, to the effect of wind and rain on the outside.

Ginger, holding up the light, looked behind, and a gasp of horror broke from his lips when he saw the vanguard of the tarantulas only a few yards away.

Algy saw them too, and it was in sheer desperation that he flung himself against the rock, near the crack. He had no genuine hope that it would widen sufficiently to allow him to go through, consequently he was utterly unprepared for what happened. The whole rock gave way under his weight, and after a vain attempt to save himself, he fell through behind it. The next moment he was clutching wildly at anything as he slid down a short but steep slope to what seemed certain destruction, for all he could see below him was a fearful void. A little avalanche of rocks preceded him to the brink. Loose boulders followed him down. He gave himself up for lost.

When his heels struck solid ground he could hardly believe his good fortune. Then, not before, did he see where he was. He was on the stairway. On either hand ran the narrow cornice. Even then he nearly went over the edge, for a piece of rock, catching him in the small of the back, sent him sprawling. He fell across the path with his legs in space. With frantic haste he drew them in, caring little that his rifle went spinning into the void.

Now Ginger's startled face had appeared at the aperture behind Algy, so he had seen everything that had happened. He also saw something which Algy did not see. Happening to glance up the steps, he saw to his amazement and alarm that somebody was coming down—running down. There was no need to look twice to ascertain who it was. It was the Tiger. Ginger let out a yell of warning.

'Here! Grab this!' he shouted, and allowed his rifle to slide down the slope.

At this moment he in turn was warned by Eddie that the tarantulas were on their heels, so half slipping and half sliding, he followed the rifle to the steps. Eddie came down behind him, and nearly knocked him over the edge. By the time they got down to him, Algy was covering the Tiger, who appeared to be unarmed, and shouting to him to go back.

Now, it must be remembered that none of them knew what had happened on the plateau, so not for an instant did it occur to them that the Tiger was a fugitive. On the contrary, they supposed that either by luck, or by judgement beyond their understanding, he had deliberately aimed to intercept them. And when a yelling horde of Indians and half breeds appeared round the bend higher up the steps, it only tended to confirm this. That the Indians were, in fact, pursuing the Tiger, did not occur to them. There was no reason why it should.

The Tiger pulled up when he saw the three white men in front of him. He threw a nervous glance over his shoulder, although this gave the impression that he was waiting for his men to come to his assistance. The situation appeared critical.

Algy addressed the Tiger. 'Get back,' he ordered. 'Get back and tell those men of yours to stop, or I'll shoot you.'

The Tiger appeared not to understand. He shouted something, either in Spanish or in a local dialect. Anyway, none of those below him knew what he said. Then he did a surprising thing. He looked up, then down the steps. Then he surveyed the face of the cliff. Before any of the watchers suspected his intention, with a cat-like leap he reached a narrow ledge above the path, a ledge that was not visible to those below. Along this ledge he made his way towards the hole from which the comrades had just emerged.

At first Algy thought he simply intended getting above them, but as soon as he realised what he was going to do, he shouted a warning. Again, either the Tiger did not understand or he took no notice. He disappeared into the hole.

He was out of sight only a moment or two. Then he reappeared, screaming, snatching and striking at a number of black hairy objects that were running over his body. He appeared to forget where he was, so it came as no surprise to the horrified watchers when he lost his balance and fell. He landed head first on the stairway amid a shower of rocks, and there he lay, limp in unconsciousness.

For a second or two Ginger stared blankly at the wretched man, his brain trying to keep pace with events. As in a dream he saw Algy bring his heel down viciously on a loathesome great spider, and shuddered. Then, remembering the Tiger's men, he looked up the steps and saw with fresh astonishment that they had stopped. One man now stood a little way in front of the others. It was a white man, in spotless ducks. He blinked and looked again. 'I'm going crazy,' he muttered.

Algy, looking rather pale, swung round. 'What are you

talking about?' he snapped.

Ginger pointed. 'Is that Carruthers, or am I beginning to imagine things?'

Algy stared. He passed his hand wearily over his forehead. 'It's Carruthers, all right,' he said. 'If he's here, then Biggles shouldn't be far away.'

'I don't get it,' muttered Eddie in a dazed voice.

'Something seems to have happened while we were away,' murmured Algy.

Then Carruthers raised his hand in greeting, and shouted: 'What are you fellows standing there for? Come on up. We were wondering where you were. It's all over.'

Algy turned a stupefied face to Ginger. 'Did you hear that?' he said incredulously. 'It's all over.'

'What's all over?' demanded Ginger, whose nerves were beginning to crack.

'Let's go up and find out,' suggested Algy.

They went slowly up the steps. Carruthers went on ahead of them. They could hear him shouting. By the time they reached the top Biggles was standing there.

'What do you fellows think you're playing at?' he inquired curtly.

'Playing!' snorted Algy. 'Playing! That's pretty good.' He laughed bitterly.

'I told you to wait until I came back.'

'So we should have done if somebody hadn't blown the place up.'

'What happened to the Tiger?' asked Biggles.

Algy told him. 'Some of the slaves are carrying him back up here,' he concluded.

Biggles nodded. 'That saves us a lot of trouble,' he observed. 'Let's go and meet him. I want to get that map. It should be in his pocket.'

'If you're thinking about the treasure you won't need it,' said Ginger with relish.

'Why not?'

It was Ginger's turn to smile. 'Because we've found it.'

Biggles started. 'So that's what you've been up to, is it? I might have guessed it. Well, let's go and have a look at it.'

'You can have a look at it—provided I can get to it again—when I've had a look at a square meal and a cake of soap,' promised Algy.

Biggles smiled. 'That's a fair proposition,' he agreed. 'Come on, I think we can fix you up.'

He led the way back to the machine, leaving Carruthers to attend to the business of sorting out the people on the plateau.

The rest of the story is soon told.

After a meal and a general clean-up, during which time Biggles ran over his adventures and the others gave him an account of what had happened during his absence, they all returned to the underground chamber. They wasted no time searching for the secret spring that actuated the idol, but with crowbars brought from the tool-store forced the panel open. The treasure was then carried into the open, where it could more easily be examined, and where Carruthers officially took possession of it in the name of the Crown.

It proved to be of even greater value than they had supposed, for there were some wonderful jewels, mostly rubies and emeralds, mixed up with the gold. It was a wonderful find, for many of the objects were unique examples of the craftsmanship of the early inhabitants of tropical America, and as such were likely to bring high prices from collectors of such things. As a matter of detail, most of the pieces later found their way into museums, the comrades, including Eddie, receiving a fair percentage in cash of the total sum they produced.

After the treasure had been examined it was taken to the *Wanderer* for transportation to the coast; and as their task was finished, the comrades flew straight back, taking Carruthers and the still unconscious King of the Forest with them. They stayed at the acting-Governor's bungalow while the official inquiry into the whole affair was held. The court, having heard the evidence, exonerated them from all blame in connection with the deaths of the leading conspirators, and unofficially congratulated them on their work in putting an end to a menace that had long been a scandal in the colony. This was very gratifying, and gave them all that satisfactory feeling of a job well done. The Tiger was still in prison, awaiting trial on several charges of murder—evidence of which had been furnished by the released slaves—when they left the colony, but they had little doubt as to what his fate would be.

The formalities over, Eddie, after trying in vain to persuade the others to go with him, returned to the United States. Dusky was given a responsible position in the native police. Then, as there was no reason for them to stay, they climbed once more into the *Wanderer* and continued their interrupted pleasure cruise, well satisfied with the result of their call at the little outpost of the Empire.